STEPHEN JONES lives in London, England. He is the winner of three World Fantasy Awards, four Horror Writers Association Bram Stoker Awards and three International Horror Guild Awards as well as being an eighteen-time recipient of the British Fantasy Award and a Hugo Award nominee. A former television producer/director and genre movie publicist and consultant (the first three *Hellraiser* movies, *Night Life*, *Nightbreed*, *Split Second*, *Mind Ripper*, *Last Gasp* etc.), he is the co-editor of *Horror: 100 Best Books*, *Horror: Another 100 Best Books*, *The Best Horror from Fantasy Tales*, *Gaslight & Ghosts*, *Now We Are Sick*, *H.P. Lovecraft's Book of Horror*, *The Anthology of Fantasy & the Supernatural*, *Secret City: Strange Tales of London*, *Great Ghost Stories*, *Tales to Freeze the Blood: More Great Ghost Stories* and the *Dark Terrors*, *Dark Voices* and *Fantasy Tales* series. He has written *Coraline: A Visual Companion*, *Stardust: The Visual Companion*, *Creepshows: The Illustrated Stephen King Movie Guide*, *The Essential Monster Movie Guide*, *The Illustrated Vampire Movie Guide*, *The Illustrated Dinosaur Movie Guide*, *The Illustrated Frankenstein Movie Guide* and *The Illustrated Werewolf Movie Guide*, and compiled *The Mammoth Book of Best New Horror* series, *The Mammoth Book of Terror*, *The Mammoth Book of Vampires*, *The Mammoth Book of Zombies*, *The Mammoth Book of Werewolves*, *The Mammoth Book of Frankenstein*, *The Mammoth Book of Dracula*, *The Mammoth Book of Vampire Stories By Women*, *The Mammoth Book of New Terror*, *The Mammoth Book of Monsters*, *Shadows Over Innsmouth*, *Weird Shadows Over Innsmouth*, *Dark Detectives*, *Dancing with the Dark*, *Dark of the Night*, *White of the Moon*, *Keep Out the Night*, *By Moonlight Only*, *Don't Turn Out the Light*, *H.P. Lovecraft's Book of the Supernatural*, *Travellers in Darkness*, *Summer Chills*, *Exorcisms and Ecstasies* by Karl Edward Wagner, *The Vampire Stories of R. Chetwynd-Hayes*, *Phantoms and Fiends* and *Frights and Fancies* by R. Chetwynd-Hayes, *James Herbert: By Horror Haunted*, *Basil Copper: A Life in Books*, *Necronomicon: The Best Weird Tales of H.P. Lovecraft*, *The Complete Chronicles of Conan* by Robert E. Howard, *The Emperor of Dreams: The Lost Worlds of Clark Ashton Smith*, *Sea-Kings of Mars and Otherworldly Stories* by Leigh Brackett, *The Mark of the Beast and Other Fantastical Tales* by Rudyard Kipling, *Clive Barker's A-Z of Horror*, *Clive Barker's Shadows in Eden*, *Clive Barker's The Nightbreed Chronicles* and the *Hellraiser Chronicles*. He was a Guest of Honour at the 2002 World Fantasy Conventi[on] the 2004 World Horror Conventio[n] his website at *www.stephenjonesedit[or]*

D0465777

Also available

The Mammoth Book of 20th Century Science Fiction
The Mammoth Book of Best British Crime
The Mammoth Book of Best Crime Comics
The Mammoth Book of Best Horror Comics
The Mammoth Book of Best of Best New SF
The Mammoth Book of Best New Erotica 8
The Mammoth Book of Best New Manga 3
The Mammoth Book of Best New SF 21
The Mammoth Book of Best War Comics
The Mammoth Book of Bikers
The Mammoth Book of Boys' Own Stuff
The Mammoth Book of Brain Workouts
The Mammoth Book of Celebrity Murders
The Mammoth Book of Comic Fantasy
The Mammoth Book of Comic Quotes
The Mammoth Book of Cover-Ups
The Mammoth Book of CSI
The Mammoth Book of the Deep
The Mammoth Book of Dirty, Sick, X-Rated & Politically Incorrect Jokes
The Mammoth Book of Dickensian Whodunnits
The Mammoth Book of Egyptian Whodunnits
The Mammoth Book of Erotic Confessions
The Mammoth Book of Erotic Online Diaries
The Mammoth Book of Erotic Women
The Mammoth Book of Extreme Fantasy
The Mammoth Book of Funniest Cartoons of All Time
The Mammoth Book of Hard Men
The Mammoth Book of Historical Whodunnits
The Mammoth Book of Illustrated True Crime
The Mammoth Book of Inside the Elite Forces
The Mammoth Book of International Erotica
The Mammoth Book of Jack the Ripper
The Mammoth Book of Jacobean Whodunnits
The Mammoth Book of the Kama Sutra
The Mammoth Book of Killers at Large
The Mammoth Book of King Arthur
The Mammoth Book of Lesbian Erotica
The Mammoth Book of Limericks
The Mammoth Book of Maneaters
The Mammoth Book of Modern Ghost Stories
The Mammoth Book of Modern Battles
The Mammoth Book of Monsters
The Mammoth Book of Mountain Disasters
The Mammoth Book of New Gay Erotica
The Mammoth Book of New Terror
The Mammoth Book of On the Edge
The Mammoth Book of On the Road
The Mammoth Book of Pirates
The Mammoth Book of Poker
The Mammoth Book of Prophecies
The Mammoth Book of Roaring Twenties Whodunnits
The Mammoth Book of Sex, Drugs and Rock 'N' Roll
The Mammoth Book of Short SF Novels
The Mammoth Book of Short Spy Novels
The Mammoth Book of Sorcerers' Tales
The Mammoth Book of True Crime
The Mammoth Book of True Hauntings
The Mammoth Book of True War Stories
The Mammoth Book of Unsolved Crimes
The Mammoth Book of Vampire Romance
The Mammoth Book of Vintage Whodunnits
The Mammoth Book of Women Who Kill
The Mammoth Book of Zombie Comics

The Mammoth Book of

WOLF MEN

THE ULTIMATE WEREWOLF ANTHOLOGY

Edited by

Stephen Jones

ROBINSON

RUNNING PRESS
PHILADELPHIA · LONDON

Constable & Robinson Ltd
3 The Lanchesters
162 Fulham Palace Road
London W6 9ER
www.constablerobinson.com

First published in the UK as *The Mammoth Book of Werewolves* by Robinson,
an imprint of Constable & Robinson Ltd, 1994

This revised and updated edition published by Robinson,
an imprint of Constable & Robinson Ltd, 2009

A copy of the British Library Cataloguing in Publication
Data is available from the British Library

UK ISBN 978-1-84901-031-3

1 3 5 7 9 10 8 6 4 2

First published in the United States in 2009 by Running Press Book Publishers

US Library of Congress number: 2008944142
US ISBN 978-0-7624-3797-9

Running Press Book Publishers
2300 Chestnut Street
Philadelphia, PA 19103-4371

Visit us on the web!
www.runningpress.com

Printed and bound in the EU

CONTENTS

Acknowledgments   vii

Introduction: Even a Man Who is Pure in Heart ...   xi

Twilight at the Towers   1
CLIVE BARKER

The Dream of the Wolf   37
SCOTT BRADFIELD

Night Beat   64
RAMSEY CAMPBELL

The Werewolf   70
R. CHETWYND-HAYES

Rain Falls   84
MICHAEL MARSHALL SMITH

Guilty Party   96
STEPHEN LAWS

Essence of the Beast   113
ROBERTA LANNES

Immortal   133
MARK MORRIS

Cry Wolf   155
BASIL COPPER

Rug   165
GRAHAM MASTERTON

The Whisperers   182
HUGH B. CAVE

And I Shall Go in the Devil's Name   198
DAVID SUTTON

The Foxes of Fascoum   214
PETER TREMAYNE

One Paris Night   239
KARL EDWARD WAGNER

Soul of the Wolf   252
BRIAN MOONEY

The Hairy Ones Shall Dance   280
MANLY WADE WELLMAN

Heart of the Beast   352
ADRIAN COLE

Wereman   367
LES DANIELS

Anything But Your Kind   374
NICHOLAS ROYLE

The Nighthawk   391
DENNIS ETCHISON

The Cell   409
DAVID CASE

Boobs   472
SUZY McKEE CHARNAS

Only the End of the World Again   493
NEIL GAIMAN

Out of the Night, When the Full Moon is Bright …   511
KIM NEWMAN

Bright of Moon   575
JO FLETCHER

ACKNOWLEDGMENTS

My thanks to Neil Gaiman, Jo Fletcher, Kim Newman, Brian Mooney, David Pringle, Dorothy Lumley and Pete Duncan for their help and advice.

*For Mike and Jan who,
I hope, will never change …*

Introduction

EVEN A MAN WHO IS PURE IN HEART . . .

Lycanthropes … Shapechangers … Loups-Garous …Werewolves … the men (and sometimes women) who hide beneath the mask of the Beast, and the Beasts who kill with the tortured soul of Man. Of all horror's pantheon of great monsters (the vampire, the zombie, the Frankenstein creature), the werewolf is perhaps the most tragic. Condemned (usually through no fault of their own) to metamorphose during the phases of the full moon into bestial killers who destroy the ones they love, werewolves exemplify the classic dichotomy of Good versus Evil which, since the publication of Robert Louis Stevenson's *The Strange Case of Dr Jekyll & Mr Hyde* in 1886, lies at the core of most great modern horror fiction.

Like its stablemate, the vampire, the werewolf has also been successfully adapted into numerous novel-length works: from such classics as Jessie Douglas Kerruish's *The Undying Monster* (1922), Guy Endore's *The Werewolf of Paris* (1933), Jack Williamson's *Darker Than You Think* (1948), Whitley Strieber's *The Wolfen* (1978) and Stephen King's *Cycle of the Werewolf* (1985), to more recent incarnations like Brian Stableford's *Werewolves of London* (1990), Michael Cadnum's *Saint Peter's Wolf* (1991), Alice Borchardt's *The Silver Wolf* (1998), Kelly Armstrong's *Bitten* (2001) and Carrie Vaughn's werewolf romance *Kitty and the Midnight Hour* (2005) and its popular sequels.

The movies were also not slow to capitalize upon the public's fascination with shapechangers, and among the earliest versions of the myth are the 1913 Canadian two-reeler *The Werewolf* (loosely based on Henry Beaugrand's story "The Werewolves") and the silent French feature *Le Loup-Garou* (1923).

Hollywood finally got into the act with *The Werewolf of London* (1935), which utilised Oliver Onions' 1929 story "The Master of the House" and starred Henry Hull as the cursed scientist. Six years later the same studio, Universal, introduced Lon Chaney Jr's doomed Lawrence Talbot in *The Wolf Man* (1941), and the character went on to meet Frankenstein, Dracula, and various mad doctors, before ending up as a foil for the comedy duo Abbott and Costello at the decade's end. Far more interesting during this period were producer Val Lewton's low-budget classics, *The Cat People* (1942) and its semi-sequel, *The Curse of the Cat People* (1944), which explored their own implied brand of lycanthropy.

Over the years cinema audiences have been subjected to countless variations on the theme, including *The Undying Monster* (1942, adapted from Jessie Douglas Kerruish's 1922 novel), *I Was a Teenage Werewolf* (1957), *Werewolf in a Girls' Dormitory* (1961), *The Curse of the Werewolf* (1961, based on Endore's book), *Werewolves on Wheels* (1971), *The Werewolf of Washington* (1973), *Legend of the Werewolf* (1974), *The Howling* (1980, from the novel by Gary Brander) and its various direct-to-video sequels, *An American Werewolf in London* (1981), *The Wolfen* (1981), *Silver Bullet* (1985), *Teen Wolf* (1985) and *Wolf* (1994), right up to more recent entries in the genre such as *Ginger Snaps* (2000) and its sequels, *Dog Soldiers* (2001), the *Underworld* (2003) series, Wes Craven's *Cursed* (2005) and Universal's remake of *The Wolf Man* (2009) starring Benicio Del Toro and Anthony Hopkins.

As always, it is in the literature of short fiction where the werewolf has flourished. However, unlike my previous *Mammoth* anthologies (*Terror*, *Vampires* and *Zombies*), this volume marks something of a departure from my usual criteria of presenting a mixture of favourite reprints and newer stories, with a greater emphasis this time on original tales. You will still discover classic novellas from the pulp era like Manly Wade Wellman's "The Hairy Ones Shall Dance" and "The Whisperers" by Hugh B.

Cave along with such modern masterpieces as David Case's "The Cell", Clive Barker's "Twilight at the Towers", the award-winning "Boobs" by Suzy McKee Charnas and, new to this printing, Neil Gaiman's revisionist reworking of the original Wolf Man, Lawrence Talbot, as a private detective battling Lovecraftian Deep Ones in "Only the End of the World Again".

However, because of lack of space, I have had to exclude a number of personal favourites by such authors as Robert Bloch, H. Warner Munn, Clark Ashton Smith, Robert E. Howard, Seabury Quinn, Anthony Boucher, James Blish, Algernon Blackwood and Ambrose Bierce, to name only a few.

In the meantime, *The Mammoth Book of Wolf Men* collects together for the first time stories by such contemporary masters of the genre as Ramsey Campbell, Basil Copper, R. Chetwynd-Hayes, Karl Edward Wagner, Dennis Etchison, Les Daniels, Stephen Laws and Scott Bradfield, as well as original fiction from Graham Masterton, Michael Marshall Smith, Mark Morris, Peter Tremayne, Roberta Lannes, Nicholas Royle, Adrian Cole, David Sutton, Brian Mooney and Kim Newman's remarkable new novella, "Out of the Night, When the Full Moon is Bright ..."

So once again, when the wolfbane blooms and the moon is full and bright, get your silver bullets ready as the sign of the pentagram reveals the Beast that lurks within the heart of Man. Prepare to howl with horror at one poem and twenty-three tales of terror and transformation. After all, you know what they say – a change is as good as a rest ...

Stephen Jones,
London, England

Clive Barker

TWILIGHT AT THE TOWERS

Author, playwright, screenwriter, artist and film director, Clive Barker could almost be a shapeshifter himself, he wears so many different hats. Since his sextet of Books of Blood *collections first appeared in 1984–85, he has published such novels as* The Damnation Game, Weaveworld, Cabal, The Great and Secret Show, Imajica, The Thief of Always, Everville, Sacrament, Galilee, Coldheart Canyon: A Hollywood Ghost Story, Mister B. Gone *and the* New York Times *bestselling* Arabat *series.*

As a film-maker, he created the hugely influential Hellraiser *franchise in 1987 and went on to direct* Nightbreed *and* Lord of Illusions. *Barker also executive produced the Oscar-winning* Gods and Monsters, *while the* Candyman *series, along with* Underworld, Rawhead Rex, Quicksilver Highway, Saint Sinner, The Midnight Meat Train *and* Book of Blood, *are all based on his concepts. Current projects in development include* Born, Tortured Souls: Animae Damnatae, The Thief of Always *and a remake of the original* Hellraiser.

As an artist he has successfully exhibited his paintings and drawings in many prestigious galleries, created the concepts for a whole slew of comic book series, and still finds time to turn out the occasional short story. Books about the author include Clive Barker's Shadows in Eden *(with Stephen Jones),* Clive Barker: The Dark Fantastic *by Douglas E. Winter and* The Hellraiser Films and Their Legacy *by Paul Kane.*

Clive Barker was born in Liverpool, England, and now lives in California with his partner, photographer David Armstrong, and their daughter Nicole.

*The tale that follows is an unusual spy thriller set during the Cold
War, in which the author opines that shapechangers would be used
by opposing governments as the best – and most deadly – undercover
agents. Perhaps not such a far-fetched idea if such creatures actually
exist …*

The photographs of Mironenko which Ballard had been shown
in Munich had proved far from instructive. Only one or two
pictured the KGB man full face; and of the others most were
blurred and grainy, betraying their furtive origins. Ballard was
not overmuch concerned. He knew from long and occasionally
bitter experience that the eye was all too ready to be deceived;
but there were other faculties – the remnants of senses modern
life had rendered obsolete – which he had learned to call into
play, enabling him to sniff out the least signs of betrayal. These
were the talents he would use when he met with Mironenko.
With them, he would root the truth from the man.

The truth? Therein lay the conundrum of course, for in this
context wasn't sincerity a movable feast? Sergei Zakharovich
Mironenko had been a Section Leader in Directorate S of
the KGB for eleven years, with access to the most privileged
information on the dispersal of Soviet Illegals in the West. In the
recent weeks, however, he had made his disenchantment with
his present masters, and his consequent desire to defect, known
to the British Security Service. In return for the elaborate efforts
which would have to be made on his behalf he had volunteered
to act as an agent within the KGB for a period of three months,
after which time he would be taken into the bosom of democracy
and hidden where his vengeful overlords would never find him.
It had fallen to Ballard to meet the Russian face to face, in the
hope of establishing whether Mironenko's disaffection from his
ideology was real or faked. The answer would not be found on
Mironenko's lips, Ballard knew, but in some behavioural nuance
which only instinct would comprehend.

Time was when Ballard would have found the puzzle
fascinating; that his every waking thought would have circled
on the unravelling ahead. But such commitment had belonged

to a man convinced his actions had some significant effect upon the world. He was wiser now. The agents of East and West went about their secret works year in, year out. They plotted; they connived; occasionally (though rarely) they shed blood. There were débâcles and trade-offs and minor tactical victories. But in the end things were much the same as ever.

This city, for instance. Ballard had first come to Berlin in April of 1969. He'd been twenty-nine, fresh from years of intensive training, and ready to live a little. But he had not felt easy here. He found the city charmless; often bleak. It had taken Odell, his colleague for those first two years, to prove that Berlin was worthy of his affections, and once Ballard fell he was lost for life. Now he felt more at home in this divided city than he ever had in London. Its unease, its failed idealism, and – perhaps most acutely of all – its terrible isolation, matched his. He and it, maintaining a presence in a wasteland of dead ambition.

He found Mironenko at the Germälde Galerie, and yes, the photographs *had* lied. The Russian looked older than his forty-six years, and sicker than he'd appeared in those filched portraits. Neither man made any sign of acknowledgement. They idled through the collection for a full half-hour, with Mironenko showing acute, and apparently genuine, interest in the work on view. Only when both men were satisfied that they were not being watched did the Russian quit the building and lead Ballard into the polite suburbs of Dahlem to a mutually agreed safe house. There, in a small and unheated kitchen, they sat down and talked.

Mironenko's command of English was uncertain, or at least appeared so, though Ballard had the impression that his struggles for sense were as much tactical as grammatical. He might well have presented the same façade in the Russian's situation; it seldom hurt to appear less competent than one was. But despite the difficulties he had in expressing himself, Mironenko's avowals were unequivocal.

"I am no longer a Communist," he stated plainly, "I have not been a Party member – not *here*—" he put his fist to his chest "—for many years."

He fetched an off-white handkerchief from his coat pocket, pulled off one of his gloves, and plucked a bottle of tablets from the folds of the handkerchief.

"Forgive me," he said as he shook tablets from the bottle. "I have pains. In my head; in my hands."

Ballard waited until he had swallowed the medication before asking him, "Why did you begin to doubt?"

The Russian pocketed the bottle and the handkerchief, his wide face devoid of expression.

"How does a man lose his ... his faith?" he said. "Is it that I saw too much; or too little, perhaps?"

He looked at Ballard's face to see if his hesitant words had made sense. Finding no comprehension there he tried again.

"I think the man who does not believe he is lost, is lost."

The paradox was elegantly put; Ballard's suspicion as to Mironenko's true command of English was confirmed.

"Are you lost *now*?" Ballard inquired.

Mironenko didn't reply. He was pulling his other glove off and staring at his hands. The pills he had swallowed did not seem to be easing the ache he had complained of. He fisted and unfisted his hands like an arthritis sufferer testing the advance of his condition. Not looking up, he said:

"I was taught that the Party had solutions to everything. That made me free from fear."

"And now?"

"Now?" he said. "Now I have strange thoughts. They come to me from nowhere ..."

"Go on," said Ballard.

Mironenko made a tight smile. "You must know me inside out, yes? Even what I dream?"

"Yes," said Ballard.

Mironenko nodded. "It would be the same with us," he said. Then, after a pause: "I've thought sometimes I would break open. Do you understand what I say? I would crack, because there is such rage inside me. And that makes me afraid, Ballard. I think they will see how much I hate them." He looked up at his interrogator. "You must be quick," he said, "or they will discover me. I try not to think of what they will do." Again, he paused. All trace of the smile, however humourless, had gone. "The Directorate has Sections even I don't have knowledge of. Special hospitals, where nobody can go. They have ways to break a man's soul in pieces."

Ballard, ever the pragmatist, wondered if Mironenko's vocabulary wasn't rather high-flown. In the hands of the KGB he doubted if he would be thinking of his *soul's* contentment. After all, it was the body that had the nerve-endings.

They talked for an hour or more, the conversation moving back and forth between politics and personal reminiscence, between trivia and confessional. At the end of the meeting Ballard was in no doubt as to Mironenko's antipathy to his masters. He was, as he had said, a man without faith.

The following day Ballard met with Cripps in the restaurant at the Schweizerhof Hotel, and made his verbal report on Mironenko.

"He's ready and waiting. But he insists we be quick about making up our minds."

"I'm sure he does," Cripps said. His glass eye was troubling him today; the chilly air, he explained, made it sluggish. It moved fractionally more slowly than his real eye, and on occasion Cripps had to nudge it with his fingertip to get it moving.

"We're not going to be rushed into any decision," Cripps said.

"Where's the problem? I don't have any doubt about his commitment; or his desperation."

"So you said," Cripps replied. "Would you like something for dessert?"

"Do you doubt my appraisal? Is that what it is?"

"Have something sweet to finish off, so that I don't feel an utter reprobate."

"You think I'm wrong about him, don't you?" Ballard pressed. When Cripps didn't reply, Ballard leaned across the table. "You do, don't you?"

"I'm just saying there's reason for caution," Cripps said. "If we finally choose to take him on board the Russians are going to be very distressed. We have to be sure the deal's worth the bad weather that comes with it. Things are so dicey at the moment."

"When aren't they?" Ballard replied. "Tell me a time when there wasn't some crisis in the offing?" He settled back in the chair and tried to read Cripps' face. His glass eye was, if anything, more candid than the real one.

"I'm sick of this damn game," Ballard muttered.

The glass eye roved. "Because of the Russian?"

"Maybe."

"Believe me," said Cripps, "I've got good reason to be careful with this man."

"Name one."

"There's nothing verified."

"What have you got on him?" Ballard insisted.

"As I say, rumour," Cripps replied.

"Why wasn't I briefed about it?"

Cripps made a tiny shake of his head. "It's academic now," he said. "You've provided a good report. I just want you to understand that if things don't go the way you think they should it's not because your appraisals aren't trusted."

"I see."

"No you don't," said Cripps. "You're feeling martyred; and I don't altogether blame you."

"So what happens now? I'm supposed to forget I ever met the man?"

"Wouldn't do any harm," said Cripps. "Out of sight, out of mind."

Clearly Cripps didn't trust Ballard to take his own advice. Though Ballard made several discreet enquiries about the Mironenko case in the following week it was plain that his usual circle of contacts had been warned to keep their lips sealed.

As it was, the next news about the case reached Ballard via the pages of the morning papers, in an article about a body found in a house near the station on Kaiser Damm. At the time of reading he had no way of knowing how the account tied up with Mironenko, but there was enough detail in the story to arouse his interest. For one, he had the suspicion that the house named in the article had been used by the Service on occasion; for another, the article described how two unidentified men had almost been caught in the act of removing the body, further suggesting that this was no crime of passion.

About noon, he went to see Cripps at his offices in the hope of coaxing him with some explanation, but Cripps was not available, nor would be, his secretary explained, until further notice; matters arising had taken him back to Munich. Ballard left a message that he wished to speak with him when he returned.

As he stepped into the cold air again, he realized that he'd gained an admirer; a thin-faced individual whose hair had retreated from his brow, leaving a ludicrous forelock at the high-water mark. Ballard knew him in passing from Cripps' entourage but couldn't put a name to the face. It was swiftly provided.

"Suckling," the man said.

"Of course," said Ballard. "Hello."

"I think maybe we should talk, if you have a moment," the man said. His voice was as pinched as his features; Ballard wanted none of his gossip. He was about to refuse the offer when Suckling said: "I suppose you heard what happened to Cripps."

Ballard shook his head. Suckling, delighted to possess this nugget, said again: "We should talk."

They walked along the Kantstrasse towards the Zoo. The street was busy with lunchtime pedestrians, but Ballard scarcely noticed them. The story that Suckling unfolded as they walked demanded his full and absolute attention.

It was simply told. Cripps, it appeared, had made an arrangement to meet with Mironenko in order to make his own assessment of the Russian's integrity. The house in Schöneberg chosen for the meeting had been used on several previous occasions, and had long been considered one of the safest locations in the city. It had not proved so the previous evening however. KGB men had apparently followed Mironenko to the house, and then attempted to break the party up. There was nobody to testify to what had happened subsequently – both the men who had accompanied Cripps, one of them Ballard's old colleague Odell, were dead; Cripps himself was in a coma.

"And Mironenko?" Ballard inquired.

Suckling shrugged. "They took him home to the Motherland, presumably," he said.

Ballard caught a whiff of deceit off the man.

"I'm touched that you're keeping me up to date," he said to Suckling. "But *why*?"

"You and Odell were friends, weren't you?" came the reply. "With Cripps out of the picture you don't have many of those left."

"Is that so?"

"No offence intended," Suckling said hurriedly. "But you've got a reputation as a maverick."

"Get to the point," said Ballard.

"There is no point," Suckling protested. "I just thought you ought to know what had happened. I'm putting my neck on the line here."

"Nice try," said Ballard. He stopped walking. Suckling wandered on a pace or two before turning to find Ballard grinning at him.

"Who sent you?"

"Nobody sent me," Suckling said.

"Clever to send the court gossip. I almost fell for it. You're very plausible."

There wasn't enough fat on Suckling's face to hide the tic in his cheek.

"What do they suspect me of? Do they think I'm conniving with Mironenko, is that it? No, I don't think they're that stupid."

Suckling shook his head, like a doctor in the presence of some incurable disease. "You like making enemies?" he said.

"Occupational hazard. I wouldn't lose any sleep over it. I don't."

"There's change in the air," Suckling said. "I'd make sure you have your answers ready."

"Fuck the answers," Ballard said courteously. "I think it's about time I worked out the right questions."

Sending Suckling to sound him out smacked of desperation. They wanted inside information; but about what? Could they seriously believe he had some involvement with Mironenko; or worse, with the KGB itself? He let his resentment subside; it was stirring up too much mud, and he needed clear water if he was to find his way free of this confusion. In one regard, Suckling was perfectly correct: he *did* have enemies, and with Cripps indisposed he was vulnerable. In such circumstances there were two courses of action. He could return to London, and there lie low, or wait around in Berlin to see what manoeuvre they tried next. He decided on the latter. The charm of hide-and-seek was rapidly wearing thin.

As he turned north onto Leibnizstrasse he caught the reflection of a grey-coated man in a shop window. It was a glimpse, no more, but he had the feeling that he knew the fellow's face. Had they put a watch-dog onto him, he wondered? He turned, and caught the man's eye, holding it. The suspect seemed embarrassed, and looked away. A performance perhaps; and then again, perhaps not. It mattered little, Ballard thought. Let them watch him all they liked. He was guiltless. If indeed there was such a condition this side of insanity.

A strange happiness had found Sergei Mironenko; happiness that came without rhyme or reason, and filled his heart up to overflowing.

Only the previous day circumstances had seemed unendurable. The aching in his hands and head and spine had steadily worsened, and was now accompanied by an itch so demanding he'd had to snip his nails to the flesh to prevent himself doing serious damage. His body, he had concluded, was in revolt against him. It was that thought which he had tried to explain to Ballard: that he was divided from himself, and feared that he would soon be torn apart. But today the fear had gone.

Not so the pains. They were, if anything, worse than they'd been yesterday. His sinews and ligaments ached as if they'd been exercised beyond the limits of their design; there were bruises at all his joints, where blood had broken its banks beneath the skin. But that sense of imminent rebellion had disappeared, to be replaced with a dreamy peacefulness. And at its heart, such happiness.

When he tried to think back over recent events, to work out what had cued this transformation, his memory played tricks. He had been called to meet with Ballard's superior; *that* he remembered. Whether he had gone to the meeting, he did not. The night was a blank.

Ballard would know how things stood, he reasoned. He had liked and trusted the Englishman from the beginning, sensing that despite the many differences between them they were more alike than not. If he let his instinct lead, he would find Ballard, of that he was certain. No doubt the Englishman would be surprised to see him; even angered at first. But when he told Ballard of this new-found happiness surely his trespasses would be forgiven?

Ballard dined late, and drank until later still in The Ring, a small transvestite bar which he had been first taken to by Odell almost two decades ago. No doubt his guide's intention had been to prove his sophistication by showing his raw colleague the decadence of Berlin, but Ballard, though he never felt any sexual *frisson* in the company of The Ring's clientele, had immediately felt at home here. His neutrality was respected; no attempts were made to solicit him. He was simply left to drink and watch the passing parade of genders.

Coming here tonight raised the ghost of Odell, whose name would now be scrubbed from conversation because of his involvement with the Mironenko affair. Ballard had seen this process at work before. History did not forgive failure, unless it was so profound as to achieve a kind of grandeur. For the Odells of the world – ambitious men who had found themselves through little fault of their own in a cul-de-sac from which all retreat was barred – for such men there would be no fine words spoken nor medals struck. There would only be oblivion.

It made him melancholy to think of this, and he drank heavily to keep his thoughts mellow, but when – at two in the morning – he stepped out on to the street his depression was only marginally dulled. The good burghers of Berlin were well a-bed; tomorrow was another working day. Only the sound of traffic from the Kurfürstendamm offered sign of life somewhere near. He made his way towards it, his thoughts fleecy.

Behind him, laughter. A young man – glamorously dressed as a starlet – tottered along the pavement arm in arm with his unsmiling escort. Ballard recognized the transvestite as a regular at the bar; the client, to judge by his sober suit, was an out-of-towner slaking his thirst for boys dressed as girls behind his wife's back. Ballard picked up his pace. The young man's laughter, its musicality patently forced, set his teeth on edge.

He heard somebody running nearby; caught a shadow moving out of the corner of his eye. His watch-dog, most likely. Though alcohol had blurred his instincts, he felt some anxiety surface, the root of which he couldn't fix. He walked on. Featherlight tremors ran in his scalp.

A few yards on, he realized that the laughter from the street behind him had ceased. He glanced over his shoulder, half-expecting to see the boy and his customer embracing. But both had disappeared; slipped off down one of the alleyways, no doubt, to conclude their contract in darkness. Somewhere near, a dog had begun to bark wildly. Ballard turned round to look back the way he'd come, daring the deserted street to display its secrets to him. Whatever was arousing the buzz in his head and the itch on his palms, it was no commonplace anxiety. There was something wrong with the street, despite its show of innocence; it hid terrors.

The bright lights of the Kurfürstendamm were no more than three minutes' walk away, but he didn't want to turn his back on this mystery and take refuge there. Instead he proceeded to walk back the way he'd come, slowly. The dog had now ceased its alarm, and settled into silence; he had only his footsteps for company.

He reached the corner of the first alleyway and peered down it. No light burned at window or doorway. He could sense no living presence in the gloom. He crossed over the alley and walked on to the next. A luxurious stench had crept into the air, which became more lavish yet as he approached the corner. As he breathed it in the buzz in his head deepened to a threat of thunder.

A single light flickered in the throat of the alley, a meagre wash from an upper window. By it, he saw the body of the

out-of-towner, lying sprawled on the ground. He had been so
traumatically mutilated it seemed an attempt might have been
made to turn him inside out. From the spilled innards, that ripe
smell rose in all its complexity.

Ballard had seen violent death before, and thought himself
indifferent to the spectacle. But something here in the alley
threw his calm into disarray. He felt his limbs begin to shake.
And then, from beyond the throw of light, the boy spoke.

"In God's name ..." he said. His voice had lost all pretension
to femininity; it was a murmur of undisguised terror.

Ballard took a step down the alley. Neither the boy, nor the
reason for his whispered prayer, became visible until he had
advanced ten yards. The boy was half-slumped against the wall
amongst the refuse. His sequins and taffeta had been ripped
from him; the body was pale and sexless. He seemed not to
notice Ballard: his eyes were fixed on the deepest shadows.

The shaking in Ballard's limbs worsened as he followed the
boy's gaze; it was all he could do to prevent his teeth from
chattering. Nevertheless he continued his advance, not for the
boy's sake (heroism had little merit, he'd always been taught)
but because he was curious, more than curious, *eager*, to see
what manner of man was capable of such casual violence. To
look into the eyes of such ferocity seemed at that moment the
most important thing in all the world.

Now the boy saw him, and muttered a pitiful appeal, but
Ballard scarcely heard it. He felt other eyes upon him, and their
touch was like a blow. The din in his head took on a sickening
rhythm, like the sound of helicopter rotors. In mere seconds it
mounted to a blinding roar.

Ballard pressed his hands to his eyes, and stumbled back
against the wall, dimly aware that the killer was moving out
of hiding (refuse was overturned) and making his escape. He
felt something brush against him, and opened his eyes in time
to glimpse the man slipping away down the passageway. He
seemed somehow misshapen; his back crooked, his head too
large. Ballard loosed a shout after him, but the berserker ran on,
pausing only to look down at the body before racing towards
the street.

Ballard heaved himself off the wall and stood upright. The noise in his head was diminishing somewhat; the attendant giddiness was passing.

Behind him, the boy had begun sobbing. "Did you see?" he said. "Did you *see*?"

"Who was it? Somebody you knew?"

The boy stared at Ballard like a frightened doe, his mascaraed eyes huge.

"Somebody ... ?" he said.

Ballard was about to repeat the question when there came a shriek of brakes, swiftly followed by the sound of the impact. Leaving the boy to pull his tattered *trousseau* about him, Ballard went back into the street. Voices were raised nearby; he hurried to their source. A large car was straddling the pavement, its head-lights blazing. The driver was being helped from his seat, while his passengers – party-goers to judge by their dress and drink-flushed faces – stood and debated furiously as to how the accident had happened. One of the women was talking about an animal in the road, but another of the passengers corrected her. The body that lay in the gutter where it had been thrown was not that of an animal.

Ballard had seen little of the killer in the alleyway but he knew instinctively that this was he. There was no sign of the malformation he thought he'd glimpsed, however; just a man dressed in a suit that had seen better days, lying face down in a patch of blood. The police had already arrived, and an officer shouted to him to stand away from the body, but Ballard ignored the instruction and went to steal a look at the dead man's face. There was nothing there of the ferocity he had hoped so much to see. But there was much he recognized nevertheless.

The man was Odell.

He told the officers that he had seen nothing of the accident, which was essentially true, and made his escape from the scene before events in the adjacent alley were discovered.

It seemed every corner turned on his route back to his rooms brought a fresh question. Chief amongst them: why had he been lied to about Odell's death?; and what psychosis had seized the man that made him capable of the slaughter Ballard had witnessed? He would not get the answers to these questions from his sometime colleagues, that he knew. The only man whom he might have beguiled an answer from was Cripps. He remembered the debate they'd had about Mironenko, and Cripps' talk of "reasons for caution" when dealing with the Russian. The Glass Eye had known then that there was something in the wind, though surely even he had not envisaged the scale of the present disaster. Two highly valued agents murdered; Mironenko missing, presumed dead; he himself – if Suckling was to be believed – at death's door. And all this begun with Sergei Zakharovich Mironenko, the lost man of Berlin. It seemed his tragedy was infectious.

Tomorrow, Ballard decided, he would find Suckling and squeeze some answers from him. In the meantime, his head and his hands ached, and he wanted sleep. Fatigue compromised sound judgement, and if ever he needed that faculty it was now. But despite his exhaustion sleep eluded him for an hour or more, and when it came it was no comfort. He dreamt whispers; and hard upon them, rising as if to drown them out, the roar of the helicopters. Twice he surfaced from sleep with his head pounding; twice a hunger to understand what the whispers were telling him drove him to the pillow again. When he woke for the third time, the noise between his temples had become crippling; a thought-cancelling assault which made him fear for his sanity. Barely able to see the room through the pain, he crawled from his bed.

"Please ..." he murmured, as if there were somebody to help him from his misery.

A cool voice answered him out of the darkness:

"*What do you want?*"

He didn't question the questioner; merely said:

"Take the pain away."

"*You can do that for yourself,*" the voice told him.

He leaned against the wall, nursing his splitting head, tears of agony coming and coming. "I don't know *how,*" he said.

"*Your dreams give you pain,*" the voice replied, "*so you must forget them. Do you understand? Forget them, and the pain will go.*"

He understood the instruction, but not how to realize it. He had no powers of government in sleep. He was the object of these whispers; not they his. But the voice insisted.

"*The dream means you harm, Ballard. You must bury it. Bury it deep.*"

"Bury it?"

"*Make an image of it, Ballard. Picture it in detail.*"

He did as he was told. He imagined a burial party, and a box; and in the box, this dream. He made them dig deep, as the voice instructed him, so that he would never be able to disinter this hurtful thing again. But even as he imagined the box lowered into the pit he heard its boards creak. The dream would not lie down. It beat against confinement. The boards began to break.

"*Quickly!*" the voice said.

The din of the rotors had risen to a terrifying pitch. Blood had begun to pour from his nostrils; he tasted salt at the back of his throat.

"*Finish it!*" the voice yelled above the tumult. "*Cover it up!*"

Ballard looked into the grave. The box was thrashing from side to side.

"*Cover it, damn you!*"

He tried to make the burial party obey; tried to will them to pick up their shovels and bury the offending thing alive, but they would not. Instead they gazed into the grave as he did and watched as the contents of the box fought for light.

"*No!*" the voice demanded, its fury mounting. "*You must not look!*"

The box danced in the hole. The lid splintered. Briefly, Ballard glimpsed something shining up between the boards.

"*It will kill you!*" the voice said, and as if to prove its point the volume of the sound rose beyond the point of endurance, washing out burial party, box and all in a blaze of pain. Suddenly it seemed that what the voice said was true; that he was near to death. But it wasn't the dream that was conspiring to kill him, but the sentinel they had posted between him and it: this skull-splintering cacophony.

Only now did he realize that he'd fallen on the floor, prostrate beneath this assault. Reaching out blindly he found the wall, and hauled himself towards it, the machines still thundering behind his eyes, the blood hot on his face.

He stood up as best he could and began to move towards the bathroom. Behind him the voice, its tantrum controlled, began its exhortation afresh. It sounded so intimate that he looked round, fully expecting to see the speaker, and he was not disappointed. For a few flickering moments he seemed to be standing in a small, windowless room, its walls painted a uniform white. The light here was bright and dead, and in the centre of the room stood the face behind the voice, smiling.

"*Your dreams give you pain,*" he said. This was the first Commandment again. "*Bury them Ballard, and the pain will pass.*"

Ballard wept like a child; this scrutiny shamed him. He looked away from his tutor to bury his tears.

"*Trust us,*" another voice said, close by. "*We're your friends.*"

He didn't trust their fine words. The very pain they claimed to want to save him from was of their making; it was a stick to beat him with if the dreams came calling.

"*We want to help you.*" one or other of them said.

"No ..." he murmured, "No damn you ... I don't ... I don't believe ..."

The room flickered out, and he was in the bedroom again, clinging to the wall like a climber to a cliff-face. Before they could come for him with more words, more pain, he edged his way to the bathroom door, and stumbled blindly towards the shower. There was a moment of panic while he located the taps, and then the water came on at a rush. It was bitterly cold, but he put his head beneath it, while the onslaught of rotor-blades tried to shake the plates of his skull apart. Icy water trekked down his back, but he let the rain come down on him in a torrent, and by degrees, the helicopters took their leave. He didn't move, though his body juddered with cold, until the last of them had gone; then he sat on the edge of the bath, mopping water from his neck and face and body, and eventually, when his legs felt courageous enough, made his way back into the bedroom.

He lay down on the same crumpled sheets in much the same position as he'd lain in before; yet nothing *was* the same. He didn't know what had changed in him, or how. But he lay there without sleep disturbing his serenity through the remaining hours of the night, trying to puzzle it out, and a little before dawn he remembered the words he had muttered in the face of the delusion. Simple words; but oh, their power.

"I don't believe ..." he said; and the Commandments trembled. It was half an hour before noon when he arrived at the small book exporting firm which served Suckling for cover. He felt quickwitted, despite the disturbance of the night, and rapidly charmed his way past the receptionist and entered Suckling's office unannounced. When Suckling's eyes settled on his visitor he started from his desk as if fired upon.

"Good morning," said Ballard. "I thought it was time we talked."

Suckling's eyes fled to the office-door, which Ballard had left ajar.

"Sorry; is there a draught?" Ballard closed the door gently. "I want to see Cripps," he said.

Suckling waded through the sea of books and manuscripts that threatened to engulf his desk. "Are you out of your mind, coming back here?"

"Tell them I'm a friend of the family," Ballard offered.

"I can't believe you'd be so stupid."

"Just point me to Cripps, and I'll be away."

Suckling ignored him in favour of his tirade. "It's taken two years to establish my credentials here."

Ballard laughed.

"I'm going to report this, damn you!"

"I think you should," said Ballard, turning up the volume. "In the meanwhile: *where's Cripps?*"

Suckling, apparently convinced that he was faced with a lunatic, controlled his apoplexy. "All right," he said. "I'll have somebody call on you; take you to him."

"Not good enough," Ballard replied. He crossed to Suckling in two short strides and took hold of him by his lapel. He'd spent at most three hours with Suckling in ten years, but he'd scarcely passed a moment in his presence without itching to do what he was doing now. Knocking the man's hands away, he pushed

Suckling against the book-lined wall. A stack of volumes, caught by Suckling's heel, toppled.

"Once more," Ballard said. "The old man."

"Take your fucking hands off me," Suckling said, his fury redoubled at being touched.

"Again," said Ballard. "*Cripps.*"

"I'll have you carpeted for this. I'll have you *out!*"

Ballard leaned towards the reddening face, and smiled.

"I'm out anyway. People have died, remember? London needs a sacrificial lamb, and I think I'm it." Suckling's face dropped. "So I've got nothing to lose, have I?" There was no reply. Ballard pressed closer to Suckling, tightening his grip on the man. "*Have I?*"

Suckling's courage failed him. "Cripps is dead," he said.

Ballard didn't release his hold. "You said the same about Odell—" he remarked. At the name, Suckling's eyes widened. "— And I saw him only last night," Ballard said, "out on the town."

"You saw Odell?"

"Oh yes."

Mention of the dead man brought the scene in the alleyway back to mind. The smell of the body; the boy's sobs. There were other faiths, thought Ballard, beyond the one he'd once shared with the creature beneath him. Faiths whose devotions were made in heat and blood, whose dogmas were dreams. Where better to baptize himself into that new faith than here, in the blood of the enemy?

Somewhere, at the very back of his head, he could hear the helicopters, but he wouldn't let them take to the air. He was strong today; his head, his hands, all *strong*. When he drew his nails towards Suckling's eyes the blood came easily. He had a sudden vision of the face beneath the flesh; of Suckling's features stripped to the essence.

"Sir?"

Ballard glanced over his shoulder. The receptionist was standing at the open door.

"Oh. I'm sorry," she said, preparing to withdraw. To judge by her blushes she assumed this was a lover's tryst she'd walked in upon.

"*Stay*," said Suckling. "Mr Ballard ... was just leaving."

Ballard released his prey. There would be other opportunities to have Suckling's life.

"I'll see you again," he said.

Suckling drew a handkerchief from his top pocket and pressed it to his face.

"Depend upon it," he replied.

Now they would come for him, he could have no doubt of that. He was a rogue element, and they would strive to silence him as quickly as possible. The thought did not distress him. Whatever they had tried to make him forget with their brain-washing was more ambitious than they had anticipated; however deeply they had taught him to bury it, it was digging its way back to the surface. He couldn't see it yet, but he knew it was near. More than once on his way back to his rooms he imagined eyes at his back. Maybe he was still being tailed; but his instincts informed him otherwise. The presence he felt close-by – so near that it was sometimes at his shoulder – was perhaps simply another part of him. He felt protected by it, as by a local god.

He had half expected there to be a reception committee awaiting him at his rooms, but there was nobody. Either Suckling had been obliged to delay his alarm-call, or else the upper echelons were still debating their tactics. He pocketed those few keepsakes that he wanted to preserve from their calculating eyes, and left the building again without anyone making a move to stop him.

It felt good to be alive, despite the chill that rendered the grim streets grimmer still. He decided, for no particular reason, to go to the Zoo, which, though he had been visiting the city for two decades, he had never done. As he walked it occurred to him that he'd never been as free as he was now; that he had shed mastery like an old coat. No wonder they feared him. They had good reason.

Kantstrasse was busy, but he cut his way through the pedestrians easily, almost as if they sensed a rare certainty in him and gave him a wide berth. As he approached the entrance to the Zoo, however, somebody jostled him. He looked round to upbraid the fellow, but caught only the back of the man's head as he was submerged in the crowd heading onto Hardenbergstrasse. Suspecting an attempted theft, he checked his pockets, to find that a scrap of paper had been slipped into one. He knew better than to examine it on the spot, but casually glanced round again to see if he recognized the courier. The man had already slipped away.

He delayed his visit to the Zoo and went instead to the Tiergarten, and there – in the wilds of the great park – found a place to read the message. It was from Mironenko, and it requested a meeting to talk of a matter of considerable urgency, naming a house in Marienfelde as a venue. Ballard memorized the details, then shredded the note.

It was perfectly possible that the invitation was a trap of course, set either by his own faction or by the opposition. Perhaps a way to test his allegiance; or to manipulate him into a situation in which he could be easily despatched. Despite such doubts he had no choice but to go however, in the hope that this blind date was indeed with Mironenko. Whatever dangers this rendezvous brought, they were not so new. Indeed, given his long-held doubts of the efficacy of sight, hadn't every date he'd ever made been in some sense *blind*?

By early evening the damp air was thickening towards a fog, and by the time he stepped off the bus on Hildburghauserstrasse it had a good hold on the city, lending the chill new powers to discomfort.

Ballard went quickly through the quiet streets. He scarcely knew the district at all, but its proximity to the Wall bled it of what little charm it might once have possessed. Many of the houses were unoccupied; of those that were not most were sealed off against the night and the cold and the lights that glared from the watch-towers. It was only with the aid of a map that he located the tiny street Mironenko's note had named.

No lights burned in the house. Ballard knocked hard, but there was no answering footstep in the hall. He had anticipated several possible scenarios, but an absence of response at the house had not been amongst them. He knocked again; and again.

It was only then that he heard sounds from within, and finally the door was opened to him. The hallway was painted grey and brown, and lit only by a bare bulb. The man silhouetted against this drab interior was not Mironenko.

"Yes?" he said. "What do you want?" His German was spoken with a distinct Muscovite inflection.

"I'm looking for a friend of mine," Ballard said.

The man, who was almost as broad as the doorway he stood in, shook his head.

"There's nobody here," he said. "Only me."

"I was told—"

"You must have the wrong house."

No sooner had the doorkeeper made the remark than noise erupted from down the dreary hallway. Furniture was being overturned; somebody had begun to shout.

The Russian looked over his shoulder and went to slam the door in Ballard's face, but Ballard's foot was there to stop him. Taking advantage of the man's divided attention, Ballard put his shoulder to the door, and pushed. He was in the hallway – indeed he was half-way down it – before the Russian took a step in pursuit. The sound of demolition had escalated, and was now drowned out by the sound of a man squealing. Ballard followed the sound past the sovereignty of the lone bulb and into gloom at the back of the house. He might well have lost his way at that point but that a door was flung open ahead of him.

The room beyond had scarlet floorboards; they glistened as if freshly painted. And now the decorator appeared in person. His torso had been ripped open from neck to navel. He pressed his hands to the breached dam, but they were useless to stem the flood; his blood came in spurts, and with it, his innards. He met Ballard's gaze, his eyes full to overflowing with death, but his body had not yet received the instruction to lie down and die; it juddered on in a pitiful attempt to escape the scene of execution behind him.

The spectacle had brought Ballard to a halt, and the Russian from the door now took hold of him, and pulled him back into the hallway, shouting into his face. The outburst, in panicked Russian, was beyond Ballard, but he needed no translation of the hands that encircled his throat. The Russian was half his weight again, and had the grip of an expert strangler, but Ballard felt effortlessly the man's superior. He wrenched the attacker's hands from his neck, and struck him across the face. It was a fortuitous blow. The Russian fell back against the staircase, his shouts silenced.

Ballard looked back towards the scarlet room. The dead man had gone, though scraps of flesh had been left on the threshold.

From within, laughter.

Ballard turned to the Russian.

"What in God's name's going on?" he demanded, but the other man simply stared through the open door.

Even as he spoke, the laughter stopped. A shadow moved across the blood-splattered wall of the interior, and a voice said:

"Ballard?"

There was a roughness there, as if the speaker had been shouting all day and night, but it was the voice of Mironenko.

"Don't stand out in the cold," he said, "come on in. And bring Solomonov."

The other man made a bid for the front door, but Ballard had hold of him before he could take two steps.

"There's nothing to be afraid of, Comrade," said Mironenko. "The dog's gone." Despite the reassurance, Solomonov began to sob as Ballard pressed him towards the open door.

Mironenko was right; it *was* warmer inside. And there was no sign of a dog. There was blood in abundance, however. The man Ballard had last seen teetering in the doorway had been dragged back into this abattoir while he and Solomonov had struggled. The body had been treated with astonishing barbarity. The head had been smashed open; the innards were a grim litter underfoot.

Squatting in the shadowy corner of this terrible room, Mironenko. He had been mercilessly beaten, to judge by the swelling about his head and upper torso, but his unshaven face bore a smile for his saviour.

"I knew you'd come," he said. His gaze fell upon Solomonov. "They followed me," he said. "They meant to kill me, I suppose. Is that what you intended, Comrade?"

Solomonov shook with fear – his eyes flitting from the bruised moon of Mironenko's face to the pieces of gut that lay everywhere about – finding nowhere a place of refuge.

"What stopped them?" Ballard asked.

Mironenko stood up. Even this slow movement caused Solomonov to flinch.

"Tell Mr Ballard," Mironenko prompted. "Tell him what happened." Solomonov was too terrified to speak. "He's KGB, of course," Mironenko explained. "Both trusted men. But not trusted enough to be warned, poor idiots. So they were sent to murder me with just a gun and a prayer." He laughed at the thought. "Neither of which were much use in the circumstances."

"I beg you ..." Solomonov murmured, "... let me go. I'll say nothing."

"You'll say what they want you to say, Comrade, the way we all must," Mironenko replied. "Isn't that right, Ballard? All slaves of our faith?"

Ballard watched Mironenko's face closely; there was a fullness there that could not be entirely explained by the bruising. The skin almost seemed to crawl.

"They have made us forgetful," Mironenko said.

"Of what?" Ballard enquired.

"Of ourselves," came the reply, and with it Mironenko moved from his murky corner and into the light.

What had Solomonov and his dead companion done to him? His flesh was a mass of tiny contusions, and there were bloodied lumps at his neck and temples which Ballard might have taken for bruises but that they palpitated, as if something nested beneath the skin. Mironenko made no sign of discomfort however, as he reached out to Solomonov. At his touch the failed assassin lost control of his bladder, but Mironenko's intentions were not murderous. With eerie tenderness he stroked a tear from Solomonov's cheek. "Go back to them," he advised the trembling man. "Tell them what you've seen."

Solomonov seemed scarcely to believe his ears, or else suspected – as did Ballard – that this forgiveness was a sham, and that any attempt to leave, would invite fatal consequences.

But Mironenko pressed his point. "Go on," he said. "Leave us please. Or would you prefer to stay and eat?"

Solomonov took a single, faltering step towards the door. When no blow came he took a second step, and a third, and now he was out of the door and away.

"Tell them!" Mironenko shouted after him. The front door slammed.

"Tell them what?" said Ballard.

"That I've remembered," Mironenko said. "That I've found the skin they stole from me."

For the first time since entering this house, Ballard began to feel queasy. It was not the blood nor the bones underfoot, but a look in Mironenko's eyes. He'd seen eyes as bright once before. But where?

"You—" he said quietly, "you did this."

"Certainly," Mironenko replied.

"How?" Ballard said. There was a familiar thunder climbing from the back of his head. He tried to ignore it, and press some explanation from the Russian. "How, damn you?"

"We are the same," Mironenko replied. "I smell it in you."

"No," said Ballard. The clamour was rising.

"The doctrines are just words. It's not what we're taught but what we *know* that matters. In our marrow; in our souls."

He had talked of souls once before; of places his masters had built in which a man could be broken apart. At the time Ballard had thought such talk mere extravagance; now he wasn't so sure. What was the burial party all about, if not the subjugation of some secret part of him? The marrow-part; the soul-part.

Before Ballard could find the words to express himself, Mironenko froze, his eyes gleaming more brightly than ever.

"They're outside," he said.

"Who are?"

The Russian shrugged. "Does it matter?" he said. "Your side or mine. Either one will silence us if they can."

That much was true.

"We must be quick," he said, and headed for the hallway. The front door stood ajar. Mironenko was there in moments. Ballard followed. Together they slipped out on to the street.

The fog had thickened. It idled around the street-lamps, muddying their light, making every doorway a hiding place. Ballard didn't wait to tempt the pursuers out into the open, but followed Mironenko, who was already well ahead, swift despite his bulk. Ballard had to pick up his pace to keep the man in sight. One moment he was visible, the next the fog closed around him.

The residential property they moved through now gave way to more anonymous buildings, warehouses perhaps, whose walls stretched up into the murky darkness unbroken by windows. Ballard called after him to slow his crippling pace. The Russian halted and turned back to Ballard, his outline wavering in the besieged light. Was it a trick of the fog, or had Mironenko's condition deteriorated in the minutes since they'd left the house? His face seemed to be seeping; the lumps on his neck had swelled further.

"We don't have to run," Ballard said. "They're not following."

"They're always following," Mironenko replied, and as if to give weight to the observation Ballard heard fog-deadened footsteps in a nearby street.

"No time to debate," Mironenko murmured, and turning on his heel, he ran. In seconds, the fog had spirited him away again.

Ballard hesitated another moment. Incautious as it was, he wanted to catch a glimpse of his pursuers so as to know them for the future. But now, as the soft pad of Mironenko's step diminished into silence, he realized that the other footsteps had also ceased. Did they know he was waiting for them? He held his breath, but there was neither sound nor sign of them. The delinquent fog idled on. He seemed to be alone in it. Reluctantly, he gave up waiting and went after the Russian at a run.

A few yards on the road divided. There was no sign of Mironenko in either direction. Cursing his stupidity in lingering behind, Ballard followed the route which was most heavily shrouded in fog. The street was short, and ended at a wall lined with spikes, beyond which there was a park of some kind. The fog clung more tenaciously to this space of damp earth than it did to the street, and Ballard could see no more than four or five yards across the grass from where he stood. But he knew intuitively that he had chosen the right road; that Mironenko had scaled this wall and was waiting for him somewhere close by. Behind him, the fog kept its counsel. Either their pursuers had lost him, or their way, or both. He hoisted himself up on to the wall, avoiding the spikes by a whisper, and dropped down on the opposite side.

The street had seemed pin-drop quiet, but it clearly wasn't, for it was quieter still inside the park. The fog was chillier here, and pressed more insistently upon him as he advanced across the wet grass. The wall behind him – his only point of anchorage in this wasteland – became a ghost of itself, then faded entirely. Committed now, he walked on a few more steps, not certain that he was even taking a straight route. Suddenly the fog curtain was drawn aside and he saw a figure waiting for him a few yards ahead. The bruises now twisted his face so badly Ballard would not have known it to be Mironenko, but that his eyes still burned so brightly.

The man did not wait for Ballard, but turned again and loped off into insolidity, leaving the Englishman to follow, cursing both the chase and the quarry. As he did so, he felt a movement close by. His senses were useless in the clammy embrace of fog and night, but he saw with that other eye, heard with that other ear, and he knew he was not alone. Had Mironenko given up the race and come back to escort him? He spoke the man's name, knowing that in doing so he made his position apparent to any and all, but equally certain that whoever stalked him already knew precisely where he stood.

"Speak," he said.

There was no reply out of the fog.

Then; movement. The fog curled upon itself and Ballard glimpsed a form dividing the veils. Mironenko! He called after the man again, taking several steps through the murk in pursuit and suddenly something was stepping out to meet him. He saw the phantom for a moment only; long enough to glimpse incandescent eyes and teeth grown so vast they wrenched the mouth into a permanent grimace. Of those facts – eyes and teeth – he was certain. Of the other bizarrities – the bristling flesh, the monstrous limbs – he was less sure. Maybe his mind, exhausted with so much noise and pain, was finally losing its grip on the real world; inventing terrors to frighten him back into ignorance.

"Damn you," he said, defying both the thunder that was coming to blind him again and the phantoms he would be blinded to. Almost as if to test his defiance, the fog up ahead shimmered and parted and something that he might have taken for human, but that it had its belly to the ground, slunk into view and out. To his right, he heard growls; to his left, another indeterminate form came and went. He was surrounded, it seemed, by mad men and wild dogs.

And Mironenko; where was he? Part of this assembly, or prey to it? Hearing a half-word spoken behind him, he swung round to see a figure that was plausibly that of the Russian backing into the fog. This time he didn't walk in pursuit, he *ran*, and his speed was rewarded. The figure re-appeared ahead of him, and Ballard stretched to snatch at the man's jacket. His fingers found purchase, and all at once Mironenko was reeling round, a growl in his throat, and Ballard was staring into a face that almost made him cry out. His mouth was a raw wound, the teeth vast, the eyes slits of molten gold; the lumps at his neck had swelled and spread, so that the Russian's head was no longer raised above his body but part of one undivided energy, head becoming torso without an axis intervening.

"Ballard," the beast smiled.

Its voice clung to coherence only with the greatest difficulty, but Ballard heard the remnants of Mironenko there. The more he scanned the simmering flesh, the more appalled he became.

"Don't be afraid," Mironenko said.

"What disease is this?"

"The only disease I ever suffered was forgetfulness, and I'm cured of that—" He grimaced as he spoke, as if each word was shaped in contradiction to the instincts of his throat.

Ballard touched his hand to his head. Despite his revolt against the pain, the noise was rising and rising.

"… You remember too, don't you? You're the same."

"No," Ballard muttered.

Mironenko reached a spine-haired palm to touch him. "Don't be afraid," he said. "You're not alone. There are many of us. Brothers and sisters."

"I'm not your brother," Ballard said. The noise was bad, but the face of Mironenko was worse. Revolted, he turned his back on it, but the Russian only followed him.

"Don't you taste freedom, Ballard? And life. Just a breath away." Ballard walked on, the blood beginning to creep from his nostrils. He let it come. "It only hurts for a while," Mironenko said. "Then the pain goes ..."

Ballard kept his head down, eyes to the earth. Mironenko, seeing that he was making little impression, dropped behind.

"They won't take you back!" he said. "You've seen too much."

The roar of helicopters did not entirely blot these words out. Ballard knew there was truth in them. His step faltered, and through the cacophony he heard Mironenko murmur:

"*Look ...*"

Ahead, the fog had thinned somewhat, and the park wall was visible through rags of mist, Behind him, Mironenko's voice had descended to a snarl.

"*Look at what you are.*"

The rotors roared; Ballard's legs felt as though they would fold up beneath him. But he kept up his advance towards the wall. Within yards of it, Mironenko called after him again, but this time the words had fled altogether. There was only a low growl. Ballard could not resist looking; just once. He glanced over his shoulder.

Again the fog confounded him, but not entirely. For moments that were both an age and yet too brief, Ballard saw the thing that had been Mironenko in all its glory, and at the sight the rotors grew to screaming pitch. He clamped his hands to his face. As he did so a shot rang out; then another; then a volley of shots. He fell to the ground, as much in weakness as in self-defence, and uncovered his eyes to see several human figures moving in the fog. Though he had forgotten their pursuers, they had not forgotten him. They had traced him to the park, and stepped into the midst of this lunacy, and now men and half men and things not men were lost in the fog, and there was bloody confusion on every side. He saw a gunman firing at a shadow, only to have an ally appear from the fog with a bullet in his belly; saw a thing appear on four legs and flit from sight again on two; saw another run by carrying a human head by the hair, and laughing from its snouted face.

The turmoil spilled towards him. Fearing for his life, he stood up and staggered back towards the wall. The cries and shots and snarls went on; he expected either bullet or beast to find him with every step. But he reached the wall alive, and attempted to scale it. His co-ordination had deserted him, however. He had no choice but to follow the wall along its length until he reached the gate.

Behind him the scenes of unmasking and transformation and mistaken identity went on. His enfeebled thoughts turned briefly to Mironenko. Would he, or any of his tribe, survive this massacre?

"Ballard," said a voice in the fog. He couldn't see the speaker, although he recognized the voice. He'd heard it in his delusion, and it had told him lies.

He felt a pin-prick at his neck. The man had come from behind, and was pressing a needle into him.

"Sleep," the voice said. And with the words came oblivion.

At first he couldn't remember the man's name. His mind wandered like a lost child, although his interrogator would time and again demand his attention, speaking to him as though they were old friends. And there was indeed something familiar about his errant eye, that went on its way so much more slowly than its companion. At last, the name came to him.

"You're Cripps," he said.

"Of course I'm Cripps," the man replied. "Is your memory playing tricks? Don't concern yourself. I've given you some suppressants, to keep you from losing your balance. Not that I think that's very likely. You've fought the good fight, Ballard, in spite of considerable provocation. When I think of the way Odell snapped ..." He sighed. "Do you remember last night at all?"

At first his mind's eye was blind. But then the memories began to come. Vague forms moving in a fog.

"The park," he said at last.

"I only just got you out. God knows how many are dead."

"The other … the Russian … ?"

"Mironenko?" Cripps prompted. "I don't know. I'm not in charge any longer, you see; I just stepped in to salvage something if I could. London will need us again, sooner or later. Especially now they know the Russians have a special corps like us. We'd heard rumours of course; and then, after you'd met with him, began to wonder about Mironenko. That's why I set up the meeting. And of course when I saw him, face to face, I *knew*. There's something in the eyes. Something hungry."

"I saw him change—"

"Yes, it's quite a sight, isn't it? The power it unleashes. That's why we developed the programme, you see, to harness that power, to have it work for us. But it's difficult to control. It took years of suppression therapy, slowly burying the desire for transformation, so that what we had left was a man with a beast's faculties. A wolf in sheep's clothing. We thought we had the problem beaten; that if the belief systems didn't keep you subdued the pain response would. But we were wrong." He stood up and crossed to the window. "Now we have to start again."

"Suckling said you'd been wounded."

"No. Merely demoted. Ordered back to London."

"But you're not going."

"I will now; now that I've found you." He looked round at Ballard. "You're my vindication, Ballard. You're living proof that my techniques are viable. You have full knowledge of your condition, yet the therapy holds the leash." He turned back to the window. Rain lashed the glass. Ballard could almost feel it upon his head, upon his back. Cool, sweet rain. For a blissful moment he seemed to be running in it, close to the ground, and the air was full of the scents the downpour had released from the pavements.

"Mironenko said—"

"Forget Mironenko," Cripps told him. "He's dead. You're the last of the old order, Ballard. And the first of the new."

Downstairs, a bell rang. Cripps peered out of the window at the streets below.

"Well, well," he said. "A delegation, come to beg us to return. I hope you're flattered." He went to the door. "Stay here. We needn't show you off tonight. You're weary. Let them wait, eh? Let them sweat." He left the stale room, closing the door behind him. Ballard heard his footsteps on the stairs. The bell was being rung a second time. He got up and crossed to the window. The weariness of the late afternoon light matched his weariness; he and his city were still of one accord, despite the curse that was upon him. Below, a man emerged from the back of the car and crossed to the front door. Even at this acute angle Ballard recognized Suckling.

There were voices in the hallway; and with Suckling's appearance the debate seemed to become more heated. Ballard went to the door, and listened, but his drug-dulled mind could make little sense of the argument. He prayed that Cripps would keep to his word, and not allow them to peer at him. He didn't want to be a beast like Mironenko. It wasn't freedom, was it, to be so terrible?; it was merely a different kind of tyranny. But then he didn't want to be the first of Cripps' heroic new order either. He belonged to nobody, he realized; not even himself. He was hopelessly lost. And yet hadn't Mironenko said at that first meeting that the man who did not believe himself lost, *was* lost? Perhaps better that – better to exist in the twilight between one state and another, to prosper as best he could by doubt and ambiguity – than to suffer the certainties of the tower.

The debate below was gaining in momentum. Ballard opened the door so as to hear better. It was Suckling's voice that met him. The tone was waspish, but no less threatening for that.

"It's over …" he was telling Cripps "… don't you understand plain English?" Cripps made an attempt to protest, but Suckling cut him short. "Either you come in a gentlemanly fashion or Gideon and Sheppard carry you out. Which is it to be?"

"What is this?" Cripps demanded. "You're nobody, Suckling. You're comic relief."

"That was yesterday," the man replied. "There've been some changes made. Every dog has his day, isn't that right? You should know that better than anybody. I'd get a coat if I were you. It's raining."

There was a short silence, then Cripps said:

"All right. I'll come."

"Good man," said Suckling sweetly. "Gideon, go check upstairs."

"I'm alone," said Cripps.

"I believe you," said Suckling. Then to Gideon, "Do it anyway."

Ballard heard somebody move across the hallway, and then a sudden flurry of movement. Cripps was either making an escape-bid or attacking Suckling, one of the two. Suckling shouted out; there was a scuffle. Then, cutting through the confusion, a single shot.

Cripps cried out, then came the sound of him falling.

Now Suckling's voice, thick with fury. "Stupid," he said. "Stupid."

Cripps groaned something which Ballard didn't catch. Had he asked to be dispatched, perhaps, for Suckling told him: "No. You're going back to London. Sheppard, stop him bleeding. Gideon; upstairs."

Ballard backed away from the head of the stairs as Gideon began his ascent. He felt sluggish and inept. There was no way out of this trap. They would corner him and exterminate him. He was a beast; a mad dog in a maze. If he'd only killed Suckling when he'd had the strength to do so. But then what good would that have done? The world was full of men like Suckling, men biding their time until they could show their true colours; vile, soft, secret men. And suddenly the beast seemed to move in Ballard, and he thought of the park and the fog and the smile on the face of Mironenko, and he felt a surge of grief for something he'd never had: the life of a monster.

Gideon was almost at the top of the stairs. Though it could only delay the inevitable by moments, Ballard slipped along the landing and opened the first door he found. It was the bathroom. There was a bolt on the door, which he slipped into place.

The sound of running water filled the room. A piece of guttering had broken, and was delivering a torrent of rain-water onto the window-sill. The sound, and the chill of the bathroom, brought the night of delusions back. He remembered the pain and blood; remembered the shower – water beating on his skull, cleansing him of the taming pain. At the thought, four words came to his lips unbidden.

"I do not believe."

He had been heard.

"There's somebody up here," Gideon called. The man approached the door, and beat on it. "Open up!"

Ballard heard him quite clearly, but didn't reply. His throat was burning, and the roar of rotors was growing louder again. He put his back to the door and despaired.

Suckling was up the stairs and at the door in seconds. "Who's in there?" he demanded to know. "Answer me! Who's in *there?*" Getting no response, he ordered that Cripps be brought upstairs. There was more commotion as the order was obeyed.

"For the last time—" Suckling said.

The pressure was building in Ballard's skull. This time it seemed the din had lethal intentions; his eyes ached, as if about to be blown from their sockets. He caught sight of something in the mirror above the sink; something with gleaming eyes, and again, the words came – "I do not believe" – but this time his throat, hot with other business, could barely pronounce them.

"*Ballard,*" said Suckling. There was triumph in the word. "My God, we've got Ballard as well. This is our lucky day."

No, thought the man in the mirror. There was nobody of that name here. Nobody of any name at all, in fact, for weren't names the first act of faith, the first board in the box you buried freedom in? The thing he was becoming would not be named; nor boxed; nor buried. Never again.

For a moment he lost sight of the bathroom, and found himself hovering above the grave they had made him dig, and in the depths the box danced as its contents fought its premature burial. He could hear the wood splintering – or was it the sound of the door being broken down?

The box-lid flew off. A rain of nails fell on the heads of the burial party. The noise in his head, as if knowing that its torments had proved fruitless, suddenly fled, and with it the delusion. He was back in the bathroom, facing the open door. The men who stared through at him had the faces of fools. Slack, and stupefied with shock – seeing the way he was wrought. Seeing the snout of him, the hair of him, the golden eye and the yellow tooth of him. Their horror elated him.

"Kill it!" said Suckling, and pushed Gideon into the breach. The man already had his gun from his pocket and was levelling it, but his trigger-finger was too slow. The beast snatched his hand and pulped the flesh around the steel. Gideon screamed, and stumbled away down the stairs, ignoring Suckling's shouts.

As the beast raised his hand to sniff the blood on his palm there was a flash of fire, and he felt the blow to his shoulder. Sheppard had no chance to fire a second shot however before his prey was through the door and upon him. Forsaking his gun, he made a futile bid for the stairs, but the beast's hand unsealed the back of his head in one easy stroke. The gunman toppled forward, the narrow landing filling with the smell of him. Forgetting his other enemies, the beast fell upon the offal and ate.

Somebody said: "Ballard."

The beast swallowed down the dead man's eyes in one gulp, like prime oysters.

Again, those syllables. "*Ballard.*" He would have gone on with his meal, but that the sound of weeping pricked his ears. Dead to himself he was, but not to grief. He dropped the meat from his fingers and looked back along the landing.

The man who was crying only wept from one eye; the other gazed on, oddly untouched. But the pain in the living eye was profound indeed. It was *despair*, the beast knew; such suffering was too close to him for the sweetness of transformation to have erased it entirely. The weeping man was locked in the arms of another man, who had his gun placed against the side of his prisoner's head.

"If you make another move," the captor said, "I'll blow his head off. Do you understand me?"

The beast wiped his mouth.

"Tell him, Cripps! He's your baby. Make him understand."

The one-eyed man tried to speak, but words defeated him. Blood from the wound in his abdomen seeped between his fingers.

"Neither of you need die," the captor said. The beast didn't like the music of his voice; it was shrill and deceitful. "London would much prefer to have you alive. So why don't you tell him, Cripps? Tell him I mean him no harm."

The weeping man nodded.

"Ballard ..." he murmured. His voice was softer than the other. The beast listened.

"Tell me, Ballard—" he said, "– how does it feel?"

The beast couldn't quite make sense of the question.

"Please tell me. For curiosity's sake—"

"Damn you—" said Suckling, pressing the gun into Cripps' flesh. "This isn't a debating society."

"Is it good?" Cripps asked, ignoring both man and gun.

"Shut up!"

"Answer me, Ballard. *How does it feel?*"

As he stared into Cripps' despairing eyes the meaning of the sounds he'd uttered came clear, the words falling into place like the pieces of a mosaic. "Is it good?" the man was asking.

Ballard heard laughter in his throat, and found the syllables there to reply.

"Yes," he told the weeping man. "Yes. It's good."

He had not finished his reply before Cripps' hand sped to snatch at Suckling's. Whether he intended suicide or escape nobody would ever know. The trigger-finger twitched, and a bullet flew up through Cripps' head and spread his despair across the ceiling. Suckling threw the body off, and went to level the gun, but the beast was already upon him.

Had he been more of a man, Ballard might have thought to make Suckling suffer, but he had no such perverse ambition. His only thought was to render the enemy extinct as efficiently as possible. Two sharp and lethal blows did it. Once the man was dispatched, Ballard crossed over to where Cripps was lying. His glass eye had escaped destruction. It gazed on fixedly, untouched by the holocaust all around them. Unseating it from the maimed head, Ballard put it in his pocket; then he went out into the rain.

It was dusk. He did not know which district of Berlin he'd been brought to, but his impulses, freed of reason, led him via the back streets and shadows to a wasteland on the outskirts of the city, in the middle of which stood a solitary ruin. It was anybody's guess as to what the building might once have been (an abbatoir? an opera-house?) but by some freak of fate it had escaped demolition, though every other building had been levelled for several hundred yards in each direction. As he made his way across the weed-clogged rubble the wind changed direction by a few degrees and carried the scent of his tribe to him. There were many there, together in the shelter of the ruin. Some leaned their backs against the wall and shared a cigarette; some were perfect wolves, and haunted the darkness like ghosts with golden eyes; yet others might have passed for human entirely, but for their trails.

Though he feared that names would be forbidden amongst this clan, he asked two lovers who were rutting in the shelter of the wall if they knew of a man called Mironenko. The bitch had a smooth and hairless back, and a dozen full teats hanging from her belly.

"Listen," she said.

Ballard listened, and heard somebody talking in a corner of the ruin. The voice ebbed and flowed. He followed the sound across the roofless interior to where a wolf was standing, surrounded by an attentive audience, an open book in its front paws. At Ballard's approach one or two of the audience turned their luminous eyes up to him. The reader halted.

"Ssh!" said one, "the Comrade is reading to us."

It was Mironenko who spoke. Ballard slipped into the ring of listeners beside him, as the reader took up the story afresh.

"*And God blessed them, and God said unto them, Be fruitful, and multiply, and replenish the earth ...*"

Ballard had heard the words before, but tonight they were new.

"*... and subdue it: and have dominion over the fish of the sea, and over the fowl of the air ...*"

He looked around the circle of listeners as the words described their familiar pattern.

"*... and over every living thing that moveth upon the earth.*"

Somewhere near, a beast was crying.

Scott Bradfield

THE DREAM OF THE WOLF

Californian Scott Bradfield divides his time between living in London and on the West Coast of America. After receiving his Ph.D in American Literature at the University of California in Irvine, he taught for five years while his short stories, reviews and essays appeared in a wide variety of magazines and anthologies. His books include The Secret Life of Houses, The History of Luminous Motion, Greetings from Earth *and* What's Wrong with America.

" 'The Dream of the Wolf' originally started out as an actual werewolf story," explains Bradfield, "but I quickly realized I wasn't interested in the physical transformation so much as the emotional one. It's about loneliness, really, and simply the saddest story I could imagine at the time."

After its initial appearance in Interzone, *the story was reprinted in* Omni *and a number of other places, including two college textbooks. It was also adapted by Patrick McGrath into an award-winning episode of the American television series* The Hidden Room. *"I think it's one of the best things I've ever done," says the author. I think you'll agree ...*

> Without the dream
> one would have found no occasion
> for a division of the world.
>
> *Nietzsche*

"Last night I dreamed I was *Canis lupus tundarum*, the Alaskan tundra wolf," Larry Chambers said, confronted by hot Cream

O' Wheat, one jelly donut, black coffee with sugar. "I was surrounded by a vast white plain and sparse gray patches of vegetation. I loped along at a brisk pace, quickening the hot pulse of my blood. I felt extraordinarily swift, hungry, powerful ..." Larry gripped his donut; red jelly squirted across his knuckles. "My jaws were enormous, my paws heavy and calloused." He took a bite, chewed with his mouth open. "My pelt was thick and white and warm. The cold breeze carried aromas of fox, rabbit, caribou, rodent, fowl, mollusc ..."

"Caroline!" Sherryl Chambers reached for the damp dish cloth. "Eat over the table, *please*. Just look at this. You've dripped cereal all over your new shoes."

Caroline gazed up intently at her father, her chin propped against the table edge. Her fist gripped a grainy spoon.

"I heard a noise behind me and I turned." Larry warmed his palms against the white coffee cup. "The mouse hesitated – just for a moment – and then quickly I pounced, pinned him beneath my paw. His eyes were wide with panic, his tiny heart fluttered wildly. His fear blossomed in the air like pollen—"

"What did you do, Daddy? What did you do to the mouse?"

Larry observed the clock radio. *KRQQ helicopter watch for Monday, March twenty-third,* the radio said. *An overturned tanker truck has traffic backed up all the way to Civic Center ...*

"I ate him," Larry said. The time was eight-fifteen.

"Caroline. Finish your cereal before it gets cold."

"But Daddy's a wolf again, Mommy. He caught a mouse and he *ate* it."

"I'm practically certain it was the *tundarum*," Larry said, and pulled on his sport coat.

"Please, Caroline. I won't ask you again."

"But I want the rest of Daddy's donut."

"Finish your cereal. *Then* we'll discuss Daddy's donut."

"I think I'll stop by the library again tonight." Larry got up from the table. His spoon remained gripped by the thickening cereal like a fossil in La Brea.

"Sure, honey. And pick up some milk on the way home, will you? *Try* and remember."

"I will," Larry said, "I'll try," recalling the brilliant white ice, the warm easy taste of the blood.

"And here – bend over." Sherryl moistened the tip of a napkin with her lips. "There's jelly all over your face."

"It's the blood, Daddy. It's the mouse's blood."

"Thanks," Larry said, and went into the living-room.

Caroline watched the kitchen door swing shut. After a few moments she heard the front door open and close.

"Daddy forgot to kiss me goodbye," she said.

Sherryl spilled pots and pans into the sink. "Daddy's a little preoccupied this morning, dear."

Caroline thought for a moment. The bitten jelly donut sat in the middle of the table like a promise.

"Daddy ate a mouse," she said finally, and made a proud little flourish in the air with her spoon.

Canis lupus youngi, canis lupus crassodon, canis niger rufus, Larry thought, and boarded the RTD at Beverly and Fairfax. The wolf, he thought. The wolf of the dream, the wolf of the world. He showed the driver his pass. Wolves in Utah, Northern Mexico, Baffin Island, even Hollywood. Wolves secretly everywhere, Larry thought, and moved down the crowded aisle. Elderly women jostled fitfully in their seats like birds on a wire.

"Larry! Hey – Spaceman!"

Andrew Prytowsky waved his *Wall Street Journal.* "Sit here." He removed his briefcase from the window seat and placed it in his lap. "Rest that frazzled brain of yours. You may need it later."

"Thanks," Larry said, squeezed into the vacant seat and recalled an exotic afternoon nap. *Canis lupus chanco,* Tibetan spring, crepuscular hour. His pack downed a goat. Blood spattered the gray dust like droplets of quivering mercury.

"*That's* earnings, Larry. *That's* reliable income. *That's* retirement security, a summer cottage, a sporty new car." Andrew shook the American Exchange Index at him, as if reproving an unhousebroken puppy. "Fifteen points in two weeks, just like I promised. Did you hear me? *Fifteen* points. Consolidated Plastics Ink. Plastic bullets, the weapon of the future. Cheap, easy to manufacture, minimal production overhead. You could have cut yourself a piece of that, Larry. I certainly gave you every opportunity. But then *my* word's not good enough for you, is it? You've already got your savings account, your fixed interest, your automatic teller, your free promotional albums. You've got yourself a coffin – *that's* what you've got. Fixed interest is going to bury you. Listen to me, pal. I can help. Let's talk tax-free municipal bonds for just one second—"

Larry sighed and gazed out the smudged window. Outside the Natural History Museum sidewalk vendors sold hot dogs, lemonade and pretzels while behind them ancient bones surfaced occasionally from the bubbling tar pit.

"– in the long run we're not just talking safety. We're talking variable income *and* easy liquidity." Prytowsky slapped Larry's chest with the rolled up newspaper. "Get *with* it, Spaceman. What are you, now? Late thirties, early forties? You want to spend the rest of your life with your head in the clouds? Or do you want to come back down to earth and enjoy a little of the *good* life? Your little girl – Carol, Karen, whatever. She may be four or five now, pal, but college is *tomorrow. Tomorrow*, Spaceman. And you want your little girl to go to college, don't you? Well, *don't* you? Of *course* you do! Of *course!*"

The traffic light turned green, the RTD's clutch connected with a sudden sledgehammer sound. Oily gray smoke swirled outside the window.

"And what about that devilish little wife of yours? Take it from me, Spaceman. A woman's eye is *always* looking out for those greener pastures. It's not their *fault*, Spaceman – it's just their *nature* ... Hey, *Larry*." The rolled up newspaper jabbed Larry's side. "You even listening to me or what?"

"Sure," Larry said, and the bus entered Beverly Hills. Exorbitant hood ornaments flashed in the sun like grails. "Easy liquidity, interest variations. I'll think about it. I really will. It's just I have a lot on my mind right now, that's all. I mean, I'll get back to you on all this, I really will." *Canis lupus arabs, pallipes, baileyi, nubilis, monstrabilis*, he thought. The wolves of the dream, the wolves of the world.

"Still having those nutty dreams of yours, Spaceman? Your wife told my wife. You dream you're a dog or something?"

"A wolf. *Canis lupus*. It's not even the same sub-species as a dog."

"Oh." Andrew discarded his newspaper under his seat. "Sure."

"Wolves are far more intelligent than any dog. They're fiercer hunters, loyaler mates. Their social organization alone—"

"Yeah – right, Spaceman. I stand corrected. I'll bet in your dreams you really raise hell with those stupid dogs – hey, Larry, old pal?" Andrew said, and disboarded with his briefcase at Westwood Boulevard.

As the bus approached 27th Avenue Larry moved back through the crowd of passengers who stood and sat about with newspapers, magazines and detached expressions as they vacantly chewed Certs, peanuts from a bag, impassive bubble gum, like a herd of grazing buffalo while the wolf, the wolf of Larry's mind, roamed casually among them, searching out the weak, the sickly, the injured, the ones who always betrayed themselves with brief and anxious glances – the elderly woman with the aluminum walker, the gawky adolescent with the bad complexion and crooked teeth. Wolves in Tibet, Montana, South America, Micronesia, Larry thought, disembarked at 25th Avenue and entered Tower Tyre and Rubber Company. He showed his pass to the security guard, then rode the humming elevator to the twelfth floor. When Larry stepped into the foyer the secretaries, gathered around the receptionist's desk, exchanged quick significant glances like secret memoranda. Larry heard them giggling as he disappeared into the maze of high white partitions that organized office cubicles like discrete cells in an ant farm.

Larry entered his office.

"Ready for Monday?" Marty Cabrillo asked.

Larry hung his coat on the rack, turned.

The Marketing Supervisor stood in front of Larry's aluminum bookshelf, gazing aimlessly at the spines of large gray Acco-Grip binders. "Frankly," Marty said, "I'd rather be in Shasta. How was your weekend?"

"Fine, just fine," Larry said, sat down at his desk and opened the top desk-drawer.

"I thought I'd drop by and see if the Orange County sales figures were in yet. Didn't mean to barge in, you know."

"Certainly. Help yourself." Larry gestured equivocally with his right hand, rummaged in the desk drawer with his left.

"Ed Conklin called from Costa Mesa and said he still hasn't received the Goodyear flyers. I told him no problem – you'd get right back to him. All right?"

"Right." Larry slammed shut one drawer and pulled open another. "No problem. Here we are …" He removed a large faded green hardcover book. One of the book's corners was bloated with dogeared pages. Larry wiped off dust and bits of paper against his trousers. *The Wolves of North America: Part I, Classification of Wolves.*

Marty propped one hand casually in his pocket. "I hope you don't take this the wrong way or anything, Larry … I mean, I'm not trying to pull rank on you or anything. But maybe you could try being just a little bit more careful around here the next few weeks or so. Think of it as a friendly warning, okay?"

Larry looked up from his book.

"It's not me, Larry." Marty placed his hand emphatically over his heart. "You know me, right? But district managers are starting to complain. Late orders, unitemized bills, stuff like that. *Harmless stuff*, really. Nothing I couldn't cover for you. But the guys upstairs aren't so patient – that's all I'm trying to say. I'm just trying to say it's my job, too. All right?"

Finally Larry located the *tundarum's* sub-species guide. *Type locality: Point Barrow, Alaska. Type Specimen: No. 16748, probably female, skull only, US National Museum; collected by Lt. P. H. Ray …*

"But for God's sake don't take any of this personal or anything. It's not really serious. Everybody has their off-days – it's just the way things go. People get, well, *distracted*."

"I knew it." Larry pointed at the page. "Just what I thought. Look – *tundarum* is 'closely allied to *pambisileus*'. Exactly as I suspected. The dentition was a dead giveaway."

Marty fumbled for a cigarette from his shirt pocket, a Bic lighter from his slacks. "Well," he said, and took a long drag from his Kool. Then, after a moment, "You know, Larry, Beatrice and I have always been interested in this ecology stuff ourselves. You should visit our cabin in Shasta sometime. There's nothing like it – clean air, trees, privacy. We even joined the Sierra Club last year … But look, I could talk about this stuff all day, but we've *both* got to get back to work, right?" Marty paused outside the cubicle. "We'll get together and talk about it over lunch sometime, okay? And maybe you could drop the sales figures by my office later? Before noon, maybe?"

That night Larry returned home after the dinner dishes had been washed. He glanced into Caroline's room. She was asleep. Stuffed wolves, cubs, and an incongruous unicorn lay toppled around her on the bed like dominoes. He found Sherryl in the master-bedroom, applying Insta-Curls to her hair and balancing a black rectangular apparatus in her lap.

Larry sat on the edge of the bed, glimpsed himself in the vanity mirror. He had forgotten to shave that morning. His eyes were dark, sunken, feral. (The lone wolf lopes across an empty plain. Late afternoon, clear blue sky. The pale crescent moon appears on the horizon like a spectre. Other wolves howl in the distance.)

Larry turned to his wife. "I went all the way out to the UCLA Research Library, then found out the school's between quarters. The library closed at five."

"That's too bad, dear. Would you plug that in for me?"

Sherryl pulled a plastic cap over her head. Two coiled black wires attached the cap to the black rectangular box. Larry connected the plug to the wall-socket and the black box began to hum. Gradually the plastic cap inflated. "Larry, I wish I knew how to phrase this a bit more delicately, but it's been on my mind a lot lately." Sherryl turned the page of a K-Mart Sweepstakes Sale brochure. "You may not believe this, Larry, but there are actually people in this world who like to talk about some things besides *wolves* every once in a blue moon."

Larry turned again to his reflection. He had forgotten to finish Cabrillo's sales figures. Tomorrow, he assured himself. First thing.

"I remember when we had decent conversations. We went out occasionally. We went to movies, or even dancing. Do you remember the last time we went out together – I mean, just out of the *house*? It was that horrid PTA meeting last fall, with that dreadful woman – the hunchback with the butterfly glasses, you remember? Something about a rummage sale and new tether poles? Do you *know* how long ago that was? And frankly, Larry, I wouldn't call that much of a night *out*."

Larry ran his hand lightly along the smooth edge of the humming black box. "Look, honey. I know I get a little out of hand sometimes ... I *know* that. Especially lately." He placed his hand on his forehead. A soft pressure seemed to be increasing inside his skull, like an inflating plastic cap. "I've been forgetful ... and I realize I must seem a little nutty at times ..." The wolves, he thought, trying to strengthen himself. The call of the pack, the track of the moon, the hot quick pulse of the blood. But the wolves abruptly seemed very far away. "I know you don't understand. *I* don't really understand ... But these aren't just dreams. When I'm a wolf, I'm *real*. The places I see, the feelings I feel – they're *real*. As real as I am now talking to you. As real as this bed." He grasped the king-size silk comforter. "I'm not making all this up ... And I'll *try* to be a little more thoughtful. We'll go out to dinner this weekend, I promise. But try putting up with me a little longer. Give me a little credit, that's all ..."

Sherryl glanced up. She took the humming black box from his hand.

"Did you say something, hon?" She patted the plastic cap. "Hold on and I'll be finished in a minute." She turned another page of the brochure. Then, with a heavy red felt marker, she circled the sale price of Handi-Wipes.

Larry walked into the bathroom and brushed his gleaming white teeth.

"Last night I dreamed of the Pleistocene."

"Where is that, Daddy?"

"It's not a place, honey. It's a time. A long time ago."

"You mean dinosaurs, Daddy? Did you dream you were a *dinosaur*?"

"No, darling. The dinosaurs were all gone by then. I was *canis dirus*, I think. I'll check on it. The tundra was far colder and more desolate than before. The sky was filled with this weird, reddish glow I've never seen before, like the atmosphere of some alien planet. Ice was everywhere. Three of us remained in the pack. My mate had died the previous night beneath a shelf of ice while the rest of us huddled around to keep her warm. Dominant, I led the others across the white ice, my tail slightly erect. We were terribly cold, tired, hungry ..."

"Weren't there any mice, Daddy? Or any snails?"

"No. We had travelled for days. We had discovered no spoor. Except one."

"Was it a deer, Daddy? Did you kill the deer and eat it?"

"No. It was Man's spoor. We were seeking an encampment of men." He turned. Sherryl was beating eggs into a bowl and watching David Hartman on the portable television. "Sherryl, that was the strangest part. I've read about it, anthropologists have suggested it – a prehistoric, communal bond between man and wolf. We weren't afraid. We sought shelter with them, food, companionship, allies in the hunt."

Larry watched his wife. After a moment she said, "That's nice, dear."

David Hartman said, "Later in this half-hour we'll be meeting Lorna Backus to discuss her new hit album, and then take an idyllic trip up the coast to scenic New Hampshire, the Garden State, as part of our "States of the Union" series. Please stay with us."

"I've always wanted to live in New Hampshire," Sherryl said.

Every day on his way home from work Larry stopped at the Fairfax branch library. Many of the books he needed he had to request through inter-library loan. He read Lopez's *Of Wolves and Men*, Fox's *The Soul of the Wolf*, Mech's *The Wolf: the Ecology and Behavior of an Endangered Species*, Pimlott's *The World of the Wolf*, Mowat's *Never Cry Wolf*, Ewer's *The Carnivores*, and the pertinent articles and symposiums published in *American Zoologist, American Scientist, Journal of Zoology, Journal of Mammalogy*, and *The Canadian Field Naturalist*. Sherryl pulled the blankets off the bed one day and three books came loose, thudding onto the floor. "I'd really appreciate it, Larry, if you could start picking up after yourself. It's bad enough with Caroline. And just look – this one's almost a month overdue." Larry returned them to the library that night, checked out three more, and xeroxed the "Canids" essay in *Grzimek's Animal Life Encyclopedia*.

On the way out the door he noticed a three-by-five file card tacked to the Community Billboard. *Spiritual Counselling, Dream Analysis, Budget Rates, Free Parking*. Her name was Anita Louise. She lived on the top floor of a faded Sunset Boulevard brownstone, and claimed to be circuitously related to Tina Louise, the former star of *Gilligan's Island*. Her living-room was furnished with tattered green lawn-chairs and orange-crate bookshelves. She required a personal item; Larry handed her his watch. She closed her eyes. "I can see the wolf now," she said. Her fingers smudged the watch's crystal face, wound the stem, tested the flexible metal band. "While he leads you through the forest of life, he warns you of the thorny paths. When the time comes, he will lead you into Paradise."

"The wolf doesn't guide me," Larry said. "I *am* the wolf. Sometimes *I* am the guide, the leader of my pack."

"The ways of the spirit world are often baffling to those unlearned in its ways," Anita told him. "I take Visa and Mastercard. I take personal checks, but I need to see at least two pieces of ID."

Before he left, Larry reminded her about his watch.

"I don't know, Evelyn. I really just don't know. I mean, I *love* Larry and all, but you can't imagine how difficult life's been around here lately – especially the last few months." Sherryl held the telephone receiver with her left hand, a cold coffee cup with her right. She listened for a moment. "No, Evelyn, I don't think *you* understand. This isn't a hobby. It's not as if Larry was collecting stamps, or a *bowler* or something. I could understand that. *That* would be understandable. But all Larry talks about any more is wolves. Wolves this and wolves that. Wolves at the dinner table, wolves in bed, wolves even when we're driving to the market. Wolves are everywhere, he keeps saying. And honestly, Evelyn, sometimes I almost believe him. I start looking over my shoulder. I hear a dog bark and I make sure the door's bolted ... Well, of *course* I try to be understanding. I'm trying to tell you that. But I have to worry about Caroline too, you know ... Well, listen for a minute and I'll tell you what happened yesterday. We're sitting at breakfast, you see, and Larry starts telling Caroline – a four-year-old girl, remember – how he's off in the woods somewhere, God only knows *where*, and he meets this female dog and, well, I can't go on ... No, I simply can't. It's too embarrassing ... No, Evelyn. You've completely missed the point. It's mating season, get it? And Larry starts going into explicit detail ... Well, maybe. But that's not even the worst part ... Hold *on* for one second and I'll tell you. They, well, I don't know how to phrase this delicately. They get *stuck* ... *No*, Evelyn. Honestly, sometimes I don't think you're even listening to me. They get stuck *together*. Can you believe that? What am I supposed to say? Caroline's not going to outgrow a trauma like this, though. I can promise you that." Sherryl heard the kitchen door opening behind her. "Hold on, Evelyn," she said, and turned.

Caroline blocked the door open with her foot. "What are you talking about?" Her hand gripped the plastic Pez dispenser. Wylie Coyote's head was propped back by her thumb, and a small pink lozenge extruded from his throat.

"It's Evelyn, dear. We're just talking."

Caroline's lips were flushed and purple; purple stains speckled her white dress. She thought for a moment, took the candy with her teeth and chewed. Finally she said, "I think somebody may have spilled grape-juice on one of Daddy's wolf books."

Larry read Guy Endore's *The Werewolf of Paris*, Hesse's *Steppenwolf*, Rowland's *Animals With Human Faces*, Pollard's *Wolves and Werewolves*, Lane's *The Wild Boy of Aveyron*, Malson's *Wolf Children and the Problem of Human Nature*. Marty gave him the card of a Jungian in Topanga Canyon who sat Larry in a plush chair, said "archetype" a few times, informed him that *everyone* is fascinated with evil, sadism, pain ("It's perfectly

normal, perfectly *human*"), recommended Robert Eisler's *Man
Into Wolf*, charged seventy-five dollars and offered him a valium
prescription with refill. "But when I'm a wolf, I never know
evil," Larry said as he was ushered out the door by a blonde
receptionist. "When I'm a wolf, I know only peace."

"I don't know, Larry. It just gives me the creeps," Sherryl
said that night after Caroline was in bed. "It's *weird*, that's
what it is. Bullying defenceless little mice and deer that never
hurt anybody. Talking about killing, and blood, and ice – and
particularly at *breakfast*."

Larry was awake until two a.m. watching *The Wolf Man* on
Channel Five. Claude Raines said, "There's good and evil in
every man's soul. In this case, the evil takes the shape of a wolf."
No, Larry thought, and read Freud's *The Case of the Wolf-Man*,
the first chapter of Mack's *Nightmares and Human Conflict*. No.
Then he went to bed and dreamed of the wolves.

"The wolf-spirit has always been considered very *wakan*,"
Hungry Bear said, his feet propped on his desk. He poked
out his cigarette against the rim of the metal wastebasket, then
prepared to light another. "Most tribes believe the wolf's howl
portends bad things. The Lakota say, 'The man who dreams of
the wolf is not really on his guard, but the man haughtily closes
his eyes, for he is very much on his guard.' I don't know what
that means, exactly, but I read it somewhere." Hungry Bear
refilled his dixie-cup with vin rosé. His grimy teeshirt was taut
against his large stomach; a band of pale skin bordered his belt.
He wore a plaid Irish derby atop his braided hair. "I try to do a
good deal of reading," he said, and fumbled in his diminished
pack of Salems.

"So do I," Larry said. "Maybe you could recommend—"

"I don't think the wolf was ever recognized as any sort of
deity, but I could be wrong." Hungry Bear was watching the
smoke unravel from his cigarette. "But still, you shouldn't be
too worried. It's very common for animal spirits to possess a
man. They use his body when he's asleep. When he awakes, he
can't remember anything ... oh, but wait. That's not quite right,

is it? You said you *remember* your dreams? Well, again, I could be wrong. I guess you *could* remember. Sure, I don't see why not," Hungry Bear said, and poured more vin rosé.

"*I* inhabit the body of the *wolf*," Larry said, beginning to lose interest, and glanced around the cluttered office. The venetian blinds were cracked and dusty, the floors littered with tattered men's magazines, empty wine bottles and crumpled cigarette packs. After a moment he added, "I don't even know what I should call you. *Mister* Bear?"

"No, of course not." Hungry Bear waved away the notion, dispersing smoke. "Call me Jim. That's my real name. Jim Prideux. I took Hungry Bear for business purposes. If you remember, Hungry Bear was the brand name of a terrific canned chili. It was discontinued after the war, though, I'm afraid." He checked his shirt pocket. "Do you see a pack of cigarettes over there? Seems I'm running short."

"You're not Indian?" Larry asked.

"Sure. Of course I'm Indian. One-eighth pure Shoshone. My great-grandmother was a Shoshone princess. Well, maybe not a princess, exactly. But *her* father was an authentic medicine man. I've inherited the gift." Jim Prideux rummaged through the papers on his desk. "Are you sure you don't see them? I'm sure I bought a pack less than an hour ago."

"This is very nice," Sherryl said, and swallowed her last bite of red snapper. She touched her lips delicately with the napkin. "It's *so* nice to get out of the house for a change. You wouldn't know how much."

"Sure I would, darling," Andrew Prytowsky said, and poured more Chenin Blanc.

"No, I don't think you would, Andy. Your wife, Danielle, is *normal*. You wouldn't know what it's like living with someone as … well, as *unstable* as Larry's been acting lately."

"I'm sure it's been very difficult for you."

"Marty Cabrillo, Larry's boss at work, got Larry in touch with a doctor, a *good* doctor. Larry visits him *once* and then tells me he isn't going any more. I say to Larry, don't you think he can help you? And Larry says no, he can't, he can't help him at all. He says the doctor is *stupid*. Can you believe that? I say to Larry, this man has a *Ph.D*. I don't think you can just call a man with a Ph.D. *stupid*. And so then Larry says *I* don't know what *I'm* talking about, either. Larry thinks he knows more than a man with a Ph.D. That's what Larry thinks."

"Here. Why don't you finish it?" Andrew put down the empty bottle and flagged the waiter with his upraised Mastercard.

"I'm sorry, Andy." Sherryl dabbed her eyes with the napkin. "It's just I'm so shook up lately. All I ever asked for was a normal life. That's not too much, is it? A nice home, a normal husband. Someone who could give me a little help and support. Is that too much to ask? Is it?"

"Of course not." Andrew signed the check. After the waiter left he said, "I'm glad we could do this."

Sherryl folded her napkin and replaced it on the table. "I'm glad you called. This was very nice."

"We'll do it again."

"Yes," Sherryl said. "We should."

Two weeks later Larry returned home from work and found the letter on the kitchen table.

> Dear Larry,
>
> I know you're going to take this the wrong way and I only hope you realize Caroline and I still care about you but I've thought about this a lot and even sought professional counselling on one occasion and I think it's the only solution right now at this moment in our lives. Especially Caroline who is at a very tender age. Please don't try calling because I told my mother not to tell you where we are for a while. Please realize I don't want to hurt you and this will probably be better for both of us in the long run, and I hope you make it through your difficulties and I'll think good thoughts for you often.
> Sherryl

"You can't just keep moping around, Larry. Things'll get better, just you wait. I sense big improvements coming in your life. But first you've *got* to start being more careful around the office."

Marty sat on the edge of Larry's desk. He pulled a string of magnetized paper clips in and out of a clear plastic dispenser. "Did I tell you Henderson asked about you yesterday? Asked about you *by name*. Now, I'm not trying to make you paranoid or anything, but if Henderson asked about you then you can bet your socks the *rest* of the guys in Management have been tossing your name around. And Henderson's not a bad guy, Larry. I'm not suggesting that. But there's been a sincere ... a sincere *concern* about your performance around here lately. And don't think I don't understand. Really, Larry, I'm very sensitive to your position. Beatrice and I came close to breaking up a couple times ourselves – and I don't know *what* I'd do without Betty and the kids. But you've got to keep your chin up, buddy. Plow straight ahead. And remember – I'm on *your* side."

At his desk, Larry made careful, persistent marks on a sheet of graph paper. The frequency of dreams had increased over the past few weeks: the line on the graph swooped upwards. Often three, even four times a night he started awake in bed, clicked on the reading lamp and reached for a pen and notepad from the end table, quickly jotting down terrain and sub-species characteristics while the aromas of forest, desert and tundra were displaced by the close stale odors of grimy bedsheets, leftover Swanson frozen dinner entrées, and Johnson's Chlorophyll-Scented Home Deodorizer.

"I'm really sincere about this, Larry. I can't keep covering for you. I need some assurances, I need to start seeing some real *effort* on your part. You're going to start seeing Dave Boudreau on the third floor. He's our employee stress-counsellor – but that doesn't mean he's like a shrink or anything, Larry. I know how you feel about *them*. Dave Boudreau's just a regular guy like you and me who happens to have a lot of experience with these sorts of problems. You and Sherryl, I mean. All right, Larry? Does that sound fair to you?"

"Sure, Marty," Larry said, "I appreciate your help, I really do," and peeled another sheet from the Thrifty pad. Abcissa, he thought: real time. Ordinate: dream time. At the top of the page he scribbled *Pleistocene*.

★   ★   ★

"I'm dreaming now more than ever," Larry told Dave Boudreau the following Thursday. "Sometimes half-a-dozen times each night. Look, I've kept a record—" Larry opened a large red loose-leaf binder, flipped through a sheaf of papers, and unclamped a sheet of graph paper. "There, that's last Friday. Six times." He held the sheet of paper over the desk, pointing at it. "And Sunday – *seven* times. And that's not even the significant part. I haven't even got to *that* part yet."

Dave Boudreau sat behind his desk and rocked slightly in a swivel chair. He glanced politely at the statistical chart. Then his abstract gaze returned to Tahitian surf in a framed travel poster. He heard the binder clamp click again.

Larry pulled up his chair until the armrests knocked the edge of the desk. "Increasingly I dream of the Pleistocene, the Ice Age. The Great Hunt, when man and wolf hunted together, bound by one pack, responsible to one community, seeking their common prey across the cold ice, beneath the cold sun. Is *that* something? Is that one hell of an archetype or what?"

Casually Boudreau opened the manilla folder on his desk.

CHAMBERS, LAWRENCE
SUPPLIES AND SERVICES DEPARTMENT
BORN: 3–6–45 EYES: BLUE

"And don't get me wrong. I'm just kidding about that archetype stuff. That's not even close, that's not even in the same ballpark. These aren't memories, for chrissakes. When I dream of the wolf, I *am* the wolf. I've been wolves in New York, Montana and Beirut. It's as if time and space, dream and reality, have just *opened up*, joined me with everything, everything *real*. I'm living the *one life*, understand? The life of the hunter and the prey, the dream and the world, the blood and the spirit. It's really spectacular, don't you think? Have you ever heard anything like it?"

In the space reserved for Counsellor's Comments Boudreau scribbled "wolf nut," and underlined it three times.

When Larry arrived at work the following Monday the security guard took his ID card and, after consulting his log, asked him to please wait one moment. The guard picked up his phone and asked the operator for Personnel Management. "This is station six. Mr Lawrence Chambers has just arrived." The guard listened quietly to the voice at the other end. He snapped his pencil against the desk in four-four time.

Finally he put down the phone and said, "I'm sorry. I'll have to keep your card. Would you please follow me?"

They walked down the hall to Payroll. Larry was given his final paycheck and, in a separate envelope, another check for employee minimum compensation.

By the time Larry returned home it was still only ten a.m. He cleared the old newspapers from the stoop, unbound and opened the whitest, most recent one. He read for a few minutes, then refolded the paper and placed it with the others beside the fireplace. He picked up Harrington and Paquet's *Wolves of the World* and put it down again. He got up and walked to the kitchen. Dishes piled high in the sink, four full bags of trash. The few remaining dishes in the dishwasher were swirled with white mineral deposits. In the refrigerator he found a garlic bulb with long green shoots, an empty bottle of Worcestershire Sauce, and an egg. He drank stale apple juice from the plastic green pitcher, then continued making his rounds. In the bathroom: toothpaste, toothbrush, comb, water glass, eyedrops, Mercurochrome, a stray bandage, Sherryl's Ph-balanced Spring Mountain Shampoo, his electric razor. All the clothes and toys were gone from Caroline's room. Over the bed the poster of a wolf gazed down at him, its eyes sharp, canny, primitively alert.

He tried to watch television. People won sailboats and trash-compacters on game shows, cheated one another and plotted financial coups on soap operas. After a while he got up again and returned to the bathroom, opened the medicine cabinet. Johnson's Baby Aspirin, an old stiffened toothbrush, mouthwash, a bobby-pin. High on the top shelf he found Sherryl's Seconal in a child-proof bottle. He took two. Then he got into bed.

Sometime after dawn he dreamed again of the wolves, but this time the dream was fragmentary and detached. He viewed the wolves from very far away. From atop a high bluff, perhaps, or hidden behind some bushes like Jane Goodall. The wolves moved down into the gully and paused before a small stream, drinking. Two cubs splashed and chased one another through the puddles. The other wolves observed them dispassionately. The sun was going down. Larry woke up. It was just past six a.m.

He stayed indoors throughout the day. In the evening he might walk to the corner Liquor Mart to cash a check and purchase milk, Scotch, Stouffer's frozen dinners. Sometimes, remembering Sherryl and Caroline, he turned the television up louder. It wasn't their physical presence he missed (he could hardly recall their faces any more) but rather their noise: the clatter of dishes, the inconstant whir and jingle of mechanical toys. Soundless, the air seemed thinner, staler, more oppressive, as if he were sealed inside an air-tight crystal vault. The silence invested everything – the walls, the furniture, the diminishing vial of Seconal, the large empty bedrooms, even the mindless chatter of the Flintstones on television. He drank his beer beside the front window and watched the dust swirl soundlessly in the soundless shafts of light, recalling the wolves and the soundless expanse of white ice where not only the noise but even the aromas and textures of the landscape seemed to be leaking from the dreamlike atmosphere from the cracks in some domed underwater city. In the mornings, now, he hardly recalled his dreams at all any more. Sporadic glimpses of wolf, prey, sky, moon, interspliced meaninglessly like the frames of some surrealist montage. He smoked three packs of cigarettes a day, just to give his hands something to do. The Scotch and Seconal compelled him to take so many naps during the day that he couldn't sleep at night. Wolves, he thought. Wolves in Utah, Baffin Island, Tibet, even Hollywood. Wolves secretly everywhere ... Eventually the dreams disappeared entirely. Sleep became a dark visionless place where nothing ever happened.

The Seconal, he thought one morning, and departed for the library. He squinted at the sunlight, staggered occasionally. People looked at him. A book entitled *Sleep* by Gay Gaer Luce and Julius Siegal confirmed his suspicions. Alcohol and barbiturates suppressed the dream stage of sleep. He returned home and poured the Scotch down the sink, the remaining

Seconal down the toilet. He lay in bed throughout the afternoon, night and following morning. He tossed and turned. He couldn't keep his eyes closed more than a minute. His heart palpitated disconcertingly. He tried to remember the wolf's image, and remembered only pictures in books. He tried to recall the prey's hot steaming blood, and tasted only yesterday's Chicken McNuggets. He wanted the map of the sky, and found only the close humid rectangle of the bedroom. He got up and went into the living-room. It was night again. In order to dream, he must sleep. In order to regain the real, he must dispel the illusion: newspapers, furniture, unswept carpets, Sherryl's letter, Caroline's toys, easy liquidity, magazines and books. He realized then that evil was not the wolf, but rather the wolf's disavowal. Violence wasn't something in nature, but rather something in nature's systematic repression. Madness isn't the dream, but rather the world deprived of the dream, he thought, selected a stale pretzel from the bowl, chewed, and gazed out the window at the dim, empty streets below where occasional streetlamps illuminated silent, unoccupied cars parked along the curbs. The moon made a faint impression against the high screen of fog. A distant siren wailed, a dog barked, and in their homes the population slept fitfully, often aided by Seconal and Dilantin, descending through soft penetrable stages of sleep, seeking that fugitive half-world in which they struggled to dream beneath the repressive shadows of the real.

A few weeks after signing Larry Chambers' termination notice, Marty Cabrillo took his wife to Shasta. "Two weeks alone," he promised her. "We'll leave the kids with your mother. Just the two of us, the trees, candlelight dinners again, just like I always said it would be." But Marty said nothing during the long drive. Beatrice put her arm around him and he shrugged at her. "Please," he said. "I can't get comfortable." At the cabin they sat out on the sundeck. Marty held paperbacks and turned the pages. Beatrice read *People Magazine*. After only a few days they returned home. "I'm sorry, honey," Marty said to her. "I'll make it up to you. I promise."

"What's the matter with you lately?"

"Nothing. Just things on my mind."

"Work?"

"Sort of."

After a while Beatrice said, "Larry," folded her arms, and gazed out the window at Ventura car-lots.

The following Sunday Marty drove to *Ralph's* in Fairfax, loaded four bags of groceries into his Toyota station wagon, and drove to Larry's house on Clifton Boulevard. The front yard was brown and overgrown. Aluminum garbage cans, streaked with rust, lay overturned in the alley. Dormant snails studded the front of the house, their slick intricate trails glistening in the sunlight. Marty knocked, rang the bell a few times. The door was ajar and he pushed it open. A pyramid of bundled newspapers blocked the door, permitting him just to squeeze through. In the living-room, torn magazines and mouldy dishes lay strewn across the sofa, chairs and floor. The telephone receiver was off the hook, wailing faintly like a distant, premonitory siren. At first the room seemed oddly disproportionate, as if the furniture had all been rearranged. Then he noticed Larry asleep on the middle of the floor, his head propped by a sofa cushion, his arm wrapped around a leg of the coffee table. "He must've lost eighty, ninety pounds," Marty told Beatrice later that night. "His clothes stank, he hadn't shaved or washed in I don't know how long. And all I could think looking at him there was it's all *my* fault. I was responsible. Me, Marty Cabrillo."

Marty followed the ambulance to St John's, wishing they would run the siren. "Dehydration," the doctor told him, while Marty paid the deposit on a private room. Larry lay in a stiff, geometric white bed, a glucose bottle hanging beside him, a white tube connected to his arm by white adhesive tape. Every so often the glucose bubbled. "We'll bring him along slow, have him eating solid food in a couple days. I think he'll be all right," the doctor said, and handed Marty another form to sign.

"It's all my fault," Marty said when Larry regained consciousness the following morning. "Look, I brought you some books to read. And the flowers – they're from Sherryl. Beatrice got in touch with her last night and she's on her way here right now. The worst is over, pal. The worst is all behind you."

Later Sherryl told him, "We missed you. Caroline missed you. *I* missed you. Oh, Larry. You just look so *awful*." Sherryl laid her head in Larry's lap and cried, hugging him. Silently Larry stroked her long blonde hair. Sherryl had been staying with her sister in Burbank, working as a secretary at one of the studios. Her boss was a flushed, obese little man who put his hand on her knee while she took dictation, or snuck up behind her every once in a while and gave her a sharp pinch. "Loosen up, relax. Life's short," he told her. Caroline hated her new nursery school and cried nearly every day. Sherryl's sister had begun bringing the Classified Pages home, pointing out to her the best bets on her own apartment. Andy had promised to help out, but every time she called his office his secretary said he was still out of town on business. And then one of the Volvo's tyres went flat, and in all the rush of moving she realized she had misplaced her triple-A card, and so she just started crying, right there on the side of the freeway, because it seemed as if nothing, nothing ever went right for her any more.

"We need you, Larry," Sherryl said. "You need us. I'm sorry what happened, but I always loved you. It wasn't because I didn't love you. And Marty thinks he can get your old job back—"

Marty leaned forward, whispered something.

"He says he's certain. He's certain he can get it back. Did you hear, honey? Everything's going to be all right. We're all going to be happy again, just like before."

Sherryl brought Caroline home a month later.

"Is Daddy home?" Caroline asked.

"He's at work now, honey. But he'll be back soon. He's missed you."

Caroline waited to be unbuckled, climbed out of the car. The front yard was green and delicate, the house repainted yellow. The place seemed only dimly familiar, like the photograph Mommy showed her of where she lived when she was born.

"All your toys are in your room, sweetheart. Be good and play for a while. Mommy'll fix dinner."

Caroline's room had been repainted, too. Over her bed hung a bright new Yosemite Sam poster. She opened the oak toy-chest.

The toys were boxed and neatly arranged, just like on shelves at the store. She went into the bedroom and looked at Daddy's bookcase. The large picture books were gone, along with their photographs of wolves and deer and rabbits and forests and men with rifles and hairy, mis-shapen primitive men. Bent paperbacks had replaced them. The covers depicted beautiful men and women, Nazi insignia, secret dossiers, demonic children, cowboys on horses, murder weapons.

She heard the front door open. "Hi, honey. Sorry I'm late. I ran into Andy Prytowsky on the bus – remember him? I introduced you at a party last year. Anyway, I told him I'd drop by his office tomorrow. I figure it's time we started some sort of college fund for Caroline. I'm pretty excited about it. Andy says he can work us a nice little tax break, too. Oh, and look what else. I bought us some wine. For later."

Caroline walked halfway down the hall. Mummy and Daddy stood at the door, kissing.

"There she is. There's my little girl."

Daddy picked her up high in the air. His face seemed strange and unfamiliar, like the front of the house.

"So how have you been, sweetheart?" Daddy put her down.

"I'll finish dinner," Sherryl said.

"Come and sit down." Daddy led her to the sofa. "Tell me what you've been up to. Did you have fun at Aunt Judy's?"

Caroline picked at a scab on her knee. "I guess."

"What do you want to do? I thought we'd go to a movie later. Would you like that?"

Caroline clasped her hands in her lap. Here is the church, and here is the steeple. When you open the doors you see all the people.

"What should we do right now? Do you want to play a game? Do you want me to read you one of your Dr Seuss books?"

Caroline thought for a while. Daddy's large rough hand ran through her hair, snagging it. Delicately, she pushed his hand away.

"I want to watch television," she said after a while.

*   *   *

Three nights each week Larry went to the YMCA with Marty. Sherryl began subscribing to *Sunset Magazine*, and over dinner they discussed a new home, or at least improvements on their present one. Finally Marty suggested they buy into his Shasta property. "Betty and I don't make it up there more than three or four times a year. The rest of the time it'd be all yours." Larry took out a second mortgage, paid Marty a lump sum, and began sharing the monthly payments. The first few months they drove up nearly every weekend. Then Larry received a promotion which required him to make weekly trips to the Bakersfield office. "I'm really bushed from all this driving," he told Sherryl. "We'll try and make Shasta *next* weekend." Caroline started grade school in the fall. Sherryl joined an ERA support group and was gone two nights a week. Occasionally Larry spent the night in Bakersfield, and drove from there directly to work the next morning.

"All I told Conklin was I've got a merchandise deficit from his store three months in a row. It wasn't like I called him a thief or anything. I just wanted an explanation. I'm entitled to that much, don't you think? It's my job, right?"

"I'm sure he didn't mean it, Larry. He was probably just upset." Sherryl sat on the sofa, smoking a cigarette.

"I'm sure he *was* upset. I'm sure he *was*." Larry sat at the dining-room table. The table was covered with inventories, company billing statements, and large gray Acco-Grip binders. His briefcase sat open on the chair beside him. "And now *I'm* a little upset, all right? Is that all right with you?"

"I'm sure you are, Larry. I was just saying maybe he didn't mean it, that's all. That's all I said."

Larry put down his pencil. "No. I don't think that's all you said."

Sherryl looked at the *TV Guide* on the coffee table, considered picking it up. Then she thought she heard Caroline's bedroom door squeak open down the hall.

"What you said was I'm imagining things. Isn't *that* what you said?"

Sherryl crushed out her cigarette. "Larry, I really wish you'd stop snapping at *me* every time you're mad at somebody." She got up and went to the end of the hall. "Caroline? Aren't you supposed to be in bed?"

Caroline's door squeaked shut. Sherryl watched the parallelogram of light on the hall floor diminish to a fine yellow line. "And turn off those lights, young lady. You heard me. Right now," Sherryl said. In high school Billy Mason had a crush on me, she thought, but I wouldn't give him the time of day. That morning she had seen Billy's picture on the cover of *Software World* at the supermarket.

"What I mean is, Larry, is that you're not the *only* person who's had a bad day sometimes—"

Sherryl was turning to face him when the telephone rang.

"Sometimes *my* day hasn't been that hot either," she said, and retreated to the telephone, picked up the receiver. "Hello?"

"Hi. Hello," the voice said. "I was hoping, well, I mean I didn't want to disturb anybody, but I wondered if Mr Chambers was in. Mr *Larry* Chambers, I think? Have I got that right?"

"This is his wife. Who's this?"

"Who is it?" Larry asked, picking up his pencil and jotting a number on his note pad.

Sherryl gazed expressionlessly over Larry's head at the dining-room window and, beyond, the 7–11 marquee. The voice on the phone filled her ears like radio static. "—I mean, I just had the article here a moment ago, let me see … Look, tell him Hungry Bear called, and by the time he calls back I'll find the article – wait, in fact here it is right here – no, sorry, *that's* not it. But still, tell him Jim called. Jim Prideux—" Sherryl looked around the kitchen. She had forgotten to clean up after dinner. The sink was filled with dirty dishes, the counter top littered with bread crumbs. Stray Cheerios from that morning's breakfast had attached themselves like barnacles to the formica table. She pulled up a chair and sat down, feeling suddenly tired. There was a television movie she had been looking forward to all week, and now, by the time she finished her cleaning, the show would practically be half over. She felt like saying to hell with it, to hell with all of it. She just wanted to go to bed. To hell with Larry, Caroline, the dishes, the vacuuming – every damn bit of it. The voice buzzed inconstantly in her ear like a mosquito, something about wolves, Navajo deities, sacred totems, irrepressible dreams of wolves, he wasn't exactly sure … Wolves wolves wolves, wolves everywhere, she thought, and strengthened her grip on the receiver. "Listen to me," she said. "Listen to me, Mr Bear, or Mr Prideux, or Mr Whoever You Are. Listen to me for just one minute, and I'll say this as *nicely* as I can. Please don't call here any more. Larry's not interested, *I'm* not interested. Frankly, Mr Bear, I don't think *anybody's* interested. I don't think anybody's really interested at all."

In Sherryl's dream the men and wolves loped together across the white plain. Larry was there, and Caroline, and Andy and Evelyn and Marty and Beatrice. Sherryl recognised the mailman, the newspaper boy, supermarket employees, former boyfriends and lovers. Even her parents were there, keeping pace with wolves under the cold moonlight. Everybody was dressed as usual: the men wore slacks, ties, cufflinks and starched shirts, the women skirts, blouses, jewelry and high heels. Caroline carried one of her toys, Andy his briefcase, Marty his racquetball racquet, and Larry one of his largest gray Acco-Grip binders. Sherryl raised a greasy spatula in her right hand, a tarnished coffee pot in her left. We forgot to schedule Caroline's dental appointment, she told Larry. When I was a child you treated me as if I was stupid, she told her father, but I wasn't stupid. The sky is filled with stars, she told Davey Stewart, her high school sweetheart. The Milky Way: the Wolf's Trail. But nobody responded, nobody even seemed to notice her. The bright air was laced with the spoor of caribou. She felt a sudden elbow in her back, she turned and awoke in a dark room, a stiff bed. I forgot the shopping today, she thought. There isn't any milk in the house, or any coffee.

Beside her in bed, the man slowly moved.

Sherryl sat up, her pupils gradually dilating. Eventually she discerned the motel room's clean uncluttered angles. The thin and fragile dressing table, the water glasses wrapped in wax paper, the hot-plate, the aluminum hot cocoa packets.

"What's the matter, baby?" Andrew sat up beside her, his arm encircling her waist. "Nightmare? Tell me, sweetheart. You can tell lover." He kissed her neck, stroked her warm stomach.

"Please, Andy. Not now. Please." Sherryl climbed out of bed. Her clothes lay folded on a wooden chair.

"Sorry. Forget it." Andrew rolled over, adjusted his pillow, and listened to the rustle of Sherryl's clothing.

Sherryl stood at the window, gazing out through the blinds. Stars and moon were occluded by a high haze of lamplight. She heard the distant hissing of streetsweepers, and pulled on her blouse. Then she heard the rain begin, drumming hollowly against the cheap plywood door.

Andrew took his watch from the end table. The luminous dial said almost two a.m. "I'll call you," he said.

"No," she said. "I'll call you this time. I need a few days to think." She opened the door and stepped out into the rain. They always do that, she thought. *They* have to be the ones who call, *they* have to be the ones who say when you'll meet or where you'll go. She pulled her coat-collar up over her new perm, gripped the iron bannister, and descended one step at a time on darkling high heels. Puddles were already gathering on the warped cement stairs. "It's as if we don't have any brains of our own," she imagined herself telling Evelyn. "And I'm sure that's just what they think. That we haven't got the brains we were born with. That we have to be told *everything*." By the time she climbed into the Volvo the rain had ceased, as abruptly as if someone had just thrown a switch. Her coat was soaked through, and she laid it out on the back seat to dry.

At this hour, the streets were practically deserted. She drove past a succession of shops and restaurants: Bob's Big Boy, Li'l Pickle Sandwiches, Al's Exotic Birds, Ralph's Market. Inside Long's Drugs empty aisles of hair supplies, pet food, household appliances and vitamin supplements were illuminated by pale, watery fluorescents, like the inside of an aquarium. 'It's not as if we couldn't do just as well without them," she would continue, awaiting Evelyn's quick nods of agreement. "I certainly didn't need to get married. I could have done just as well on my own. It's not as if it's some *man's* secret how to get by in this world. It's just a matter of keeping your feet on the ground, being objective about things, not fooling yourself. That's all there is to it. That's the big secret."

As she turned onto Beverly Glen her high-beams, sweeping through an alleyway, reflected off a pair of attentive red eyes. Being realistic, she thought, and heard the wolves emerge from alleyways, abandoned buildings, underground parking garages, their black calloused paws pattering like rain against the damp streets. They loped alongside her car for short distances, trailed off to gobble stray snails and mice, paused to bite and scratch their fleas. She refused to look, driving on through the deserted city. The alternating traffic lights cast shifting patterns and colors across the glimmering asphalt, like rotating spotlights on aluminum Christmas trees. Wolves, men, lovers, cars, streets, cities, worlds, stars. The real and the unreal, the true and the untrue. Unless you're careful it all starts looking like a dream, it all seems pretty strange and impossible, she thought, while all across the city the wolves began to howl.

Ramsey Campbell

NIGHT BEAT

Ramsey Campbell is the most respected living British horror writer. He is a multiple winner of the World Fantasy Award, the British Fantasy Award and the HWA Bram Stoker Award. After working in the civil service and public libraries, he became a full-time writer in 1973.

He has written hundreds of short stories (most recently collected in Ghosts and Grisly Things, Told by the Dead *and* Inconsequential Tales*), while his novels include* The Doll Who Ate His Mother, The Face That Must Die, The Parasite, The Nameless, The Claw, Incarnate, Obsession, The Hungry Moon, The Influence, Ancient Images, Midnight Sun, The Count of Eleven, The Long Lost, The One Safe Place, The House on Nazareth Hill, The Last Voice They Hear, Silent Children, Pact of the Fathers, The Darkest Part of the Woods, The Overnight, Secret Stories, The Grin of the Dark *and* Thieving Fear.

His reviews of obscure DVDs, "Ramsey's Rambles", appears in each issue of Video Watchdog, *and "Ramsey Campbell, Probably" is a regular non-fiction column in* All Hallows *magazine.*

The following, EC comics-inspired story makes its book debut here for the first time.

Almost exactly three weeks ago. Constable Sloane had visited the exhibition. Now, as he stood outside the museum at midnight, his thoughts were elsewhere. Streetlamps marched up the hill on which he stood, their lights padded by mist; cars laboured up the carriageway, reached the summit and sped away – but he hardly noticed their speed or their numbers, for his thoughts had returned to the murder.

It had been the night of the day on which he had visited the exhibition. What mattered, though, was that it had been his first month on a beat: and it mattered more that when his radio had called him to view the corpse thrown broken among the bricks of a disintegrating alley leading from one of his main roads, the older policemen who had discovered the body had had to drive him back to the station, where he had sat white and shaking, gulping cups of tea. Of course his superiors had been sympathetic: he was young, he had never seen death before – they had even excluded him from the investigation which would be concentrated on his beat, and insisted that he confine himself to the calmer city centre for a while. He had barely been able to persuade them not to give him a companion, for he knew that it had not been the corpse which had left him shaking, not the mutilations or the blood. When he looked back on that night, he felt that he had been shaking with shame and fury: for he could have led them to the murderer.

And he had been furious because he knew that they would never have countenanced his method. Intuition was no part of police procedure. Yet ever since his childhood he had been able intuitively to sense sources of violence. He felt profoundly what his superiors wearily accepted: that violence surrounds us all. His first beat had led him through both suburbia and slums; and if each broken bottle outside a pub hinted terror to him, equally he felt the presence of violence in quiet suburban roads behind the ranks of sleeping cars, knew instinctively which set of patterned curtains concealed shouts of rage, the smash of china, screams. Sometimes he was honest with himself, and admitted that it was the violence buried in him that recognized these sources, reached out to them. But now this was forgotten, for never had he felt the imminence of violence so powerfully as here. When they'd moved him to the city centre neither he nor they had realized what they had done. Last night he had passed the museum and had come alert; tonight he knew. Within the museum lay the source of that murder.

His radio hissed and spat. For a second he thought of calling Central for help, but then he half-smiled bitterly: he had no evidence, they would only think that the murder had unbalanced him completely. Yet he was determined to act; once he had conquered his fear of the surrounding violence he had become obsessed with the suppression of violence – and as well, this murder had stained his beat. He thrust the radio into his pocket and started up the steps to the museum.

When he knocked on the doors the glass panes shuddered. They were a meagre protection against the violence within. After a minute Sloane saw a light bobbing closer through the wide dark foyer. As the light found Sloane and held him, a figure formed darkly about it; a face swelled from the shadows like a wrinkled half-inflated balloon. At a childhood party Sloane had dulled and grown more taciturn as the evening wore on; tired of trying to rouse him to play, the other children had buffeted him with balloons. "What's all this about, son?" the caretaker demanded.

Now that the doors of the museum were open the sense of violence seemed stronger; Sloane could scarcely remember his lies. "A routine check, sir," he said.

"What routine's that, son? What's up?"

"We've had a few robberies around here recently. I'd like to look around, if you don't mind. Just to check."

The watchman hawked and gave Sloane room to pass. The foyer was high, reaching above the light; Sloane felt the cold arch of the ceiling. The walls were walled by darkness; painted faces glimmered dimly in the void. "Can we have the lights on, please?" Sloane asked.

"You'd have to ask the curator for that, son. But he'll be home in bed." He was obviously triumphant. Sloane frowned and the man came closer, nipping Sloane's arm with his fingers and apologizing with a lopsided alcoholic smile. "You can have my torch for a few minutes if you ask nicely."

"I'm sure you don't want to obstruct the law. You seem a bit unsteady – perhaps you ought to sit down."

"You can't have it unless I've got a spare battery." The caretaker sidled into his office behind the marble staircase and rummaged in the drawers of a dark table. Above the table a white lampshade was bearded with a single strand of cobweb; on the table, next to a sagging moist rectangle outlined in rum, lay an open copy of *True Detective Confessions*. "You're lucky," the caretaker said, passing Sloane the torch.

Sloane felt violence massing in the room. "I won't be long," he said.

"Don't you worry your head about that, son. I'll come round with you."

As Sloane emerged from the office the torch's beam touched a globe of the world standing at the entrance to the Planetarium. Above the globe a moon was balanced on a wire; a dim crescent coated its edge. Sloane crossed to the staircase and the crescent expanded. At the same time the caretaker moved behind him. Sloane flexed his shoulders as if to shake off the violence which he felt looming.

The staircase climbed through a void across which their footsteps rang. The marble was slippery and sharp; Sloane glanced back at the caretaker and hurried to the top. A finger on a marble pillar pointed to THE HISTORY OF MAN. The torch-beam led him through an archway and fastened on a crumpled yellow paper mask inexpertly smoothed: a mummy's face.

"These are their specimens, here," the caretaker said behind him. "This is where thieves would be hiding, son, among the bodies, eh?"

He can move faster than I thought, Sloane realized. He peered at the man behind him, redolent of alcohol, one hand on a case containing the dark handle of a Cro-Magnon jaw. The air was thick with inertia; even the violence hung inert, and the caretaker seemed embalmed as the mummy. "Not here," Sloane said.

As he crossed the marble landing, his heels clanking like boots of armour, Sloane felt the violence swell to meet him. He halted, afraid. "I'll show you this room, son," the caretaker said. "It's where I take my pride."

The torch-beam splayed out beyond the figure of the caretaker, a star of darkness shone from his limbs; Sloane moved aside to see at once what was beyond the second archway. As the light plunged in, moons sprang up in glass cases, slid from the blades of swords and axes. "Tell me those aren't good as new," the caretaker said. "They can't say I don't keep these clean, son, that's a fact. I'd be in here like a shot if I heard a thief. Take his head off quick as that, I would."

Aggression stirred. "You wouldn't need me, then," Sloane said.

"When you've seen as much as I have, son, then I'll need you."

Although he could feel the violence mounting Sloane half-laughed: here they were quarrelling among the ready naked blades, yet no word was ever worth a blow. And as the violence ebbed from him, he located its source at last. It lay beneath his feet. "I haven't time to argue," he said, and ran.

The void beyond the staircase clanged about him; the caretaker shouted; Sloane's radio crackled and called out; in the shaft of light paintings, pillars, stairs leapt and swayed. Sloane's ankles trembled as he landed on the marble of the foyer. Then he ran past the moon on the globe, which vibrated and began to swing as he rushed by, into the Planetarium.

The arc of the torch-beam streaked across the false sky like a comet; on the ceiling stars sparkled and were gone. Beyond the ranks of benches leading down to the stage, Sloane saw a glass case. At once the air snapped taut. Within the case violence was trapped. Outside, in the foyer, the caretaker swore and clattered closer. Sloane switched off the torch and felt his way forward down the aisle.

He had never been afraid of darkness; it had been the moon that he had feared in childhood, never more so than on the night of the party. But now the darkness seemed a mass of weapons, any one of which might mutilate him. His entire body prickled; each nerve felt the imminence of some poised threat. He could hear faint footsteps, but the room was full of echoes; his pursuer might be at any distance on either side of him. Sloane had failed to count the benches. His hand groped forward from what he had assumed to be the last bench. His fingers touched another, rose and felt the darkness. Moist breath clung to them, and they recoiled from a face.

As Sloane fell back, struggling with the torch, the beam sprang between his fingers. He was close to the glass case, and the caretaker was inches from him. "I thought you'd be here, son," the caretaker said. "What's the game? Trying to twist an old man?"

The caretaker moved in front of the glass case. His face came at Sloane, nodding like a balloon. Instinct leapt and Sloane struck out, punching blindly as he had the children at the party. Gasping, the caretaker fell beside the case. And Sloane saw the sign which the man's body had concealed.

He had seen the sign before, on the day of the murder. Before his mind was overwhelmed he had time to remember and realize. Last time had been in daylight; the sun had helped him for a few hours, but they hadn't won. Already the sign was meaningless; all meaning was contained in the grey stone within the case, beneath the sign LUNAR ROCK.

Sloane felt his mouth forced open from within. His skin ached as if a million needles were being forced through. But they were hairs; and his shoulders slumped as his hands weighed down his arms, formed into claws, and dragged him at last to stare down at the unconscious caretaker.

R. Chetwynd-Hayes

THE WEREWOLF

Ronald Chetwynd-Hayes (1919–2001) was known as "Britain's Prince of Chill" at a time when horror fiction was a more genteel genre. During a publishing career that lasted more than forty years, he produced eleven novels, more than 200 short stories, and edited twenty-five anthologies.

His stories were widely anthologised and collected in such volumes as Cold Terror, Terror by Night, The Elemental *(aka* From Beyond the Grave*),* The Night Ghouls and Other Grisly Tales, The Monster Club, Tales of Fear and Fantasy, Shudders and Shivers, The Vampire Stories of R. Chetwynd-Hayes *(aka* Looking for Something to Suck and Other Vampire Stories*),* Phantoms and Fiends *and* Frights and Fancies, *while the anthology movies* From Beyond the Grave *(1973) and* The Monster Club *(1980) were based on his work.*

The house was old and tucked away behind a curtain of trees; a lonely place that had been built by a man who loved solitude.

Mr Ferrier liked the company of his fellow beings as much as the next man, but he did not have much money, and The Hermitage – due, possibly, to its isolated position – had been very cheap. So he bought the property, moved in with his furniture and family and began to extol the virtues of a rustic life.

"Room to move around," he informed a sceptical Mrs Ferrier. "A chance to breathe air that isn't contaminated by petrol fumes."

"But it's such a long way for Alan to go to school," his wife protested. "And the nearest shop is five miles away. I tried to warn you, but I might as well have saved my breath."

"Ten minutes' car ride," Mr Ferrier retorted impatiently. "Besides, there's a travelling salesman who has everything you'll ever need in his van."

"And what about social life?" Mrs Ferrier demanded. "How will we get to know people, stuck in this out-of-the-way place?"

"Other people have cars, haven't they? At least give the place a chance. If at the end of three months we find the solitude a bit too much, well – I suppose I'll have to look for another house nearer town."

Alan was more than content with his new home. After years spent in a large industrial town, he found the rolling moors had much to commend them. He also discovered ruined farmhouses with frameless windows and gaping roofs, the exposed inner walls still retaining patches of flower-patterned wallpaper; and he wondered how long ago the last family had moved away, leaving their home to fall into decay.

But one of these relics from a bygone age was not completely deserted. According to an old map which Alan borrowed from the public library, this particular ruin had been called High Burrow: a very suitable name, as the house stood on the summit of a fairly steep hill and commanded a splendid view of the surrounding countryside. Alan climbed the slope, clambered over a low wall, then walked across an expanse of weed-infested ground that had probably once been a front garden.

He mounted three crumbling steps and passed through an open doorway, then entered the narrow hall, where the stone floor was coated with dust, and a large rat jumped down from a window-ledge and went scurrying into a side room. The ceiling had either fallen down or been removed, and Alan could see the room above, which had an iron fireplace clinging precariously to one wall. Higher still were massive beams, each one festooned with writhing cobwebs; the naked bones of a dead house.

Alan was about to leave, for there was an indefinable, eerie atmosphere about the place, when he heard the sound of ascending footsteps, which seemed to come from beyond a gaping doorway situated to the left of a dismantled staircase. The footsteps became louder and were intermingled at irregular intervals by an exceedingly unpleasant barking cough.

Presently a figure emerged from the doorway and walked slowly into the hall. Alan saw a tall young man with a heavily bearded face and long matted hair that hung down to his slightly bowed shoulders, deep sunken eyes that were indescribably sad and a set of perfect teeth which were revealed when he again coughed and gasped in a most alarming way.

Alan waited until the man had regained his breath, then said: "I didn't realize there was anyone here. I was just exploring."

The man wiped his brow on the sleeve of his ragged shirt, then spoke with a surprisingly cultivated voice.

"That's all right. But I heard you come in and wondered who it could be. Haven't had a visitor for years. This place is rather off the beaten track."

"Do you live here?" Alan enquired.

The man jerked his head in the direction of the doorway.

"Yes, down there. The cellars are still intact, if rather damp." He sighed deeply. "There's no other place I can go."

Alan thought there were many places he would rather live than in a damp cellar of a ruined house, particularly if he had such a bad cold. In fact, the man probably had bronchitis, or even pneumonia, for, despite the perspiration that poured down his face, he was shivering and could scarcely stand upright. Alan felt a twinge of pity for this strange, lonely person who appeared to have no one to look after him.

"Look, I know it's none of my business – but shouldn't you be in bed?"

The man nodded and leaned against the wall.

"Yes, I suppose I should. But my stores are running low and I must somehow get to the village before ..."

Another fit of coughing interrupted his next words, and Alan made the only suggestion that was possible under the circumstances.

"Would you like me to do your shopping?"

The man groaned and shivered so violently that Alan became quite alarmed.

"It's a long way for you to go and come back," said the man.

"I've nothing else to do," the boy replied, although the prospect of tramping back across rugged moorland carrying a heavy shopping bag was not all that attractive.

"Well, if you're sure you don't mind. Come downstairs and I'll give you some money and some idea of what I require."

Alan followed the tall figure through the doorway, down a winding flight of steps and finally into a large underground room, dimly lit by an ancient hurricane lamp. So far as he could see, this dismal place contained little more than an iron bedstead and a rickety chair.

"The nearest village is Manville," the man said, pulling a tin box from under the bed. "About five miles as the crow flies. Get some tinned stuff. Soups and stewed steak. I suppose you couldn't carry a gallon can of paraffin?"

"I could try," Alan said ruefully, determined never to explore empty houses again.

"I'd be greatly obliged if you could. Otherwise I'll soon have to lie down here in the dark. Here's five pounds – that should cover the cost of all you can carry."

"Right." Alan cast a glance at the untidy bed. "You cover yourself up and keep warm. I'll be back as soon as I can."

"Thank you very much," the man said. "You are exceedingly kind."

Actually, Alan thought he was, too, but just murmured: "Nonsense, no trouble at all," before walking towards the steps, carrying a leather shopping bag in one hand and an old rusty paraffin can in the other.

The greater part of four hours passed before Alan arrived back at the ruined house.

He ran down the steps and found the sick man sitting up in bed, his face lit by a smile of intense relief.

"And I thought you were not coming back! I should have known better."

Alan frowned and put the heavy bag and paraffin can down on the floor. "Of course I've come back! But it took me a long time to find that village and I lost my way coming back."

The man shook his head in self-reproach.

"Sorry, I shouldn't have said that. And it must have been very hard work lugging that bag and can over the moors. What have you got?"

Alan began to remove tins of food from the leather bag.

"I spent most of your five pounds. There's tins of stewed steak, mixed vegetables, soups and some nourishing rice pudding. Now, where's your cooking stove?"

The man nodded in the direction of a dark corner. "Over there. You'll find a saucepan and a few odds and ends of crockery."

Alan found the oil stove – and a very smelly, decrepit piece of apparatus it was, too – and, after lighting it, heated some oxtail soup, which the sick man consumed with every sign of satisfaction.

"That's marvellous!" he said. "I'm beginning to feel much better already."

"Would you like some stewed steak now?" Alan asked.

The man shook his head. "No, this will keep me going for a bit. Maybe I'll heat something up myself a little later on. But I must thank you for all your trouble. Not many lads of your age would have been so kind."

"That's all right." Alan began to back towards the steps. "I'd better get back now or my parents will start worrying. Would you like me to pop in tomorrow?"

For a while the man did not answer, then he said quietly: "I don't think you should. No – definitely not. Go away and forget you ever saw me. That would be best."

Alan wondered if the man had done something wrong and was hiding from the police. It might well be the reason why he was living in this awful place. But he did not look like a criminal, nor act like one. After all, he apparently went into Manville to do his shopping. So, just before he ran up the steps, Alan said:

"Don't worry – I won't tell anyone you're here. And I will come to see you again."

*   *   *

Mr Ferrier brought Charlie Brinkley back from the Grape and Barleycorn, for he was determined to make friends with his nearest neighbours, even if they did live miles away. Charlie was a youngish man with a full red face, a mop of flaxen hair and a hearty, familiar manner which did not go down all that well with Mrs Ferrier.

He sank into a chair, accepted a glass of brown ale, winked at Alan, then directed a slightly bovine stare at the good lady.

"Must be rather lonely for you out here, mam. Not a sight or sign of another body for miles. Wouldn't suit my missus. Likes a bit of company, she does."

"It takes all sorts to make a world," Mrs Ferrier remarked coldly. "It wouldn't do if we were all alike."

Charlie emptied his glass, then held it out for replenishment. "Ah, you're not wrong there, mam. Right nice drop of beer, this is."

Mr Ferrier smiled amicably, rubbed his hands together and all but pleaded with his wife to like their guest.

"Charlie's in the way of being a sheep farmer," he said heartily.

Mrs Ferrier was clearly not impressed. "Really! How interesting."

Charlie shook his head with mock modesty.

"I wouldn't go so far as to say that, mam. Maybe I've got a few hundred head out there on the moors. Got grazing rights, see. Not much money in sheep these days. Just enough to let me have a scrape of margarine on me dry crust and maybe a spoonful of jam on Sundays."

"How distressing for you," Mrs Ferrier commented.

Conversation lagged for a little while after that, until Mr Ferrier said desperately:

"Tell Ethel about that dog, Charlie. The one that's been killing your sheep."

"Oh, ah! Must be a monster, man. Skulking great brute. Do you know I've found six of my best rams with their throats torn out, over as many months?"

Mrs Ferrier grimaced and gave the impression that such information was not to her liking. But Charlie was not to be deterred from a subject that was clearly of great interest to him.

"Three were ripped to bits, mam. Never seen anything like it. Blood and wool everywhere, there was."

Mrs Ferrier did not comment, but dabbed her lips with a lace handkerchief, and Alan knew she would speak most sternly to his father, once their guest had departed.

"But you did catch a glimpse of the beast, didn't you, Charlie?" Mr Ferrier prompted.

"Ah, that I did! One bright moonlit night last week it were, and a body could see for miles. I was on top of Manstead Tor and I see'd this thing go prancing across the moors. Must have been two mile or more away, so there was no chance of me having a pot-shot at it with me old rabbit gun."

He took a deep swig from his glass, then continued.

"But this is the bit which makes the chaps down at the Grape and Barleycorn curl up. Mind you, it's as true as I sit here. It stopped and stood up on two feet. May I be struck down if it didn't. Reared up on its hindlegs, and ..."

"Howled, I dare say," Mrs Ferrier interrupted. "Howled at the moon."

"No, mam. Begging your pardon for contradicting such a forth-right lady as yourself – but it coughed. Sound travels on those moors when the wind is in the right direction, and I distinctly heard a barking cough. Like a chap who's got a nasty cold on his chest. Then it ran – still on two feet, mam – over Hangman's Ridge, and I didn't see it any more."

Mrs Ferrier glanced at the clock and assumed an expression of great surprise.

"Good gracious! Is that the time? I never realized it was so late."

Charlie, in no way put out by this broad hint, emptied his glass and stood up. "Ah, I must be pushing on. The missus will think I'm up to something I shouldn't. But I'll get the varmint, never you fret, mam. Then everyone will laugh t'other side of their faces."

"I'm sure we wish you all good fortune, Mr Brinkley," Mrs Ferrier remarked, before crossing the room and opening the door. "I do hope you get home safely."

"That I will, mam. Unless me old boneshaker blows a gasket."

Charlie Brinkley departed and Alan – without being told – went upstairs to bed. He had a lot to think about.

Three days later, Alan Ferrier once again paid a visit to the ruined High Burrow. He had intended never to go near the place again, but the memory of that poor sick man, lying all alone in a damp cellar, had haunted his dreams and spoilt his enjoyment of the perfect summer days. The man might have died – or be on the verge of death – all because a boy had been too frightened by a silly story to keep his promise.

So he now climbed over the low wall, walked very slowly across the neglected garden and entered the house. He called out:

"Excuse me … is it all right for me to come down?"

Presently he heard the sound of a match being struck, then a voice that said:

"Yes, come on down, lad."

Alan crept down the steps, not knowing what he was going to see, determined to turn and run should there be the slightest sign of anything alarming. But to his gratified surprise he found the man standing up and adjusting the flame of the oil-lamp.

He greeted the boy with a sad smile.

'I've been for a little walk and only just got back. I thought I told you to keep away."

"I was worried about you," Alan replied, relieved that his one-time patient looked so well – and normal. 'Are you better?"

"It's very nice of you to be so concerned. Yes, I'm much better. There's no fear of my dying – not from a cold."

Alan looked around the room. So far as he could see some effort had been made to tidy it up, for the floor had been swept, the bed stripped and the blankets folded into neat squares.

"What about your stores?" he asked. "Do you want me to fetch you some more?"

"No, thank you. I'm well able to look after myself now. I cook my meals upstairs in one of the empty rooms."

Alan took a deep breath and braced himself to ask the question that had been partly responsible for the fear which had haunted him for three days.

"Why do you live in this awful place? You have plenty of money. I saw lots of banknotes when you opened that tin box."

The man sighed and pushed him gently towards the flight of steps.

"Let's go up into the light of day and I'll try to explain."

They went up into the devastated hall and out into the overgrown garden. The man led his young friend over to the low wall.

"Sit down, son, and listen very carefully. Once, I lived in this house with my parents. That was a long time ago and, believe it or not, this was a very pleasant place then. My father farmed the entire expanse of this high ground, and although we were by no means rich, we were quite comfortably off. Then one day a stranger came to High Burrow."

The man stopped and stared sadly out across the wild moors. Alan knew he must not speak, but had to wait for the story to be completed.

Presently the man continued.

"Ah, a stranger! A tall, dark man with haunted eyes. He was lost – or so he said – and my father invited him to spend a night here. One full-moonlit night. Never has anyone been so ill-paid for an act of kindness."

He lapsed into silence again, and Alan prompted gently.

"What happened?"

"What happened indeed! The stranger had a rare disease. And during that one night I was ... oh, most merciful God! ... I was infected. I became as he was. He went away next morning, but I remained. Remained to see my parents die of grief and horror, my old home crumble slowly to the ruin you see now – and watch a hundred summers fade into autumn."

"A hundred!" Alan gasped.

"Yes. Maybe more. For the rare disease has a strange side effect. I cannot grow old. Or – so far as I know – die a natural death. But I can't expect you to believe that."

"Then ..." Alan hesitated, then blurted out what he now knew to be the awful truth. "Then ... you must be a werewolf."

The man jerked his head round and looked down at the boy with shocked surprise. "You believe that! You can actually accept that I'm cursed with the mark of the pentagon! Indeed, must your generation be gifted with great knowledge!"

"I've seen lots of horror films," Alan explained, "and I always thought they were just fantasies. But a man called Charlie Brinkley saw what he thought was a large dog standing up on two feet – and it coughed as you did. So I put two and two together and … It must be awful to be a werewolf."

The man nodded and recited the following words:

> *"A man may be pure of heart,*
> *And say his prayers at night,*
> *But into a wolf he will turn,*
> *When the moon is full and bright."*

"You've never killed *people*, though – have you?" Alan asked.

The man frowned. "No, of course not. Wolves don't unless they're starving and there's no wild life for them to hunt. But I appear to be rather partial to sheep. Disgusting, isn't it."

Certainly, Alan thought that tearing-sheep to pieces was not very nice, and he could only hope they had been killed first. However, he said gently:

"You can't help doing – what you do. But that man called Charlie Brinkley says he's going to shoot you. Doesn't he have to use a silver bullet?"

The man shook his head. "Shouldn't think so. An ordinary bullet can kill a werewolf – or at least injure him. Now, you have heard my story and know why you must not come here again."

"But you only – well – turn into a wolf when there's a full moon," Alan protested. "There's no reason why I shouldn't visit you during the day."

"I'm sure your parents wouldn't approve of you associating with a werewolf," the man said sternly. "I know I wouldn't if you were my son. So – thank you once again for your help and kindness. Now you *must* go."

And without so much as another word, he got up and walked quickly back to the house. Presently, Alan climbed the low wall and wandered dejectedly down the hill and out across the moors.

* * *

The summer days slipped by, and the moon, from resembling a sliver of Edam cheese, began to assume the proportions of a ripe melon. Every evening Alan would peer up at the gradually increasing disc of bright light and try to imagine how his friend in the ruined house was feeling, knowing he must soon be transformed into a dreadful monster.

Then came the night when a full moon rode a cloudless sky and Charlie Brinkley paid another visit to The Hermitage.

"That awful man has just parked his dreadful car in our drive," Mrs Ferrier informed her husband. "I saw him from the bedroom window. And I'm sure he's drunk. Ah, that must be him ringing the doorbell now. Tell him I've got a headache."

Charlie was not drunk but very excited.

"Saw the brute again," he gasped. "Running across Black Heath. Had to come back for me gun – in fact two guns. Thought you'd like to come with me, old chap. You can take up a position on Manstead Tor, and with me patrolling Hangman's Ridge, one of us should be able to pot him."

Mr Ferrier's eyes sparkled with excitement.

"Count me in. Hang on a second and I'll have a word with the wife, then I'll join you. Do we need my car?"

"No. Have to walk most of the way."

Alan, who had stationed himself in the hall, did not hesitate. He slipped out of the back door and ran up the narrow path which led to the moors.

The wind, which in this wild place was like a wailing, never-resting ghost, tore at Alan's hair and seemed to be trying to hold him back with invisible arms. But he continued to trot forward, even though his labouring heart and rasping lungs warned him that the limit of endurance would soon be reached. He had no idea what would happen when – or should – he come face to face with a raging werewolf. There was only the overwhelming urge to warn his friend that two hunters would soon be on his track, each one armed with a loaded rifle.

Manstead Tor stood out against the moonlit sky, a gently sloping hill that flowed up from a sea of heather to a grass-covered crown. Opposite, and about a quarter of a mile away, was Hangman's Ridge, a long, high mound that, according to local tradition, had at one time been a place of execution.

Alan stopped running when he saw the sheep. They were bunched together on the lower slopes of the ridge, looking like a large, grey shadow. They stirred uneasily when the boy approached them. Suddenly he knew what must be done.

The sheep were the only reason why the werewolf would come to this part of the moor. If he could drive them from the valley before his father and Charlie Brinkley arrived, then his friend might live to see another sunrise. He shouted, uprooted a clump of heather and waved it from side to side.

The sheep became a protesting, heaving mass that began to slowly move down into the valley as Alan raised his voice to a higher pitch. His was not an easy task, for the disturbed animals insisted on milling round in circles, and one or two would not budge at all, but stood still and stared at him with pathetic reproach.

He finally managed to get them all on the move and might well have succeeded in driving them from the valley, had not a sudden terrifying howl shrieked out from Hangman's Ridge. There was no controlling the sheep after that. They ran in every direction; they burrowed deep into the heather, bumped into each other and raced up and down the slopes. When Alan raised his eyes he all but turned and ran away himself.

Long afterwards, he decided that not one film producer had ever laid eyes on a werewolf, for the creature that was advancing towards him bore not the slightest resemblance to any of the monsters he had seen in the cinema.

The head was round, the ears large, hairy and tapering to sharp points. The face – which was narrow and sloped down to the slavering mouth – was covered with black, matted fur. But it was the eyes that made Alan wish he had stayed at home. They were sunken and bright red. Little pools of liquid fire that appeared to gleam with ferocious hate. The body was that of a deformed man. Bent shoulders, long arms that terminated in curved claws, the ghastly white skin sparsely covered by long strands of reddish hair. The creature still wore a torn shirt and a pair of stained grey trousers.

The werewolf ran forward, its claws brushing the ground, then stopped when it reached a point that was just a few feet from the terrified boy. The grotesque head went back, the jaws slowly parted to reveal sharp, pointed teeth, then a low growl rose to a full-throated roar.

Alan screamed.

"No ... no ... I'm your friend! Don't you know me?"

The roar died away, and the monster became still, a dark, menacing figure that gave the impression it might explode into lethal activity at any moment. Then it shuffled forward, lowered its head – and sniffed. Alan shuddered when the long snout travelled up his left arm, across his chest and finally muzzled his right ear.

Then the werewolf whined.

A dog that wishes to be patted, fed or taken for a walk, might have made some such sound. It could also have come from any unhappy creature, who, through no fault of its own, has been cursed with the stigma of a monster. Alan's fear drained away and was replaced by a warm flood of pity. His friend – the gentle, kindly man with the sad eyes – was imprisoned in that hideous form, pleading for understanding – forgiveness – a morsel of affection.

Alan was about to lay his hand on that unlovely head – when there came the sound of a rifle shot. A single, muffled report that came from the ridge. The werewolf jerked upright, gave one terrible cry of despair, then went bounding across the valley and disappeared behind Manstead Tor.

Alan was crying when Charlie Brinkley and Mr Ferrier reached him. His father put an arm round his shoulders and said:

"Thank God you're all right, son. When I saw that awful creature so close to you ..."

"I got him!" Charlie Brinkley interrupted, his voice trembling with excitement. "Right between the shoulders. He won't last long. Biggest dog I ever saw ... and did you see? It stood up on its hindlegs! You'll tell those nincompoops down in the Grape and Barleycorn, won't you? It stood upright!"

"I think," Mr Ferrier said, leading his young son away, "the least we say about this night's work the better. I would rather not believe what I saw."

But Alan could only repeat over and over again: "He couldn't help being a werewolf. He wouldn't have harmed me."

It was two days before Alan was allowed to go out on his own, for the doctor said he was suffering from shock and needed time to recover.

When he reached High Burrow he found it sleeping under a benign sky, with moths fluttering among the hare-bells in the overgrown garden and the wind breathing through the grass, and knew that tranquillity had returned to this once happy homestead.

He walked slowly down the stone steps and directed the beam of his torch round the desolate cellar. The man who had been a werewolf lay on the bed. He was dead – but on his face was the most beautiful smile that Alan had ever seen.

Presently he covered the body with a blanket, then remounted the steps.

He never went back.

Michael Marshall Smith

RAIN FALLS

Michael Marshall Smith's first novel, Only Forward, *won the August Derleth and Philip K. Dick Awards, and his next two –* Spares *and* One of Us *– were both optioned by major Hollywood studios. His* Straw Men *books, written under the name "Michael Marshall", were* Sunday Times *and international best-sellers, and his most recent thriller –* The Intruders *– is currently under series development with the BBC. 2008 saw the publication of a short novel* The Servants *under a further name, "M.M. Smith". He has also worked extensively as a screenwriter for clients in London and Hollywood, both individually and as a partner in Smith & Jones Productions. He lives in North London with his wife, a son, and two cats.*

The writer reveals that the idea for the following story "leapt full-grown into my head while spending an evening in a certain pub in London's Camden district. Though the atmosphere was not as described, there was a group of lads milling about the pub, and one in particular who had an awful fascination about him. I was glad I had a story to think about, a) because I was stuck at the end of a table out of hearing distance from the people I was with, and b) because the only people I could hear were a couple sitting opposite. It sounded as if they'd met through a Time Out *ad, and they spent nearly three hours talking about Astrology in terms of the most tragic conviction. Sadly, the guy blew it by drinking too much, but on the other hand the woman never took her jacket off the entire evening, so he was probably onto a loser anyway. The story about the narrator getting his nose broken is completely accurate."*

I saw what happened. I don't know if anyone else did. Probably not, which worries me. I just happened to see, to be looking in the right directions at the right times. Or the wrong times. But I saw what happened.

I was sitting at one of the tables in The Porcupine, up on the raised level. The Porcupine is a pub on Camden High Street, right on the corner where the smaller of the three markets hangs its hat. At least, there is a pub there, and that's the one I was sitting in. It's not actually called The Porcupine. I've just always called it that for some reason, and I can never remember what its real name is.

On a Saturday night the pub is always crowded with people who've stopped off on the way to the subway after spending the afternoon trawling round the markets. You have to get there very early to score one of the tables up on the raised level: either that or sit and watch like a hawk for when one becomes free. It's an area about ten feet square, with a wooden rail around it, and the windows look out onto the High Street. It's a good place to sit and watch the passing throng, and the couple of feet of elevation gives an impression of looking out over the interior of the pub too.

I didn't get to the pub until about eight o'clock, and when I arrived there wasn't a seat anywhere, never mind on the upper level. The floor was crowded with the usual disparate strands of local colour, talking fast and loud. For some reason I always think of them as beatniks, a word which is past its use-by date by about twenty years. I guess it's because the people who hang out in Camden always seem like throwbacks to me. I can't really believe in counter-culture in the '90s: not when you know they'll all end up washing their hair some day, and trading the beaten-up Volkswagen for a nice new Ford Sierra.

I angled my way up to the bar and waited for one of the Australians behind it to see me. As I waved some money diffidently around, hoping to catch someone's eye, I flinched at the sound of a sudden shout from behind me.

"Ere, you! Been putting speed in this then 'ave you?"

I half-turned to see that the man standing behind me was shouting at someone behind the bar, gesticulating with a bottle of beer. He was tall, had very short hair and a large ring in his ear, and spoke – or bawled – with a Newcastle accent of compact brutality.

My face hurriedly bland, I turned back to the bar. A ginger-haired bar person was smiling uncertainly at the man with the earring, unsure of how seriously to take the question. The man laughed violently, nudged his mate hard enough to spill his beer, and then shouted again.

"You 'ave, mate. There's drugs in this."

I assume it was some kind of joke relating to how drunk the man felt, but neither I nor the barman were sure. Then a barmaid saw me waiting, and I concentrated on communicating to her my desire for a Budweiser, finding the right change, that sort of thing. When I'd paid I moved away from the bar, carefully skirting the group where the shouting man stood with three or four other men in their mid-twenties. They were all talking very loudly and grinning with vicious good humour, faces red and glistening in the warmth of the crowded pub.

A quick glance around showed that there was still nowhere to sit, so I shuffled my way through the crowd to stand by the long table which runs down the centre of the room. By standing in the middle of the pub, and only a few feet away from the steps to the raised area, I would be in a good position to see when a seat became available.

After ten minutes I was beginning to wonder whether I shouldn't just go home instead. I wasn't due to be meeting anyone: I'd spent the day at home working and just fancied being out of doors. I'd brought my current book and was hoping to sit and read for a while, surrounded by the buzz of a Saturday night. The Porcupine's a good pub for that kind of thing. The clientele are quite interesting to watch, the atmosphere is generally good, and if you care to eavesdrop you can learn more about astrology in one evening than you would have believed there was to know.

That night it was different, and it was different because of the group of men standing by the bar. They weren't alone, it seemed. Next to them stood another three, and another five were spread untidily along one side of the long table. They were completely unlike the kind of people you normally find in there, and they changed the feel of the pub. For a start they were all shouting, all at the same time, so that it was impossible to believe that any of them could actually be having a conversation. If they were all talking at the same time, how could they be? They didn't look especially drunk, but relaxed in a hard and tense way. Most of all they looked dangerous.

There's a lot of talk these days about violence to women, and so there should be. In my book, anyone who lays a hand on a woman is breaking the rules. It's simply not done. On the other hand, anyone who gets to their twenties or thirties before they get thumped has had it pretty easy, violence-wise. It's still wrong, but basically what I'm saying is: try being a man. Being a man involves getting hit quite a lot, from a very early age. If you're a teenage girl the physical contact you get tends to be positive: hugs from friends and parents. No one hugs teenage boys. They hit them, fairly often, and quite hard.

Take me, for example. I'm a nice middle-class bloke, and I grew up in a comfortable suburb and went to a good school. It's not like I grew up on an estate or anything. But I took my fair share of knocks, recreational violence that came and went in a meaningless second. I've got a small kink in my nose, for example, which came from it being broken one night. I was walking back from a pub with a couple of friends and three guys behind us simply decided they'd like to push us around. For them the evening clearly wouldn't be complete without a bit of a fight.

We started walking more quickly, but that didn't work. The guys behind us just walked faster. In the end I turned and tried to talk to them, idiot that I was at that age. I said we'd had a good evening and didn't want any trouble. I pointed out that there was a policewoman on the other side of the street. I advanced the opinion that perhaps we could all go our separate ways without any unnecessary unpleasantness. Given that I was more than a little drunk, I think I was probably quite eloquent.

The nearest of them thumped me. He hit me very hard, right on the side of the nose. Suddenly losing faith in reason and the efficacy of a logical discussion, I turned to my friends, to discover that they were already about fifty yards up the road and gaining speed.

I turned to the guys in front of me again. Two of them were grinning, little tight smiles under sparkling eyes. The other was still standing a little closer to me, restlessly shifting his weight from foot to foot. His eyes were blank. I started to recap my previous argument, and he punched me again. I took a clumsy step backwards, in some pain, and he hit me again, a powerful and accurate belt to the cheekbone.

Then, for no evident reason, they drifted off. I turned to see that a police van was sitting at the corner of the road, but I don't think that had made any difference. It was a good eighty yards away, and wasn't coming any closer. My two friends were standing talking to a policeman who was leaning out of the passenger window. There was no sign that any action was going to be taken. There didn't need to be. That's what violence is like, in its most elemental, unnecessary form. It comes, and it goes, like laughter or a cold draught from under a door.

I trotted slowly up the road, and my friends turned and saw me with some relief. The policeman took one look, reached behind into the cab, and passed out a large roll of cotton wool. It was only then that I realized that the lower half of my face, and all of my sweatshirt, was covered in blood.

My face was a little swollen for a couple of days, and my nose never looked quite the same again. But my point is, it was no big deal. The matter-of-fact way in which the policeman handed me something to mop up with said it all. It wasn't important. If you're a man, that kind of thing is going to happen. You wipe your nose and get on.

And that's why when a man walks into a pub, he takes a quick, unconscious look around. He's looking to see if there's any danger, and if so, where it's likely to be located. Similarly, if a fight breaks out, a woman may want to watch, a little breathless with excitement, or she may want to charge fearlessly in and tell them all to stop being silly. Both reasonable reactions, but most men will want to turn the other way, to make themselves invisible. They know that violence isn't a spectator sport: it has a way of reaching out and pulling you in. It won't matter that you don't know anyone involved, that you're just sitting having a quiet drink. These things just happen. There's generally a reason for violence against women. It'll be a very bad reason, don't get me wrong, but there'll be a reason.

Amongst men violence may be just like an extreme, cold spasm of high spirits. There may not be any reason for it at all, and that's why you have to be very, very careful.

The string of guys standing and sitting near the bar in The Porcupine were giving off exactly the kind of signals that you learn to watch out for. Something about the set of their faces, their restless glances and rabid good humour, said that unreason was at work. The one by the bar was still hollering incomprehensibly at the barman, who was still smiling uncertainly back. Another of the group was leaning across his mate to harangue a couple of nervous-looking girls sitting at a table up against the bar. One of them was wearing a tight sweater, and that's probably all it had taken to kick-start the man's hormones. The look on his face was probably meant to be endearing. It wasn't.

After a couple of minutes the two girls gathered up their stuff and left, but I didn't swoop over to their table. It was too close to the men. Just by being there, by getting too close to their aura, I could have suddenly found myself in trouble. That may sound paranoid, or cowardly: but I've seen it happen. I had every right to sit there, just as a woman has every right to dress the way she wants without attracting unwelcome attention. Rights are nice ideas, a comforting window through which to view the world. But once the glass is broken, you realize they were never really there.

So I remained standing by the long table, sipping my beer and covertly looking around. I couldn't work out what they were doing here. One of them had a woolly hat, which was doing the rounds and getting more and more grubby and beer-stained. I thought it had the letters "FC" on the front somewhere, which would almost certainly stand for Football Club, but I couldn't understand why or how a group of football supporters could have ended up in the Porcupine when it's not near any of the major grounds. One of the groups linked arms to shout some song together at one point, but I couldn't discern any of the words.

I was glancing across to the bar, to see how long the queues were and decide whether it was worth hanging round for another beer, when I saw the first thing. It was very unexceptional, but it's one of the things I saw.

The door onto the main street had been propped open by the staff, presumably in a vain attempt to drop the temperature in the crowded room to something approaching bearable. As I swept the far end of the bar with my gaze, trying to judge the best place to stand if I wanted to get served that evening, a large grey dog came in through the door, and almost immediately disappeared into the throng. I noticed and remembered it because I was sort of expecting its owner to follow him in, but nobody came. I realized he or she must already be in the pub, and the dog had simply popped out for a while. The owner would have to be a he, I decided: no woman would want a dog like that. I only got a very quick sighting of it, but it was very large and slightly odd-looking, a shaggy hound that moved with a speed that was both surprising and somehow oily.

At that moment I saw a couple who were sitting at a table in the raised area reach for their coats, and I forgot about the dog. The couple had been sitting at the best table in the pub, one which is right in the corner of the room, up against the big windows. I immediately started cutting through the mass of people towards it.

Once I'd staked the table out as my territory I went to the bar and bought another beer. It may have been my imagination but it looked to me as if the staff were very aware of the group of men too: though they were all busy, each glanced out into the body of the pub while I was there, keeping half an eye on the long table. I avoided the area completely and got myself served right at the top of the bar, next to the door.

I settled myself back down at the table, glad that the evening was getting on track. I glanced out of the window, though it was mid-evening by then, too late for much to be going on. A few couples strolled by outside in a desultory fashion, dressed with relentless trendiness. Some kind of altercation was taking place in the Kentucky Fried Chicken opposite, and a derelict with dreadlocks was picking through a bin on the pavement near the window. If I can get the window seat early enough I like to sit and watch, but the strong moonlight made the view looked distant somehow, unreal.

A fresh surge of noise made me turn away from the window and look out across the pub. One of the men had knocked over his beer, or had it knocked over. Those nearby were shouting and laughing. It didn't look like much was going to come of it. I'd opened my book and was about to start reading when I noticed something else.

There was one more person in the party than there had been before. Now you're probably going to think that I simply hadn't registered him, but that's not true. I'd looked at them hard and long. If I'd seen this man before, I would have remembered it. He was standing with the group nearest the steps which led up to the area where I was sitting. I say "standing with", because there was something about him that set him apart slightly from the other men, though he was right in the middle of them, and had the cocky pub charisma of someone who's used to respect amongst his peers. He was wearing jeans and a bulky grey jacket, typical sloppy casual, his dark hair was slightly waved, and his face came to a point in an aquiline nose. He exuded a sort of manic calm, as if it was the result of a bloodstream coursing with equal quantities of heroin and ecstasy, and he was listening to two of the other men with his mouth hanging slackly open, head tilted on one side. When there was another wave of noise from the other part of the group he raised his head slightly, the corners of his mouth creased in a half-smile of anticipation, keen to see what was going on, what new devilry was afoot. He was at home here. This is what he knew, what he was good at. This was where he lived.

He had weird eyes, too. They weren't too big or small, and they weren't a funny colour or anything. But they were dead, like two coins pushed into clay. They weren't the kind of eyes you would want to see looking at you across a pub, if you were a woman. If you were a man, they weren't eyes you wanted to see at all. They were not good eyes.

I watched with an odd sort of fascination as the man stood with a loose-limbed solidity, turning from side to side to participate in the various shouting matches going on around him. And all the time he had this half-smile, as if he was enjoying every epic moment. I caught a momentary look on the face of one of his mates, a look of slight puzzlement, but I couldn't interpret it any more closely than that. Not at the time, anyway.

After a while I lost interest and finally started reading my book. The pub was warm, but the window next to me was cool, and I can tune out just about anything when I'm reading. I don't wear a watch, so I don't know how long it was before it all went off.

There was the sudden sound of breaking glass, and the noise level in the pub dipped for a moment, before shooting up into pandemonium. Startled, I looked up, still immersed in my book. Then my head went very clear.

A fight had broken out. That's what they do. They break out, appear like rain from clear April skies. Virtually all of the men around the table seemed to be involved, apart from a pair who were gloatingly watching from the sidelines. The rest of the pub were doing what people always do in these situations. The bar staff were either cowering or gearing themselves up to do something, and the other customers were shifting back in their seats, watching but trying to move out of trouble. I couldn't really see what was going on, but it looked as if the men had taken on another, smaller, group who'd been sitting affably at the bar.

Amongst the general noise and chaos, I saw that the man with the bulky grey jacket was right in the thick of it. In fact it looked rather as if he'd started the whole thing. Once I'd noticed him again the rest of the action seemed to shade away, and I saw him loop a fist into the mêlée. A couple of the male bar staff emerged into the body of the pub, holding their hands out in a placatory way, trying to look stern. The ginger-haired one in particular looked as if he wished this wasn't his job, that he was a waiter in some nice bistro instead. A couple of men responded by ploughing into them, and the fight immediately leapt up to a new level of intensity. People nearby hurriedly slipped out of their chairs and fled to the sides of the room. A beer bottle was smashed and brandished, and it all looked as if it was going to get very serious indeed.

As everybody was watching the new focus of attention, I happened to glance down towards the other end of the long table. The man in the grey jacket, I was surprised to see, had stopped fighting. He had his arm round the tall man with the earring, who'd been hurt, and was leading him towards the toilets at the back of the pub. I clocked this, and then turned to look back at the other end. The manager, a large man with forearms the size of my thighs, had come out from behind the counter. He was holding a pool cue and looked as if he had every intention of using it.

Luckily, I wasn't the only person who thought so. The man waving the broken bottle faltered, only for a moment, but it was enough. The guy he'd been threatening took a step back, and suddenly the mood dropped. It happened as quickly as that. A gust of wind dispersed the cloud, and sparks stopped arcing through the air. The fight had gone away.

There was a certain amount of jockeying as the two groups of men disentangled and took up their previous positions. The manager kept a firm eye on this, cue still in hand. The other customers gradually relaxed in their seats and slowly, like a fan coming to rest, the evening settled.

When I'd finished my beer I started towards the bar for another, and then elected to go to the toilets first. It was a bit of a struggle getting through the crowd towards the far end of the bar, and my route took me a little closer to the men that I would have liked. When I passed them, however, I relaxed a little. They were still up, still feisty, but the main event of the evening was over. I don't know how, but I could sense that. The mood was different, and something had been satisfied. The funniest joke had been told.

I hesitated for a moment before entering the toilets. As far as I knew, the man with the grey jacket and his wounded colleague were still in there. The Porcupine's toilet is not big, and I'd have to walk quite close to them. But then I thought "fuck it", and pushed the door open. You can be too bloody cautious. Quite apart from anything else, the mood in the aftermath of a fight tends to be one of fierce good humour and comradeship. A nod and a grunt from me would be enough to show I was one of the lads.

I needn't have worried, because it was empty. I took a leak into one of the urinals, and then turned to wash my hands at the minuscule washbasin. There was a certain amount of blood still splattered across the porcelain, the result of a bad nosebleed, by the look of it.

Then I noticed that there were drops of blood on the floor too, leading in the direction of the cubicle. The door was nearly shut, but not actually closed, which was odd. It didn't feel as if anyone was behind the door, and people don't generally pull a cubicle door to when they leave. Not knowing why I was doing so, I carefully pushed it open with my finger.

When it was open a couple of inches I nearly shouted, but stopped myself. When it was open all the way I just stared.

The walls of the cubicle were splattered with blood up to the level of the ceiling, as if someone had loaded dark red paint onto a thick brush and tried to paint the walls as quickly as possible. A couple of lumps of ragged flesh lay behind the bottom of the toilet, and the bowl was full of mottled blood, with a few pale chips of something floating near the top.

My mind balked at what I was seeing, and I simply couldn't understand what might have happened until I saw a large metal ring on the floor, nearly hidden behind one of the lumps.

Moving very quickly, I left the toilet. The pub was still seething with noise and heat, and the way through to the raised area was completely blocked. Suddenly remembering you could do such a thing, I ducked out of the side door. I could walk around the pub and re-enter at the front, much closer to my seat. Or I could just start running. But I didn't think I should. I had to get my book, or people might wonder why it was still there.

The air outside the pub was cool, and I hurried along the wall. After a couple of yards I stopped when I saw a movement on the other side of the road.

The dog was sitting there. Now that it was still, I could see just how large it was. It was much bigger than a normal dog, and bulkier. And it was looking at me, with flat grey eyes.

We stared at each other for a moment. I couldn't move, and just hoped to God it was going to stay where it was. I wanted to sidle along the wall, to get to the bit where the windows started so that people could see me, but I didn't have the courage. If I moved, it might come for me.

It didn't. Still looking directly at me, the dog raised its haunches and then walked slowly away, down towards the dark end of the street where the lamps aren't working. I watched it go, still not trusting. Just before the corner it turned and looked at me again, and then it was gone.

I went back into the pub, grabbed my book and went home. I didn't tell anyone what I'd found. They'd discover it soon enough. As I hurried out of the pub I heard one of the men at the table wonder where Pete was. There was no point me telling him, or showing him what was left. I had to look after myself.

I noticed all of those things. I was looking in those directions, and saw what I saw. I saw the earring on the floor of the cubicle, still attached to the remains of its owner's face. I saw that the man in the grey jacket wasn't there when I left, but that nobody seemed to be asking after him. I saw the look one of the other men had given him, a look of puzzlement, as if he was wondering exactly when he'd met this man with grey eyes, where he knew him from. And I saw the look in the eyes of the dog, and the warning that it held.

I didn't tell anyone anything, but I don't know whether that will be enough. It wasn't my fault I saw things. I wasn't looking for trouble. But I understand enough to realize that makes no difference. Rain will sometimes fall, and I was standing underneath.

I haven't been to The Porcupine in the last month. I've spent a lot of time at home, watching the street. In the last couple of days I've started to wonder if there are as many cats around as usual, and I've heard things outside the window in the night, shufflings. They may not mean anything. It may not be important that the darkness outside my window is becoming paler, as the moon gets fuller every night. All of this may amount to nothing.

But it makes me nervous. It makes me really very nervous.

Stephen Laws

GUILTY PARTY

Stephen Laws' early short stories in the genre won a number of awards and led to his first novel, Ghost Train *(1985), which achieved a degree of notoriety when posters advertising the paperback were banned by British Rail from their mainline stations for fear of alarming passengers. His subsequent books have included* Spectre, The Wyrm, The Frightners, Darkfall, Gideon *and* Macabre.

His short stories have been published in various anthologies, magazines and newspapers, winning awards on BBC Radio and in the Sunday Sun.

As the author explains, the story which follows is taken from real life: "Years ago, when I worked for the now-defunct Tyne and Wear County Council, my fellow office cronies and I would hire a mini-bus for a jaunt to Stamfordham (a small hamlet outside Newcastle) about twice a year. We'd go up there, take over the pub, have a buffet, get drunk and incur the wrath of the locals (remember those first scenes in An American Werewolf in London *when the two American guys walk into the pub … ?) The story was my attempt to place fellow-worker 'Stuart' in a dangerous situation. Just how much is fact and how much is fiction we can leave to the reader's imagination …"*

> *I've been a wild rover for many a year*
> *And I've spent all me money on whisky and beer*
> *But now I've returned with gold in great store*
> *I won't play the wild rover. No never.*
> *No more.*

The last chorus of the old song reverberated from the swaying occupants of the battered bus as it sped down yet another country lane. As if on cue, a sudden turn in the road sent the chorus leader, who had been standing in the aisle, crashing across two of the seats.

There was a roar of drunken laughter.

It had been a good night. The usual office Christmas party with hired bus and a pub far out in the wilds. Stamfordham was usually a quiet little spot. Not really too remote, but "countrified" enough to appeal to the most hardened of "city" types and to arouse the irritation of local residents when the "townies" arrived en masse to take over the only two pubs in the area.

Stuart heaved himself from the seat and struggled past Mark towards the back of the bus. Mark by this time had begun to lead the others in another typical "Oirish" folk song, "The Wild Colonial Boy," and the strains of the boozy singers echoed in Stuart's whisky-befuddled brain as he slumped next to Steve, who was near to falling asleep, partly because of the rocking of the bus but mainly because of the ten rum and cokes which had passed through his system.

Moonlight occasionally flashed through the ragged trees which reared and loomed past the windows as the bus rattled on its way, city-bound.

"Hello, my good man," said Steve slurrily. "What brings you down here then?"

"Just had an idea," said Stuart. "An idea for a story."

Both men were fanatical dreamers and film buffs. Ideas for scripts and screenplays were often shouted across the office in between writing reports and drafting committee minutes.

"Just supposing," Stuart went on after a slight pause. "That there's been an office party just like this one, and we're on our way home. Just like this. Then, suddenly, one of the people on the bus sees something ... *something* ... outside in the trees, by the glare of the headlights."

Steve pursed his lips thoughtfully and screwed up his eyebrows. Then, after another pause, he looked at Stuart.

"You mean ... something vague. Something ... not quite *right*."

"Yeah. That's right. Something pretty weird. So that he's not sure whether it's the booze or not."

"It would be a good starting point for ..."

"... a horror film. Yeah."

They continued to bounce ideas off each other. Clichés abounded. Stock situations seemed to spring readily to mind. Completely absorbed, they'd forgotten everything else. Suddenly, a chorus of voices brought Stuart back to reality.

"Stuart! Hi, man! You don't want to sleep on the bus tonight, do you? It's your stop!"

"Is it?"

Stuart bundled to his feet and pulled his coat on.

"Don't forget, Steve! This is one we can take up on Monday! See you!"

As he bustled to the front of the bus, a flurry of arms slapped him amiably across the shoulders.

"Get a move on, Stu! We've got to get home as well, you know!"

The hiss of the pneumatic bus door. The bite of the cold winter air. With breath turning to steam, Stuart turned on the step and waved his arm in a mock dramatic gesture of farewell.

As he stepped down from the bus and into the night, the cries of farewell were snuffed out as the door snapped shut. With a coughing roar of the engine, a shifting of gears and a crunch of gravel, the bus sped off rattling into the blackness of the country lane.

Country lane?

What the hell am I doing in a country lane? thought Stuart, spinning none too steadily on one heel and surveying the blue blackness of his surroundings. In the cold moonlight he could just make out the row of hedges bristling on each side of the road.

Clutches of trees like gnarled giants crouched along the roadway, their spiny fingers dancing in the freezing air as if conducting the weird melody which the wind was playing amongst them.

"The stupid idiots have dropped me off in a country-bloody road! Miles from anywhere."

It was a little while before he realized that he was standing directly under a rusted signpost and when he squinted up at the weatherbeaten lettering, he realized what had happened.

"Don't forget," he had said in the Bay Horse Pub, "I've got to be dropped off at Crawpost when we head back. My mate's picking me up there and taking me on home."

The signpost had only two placenames on it … Newcastle 13 miles: Crowfast Farm 2 miles. Maybe Crawpost *had* sounded like Crowfast after ten whiskies but it didn't make Stuart feel any better disposed towards his fellow man as he started to walk down the lane. Turning up his collar he looked for a telephone box or the tell-tale flashing headlights of an approaching car. Nothing. Not even the distant glow from a farmhouse window.

Nothing.

He began to curse under his breath that the party had been organized so far away from Newcastle. Why couldn't it have been held in the town? Or at least near to a bus route. Here he was, miles from anywhere on a lonely country road. Anything could happen. He could fall into a ditch and break a leg or something. Unnoticed for weeks maybe. That was a good idea for a story …

Stories later. The first matter of priority was a phone box or a farmhouse with a telephone.

It seemed that only ten minutes had passed before a gradual feeling of unease began to creep over him. Continually, he found himself glancing over at the other side of the road as the hedges hissed and swayed with the wind. Stuart was not a nervous man. Admittedly, being stranded out in the wilds was an irritating experience to say the least, but no reason to suppose that someone was …

Damn it, someone *was* following him! Creeping along behind the hedge on the other side of the road.

Stuart stopped. This was bloody stupid. There wasn't anyone there. *This is what comes of getting ideas for horror films*, he thought. He continued to walk, the lonely sound of his footsteps on the road somehow challenging the darkness. But he still couldn't lose the feeling that something was moving over there.

Must be a cow.

Another five minutes or so passed as he walked. For an instant, he thought he saw something slinking past a gap in the hedgerow. Again, he stopped and stared at the hedge. There wasn't anybody there, surely? Funny thing though, standing there in the moonlight staring at the hedgerow, Stuart had to admit that by a trick of the light it *did* look as if something was just visible on the other side. Something that crouched and watched.

Stuart laughed and kept on walking. He conjured up pictures of Cary Grant in a similar situation. Alighting from a bus in the film *North by Northwest*, he had found himself out in the open. Isolated and vulnerable. And there he'd been attacked by a crop-dusting aeroplane.

But that was in the daytime. No homicidal plane pilot in sight here. Just a rustling in the hedgerow which seemed to be keeping pace with him as he walked.

Unconsciously, he found himself walking slightly into the road; away from the gravel at the roadside which had been crunching underfoot. Was he afraid of giving away his position? Could that be his own shadow somehow reflecting in the shrubbery? No … his own shadow was right there in the middle of the road. The foolishness of the situation stopped him from crossing the lane and peering over the hedge.

A scudding cloud covered the moon like a giant veil and the countryside was plunged into an even greater darkness.

Stuart had read the clichés about fear jolting a person's nervous system like an electric shock. He had heard how a person's blood could "turn to ice" and of how his heart could "leap into his mouth". But he was totally unprepared for it to happen to him.

As if waiting for the moon to disappear, something large crashed through the hedge and was bounding across the road. What happened next seemed to be a series of impressions … of "frozen frames" in a film. Everything happened so quickly.

Something came dashing at him through the dark. Something which panted and grunted as it approached. Stuart was frozen in his tracks. In an instant, there was the horrific impression that something wanted to catch him very badly. Something altogether bestial, hungry and decidedly unpleasant. A glint in the dark from what seemed to be an eye or a tooth made him realise that his assailant was almost on top of him. Almost at his ear there came an animal-like snarl as he ducked down instinctively onto his haunches.

A brush of hair on his cheek.

A savage, tearing blow on his back.

The ripping of cloth.

The crash of undergrowth as his attacker burst through the other hedge behind him.

Stuart wheeled around to face the hedge just as the moon reappeared, throwing out everything around him in crystal clear vision. A gaping hole had been torn into the hedge, the inner fringes of which still twisted and writhed from the passage of … whatever it had been.

Stuart could actually feel his heart pounding in his chest. His throat seemed dry and constricted. He was no longer drunk.

An impression remained in his mind of a man-like shape. But not a man.

"No …" Stuart muttered under his breath, his eyes flickering the length of the hedgerow "… not a werewolf either. More like some stupid bugger dressed in a ridiculous werewolf costume from a very bad horror B-feature."

It all seemed perfectly clear. Somebody was dressed up and trying to scare the hell out of him. Well … he'd done a pretty good job so far. If Stuart hadn't left Steve on the bus, he would have sworn that this would be the sort of trick *he* would pull after their conversation on film plots.

Stuart started to run, still scanning the bushes at his left, not sure whether the sound of his own gasping was covering the horrific panting and growling of something keeping abreast with him on the other side of the hedge. Hardly even altering his speed, he stooped and grabbed half of a housebrick from the grass verge. Still running, he weighed the brick in his hand. The very fact that it was a housebrick and not just some rock was a comfort. A brick made by a builder for a house. For people. Out in the wilds, it was a comfort to know that his grab for a weapon had given him something which was man-made. Now, even the lonely stretch of road didn't seem quite so cut off from civilization as before, and the feeling that there was nothing more supernatural than a lunatic in a halloween costume following him, made Stuart's fear re-channel itself into something approaching rage. Just one more glimpse of the bastard, and he'd have a skull fracture to laugh off.

Stuart's anger reached a peak. Veering in towards a gap in the hedge where anyone on the other side would have to pass, he suddenly halted, whirled and raised the brick ready to throw.

Just show yourself for one second …

Sucking in lungfuls of air, he tensed … waiting for his assailant. His own heartbeats thudded like the footsteps of an approaching giant.

Nothing.

Clouds of breath streamed around his face.

Nothing.

The branches of a nearby tree shook and rattled in the wind.

Nothing.

Slowly, Stuart began to move along the road again, still with the brick half-raised in his hand, ever watchful for any sign of movement. A flicker of light between the trees suddenly caught his eye.

A farm! Crowfast Farm!

He realized that he'd run almost two miles. Normally, running for a bus would have completely winded him. But the circumstances here were entirely different. If the farm had a telephone – which it surely must have – he could phone for a taxi and be on his way home in no time at all. On instinct, Stuart turned quickly as he ran. About twenty-five yards behind him something suddenly dashed across the road from right to left and vanished into a copse of trees. Something which crouched as it ran, but with extremely broad shoulders and long arms. And … pointed ears?

Stuart began to run even faster than before. The road twisted to the right and, just at the turn, he saw on the left-hand side a twisted, roughly hewn gate bearing a hand-etched inscription ... "Crowfast Farm".

Deep in the trees he could see the glow which had first caught his eye. Reaching the gate, Stuart took a running leap by bracing one hand on the topmost bar of the gate. Years of sitting behind a desk and insufficient exercise suddenly caught up with him as his foot caught against the bar and sent him cartwheeling into the deep grass on the other side of the gate. Spitting out soil, he pulled himself up to his feet. His leg felt about six inches longer than the other one. The thought of being hemmed in by trees was suddenly unnerving. At least in the open road he could almost see if anyone was lurking nearby. But with all of those trees ...

Crashing into the copse, Stuart dodged in and out around the tree trunks with his eyes fixed steadfastly on the glowing light up ahead. No less than ten yards into the trees he heard something blundering into the gate behind him.

Bastard!

Spinning around, Stuart swung his arm back to throw the brick and for the first time really saw his pursuer, crouched at the gate and with the moonlight shining full on its face.

As a child, Stuart had once dreamed that someone was standing in the shadows at the foot of his bed. Frozen by some strange force, he had watched as the figure silently moved around the bed and approached him. It was only when the figure had suddenly thrust itself forward into the moonlight that he had been able to scream and pull the bedclothes over his head. The same immobility now came over him as he saw the slavering jaws, the balefully glowing red eyes, and the hideously pointed wolf's ears. This was no lunatic in a halloween costume ...

The stooped figure paused at the broken gate and swung its head backwards and forwards, looking for him. The clawed arms swung restlessly like some horrific ape. The figure suddenly became rigid and Stuart realized that it had seen him. As the horror, with terrible strength, loped over the gate and lunged into the trees towards him, the spell was broken and Stuart heaved the brick with more strength than he thought he possessed. At once, he knew that he had thrown wide of the mark. He watched as the projectile twisted through the air, as if in slow motion. The man-beast thrashed between the trees and it seemed as if the missile would hit one of the tree boles. Unaware of the projectile, the beast stepped straight into its path.

The brick struck the animal full on the temple with an audible crunch of bone and sent it reeling into the undergrowth. Turning, Stuart dashed through the trees and was suddenly aware of the most chilling howl of rage and pain from behind him. He had never heard a wolf howl before. Only on film. Never in real life. Again, the thought came back to him that he had been caught in the fantasy world of a B-film character.

But for no more than an instant. This nightmare was real. The iced air tore at his lungs as he charged through the undergrowth. The tangled grass and weeds seemed to deliberately clutch at his legs, slowing him down.

The farmhouse *must* be up ahead somewhere. The light flashed clearly through the trees only twenty yards away. From somewhere behind him came the sound of crashing vegetation. Only ten yards to go. A thicket obscured the light. Clawing fingers. Twigs tearing at his clothes. Thrusting through the shrubbery, Stuart came into a small clearing and saw the source of the light.

"What the bloody hell … ?"

A lantern hung from the low limb of an ash tree, throwing out the surrounding trees in bright relief. A lantern, but no farm house.

Jesus! There had to be a farmhouse somewhere. Realizing that he'd run into the copse only to find that there was no sanctuary and that the thing behind him was still approaching rapidly made panic clutch at his throat. There *must* be a farmhouse nearby. Who had put the light there? And why? Stuart dashed around the clearing frantically searching for some sign of human habitation.

The farmhouse was up ahead, surrounded on all sides by thick undergrowth and twisted trees. Stuart had a fleeting glimpse of dilapidated buildings, a crumbling wall and rusting farm equipment as he launched himself towards the main thatched building. A dull light shone through one of its windows. The solid oak door seemed to swing towards him at a crazy angle as he pounded into a small paved yard, leapt over the rusting plough and crashed against the panelling. Grasping the large gargoyle doorknocker, he pounded on the door.

"Let me in!"

Looking over his shoulder as he hammered on the solid oak, he saw a dark shadow lurching through the trees just beyond the glow of the lantern in the clearing.

"*Let me in!*"

As he pounded, he realized that the creature could easily find him by the noise he was making. They were the longest moments Stuart had ever experienced in his life. A crash from somewhere behind, and the yellow glow of the lantern was extinguished.

"LET ME IN!"

Suddenly, there came the judder and rattle of a large bolt being thrown on the other side of the door, and Stuart practically fell inside as the heavy door swung inwards. A hand grasped his arm to steady him as he staggered across a musty room and into a chair. The door slammed shut and he heard the bolt being pushed back into position. Gasping for breath, Stuart looked up and saw a small and very wrinkled old man with an extremely benign face and faded-blue eyes standing at the door holding a small lantern above his stooped head. Its guttering light made shadows loom and sway throughout the room.

The old man smiled.

"Happy Birthday, son. We've been expecting you."

Stuart pointed at the window, unable to speak, as he sucked in lungfuls of the stale air. The old man slowly followed his pointing finger, smiled again, and crossed to the far side of the room to a battered door. In the gloom, Stuart could just make out the ancient furniture in the room. A gigantic cobweb stretched from an old spinning wheel in the corner to a dust-covered sideboard.

The old man opened the door and without taking his eyes from his visitor, called to someone beyond.

"Violet. He's come."

Stuart stood up, chest heaving, and moved to the fly-stained window. The faint light from within the room cast a glow into

the yard, but the blackness beyond hid anything that might …
that *was* lurking outside.

"Listen," Stuart said and turned again to the old man, who
had shut the door and moved to the table in the centre of the
room. "Have you got a telephone?"

The old man smiled.

"A phone? Have you got a phone?" Stuart demanded angrily.
"There's a dangerous animal out there. Somebody's got to
phone the police!"

"You know we haven't got a phone, Matthew," said the old
man.

The door behind him opened with a slight creak and an old
woman appeared, stooped and shambling. Stuart could see that
her face held the same indulgent smile as that of the old man. Her
eyes lit up as she looked at Stuart from under a furrowed brow.

"Matthew," she said. "We knew that you'd come back to us.
Happy Birthday, son."

Stuart braced himself and looked at the couple, anger
beginning to swell inside.

"I'm not Matthew, whoever he is. And if we don't do
something …"

Another figure entered the room. A younger man with a
checked shirt and a notably extravagant expression of grim
determination. However, the most notable thing about him was
the twelve-bore shotgun which he held pointed at Stuart's chest.

The old man placed a hand on Stuart's shoulder.

"Sit down, my boy."

As he sat, the younger man shut the door with his foot and
hissed at the old woman: "Is it him?"

The old lady smiled, nodded and pulled up a chair at the
table across from Stuart and the old man.

This is crazy! thought Stuart.

"Ten years to the day, Matthew," croaked the old man. "And
here you are, just as you said you would be. You always were
true to your word. Punctuality. Punct-u-ality."

Stuart began to stand again. The younger man waved the
shotgun in a gesture which made Stuart realize that not only
was there great danger outside, but also a very real danger *inside*.

"Would you mind telling me just what's going on?" he asked.

"You *know*, Matthew. It's been a long time now since we last saw you. And I suppose we should really explain a few things. You have every right to be angry with us for what we did, but it was all for the best. All for the best." Stuart sat down again and the old man crossed his arms on the table, before continuing. "If you hadn't been such a wild rover in the first place, Matthew, nothing would have come of it. Never mind – when you returned to your mother and I after all those years abroad we were glad to see you again." The old man pointed at the younger man with the gun. "Arnold always missed his brother, didn't you Arnold? And as for all that money you brought back with you … It's still here, you know. We've never touched a bit of it. Locked up in the cellar for ten years, 'Matthew's money' – that's what your mother calls it. We've been keeping it for you."

Stuart shifted uncomfortably in his seat and glanced at the window.

The old man continued: "So we've never stolen anything, son. You've got to understand that we didn't kill you for your money."

Stuart looked at the old man again. He *must* be mad.

"We really didn't want to kill you in the first place. But you know how it was when you came back to us. You were changed. And when the killings started, we had to shelter you, didn't we? We would never have given you away, would we, mother? We suffered far a long time, Matthew. The old gypsy lady told us what was happening and what we should do. When the little boy was killed, we had no alternative …"

The old lady leaned forward. "We were never cruel parents, Matthew. Were we, father?"

"No of course we weren't." The old man shook his head slowly and earnestly. "But anyway … you're here now, just like you said you would be. And you're not angry with us anymore for what we did."

Stuart turned to the younger man. "Listen, mate. There's an animal out there. It looks like a … well, it's … You've got to get a message to the police or something. Have you got a car?"

The young man remained impassive, shotgun still pointed at him.

"We can't have a birthday without a birthday party, can we, Violet?" said the old man.

Smiling like a small child who has just thought of a new game to play, the old woman scurried past the shotgun-wielding Arnold and into the darkness beyond.

"I'm not your son" protested Stuart. "You should know that. My name's …"

"Of course you are, Matthew", replied the old man indulgently.

"Look, I don't even … Have you got a picture? A picture of your son?"

Arnold stood slightly to one side and motioned with the shotgun at a picture hanging over the spinning wheel.

"I can't see it clearly."

Stretching across, Arnold took down the picture and gingerly placed it in front of Stuart, the barrels of the shotgun coming uncomfortably close to his face. Wiping the dust from the glass frame, Stuart saw that the face was of a very ordinary looking young man in his mid-twenties. Glassy eyes. Dark hair. The likeness to the threatening young man with the gun was unmistakeable.

"Brother?" Stuart asked.

For the first time, Arnold spoke. In a voice that quivered with fear.

"Yes."

"Listen, old man," said Stuart. "This picture doesn't even remotely look like me."

The old man wagged a reproachful finger at Stuart. "The gypsy lady said that you would be changed when you came back. Being able to change was always one of your tricks, you know."

The woman returned from her mission carrying a wooden tray. On the tray rested a cake. A huge birthday cake covered in candles, many of which were cracked and broken. A wickedly sharp cake knife lay alongside it. Stuart could see that the cake itself was old. Very old. Cobwebs fluttered on its surface. Through the mould, he could just make out that the cake had once been decorated with the legend, "Happy Birthday Matthew".

The old man gestured to Arnold to sit down with them at the table. As he sat, the woman handed him a paper party hat and then, reaching across the table, gave another to Stuart and the old man. The old man smoothed it onto his balding pate. A green hat with long spikes that rustled in the still air like a strange crown.

"Come on, Matthew. Join in the fun."

Stuart again rose to his feet, pushing the chair back as he did so.

"If you think ..."

Arnold leapt to his feet and swung the shotgun up.

"Sit down, Matthew."

The old man gripped Stuart by the coatsleeve.

"Sit ... *down* and join in the fun," he hissed vehemently through clenched teeth, the air of gentility completely gone from his voice. Stuart sat, slowly and reluctantly, putting the orange paper hat on his head. The old lady had begun to light the candles on the cake.

"It has to be done this way," hissed the old man. "The old lady said so. When you promised to come back to us, Matt ... as you were dying ... you were very angry. You would have killed us. The old lady said that you would come back on your birthday. Today. And that if we didn't arrange things properly, there wouldn't be ... wouldn't be any stopping you. You do see that, don't you son?" The tone of the old man's voice had changed again. Now he was imploring Stuart, explaining something and trying to make him understand.

"You've got to have a special cake ready for him when he returns. That's what the old lady said. A special cake. And you've got to make him welcome. That's important. You must always keep a special lantern burning out there in the clearing where the deed was done. And you can see, can't you son? We *have* made you welcome. You'll always be our boy. Nothing can change that."

Stuart banged his fist down hard on the table in anger, making the guttering candles on the cake shake, creating new shadows which leapt threateningly from the corners of the room. The old woman cried out in alarm, and the old man seized him by the wrist.

"Matthew! We've done everything that the gypsy woman said. But I should warn you. Arnold has put pieces of silver into the cartridges of his shotgun. Violet! Cut the cake!"

This is absolutely bloody crazy! thought Stuart. And then the nightmare and its logic suddenly fitted together perfectly. The whole insane sequence of events began to make sense.

Quietely, Stuart leaned across to the old man.

"I'm not Matthew. But he *is* out there – somewhere in the dark. I know he's a werewolf. He attacked me out there on the road and followed me up to the farm. He's come back alright and he's out there prowling around the house. I don't know whether this … this … ritual is supposed to placate him or something. But *believe* me … you've got the wrong person!"

The old woman shoved a plate across the table with a wedge of cake on it. It came to rest with a rattle, right in front of Stuart. Two warped candles flickered madly from the concrete-hard icing.

"Eat!"

"What?" gasped Stuart incredulously, "You must be joking…" A grey worm, cut in half by the cake knife, writhed and squirmed its way free from the cake mixture onto the plate.

"Eat!"

A gossamer thread of cobweb was caught in the flame of one of the candles and hissed as it dissolved. With stomach heaving, Stuart picked up the piece of cake and looked at the trio sitting around the table. Sitting there, in their paper hats, the shadows from the candles creeping and fluttering on their faces. For all the world it looked as if they were engaged in some weird grimacing competition.

"Eat!"

The room vibrated to the ullulating howl of a savage wolf.

Stuart dropped the cake and leapt backwards in his chair from sheer fright – which probably saved his life. As he fell to the floor, there was an ear-shattering roar as the shotgun spat bright yellow flame and sparks across the table and huge slivers of wood were ripped from the wall where Stuart had been sitting. The recoil sent Arnold hurtling backwards.

Hell had suddenly erupted in the cottage.

The fly-blown window beside the oak door suddenly exploded into a thousand glittering fragments, and as Stuart rolled on the floor he had the impression that a long clawed arm had come thrusting through the window.

The old woman screamed again as a howling wind blasted through the gaping aperture and blew out all the candles on the cake. The lantern crashed to the floor and fizzled out. Above the noise of the howling wind, and the reverberating echo of the shotgun blast, Stuart could make out the old man's voice sobbing in the darkness.

"Matthew! Matthew! We *did* love you."

The large oak door shuddered violently under the massive weight of something outside. Hammering. Scratching. Ripping. The bolt of the door rattled and clattered noisily. With the rending noise of a tree being felled, the hinges on the door screeched in protest as the oak burst inwards. Lying nearby, Stuart tried to avoid the oak panelling as it crashed to the floor. But a length of wood struck him on the shoulder as he tried to rise, and knocked him to the ground yet again. For an instant, the doorframe was blackened by something entering. And then Stuart could see the moon shining brightly in the sky as the figure passed.

Something had come into the room.

But as it passed, Stuart heard a voice. Not a human voice. More like an inhuman snarling from behind a mask. Muzzled. Spoken through lips that were never meant to speak.

Stuart kicked the oak panelling to one side and leapt through the shattered doorway. Trees swam at him crazily as he blundered panic stricken through the undergrowth, expecting the nightmare padding sound of clawed feet and inhuman panting which would mean that the thing was pursuing him again. Out into the main road again, he never looked back for fear of seeing that abominable shape crashing through the bushes after him.

Of his flight back into civilization, he could never really remember very much – and would never have thought it possible that he could run twelve miles back into the town. But he did.

In the months to come, the fact that Crowfast Farm didn't appear on any map didn't really surprise him. And when, three years later, he passed that bend in the road again where he had crashed over the gate, he wasn't at all surprised to find that there was no gate in evidence. He didn't even bother to look for the signpost which indicated that Crowfast Farm was two miles up the road. He knew it wouldn't be there.

He would have doubted his own sanity if it hadn't been for one thing. The warped birthday candle which he had found in his pocket.

The whole sequence of events would never be very clear again. But the voice which Stuart had heard in the doorway would stay with him for ever. Inhuman it may have been. And spoken in a horribly distorted voice. But the words were clear enough.

Matthew had returned home to even the score.

"*Many Happy Returns.*"

Roberta Lannes

ESSENCE OF THE BEAST

Roberta Lannes is a native of Southern California. She has been teaching junior high school English, art, and related subjects for over thirty years. Her writing career began early in college with a few sales to literary reviews. In 1970 she began a short career in stand-up comedy, doing improv, and wrote for several other comedians.

In 1985, she turned to the genre of science fiction and dark fantasy. Her short fiction has appeared in such anthologies as Cutting Edge, Lord John Ten, Fantasy Tales, Splatterpunks *and* Splatterpunks II, Alien Sex, The Bradbury Chronicles, Still Dead, Dark Voices 5, Deathport, Best New Horror 3 *and* The Year's Best Horror Seventh Annual Collection. *She claims she has every intention of finally completing a novel as retirement from teaching approaches.*

As she explains, " 'Essence of the Beast' evolved from a dream I had about burning eyes at the end of my hallway and mad dogs shifting into human form in order to hide their insanity. I'd never written about werewolves, nor do I truly understand the legend and lore of their kind. So, I summoned up four of my friends, set us out at the end of the road, gave us guises and purpose and, amazingly, I had werewolves, of a sort. I am fascinated by innocence and its loss, and this story took me down that path, once again ..."

It had been too long since our last visitor. Living in a ramshackle house nestled in the folds of low rolling hills, not many wayfarers made it out to us. If they did, we'd baited them or they arrived lost. The UPS man was the last. Of late, our hunger has been making us irritable. Each of us threatens in lean times to go off on our own again – an idle threat since the four of us are bonded in a most unusual way.

Then the young man in his van came, begging for work fixing up the house. Our hunger must have created a vacuum, sucking him from whatever errand he had found himself on along our long road.

The moment we set our eyes on him ambling up the drive, we began our transformations. I grew into Chelsea Wiggens – twenty years old, my eyes a bright yellow-green, set wide apart, my skin olive pale and flawless, my hair auburn, long and soft with curl, and my body the right kind of perfect to create a child. "Ripe", Quinell would call it. Fromme shifted into my grizzled but soft-hearted Pa, Lyla my jealous (as usual) sister – at once pretty and daunting, and Quinell got his jollies once more playing Ma, his once acute dramatic skills turned shrill and unreliable.

Randall Buss found his way into our parlour after we'd all hurried out to greet him. This fellow had a scent that inspired thoughts of a good meal in the others, but somehow not in me. I found myself hungering for him with a strange visceral longing. The feeling was unfamiliar and it put a host of fears to work in me. I wanted to understand it, but in order to do that, I would have to protect the object of my obscure desire from the feeding frenzy in which my companions were preparing to indulge. No easy task. I saw the ravenous looks on Quinell, Fromme and Lyla's faces, and confused, I wondered why I, too, wasn't slavering ghoulishly. His coming disturbed and intrigued me, changed me, though I had no idea why.

He seemed to struggle with an obvious discomfort with strangers. We stood around, waiting to take our cues from Fromme. When he took a seat on the lumpy sofa, we took our places around him.

Fromme eyed the young man up and down. "Sit yourself down. What's your name, boy?"

"Randall Buss, sir, but everyone's always just called me Buss." Buss sat down in the new recliner, Quinell's latest acquisition.

"So Buss, you say you want to fix this place up for us? You a carpenter? Painter?"

Buss folded his hands in his lap. His paint-spattered khaki pants were short enough to expose bare ankles over well-worn moccasins. I watched his muscles ripple under his faded blue T-shirt as he flexed nervously.

"Yes, sir. I've rebuilt eleven houses from foundation to roof since I was thirteen and I have licences to do just about everything from wiring to plumbing. Lots of experience. Have references, too, if you want to see them."

Out of the corner of my eye, I saw Lyla wipe drool from the corner of her mouth. She scared me most of all. Her hunger had always been the fiercest among us.

I stepped in. "Pa, you've been complaining about this relic for the last five years, saying it looks like it should be torn down. Give him the chance. What's there to lose?"

Fromme cleared his throat. "Well, Chelsea, if you and your sister want to do the extra housework for this boy now as well as for your Ma and me, I suppose we can try him out." "Pa" glanced back at Buss. "What's a boy like you going cost me?"

Quinell arched "her" back. "Now Pa, we must be careful with the inheritance. Can't go spending it all on an impulse."

Fromme frowned at "her". "I'm the one who signs the cheques. You keep your worries to yourself. If you think this boy is out to gouge us, just say so."

Quinell sniffed the air, sighing with resignation. "Whatever you say."

Buss grinned. "Sir, I think you'll be pleased with my estimate. Why don't I take a look around and figure out what needs attention and write you up a list with costs?"

"Why, that's a great idea, boy. Then we'll make us an educated decision. How's that Ma?"

Quinell looked away. "Fine."

Buss rose up, nodded to each of us, his eyes taking me in just a little bit longer than the others, then went off outside to make his calculations. Inside, we began making our own.

Lyla was the one who detested the ritual of dancing with the prey. She was anxious to just get to it. Quinell enjoyed the dance more than the meal. And Fromme and I had always found ourselves adaptable. How we'd ever managed together and keep ourselves satisfied, I'll never be sure, but now the stakes were different. I wanted the dance to go on as long as possible. I wanted the opportunity to know the forces driving me and what would come of them.

"I can just taste him." Lyla slipped back into her bestial ugliness.

Quinell shook his head. "You're so ... repugnant when you're like this. Don't you want the taste of fear on his blood when you rip the flesh from his bones, dear?" "Ma's" snout lengthened a little as Quinell's control slipped, too.

Fromme stood up and growled. "Oh, shut up you two. We have a meal hovering about outside like a fish ready to take bait, so stop this posturing. Chelsea, you've got a way with the young ones. Why don't you go on out there and do some charming?"

"I don't know, Fromme." I sat still, the power of being the baby among us settling in my stomach. "I got a feeling about this one. Something's wrong. Off." I stared outside, my brow wrinkling. "He's trouble, this Buss."

"Don't listen to her!" Lyla barked. "She just wants him all to herself."

I stayed put and watched the hierarchy working. Quinell tsked. "Lyla, Lyla, Lyla. Always the jealous one. You're an old hag and you just refuse to face it."

Fromme let his head fall back to the chair, exasperated. "None of us has ever seen Chelsea go after large prey on her own, and I will not entertain thoughts of her doing so now. She was right with the runaway wife and the home teacher. Both brought repercussions, but without her warnings, we might have been found out. Destroyed. So stop this and listen to her."

"I don't care what Chelsea says, I'm hungry and I'm going to have me some Buss stew." Lyla hurried out of the room and down the hall to her room. Her claws clacked on the hardwood floor until her door slammed.

"I'll listen, Chelsea, dear. I'm the eldest and have no desire for trouble here." Quinell stuffed grey hair into a dishevelled bun on his "Ma" head.

"Go on." Fromme nodded to me.

"I know we're all hungry. The next visitor isn't expected for another week, so I'd better have a good reason if I want to hold off. I think I do." I closed my eyes, hoping for a reason to pop into my head. "I think he knows what we are. I think he's a very intuitive boy. Sort of psychic. That and … perhaps he's been sent here to check us out. Sort of a front man for …"

"The home teacher's family!" Quinell shrieked. "She's right! We keep wondering when the other shoe's going to drop on *that* scandal."

Fromme's brow knit. He looked to Quinell, then me. "Is he right?"

The fates were favouring me. "That's the feeling I had. It's only been ten months. The company could have hired a private detective by now, and sent out someone …" I wrung my hands. "I remember when that woman showed up, the wife, how agitated and paranoid she was. I *knew* there was someone not far behind her, searching for her. She was running away, for god's sakes. The teacher wasn't so obvious. Who'd have thought his company sent out a supervisor to check on the progress of the student-teacher relationship. There wasn't much to bank my sense of dread on, there. And now my assertion is even thinner than that, so I understand why everyone's so sceptical. But, the ominous feeling is no less strong."

"Then it's settled. We send him away." Fromme bit his lip.

"No!" I countered. Quinell and Fromme looked at me, startled. "If he *is* the man sent to check us out, then we need to let him stay here, snoop around, and find that we are only what we claim to be. The Wiggens at the end of Bradford County Road. And if the subject of the teacher comes up, we say what we said then, that the man never showed up. When Mr Buss is pleased, he'll surely say his work is done and be off. We send him away now, we may let on we're scared."

Fromme, the ever-cautious and wise, opened his palms and cocked his head. "We'd have to be so careful, Chelsea. What about our shape-shifting? The cycles and rhythms we respect. Our condition. Over time, we'll be found out, surely." Quinell nodded in agreement.

"Our lives are at stake. We've grown lazy out here. We can

hold our shapes at will for days. Weeks if we want. We'll have to."
I frowned then, thinking of Lyla.

"Lyla won't do it. I know her. But she'll go off and find some large game in town, I'll bet. Anything but hold her shape for days until she can feed here." I prayed it wouldn't be so. She'd put us all off our dance before, inviting unwanted attention to us with a mysterious death too close to home.

"And what if he turns out to be nothing more than a carpenter?" Fromme asked.

I smirked. "We feast."

Quinell lurched out of the chair and minced to the hallway. "I'll inform Miss Fur-face of our decision."

Fromme looked doubtful, but acquiescent. "Go on, then." He turned to me. "This is your dance, Chelsea, so go out there and charm him."

I went to Fromme and hugged him. I felt his affection and acceptance, and hated to be taking advantage of it.

Buss was crouched down at the side of the house, his head inside the hole where a metal grille once protected a crawlspace. I tried humming as I approached so as not to startle him. He pulled his head out and stared up at me.

"Well, hello, Mr Buss. Don't mind me. I was just checking that you didn't fall into the old well or trip over one of those nasty vines from the banyan tree." I smiled my best.

"I'm all right." His head disappeared again into the hole.

"What's so interesting in there?"

He mumbled something. I went and stood right beside him.

"I can't hear you. You want some lemonade or something? It's hot out here, today."

He leaned out of the hole and gazed up at me, grinning. He shielded his eyes from the sun. "Water, please. No ice."

I nodded, turning to go before I let him see the flush I felt coming up my neck to my face.

When I returned, he was resting on an overturned washtub that sat by the path down to the glen. The view was best at sundown, but he seemed to like it just then. He emptied the glass and set it on the ground before speaking a word.

"Thanks." He drank me in with his eyes a moment, then looked away.

"I'll bet we've got hundreds of dollars worth of repairs around here."

"Yes ma'am, you do."

"Are we going to make you rich?"

He smirked. "I take my time and do a good job, but I don't make a lot doing it that way. I usually get a set fee."

"So why do you do it?" I sat down beside him on the washtub. There wasn't much room and our hind ends touched.

"I love it. Simple as that. I've loved building and repairing things since I first could grab onto a crib rail. My folks like to tell of a time I wasn't even two years old, I tried to fix my night light."

"Did you fix it?" I could smell him, his sweat had a scent like verdigris and musk and skin too long in the sun.

"Burned myself. It wasn't broken." He chuckled. It was a nice sound. Sincere. Not what I was used to hearing day in and out.

"If you don't make much, how do you live?" He smelled me, now. I saw his nostrils flare at the first hint of pheromone.

"Ah … I'm happy if I have food to eat, a roof over my head, and my health. That doesn't take much if you live simply. All I want is some comfort and doing what I love."

My human side wallowed in guilt, listening to him talk of the good work he does, what little he wants, while all I've done for most of my life was leave people in ruins, broken beyond repair. I didn't know anything else, until now. Now I wanted to spare a man, go hungry, and dance into the darkness. The unknown.

"You must know a lot of peace." I sighed.

He turned and really looked at me then. "What about you? Out here in the middle of nowhere."

"Me? I cook. Clean. Read a lot. Voraciously, actually. I watch the seasons pass." I didn't want to lie to him. His honesty made lies seem vulgar.

"That's not much. What're you waiting for?" His eyes finished taking me in and wandered off over to the fence. It looked like so many greying loose teeth about to fall.

"Maybe all I need *is* to be out here in the middle of nowhere." He blinked at me, blankly. I smiled, stood. "You want to take a walk, see what's at the bottom of the glen?"

He nodded. As we walked, he scratched his head, fidgeted with his clothes, nervously. "Your Pa own this place?"

"Well, it's a long story, but the short end of it is that we inherited the house and some money from Pa's brother a while back. A lucky visit right when his brother was dying and had no one to leave it all to. Pa called for us and we've been here ever since."

"You go to school in town?" He grabbed a switch and began whipping it through the air, making a sound like the wind screaming through the oaks.

"No. I've been home taught since I was young. I love to read and it just follows that I'd end up knowing as much as a person who went to school. What about you?"

"Huh. Well, I went to Duke University and got a bachelor's degree in general science, but that was only to please my folks. They'd saved all of their lives to send me and my sister to college. My sister teaches at Rutgers. When I was done with school, all I wanted was to get back to fixing things."

I was impressed. I wished I could have told him I'd spent six years at Oxford and had a master's degree in English Literature, but that was too long ago and my ruse was so rigid, I often forgot my past.

"Why science?"

"Science explains how things are made up and function. And if I'd taken to school, I'd have gone on to study to be a doctor."

"Well, then we would have never met." I blushed. "And Pa wouldn't have the house repaired. You think you have an estimate yet?"

He smiled. We'd come to the bottom of the glen. Trees sheltered the path from the sun and it was twenty degrees cooler. I leaned too far into him, feeling the heat of his body. I nearly fell.

"Oooh. Sorry." He grabbed me. Our faces were inches apart. "We'd better get back."

"Yeah." He pulled me up, his mouth coming down on mine suddenly. His mouth tasted sweet and coppery, of silver, water.

I lost my breath as we kissed. I hadn't thought I'd know how. It came right back to me.

I struggled weakly, then broke away. I was faint, worried I'd lose my form. It was becoming clear that fear wasn't the only feeling that affected the enchantment.

He apologized and said something about my being so beautiful, how could he be so close and not show how he felt? I was hardly a woman of the world, but a line hadn't changed much over the years. Though he hardly seemed the type.

"You must've lost your mind in this heat, Mr Buss." I grinned over my shoulder as I skipped away up the path back home. I didn't look back, but I could hear him jogging behind me.

Everyone, even Lyla, held their forms and manners through dinner. I'd prepared a large casserole of rabbit meat with millet and vegetables. We had fresh-baked bread, beans and a blueberry pie for dessert. The rabbit meat was underdone, as we like it, but Buss never complained.

Quinell brought out two bottles of wine and we began our usual after-dinner dance with the prey.

"I was pleasantly surprised by your bid, boy." Fromme sucked on his pipe, letting the spiral of smoke snake upwards. The smoke was the same shade of pale as his hair and just as wavy. In the dim light, it looked as though his hair was leaving his head, dissipating into thin air.

"How's that?" Buss sipped at the wine, grimacing slightly after each swallow.

"It's reasonable. I'd expected something much higher, but then someone would have to pay me a fortune just to *consider* lifting a beam or sanding a post. When can you start?"

"Right first thing tomorrow. I'll make up a list of the few things I'll need to start, and drive back to Haywood to get them. I want to begin with the foundation. No bugs that I could find, but you've got some rot."

"No doubt. House is close to a hundred years old." Fromme nodded to me.

I put my hand on Buss's forearm as it lay on the table beside mine. "Will you need any help?"

He shivered slightly at my touch. I noticed Quinell stifling a look of extreme pleasure at my effect on Buss.

"I work alone. But, thanks for asking."

"Oh, I was just thinking I would ask someone in town if he wanted some extra work. After all, it's a big job."

He moved his arm away and grew quiet. He stared out the dining room window into the inky night. All I saw was our reflections in the glass.

Lyla stood and began clearing dishes. She growled at my ear as she removed mine.

"Ma" cleared her throat. "So Mr Buss, what brought you down our long stretch of road?"

Buss sat up straighter and finished off his wine. I poured him another glass.

"I don't know. Curiosity. I suppose I figured anything this far out would probably need fixing. If there wasn't anything along the way, I'd have kept on driving."

"You must do a lot of driving." I brushed his leg with mine as I crossed one long leg over the other. He noticed.

"Uh, yes, some. Seems I stay in a place longer than I ever took driving there."

"You like remote places, especially?"

"I don't know. Probably. I like quiet. Nature. Isn't much of that in the middle of a town. The suburbs."

"Yes, we're very lucky here." Fromme poked at his ashes with an ivory tamper, eyeing Buss and I. "Chelsea, why don't you show Mr Buss a room upstairs. The one next to the bath in the front'll do."

Buss glanced at me. "I *am* kind of tired. I don't usually ..." He pointed to the wine.

"All settled, then. We'll say goodnight." Everyone stood.

"Thanks for a really good meal. Home cooking is always the best." He grinned. Lyla swept in to grab more dishes and licked her lips as she looked Buss over.

"Come on, Buss. I'll show you to the room." I took his arm and hurried him away from more discussion and Lyla's chops.

The room was ten by ten and the ceiling was low by the window, giving it a claustrophobic feel, but Buss didn't seem to mind. The dusty dark-stained oak furniture and twin bed covered with a green and white chenille spread were better than the mattress in the back of his van. I'd have chosen the L-shaped room in the back for Buss, but I knew Fromme was thinking of how Lyla or Quinell might run out to forage during the night. They took off out the back way every time.

"I'll open this window. This room's still hot and awfully stuffy from the day." As I leaned into the recessed window box and tugged on the window frame, I felt my skirt slide up my thighs. The window went up in jerky spurts, my face growing red with the thought of him looking at my backside.

"There." I turned. His eyes were on me, his face soft and dear with lust and sweet vulnerability. "I'll be getting you some sheets and towels." I walked by him, knowing my scent was growing stronger with the coming of the moon, letting him breathe me in.

"All right." He sighed. "I'm close to sleep, so don't be long."

"You may want to wash up. Bath's just next door. The shower grunts when you turn the water up too high." He just looked at me, a man's hunger in his eyes. I hurried out.

Lyla caught up with me at the linen cupboard. "You're hogging that boy for yourself. I *know* it. I've been wrong before, but this time I'm sure."

I took a chance. "You're right, Lyla, but not the way you're thinking. I want him all right, but not for the feasting. I think I want to lay with him." I looked away from her just then, not wanting her to see how fervently desire smouldered in me.

"You want to what?"

"Shush! You want to ruin it for me?"

She whispered and growled at the same time. Only Lyla could make that eerie sound. "What could you possibly want by laying with him? He's not one of us."

"I … I don't know. I've got this feeling … and I want to find out what it's about." I looked back at her.

"Then eat him, right?" She did a twisted metamorphosis before my eyes, turning beast and monster and Lyla in one. Her anger always cost her control.

"No, damn you. Don't you hear me? I don't even want to *taste* him." I stared at the light under Buss's room's door. "Not that way."

"I don't believe you."

"Lyla, I've never lied to you. Think it over. You have my word you can do whatever you want with him … after."

She stared at me, incredulous. "What could you possibly want to know?"

"I'd better go. He'll wonder …" I rushed away as Lyla transformed into wolf, her eyes like two golden embers floating at the end of the dark hall behind me.

Buss was lying on the bed, eyes closed, his shirt off. I stood over him, aching to run my hands over his hairless chest and tautly muscled arms. I wanted to taste his skin, so tanned and smooth. His legs were splayed, the fabric showing the outline of his thighs, his groin. I set the linens on the chiffonnier.

"Chelsea." He whispered my name. "I think I drank too much wine." He pulled himself up on one elbow. His eyes were heavy-lidded now, his smile crooked.

"I'll go. You get some sleep. You start work tomorrow." I turned to go. "I'll leave the stuff here for you." I motioned to the chiffonnier.

He got up, went to the door, shut it quietly, then put out a hand to me. "I want to say goodnight."

"Mr Buss, I …" I wanted to refuse his touch, to lengthen the dance, but I was driven to him, just as I am to prey. I folded into his arms, into him it seemed. I forgot my skin, sensing his heart beating, or was it mine? Our lips made contact, moving apart as our tongues met. I swooned. The fear of losing my shape pricked the edge of my consciousness, was lost in the moment, then returned.

"Please." I pulled away. "Too quick. I …" The fear pierced my lust, tempering it.

He pulled me close again, as if he hadn't heard me. It was then I could feel the warmth and bulk of his cock against my hip. His lips went to my neck. I growled.

"Hey." He backed away. "Jesus." His eyes were wide.

I thought for an instant I'd lost my form, my hands felt for telltale signs. There were none. It was my growl that stopped him. "I just want … to go slowly. This is my first … first time … you know."

He chuckled softly and hit himself in the forehead, animatedly. "I didn't think … my god, I'm sorry." He went to the bed and flopped onto it. "You have this effect on me. I don't know. Forgive me. I'll be more careful, Chelsea."

I didn't know what to say. I nodded numbly. We stared at one another for a few seconds. Then I caught my breath, smiled weakly and left.

I slept on the floor in my bestial form, the door locked and barred with my oak wardrobe. I laid awake a long time in the night, listening to the house creaking, shifting, the sounds of claws clattering on hardwood, waiting for the sound of human footsteps by my door. I hadn't been able to find the energy to manifest my form all night.

Morning light rose up through my bedroom window until its heat found me. I stretched. Yawned. Rarely did I wake hungry as I did this day. I'd forgotten the beast's, *my* extraordinary appetite. I knew I would have to go into the glen and beyond to the woods, and dance with animal prey for now.

I put my paws on the window ledge, searching the grounds for a sign of Buss. I heard Quinell in the kitchen arguing with Lyla. The knoll outside my corner window was brown with dry grass. I leapt onto it, scurrying over the top as quickly as I could to avoid detection. I snuck a look back and saw no one.

My hunger drove me deep into the woods. It was cool under the dense foliage, and I loved the feeling of moss and fern beneath my paws. As the beast, I smelled everything much stronger. Earth and loam, sap and water, bird, insect and prey. Sunlight came in bright spears through the thick leafy canopy. The buzzing of wasps and tinkling of stream filled the air around me. When I was here, in my element, I was animal and no other.

I picked up the scent of rabbit and followed it. A new mother and her young were nestled in the elbow of tangled roots at the base of a tree. She sensed me right away, and her scream pierced the stillness. Her choice would be to protect her brood and fight, I guessed, but instead she ran. Instinct drove me past her offspring, after her. Cunning bitch.

In no mood for toying with her, I focused my appetite and chased her into a bowl of earth beneath a fallen tree. Cornered, she leapt at me. My jaws snapped around her, killing her instantly. I devoured her quickly without really tasting her, leaving little for the carrion beetles to work on. And as I turned to lumber off toward the stream to wash, I saw Fromme on the hillside watching me. He nodded and ran off in the direction of home.

Sometime before noon, I gathered up my female form and ambled up the path from the glen. Quinell was "Ma", gardening in the small patch of land he liked to grow herbs. I looked for Buss, but saw that his van was gone. Quinell caught me looking.

"He's gone off to Haywood, but should be back any minute."

"Ah. I was hoping I wouldn't get caught. I went off into the woods this morning."

"Ha. Lyla was out half the night. I met her coming in on my way out before the sun came up. Gave her a piece of my mind about giving that boy cause to suspect us. Fromme was wandering out as I came in. Perhaps we're all too hungry to let Buss make us too cautious."

"You're right. We'd better be more careful." My stomach clenched with fear around my breakfast.

"Well, it won't be long before we feast." "Ma" gingerly pulled some rosemary up by the roots.

"I'm telling you, there's something we don't know about this one. He's dangerous."

"Maybe to you, he is. I've known you an awfully long time and I can't say I've ever seen you with less guile or more lust. You'll bring us all down, dear, if you give in to those human pleasures."

I blinked, stunned. I think of my self as so opaque, hidden. "You mean you …"

Quinell winked at me. "I see right through you, darling. I don't think Lyla or Fromme do. Neither of them would let their carnal desires eclipse their carnivorous natures. Fromme's too staid, phlegmatic, when not a beast. And Lyla is an angry, most suspicious animal in any form. She'd never let herself get close to a human enough to … to let them have a part of *her*."

"Have you ever … you know … given in to the feelings?"

"Oh, yes, love. In my youth, before I was bitten by the brute who made me what I am. I was quite … promiscuous. After all, I was the darling of the theatre set, with my Byronesque appearance and princely manner. I could have any swain or damsel I chose."

"I mean since. Since becoming."

"Why, of course. With others of our kind. And once. Once with a man I fell in love with." He stared off into the woods and sighed. "He didn't know … about me." Quinell bowed his head and "Ma" began to weep. I knelt beside him and tried to comfort him. He shrivelled in my arms, transforming into something small and bleating.

I heard the sound of the van and stood up. Quinell turned beast, then "Ma", wiping his face with his apron.

"I'm sorry, Quinell. I hope we can talk …"

We heard the side door slap closed. Fromme looked concerned, catching us in such an emotional pose, then he walked away up the drive.

I went inside, afraid to let Buss see me so soon after I'd gone on a feeding. I was sated, yet I felt the yearning for him just as intensely as I had the night before. I also felt how the yearning was turning Chelsea from soft and pretty to desperate and waggish. Outside, Fromme watched Buss stack lumber as Quinell tended his garden. Inside, I would feel safe, for a while.

I went around the back of the house to my window, remembering I'd barricaded myself in the night before. The window ledge was too high. I looked past Quinell, watching the corner of the house, waiting to see anyone, movement, anything. Quinell signalled it was safe. I shifted, feeling drained by the changes in too quick a succession. I loped up the knoll and leapt into my room, hitting the floor wrong, sliding into the wardrobe, cracking the mirror and turning an ankle.

Exhausted from shifting shape again, I moved the wardrobe back to its regular position and made my way down to the kitchen to put ice on my pains. Lyla swaggered in. "Did Chelsea fall down and go 'boom'?"

"Oh, shut up, you old cow. You don't care about any of it."

"I care about getting my big meal, girly. I want to taste that huge steak that's outside propping up our foundation. Why should I care what you want?"

"Because there might still be a human heart beating beside the beast's in you."

She chortled. "You know what your problem is? You and Quinell and Fromme? You haven't accepted that you're beasts. You still long to be what you were. All human. Not me. I relish my bestial form, and all the animal instincts that go with it. No more being some vulnerable little lady – all form and manners and no power. You all hold onto the past." She spat on the floor. "That's what I think of the past."

"If you detest us all so much, why don't you leave, Lyla?"

"Believe it or not, you fools serve your purpose." She twirled and danced away, leaving me with a rage in my gut.

Poetry books piled on my bed, a pitcher of lemonade and a half-empty glass on my nightstand, I sat curled up under my window catching whatever breeze wafted in this late afternoon. My ankle felt better, but my head still ached. I was deep into Elizabeth Barrett Browning, when someone tapped on my door. I hoped it was Quinell, wanting to finish our discussion.

"Come in."

Buss stuck his head in. "I'm done for the day." He grinned at the sweating pitcher. "Mind if I have some of that lemonade?"

I sat up, patting down my sundress and fanning myself. "I suppose." I could smell his sweat and musk as he came in. I closed my eyes and could taste him.

He poured himself some lemonade in my glass. "It's cool under the house, but hot as hell moving all the lumber and supplies back and forth."

Buss sat opposite me on the end of the bed. "Oh, I shouldn't sit here after being under the house …" He stood up suddenly. "I'm going to shower, clean up. Then I'll stop back. How's that?"

"All right." He smiled at me, and I wanted to follow him into the shower. Whatever forces were at work in me were growing in strength. "Wait. I have an idea."

"Yeah?"

"Let me show you the stream and the falls. It's a hike into the woods a ways, but it's worth it. You could wash there. The water's cool and clean and it's so pretty."

He took my hand and yanked me off of the bed, my ankle turned with a sharp pain. "Ow." He looked back at me as he let my hand go.

"Sorry. Come on." He was like a giddy kid.

We raced to the stream. I fought the urge to shift and go the distance on all fours, the earth under my bare paws. When we got close, I slowed and he ran on ahead. My ankle hurt. I could barely wait until the cool water was rushing over the pain.

When I got to the stream, he had rolled up his pants and was knee-deep in it. "Hey, Chelsea, this is great!"

I stepped in beside him, shrieking at the cold *and* welcoming it. "Come on. Let's go in."

Buss hurried to the bank, peeled off his T-shirt, dropped his pants and stepped out of his shoes in one sweeping movement. I was startled by how white his body was where the sun hadn't tanned him. He saw me looking and chuckled.

"You just going to watch or were you thinking you might join me?" He walked into the shallows, shivered, then dunked himself to the neck.

I closed my eyes, grabbed the hem of my dress and pulled it over my head. I tossed it to the bank and let myself fall backwards into the water. I felt the bruise on my head as the cold water touched my scalp.

"It's freezing! Whew!"

Buss waded upstream to where I curled myself, back against the current. When he was beside me, I let him take me in his arms.

"I'll warm you up." He held me tightly, his lips brushing over my head and face.

I twisted my body so he was wrapped around me. The water and his tongue and the moment took over. I concentrated on holding my form in a corner of my mind, while the remainder of me turned to putty.

We rolled over well-worn rock until we were on the wet bank. I felt the cool of our skin from the water, the earth beneath us, the dappling of sunlight through the trees and the warmth of his tongue and lips and hands as they gently played over my body. I knew nothing but the sensations, the smell of him, the sound of his breathing, our moans accompanied by the babbling of the stream. When he entered me, I felt his warmth there, too.

My instincts kicked in and I moved so that he was behind me. He didn't mind, his hands going over my breasts, kneading the nubs of my nipples. He began making growling noises, his teeth and lips taking nips at my back and neck. I could feel the muscles inside me closing around him, milking him. My breath came in hurried gasps as I felt myself sinking into a kind of dusk, a sur-reality. I wasn't Chelsea, nor was I the beast. I was both, rutting in the woods, grunting and moaning, an animal and a woman, body and heart, feeling, falling. Falling.

When he came, his cry was so loud, the birds flew off their branches in a sudden cacophony of thrashing wings. I howled as the bucking stopped and that dusk slowly grew into lucidity and light. Buss's full weight fell on me. My legs gave way and we lay there, he still locked inside me. The air was alive with birds in song, and the frogs began to croak. I listened to his breathing, the sound rasping from deep in his throat. An animal sound.

I followed my first impulse, to release him and lick him clean. He lay back, a half-sleep overtaking him. Soon he was aroused again and once more we coupled. More lazily, as if time were suspended for the sake of pure pleasure. He touched me in ways I had only read of, my body knowing exactly what to do, though my mind reeled.

I was released in some way that reached into the core of me, threatening my shape. For a few moments, I shifted, thankful that Buss's eyes were shut. But his hands knew – my fur lengthening, my muscles growing, rippling. I held his face to my neck as I strained to return to form. It was Chelsea who let him go, the beast finally settling somewhere inside of me. He seemed to search me with a muted fear. I let him, his eyes scanning me, his fingertips lightly tracing my curves. When he was done, he lay back, satisfied, but wary.

My slow grin warmed him and when we kissed, I saw

something tender and sweet in his eyes. I had the urge to weep, but tears didn't come.

We rinsed ourselves in the stream as the light grew amber then crimson. We said nothing, our eyes speaking the language of two connected by a special union.

I walked just behind him all the way back home. He turned often, smiling at me. I grinned back. Something had grown between the two of us. The longing I'd felt before had been transformed into a feeling of connection, warm and nurturing. It was very different from the bond I had with the others – a bond forged by shared sins and harbored secrets. Thinking of the others suddenly left me with a chill in my bones. As we neared the house, I could see the peeling white clapboard across the glen, and my gut knotted.

They'd take one look at me, at us, and *know*. Lyla knew what I'd wanted, as did Quinell. Surely, Lyla had said something about it to Fromme. Once I'd had my way with Buss, they'd be waiting – appetites raging and ready for the feast. I didn't want them to take him away from me so soon. Not yet.

"Buss, stop." He took a step and turned to me, his arms open. I went to him. "I ... I don't want them to know. You know."

"Oh." His face fell. "Yeah. Your father would fire me and then he'd kill me. What do you want me to do?"

I kissed him. "Can you act? Pretend that we just had a walk in the woods and that nothing's different?"

"I guess. Can you?"

I doubted he could. He epitomized simple honesty, sincerity. "I'm a pretty good actress when I have to be. Just don't let them know. You're right about him wanting to kill you."

His brow knit. I stared at him in wonder. I'd come to care so much about what happened to him. To our *prey*. I thought about wounding him, making him one of us. At least he'd have a chance of being spared and we might spend eternity together, in immortality. But I recalled how I felt about the beast who'd nearly killed me, left me for dead, transforming me into something not human, not animal, unfit for the life either might have lived well. I loathed that beast. I *still* loathed him. I couldn't stand the thought of Buss hating me. Not for a moment, let alone forever.

He regarded me with sudden urgency. "We could leave, Chelsea. Just pack up and go. I can get work anywhere." He seemed surprised by his own suggestion.

"No. I can't. Not now. Just promise you won't let on."

"Chelsea, I love you. I'll do anything."

I heard the words and felt myself shifting, my edges growing soft with a growing ache in my heart. I hugged him tightly, struggling to keep my form. I mumbled the same to him.

"Now go. Walk in on your own. I'll follow in a bit. Tell them you saw me wander up into the woods and went looking for me. Say you couldn't find me."

"Right. See you." We kissed again. I tasted myself on his tongue, sweet, musky. It made me giggle.

He waved, then made his way down the path into the glen.

I wrapped my arms around myself, still feeling Buss inside me. When he was out of my range of vision, I threw back my head and howled. Tears came then. Even as I shifted onto all fours, I bayed my heart out. So this was love. Hope. Pain.

They took him that evening, before I returned. They saved me some, but I wouldn't eat. I'd lost my hunger. I'd changed, forever, knowing love. Quinell understood.

I'm not like them any longer. Fromme, Lyla, even Quinell. Perhaps I never was. I'm with child, now. Buss's child, and mine. I've chosen to stay with them, though, for now. They're all I've known. My family. I know I'll have to leave eventually, when the child is born. The child won't be like them, either. And they will always have their hunger.

They still speak of Buss, but always as prey. To me, he was my lover, my friend, the man who loved to fix things, the father of my baby, honest, good and trusting. That's the way I want my child to know him, his father. A loving man. Never the prey.

Mark Morris

IMMORTAL

Mark Morris became a full-time writer in 1988 on the British government's Enterprise Allowance Scheme, and a year later saw the publication of his first novel, Today *(aka* The Horror Club*). Since then he has published more than a dozen others, including* Stitch, The Immaculate, The Secret of Anatomy, Mr Bad Face, Longbarrow, Genesis, Nowhere Near an Angel, The Deluge *and four* Doctor Who *novelizations.*

He has recently published a Torchwood *novel,* Bay of the Dead, *and he is editor of the HWA Bram Stoker Award-nominated* Cinema Macabre, *a book of fifty horror movie essays by genre luminaries.*

The author reveals that "Immortal" came about as the result of a three-way collision of desires: "Firstly, and most obviously, was my desire to write a story that would pander to the thematic requirements of this particular anthology. Secondly was my desire to write a police procedural, inspired largely, it must be said, by a number of recent excellent television series. Thirdly was my desire to make use of a particular location, in this case the railway platform at Stalybridge in Cheshire.

"I went over there to do a talk and reading at the local library. I arrived in an almost deserted town to find a huge banner plastered across the front of the library with my name written on it in three-foot high, blood-red letters. Weird. After the talk, which was surprisingly well-attended, I sat on the railway platform with a friend who had travelled over from Warrington to see me. There was an excellent bar on the platform and we sat and got slowly pissed as we waited for

our respective trains home. I've always loved macabre tales centered around railway stations and this seemed the ideal location for just such a tale – still in use but somehow lost and forgotten.

"We sat there for a good while as it got gradually colder and darker, but though we saw a number of trains pulling into and then speeding out of the station, I don't think we ever saw anyone alighting or ascending. Very strange … but, then again, we had had a few pints …"

I feel him inside me, and I know that he is hungry. He whispers to me. He says: What you do is not murder. It is instinct. Survival. These creatures are not your kind.

I know what he says is true, and I know that I can't stop until it is over, that it is out of my control, but that doesn't make it any easier to bear. I ask him: Don't they have a right to survival too?

And he says: Hush. Listen to your blood.

Most people were still asleep, locked into forgetfulness. As George Farrow stepped from the car and crossed the pavement, early morning frost crackling beneath his feet, he glanced up at curtained windows and felt a stab of envy so acute he had to deep-breathe it away.

Half an hour ago he'd been wrenched from his own warm and welcome oblivion by the clamouring of the telephone. Even as his hand groped from beneath the duvet, he'd felt the chill of the morning settling on his skin, seeping into his bones.

Detective Sergeant Jackson's briskness, as ever, infuriated him. "We've got another one, sir, Cumberland Street. Less than a mile from where Louise Castle was killed. I've taken the liberty of sending a car round for you, sir. Save you driving. Should be there in fifteen minutes."

Shit, thought Farrow, and murmured something in reply before dropping the receiver none too gently back into its cradle. He suspected that Jackson was sending a car because the younger man thought he might otherwise dawdle, or even turn over and go back to sleep.

By the time Banks tapped on his door, Farrow was washed and dressed and making toast, which he ate in the car on the way over.

Despite his hasty ablutions, he was still uncomfortably aware that he must look how he felt, which was like several different kinds of shit. Banks, however, was as courteous and respectful as ever, as was the uniformed constable standing outside the high wooden doors of the builder's yard on Cumberland Street. However the instant Farrow set foot inside the yard, Jackson shot him the kind of look he might normally reserve for some smelly old dosser who'd just wandered in off the street to scrounge the price of a cup of tea.

Farrow bridled. He was aware that he did not look his best at the present time, but he had his reasons. Besides, who was this *boy* to pass judgement on him? He could imagine what Jackson and his cronies were saying about him behind his back – that he was washed out, that the strain of handling such a serious investigation was getting too much for him.

Jackson was smiling now, offering a brisk, "Morning, sir," a small balloon of white breath curling away from his face. With his double-breasted suit, expensive haircut and bright questing eyes, he looked more like an advertising executive than a policeman.

Even as Farrow was mustering a response, Jackson was striding towards a large yellow plastic construction at the end of the yard, calling over his shoulder, "Deceased is in here, sir."

Farrow, aware that in the eyes of his colleagues he was already trailing by several points, perfunctorily smoothed down his thin but wayward hair, and said, loud enough to draw the attention and smiles of the other dozen or so people in the yard, "Really, Christopher? You do surprise me."

Jackson at least had the decency to blush and mutter an apology. He even held the flap of the incident tent open so that Farrow could enter without taking his hands from his pockets.

The killer's work was several hours old. The girl's innards, exposed for all to see, had long ago stopped steaming.

"Careful, sir," Jackson said, placing a restraining hand on Farrow's arm and nodding down at the floor as the Detective Inspector lifted a foot to step forward. Farrow paused, following his Sergeant's gaze. He'd been about to trample a piece of the girl underfoot, he realized; some unrecognizable gobbet of bloodied flesh, torn from the body and now ringed in yellow chalk. Despite the bitterly cold October morning, the inside of the tent was oppressively warm and smelled like an abattoir.

"Do we know who she is?" Farrow said, narrowing his eyes against the red glare of the girl's blood.

"We're not one hundred per cent sure, sir. The killer took her face again as you can see. But we're almost certain she's a 23-year-old barmaid called Sarah-Jane Springer. She was reported missing by her boyfriend just before one a.m. after failing to return from her seven to eleven shift at The Crow's Nest."

"The big pub on the corner of Maddeley Road?" said Farrow.

"That's right, sir. According to the landlord, Miss Springer normally got the twenty-five past eleven bus just across the road from the pub, which got her to the corner of Juniper Street at about eleven-forty. She would then walk up Juniper Street, take a left on to Cumberland Street, and then a right on to Markham Road, which is where she lived. Number 42."

"So she'd normally get home ... what? About quarter to twelve?"

"About that, sir."

"What's the boyfriend's name?" said Farrow. His head felt thick with the smell of blood.

"Ian Latimer, sir."

"Ian Latimer." Farrow repeated the name as if tasting it. "Any form?"

"No, sir. He works at Whitworth's Brewery, and has done since he left school nine years ago. He and Miss Springer have lived together for the past two and a half years."

"And did Mr Latimer have a reason for not reporting Miss Springer's disappearance before one a.m.?"

"The call was logged at oh-oh-fifty-one, sir," said Jackson pedantically, and then hastily added, "He says he fell asleep watching the football, sir."

"*Hmm*," said Farrow and turned his attention back to the girl. From the waist upwards she had been ripped apart, just like the others. All that identified her as human were the out-flung arms and legs and the blood-matted blonde hair. Her fingernails were long and varnished as red as her blood. On her left wrist was a thin gold-coloured bracelet and a watch.

"I assume this is just like the others? No obvious motive? No sign of robbery, sexual assault?"

"None, sir. Whoever did this just likes killing people. Correction: killing young women."

"Quite," said Farrow. He frowned; he was finding it hard to concentrate. What he wouldn't give for a cup of strong, dark coffee to kick-start these tired old cells of his into life, or preferably another hour's kip.

"Are you all right, sir?" said Jackson, not bothering to lower his voice.

Farrow was aware of people turning to look at him. He turned his frown into a scowl of annoyance.

"Perfectly, thank you, Christopher. I was just thinking. You should try it some time."

"Sorry, sir," said Jackson woodenly.

Farrow glared at Jackson just long enough to re-assert his questionable authority, and then turned to a fussy-looking man in white coat and skin-tight latex gloves, who had been hovering around the body like an albino vulture.

"What's your verdict this time, Doctor Quinn?" he asked.

The little man looked unhappy. "It's all very perplexing, Detective Inspector, very perplexing indeed. Same m.o. as the others, of course, which means that she could have died from any one of a number of injuries. It appears – just like the others – that the killer came at her in a frenzy, rendered her unconscious and probably even killed her before she had a chance to fight back. Whoever this man is, he's got tremendous strength. I only wish I could determine what type of weapon or weapons he uses."

"Any new ideas?" asked Farrow.

The pathologist pulled a face. "Not really. As before, the injuries are ragged, so it isn't a blade, unless it's a very jagged, very uneven one. If pushed, I'd guess that he's using something like … like a rake-head, but much sturdier, much more compact, more lethal. It might be worth checking locally whether anyone's had some kind of … metal claw or unusual tool built recently. I know it's a long shot, but …" He shrugged.

"Yes, I think that particular investigation is already under way. Christopher?"

"No results so far, sir," said Jackson smoothly.

"And the killer left nothing behind? No hairs, no footprints, no stray buttons with bits of thread attached?"

The pathologist offered a watery smile. "Nothing at all, which again is unusual, although as I say, the girl died before she could fight back."

"Okay." Farrow sighed. "Well, give me a shout when you're ready to do the post-mortem. I'll try to pop along for the matinee." He took a grubby handkerchief from his pocket and used it to dab beads of sweat from his forehead. Quietly he said, "Let's leave the good doctor to his work, Sergeant."

Outside the tent, Farrow breathed in the icy air for a moment and watched uniformed constables ranging about the yard, searching painstakingly for evidence. They looked as though they were helping a colleague search for a lost contact lens. The thought prompted a snigger, which he barely managed to stifle. He saw Jackson looking at him curiously and made an over-elaborate show of clearing his throat as he attempted to pull his thoughts together.

Procedure, he thought. What needs to be done? "Who have we spoken to so far, Christopher?"

"Sir?" said Jackson, who was making the word sound increasingly like a weary, puzzled rebuke.

"Who have we spoken to? In detail, I mean. The landlord, the boyfriend? Who found the body?"

Farrow clamped his lips together, aware that he was beginning to bluster. Jackson's face remained dead-pan.

"A Mrs Esther Norwood, wife of the man who owns the yard, found the body, sir, at 6.15 a.m. She says she came in early to sort out some orders."

"And where is she now?"

"She's sitting outside in a panda with Constable Butlin, sir, having a cup of tea."

"Very cosy."

Jackson turned his steely gaze on his superior. "She was very upset, sir. As you can imagine."

"Yes. Yes, of course, she must have been," said Farrow, somewhat cowed.

"As for the boyfriend, sir, PC Platt and WPC Munro are with him at the moment. He was very upset too. The landlord of The Crow's Nest, a Mr David Smithers, has only been spoken to briefly, sir, so far."

"And was he also upset?"

Jackson's expression seemed to indicate that he found Farrow's attempts at humour tiresome. "I don't know, sir."

"Right," said Farrow, trying to sound and look purposeful. "Well, I think I'll go and have a chat with our Mr Smithers, and from there move on to some of his regulars, see if any of them heard or saw anything or anyone unusual in the pub last night. What I want you to do, Sergeant, is to get statements from the boyfriend and Mrs … the woman who found the body …"

"Mrs Norwood, sir."

"That's right: Mrs Norwood. Then I want you to trace the driver of the bus that Miss Springer would have caught last night, and as many of the passengers as you can, and find out what you can from them."

"That's already being done, sir," said Jackson smugly.

"Is it? Good. Well then, I'll leave you to it. Perhaps we can rendezvous at the p.m. later? Buzz me when the doctor's ready for us, will you?"

"Yes, sir," said Jackson with an icy patience that bordered on the facetious.

"Oh, and Sergeant?"

"Yes, sir?"

"Smarten yourself up a bit, will you? Your tie's crooked."

Jackson had raised his hand to his throat before he saw Farrow's grin replicated on the faces of almost everyone else in the yard. As the Detective Inspector turned and ambled away, he wondered whether the reddening of Jackson's face was a blush of embarrassment or a flush of rage.

I admit to him that I'm scared. I ask: Will it hurt?

He moves inside me. Pain is nothing, he says. Think of it as life. As re-birth. Who would not die for that?

His words confuse me. I feel so tired. How much longer? I ask him. How much longer before it's over?

Not long, he whispers, not long now. Do you not remember?

No, I tell him. No, I remember nothing.

He whispers inside me: It is strange how one forgets.

Jackson switched off the computer and pushed himself back in his seat. His spine crackled; his shoulders felt as if someone were pressing down on them from above. He looked at his watch and groaned. Eleven-fifteen. He'd told Janice he'd try to be home by ten. She'd promised to have a turkey curry on the table by ten-thirty, and then something even spicier for him afterwards.

He thought of how he'd kissed her wicked smile goodbye as he'd slipped from between the sheets after receiving the call at half past six that morning. He thought of her warm softness, her tousled hair, the thick sleepy perfumed smell of her. Then he thought of the dead girl, her stomach ripped open, her face gone, the hot stink of her scattered organs. As he reached for the phone, he felt a cold steel pulse of angry determination. I'll get you, you vicious bastard, he promised silently, punching in his number.

"Hello?" said Janice, sounding tired or wary.

"Love, it's me. I'm really sorry I'm not home yet. I've been tied up with paperwork at the station for the past two hours."

"Chris!" she said, and this time there was definitely relief in her voice, which then dropped an octave. "I was starting to get worried."

"I know, love, I'm really sorry. Time just got away from me. I didn't realize how late it was."

"I heard about that poor girl on the news. Was it awful?"

She was not being ghoulish, Jackson knew. She was just concerned about what he had to expose himself to every day.

"Yeah," he said quietly, "it was pretty bad. Listen, Jan, I'll try not to be too much longer, okay?"

"Okay. I'll keep your dinner warm for you. That's if you haven't already eaten?"

"I had a doughnut about eleven this morning, and I've drunk more coffee than my bladder can cope with."

She tutted. "Well, that's not very good, is it? You sound really tired."

"I'm utterly shagged," said Jackson, though it was only now that he was realizing it. "It's been all hell on today. Not that you'd think so looking at our D.I."

"Is he still not pulling his weight?"

"He turned up an hour after everyone else this morning looking like something the cat dragged in, spent most of his day in the pub, showed up briefly at the post mortem and then sloped off home about six."

He convinced himself he wasn't exaggerating all that much as Janice said, "You really ought to report him, Chris. It's not fair that you get all his work to do as well as your own. You've got enough on your plate as it is."

"Yeah," said Jackson vaguely. "Anyway, that's not your problem. I'll see you later."

He sat with his hand on the phone for a minute or so after putting it down and wondered whether in fact he was being unfair to Farrow, and if so to what degree. In Jackson's eyes the Detective Inspector seemed to be stumbling through much of this investigation as if sleepwalking, but did he really lack the urgency, the drive, the commitment that Jackson saw as essential to the job, or was it simply that he was older and wiser and thus favoured a calmer, more methodical approach? Could Jackson's problems with the D.I. simply be put down to a clash of personalities? The Detective Sergeant was aware that there were still plenty of good coppers within the station, particularly among the old guard, who held faith with Farrow and his methods, who indeed resented his own dynamism, saw him as little more than an upstart, too clever for his own good, still wet behind the ears.

And yet it wasn't as though Jackson hated his superior officer, or even wanted to oust him to aid his own career, as Farrow seemed to think; what got to him was the simple fact that the man was *so* bloody sloppy. Had he always been like this – passing the buck, failing to meet appointments, wandering around looking like death warmed over? Was it simply the high profile nature of this case that was highlighting deficiencies that Farrow had previously been able to cover up? It certainly seemed as though the strain of the investigation was taking a physical toll on the older man. Admittedly Farrow had always had a face like a bag of spanners, but now his skin was grey and blotchy, his eyes bloodshot, his shoulders stooped. In truth he looked broken, defeated, which was hardly surprising after five unsolved murders, and precious few leads, in less than a month. Perhaps it would be kinder if Farrow was pensioned off, as one or two people in the department seemed to think. Otherwise he might end up dropping down dead on the job.

Jackson let his gaze wander to the incident board that had been set up on the far side of the room. It covered the whole of one wall and was intended to inspire him and his colleagues to greater efforts, to sting and harry them into catching the bastard who had reduced a quiet, community-minded Northern town into a dark arena of terror and hostility and suspicion. Jackson found it hard to believe that even now, even after what had happened, even after repeated police warnings that young women should not go out alone at night, there were still those who ignored the advice; who seemed to hold the blinkered view that violent death happened to other people, or who insisted that no man, no matter how much of a maniac he was, was going to dictate where they could and couldn't go.

Jackson sympathized with the sentiment, but he couldn't condone it. Yesterday, however, he had come down very hard on a young PC who he'd overheard telling a colleague in the locker room that as far as he was concerned any woman walking on her own at night deserved whatever was coming to her. Jackson had given the boy the whole bit about how it was up to people like him to ensure that the streets were safe for anyone to walk anywhere at any time, and if he didn't share that opinion then he was in the wrong bloody profession! However to be truthful, although he had made the bollocking sound convincing enough, his heart hadn't really been in it. In many ways he could understand the boy's attitude, the frustration behind it. It was just symptomatic of the low morale that was creeping through the station like a dose of flu.

Five women. All young, all pretty, all torn apart in quiet dark places in the dead of night without, it seemed, even having time to scream or raise so much as a finger in defence. Their celluloid faces gazed back at Jackson from the incident board, their frozen smiles turning seemingly more mocking each day. If there was any chink in the killer's armour at all – whom local and now national newspapers had gleefully dubbed "The Wolfman" – it was that his blood-lust seemed to be increasing; the gaps between his murders were getting less and less. It was surely only a matter of time before the sheer frenzy of his desires led to him making a mistake. But how many more women would be killed in the meantime? How many more photographs would have to be tacked to the incident board?

Jackson groaned and pushed himself to his feet. Despite the caffeine still buzzing in the back of his skull like an electricity pylon, he felt utterly wasted. The station was quiet, the office in semi-darkness. He lifted his jacket from the back of his chair, and yawned so hugely that his jawbone cracked.

The telephone rang. Janice again probably, telling him that the curry was bubbling on the stove and a couple of poppadoms warming under the grill. He picked up the receiver.

"Moorfield Police Station. Detective Sergeant Jackson speaking."

The man on the other end of the line either had laryngitis or was disguising his voice.

"I need to see you," he rasped.

Instinctively Jackson thought: This is it. A shudder of anticipation passed through him. He shed his fatigue like snake-skin and was all at once alert.

"What about?" he asked tentatively, wishing there was someone in the office with him who he could mime at to trace the call.

"No time for … games," hissed the caller, sounding as though he was in pain, as though he was finding it difficult to talk. "I want you to meet me. I … I want you to come alone. Don't bring anyone with you, otherwise … otherwise your last chance … will be gone."

Jackson felt a pulse beating in his throat, but his voice was steady. "Why should I want to meet you at all?" he said.

The caller groaned as if in pain. When he next spoke his voice was weaker than ever, almost inaudible. "You've been ... looking for me ... I'm the Wolfman. I killed another one tonight. I want it to be the ... the last one. The last one ever."

The pulse was really hammering now. Jackson swallowed. "How do I know you're telling me the truth?"

"I tear them open ... from stomach to throat," the caller wheezed. "I take their faces."

Jackson went cold. This information had not appeared in the newspapers. "Why should you want to meet me?" he said.

"Need to talk to you. Need you to ... to ..." The voice tailed off.

"You know I can't meet you alone," Jackson said.

"Has to be. Alone ... or not at all. No tricks. I'll know. Please believe me ..."

Jackson thought hard, and in the end said, "Okay. Where do you want to meet?"

"Old railway station ... Be there in ... ten minutes. If you're not, I'll know you've ... arranged reinforcements, and your ... last chance will ... be gone ..."

There was a clatter and a buzz.

"Wait!" called Jackson, but he was already speaking to a dead line.

I feel him growing inside me, stretching me. I feel myself dwindling. He pleads with me, howls at me, curses me, but I remain silent in the hope I can preserve my strength.

We are the same, he tells me, wheedling. Soon we shall be renewed. Together we may seem divided, but divided we will come together.

I try not to listen to him, but his words are part of me. I cannot block them out.

Finally I react. I say to him: There will be no more killing. Six lives for my one cannot be justified.

It is the price of survival, he says.

The railway link between Moorfield and its neighbours had been severed, despite vigorous local opposition, back in the mid-seventies. Oddly, however, the station building itself had never been pulled down or even converted into offices or shops, but instead had fallen into disrepair over the years, become prey to vandals and weeds and harsh weather. Situated at the edge of a newish industrial estate, it was a lonely place, retaining a sense of sad nostalgia by day and an atmosphere of brooding eeriness when darkness set in.

The pulse in Jackson's throat was still beating ten minutes after speaking to the man who claimed to be the Wolfman, and quickened as he pulled in to the station car park, which was rutted, and infested with clumps of spiny grass. The car headlights lurched over a long rectangular building with crumbling, grime-blackened stonework, boarded windows and doors, sagging drainpipes and rusting lamp standards. When Jackson brought the car to a halt and switched the headlights off, these details winked out as if only the light had created them. Now the terrain was simpler, albeit instantly more treacherous. Beneath a night sky freckled with stars, the building had become a block of impenetrable darkness.

For a minute or so the young Sergeant remained in his car, breathing long and deep, clenching and unclenching his hands. Calm down, he urged himself silently, and began to chant the instruction in his head like a mantra: calm down, calm down, calm down. There was no stopping the adrenalin surging through his body, but he wanted to be controlling it as much as possible when he went in there. If the killer was going to be waiting for him, as he had promised, then the next half-hour or so would almost certainly be the most crucial of his career, if not his life.

At last he was ready. He opened the car door and stepped out into a biting cold wind. His legs were shaking, but not too much. He swallowed to control the juddering in his stomach as he reached into his overcoat pocket and took out a torch which he turned on after a moment's hesitation. Holding the torch made him feel conspicuous, but Jackson reasoned that if the killer *was* here, then he could hardly expect him to be unaware of his arrival.

The torch beam ballooning before him, he walked through a stone arch into the body of the station, past the cobweb-strewn ticket-windows and deserted newspaper stall on his right, and the tea bar on his left, which was now nothing more than an empty black space. His senses were so attuned that grit seemed to detonate beneath his feet; his breath, slow and steady though it was, seemed to fill the air around him as though it was the building that was breathing. The inside of the station was like a black tunnel containing many crevices in which a killer might hide. Shadows seemed to loll and nod just beyond the range of his torch light as he walked forward. His head moved from side to side as if jerked by his flickering eyes.

Ahead, no more than twelve paces away, he could see the turnstile of the ticket barrier which led out on to the Southbound platform. A faint gleam of starlight was shining through from the platform itself, and this, together with the light from his torch, illuminated a shimmering swathe of unbroken cobweb stretching across the narrow gap. Jackson realized immediately that the killer couldn't have come this way. If he had, then the curtain of cobweb would have been hanging in shreds. So what did that mean? Either the killer was leading him on a wild goose chase or he had reached the station by following the line of the old track, much of which was now overgrown. Or – third possibility – he was lying in wait for Jackson between here and the turnstile, or was even now creeping up behind him, having watched him enter the station from some unseen vantage-point.

Though these thoughts hardly reassured him, it felt almost comforting to be thinking like a policeman again. As he spun round to check behind him, he thought that perhaps it was about time he acted like one too and announced his presence, rather than creeping about like a victim in a cheap horror movie.

"This is Detective Sergeant Jackson, Moorfield Police," he called, his voice booming around him. "I'm here as arranged. Please show yourself."

There was no reply, only the fading echoes of his voice which sounded reassuringly authoritative. After a moment he tried again.

"If you don't show yourself, I'll be forced to radio for reinforcements. It's entirely your choice."

Ten long seconds passed, and Jackson was beginning to wonder whether this would prove to be a dead end, after all, when a black shape appeared beyond the ticket barrier, blotting out the starlight.

Jackson swallowed. He suddenly seemed aware of the hot, juicy rhythm of his blood pulsing round his body. He shone his torch at the figure, but it flinched back as if afraid of the light.

"Stay where I can see you," Jackson called.

The figure spoke. Its hoarse whisper seemed contained within the mist that curled from its mouth. "Turn … off … the torch."

Jackson hesitated, then did as requested. He gave himself a moment to re-adjust to the darkness, then moved towards the turnstile beyond which the black bulk of the figure was waiting, like an unwanted visitor just alighted from a train.

"Move back," he ordered as he reached the turnstile and put out a hand to claw some of the cobwebs aside. The figure complied, shuffling back towards the edge of the platform.

Jackson pushed at the turnstile. It was stiff from years of disuse, and squealed as if in pain as he struggled with it. It gave inch by inch and at last he was through and standing on the platform, grimy shreds of cobweb clinging to his expensive overcoat. The figure was maybe twelve yards away, facing him, poised at the edge of the platform beside the overgrown track like a high diver about to attempt a back flip. The figure's face was indistinct with shadow, masked by a constant swirl of white breath. For a moment Jackson and the figure stood facing each other like gunslingers.

At last Jackson said, "Well, I'm here. What now?"

A shudder seemed to pass through the figure as if it was drawing itself together. It was breathing stertorously, almost panting. "We don't … have much … time," it rasped.

"Are you ill?" asked Jackson.

The figure made a wheezing, gulping sound that could have been anything from amusement to an articulation of pain. "I'm …" It seemed to grope for a suitable phrase. "… *changing*," it said at last.

Without knowing why, Jackson thought of a caterpillar pupating into a butterfly. He shuddered. "Changing into what?"

The figure groaned. "Rebirth ... Renewal ... Regeneration ..."

The three R's, Jackson thought crazily, and stammered, "I don't know what you mean."

"Listen to me ... so little time ... I'm not like you ... I'm not ... human."

"Of course you're not," said Jackson soothingly.

"*Listen to me!*" The response was momentarily energized by fury before the voice dwindled to a croak once again. "Forty-year cycle ... then renewal ... preceded by instinct to feed ... to take blood ... life energies ... identities ... Can't control change ... Too much killing ... But no more ... no more ..." The figure groaned, made a gulping sound, then sagged as though about to faint.

"Look," said Jackson, "you're hurt or ill. Come with me. I'll get you to a hospital."

"No," the figure croaked, "no hospital." It seemed to make a supreme effort and straightened up. Its voice was little more than a hoarse whisper now. "I don't want ... to go on," it said. "Don't you understand, Jackson? I have so ... little time. I want you to help me ... help me stop it all ... happening again."

Jackson had come here prepared to listen to what the man had to say, but all he was hearing was gibberish. He wondered whether the man really was as crazy and as hurt as he appeared or whether it was a ploy to catch him off guard. It was not uncommon of killers to pretend to be weaker than they actually were or incapacitated in some way. Latching on to the last thing the man had said, he asked, "How can I help you to stop it?"

The asthmatic wheeze of the man's breath certainly sounded genuine. "I want you ... to kill me. Can't do it ... myself. He won't let me. Too much ... control now. Almost through. *Quickly!* ..."

"Kill you!" Jackson exclaimed, and then forced his voice back to calmness. "You know I can't do that. It's against the law. But look, if you come with me, I can get you help. You can talk to people about your problem. Professional people. They'll help you."

The figure gave a gurgling roar of frustration. "No, Jackson ... listen to me ... I'm not human ... If you don't ... kill me, the cycle will ... complete itself ... Mind will ... repair damaged thoughts ... renew ... survival instinct ... and then I won't ... want to die. And in forty ... years the ... killings will ... start again ... You must ... do it now ... Jackson ... while I'm ... willing ... Petrol ... under bench ... matches ... do it now ... soon ... too late ..."

The croak became a slur and the figure collapsed. Jackson took two instinctive steps forward, then stopped. The figure was lying motionless on the edge of the platform, but how could Jackson be sure that he wasn't being duped? He imagined himself bending over the figure, the man's eyes snapping open, his hand – clutching whatever hideous weapon he used to kill his victims with – whipping round to take off his face. He closed his eyes briefly and shuddered, then switched on the torch which he still held in his hand and directed it at the prone figure.

The man was lying on his back, his head and his left arm hanging over the edge of the platform. If he had really fainted, then it was lucky he hadn't fallen off the platform on to the tracks. Or maybe it wasn't so lucky; at least if he'd fallen down there, Jackson would have had a territorial advantage over him. He remembered what the man had said about petrol and turned to shine his torch at the nearest dilapidated bench.

He was frankly surprised to see that there was indeed a petrol can beneath it, a slim yellow box of safety matches propped up by its side. But was this evidence that the man really wanted to die as he'd claimed or was he just being thorough? Were the petrol can and matches simply designed to persuade Jackson to lower his guard still further?

He paused for a moment, thoughts racing through his mind. Why had the killer requested this meeting with him specifically? If the killer had wanted simply to kill him, then surely there were better ways of going about it. But why *should* the killer want to kill him? Because he was working on the case? Because he feared that Jackson was coming close to catching him? Could there be any truth in the killer's claim that he wanted to die at Jackson's hand? The young D.S. found that hard to accept. If the killer was so desperate to die, why didn't he just kill himself? Jackson tried to recall what the man had said – something about he wouldn't let him because *he* had too much control. What did that mean? Who could the killer be talking about? A brother, a father, a lover, an accomplice? Or perhaps it was simply another facet of the man's personality, the part of him that made him kill.

Jackson realized he was venturing into tinpot psychology country here, but maybe the man was schizophrenic and maybe the passive, guilt-ridden side of him was dominant at the moment and wanted to end it all before the violent side reasserted itself. Perhaps he had called Jackson because he had seen him on the news and identified him as a potential ally against the dark side of himself, or as an authority figure, someone on who he could rely, on to whom he could shift his responsibility.

But what about all the other stuff about not being human and about having to kill in forty-year cycles to renew himself? That, surely, was just an example of the man's craziness. Jackson knew it was not uncommon for killers, particularly multiple killers, to consider themselves more than human. Sometimes the act of murder was seen by the killer as a step towards their transformation into something divine, God-like.

Sensing a vague flicker of movement to his right, Jackson turned his head. Far away, approaching silently along the track, he saw a number of dark bobbing shapes, hunched over in an attempt to blend with the darkness. He looked left, and saw more hunched shapes approaching from the other side. At once relief washed over him. They were here, and sooner than he'd imagined they would be. Constable Banks had done his job well.

He waved, but got no response. They were still too far away. It would take them five or ten minutes to reach the station. Nevertheless there wasn't much that could go wrong now. He imagined the headlines tomorrow: KILLER CAUGHT BY BRAVE SERGEANT.

Just then the figure groaned, began to move its limbs feebly, to raise its head. At once Jackson reached into his jacket and took out the handgun Banks had suggested he bring with him. It was a long time since Jackson had carried a gun, and at first he had been reluctant. But the Constable had insisted, despite his inferior rank, that if Jackson was going to rush in without immediate back-up to avoid the killer getting suspicious and fleeing the scene, then he had to have some form of protection. Hence the gun and body armour which Jackson had hastily strapped to himself before rushing out to his car. Jackson's aim had been to play for time, and hopefully to win the killer's confidence, to get as much out of him as he could before reinforcements arrived. All he'd been offered, however, was nonsense, the rantings of a fractured mind. He only hoped that once the killer realized the game was up, that he had no more room to manoeuvre, he would provide Jackson with rather saner responses to his questions back at the station.

Jackson held the gun in his right hand and the torch in his left, both of which he pointed at the killer. "Don't move!" he ordered. "I've got a gun pointing at you and reinforcements on the way. I'm placing you under arrest for the murders of Sylvia Hughes, Louise Castle, Amanda Barrie, Melanie Whitman and Sarah-Jane Springer. You don't have to say anything, but anything you do say may be taken down and used in evidence against you."

The man, as though still too dazed to hear, raised his head and squinted directly into the beam of Jackson's torch, allowing the Detective Sergeant, for the first time, to see his face.

It was the face of a man in his late teens or early twenties, and seeing it had a strange effect on Jackson. For a second or two he experienced an acute sense of dislocation, almost of shock. He felt certain he had never seen this man before, and yet at the same time he looked strikingly familiar.

The man smiled, shook his head and spoke, and this time there was no trace of tiredness or suffering or desperation in his voice at all. He spoke in a clear, strong voice, his tone almost conversational.

"You lied to me, Christopher," he said. "I should have known, shouldn't I? You've always been a model policeman, always played everything strictly by the book."

This time it was shock that jolted through Jackson. Suddenly everything seemed to fall sickeningly into place. But it was impossible. *Impossible*.

"Farrow?" he said wonderingly.

The man who looked and sounded like a younger, more vibrant version of the bedraggled Chief Inspector laughed.

"Starting to get it now, are you, Christopher?" he said mildly.

Jackson's arms were shaking, the gun jittering in his right hand, the torch beam wavering over Farrow's impossibly young face. His voice was a dry croak. "Get what?" he said stupidly.

The approaching marksmen were still too far away to be of any use as the rejuvenated Farrow said, "Watch."

Lit by the unflinching glare of white light from Jackson's torch, the man's face began to change. The features flowed like oil, altered before Jackson's disbelieving gaze, and then altered again, and again. It took Jackson a moment to identify what he was seeing, and then all at once, with awful clarity, it struck him: it was a shifting montage of the faces of the Wolfman's murder victims. Here was Louise Castle, here Melanie Whitman, here Sarah-Jane Springer.

The torch slipped from Jackson's nerveless fingers and smashed on the floor, mercifully plunging the killer's writhing features into darkness. Jackson staggered back two paces, gripped his gun in both hands to avoid dropping that too and levelled it at the killer. His voice was shrill with terror, the words accompanied by ragged gouts of vapour. "*What the fucking hell are you?*" he screeched.

Farrow's voice was almost sympathetic. "I did tell you I wasn't human, didn't I, Christopher? Actually, the name that the newspapers came up with for me was uncannily accurate when you think about it, though to be honest I'm not one of a species as such. If anything, I suppose you'd say I'm a sort of … sophisticated chameleon, able to blend into my surroundings, integrate myself into any situation."

"Where are you from?" Jackson demanded.

Farrow pursed his lips, shrugged. "I'm not *from* anywhere. I've always been here, on this planet I mean. I've lived here longer than mankind, longer than I can even remember. I move around a lot. I take whatever shape seems appropriate at the time."

"*Why* are you here?" Jackson said, the words catching in his dry throat.

"Because I like it," replied Farrow simply. "I like human beings, I like being one, thinking like one, living amongst them.

There's no great purpose to my existence, Christopher. I'm just surviving, like you. Like everyone."

"Not like those girls you killed."

"Ah, no. Look, I'm sorry about that, really I am. Would it help if I told you the killings were instinctive, that I don't actually have much control over what I do? No, I don't really suppose it would, and I can't blame you for thinking badly of me. What can I say? Every so often it happens. I need to kill to renew myself. Sorry." Farrow's shoulders rose in a sheepish shrug; it was like the gesture a schoolboy might make who'd been caught putting frogs in his teacher's desk. Jackson saw Farrow's head turning left and right, imagined him looking along the track. "Your reinforcements are getting awfully close," the shape-shifter said. "I think I've overstayed my welcome here. It's time. I was moving on."

He sat up. Jackson snarled, "Stay where you are, you bastard! You're not going anywhere!"

Mildly Farrow said, "Look, let's call it quits, eh, Christopher? I became a policeman as a sort of trade-in for what I knew was coming later. Over the years I've stopped lots of other people getting hurt, getting killed. I think I've payed my dues."

"*Don't fucking move!*" Jackson repeated, his voice hoarse, fierce, verging on panic. "If you do, I swear I'll blast your fucking head off!"

"Clint Eastwood. Am I right?" said Farrow mildly. He stood up.

"I said don't move!"

"Goodbye, Christopher," said Farrow, and took a step forward.

Jackson pulled the trigger, once, twice, three times. When the din and the smog of his breath had cleared, he saw Farrow still standing there, apparently unharmed.

"Don't you know it takes silver bullets to kill a Wolfman?" Farrow said apologetically.

"I hit you," said Jackson in a high, wavery, almost petulant voice. "I know I hit you."

"You did," said Farrow, "but I'm afraid it would take a massive disruption of my cells to destroy me, hence the petrol and matches earlier. I self-heal from localized wounds almost instantaneously."

"But you *wanted* to die," Jackson said, his gun arm drooping. He sounded like a little boy who'd been denied the chance to play the goodie.

"That was before. A period of confusion, of weakness caused by the change. That's all forgotten now."

Because of the gunshots, Jackson's reinforcements were now racing down the track towards them, their leaders barking orders. The group on the right were no more than thirty yards away.

Farrow gave them a quick, though casual, glance. "Time to go," he said. "Goodbye, Christopher. Have a nice life."

Before Jackson's astonished eyes, Farrow's body ran like oil once again. It seemed to hunch and darken, clothes splitting beneath broadening shoulders and bulging legs, falling away like the pieces of a discarded chrysalis. Just for an instant Jackson glimpsed what must have been the creature that had torn the girls apart. He saw muscles rippling beneath a shaggy pelt, teeth and eyes flashing like knives. Then Farrow's body seemed to compress, to rush towards a dark point in its centre. Suddenly, instead of a man or a beast there was a dark bird, a crow perhaps, which rose flapping into the sky and was quickly swallowed by the night.

The first of the police marksmen climbed up on to the platform and ran towards Jackson, assault rifle held diagonally across his body, barrel pointing upwards.

His head whipping this way and that, he shouted, "Where is he? Sergeant Jackson? Where's our man?"

But Jackson, unable to answer, could only gaze up at the sky.

Basil Copper

CRY WOLF

Basil Cooper: A Life in Books *was published in 2008 by PS Publishing. The biblio/biography includes listings of all the author's macabre and supernatural novels, collections and short stories, his "Solar Pons" series of Sherlock Holmes pastiches and other works, along with various essays and the complete script of his adaptation of M.R. James' Count Magnus. Richard Dalby also contributed a detailed overview of the author's life and career.*

Copper's first story in the horror field was "The Spider" in The Fifth Pan Book of Horror Stories *(1964), and he became a full-time writer in 1970. His short fiction has been collected in* Not After Nightfall, From Evil's Pillow, When Footsteps Echo *and* Afterward the Dark, *while recent anthology appearances include* The Mammoth Books of Vampires, The Mammoth Book of Zombies, Dark Voices 3, Shadows Over Innsmouth *and* Horror for Christmas.

He has written more than fifty hard-boiled thrillers about Los Angeles private detective Mike Faraday, and his other novels include The Great White Space, The Curse of the Fleers, Necropolis *and the werewolf chiller,* The House of the Wolf. *In 1977 he published the non-fiction study,* The Werewolf: in Legend, Fact and Art.

The village is very quiet. But then that is to be expected at this time of year. It stands in a notch of the frowning mountains far from the nearest town. And after all, it is the main reason we bought the house. In summer the meadows are carpeted with red and yellow flowers while in the winter the majesty of the snow and the unearthly beauty of the mountains against those changing skies more than compensates for the cold and the lack of modern amenities.

The wolf came early in November. That in itself was curious because the weather had been mild until then. It was first reported by Jaeckel, the frontier guard. He had seen the trace of its paws down by the stream in the moonlight, he said. Even an outsider like myself could not resist chaffing him. Wolves had not been known in these mountains for generations, said the older heads of the village. Now if it had been much higher up or on the Italian side and January as well, and one of the hardest winters on record. But a mild November! They flung up their hands with laughter and continued smoking their long pipes.

Jaeckel just smiled and said he knew what he knew and he trusted the evidence of his own eyes. A big dog, perhaps, said Jean Piotr, who owns the largest general store in the village. Jaeckel derided the suggestion. Quite impossible, he said firmly. It was a wolf's print, coming down a path from the village to the stream. In fact he'd seen the animal, or at least its shadow passing over the snow, a few seconds before. Even allowing for the moonlight and the elongation of the shadow it had been too big for a dog. And the pads were enormous.

Jaeckel said that, to settle it, why didn't we all come down to have a look at the prints ourselves. We were gathered in the auberge at the time and it was warm and friendly and the vintage was uncommonly good that year. So only a few of the less comfort-addicted spirits said they would go along. I went too, together with my son Andrew, who was eager to see the track of this fabulous beast.

We had a disappointing afternoon. The village children were using the path as a toboggan slide after the new snowfall and nothing remained by then.

"Let us try by the stream," said Jean LeCoutre, who apart from owning a logging company, was also maire of the village.

So aside from his natural authority, coupled with that of his office, it was also his duty to look into the matter. We drew a blank there too. Jaeckel was puzzled and humiliated. He looked at the turned-up snow in disgust and scratched his head. He spat thoughtfully.

LeCoutre remained on his knees for a moment, staring at the ground.

"You are certain this is the place?" he asked the frontier guard.

The latter turned and surveyed the length of the stream.

"As you can see, the remainder of the banks are covered in virgin snow," he said simply.

The maire got to his feet and brushed down his trousers.

"It seems as though someone has obliterated the tracks with a rough broom," he said in a puzzled voice.

There was a general laugh among the men who had accompanied us but I noticed we all went back to the village in a thoughtful frame of mind. That was the simple beginning and nothing else happened for more than two weeks.

Then a frightened child came running into the hamlet one evening to say he'd been chased by a big dog. The child was obviously terrified and his clothes had been torn by something sharp and jagged so his family were forced to take the story seriously. They sent for the maire and the doctor and within half an hour a search party was organised. I joined it, naturally and though Andrew was anxious to go, I told him to stay behind. He was only fifteen and I knew that he might do something foolish in his excitement.

We all got lanterns and big electric torches and thoroughly searched the track along which the boy had been coming. Sure enough, there were large paw marks right behind the half-impressions of the boy's running feet. There was no joking that night and a noticeable tremulousness in the voices of some of those who made suggestions.

LeCoutre sent back to the village for his rifle and a message summoning the best shots in the community. We left two men to guide them down. After the attack on the boy, the paw marks circled aimlessly and then started to go downhill. They followed the path the village children used as a slide and then went into the stream and disappeared. This was strange in itself, as wolves avoid water, except for drinking purposes.

We were circling up and down when there was the crack of a rifle.

"The opposite bank," shouted Jaeckel, his eyes bright with excitement. Smoke curled thinly from the barrel of his rifle. He pointed into the thicket on the opposite bank. We all distinctly heard a crackling noise following the shot.

"Now perhaps you'll believe me," said Jaeckel with quiet triumph.

"If it satisfies you, this is serious enough," the maire agreed.

By now the riflemen from the village had arrived, alarmed by the shot and disappointed at being cheated of a chance at getting the animal.

The maire led the way back in, having decided that it was too dark and dangerous to attempt to ford the stream and seek the beast out that night. He consulted with the doctor over the boy, who was found to have only minor scratches and then telephoned the civil authorities to put them on their guard. The auberge was packed that evening, while we all debated the events of the day.

When we got back to the house I found the door locked. Andrew's voice, shaken and hushed, sounded from inside. He opened up when I called to him.

"I was frightened, father," he said. "I think the wolf was here about half an hour ago. I heard something padding round the house and a snarl like a dog so I locked the door quickly."

"You were very wise, son," I comforted him.

"Shall we go and look for it?" said Andrew.

I got angry then. After all, Andrew was the only thing I had left in the world, now that his mother had gone.

"That is what we won't do," I said. "If you've had your supper, get off to bed. The authorities will handle this."

I telephoned the maire and presently another party arrived. We went over the ground minutely. We found the wolf tracks outside the main balcony windows of the house. LeCoutre looked grave.

"We'll have to keep the young people indoors after dark until this is over," he said. "I'll see if we can get some extra rifles up from the militia until the beast is shot."

We followed the tracks half-heartedly for a few hundred yards. We saw they went in the general direction of the village path before we turned back.

A party sat up at my house drinking cognac into the small hours discussing the affair.

Nothing happened for a week. Then there were further scares. Two little girls had looked from their window one night and had seen the wolf – as big as a cow, they said, though everyone allowed for their childish imagination – running across the meadow near their house. When their mother had come, alarmed by their screams, all she could see was a thin man running across the field, probably in pursuit of the wolf.

Then two goats, which were kept under cover at Papa Gremillon's, one of the last farms at the edge of the village, were found half-eaten and with their throats torn out. A minor wave of panic swept the district. One of the most alarming aspects of the business was that the outhouse in which the goats were kept had been padlocked and the key left in the lock.

Whoever had killed the goats – and the prints and evidence of the fierce struggle among the beasts pointed unmistakably to a wolf – had first unlocked the padlock and then turned the key again on leaving. When these facts became generally known the unease became tinged with terror. LeCoutre and I and some of the more undaunted members of the community talked the affair over for long hours in the auberge. It was while we were there one bitter afternoon shortly after Christmas, that the rumour of "le loup-garou" first came to be mentioned.

"A lot of superstitious nonsense among the hill people," snapped LeCoutre. "The legend of a man-wolf is as old as these mountains," he added, turning to me.

"There may be something in it," said someone farther down the table. "The story of a man who can change into a wolf to kill his prey and then turn back into a man again, has come from classical times."

"So have many things," said LeCoutre, his face purple with outraged indignation. "But that doesn't mean we have to believe minotaurs are still running about."

"But how do you account for this beast's cleverness?" said Jaeckel disarmingly. "And what about that padlock at Papa Gremillon's?"

The maire stroked his chin before downing his glass of water spirit. "I don't doubt we've got something serious here and something fiendishly clever," he said. "But I exclude the supernatural. We've enough to think about at the moment."

There was not one of us who disagreed with him on dispersing. But after that things gradually got worse. Some soldiers on winter manoeuvres in the mountains came for a bit, boosted the custom in the cafes and escorted the children to and from their various errands. Nothing happened of note. Some of the younger national servicemen fired off their rifles at shadows, alarming the countryside. And when the weather closed in, blocking the pass, the militia were, of course, withdrawn. We were left to our own resources.

The first deaths occurred in March, with the warmer weather. There was little Rene Fosse, a 12-year-old schoolboy who was found with his throat torn out one night only a few yards from his back door. He had been on his way to the barn to see that the stock were all right. With the deaths of two small sisters later the same week then truly began the reign of terror. Paw-prints of the wolf were found on each occasion but the creature was fiendishly cunning, as the maire had hinted. Despite the combing of the foothills by massive search-parties, aided by militia, the prints always ceased at the stream.

And searches up and down the banks always failed to find the place where the beast had once again regained the ground. During all this time hardly anyone had spotted the animal which fed the legend of the werewolf; a legend which was seized on first by the regional and then the national press. Hordes of journalists came with their cameramen, everyone was interviewed, old griefs disinterred and any clues there might have been of the beast's whereabouts were soon obliterated by the boots of hundreds of sightseers.

Then, at the end of March or early April, just before the snow was due to disperse, we had a report that an adult this time had been attacked. He was a man named Charles Badoit, a mechanic at the village's only garage, who lived in one of the smaller houses at the end of the settlement. The beast had jumped on his back from an embankment as he was returning on foot from work and had torn a piece out of his neck. With great courage Badoit had fought it off; fortunately for him he was still carrying a box of tools and as he was a big man and made such a threatening sight as he whirled the box around his head with the strength of despair, the wolf had given up the attack and slunk off.

Swathed in bandages and fortified by cognac, Badoit reclined on a sofa at the doctor's house and told his story. LeCoutre swiftly organised one of his biggest search parties and this time I allowed Andrew to join it on condition that he kept close to me and didn't handle any firearms. Two burly gendarmes from the *police de la route* had been left in the village and they added a useful stiffening to our party. The wolf had torn away a piece of flesh from the neck of Badoit and had apparently stopped to eat this no more than a few yards away from the scene of the attack for we found bloodstains and an area of disturbed snow in a nearby thicket.

"This is an audacious brute, all right," gritted LeCoutre grimly as we pressed on, following the clear trail in the snow. But after going in the familiar direction, the paw marks diverted from the track and started up a nearby hill. The wolf may have had its appetite whetted and might be trying for another victim the other side of the village, I said. LeCoutre nodded assent.

We plunged uphill for twenty minutes, through quite thick snow, following the clearly defined trail. We all heard the cracking branch at the same time. Andrew gave an excited cry and the wolf bounded out from behind a clump of fir trees about fifty metres ahead. Several rifles cracked out in a ragged volley and puffs of disturbed snow made plumes in the air around the big grey animal. One of the shots had apparently connected for the brute gave a whimpering cry and limped off back into the trees.

Encouraged, we plunged after it. I told LeCoutre and the gendarmes I thought one of us had hit it on the front offside paw and they were inclined to agree. But half an hour later, with the bloodstains growing fainter and dying out before the trail ended at the stream, we had to give up once more.

Next morning Andrew was pale with shock. I had been out for a talk in the village and on my return found him lying on his bed, immobile with pain. There was a bandage on his right hand.

"Don't be angry, father," he said. "I cut my fingers chopping wood. It's not serious."

"Have you been to see Dr Lemaire?" I said, alarmed.

"Yes," Andrew assured me. "And he says it's nothing to be concerned about. More painful than anything else."

"I'm glad to hear it, my boy," I said. "But you really must be more careful."

Truth to tell, I was more worried than I cared to admit, but at suppertime the colour had come back into Andrew's cheeks and he was eating with all his old appetite. The matter slipped my mind as the jangled state of nerves of the villagers gradually came to crisis point. Not that I blamed them, because I was by now almost as nervous at night-time as anyone, despite the heavy Mauser pistol I kept by my bedside. The maire had issued a ration of ammunition to every responsible male adult. Like him I had no patience with the werewolf theories which many of the villagers were quite openly advocating, but I had to admit that there were many terrible and unexplainable things about this horrifying series of events.

Poor Badoit's neck was taking a long time to heal and he had to be removed to hospital in a major town fifty kilometres away. But for a miracle we would have been following his cortège to the local cemetery as the latest in that series of pathetic funerals of earlier victims. We were hoping that the wolf had had the fight knocked out of it by the flesh wound inflicted by our shots and had retired to the higher mountains. But it was not to be.

It was only two nights later when the beast struck. In some way known only to itself it had secreted itself in a locked woodshed almost in the heart of the village. Its audacity was such that it had apparently stayed there all day. In the early evening the unfortunate old woman who owned the nearby house had run short of fuel for her stove. Opening the door in the semi-darkness of the courtyard she had her throat torn out in the first onrush of the wolf and had died immediately. The beast, not at all incommoded by its wound of three nights earlier, had dragged her off to another backyard nearby and had commenced its meal. This delay had enabled the hurriedly summoned shooting party to come up while the beast was still in the vicinity. LeCoutre was arguing with some of the more superstitious villagers as Andrew and I got there.

"I tell you, could an animal have done this?" said a stolid, elderly villager with a walrus moustache, after the problems of the locked shed had been explained. "C'est le loup-garou!"

"Werewolf be damned!" said LeCoutre, choking with rage. "Bullets will put paid to it, the same as any other wolf."

I had just pointed out that the missing woman might still be alive and that we ought to be following up the trail when the most dreadful growl came from the shadows. This was followed by a worrying noise mixed with the sound of snapping bone which made several members of the party feel sick. We all set off through the maze of courtyards. Someone wheeled a motor cycle with a bright headlamp on to the scene.

A grey shadow leaped over a wall as a gun flamed, leaving a scene of Goyaesque horror behind it. While some of the party remained to take charge and to cover the mangled remains with a tarpaulin a dozen of us rushed forward to take revenge on this devilish animal. LeCoutre and I pressed shead of the two gendarmes. I had brought Andrew with me, to spare him the scenes behind us, and he was well up with the maire and myself. We heard a snarl from the thicket in front and Andrew dashed ahead with a torch and a thick stick, despite my shouts. I called to him to come back but the party was now widely spread out. My main fear was flying bullets from excitable trigger fingers as I didn't imagine that the wolf would stop.

It suddenly appeared, eyes blazing, and several shots rang out but the animal ran off. When we got to the spot there were no blood marks. Then Jaeckel appeared behind me, his eyes inflamed with excitement. His chest heaved with his exertions.

"There," he said excitedly. "There!"

I followed his pointing finger, saw the branches of the thicket moving and undulating.

"There he is," Jaeckel screamed. "The wolf-man!"

He raised his rifle before I could stop him. The explosion fell like a heavy wound on my heart. A large body lurched from the thicket and rolled almost to our feet. I ran forward in horror. Andrew sprawled on the ground, darkness running from his mouth, soaking the snow.

I lifted his head, hardly knowing what I was doing. His bandaged hand fell forward over his chest. There was a gasp from the search party behind us.

Andrew opened his eyes.

"I cut my hand chopping wood, father," he said very deliberately in English. "That is the truth."

Then he died.

"I believe you, my boy," I said.

The group around us made way for Dr Lemaire. Powerful electric torches illuminated the scene.

Jaeckel, the frontier guard, was stammering in my ears. "Pardon, monsieur, a terrible tragedy, but I was right. Le loup-garou! The bandage on his hand."

I hardly heard him. There was a strange look of triumph in Jaeckel's eyes and I understood many things.

As he turned away I saw he too had a bandage on his right hand.

Graham Masterton

RUG

Graham Masterton was born in Edinburgh, Scotland. He was a newspaper reporter and editor of Mayfair *and* Penthouse *before becoming a full-time novelist with his 1976 book* The Manitou *(filmed two years later).*

Since then he has written numerous horror novels and short stories, as well as historical sagas, thrillers and best-selling how-to sex books. His many titles include The Djinn, Charnel House, The Sphinx, The Devil's of D-Day, The Wells of Hell, Revenge of the Manitou, Tengu, The Pariah, Sacrifice, Death Trance, Night Warriors, Nightspawn, Mirror, Death Dream, Walkers, Night Plague, Prey, The House That Jack Built, Rook, The Devil in Gray, Manitou Blood, Ghost Music *and* Death Mask. *His short fiction has been collected in* Fortnight of Fear, Flights of Fear, Faces of Fear, *the British Fantasy Award-winning* Manitou Man: The Worlds of Graham Masterton, Feelings of Fear *and* Charnel House and Other Stories. *In 1989 he edited* Scare Care, *an anthology of horror stories to benefit abused and needy children.*

Masterton is the son of an Army officer, and the setting of "Rug" will be familiar to all those one-time children of BAOR who were schooled in England and visited their parents in Germany in the holidays. As the author reveals: "The real wolfskin rug hung in a shop filled with antique bric-a-brac in Munster, Westphalia. The house and the horse are real. Only the family have been changed to protect those who are frightened by claws scratching at the window ..."

Two days later, and nearly 75 kilometres away, a tall woman entered an antique shop close to the thirteenth-century Buddensturm, in the cathedral town of Münster. The doorbell jangled on a spring; the morning sunlight illuminated antlers and stags' heads and display cases of stuffed foxes.

The shopowner appeared from behind a curtain, smoking a cigarette. The woman was standing against the light, so that it was difficult for him to see her face.

"*Ich möchte eine Relsedecke*," she said.

"*Eine Relsedecke, gnädige Frau?*"

"*Ja. Ich möchte ein Wolfshaut.*"

"*Ein Wolfshaut? Das ist rar.* Very difficult to find, you understand?"

"Yes, I understand. But you can find me one, yes?"

"*Ich weiss nicht.* I can try."

The woman took out a small black purse, unfastened the clasp, and gave the shopowner 1,000DM, neatly folded. "Deposit," she said. "*Depositum.* If you can find me a wolfskin rug, I will pay you more. Much more."

She wrote a telephone number on the back of one of his cards, blew it dry and gave it to him.

"Don't fail me," she said.

But when she had left the shop (the doorbell still ringing) the shopowner stood still for a very long time. Then he opened one of the drawers underneath his counter and took out a dark, tarnished nail. A steel nail, heavily plated with silver.

They didn't come looking for wolfskins very often, but when they did they were usually desperate, which made them even more vulnerable than ever. Still, he needed the practice. He needed to tease her along. He needed to build up her hopes. He needed to make her believe that here, at last, was a man that she could trust.

Then it would be tree time. The hammer and the heart.

The woman didn't look back at the shop as she left it. Even if she *had* done, she may not have understood the significance of its name. After all, one beast simply passed on his ferocity to the next; not caring about names or heritage or marital vows. The only thing that was important was the skin, the *Wolfshaut*, the hairy covering that gave everything meaning.

But the name of the shop was "Bremke: Jagerkunst," and its business was not only the art and artefacts of hunting, but the relentless pursuit of the hunters themselves.

John found the wolf on the third day, when everybody else had gone to Paderborn for the horse trials. He had pleaded an earache (earaches were always best because nobody could prove whether you really had one or not, and you were still allowed to read and listen to the radio.) The truth was, though, that he was already homesick, and he didn't feel like doing anything but sitting by himself and thinking miserably about mummy.

The Smythe-Barnetts were very kind to him. Mrs Smythe-Barnett always kissed him goodnight, and their two daughters Penny and Veronica tried their best to involve him in everything they did. But the truth was that he was too sad to be much fun, and he shunned affection because it made a terrible prickly lump rise up in his throat, like a sea-urchin, and his eyes fill with tears.

He stood in the bay window in the front of the house watching the Smythe-Barnetts drive away with their smartly-varnished horse-box in tow. The exhaust from Col. Smythe-Barnett's Land Rover drifted away between the scabby plane trees, and the street fell silent again. It was one of those colourless autumn mornings when he could easily believe that he would never see blue sky again, ever. From Aachen to the Teutoburger Wald, the north German plains were suffocating under a comforter of greyish-white cloud.

In the kitchen, John could hear the German maid singing as she mopped the beige-tiled floor "Wooden Heart" in German. Everybody was singing it because Elvis had just released *GI Blues*.

He knew that everything would be better next week. His father had ten days' leave, and they were going to take a Rhine steamer to Koblenz, and then they were going to spend a week at the Forces recreation centre at Winterberg, among the pine forests of the Sauerland. But that still couldn't ease the homesickness of staying with a strange family in a strange country, with his parents so recently divorced. His grandmother had said something about "all those long separations … a man's only human, you know." John wasn't at all sure what she meant by "only human". It sounded to him like only *just* human – as if beneath those pond green cardigans and those tattersall-check shirts there throbbed the heart of a creature far more primitive.

He had even heard mummy saying about his father "he can be a beast at times", and he thought of his father arching back his head and baring his teeth, his eyes filled up with scarlet and his hands crooked like claws.

He went into the kitchen, but the floor was still wet and the maid shooed him away. She was a big-faced woman in black, and she smelled of cabbagey sweat. It seemed to John that all Germans smelled of cabbagey sweat. Penny had taken him on the bus to Bielefeld yesterday afternoon, and the smell of cabbagey sweat had been overwhelming.

He went out into the garden. The lawns were studded with fallen apples. He kicked one of them so that it hit the side of the stable. John had already been told off for trying to feed the Smythe-Barnetts' horse with apples. "They give him gripes, you stupid boy," Veronica had snapped at him. How was *he* supposed to know? The only horse he had ever seen at close-quarters was the milkman's horse from United Dairies, and that wore a permanent nosebag.

He sat on the swing and creaked backward and forward for a while. The garden was almost unbearably silent. Still, this was better than being introduced to all of the Smythe-Barnett's haw-hawing friends in Paderborn. He had seen them packing their picnic lunch and it was salami and fatty beef sandwiches.

He looked up at the huge suburban house. It was typical of large family residences built in Germany between the wars, with an orange-tiled roof and fawn concrete-rendered walls. There must have been another similar house next door, but Bielefeld had been badly bombed, and now there was nothing left but a wild orchard and brick foundations.

John heard a harsh croaking noise. He looked up and saw a stork perched on the chimney – a real-live stork. It was the first one he had ever seen, and he could hardly believe it was real. It was like an omen, a warning of things to come. It stayed on the chimney for only a few moments, turning its beak imperiously from right to left, its feathers ruffled. Then it flew away, with an audible *flap, flap, flap* of its wings.

While he was looking up, John noticed for the first time that there was a dormer window in the roof: only a small one. There must be an attic or another bedroom right at the top of the house. If there was an attic, there might be something interesting in it, like relics from the war, or an unexploded bomb, or books about sex. He had found a book about sex in the attic at home, *Everything Newlyweds Should Know*. He had traced Fig. 6 – The Female Vulva and coloured it pink.

He went back inside the house. The maid was in the living-room now, polishing the furniture and filling the air with the aroma of lavender and cabbagey sweat. John climbed the stairs to the first landing, where the walls were hung with photographs of Penny and Veronica on Jupiter, each photograph decorated with a red rosette. He was glad he hadn't gone with them to Paderborn. Why should he care if their stupid horse managed to jump over a whole lot of poles?

He climbed the second flight of stairs. He hadn't been up here before. This was where Col. and Mrs Smythe-Barnett had their "sweet." John didn't know why they felt it necessary to eat their pudding in their bedroom. He supposed it was just another of those things that snobby people like the Smythe-Barnetts always did, like having silver napkin-rings and serving tomato ketchup in a dish.

The floorboards creaked. Through the half-open doors, John could see the corner of the Smythe-Barnetts' bed, and Mrs Smythe-Barnett's dressing-table, with its array of silverbacked brushes. He listened for a moment. Downstairs, the maid had started to vacuum-clean the living-room carpet. Her cleaner made a roaring drone like a German bomber. She wouldn't be able to hear him at all.

Cautiously, he crept into the Smythe-Barnetts' bedroom, and across to the dressing-table. In the mirror, he could see a solemn, white-faced boy of 11 with a short prickly haircut and sticky-outy ears. This of course was not him but simply his external disguise, the physical manifestation he adopted in order to put up his hand during school register and say "Present, miss!"

On the dressing-table lay a half-finished letter on blue deckle-edged notepaper, with a fountainpen lying across it. It read "very disturbed and withdrawn, but I suppose that's only natural under the circumstances. He cries himself to sleep every night, and suffers nightmares. He also seems to find it very difficult to get along with other children. It will obviously take a great deal of time and"

He stared at his pasty face in the mirror. He looked like a photograph of his father when his father was very young. *Very disturbed and withdrawn.* How could Mrs Smythe-Barnett have written that about him? He wasn't disturbed and withdrawn. It was just that what was inside him, he wanted to *keep* inside. Why should he let Mrs Smythe-Barnett know how unhappy he was? What did it have to do with *her*?

He tiptoed out of the Smythe-Barnetts' bedroom and quietly closed the door. The German maid was still leading a full-scale raid over London Docks. He walked along to the end of the corridor, and it was there that he discovered a small cream-painted door which obviously led up to the attic. He opened it. Inside, there was a steep flight of hessian-carpeted stairs. It was very gloomy up there, although a little of the grey, muted daylight managed to penetrate. John could smell mustiness, and dust, and an odd odour like onion-flowers.

He climbed the stairs. As he did so, he came face to face with the wolf.

It was lying flat on the floor, facing him. Its eyes were yellow and its teeth were bared, and its dry, purplish tongue was hanging out. Its hairy ears were slightly motheaten, and there was a baldish patch on the side of its snout, but that did nothing to detract from its ferocity. Even if its body was utterly empty, and it was now being used as a rug, it was still a wolf, and a huge wolf at that – the biggest wolf that John had ever seen.

He looked around the attic. Apart from a partitioned-off area at the far end, to house the water-tanks, it had been converted into a spare bedroom which ran the whole length and breadth of the house. Behind the wolf there was a solid brass bed, with a sagging mattress on it. Three ill-assorted armchairs were arranged by the window, and an old varnished chest-of-drawers stood beneath the lowest part of the eaves.

There was a framed photograph hanging by the side of the dormer window. The top of the frame was decorated with dried flowers, long ago leached of any colour. The photograph showed a fair-haired girl standing by the side of a suburban road somewhere, one eye closed against the sunlight. She was wearing an embroidered halter-top dress and a white blouse.

John knelt down beside the wolf-rug and examined it closely. He reached out and touched the tips of its curving teeth. It was incredible to think this had once been a real animal, running through the woods, chasing after hares and deer, maybe even people.

He stroked its fur. It was still wiry and thick, mostly black, with some grey streaks around the throat. He wondered who had shot it, and why. If *he* had a wolf, he wouldn't shoot it. He would train it to hunt people down, and tear their throats out. Particularly his maths teacher, Mrs Bennett. She would look good with her throat turn out. Blood creeping across the pages of *School Mathematics Part One by H.E. Parr.*

He buried his nose in the wolf-rug's flanks and breathed in, to find out if it still smelled at all like animal. All he could detect, however, was dust, and a very faintly leathery odour. Whatever wolf-scent this beast had ever possessed, it had been dried up with age.

For an hour or two, until it was lunchtime, he played hunters. Then he played Tarzan, and wrestled with the wolf-rug all over the bedroom. He clamped its jaws around his wrist, and grunted and heaved in an effort to prevent it from biting off his hand. Finally he managed to get it onto its back, and he stabbed it again and again with his huge imaginary jungle-knife, ripping out its guts, and twisting the blade deep into its heart.

A few minutes after twelve, he heard the maid calling him. He straightened the rug, and hurried quickly and quietly downstairs. The maid was ready to leave, in hat and coat and gloves, all black. On the kitchen table there was a plateful of cold salami and gherkins and buttered bread, and a large glass of warm milk, on the surface of which the yellow cream had already begun to form into blobby clusters.

That night, after the Smythe-Barnetts returned, all tired and noisy and smelling of horses and sherry, John lay in his small bed staring at the ceiling and thinking of the wolf. It was so proud, so fierce, and yet so dead, lying gutted on the attic floor with its eyes staring at nothing at all. It had been a beast at times, just like his father; and perhaps one day it could be a beast again. There was no telling with creatures like that, as his grandmother had once said, with her hand cupped over the telephone receiver, as if he wouldn't be able to hear.

The wind was getting up and clearing away the cloud; but at the same time it was making the plane tree branches dip and thrash, so that strange spiky shadows shuddered and danced across the ceiling of John's bedroom, shadows like praying-mantises, and spider-legs, and wolf-claws.

In the eye of the coming gale he closed his eyes and tried to sleep. But the spider-legs danced even more frantically on the ceiling, and the praying-mantises dipped and shivered, and every quarter-hour the Smythe-Barnetts' hall clock struck the Westminster chimes, as if to remind themselves all through the night how correct they were, both in timing and in taste.

And then at quarter past two in the morning he heard a scratching sound coming down the attic stairs. He was sure of it. The wolf! The wolf was climbing down the attic stairs with arched back and bristled tail, its eyes gleaming amber as garnets in the darkness, its breath panting *hah-hah-HAH-hah! hah-hah-HAH-hah*! ripe with wolfishness and bloodlust.

He heard it running along the corridor, past the Smythe-Barnetts' sweet, hungry, hungry, hungry. He heard it sniffing at doorlocks, growling in its throat. He heard it pause at the head of the second-floor staircase, and then plunge downwards, coming his way.

It began to run really fast now, its tail beating against the walls of the corridor. Its eyes opened wide and yellow, and its ears stiffened up. It was coming after him, coming to take its revenge. He shouldn't have fought it, shouldn't have wrestled it, and for all that his jungle-knife was imaginary, he had still intended to cut its heart out, he had still *wanted* to do it, even if he hadn't.

He heard the wolf thudding toward his bedroom-door, louder and louder, and then the door burst open and John shot up in bed and screamed and screamed, his eyes tight shut, his fists clenched, wetting his pyjamas in sheer terror.

Mrs Smythe-Barnett came into the room and took him in her arms. She switched on his bedside lamp and cuddled him and shushed him. He put up with her cuddling for two or three minutes and then he had to pull away. His wet pyjama trousers were rapidly chilling, and he felt so embarrassed that he could have happily died at that moment. Yet he had no alternative but to stand shivering in a dressing-gown while she patiently changed the bed for him, and brought him clean pyjamas, and tucked him up. A tall big-nosed woman in a tall nightdress, wearing a scarf to cover the rollers in her hair. Saintly, in a way, but a Bernini saint; marble-perfect, always able to cope. He so much missed his mummy, who couldn't cope with anything, or not very well.

"You had a nightmare," said Mrs Smythe-Barnett, stroking his forehead.

"It's all right. I'm all right now," John told her, almost crossly.

"How's your earache?" she asked him.

"Better, thanks. I saw a stork."

"That's nice. Actually, storks are quite common around here; but the local people think they're bad luck. They say that if a stork perches on your roof, somebody in the house will get the very worst thing they ever feared. I think that's why they say that storks bring babies! But I don't believe in superstitions like that, do you?"

John shook his head. He couldn't understand where the wolf had gone. The wolf had come running down the stairs and along the corridor and down the second flight of stairs and along the corridor and—

And here was Mrs Smythe-Barnett, stroking his forehead.

He took the bus into Bielefeld the next day, on his own this time. He suffered the cabbagey sweat and the Emte 23 cigarettes, squashed between a huge woman dressed in black and a thin youth with a long hair growing out of the mole on his chin.

He went to the cake-shop and bought an apfel-strudel with piles of squirty cream on it, which he ate as he walked along the street. When he saw his reflection in shop windows he couldn't believe how young he was. He went into a bookshop and looked through some illustrated art books. Some of them had pictures of nudes. He found an etching by Hans Bellmer of a pregnant woman being penetrated by two men at once, her baby crowded to one side of her womb by two thrusting penises. Her head was thrown back to swallow the penis of a third man, faceless, anonymous.

He was about to leave the bookshop when he saw an etching on the wall of a wolf. On closer inspection, however, it wasn't a wolf at all, but a man with the face of a wolf. The caption, in black Gothic lettering, read Wolfmensch. John went up and peered at it more closely. The man-wolf was standing in front of an old German town, with crowded rooftops. On one of those rooftops perched a stork.

He was still staring at the picture when the bookshop proprietor approached him – a small, balding, thin-cheeked man with yellowish skin and a worn-out grey suit, and breath that was thick with tobacco.

"You're English?" he asked.

John nodded.

"You're interested in wolf-men?"

"I don't know. Not specially."

"Well, anyway, this picture in which you show so much interest, he is our famous local wolf-man, from Bielefeld. His real name was Schmidt, Gunther Schmidt. He lived – you see the dates here – from 1887 to 1923. He was the son of a schoolmaster."

"Did he ever kill anybody?" asked John.

"Yes, they say so," nodded the bookshop proprietor. "They say he killed many young women, when they were out walking in the woods."

John said nothing, but stared at the wolf-man in awe. The wolf-man looked so much like the rug in the Smythe-Barnetts' attic – eyes and fangs and hairy ears – but then he supposed that all wolves looked much the same. Met one wolf-man, met them all.

The bookshop proprietor hooked the picture down from the wall. "Nobody knows how Gunther Schmidt became a wolf-man. Some people say that his ancestor was bitten by a wolf-man mercenary during the Thirty Years' War. There's a legend, you see, that when the Diet of Ratisbon called back General Wallenstein, he brought in some very strange mercenaries to help him. He was beaten by Gustavus at the battle of Lützen, but many of Gustavus' men had terrible wounds, throats torn open, and suchlike. Well, perhaps it isn't true. But it's true that the battle of Lützen was fought under a full moon, and you know what they say about wolf-people. Women, as well as men."

"Werewolves," said John, feeling awed.

"That's right, werewolves! Here, let me show you this book. It has pictures of all of the incidents of werewolves, during the past fifty years. It's a very interesting book, if you like to be scared!"

From the shelf just above his desk, he took down a large album, covered with brown paper. He opened it out, and beckoned John to take a look.

"Here! This is one for the werewolf enthusiast! Lili Bauer, killed on the night of April 20, 1921, in Tecklenburg, her throat was torn open. And here is Mara Thiele, found dead in the Lippe, July 19, 1921, also throat torn open … *und so weiter, und so weiter.*"

"Who's this?" asked John. He had found a photograph of a girl in a halter-top dress, with a white blouse, and blonde hair, standing by a suburban road, one eye squinched against the sunlight.

"This one … Lotte Bremke, found dead in the woods close to Heepen, August 15, 1923. Again, throat ripped out. The last victim, this is what it says. After that, nobody heard from Gunther Schmidt anything more … although here, look. A human heart was found nailed to a tree in Waldstrasse, with the message, here is the heart of the wolf."

John stared at the photograph of Lotte Bremke for a long time. He was sure that it was the same girl whose photograph was nailed up in the attic at the Smythe-Barnetts' house. But could that mean that Lotte Bremke had lived there once? And if she had – where had the wolf-skin come from? Had Lotte Bremke's father killed the wolf-man, perhaps, and nailed his heart to a tree, and kept his skin as a gruesome souvenir?

He closed the book and handed it back. The bookshop proprietor was watching him with pale, disinterested eyes, their pupils the colour of cold tea.

"Well?" said the bookshop proprietor. "*Wass glaubst du?*"

"I'm not really interested in werewolves," John told him. There were far worse things than werewolves, like wetting the bed in front of Mrs Smythe-Barnett.

"But you stared at this picture," the bookshop proprietor smiled.

"I was just interested."

"Well ... of course. But don't forget that the beast is not inside us. This is important to remember when dealing with wolf-men. The beast is not inside us. *We are inside the beast, versteh?*"

John stared at him. He didn't know what to say. He felt as if this man could read everything that he was thinking, like an open book lying on a shallow riverbed. All that was required to turn the pages was to get one's fingers wet.

John took the bus back to Heepen. It was nearly half-past five and the sky was indigo. The moon hung over the Teutoburger Wald like the bright face of God. When he arrived back at the Smythe-Barnett's house, all the lights were lit, Penny and Veronica were giggling in the kitchen, and Col. Smythe-Barnett was entertaining six or seven fellow-officers in the living-room (roars of laughter, clouds of cigarette-smoke).

Mrs Smythe-Barnett came into the kitchen and for the first time John was pleased to see her. She was wearing a glittery cocktail-dress but her face was dark with rage. "Where have you been?" she shouted, and she was so angry that it took him a moment or two to understand that she was shouting at him.

"I went to Bielefeld," he said, weakly.

"You went to Bielefeld without telling us! We've been frantic! Gerald had to call the local polizei, for God's sake, and you don't have any idea how much he hates asking for help from the locals!"

"I'm sorry," he said. "I thought it was all right. We went on Tuesday. I thought it was all right to go today."

"For God's sake, isn't it enough that we're wetnursing you? You've only been here four days and you've been nothing but trouble! No wonder your parents broke up!"

John sat with his head bowed and said nothing. He didn't understand adult drunkenness. He didn't understand that people could exaggerate things that irritated them, and not really mean it, and say sorry the next morning, and it was all forgotten. He was eleven.

Veronica set his supper in front of him. It was a cold chicken leg, with gherkins. He had asked especially not to be given warm milk, because he didn't like it. Instead, Veronica had poured him a glass of flat Coca-Cola.

In bed that night, he crunched himself up and cried as if his heart would split into pieces.

But at two o'clock in the morning, he opened his eyes and he was perfectly calm. The moon was shining so brightly through his bedroom curtains that it could have been daylight. Dead daylight, the world of the dead, but daylight all the same.

He climbed out of bed and looked at himself in his little mirror. A boy with a face made of silver. He said, "Lotte Bremke". That was all he had to say. He knew that she had lived here, when the house was first built. He knew what had happened to her. Some things are so obvious to children that they blink in disbelief when adults fail to understand. Lotte Bremke's father had done what any father would do, and hunted down the wolf-man, and killed him, somehow, and nailed his heart (*smash*! quiver! *smash*! quiver) to the nearest plane tree.

John glided to the bedroom door, and opened it. He walked along the corridor with feet like glass. He walked up the stairs, and along the second corridor, with feet like glass. He opened the cream-painted door that led to the attic, and opened it.

He climbed the stairs.

Sure enough, the wolf-rug was waiting for him, with gleaming yellow eyes and bristly fur. John crawled across the rough hessian carpet on hands and knees and stroked it, and whispered, "Wolfman, that's what you were. Don't deny it. You were on the outside, weren't you? You were the skin. That was the difference; that was what nobody understood. Werewolves are wolves turned into men, not men turned into wolves! And you ran round their houses, didn't you, and ran through their woods, and caught them, and bit them, and tore their throats out, and killed them!"

"But they caught you, didn't they, wolf, and they took out the man who was hiding inside you. They took out all of your insides, and left you with nothing but your skin.

"Still, you shouldn't worry. I can be your man now. I can put you on. You can be a rug one minute, and a real wolf the next."

He stood up, and lifted the rug up from the floor. It had felt heavy when he had been wrestling with it this afternoon, but now it felt even heavier, almost as heavy as a live wolf. It took him all of his strength to lift it around his shoulders, and to drape the empty legs around him. He perched the head on top of his own head.

He trailed around the attic, around and around. "I am the wolf, and the wolf is me," he breathed to himself. "I am the wolf, and the wolf is me."

He closed his eyes. He flared his nostrils. I'm a wolf now, he thought to himself. Fierce and fast and dangerous. He could imagine himself running through the woods of Heepen, in between the trees, his paws padding soft and deadly over the thick carpet of pine-needles.

He opened his eyes. Now was the time to get his revenge. The wolf's revenge! He climbed down the stairs with his tail beating thump, thump, thump on the treads behind him. He pushed open the attic door and began to lope along the corridor, toward the slightly-open door of the Smythe-Barnetts' bedroom.

He growled deep down in his throat, and saliva began to drip from the sides of his mouth. He made hardly any sound at all as he approached the Smythe-Barnetts' door.

I am the wolf, and the wolf is me.

He was only three or four feet away from the door when it suddenly and silently opened, and the corridor was filled with moonlight.

John hesitated for a moment, and growled again.

Then something stepped out of the Smythe-Barnetts' bedroom that made the real hair rise on the back of his neck, and turned his soul to water.

It was Mrs Smythe-Barnett, and yet it wasn't. She was naked, tall and naked – but she was more than naked, she was *raw*. Her body glistened with white bone and tightly-stretched membranes, and John could even see her arteries pulsing, and the fanlike tracery of her veins.

Inside her long, narrow ribcage, her lungs rose and fell in a quick, obscene panting.

Her face was horrifying. It seemed to have stretched out into a long bony snout, and her lips were drawn tightly back over her teeth. Her eyes glittered yellow. Wolf-yellow.

"*Where's my skin?*" she demanded, in a voice that was halfway between a hiss and a growl. "*What are you doing with my skin?*"

John let the wolf-rug drop from his shoulders and slide down onto the floor. He couldn't speak. He couldn't even breathe. He watched in helpless dread as Mrs Smythe-Barnett dropped down onto her hands and knees, and seemed to slither into the wolf-rug like a naked hand slithering into a furry glove.

"I didn't *mean* to—" he managed to choke out, but then the claws burst into his windpipe, knocking him backward against the wall. He swallowed, so that he could scream, but all that he swallowed was a half-pint of warm blood.

The wolf-rug came after him and there was nothing he could do to stop it.

John's father arrived at the house shortly after eight-thirty the following morning, as he did every morning, so that he could see John for five or ten minutes before he went to work. His German driver kept the engine of the khaki Volkswagen running, because it was so cold this morning, well below five degrees.

He went up the steps, his swagger-stick tucked under his arm. To his surprise, the front door was wide open. He pressed the doorbell, and then stepped inside the house.

"David? Helen? Anyone at home?"

He heard a strange mewing noise coming from the kitchen.

"Helen? Is everything all right?"

He walked through to the back of the house. In the kitchen he found the German maid sitting at the table, still dressed in her hat and coat, her handbag in front of her, shaking and shivering with shock.

"What's wrong?" John's father demanded. "Where is everybody?"

"*Etwas shrecklich*." the maid quivered. "All family dead."

"What? What do you mean, 'all family dead'?"

"Upstairs," said the maid. "All family dead."

"Call my driver. Tell him to come inside. Then telephone the police. *Polizei*, got it?"

Filled with terrible apprehension, John's father climbed the stairs. On the first-floor landing, he found the bedroom doors ajar, and spattered with blood. The smiling photographs of Penny and Veronica lay smashed on the carpet, the red gymkhana rosettes trampled and torn.

He went close to the girls' bedroom doors and looked inside. Penny lay sprawled on her back, her neck so furiously ripped open that her head was almost separated from her body. Veronica lay face-down, her white nightgown stained dark red.

Grim-faced, John's father went to the bedroom where John was sleeping. He opened the door, but inside the bed was empty, and there was no sign of John. He swallowed dryly, and said a prayer to himself. Please God, let him still be alive.

He climbed further. The second-story corridor was sprayed with squiggles and question-marks of blood. In the Smythe-Barnetts' bedroom, Col. Smythe-Barnett lay on his back staring at the ceiling, his larynx torn out. He looked as if he were wearing a bib of blood. No sign of Helen Smythe-Barnett anywhere.

The door that led to the staircase was decorated all over with bloody handmarks. John's father opened it, took a deep breath, and slowly climbed up to the attic.

The room was filled with sunlight. As he entered, he found himself confronted by a rug made of wolfskin, with the wolf's head still attached. The wolf's jaws were dark with congealing blood, and its fur was matted.

There was something concealed by the rug that raised it in a slight hump. John's father hesitated for a very long time, and then took hold of the edge of the rug and lifted it up.

Underneath it were the half-digested remains of a young boy.

Hugh B. Cave

THE WHISPERERS

Hugh Barnett Cave (1910–2004) was born in Chester, England, but emigrated to America with his family when he was five. He sold his first fiction in 1929, and went on to publish around 800 stories (often under various bylines) to such pulp magazines as Weird Tales, Strange Tales, Ghost Stories, Black Book Detective Magazine, Spicy Mystery Stories *and the so-called "shudder" or "weird menace" pulps,* Horror Stories *and* Terror Tales.

Cave left the field for almost three decades, moving to Haiti and later Jamaica, where he established a coffee plantation and wrote two highly-praised travel books, Haiti: Highroad to Adventure *and* Four Paths to Paradise: A Book About Jamaica. *He also continued to write for the "slick" magazines, such as* Collier's, Cosmopolitan, Esquire, The Saturday Evening Post *and many other titles. In 1977, Karl Edward Wagner's Carcosa imprint published a volume of Cave's best horror tales,* Murgunstrumm and Others, *and he returned to the genre with new stories and a string of modern horror novels:* Legion of the Dead, The Nebulon Horror, The Evil, Shades of Evil, Disciples of Dread, The Lower Deep, Lucifer's Eye, Isle of the Whisperers, The Dawning, The Evil Returns *and* The Restless Dead.

The story that follows is a revised version of one which originally saw print in 1942 in Spicy Mystery Stories *under the author's jokey pseudonym "Justin Case".*

It was a very old, very forlorn house. To reach it we had to climb over a broken gate on which hung a FOR SALE sign, and then wade through a sea of grass that had grown rampant.

"Darling," Anne said, "This is *it*! Let's buy it!"

I stared at her. We had been married a week, but I still could not even glance at her without wanting to take her in my arms. We could fix the house up and come here weekends, at least, she insisted. I was thinking we might actually live here full time because, being a writer, I could live anywhere.

An hour later we were in the village, talking to Jedney Prentiss, whose name and address were on the sign.

The price he quoted was reasonable enough, I thought. "And it's still a mighty fine house, even though it's been empty for six years," he said. We drove to Harkness, then, to arrange the transfer.

That afternoon we lit a fire in the big fireplace and burned the road-maps. Then we picked out the room we wanted for our bedroom and went to work, determined to have at least that much done by nightfall. Anne had bought bedding and some furniture in Harkness, and the store people had promised to deliver them at once.

It was great fun. To save her dress, Anne peeled down to shorts and a halter, and there she was, running around in the almost-nude with mops and brooms, dusters, and buckets of water. I watched her out of one eye and realized what a lucky man I was.

It was about six o'clock when our "company" arrived. Anne had gone out into the yard for some birch twigs to make an auxiliary broom. I was on my knees in bedroom debris. Suddenly, from the doorway at my back, a voice said, "You ain't gonna *live* here, are you, mister?"

I swung about, startled half out of my skin. There on the threshold stood a sickly, emaciated little girl about twelve years old. Pity for the poor creature overwhelmed me, and I stood up slowly for fear of frightening her. "And who are you?" I asked. "A neighbour of ours?"

"I used to live here. I'm Susie Callister."

Jedney Prentiss had mentioned the Callisters. They were local people who had rented the place for a time. After the death of Jim Callister, his wife and little girl had moved out.

"You people must be crazy, movin' into this place," the child said. "My ma says it's haunted."

"Really?"

"She'd lick the tar out of me if she knew I was here!"

"And do you come here often?" I asked.

"Yep. Pa died here. He was swell. I come here to talk to him."

"You come here to what?"

"Well," she said defiantly, "maybe I don't talk to him like me and you are talkin'. But I talk and he listens. I sit on a box down in the cellar and tell him how ma won't let me come here. He whispers back, sometimes. He died there in the cellar, from a heart attack."

"Peter!" That was Anne's voice from downstairs. "I've made coffee and sandwiches. It's after six, and I'm starved!"

"Gee!" Susie Callister whispered. "Is it that late? I'll get kilt!" She turned like a frightened rabbit, then stopped. In a low, pleading voice she added, "Can I – can I come here sometimes to talk to pa? Can I? Please?"

Something told me there was a story in this little girl, so I said she could come as often as she liked. She fled downstairs and out the front door, slamming it behind her. When I got downstairs, Anne was standing in the hall shadows, a queer look on her face.

"Who was that, Peter?"

I told her, and she seemed relieved. We sat down to our supper in the kitchen. Anne was oddly quiet.

She was tired, I supposed. Walking around the table, I put my hands on her shoulders and said, "You're working too hard."

She smiled a little and relaxed against me. But she was trembling, and suddenly looked up at me.

"Peter – before we do anything else after supper, will you go down into the cellar and look around? I was down there a while ago and I think we have rats. I heard the strangest whispering sounds over near an old work-bench …"

"I'll exterminate the vipers," I said lightly. But Anne was afraid. I knew it by the way she clung to me.

I didn't go into the cellar right away. Our purchases arrived and we had to arrange furniture. Night was upon us in earnest before I got around to the rats.

Clutching an antique oil-lamp, I groped down the steep, treacherous cellar stairs, put the lamp on the work-bench, and looked around.

It was a huge room with floor and walls of rough concrete, the floor unfinished, or long ago torn up for some reason, in the corner under the bench. My mind played with a distressing mental picture of Susie Callister, poor child, sitting here alone in the dark, pouring out her sorrows to her dead father. Something would have to be done about Susie Callister, and about the rats whose whisperings she believed to be her father's voice!

The rats? Seated on an upturned box, I waited. Presently I, too, heard a furtive whispering. It seemed to come from that section of the cellar where the floor had been torn up.

Noiselessly I stalked the sounds. Rats? I was not so sure. This odd, subtle whispering was too – seductive. I could have sworn it was trying to tell me something.

On hands and knees I crept toward the corner where the floor was bare. The sounds ceased. Carefully I explored every inch of the packed brown earth, but found nothing. Had the rats bored a tunnel beneath this part of the cellar? *Did* rats make tunnels?

I took a step toward the lamp, and stopped. Something unbelievably cold, yet soft – soft as the touch of a woman's lips! – caught at my left ankle. My heart missed a beat. Through me swept the kind of thrill that might seethe in a man if a beautiful woman were suddenly to appear naked before him out of nowhere.

I looked down and could have sworn, *though nothing was there*, that something like a human hand had hold of my foot. Then a dull, creaking noise stiffened me. I jerked loose, raised my head, and saw that the bulkhead at the far end of the cellar was being raised. There was the explanation of my "clutching hand" – simply an inrush of cold air from the night outside.

I stared. Framed in the aperture was a pair of legs garbed in coarse black stockings. Then a groping hand appeared, followed by a woman's face. Furtively the intruder descended the old wooden steps to the cellar floor.

Apparently she did not see me – and that was strange, for the lamp still burned. Slowly she advanced. Her dress was a cheap black rag that accented the paleness of her face and throat. Prowling past the bench, she stopped. Her voice, a sibilant whisper, scratched along the cellar walls.

"She's been here again, Jim Callister, hasn't she? I know it! I could tell by the look in her eyes when she got home. She comes here more often than I know, and you talk to her, you put ideas into her head. But you ain't goin' to get her, damn you! I'll take her so far away, you won't never get your hellish hairy hands on her! You hear? I'm defyin' you! I stood up to you once, and I'm doin' it again!"

She shook her fist. Her calcimine face was shapeless with hate. I swear I could hear the machine-gun beat of her heart beneath that ragged black dress. Sharply I said, "Wait, Mrs Callister!"

She stopped as though stabbed. Her glittering eyes searched for me and finally found me. I realized then why she had not seen me before. She was half blind.

"It's quite all right, Mrs Callister," I said. "I'm Peter Winslow and I've bought this house. I'd like to talk to you if—"

Flinging herself backward, she whirled toward the bulkhead, and before I could make a move to stop her, the darkness outside had swallowed her. Bewildered and afraid, I went upstairs.

That night we heard the rats. Anne pressed herself against me, her sweet body trembling with terror. I tried to comfort her, but even while doing so I thought darkly, *The rats are in the cellar. Susie Callister's father died there. Susie is a strange child and her mother is a strange woman. No ordinary rats ever whispered like that …*

In the morning I drove alone to the village, to buy traps. The proprietor of the general store was a thin, bony man. "So you're the feller bought the old Prentiss place," he said when I introduced myself. "Like it there, do you?"

"I think we might when it's fixed up."

He gave me an oblique look. "Paint and repairs will help a heap, but they won't alter what happened to Jim Callister. I'm the undertaker here, and I prepared Jim for buryin'. You can't tell *me* he died natural, and I said so till I was hoarse, but nobody'd listen."

"What do you mean?" I demanded.

"Well, he was workin' down in the cellar the night he died. Seems he spent most of his spare time workin' there. So this night it was mighty quiet down there and his wife got worried, and she went down and found him layin' there. *Or so she said.*" He snorted. "Doc Digby called it a heart attack. But I took care of the body, like I said, and I never heard of a heart attack growin' hair on a man."

"Hair?"

"Outside of his face, there wasn't an inch of Jim Callister that didn't have hair on it. Hair like you'd see on a dog, or a wolf!"

I gave him a long, hard stare, trying to figure him out.

"Another thing," he said. "When I pumped Jim Callister clean, I didn't like what came out of him."

I could only stare at him and say weakly, "I don't understand."

"Smelled funny and looked funny. If you ask me, he was poisoned."

"But what – why—?"

"Can't talk to you no more. Said too much already, I expect." Abruptly he turned his back on me.

I thought about it on the way home, and decided to have another look at that cellar. *And* to have a talk with Dr Digby at the first opportunity. Then I found a car of rather ancient vintage parked at our gate, and its doctor's emblem indicated our caller was a medical man.

He was. A bald little man in his sixties, he stopped talking to Anne and introduced himself as Everett Digby. The hand he offered me was like a wet rubber glove.

"Thought I'd drop in to say hello," he said with a mechanical smile.

You thought you'd drop in to see if we actually intend to live here, I mentally corrected. *You know something about this house – about Jim Callister – that you don't want us to find out.*

We talked for half an hour about nothing. Finally, after a cautious build-up, I said, "The fellow at the store seems to think there was something strange about Jim Callister's death."

Digby laughed. "Better take Ben with a grain of salt. He makes his own liquor and it docs queer things to him."

I thought, *One of you is lying.* Anne excused herself and went to prepare lunch. Then Digby suddenly changed his manner.

Leaning toward me, he said in a low voice, "You were insane to buy this place, Winslow. What Ben Nevins told you is right, or partly right, anyhow. There *was* something odd about Callister's death, and this house was the cause of it. If I were you, I'd clear out!"

"Why?"

He shot a glance at the kitchen door. "I'll tell you what I know, and leave out what I think. Jim Callister came here to live three years ago. At first everything went fine. Then he built a work-bench down in the cellar and things began happening. He got thin and worried. His wife begged me to look at him and I did, and it stumped me. There wasn't a thing wrong with him that I could discover, yet his skin was turning soft and white, and little clumps of hair were growing out of it. And he was changing mentally. Jim had been a fine fellow with a big, hearty laugh. Now he was grim as a grave and becoming sort of sly and stealthy."

"He got worse before his death?" I asked.

"Well, I wouldn't know about the condition of his body. After that first examination, he wouldn't let me look at him again. But according to his wife, he got more surly by the day. She and their little girl went through hell."

"And you believe this house had something to do with it?"

Digby looked away, moistening his lips. "*Something* changed him. I don't know what. All I say is, you ought to clear out of here for your own safety. There are things in this world we don't understand, Winslow. I don't *know* what turned Jim Callister into a vicious, hairy beast, but—" He caught himself, but it was too late. Anne was there in the doorway.

Digby stood up, little lines of sweat forming on his bald head. "Got to be going," he mumbled. "Said more than I meant to." He hurried out to his car.

When he had gone, Anne turned to me and said quietly, "What did he mean about Jim Callister, Peter?"

"Nothing, darling."

"I want you to tell me."

I told her, selecting with care the words I used. "I've a feeling something unpleasant happened in this house and he may have had a part in it," I concluded. "My hunch is that he wants to scare us out of here before we find out about it." But even as I put my arms around her and kissed her, I was thinking of something else. Of those whispers in the cellar.

That evening while knocking down some old shelves in the kitchen, I felt a sharp, shooting pain in my ankle. It disappeared almost at once, but at the first opportunity I went upstairs, shut the bedroom door behind me, and removed my sock.

A patch of graying white skin, peculiarly soft, extended from my instep to a point an inch or so above the shin bone. Thoroughly scared, I smeared it with salve and bound it, replacing sock and shoe. Then I began thinking of the cellar again. I had to go down there! Furtively I began seeking some excuse for leaving Anne upstairs, so that I might be alone down there, to wait.

Wait for what? The whispers?

The opportunity came just before bedtime. Anne had undressed and donned her pyjamas. We were having a nightcap in the kitchen. As a bridegroom, I should have been gazing at my wife and thinking something like *This lovely woman is mine, to have, to hold and to love.* But what I said to her was, "You go on upstairs, darling. I have to set those traps in the cellar."

She looked at me queerly, but I turned away and went down the cellar stairs, closing the door behind me.

Unerringly my feet took me to that patch of brown earth near the work bench. There I waited. Ten, fifteen minutes I waited. Then – the whispers again! Out of the earth they came, or out of the walls – sibilant, seductive sounds that seemed almost to be words.

My hands trembled. My whole body quivered with excitement. Dropping to hands and knees, I crawled toward the source of the sounds. And suddenly my hands were claws, frantically digging in the earth!

Now the whispers mocked me. They beat against my brain, tormenting me, spurring me on to greater efforts. I clawed like an animal, like a dog digging for a bone. Before long I had dug a hole nearly two feet deep and encountered wood.

It was a cistern cover. I could not budge it. But I found a crowbar back of the furnace and worked like a madman, with sweat rolling down my face and arms, until slowly, bit by bit, I broke the seal of concrete that held the cover in place. Then, using all my strength, I pried it up and managed to move it to one side.

There in the black depths of the cellar I dropped to my hands and knees to peer into a yawning pit, and from the depths of it rose a sigh, half human, half animal, that seemed to convey all the world's sadness.

I seized my flashlight and aimed its beam into the pit. The walls leaped into frightening prominence. Gray, wet walls they were, covered with a fungus growth that seemed to writhe in agony as the light touched it. But the depths of the cistern still tenaciously held their secret. Powerful as the light was, it revealed only vertical walls vanishing into a deep, seemingly impenetrable darkness. A whispering darkness. A darkness full of nameless rustlings *that called to me!*

The cellar had grown unbearably cold. My flesh crawled. I retreated in dismay from the pit's edge, but a clammy, freezing chill enveloped me as though invisible hands had stripped me naked and were rubbing me with ice.

Sharp, biting pain attacked my chest and arms. Then came the fear – fear of the dark, of the pit, of the crowding cellar walls. Sobbing out my terror, I swung the cistern cover back into place and clawed some earth over it. Then I fled.

When I entered the bedroom, Anne was lying there in bed with a magazine, waiting for me. "Peter!" she cried. "You're so pale! What's wrong?"

I crept into bed and crushed her against me, desperately afraid that something might come between us.

"Darling," she whispered without complaint – though God knows I must have been brutally hurting her – "darling, you're upset." Then her lips found mine and my fears at last subsided.

*   *   *

In the morning Anne rose quietly, thinking me asleep and wanting not to wake me. But I was awake. I lay with one eye half open, watching her.

I remembered the whispers, and what they had commanded me to do.

She had planned to drive to Harkness that morning for curtain material and a few other things we needed. I heard her go. Then stealthily I slipped out of bed, peeled off my pyjamas and studied myself, naked, in a mirror.

God help me, I *liked* what I saw.

I dressed and went downstairs. Anne had left breakfast on the table. I ate slowly, filled with thoughts of her, of what was going to happen – *had* to happen – when she returned. Suddenly I heard the front door open and the voice of Susie Callister calling anxiously, "Is anybody home?"

The voice with which I answered her was not *my* voice. Oh, no. *They* told me what to say. They told me to invite the child in and humor her.

I called to her and she came timidly into the kitchen and stood staring at me. "You–you said I could come sometimes," she reminded me. "You said I could talk to pa."

"My dear child – of course!"

"If I go downstairs, you won't tell ma I done it, will you?" Her deep-set eyes were pleading with me. Her lips trembled. "She licked me somethin' awful the last time. She–she says we're gonna move away from here. Tomorrow, maybe. I want to say goodbye to pa."

Smiling, I took her by the arm and led her down the hall to the cellar door and opened it, then stood there at the top of the treacherous cellar stairs watching her while she slowly descended into the darkness. She was young, of course. Her frail little body was not very attractive. Still, her skin was white and clear; she had arms and legs and the beginnings of breasts. She was better than nothing.

I heard the whispers, and they were evil. Never before had they been so loud, so commanding. They told me what to do next.

I closed the door softly and turned the key. Then I went back to the sitting-room and sat to wait.

It came at last, and every expectant nerve in my body thrilled to it, as a lover to a subtle caress. A scream of terror pulsed up from the dark cellar. A sudden rush of footfalls sounded on the stairs. Frantic fists beat against the locked door.

Then the scream soared again, this time a wailing, tenuous cry that fluttered for a moment in space, then died. And I sat there smiling, with my twisted mind and sated senses soaking up every last lingering echo, until the house was again quiet.

There were no whispers when I opened the cellar door. Descending, I looked about me. My little friend had said farewell to more than her dead father. She had vanished.

"There will be another soon," I promised softly. "Just be patient."

The woman came about an hour later. Angrily she strode up the porch steps and banged on the front door, and when I opened the door to her she thrust her contorted face at me and said shrilly, "Susie came here, didn't she? Where is she?"

"My dear Mrs Callister," I murmured. "What on earth makes you think—?"

"Don't lie to me! I know that child like a book!"

"Come in, Mrs Callister," I invited. "Look for yourself."

She stormed into the house, stabbing a quick glance into the sitting-room and dining-room. She strode down the hall to the kitchen. "Susie! Susie! Are you hiding from me, you little she-devil? Susie! Where are you?"

I followed her from room to room, slyly watching her. *She* would please them. She was shapely. Her legs were nicely rounded. Her mature body gleamed white as snow through the gaps in her worn-out black dress.

Upstairs we went, down again, and finally to the cellar door. There she hesitated. For one brief instant the anger on her wretched face was supplanted by fear.

I opened the door.

"I–I ain't goin' down there!" she whispered.

"My dear Mrs Callister, why not?"

"I just ain't!" Her voice rose to a screech. "Susie! Are you down there?"

It seemed strange to me that she could not hear the whispers. I could hear them. In fact, they were more than merely whispers, for mingled with them now was a kind of unearthly howling, as though down there in the gloom of the cellar a pack of wolves had gathered for some sort of feeding frenzy. I could hear them plainly, and knew exactly what was being demanded of me.

Very carefully I stepped back – so carefully that Mrs Callister did not notice. I looked at my hands and raised them, slowly, slowly, until they were poised only a few inches from her shoulders. One savage thrust, and Susie Callister's mother would go screaming down the stairs. Then I would wrench the door shut, turn the key again, and—

But at that moment I heard the front door open, and my wife's voice called, "Peter! Will you help me get the things out of the car, please? There's more than I can manage by myself!"

I closed the cellar door and went along the hall. Mrs Callister followed me. Anne, her arms laden, stopped short.

"This is Mrs Callister, Anne. She – er – she is under the mistaken impression that her daughter is here. I've been having a difficult time trying to convince her otherwise."

Mrs Callister said something under her breath and went past us to the door. Then she stopped. Too late I saw the tiny, frayed handkerchief lying there on the hall table.

She snatched it up and looked at it, her eyes yellow with venom. Fiercely she turned to confront me. "I know!" she whispered. "I know what you've done! You've turned into one of *them*, like Jim did!" Then, with a shriek, she fled.

"The woman is mad," I said to Anne. "This is the damndest village, full of the queerest people. Well, she's gone. That's something to be thankful for."

Anne was silent, but the look she gave me was strange. All morning she kept an eye on me. In the afternoon she said, "Peter, why don't you lie down and rest a bit? I think you've been working too hard."

"I think I will."

"Please. You're not yourself, darling. You – frighten me a little."

I went upstairs and shut the door. To sleep? Ah, no. I lay on the bed, thinking of the promise I had made. When night fell, I would keep it.

But night came so slowly! I lay there counting the minutes. I watched the room grow dark. I thought my wife would never stop puttering around downstairs. Hungrily I listened to every sound she made, to the soft tap-tapping of her heels as she went from room to room, to the murmur of the portable radio on the fireplace mantel. I cursed her for being so stubborn.

When she entered the bedroom at last, I pretended to be asleep. She set a lamp on the chest of drawers and turned the wick low, so not to wake me. Obliquely I watched her undress.

Pretty! Ah, so pretty! Did she know I was watching? Once, just once, she turned abruptly to look at me, and for a moment stood absolutely motionless, as though my furtive gaze had actually caught her attention. Then she put out the lamp and groped toward me in the dark.

And got into bed with me.

By the sound of her breathing I knew that her back was toward me. I became aware of the warmth and subtle fragrance of her body. I waited with devilish patience until I was certain she slept.

Then I seized her.

She screamed only once as my hands closed about her lovely throat. Her eyes flew open and I saw the whites of them staring up at me in the dark. Her lips whispered my name as I tore at her pyjamas.

Dragging her from the bed, I gathered her up in my arms and prowled to the door, leaving the torn remnants of her night-garb in a pitiful heap on the floor. If I kissed her mouth and crushed her against me in a wild, hungry embrace, it was not for love, for by that time I was laughing, and the low, bestial laughter that poured from my throat was not even remotely human.

"*They* want you!" I howled.

Down the dark stairs I carried her to the lower hall, and now the old house was alive with howlings and echoes of howlings, urging me on. Down the hall toward the cellar stairs I went.

All at once I heard voices and heavy footsteps on the porch.

I stopped. A snarl curled my lips. Lowering my limp burden, I prowled stealthily through the sitting-room to a window and crouched there, peering out.

There were many of them and they carried every conceivable kind of weapon. Up from the village they had come, led by the mother of the girl I had locked in the cellar and by Everett Digby, the doctor who knew more about this house than he had admitted.

Even as I watched, Digby hammered the door with his fist and demanded admittance, while the others crowded closer, their faces grim and gaunt in the glare of flashlights and lanterns.

"Open the door or we'll break it down!"

I slunk from the window. For a moment I thought wildly of confronting them, but the beast I had become was afraid. And yet, there might still be time to thwart them. If I could reach the cellar in time …

Trembling and afraid, I crept into the hall. There lay my wife, mercifully unaware of my intentions, her sweet body a white, soft heap on the floor. And the howlings were thunder in my brain, lashing me, driving me on. I stooped to seize Anne's arms, to drag her. But there was not time enough.

The door crashed inward and I wheeled in a crouch, snarling like a predatory beast driven from its prey. For one terrible moment I faced the mob, faced the awful accusation in the eyes of Everett Digby and the burning hatred in the stare of Mrs Callister. Then a rifle cracked and a bullet splintered the ancient timbers of the cellar door behind me. I whirled and ran, leaving my wife there on the floor.

With animal strength and cunning I sped through the kitchen, tore open the rear door and fled into the night. Darkness closed around me. At top speed I fled through the rank grass of the yard to the vast black shelter of the woods, easily escaping the frenzied swing of their searchlights.

There, exhausted, I lay snarling. And watched.

That night will live long in the memory of those people. An ambulance came from the Harkness hospital. Men in white rushed into the house with an empty stretcher and rushed out again with someone – my wife, I desperately hope – lying on it. The ambulance raced away. Lanterns moved in weird procession through the blackness as men from the village hunted me. Flashlights were glittering fireflies swarming in the night. Voices, some angry, some fearful, rode the breeze, and heavy feet tramped through the underbrush, sometimes within yards of the patch of brambles in which I cowered.

I waited. *They will give up soon,* I thought. *Then I can go back.* But in that I was mistaken. For as the first dull gray of dawn appeared, a crimson glow sprang up to rival it. Flames rose to the sky, devouring the ancient timbers of my honeymoon house. Huge clouds of smoke billowed up from the inferno.

I crept as close as I dared, and from the fringe of the woods I cursed the flames and the grim-faced men who stood by, watching the house burn. I cursed the truck that came at daybreak, when the blackened foundations had cooled. I silently reviled the men who sweated there in the dawnlight, mixing concrete with which to fill the cistern in the cellar.

When they departed, I crept into the woods again, bitterly cursing my fate. For this I knew: in the cellar of that house had existed the doorway to another world – one to which I was now irrevocably committed but to which, God help me, I could never return. The taint of that world, its foulness, its corruption, had touched me as it had touched the father of little Susie Callister.

Susie was part of that world now, too – unless they had wanted her for something else. But even if she lived as one of them, I would never see her again. I was doomed to spend the remainder of my existence alone, unable to return to *them* and never to see my beloved Anne again.

With that understanding came another, which must have been lurking just under the surface of my consciousness. How clear it all seemed now! Working there in the cellar, Jim Callister, too, must have fallen prey to the whisperers. They had turned him into the kind of creature I had now become. His wife had seen it happening.

Had he actually died of a heart attack? More likely of poison, as she tried desperately to save his soul and protect herself and the child. Poison, as the undertaker fellow had suspected. And if so, Dr Digby must have helped her, for she was a simple woman who would have had no knowledge of poisons and no access to them.

How I wish my wife had poisoned me!

And so … this letter, this manuscript, this confession or whatever you may choose to call it. I have written it laboriously, using pencil stubs and scraps of paper gathered from trash cans in the village, where I prowl at night in search of food. I will leave it tonight under a stone on the steps of the Harkness church, where someone – perhaps the pastor – will be sure to find it. Then I shall go away.

Where to? God knows. The world of the whisperers is forever closed to me, and in the world of men I have no place. Day by day the lines of my face change, my lips recede over teeth that are slowly becoming fangs, my eyes grow smaller and more luminous, my head shrinks into the bulge of my shoulders. Day by day the cold white skin of my misshapen body becomes more hairy.

Pray for me, please. I did not ask for this to happen.

David Sutton

AND I SHALL GO IN THE DEVIL'S NAME

David Sutton has edited, produced and contributed to a wide range of small press publications over the past forty years, most notably with his own magazine, Shadow, *and through periodicals for The British Fantasy Society.*

A winner of the World Fantasy Award and multiple British Fantasy Awards, he is the editor of the anthologies New Writings in Horror and the Supernatural 1 *and* 2 *and* The Satyr's Head and Other Tales of Terror, *and co-compiler of* The Best Horror from Fantasy Tales, The Anthology of Fantasy & the Supernatural, *and the* Dark Voices *and* Fantasy Tales *series.*

His own short fiction has been published widely in such anthologies and magazines as Best New Horror 2, The Mammoth Book of Zombies, Final Shadows, Cold Fear, Taste of Fear *and* Skeleton Crew, *and his fiction has recently been collected in* Clinically Dead and Other Tales of the Supernatural.

As the author explains: "As with a number of my stories, the present yarn came out of a visit to a weird, inspirational place. Bute is a quiet, picturesque Scottish island dotted with megaliths and ruins. From the hills you can invariably observe the sea, the mainland or other islands, and often all three. Yet you seem to be lost or trapped in another world.

"The Celtic monastery ruins and their location are real, so is some of the witchcraft lore. If this particular anthology wasn't about werewolves I'd probably have written a story about jellyfish – the whole of the island's shoreline was absolutely clotted with their corpses – big ones!"

And I shall go in the Devil's name,
Ay while I come home again.

Isabel Gowdie, Scottish witch, 1662

Samantha stepped through the meadows with long-legged strides, her calf and thigh muscles aching slightly as she negotiated the slopes of Lubas Crag. For a moment, as she glanced down the way she had come, she glimpsed between gently rolling hills the calm blue waters of Dunagoil Bay. The hills of Arran were a faded blue-grey in the distance beyond. Then they vanished behind gorse and grassy hummocks as she climbed higher. The day's heat was hoping to stall her booted step.

But she would not let it.

Beyond a stile, the indeterminate footpath skirted a farmer's field in which sheep had latterly grazed. Their wool lay scattered in little patches, as if someone had grabbed handfuls and thrown them to the wind.

Like remnant smears of melting, grubby snow, she thought.

This was early Summer though, and as if to emphasize the point, a hare darted carelessly across Samantha's path. A friend to witches and supernatural beings, she recalled, as the jack swerved upon seeing her and turned a right angle. He leapt ten feet at one and the same time, landing on higher ground beyond the footpath in the next field.

Leaping without furry feet touching earth in between.

Samantha wished her trek were as easy as the hare's. The animal's feet and the long, muscular hind legs propelled the mammal into the air, its black-tipped ears swept back, streamlined by its speed.

Tortoise-like, she would be the last of the two of them to reach St. Blane's Chapel, higher up, nested in a natural bowl at the summit of the hill. An old site, and similar to the hare's form, hollowed and hidden somewhere in the meadows. Likewise the granite stones of the Celtic ruin: weathered into the grass in a depression a thousand years' ancient.

Samantha sat for a moment on an outcrop of grey rock and examined her hiking books. The wetness of the grass had somehow penetrated beyond the wax she had that morning applied in her hotel room in Port Bannatyne. She almost wished she could take off her boots and proceed barefoot, wanting the caress of rough and uneven turf.

There were things she craved beyond rational thought. Beyond the grime of everyday life. Sitting here in the warm breeze, she now understood that her boyfriend would not have appreciated the inexplicable desires. She was glad he wasn't with her.

Damon had already complained that morning that they were pursuing their walking holiday as if the whole island and its mysteries must be explored in a brief couple of days; when in fact they had two whole weeks. And much more to explore than merely the island of Bute itself, he'd added. With no further comment she'd known he was silently dissociating himself from her interest in the island's history.

"I'm taking the bus to Rhubodach," he'd announced after breakfast, flinging an empty rucksack on the bed, "and taking the quick ferry. Then I might see if I can't get up to loch Fyne. You coming?"

His question was a veiled threat. Don't accompany me, and that's it: some undefined punishment looming as if she were an unruly child. Samantha had wanted to ask if he were prepared to walk to the loch from the mainland, quite a distance; or if he were, as his mood now implied, inclined to public transport.

Instead she said, "I'd rather stay on the island."

"Where will you go?" he asked, now dropping the indignation from his voice, if not the frown from his features. The frown that now reminded her of the hare's face and its bulbous, startled eyes.

Samantha had edged around the side of her bed, a bath towel wrapped modestly across her breasts. Her thighs were squeezed by the narrow space between the bed and the wardrobe. "St Blane's," she'd answered. "As we'd *planned* for today, if you remember." She grabbed a hairbrush off her bedside cabinet and swept it through her short, damp hair, cold droplets of water cascading against her back.

The water made her skin goosebump, although it might have been caused by her contemplation of seeing the mysterious chapel. She wasn't prepared to admit that there was something undefined in her mind that was nonetheless curiously compelling and at the same time distinctly uneasy about wanting to go to the chapel.

As Samantha was finishing her hair, she was about to try to persuade Damon to change his mind and accompany her, but there were his legs to think about. Suddenly, on this holiday, Damon had become lame. His customary stamina and his inexhaustible energy had ebbed away as if he were an animal caught in a gin trap, its wide shark teeth sucking on the blood, cracking the bones, tearing the sinews and exhausting the creature. Draining not only his body's potency but his mind's, too.

He wasn't about to admit it, but age, his diet and drink were immobilizing him, slowly but surely. The result was plain to see on this holiday, in which pub lunches had already been favoured to traipsing heather-purpled hills.

During their days here, Samantha had been the one who set the pace, much to her surprise. At first she thought he was coming down with the flu, but he was angry with her when she had suggested the previous evening that he might be.

An irrational argument had flared between them in the darkness of their cheap hotel room, as if a flame was igniting the space between the beds.

"A good job the owner gave us a twin-bedded room by mistake!" had been Damon's final goodnight communication.

Samantha waited in the darkness. For the three years she had been with Damon, she never had been able to sleep properly in a separate bed. Finally she did sleep, though, but warned herself on the edge of slumber that she was not an arm of Damon's personality; not a withered twin, about to follow the stronger half because if she didn't, she would be lost.

Damon was not the stronger half. They weren't even halves. She was not a fraction, she told herself. She was a whole.

In the morning Damon remained sullen. His dark hair was greasy, but he'd refused to shower when Samantha had shouted from the bathroom that she was finished and he could take his.

Well, he could stay greasy and fat, for all she cared. Podgy was how she now viewed his stocky figure. She was eyes and forehead taller than him, but with his broad shoulders she hadn't cared, up until today. Now, well now there was something pathetic in a taller woman being around such a fat slob of a man …

Samantha's heart was beating fast, driving her lingering irritation with Damon. More brisk walking would settle her down.

Lifting herself from the rock, she pulled up her socks, forgetting how damp her toes were, hefted her rucksack onto one shoulder and set off again. The steep slopes of the hill ducked and dived, but she was unable to use the rusted barbed wire lines and posts of the fence on her left to pull her along: they were too high up, raised along a natural bank dividing the meadow she was in from the one adjacent.

Up above, she thought she could see the jack staring down at her from behind gorse, waiting for her to follow, perhaps? Peeping out as if he were the white rabbit and she Lewis Carroll's Alice, being invited to visit curious and bizarre places.

She even felt a little odd. As if the sands of Strathavan in the west and Kilchattan bay in the east were squeezing the peninsular of Garroch Head, cutting it off from the main part of the island to the north. Cutting, squeezing, isolating her on a new island in a strange new time. She wondered if she wasn't overdoing the hike. Walking too briskly might be making her light-headed. Yet the peculiar tenor of her thoughts was striving to make her apprehensive. Of what, she was at a loss to understand.

The hare, though, turned out to be a small stone simulacrum, its contours defined and shaped by lichen.

A kissing gate grabbed at her rucksack as she manoeuvred through it, and she heaved herself up the final steep part of the hill. In front of her, Samantha could now see the grey, dry stone of St. Blane's perimeter wall. The ramparts were built on a high dyke, making it both impossible to see the ruins of the chapel itself, and difficult to climb over. She crossed through a stand of trees and began to follow the line of the wall until she came to a wrought iron gate blanketed by heavy shade. Nearby was a National Trust for Scotland's information notice, where she learned that marauding Norsemen had burned the chapel in 790 when they swept across the country.

Yet the place exuded an atmosphere that reeked of a time more ancient, beyond the time of the Celtic monks and rape and pillage. Though contemplation of that bloody event alone, never mind the general and unwelcome sense of disquiet she was suffering, gave Samantha a shiver.

Inside the wall, she was impressed by the huge elm and ash trees which crowded the pathetic ruins of the chapel itself. Grey walls stood in half or full measure, a single remaining Norman arch announcing the building's one-time restoration. Completely exposed to the elements, the blocks of the floor were worn into dips by the tread of many feet, hers soon to be part of that nameless company of lost souls.

Sitting on a block which was once part of a wall, Samantha began to think that the strenuous walk here might not, after all, have been worth it. The chapel ruins lacked interest, she decided. No doubt Damon would have been furious at the wasted effort if he had come. However, she was here now and decided to examine all the archeological features.

Crossing to the north, down the slope and back through the entrance, she came to the so-called Devil's Cauldron. A ruin whose few remaining stones suggested a circular structure. Samantha saw that they were megalithic. Although, she recalled from the information notice, no one knew what the structure was for, it suggested that the building might have been a tower, similar to the Irish and Scottish round towers or brochs. Inside its truncated walls, shade and dampness allowed lichen to flourish.

On the floor, emerging from an undergrowth of ferns, several large mushrooms bloomed, apparently out of their normal season. They stood out against the uniformity of grey stone and dark green-grey leaves as if tempting her with their flesh. The caps were a brilliant blood-red, mottled with white flecks. Instantly she was reminded of fairy stories, for weren't these traditionally the toadstools upon which the fairy-folk invariably sat in innumerable illustrated children's books?

The mushrooms were unusually attractive and at the same time distinctly creepy. Samantha's suspect and unwilling memories were attempting, unsuccessfully for the moment, to clamber forth, with all kinds of mythological half-truths to tell.

Don't touch them. That was what common sense told her. Old Wives' Tales or no, these toadstools looked uncommon enough to be dangerous.

A few minutes later Samantha had retraced her steps and was within the confining wall again, examining the foundations of what was thought to be the original chapel. These consisted of several large slabs almost buried and overgrown by grasses.

She sat nearby and took off her rucksack, intending to have lunch, using one of the slabs as her table. It was ideal. Looking up, the view over and beyond the wall from this vantage point allowed her to see the hills of the mainland streaked with low cloud like smoke, whilst she and her surroundings were bathed in clear sunlight.

As she unpacked her lunch and a bottle of cola, Samantha noticed something on one of the rocks nearby. Something left there, apparently, as if it were an offering placed on a recumbent altar stone. Scrambling across, she examined what were the brownish, desiccated remains of several of the mushrooms she'd seen in the ruined tower.

Someone must have been here recently, picked some from the broch, and left them to dry out, as if the next visitor would find them useful. Samantha searched her memories, knowing her unconscious mind could share with her some knowledge she'd forgotten. Wasn't it that if eaten, these fairy mushrooms were supposed to cause hallucinations? She wondered if some New Age folk might have been here recently, sampling nature's pharmacy, trying to convene with something higher. With the shamanists, perhaps, who used the Soma in ancient times and, according to legend, metamorphosed into bird and beast.

Samantha's earlier sense of displacement returned, as if the ancient world was slipping into the present and her mind and body could perceive the transition somehow. The hare might almost have been the catalyst. A symbol of the moon, of fecundity and resurrection.

And madness.

She shivered in spite of the naked sun.

Then she remembered that she was no longer held back by Damon's selfishness, nor his down to earth boorishness. The rustic coarseness she had once found so attractive. She was free with the wild breeze and the sun. As free *as* them. Her thoughts turned into a thousand feelers, resembling the crowded, entangled mass of twigs, sticking out of a nearby birch.

A witch's broom.

A *witch* ...

The mass of her thoughts uncurled as a tangle of serpents loosened from their basket, and she began to recall the importance of being here. It was one of the reasons why she wanted to visit the chapel. St. Blane's had once been the site of a local coven. In Bute's museum, she remembered the displays lucidly presenting the island's history.

Old English lettering described, with woodcut type illustrations on wall-mounted boards, the seventeenth century. The baptism of a local witch. Her coven dancing in a ring around the broch. Hysteria and convulsions. The writhing and swelling of the witch's body and changes in its height and weight.

And then there were the trials and tortures. Here on the island were preserved samples of the instruments used by the witch-finders: the witch-bridle, the capsie-claws, the thumbscrews ...

Seeing again the rusty tools from the museum in her mind's eye, Samantha shuddered.

Yet there was more her recessed memories had to reveal. The ointments, the substances that induced in the witch the hallucinatory experience of flying, or of changing shape.

The witch-hunters, on the other hand, were simply sadists and murderers, wallowing in their mundane depravity. But their victims? Merely unfortunate, innocent women? All of them?

Or gifted individuals?

Samantha placed her sandwich back in its wrapper uneaten. Her hands shook nervously, but there was a craving inside her, navigating her with a persistence greater than her fear of the unknown.

Quickly, she picked up a shrivelled mushroom, broke off a large piece, and placed it between her lips. The tip of her tongue picked up the flavour, touching the fungus much as she would touch Damon's tongue, before making love. Her lips closed. She ate it, washing it down with cola to mask the bitter taste.

"And how was *your* day?" Damon asked, still nursing his resentment at Samantha's independence. He was lying on his bed as if he had been there all day, hiding like a slug from the drying heat of the sun.

She had hardly dropped the rucksack from her shoulders before he'd pounced with his sarcastic question and immediately her hackles rose at his stupidity. The next second she allowed the vitriol she was about to unleash to dissipate. She was wide awake, healthy. The day's walk had not tired her at all; there was no need to allow anger to spoil her euphoria.

"Fine," she stated, her voice measured, affable. "And yours? Did you make it to Loch Fyne?" The real curiosity she displayed would sedate Damon's skewed attitude.

"I decided not to go after all," he stated, only mildly embarrassed by the admission.

"You mean, you've stayed in the hotel *all* day?" Her nearly shouted response made Damon flinch. Looking around the room, she saw a paperback carelessly tossed at the bottom of his bed, a half-open newspaper lying on the floor near the bedside table. On the window ledge a polystyrene container with the remains of a fish and chip meal stuck to it made the room smell of vinegar.

Well, he had been out, she sneered internally. For a distance of maybe a couple of hundred yards to the newsagent's and the chippy! But that hardly counted.

"What a waste of a day."

A thin smile appeared on his face and disappeared as quickly as it had come.

Damon appeared to be trapped, held here by more than his lethargy. Had he done this to spite her, Samantha wondered?

"Don't concern yourself." He shifted sluggishly on the bed, its springs quietly squeaking as though miserable with age and rust. "It was *my* fucking day, not yours." Damon smiled again, apologetically this time. "Look, how about we go down to Rothesay for dinner at the Black Bull? You liked it there before."

She *was* hungry. And maybe he was trying to heal the growing rift between them before it became a canyon. Or was he merely thinking about filling his fat stomach? Samantha was only half convinced.

"And," Damon continued, "you can tell me all about Blane's Chapel over dinner." Conciliation softened his voice.

Rothesay was a mile's walk from their hotel and as soon as they started out, Damon began trailing behind.

"What's the matter?" Samantha asked, before she noticed he was limping slightly.

"Sprained my ankle, I think."

"What? On your hike to the chip shop!" she laughed at her wisecrack. She was fresh, alert even after a full day of strenuous walking, and now the idea of Damon as an infirm old man made her giggle.

"Thanks for the sympathy!" Then, "Just walk a bit slower. I'm sure it'll be all right in a bit."

But she did not *want* to walk more slowly. Her body longed for the adrenalin rush, the blood pumping to serve eager muscles. So she had to demand that her legs take shorter steps. She imagined herself as the hare, bounding away into the fields, turning on a sixpence, ears swept back, hind legs long and lithe, thrusting backwards, leaping, leaping, the wind blowing freely across her fine silky hair …

In the Black Bull, Damon consumed haggis, mashed potatoes and turnips and washed it down with four pints of beer. In a short space of time he was smiling, merry from intoxication.

Samantha looked at him over her unfinished plaice and fries and wondered if she should tell him she'd eaten the mushroom and had discovered she wasn't really hungry after all. He'd think her completely mad and lucky not to have been poisoned. Even though he poisoned himself repeatedly with alcohol. He might also become argumentative again. She could do without that two nights' running.

Darkness had fallen by the time Damon had decided he'd drunk enough and wanted to go to bed. She resigned herself to another sexless night.

"Shall I call a taxi?" Samantha asked, assuming the short walk back to the hotel would be far too much for him, what with his ankle and the beer sloshing around in his system.

He dismissed the very idea, the drink supplying him with bravado. They headed along the path by the foreshore, the black waters to their right and below them lapping at the shingle as they walked. Just the two of them, alone under the stars.

It could have been romantic.

But it wasn't long before Damon needed a rest. Samantha could see it coming. He was staggering from his sprain and the beer. It was unbelievable that a few days earlier he had been a fit hill-walker.

Now he behaved like an arthritic pensioner.

She wanted to leave him sitting on the sea wall, where he'd decided to rest, and dash off, use up some of the energy bursting through her. She wanted to say: "last one to the hotel's a slug", and race off, knowing in her heart that she was swift and tireless and unbeatable.

"Just a couple of minutes," Damon suggested, dampening, momentarily, her wayward thoughts.

Impatiently, Samantha stamped through a gap in the wall and down concrete steps onto the beach. Underfoot, pebbles squeaked against one another and the dark water close by reflected the distant lights of the town around the bay.

A full moon bobbed out to sea, shimmering. Above, in the sky overhead, its real self gleamed as brightly as a freshly minted bronze coin.

She turned to face her partner. "If we use the beach it'll be quicker." Pointing to the diverging of the road ahead, which would take them out of their way, she displayed with her other arm the sharper curve of the beach, leading to Port Bannatyne and the hotel on the front. "It's more direct."

"And we'll probably get our feet soaking wet into the bargain," Damon replied morosely. "Besides, do you really think walking on a pebble beach is going to be any good for my ankle?"

He never used to be like that!

"My god, Damon, that's the first time I've ever heard you complain about wet feet. And that coming from Mr Mountainer himself!" Samantha's words were freeing themselves, criticism a sharp instrument, inflicting the necessary irony.

Deciding not to allow him to challenge her decision, Samantha began to walk along the shingle without a backward glance.

The moon bathed her, baptizing her with cool radiance, its borrowed light penetrating her soul. So good, she felt *so* good.

Damon stood up and began to follow her. She sighed with a sense of satisfaction as she heard him clambering down the steps, and she stomped ahead. After several minutes walking, enjoying the pressure of pebbles under her feet and the interactive play of muscles in her legs, Samantha turned to see how far behind Damon had lagged.

He was way back, stumbling along. He appeared to be a black blob. A hunched, fat shape staggering under the weight of booze.

He really looked as if he'd put on weight. Perhaps he had, Samantha thought, and she'd failed to notice.

"Come on!" she shouted, amused, yet puzzled at his gait, which was more awkward and lopsided than a sprained ankle might suggest. She was willing to wait exactly thirty seconds for him to catch her up and then she would be gone, swiftly to the hotel.

Laughing. She would laugh all the way …

Instead of speeding up, however, Damon slowed even more, as if the surface of the beach was adhering to the soles of his boots with each step he took.

An expletive was on her lips, ready to explode, when Damon stopped moving completely. Another damn rest, she mouthed silently.

He sat heavily on a rock.

There was nothing for it, she had two options. To let him stay there until the tide came in and forced him to sink or swim, while she carried on. Or go back and help the invalid.

Just like dealing with a naughty child, Samantha decided. There was little sympathy in her heart as she began to trot resignedly along the strand towards the crumpled figure.

He appeared to be mumbling something as she approached and it sounded as if he were rubbing two pebbles together in the palm of his hand. A cloud drifted clear of the moon's bright face as she neared him and the dark hump took form.

Yes …

No, he was formless …

Damon had become so listless that he appeared to have transformed into a rock, a rounded, sea-washed piece of basalt that the gulls would use as a perch and shit on for a thousand generations.

Moonlight gilded the beach with wheat-coloured light. Even with the illumination, Samantha could not distinguish between Damon and the rock on which he was sitting, as if her eyes were no longer focusing the way they should.

When the scraping pebble noise came again, she realized, with exasperation, that he had fallen asleep.

In her heart Samantha knew that Damon no longer wanted to move, asleep or not. He was contented with his new lifestyle. And if that was what he wanted, so be it. His decision freed her completely. She could allow the lurking chemical in her brain its liberty at last.

She turned her eyes up to face the sky and as her head swept back, arching her neck, bangs of long hair she didn't have, like silky ears, fell about her shoulder blades. They were kissed by the soft current of air off the sea. She crouched low and twitched her upper lip, sniffing. The breeze was heavy with the smell of salt and seaweed.

Should she be here? But where if not here?

Abruptly, fear skewered her heart. Terror began to swell inside her head, squeezing her eyes until her vision became blurred. As if … As if her face was changing shape, forcing her eyes to bulge. Her hands and feet twitched with increasing panic and something else was happening to them, but the lustre of the moon was now veiled by cloud and she was unable to make out anything.

Damon was immobilized nearby and might drown if he didn't wake up. Samantha reached out towards the black shape with the pebbly voice of its snores, thinking that if she could only touch him, wake him, everything would be all right. The glamour that terrorized her would fade away and normality would return and she would cuss him good-naturedly about his injury. And bathe his foot and bandage it when they reached their hotel …

Then the other life beckoned more strongly, overwhelming her. Damon was all but forgotten.

Samantha's anxiety intensified even as she realized that he no longer mattered.

Her skin was becoming prickly all over, and she rubbed herself, thinking it might be merely goose pimples. The curious touch of her hands against her sweater. Wool on wool? She felt the urge to throw off her clothes, but before she could do so her skin began to lift, pulling itself against tenacious inner nerve endings, hair follicles and blood vessels.

Suddenly, shockingly, a cry rang against the beach and dispersed quickly into the night. Damon was heaving himself out of his complacency, but only in order to flee from what he was witnessing. He cried out again, a mixture between a scream and a raucous yell. Then he was hobbling as fast as he could back towards the distant town.

Samantha watched him, a shadow-shape lurching away, becoming smaller as each second passed, and it helped take her mind off what he had seen was happening to her. Then came an agonizing pain that flowed from her head, down her neck, arms, body and legs. As sharp as several scalpels cutting simultaneously and deeply beyond the subcutaneous tissue into the soft, unwilling, fatty red flesh that lay beneath her surface. A hollow tearing sound assaulted her ears, resembling the paring of a strip of thick, stubborn wallpaper from plaster in an empty room. Samantha bit her lower lip, fighting waves of hurt, and she sensed long incisors growing, clogging her too-small mouth. Finally, with one prolonged and graceful movement, as a stripper swirling off her last veil, or a shaman his earthly raiment, Samantha's old flesh corkscrewed onto the beach along with her torn, ruined clothes.

She took a tentative step backwards. Gazing down, she watched as flaps and folds of skin collapsed within her outer garments. A thick film of blood dribbled from the livid white interior of the exposed shapeless mass. It was as if some recently eviscerated, decomposing cetacean had been washed ashore.

But the shed flesh was hers. Lying there, heat steaming off its exposed blood.

With a tremor and a fresh prickling of her new, drying skin, Samantha's torment ceased as abruptly as it had begun.

Sitting up on hind legs, she preened her blood clotted whiskers and nose with the soft, tongue-wetted fur of her hands.

Her *paws*.

Samantha discerned that there was no longer any need to be frightened. She had taken the first step, a large one. Had she the time to contemplate, she might wonder whether there was any going back. She didn't, because her thoughts were full of new possibilities. There was Damon and eternal boredom. Life weighted down and as grey as the leaden sky of winter. Samantha didn't want that. She hadn't wanted any of Damon's tedium since coming here. Not his monotonous life which she had felt obliged to put up with. To which she had been bound.

Preferable, far more was what beckoned. She could transform herself now, one shape to another at will and with only transient pain. It was worth a little of that. To greet each new day with a deeper understanding of the enigmatic world of nature, and be able to mould herself to it in a thousand new ways.

It was freedom. Real emancipation at last. Nothing, but simply nothing and no one might lure her back from this most beguiling, glorious certainty. Least of all Damon.

And with the surging of her new heart, she once more listened to the voice in her soul. The voice began to recite in the ancient Scottish vernacular, only half understood, that witch's spell she'd read in the museum:

"I shall go intill a hare, With sorrow and sych and meikle care; And I shall go in the Devil's name, Ay while I come home again. Hare, Hare, God send thee care. I am in a hare's likeness now, But I shall be in a woman's likeness even now".

With a mighty leap that earlier would have been beyond her wildest imagining, Samantha bounded off the beach and away from its stench. Across the road she skittered, racing south through heavily wooded valleys, scented with the heady musk of its inhabitants, as she headed for the hills and the new dawn rising over the primeval ruins on Lubas Crag.

Peter Tremayne

THE FOXES OF FASCOUM

Peter Tremayne is one of the pseudonyms of historian and bestselling Celtic scholar Peter Berresford Ellis. In the horror and fantasy genres he has published more than twenty-five books under the Tremayne alias, beginning with Hound of Frankenstein *(1977) and including* The Curse of Loch Ness, Zombie!, The Morgow Rises, Swamp!, Nicor, Angelus!, Ravenmoon, Snowbeast *and the recent omnibus* Dracula Lives! *His short stories have been collected in* My Lady of Hy-Brasil *and* Aisling and Other Tales of Terror.

More recently he has written a number of short stories and novels detailing the investigative exploits of Sister Fidelma which, like the tale that follows, are firmly rooted in Irish history and mythology, as the author explains: "In this story, based on folktales heard in the lonely Comeragh Mountains (pronounced 'Cu'mra') of Co. Waterford, Ireland, it is were-foxes that concern us. The 'vengeance tale' is one often found in Irish folklore. Such motifs occur frequently in countries that suffered conquest and colonization and nowhere more so than Ireland.

"The serf-like conditions of the Irish peasantry were not alleviated until the Irish Land War of the 1880s when, finally, the feudalism of English landowners in Ireland was broken. It is hard to believe the absolute power these landowners had – a power equal to the aristos of France before the French Revolution.

"Small wonder, under such conditions, that revenge stories became a sub-genre of the folktales told around Irish hearths at night while

*others plotted and planned for the day when they could rise up and
throw out the invader."*

The guide book had told me that the Comeragh Mountains in
Ireland were one of the last unspoiled wildernesses in Western
Europe. The guide book was right.

How did I come to be camping in those mountains in early
September?

Well, I am secretary of our local rock-climbing and walking
club back in Sheffield and our members were eager to widen
their forays in search of good walking and climbing country.
That was why I came to be in the south of Ireland. I had been
delegated to check out the area for the club and, should it
prove suitable, make arrangements for the club's annual outing
there during the following spring. I was going to go with our
president, Tom Higgins, but, at the last minute, Tom went down
with flu and I wound up going to Ireland alone. Not that I really
minded. Matter of fact, I preferred it that way. I enjoy walking
and climbing alone. Maybe it stems from a solitary childhood.

Anyway, the point I am making is that as soon as I arrived in
the area I knew that it would be ideal territory for our club. Not
only did it offer good trekking country but provided marvellous
rock faces for climbing. The Comeragh Mountains constitute
over two hundred square miles of mountainous wilderness.
When I started into the area, south from Clonmel, I realized
that the recommendation to our club had been correct. The
mountains offered splendid walking country but were trackless
and needed care and preferably previous mountain experience.
The mountains here averaged about two-and-a-half thousand
feet in height, the highest being a mound of a summit called
Fascoum at 2,597 feet.

I was in the area a few days before I came to Fascoum. I
carried with me a lightweight tent and sleeping bag and so could
wander as I chose. There were plenty of fresh mountain streams
and springs, even sedate rivers and lakes. No one would ever
starve here for there was wild life in plenty and in several places
I could see brown trout near the surface of the waters, basking

as if begging to be taken. However, I was well prepared with my own provisions without recourse to hunting the wild life. If I miscalculated, there were always one or two farms or cottages in the area, though not very many, where I could buy supplies.

Just beyond the broad sunlight-dappled slopes of Fascoum, with its jutting grey granite rocks ripping through the green carpet of grass and moss, I came across an overgrown path which meandered through stretches of brilliant gorse and fuchsia. The wild life seemed abundant and unthreatened by the presence of man the great predator. While the occasional deer, red squirrel, and grey mountain hare, raised their heads warily at my passing, they did not flee from my presence. At one point I was surprised to pass near a rock a little way above me on the mountain side on which sat a dog. It was only when I gave it a second glance that I realized it was a wild fox, a large vixen staring down at me with pointed features and brightly reflecting grey-green eyes, the head surmounted by silver greying fur until it blended into the rusty red of its hide. I halted, delighting in the scene, staring back at the animal. It held its ground for a long while before throwing back its head, giving a sharp bark of disgust at being disturbed and then abruptly disappearing.

I continued on down the mountain path accompanied by the music of September bird calls which would now and then fall silent as I saw the black and white form of a darting hooded crow scavenging for food.

It was a beautiful, peaceful landscape.

It was nearing lunchtime and I had passed the skirts of Fascoum and traversed the valley towards the neighbouring height of Coumshingaun when I saw a small whitewashed cottage, with heavy weather-grey thatch. To my unexpected joy I saw it bore a brightly painted sign with the word's "Dan's Bar" on it and I immediately decided to stop for lunch.

There were only two men in the bar as I entered. The barman, who turned out to be none other than Dan the owner himself, and a man clad in workman's clothes. Ireland is a friendly place to the visitor and they greeted me in amiable fashion. We immediately fell to talking about the countryside, its merits for walkers and climbers, and they recommended me to some out of the way spots which they thought I might gain profit by visiting.

Dan was a tall, lean, hooked-nosed sort of man. The type you would expect to see wearing an eye-patch and a pirate costume. The other, he introduced himself as Shawn Duff, was diminutive and whimsical, a man who looked so familiar that I had to think where I could have seen him before. It was only after some moments of concentrated thought that I finally realized that he was the image of the late Barry Fitzgerald, the movie star.

The conversation progressed, as passing conversations in pubs do, and Dan, hearing that I was surveying the countryside for our walking and climbing club, mentioned that he owned some property nearby which could be rented as a base for our prospective tour of the area. We discussed the matter and Dan was more willing to add to his income in this manner. We conferred on prices and then decided to exchange names and addresses for the official correspondence.

It was when I wrote down my name and address and handed it across the bar to him that a strange thing happened.

He took it, glanced at it and his whole face changed. His good-natured smile vanished, his mouth went slack and his eyes widened. Then he stared at me searchingly. Finally, without speaking, he pushed the paper across to Shawn Duff. The little man nearly fell from his precarious perch on the bar stool. His face wore a look of utter astonishment.

"It's surely joking you are, mister?" he said softly.

I frowned, having no understanding of what was wrong.

"About what?" I asked bemused.

"What is your name?" demanded Dan. His voice was slow as if he were framing his words carefully.

"It's there on the paper. My name is Trezela."

I thought that I began to see why they might be surprised. I am used to astonishment or some slighting comment when I tell people my name. I gave a deep sigh.

"My name is Harlyn Trezela. It's an old Cornish name."

But their expressions carried more than simply a questioning of my odd sounding name. There was awe on their faces and something else … something I couldn't quite fathom nor understand.

I gestured in irritation.

"I'm not Cornish," I went on, endeavouring to explain. "But my grandfather was. He settled in Sheffield at the turn of the century. That's where I come from."

Dan seemed to recover himself first and gazed intently on the piece of grubby envelope on which I had jotted down my name and address.

"Tell me, sir," he said softly, "how long ago was it that your family connected was with this place?"

I asked him what he meant by the question and when he repeated it I replied that my family had no connection with Ireland. In truth, I began to think he was rather weird and decided that I should drink up and be on my way. But he was staring at me in that curiously awed way. The little man, Shawn Duff was silent. It was then that I identified the look in his eyes. It was almost a look of animosity; a look of angry hate.

"No connection? Are you sure? No connection at all?"

"None at all," I said slowly, as if I were dealing with someone hard of comprehension. "The name's Cornish, not Irish. Why should there be a connection?"

The bar owner shook his head slowly.

"Mister, are you saying that you have never heard of the old Mountmayne house down the road here?"

"Never," I affirmed. "Now what is all this about? Is it some kind of joke?"

Both men exchanged a long glance.

" 'Tis no joke, mister." It was Shawn who spoke now. "Castle Mountmayne is one of those old Anglo-Irish houses built in the eighteenth century. The earls of Mountmayne lived there until the days of the Land War. That was in the late nineteenth century when the old feudal landlord system was overturned in Ireland. You must remember … the times of the terrible evictions, the Land League, Captain Boycott, whose name has become part of the English language, and the dreadful happenings at Lough Mask?"

I sighed impatiently.

"I am not well up in history. To be honest, I fail to see what Castle … whatsitsname? … has to do with me."

"Aren't I telling you? Castle Mountmayne has been empty now these last hundred years. It is being demolished now and aren't I working on that demolition?"

Dan nodded agreement at the little man's annoyance, still staring at me strangely.

"Shawn has been working up at the old place these last few weeks," he said, as if explaining everything.

"Only this morning," interposed Shawn Duff, "I was pulling down some cupboards in the old house when I found a tin box."

He paused and licked his lips. They seem to have suddenly gone cracked and dried. He took a swallow of his drink and wiped his mouth with the back of his hand.

"It was an old box, tucked away at the back of a wooden cupboard. The tin box had the name Trezela on it. Harlyn Trezela."

I started chuckling.

Now I knew that it was a joke. A tin box with my name in a house in Ireland, where none of my family had ever been before, and which just happened to have been found when I was walking through one of the most desolate spots on my very first visit to the country. Who were they kidding?

"Come on, then," I smiled. "What's the punch line?"

" 'Tis true, I swear it," replied Shawn Duff.

"What's the catch?" I insisted.

Shawn half rose in temper but Dan motioned him to stay where he was.

Dan glanced at me and shook his head seriously.

"What Shawn says is true. In fact, he brought the tin box here not an hour since, wondering what to do with it."

I had a superior smile on my face now.

"In that case, perhaps you'll show it to me."

That would put paid to this nonsense, I thought in satisfaction. We would come to the meaning of their silly joking now.

Without a word, the bar owner reached under his bar and placed an object on the top of the counter before me.

It was a small metal box, some nine inches by six inches by three inches deep. It was rusty and dirt covered and had obviously lain discarded for many years.

My eyes went to the still legible calligraphy on top of the box. They grew wide and my mind began to race.

There was no doubting the truth of the men's statement.

There was emblazoned the name: "Harlyn Trezela, 1880."

I shook my head with disbelief.

"It's not possible."

Shawn Duff was still annoyed.

"You might be right, mister. We find a box a century old and the very morning we find it, along you come, claiming the same name and yet saying that you are a stranger to the country. Just who are you, mister?"

"I am who I say I am," I said, almost whispering, trying to understand the bizarre coincidence.

Dan smiled ruefully, scratching the tip of his nose.

"Perhaps now, mister, we should ask you to prove that you are who you say you are?"

In a stupor I reached into my pocket and handed across my driving licence. Both men bent to examined it. Shawn Duff let out a long, low whistle. Indeed, I saw his hand go up as if he were going to perform a genuflection. Then he let it fall.

" 'Tis true, then. True, right enough. But what can it mean?"

I was staring at the box a long time.

Eventually, Dan continued: "It bears your name. Perhaps you should open it. We have already done so. It contains a letter. I was only saying to Shawn before you came in that he should take it down to the Guards at Lenybrien."

"The Guards?" I tried to draw my mind away from the hypnotic attraction of the box.

"The Garda Siochana, the po'lis," explained Shawn Duff in irritation.

"Is there anything inside besides the letter?" I asked.

"Only the letter in a packet. A packet in oilskins. We replaced it after we read it," Dan said.

I leant forward, rather in a dream, and eased open the rusty hinges. It was obvious that it had recently been inspected for the lid opened easily enough. And it was true what they had told me. Inside lay an oblong packet of oilskin. I carefully unfolded it onto the bar and out fell a yellowing envelope.

It was addressed to Peggy Trezela. The name meant nothing to me. I knew of no one in my family of that name.

Carefully, I drew out the folded sheets of paper which were inside the envelope and opened them. They, too, were yellowing and faded, and covered in brown spidery calligraphy. It was easy to read and I read, fascinated and oblivious to the impatient sounds from my two curious companions.

Castle Mountmayne,
Co. Waterford.
September 11, 1881

Dearest Peggy,

I am afraid that this will be the last letter that you will receive from me. I fear that my remaining days on this earth are not long. Forgive me, darling, therefore, if I write with brevity of my affection for you. Know, too, that my thoughts are ever with you. God keep you.

Darling, you know the circumstances of my coming to this place. However, I must needs repeat the occasion of my arrival here, in order, perhaps, to clarify matters in my own troubled mind.

I was invalided out of my regiment in November, 1880, having been wounded in the disaster which overtook our British garrison at Maiwand, in that accursed country of Afghanistan. In July, the rebel, Ayub Khan, had stormed Maiwand, just west of Kandahar, and killed nearly a thousand of our men. I was one of a mere 160 left wounded who managed to escape to the besieged town of Kandahar. Kandahar was relieved by General Roberts some time later and I was transported to India and back home. But such was my wound, I was no longer deemed capable of service in Her Majesty's army.

What was I, an ex-infantry captain with a permanent limp, to do in life? What could I offer you, whom I had promised to marry and support on my return as a victorious hero from the Afghan war? Indeed, what could I offer now that I had returned merely a crippled man with no private income to sustain me?

That was when I renewed the acquaintanceship of Justin Mountmayne, who had been the colonel of my regiment. He was a good sort. A man of sensitive humour and joviality who, assessing correctly my predicament, immediately offered me a job on his Irish estates as his agent. He owned three thousand acres in Co. Waterford which produced an income of nearly nine hundred pounds a year. Apparently, Mountmayne had an intense dislike of Ireland and never went there, not even to visit his estates. Therefore, my task and duty was to ensure the estates were kept in order, live in the Mountmayne mansion, a strange, brooding pile called Castle Mountmayne, though anything less like a castle you cannot imagine. It is simple a grandiose 18th Century manor. In addition to this it was also my task to collect the rents from the tenant farmers.

How I jumped at the chance for it not only offered me a rent free mansion but also an income of one hundred pounds a year.

You'll recall, my dear Peggy, how we decided that we should marry immediately and then I should set out for Mountmayne alone to prepare the way before you followed to our new home.

I was glad that I had gone on alone, as matters turned out.

Castle Mountmayne was a grim, dour and deserted place. The peasantry were suspicious and sullen. There were rumours of the illegal Land Leaguers active in the area but generally there was no trouble. No evictions. The rents were fair and Mountmayne gave as much security of tenure as could be expected of him to the poor tenant farmers. Yet there was a feeling of gloom and foreboding about the estate. The very name of Mountmayne seemed to inspire sullen hatred among the local people. I was appalled for there was never a more worthy man than Colonel Justin Mountmayne.

To give you an example of the depth of feeling, when my carriage passed through the gates of the estate, there was a bunch of sullen peasants lined up to watch its conveyance to the house. I saw several fists shaken and one old woman leapt forward almost into the path of the horse and spat, crying: "Remember Black John's curse, Mountmayne."

It was then I discovered that the people had mistakenly thought I was the new heir to Mountmayne and when my true identity became known, the people became less hostile but still retaining a great deal of reserve.

It was only after I had been here several weeks that I uncovered the dark secret of Mountmayne's family and the reason why Justin Mountmayne had never come to claim his inheritance in person. Three generations of his family had met violent deaths here. Jasper Mountmayne had been killed in a hunting accident in 1846; Jervis Mountmayne had drowned in a nearby lake in 1857 and Justin's elder brother, Jodocus, had died of a heart attack on Fascoum mountain in 1879.

The local peasants firmly believed there to be a curse on the Mountmayne family.

Well, as I say, things began to improve a little when I made clear that I was in no way related to Justin Mountmayne and that I was merely employed as his agent. Eventually, the overseer, a dour man called Roe, began to speak with me more freely and it was from him that I eventually learnt of the local belief concerning the Mountmayne curse.

It seems that during the years the locals refer to as "An Gorta Mór" or "The Great Starvation", a period in the mid 1840s, when a terrible famine gripped Ireland and destroyed two-and-a-half million of its population, Jasper Mountmayne lived on his estate. He was the 9th earl of Mountmayne, a family who had won their title and lands at the battle of the Boyne while fighting for William of Orange. By all accounts, Jasper was given to an evil temper, was a wild, profane man who delighted in his feudal grip over the surrounding countryside. He was absolute lord of life and death on his estate.

The story went that one day, while out riding to hounds, which was a favourite occupation, his pack picked up the spoor of a fox and followed it across the mountain of Fascoum, which overshadows the estate. The chase was tough but the fox was a young vixen and she was pregnant. The beast eventually went to earth, exhausted, and was soon surrounded.

Mountmayne and his hunting cronies gathered in for the kill.

It was then that a young peasant girl, Síle, appeared. She was pregnant herself, the wife of one of the tenant farmers named Seán Dubh, the name means Black John, Sheehan. She cried out, rebuking the huntsmen for chasing a pregnant beast and she placed herself before the pack of hounds, shielding the fox for a while and so managed to divert their attention that the vixen succeeded in slipping away to freedom.

The anger in Mountmayne, deprived of his sport, was so great that he slashed out in uncontrolled rage at the young woman with his whip, cutting open her face. The blood began to run. This terrible deed excited the hounds and they, thinking the poor woman to be a kill, leapt upon the unfortunate in attack. By the time Mountmayne's horrified companions managed to drag the hounds away, she was in a bad condition. One of Mountmayne's hunting colleagues took her in his own carriage to Waterford where she died within a few days not only from her terrible injuries but raving and insane from the experience.

Now a strange thing happened. Mountmayne had always seen human life on his estate as cheap, as, indeed, had his forebears before him, for they say that there had been no less than two hundred executions on his estate in the wake of the uprising in 'Ninety-Eight with the captured rebellious peasants being killed by boiling pitch being poured on their heads. Locally, this was called, in the Gaelic, a *cáip báis*, or death cap. The words have since entered English currency as putting the "kibosh" on something. Meaning to "end it". Therefore, Jasper Mountmayne did not see the death of Black John's wife as anything to fret over, nor the death of her unborn child as a matter of concern. Had they not ruined a good day's sport?

One evening, however, Black John stood before the house and called out Mountmayne. The man was hysterical from his grief. He cursed Mountmayne to the seventh generation. Fear and death would haunt the generations from Jasper through all his offspring. Jasper, laughingly, called for his overseer, had Black John whipped and thrown off his estate.

The next day Jasper went riding by himself across the mountain of Fascoum, a place where he usually rode. The estate workers swore that day they heard the curious yelping cry of foxes on the mountain. That was unusual as foxes are a quiet, almost silent species which have come to fear man who hunts and destroys them. They are quick to avoid announcing their presences. Yet people swear they heard the wailing bark echoing a long, long time across through the mountain stillness.

When Jasper Mountmayne failed to return by evening, his overseer and some estate workers conducted a search for him. They found him in a hollow below the mountain, his horse standing nervously by. He had been ripped to pieces as if by savage animals. One worker swore that only a pack of wild wolves could inflict such damage. But the wolf packs had been depleted in Ireland. In the 17th Century the English authorities had offered rewards: an English soldier could claim £5 for the head of a wolf or, incidentally, for the head of an Irish rebel. By the 19th Century wolves had vanished from the countryside.

The Royal Irish Constabulary, knowing of the curse of Black John, were not so superstitious about the matter. Black John was found in Waterford that evening, boarding a ship for America and arrested. Eventually he was released when the doctor made it clear no human agency could have torn Mountmayne limb from limb in such a manner. On his release, however, Black John repeated the curse that seven generations of the Mountmaynes would have to pay the price for the death of his wife.

Eleven years later, Jasper Mountmayne's son, Jervis, who had inherited his father's estates but only then came to the area, arrived with a crowd of rowdy friends and a mistress, whose name, recalled Roe, my overseer, was Ella. Apparently, Jervis was already married to some titled English lady and had two sons, Jodocus and Justin, living in London. Jervis seemed as profligate as his father, Jasper.

A week after his arrival, Jervis disappeared and a search was made.

The search party eventually made their way across Fascoum to Coumshingaun where lies one of the most impressive sights in these mountains, an upland lake set among a cirque of cliffs rising sheer from the water on three sides to a height of thirteen hundred feet. Locals will tell you that the dark waters are bottomless. That's as maybe. The lake is certainly very deep, dark and dank. Some bolder spirits have fished there for brown trout but they are no good to the taste. Locals will tell you that the place is haunted and that the trout are the reincarnation of lost souls. No local would eat them.

It was in that dark, isolated lake that they found Jervis Mountmayne, floating face downward, fully clothed.

A local sergeant of the Royal Irish Constabulary reported that Jervis, judging from a series of footprints he had discovered nearby, had actually walked into the lake. The local doctor pointed to the fact that only the toes of his boots made an impression on the muddy shore which indicated that he went on tiptoe. No one could quite work out the reason why. The curious thing is that around the footprints, indeed, overlapping them were the prints of what were taken to be dogs. Yet the overseer swore that the Mountmaynes' pack of hounds were in their kennels that day. The inquest found that Jervis, in walking or tiptoeing into the lake, had committed suicide while the balance of his mind was disturbed. But the coroner failed to mention what had caused that disturbance and why a man in the prime of life, with no worries whatsoever, had taken his life.

Roe, the overseer, told me that Mountmayne's mistress, the lady called Ella, had soon after returned to London and rumour had it that she later gave birth to Jervis' illegitimate brat.

Finally, and this is now only a few years ago, Jodocus Mountmayne had grown to manhood and went to Ireland to claim the estate. He was Colonel Justin's elder brother. He was barely on the estate two weeks when search parties were called out again for he was missing. He was found the next morning on the slopes of Mount Fascoum – dead. His face an immobile mask of fear. The local doctor was called out and averred that the man had died from a heart attack and that there was nothing sinister in the manner of his death.

The locals, who like to embellish a good tale, reckoned that they heard the jubilant bark of foxes all through the night.

And so, my dear Peggy, the Mountmayne estate, across the slopes of Fascoum, has became the inheritance of Justin Mountmayne. I cannot blame the Colonel for not wanting to claim that inheritance in person. He did well to employ an agent, myself, to act as his representative while he remained in the safety of London where Black John's curse does not appear to extend.

That much I thought only a few days ago. Now I am not so sure. Things are happening which I do not understand.

I was out walking a few days ago when I saw, on the mountain slope about fifty yards above me, a large dog … or so I thought. Looking more closely, I saw it was a fox, slightly larger than the usual run of foxes. Its sharp features stared keenly down at me. It was a beautiful creature and I realized that it was heavy in pregnancy. A great vixen with steely, bright eyes.

I halted and examined the creature. After a while, it rose languidly, gave a yelp, and moved off sedately.

That night, I awoke from my sleep, and lay in my bed with sweat pouring from me and wondering what had disturbed me. To my ears came curious wailing sounds. At first I thought it might be a child screaming in the night, then I imagined a group of cats crying. The sound created such a weird tingling feeling on the nape of the neck. I lay fearful for a while. The noise died away and eventually I returned to sleep.

In the morning, my overseer looked troubled. He inquired whether I had heard the sound of foxes echoing from the mountain nearby. I replied that I had not realized that the sound was that of foxes, never having heard the like before.

Then he said a curious thing: he asked me whether I was sure that I was not a Mountmayne.

I did not understand then. I laughed and replied that I wished I was and that this beautiful estate actually belonged to me. I might then have no more financial worries.

The following night the sounds once more roused me from slumber, disturbing my sleep yet again.

That afternoon I was walking across the mountain side to one of the cottages of the tenant farmers when I encountered a girl sitting on a rock by the roadside. It was obvious that she was a local girl, dark of hair, white of skin, with natural red on her cheeks and eyes of bright grey-green. She had those attractive Irish looks for which the colleens, as they are locally called, are renowned. Her feet were shoeless, her thin dress worn and she made no attempt to hide her pregnant condition.

"Good afternoon," I said politely, raising my hat.

"Bad cess to you, Mountmayne," she replied, so sweetly that for a moment I thought she had politely returned my greeting until the meaning of her words sunk into my brain.

I frowned in irritation.

"Now what call do you have to abuse me?" I demanded, angrily. "My name is Harlyn Trezela. I work for Colonel Mountmayne and am not of his family."

Her sweet, smiling expression did not alter.

"I have the right to curse all Mountmaynes no matter what guise they present themselves in."

"I am not a Mountmayne!" I stormed, my anger increasing. "When will you people get that into your head? I have had enough of people making mistakes. I am Mountmayne's agent and no relation."

She chuckled. I have seldom heard a sound so devoid of humour.

"Remember the curse of Seán Dubh? Even unto the seventh generation."

Then she rose and walked away with a rapid pace which seemed incongruous to her condition.

I stood staring after her a moment or two and then shrugging continued my journey.

These are a strange and stubborn people, Peggy. You do not realize just how foreign these Irish are to we English and yet we pretend they are part of the nation we are pleased to call "British".

Returning from my visit to the tenant farmer, I was passing along the same road when something made me look up the hillside. The sun was lowering in the sky and its feeble pale rays were spreading themselves over the grey boulders and the now muted colours of the gorse.

I halted in surprise.

Not far away, seated on its haunches on a rock, was a fox. I swear, it was the same large, pregnant vixen which I had seen a few days earlier. It was looking at me keenly with its sharp, bright eyes. For the first time, a thrill of fear ran through me. Yet I held my ground, raising my chin defiantly, and stared back. After a while, it rose languidly. This time it opened its jaws, showing its rows of sharp white incisors. My lips came together tightly as I saw the tiny flecks of blood on those white razor teeth. I glanced nervously about for something to defend myself with for I felt a terrible menace.

Then with a sharp yelp, it turned and disappeared.

It look me a while to return to Castle Mountmayne for my heart was pounding and I had a feeling any time that I might collapse with the strain of the blood surging through my head.

I reached the house and went straight into the study, pouring myself a large brandy and slumping in a chair. The sweat poured freely from me. But gradually my heart ceased its cannonade and my pulse became less rapid.

I knew that something, evil was dogging my footsteps. Dogging! The word had come ironically to my mind. That Mountmayne was haunted by evil, that the Mountmayne curse was real, I have little doubt now. But what can it mean, Peggy, that I have seen these things, can feel these things, and I am not a Mountmayne? Does Black John's curse apply to all who come to live in Castle Mountmayne? I do not understand it. All I know is that I, too, am cursed, and shall meet an awesome fate which rolls remorseless and inexorably towards me; I know that I am helpless against it. I am doomed.

I scribble these lines now, in my study, as darkness approaches. I shall not survive long here.

But I do not understand why. Why me? Why me? Why should I inherit the Mountmayne curse?

My last thoughts will be for you, dearest Peggy.

Your loving husband,

Harlyn Trezela

I sat back, shaking my head in wonder at this astonishing document.

Dan and Shawn were examining my expression curiously.

"Is it a relative of yours?" demanded Dan.

I shrugged, more bewildered than certain.

"None that I know of. And I know my ancestry back to my grandparents. My grandfather was a Harlyn Trezela but his wife was named Cynthia and he died in 1956 at the age of seventy-five. So he could not have been this Harlyn Trezela who calls his wife Peggy."

"True enough," remarked Dan, scanning the yellowing pages again. "Your grandfather would not be born at this time. And this Harlyn Trezela had no children when he was writing. It seems that he had only just married before coming to Mountmayne."

"Nevertheless, it is a curiosity," I conceded. "Is it true what he says about Mountmayne?"

Shawn Duff grinned wryly.

"Sure, there were stories of a curse which the old ones used to talk of. But they were stories. Mind you, it was about this time when Castle Mountmayne and the estate fell into disuse and broke up. Several people grabbed the land after the Land Purchase Acts at the end of the last century. They managed to get advances to buy their own small plots. Come to think of it, the last time Castle Mountmayne was used was in 1921 when it was converted into a barracks for the 'Black and Tans'. It was attacked by the republicans and set on fire. Several people were killed there, including the commander of the Tans, a Major Mayne. There was some talk that he was related to the Mountmaynes. But Castle Mountmayne has been empty ever since."

While he was speaking, my mind was still racing as to whom this Harlyn Trezela could have been? Some relative, that seemed likely. That much was obvious by the name. But what relation was he to me?

"Do you have a phone?" The idea came into my mind quite suddenly and I acted on it.

Dan nodded to a cubicle in the corner of the bar.

It did not take me long to get through to my Aunt Rita in Sheffield.

"What? You're ringing from Ireland? Isn't that expensive, Hal?" she demanded. The family always called me Hal.

I suppressed a smile.

"Not really, aunt. Look, you know a bit about the Trezela family, don't you. I mean, have you heard of another person called Harlyn Trezela?"

"My father, your grandfather, of course …" she began but I cut her short.

"No, not him. This Harlyn Trezela would have lived before grand-dad. His wife was, Peggy. But I don't think he had any children."

There was a pause.

"No," Aunt Rita spoke slowly and was clearly thinking. "No. All I know is that your grand-dad came to Sheffield from Truro. He was in his early twenties, and that was about Nineteen-oh-five."

"Do you know anything about his family before that?"

"No. Why is this important? You've hardly shown an interest in your family while over here and then you go to Ireland and start ringing up wanting your family history. What's happened to you?"

"Nothing, auntie," I replied patiently.

There was an audible sniff.

"Well, the only other thing I know about your grand-dad was that his mother was called Maggie and that his grandmother was called Pernel."

"Pernel?"

"That's right."

"There's some strange names in our family," I commented reflectively.

"Look, I have some old papers belonging to your grand-dad. If it's that important, I'll look through them. Why don't I call you back later this evening?"

Not knowing where I would be, I agreed to call her back later and then returned to join Dan and Shawn at the bar. But Shawn Duff had already left. He had, apparently, had to return to his demolition job.

"Well? Have you solved the mystery?" asked Dan with open interest.

I shook my head with a wry smile.

"Not much of a mystery," I said. "This Harlyn could only have been some distance relative, if that."

"Yet you share the same name?"

"I know. It's odd. But a lot of people have the same name."

"Not one as distinctive as yours," grinned Dan. He glanced down at the letter, oilskin and tin box. "What will you do with these?"

"Well, it's not mine."

"But the name … ?"

I sighed and thought for a while.

"Tell you what. I shall be in this area for the next few days. I'll return here soon. If you keep it, I'll come by here in a day or two and might have made up my mind. I'm asking a relative to do a little research on the family. We might be able to sort it out then."

Dan agreed and together we rewrapped the letter into the oilskin and returned it to the box.

It was late afternoon when I left Dan's bar and began to wander along the valley road. The curious letter was on my mind. Had my namesake gone insane? Had his mind been turned by the tales of a curse? Indeed, what had happened to him? Perhaps he had returned to his beloved Peggy.

Peggy! I suddenly halted. Peggy was a diminutive, a diminutive of Margaret. And Maggie was also a diminutive of Margaret. Maggie. Aunt Rita said that grand-dad called his mother Maggie. Could it be possible?

Was Harlyn Trezela's wife really called Margaret, and he called her Peggy? Had he not returned from Ireland? Had she borne him a son whom she also called Harlyn? And that son had grown up without knowing his father but hearing friends call his mother, Maggie?

My mind spun in confusion.

I had meant to leave the Fascoum area that afternoon and make my way into the neighbouring Monavullagh Mountains, the next range to the Comeraghs, to examine their highest peak at Seefin, but something kept me in the area. Perhaps it was a longing to clear up the mystery. I spent the next few hours walking around the old Mountmayne estate. Castle Mountmayne was never a castle but a grand Georgian country house – or had been once. Now it was gaunt, blackened, with charred timbers, standing desolate and lonely in the countryside.

I spent a little time examining it from a distance, for I could see workmen employed on demolition work there and did not particularly want to fall in with Shawn Duff again.

Realizing that evening was approaching, I decided to pitch my tent on the lower slopes of Fascoum and began searching for a good spot.

The girl was young and pretty and I did not see her until I came abreast of the rock on which she was sitting in the pale early evening sun. She had dark hair, pale skin and bright eyes whose colour was difficult to determined, changing between grey and green as the light slanted against them.

"Good evening," I smiled, as I realized her presence.

She stared at me but made no reply. Unusual, I thought, for the Irish were usually courteous to strangers.

"I'm looking for a spot to camp near here. Is there a place with a fresh spring or stream?"

She continued to watch me silently, until I grew uncomfortable and was about to say something else, wondering whether she was deaf or dumb. But then she raised a languid hand and wordlessly pointed along the track.

I thanked her politely, thinking that I must be right, that she was dumb, and made on.

I'd gone only a few yards when I heard a female voice distinctly say: "Even unto the seventh generation, Mountmayne."

I turned swiftly round, confused.

The girl was no longer on the rock. It was as if the earth had swallowed her. I bit my lip wondering why my imagination was playing me tricks. I'd had a long tiring day, it was true, and the curious events at Dan's Bar must have set my imagination rioting.

Time for rest.

I found a spot by a stream a little further on and, a short way down the hill, I spied a small roadway and, of all things, a telephone kiosk. The Irish seem to have a habit of sticking telephone kiosks in unexpected, desolate places by roads that come from nowhere and lead to nowhere. The sight of the phone box reminded me of my promise to telephone Aunt Rita. I decided to pitch my tent and have a meal first.

It was a nice, scenic spot to camp, overlooking the ruins of Castle Mountmayne, still standing out dark and gaunt in the gathering dusk. A little way behind the house, quite near to the road where I had spotted the telephone kiosk was a clump of trees in which I could see another ruin, an odd affair like an old church. I wondered whether it could be a family chapel or perhaps a grandiose piece of architecture for the stables of the house.

It was almost twilight when I went into the cream and green box marked "Telefon", the interior lit by a dim, dirt covered light-bulb, and checked the direct dialling for Sheffield, England. I fed the coins and dialled. Aunt Rita answered.

"Well, you made me spend an interesting few hours with your grand-dad's papers. What's more it seems that we have a skeleton in the family closet."

"What do you mean, aunt?" I demanded.

"Well, grand-dad's father seems to have been illegitimate."

"Yes," I sighed, slightly impatiently, "but that doesn't sort out my problem, does it?"

"Hang on, Hal. I have your grand-dad's birth certificate. He was born in March, 1882. His father was Harlyn Trezela, deceased, and his mother was Margaret Trezela. Not Peggy but Maggie."

I groaned for it didn't really solve anything.

"But Peggy is a diminutive of Margaret," I pointed out.

"Is it, dear?" she replied absently. "Well, the main thing is that I found a birth certificate for another Harlyn Trezela. He was born in 1857. His mother was a Petronella Trezela. The boy was illegitimate. She named her son Trezela, her own name, for there is no father registered. That means he was illegimate."

She sounded quite proud of the fact. I sniffed.

"Well, that was happening all the time in the so called Victorian age of morality. Was he the Harlyn Trezela who I'm looking for?"

"Well, whoever he was, dear, it would mean that he was only twenty-four when grand-dad was born but according to grand-dad's birth certificate, his father was already dead. It ties in but grand-dad called his grand-mother Pernel not Petronella. It's a different name. There's a reference to her in his papers …"

The beeps sounded and I had no more money, so I quickly bade Aunt Rita goodbye and said I would be in touch soon.

I turned out of the dimly lit public telephone kiosk into the darkening September evening.

I began to turn my steps back slowly towards my encampment. I realized that it would be dark before I reached it but, thankfully, I had brought my flashlight with me.

I did not think there could be any doubt that Harlyn Trezela, who died when he was twenty-four, was the person who had written the curious letter. Could he have been grand-dad's father? His wife was Peggy, a diminutive of Margaret. Grand-dad's mother was called Maggie, also a diminutive. Harlyn son of Petronella was dead when grand-dad was born in 1882. So, too, was Harlyn, grand-dad's father. They had to be one and the same person. Which meant that Harlyn Trezela had not returned from Ireland. Grand-dad had been born and brought up without knowing what had happened to his father.

So what had happened to Harlyn Trezela at Mountmayne? Had he fallen to the fabled curse? Had he been driven insane by a morbid fascination with the fate of the Mountmaynes, a morbidity clearly demonstrated in the document which I had been shown? But if he had felt threatened by the Mountmayne curse … why? Why was he a victim of a curse which was only to affect the Mountmaynes? It seemed to make no sense at all, even if one believed in the curse of the Mountmaynes.

I suddenly realized that I had been so deep in thought that I had made a wrong turn at the stone wall which led up to where I had pitched my camp and, in the dusk, came to the old overgrown copse which I had spied from the hillside.

I stood, squinting into the darkness. I could just make out the dark shadows of the ruined building, Gothic in form, like an old chapel.

I realized that I been right in my original assessment of what the building was and that I had wandered into what was once the private chapel and graveyard of the Mountmaynes situated behind the great house.

I was turning away when a headstone obviously newer than the rest of the ancient cracked and decaying memorials caught my eye.

I turned towards it, reaching for my flashlight, for the darkness had descended so quickly that it was no longer possible to read anything in the gloomy twilight.

A simple headstone. It was simply inscribed.

HARLYN TREZELA, 1857–1881.

Surprise went through me. Here was the grave of the very man whose letter I had read. The man who had borne my name. The grave, I now had little doubt, of my great-grandfather.

I heard a whisper in the shadows. The voice of a woman mocking me.

"Even unto the seventh generation, Mountmayne."

I swung round, heart pounding, but could see nothing.

The hairs on the nape of my neck rose.

"Ridiculous!" I said aloud, almost to give courage to myself. "If there was a curse on the Mountmayne family, it had nothing to do with the Trezelas."

I returned my gaze to the headstone.

I felt sorry for the man, this unknown ancestor of mine. If Aunt Rita had been right, he had a half life. Illegitimate, yet he managed to become an officer in the army. Someone with influence, in those days, would have had to buy him a commission. Wounded in the Afghan wars, crippled and invalided out. Married. Given a job in Ireland as a land agent. He had died without seeing his wife again, nor knowing that she was pregnant and would give him a son. A sad sort of life.

My mind suddenly seemed to stop at one thought.

My mouth went dry.

The word "illegitimate" had stayed in my mind, clanging like an alarm bell.

What was it that he had written? Jervis Mountmayne had arrived on the estate in 1857 "with a crowd of rowdy friends and a mistress, whose name recalled Roe, my overseer, was Ella … Ella had soon after returned to London and rumour had it that she later gave birth to Jervis' illegitimate brat".

Ella! Ella! Petronella! Petronella Trezela!

Oh God!

And grand-dad called his grand-mother Pernel. And what was Pernel, I suddenly recalled, but one of the accepted contractions for Petronella!

Harlyn Trezela had been a Mountmayne without knowing it. The illegitimate son of Jervis!

"Even unto the seventh generation!" came the mocking sibilant laughter in the darkness.

Harlyn was the fourth to suffer the Mountmayne curse.

He was my great-grandfather. Grandfather, Father and me – three more generations. I was the seventh generation! Even unto the seventh generation! The curse spoke of "generations" and not "heirs" of Mountmayne.

I felt a terrible icy fear grip me. Panic sent my limbs into action. I turned and began to run from the decaying old burial ground.

I stumbled and almost fell into a large hole which lay across my path. I regained my balance and, thankfully, I did not loose grip of my flashlight but shone it before me.

The hole was long and narrow. It had the appearance of a freshly dug grave.

There was a stone at the head. A fairly new quarried stone.

A man was standing behind it grinning in the darkness. It was old Shawn Duff. Seán Dubh? Black John! He stood pointing,

pointing and grinning. In the curious light his face seemed to take on a sharp pointed aspect, the eyes bright and unblinking … almost fox-like. I followed the indication of his finger.

Inscribed on the stone was: *Harlyn Trezela. 1953–1993*.

I strained my eyes back to where Shawn Duff stood but he was no longer there. Instead, in the darkness, there sat a lean looking dog fox, its mouth seemed to grin evilly at me. At its side was a larger fox; a great pregnant vixen which regarded me keenly with its sharp, bright eyes, the jaws slightly open, displaying rows of razor-like incisors on which were tiny flecks of blood.

Around me from the encompassing blackness of the mountains came a series of wailing barks, strange child-like cries in the night.

Karl Edward Wagner

ONE PARIS NIGHT

Karl Edward Wagner (1945–1994) is remembered as the insightful editor of fifteen volumes of The Year's Best Horror Stories *series (1980–94) and an author of superior horror and fantasy fiction. While still attending medical school, Wagner set about creating his own character, Kane, the Mystic Swordsman. The first novel in the series,* Darkness Weaves with Many Shades, *was published in 1970. It was followed by* Bloodstone *and* Dark Crusade, *and the collections* Death Angel's Shadow, Night Winds *and* The Book of Kane. *Wagner's horror fiction was collected in* In a Lonely Place, Why Not You and I?, Author's Choice Monthly Issue 2: Unthreatened by the Morning Light *and the posthumous* Exorcisms and Ecstasies.

The story that follows was one of two that the author wrote featuring gunslinger Adrian Becker: "He is supposedly a distant offspring of Kane," explained the writer, "and was conceived about the same time in my imagination in the early 1960s." Wagner intended to write a novel about the character, entitled Satan's Gun, *but only a fragment survives.*

"I can't understand how you came to be shot *there*."

Adrian Becker was in a foul mood. He paced about the rubble of the shelled cathedral. In the distance they could hear the Prussian shells hammering Paris.

"What's so odd about being shot in a sporting house?" Sir Stanley examined the dressing.

"I meant being shot in the arse!" Becker had performed the attendant surgery and applied the dressing himself. While he had some medical education, he had gained extensive practical experience while riding with Quantrill during the recent American Civil War.

"I imagine it was the first target the Communard saw," Sir Stanley argued. "You saw how they burst in upon us. Paris is in chaos. There is no respect for any institution."

"You should have guarded your backside." Becker retained the Prussian zeal for order, despite the fact his former fellow Uhlan Lancers would now shoot him on sight.

"Well, it was her backside I had in mind just then, old man," Sir Stanley pointed out. He had found most of a cigar in his coat, and he lit it from their lamp. Despite the risk, Becker had demanded proper light to dress the bullet wound. "Furthermore, one doesn't expect a husband or angry suitor to make an outraged entrance into a whore's bedroom."

"Why then did he shoot you?"

"He shouted that I had devoured his sister." Sir Stanley sucked on the bedraggled cigar.

"He said what?"

"Well, my French isn't all that good, and he was in a state. But I believe that that was what he said, before I shot him dead."

Becker observed Sir Stanley with suspicion. "Well. Had you?"

Sir Stanley was affronted. "Well, certainly not. It's the Parisians who have resorted to cannibalism during the siege, not us. P'raps I didn't fully understand him. You should understand: One instant I was furiously at work on Mimi or whatever her name was; the next, a crazy Frenchman kicks in the door and begins shooting his revolver at me. Yes, and another thing I recall. He called me Bertrand."

"So, then. A quarrel of some sort. The wrong room. The wrong man. Now we are caught between the Communards and the Prussians. This is not good."

Colonel Adrian Becker, late of the Army of the Confederacy under General Quantrill, had found it expedient to leave the Confederate States of America shortly after the truce was declared in 1868. Born during the tumult of an emerging

Germany to a Bavarian countess and a Prussian officer, Becker had returned to his fatherland to join a Prussian Uhlan regiment. His experience had taught him the suicidal futility of cavalry charges against Gatling guns – in this case, mitrailleuses. As the siege of Paris reached its inevitable bloody conclusion this May of 1870, Becker looted the regimental treasury while the rest were looting Paris.

In the process Becker had freed Sir Stanley Sutton, supposedly of the something Lancers and a British observer. While none of the above credentials could stand the test of evidence, it was proved that Sutton was a spy of some sort, and he was awaiting the firing squad when Becker killed his guards. Becker had known him as British liaison to Quantrill's Army of the West near the close of that war. Becker also knew him as a ready adventurer and an expert killer, and Becker needed help robbing the regimental treasury.

A stray shell – French or Prussian, Becker never decided – had blasted their wagon and its concealed treasure. With whatever gold they had earlier pocketed, the two had crept into the wreckage of Paris. In civilian clothes and with enough gold to buy anything they couldn't steal, or bribe anyone they couldn't kill, Becker reckoned they could blend into the chaos of looting and destruction until time to slip away to England. Becker had seen towns sacked from Lawrence to the burning of Washington, and he knew how to blend.

Then a crazy Frenchman had shot Sir Stanley in the arse while they were enjoying themselves in a sporting house. Sutton couldn't sit a horse or walk a dozen steps. Becker was a ruthless killer, but he wouldn't leave a comrade. They needed a carriage or wagon, and instead they were hiding out in a shelled-out cathedral in a Paris that was in its death throes.

Becker wondered which side would try to kill them first. He wasn't even sure how many sides there now were, at work at the slaughter. The cathedral was ringed with the bodies of priests and nuns shot down by the Communards before the shells had struck.

"What's that howling?" Becker peered through the ruins of an eleventh-century window.

"That's a dog, Adrian." Becker had given Sutton a bottle of brandy he'd found in the rubble. Sutton was killing his pain with liberal swallows.

"No. It's a wolf." Becker had lived in the Harz Mountains as a child.

"Wolf or dog, it's more likely to be the wind. The Communards have eaten even the zoo animals. Have you priced rat meat?"

"And I say that it is a wolf. I know that sound."

Adrian Becker was in his late twenties, but years of war on two continents had aged him, as surely as the saber cut that faintly scarred his left forehead. He was tall – just over six feet – and had the broadshouldered, hardmuscled swagger of a cavalryman. His face was handsome enough to the ladies, although just now his blond hair and goatee were unkempt. His eyes were of a blue-grey shade, and their full stare was unnerving. He had been trained in martial skills since a child in 1848, after his parents had fled the failed revolution. Sutton had seen Becker draw, but he could never see the movement of his left hand between the instant of deciding to kill and the impact of his bullets.

"Why did he call you Bertrand?" Becker had drawn one of his pair of .36 Colt Navy revolvers and was wishing for a Henry rifle.

"Who knows? All cats are grey in the dark."

Sutton had readjusted his clothing and was feeling quite a bit better, thanks mostly to the brandy. At least he'd had the presence of mind to snatch up his clothing as they'd fled. While the wound had bled profusely, his trousers, clutched under one arm, had been spared. The cathedral had been close by, and, with Becker supporting him, they had reached its cover just as the shelling resumed. Sutton doubted anyone would have pursued them in the ensuing chaos.

Sir Stanley Sutton, as he styled himself, was half a foot shorter than Becker and rather leaner. He had a polished military bearing that came of being drummed out of several crack regiments, and an easy aristocratic air that came of being born into a noble house whose name he had agreed never to disgrace by claiming it as his own. He had wavy brown hair, a bristling beard, innocent hazel eyes, and a brooding romantic face that the ladies would swoon for. His skill with pistol and sword had kept him alive thus far in his twenty-some years, although luck had helped a great deal. Which was why, instead of having faced a firing squad, Sir Stanley Sutton was merely holed up in the rubble of a Paris cathedral with Colonel Adrian Becker, a bullet hole in his bum, shells falling all about, with the certainty that either side would happily shoot down the both of them.

Becker fired his pistol twice. Sutton drew his Adams double-action revolver and strained to see what his friend was shooting at. Knowing Becker, it was either dead or dying.

"Where are they?" Sutton whispered, seeing nothing.

"There was something by the break in the wall there," Becker said, "I could not have missed. The full moon backlighted him."

"How many?"

"Just the one, I think. He did not fall."

"Use my fifty-four bore," Sutton suggested, holding out his Adams revolver. "More stopping power."

"Same bullet as the American .44 calibre," Becker said. "I think the .36 ball is more accurate."

"All right then, Adrian. Where's your Communard?"

"I'll just go finish him."

Becker stepped carefully over the rubble, pistol cocked, and leaving Sutton a line of fire. There had been something wrong with that silhouette. The man had crouched like an ape, then had sprung away when shot, as though he were unhit. Becker was certain of his aim.

A shell screamed through the night. Becker flung himself headlong beneath a pew. The cathedral foundations shook, hunks of debris pelted through the breached wall, dust and slabs of plaster scattered across the pew. Almost deafened by the near hit, Becker barely heard the scream of the next shell in time to burrow deeper beneath the pew. This shell struck cleanly through the Norman Gothic arches and exploded somewhere about the altar.

Large things fell upon Becker's scant shelter. One of them wore many petticoats and smelled of gardenia perfume.

Becker wiped away dust and petticoats from his face, still holding his pistol which he had managed not to fire. The next shell struck some distance away. Stunned by the concussion, Becker became vaguely aware that he was being held by an equally dazed woman who had parted from her outer dress at some point. She was a lovely mass of lace and stockings and corset, and she was clinging to him fiercely. For an instant, Becker wondered whether she might be an angel, dragging him to Heaven. However, this seemed an unlikely destination for him, and no angel would wear a whore's perfume. Besides, he recognized the face beneath the grit and tousled black hair.

"Jacqueline?"

"Oh, Adrian!" She clung to him with far more ardor than she had shown him earlier that night. "It is horrible out there! I followed you when you two fled. There was much blood!"

Becker lowered the hammer on his Colt. He struggled upward, dragging both of them to their feet. His ears rang, and his head throbbed. From the shudders beneath his feet, he sensed that the shelling was moving away – for now.

"You should have taken refuge in the cellars." Becker was trying to ascertain Sir Stanley's earthly presence. The lantern had somehow remained intact and alight. Something was stirring amidst the debris.

"Bertrand was hiding there!" Jacqueline hissed.

Lucky for him," Becker said. He led Jacqueline over to where Sutton was cursing, and he pulled away some wainscoting that had probably been in place for five centuries until a minute ago. The Englishman was unhappy but unhurt. He thanked Becker with scant courtesy, then favored Jacqueline with a begrimed smile.

Jacqueline pressed back against Becker. "It is not Bertrand! But with his beard he *looks* like Bertrand!"

"*Sehr Gut*," said Becker, still stunned and struggling with his English. "At least we have one thing here tonight settled. This Bertrand. Who is he that someone shoots my friend by mistake?"

Jacqueline's eyes widened. "Bertrand is a … *loup-garou!*"

"I … I believe she means werewolf," Sir Stanley supplied.

"Is there any of that brandy left?" Becker asked.

Sir Stanley surrendered the bottle. "This is a lot of rot."

Becker took a swallow, handed the bottle to Jacqueline. "I told you I heard a wolf. I was a child in the Harz Mountains. I do not miss when I shoot a man."

Jacqueline coughed a bit after her liberal swallow. Sir Stanley gallantly arose and presented her with his coat. Becker was mumbling to himself in German, watching the openings in the walls.

Finally he said: "Yes. I know what a werewolf is."

"Come on, old man!" Sutton suspected shell-shock. "This *is* the nineteenth century, after all."

"Adrian is correct!" Jacqueline interceded. "I have seen this thing! He killed Yvonne! Bit her through the throat! Chewed her flesh horribly! He was Bertrand when he entered her room, but when we broke down the door, it was a wolf that leapt from her window!"

"A wolf escaped from the zoo," Sir Stanley explained. "It was famished and lucky not to have been eaten itself by the Communards." He put his arm around Jacqueline, purely to reassure her.

"How did you find us?" Becker asked suddenly. He was recovering from the shell blast.

"I saw in which direction you had fled. Then I followed the trail of blood. The moon is quite bright."

From outside the cathedral echoed a long bestial howl. A shell hit in the near distance, muffling the cry.

Becker searched his pockets. "Who has silver?" He found a few gold coins and some copper.

"Afraid I'd paid Mimi in advance," Sutton apologized.

Jacqueline had obviously fled in haste. "A cross?" Becker asked her. "Some rings?" But she only shook her head and pressed closer to Sir Stanley.

"We must have silver to kill the werewolf." Becker looked all about. "Perhaps a crucifix from the altar?"

"You won't find as much as a biscuit," Sutton said. "This cathedral was thoroughly looted while the Communards were at work butchering everyone from Mother Superior to altar boy."

Becker peered through the broken wall carefully. "Well, we'll have to look for silver. I can't say how long Bertrand will be content with the nun."

"What?" Sir Stanley joined him at the breach.

The full moon glared down upon the churchyard beyond. Tombstones and funeral monuments shone white and shattered like a scatter of broken teeth. The corpses of the executed clergy lay in rows. Something was moving upon the body of one nun.

Sutton's first thought was of a man in a fur coat. Then he saw that, while it was male, it wasn't a man. It was a man-shaped creature, covered in dark fur. Its face was the muzzle of a beast. The nun's habit had been ripped apart, her legs outflung. As the creature hunched obscenely between her thighs, its wolfish muzzle gnawed at her dead breasts.

Sutton turned away, stunned for once in his checkered career.

"It is Bertrand," Jacqueline said.

"Don't look!" Sir Stanley pulled her away.

"She is a whore in a city gone mad," said Becker. "What now can shock her? But why has nothing been done to destroy this Bertrand?"

"We only recently suspected." Jacqueline was in a near faint. "With all this killing, the riots … How easy to hide his crimes amongst so many!"

"Shoot the thing, man!" Sutton relinquished the collapsing girl and drew his revolver.

"It will only return his attention to us." Becker pushed away the other man's gun. "We must have silver."

"And if we can't find silver?"

"Then we must hope that he will be content amidst the dead until daylight. Unfortunately the werewolf prefers the blood and flesh of the living, and you, my friend, have left a recent bloodtrail. I think that very soon he will come for us, and you are unable to run."

"Then I say give him a belly full of lead right now!"

"Sir Stanley, I tell you that I shot him. As you can see, there was no effect. Watch him now, while I search for silver."

"And what if he moves toward us?"

"Then you must shoot him and pray that I am wrong."

"What about fire?" Sutton wondered, watching the necrophilic feast with growing horror.

"Well, first you catch and skin him," Becker suggested. "I'll get a fire started to roast him over."

"Firebrands!" Jacqueline said. "Wild beasts fear fire."

"Werewolves are only part beast." Becker picked up the lamp. "And they move very fast."

Jacqueline gathered up her petticoats to follow him across the rubble. "You seem to be very well informed of the *loup-garou*: Have you bagged very many?"

"One is sufficient," said Becker, and she thought she saw him shiver. It was probably only the difficulty of walking over the rubble-strewn floor, as they approached the ruined altar.

Becker held high the lamp. "Look for a crucifix, a chalice, silver plate, anything the looters missed."

The shell had blasted the altar into hopeless debris, piercing the cathedral floor and disgorging the crypts beneath. The bones of crusaders and bishops were heaped together in shattered and moldering piles, like the wreckage of unstrung and rotted puppets. Broken swords and rusted armor lay amidst desiccated flesh and tatters of worm-eaten finery. The smell was of dust and mold – the stench barely noticeable against the greater stench of smoke, burnt powder and recent death that pervaded Paris this night.

"I can't bear this." Jacqueline shuddered and covered her face with her hands.

"Then hold this lamp." Becker thrust the lantern toward her, waited until she had it in her grasp, then carefully clambered down through the rubble into the exposed crypt. He had seen far worse too many times before, and the moldering skeletal remains of the centuries-dead held neither terror nor awe, so long as they didn't move.

"Here! Shine the light here, Jacqueline!"

The wreckage from the shelling made it impossible to be certain of anything – everywhere bones and fragments of rusted armor and rotted vestments – but Becker judged the crypts dated from the Crusades. There was a black chalice lying intact amidst the rubble, evidently dislodged from the crypt by the explosion. Becker recognized age-blackened silver, and he snatched it from the debris.

A skeletal hand clutched at its stem, refusing to relinquish its grasp. Becker swore as the chalice was pulled away from his fist. Drawing his bowie knife, he hacked frenziedly at the leathery knots of desiccated flesh and bone, prying the dead fingers one by one from their grip. Steel prevailed, and in a moment he was scrambling out of the crypt, carrying his prize.

"Now we must have a fire. Gather some of this wood, please. We must hurry, Jacqueline!"

"The beast has moved away into the shadow," Sir Stanley warned, as Becker busied himself with his kit. "I can't spot him!"

"Keep looking!" For his pistols, Becker carried percussion caps, a flask of black powder, a tin of grease, wadding, spare balls, a capping tool, and a bullet mold. While Jacqueline made a fire from the smashed woodwork, Becker quickly removed powder and ball from the cylinder of one Colt Navy revolver.

With his bowie knife he hacked the ancient silver chalice into chunks. Becker was pleased to see that it was indeed of silver, a plain chalice, obviously quite old. Becker had no time to appreciate its antiquity.

By the time the fire was going well, he had recovered a rusted scrap of a crusader's helmet from the crypt – sound enough to serve as a melting pot. Becker dropped in the mutilated chalice and waited for the silver to melt.

A wolf's howl reminded him of the need of urgency.

"Can you see him?" Becker fanned the coals.

"The clouds are across the moon," Sutton told him. "I can't see anything."

"Jacqueline." Becker pointed to some smashed paneling. "Make firebrands!"

"But can these kill the beast?"

"They might discourage him from further courses of his dinner."

Becker blew on the coals. Silver melted at almost three times the melting point of lead, but the fragments of the chalice were at last beginning to slump and mingle together. Looking about, he found sections of a medieval tapestry crushed beneath the rubble. Quickly he hacked away pieces with his knife to make padding for his hands.

Positioning his bullet mould, Becker clumsily gripped the glowing fragment of helmêt, removed it from the fire and poured – trying not to spill much of the molten silver. Replacing the makeshift pot, he flicked the spilled pools of silver back into it, waiting for the mold to cool.

"Any sign of the beast?" Becker opened the mold. Three glinting balls of silver shook out.

"The moon is clear, but I can see nothing," Sutton called back.

"Perhaps Bertrand has eaten his fill," Jacqueline said.

"While the moon is full, nothing can sate his bloodlust." Becker poured again into the mold, then trimmed the flashing from the three .36 calibre bullets, cursing as the hot metal burnt his fingers. They must cool a bit more, or he'd risk their igniting the powder as he charged his pistol. Becker poured a little of the brandy over the hot balls. He opened the bullet mold and cracked loose another three bullets. There remained a good quantity of silver, but time was the essential matter now.

Becker now had six silver bullets. He decided to risk the first three and began to load his revolver, hoping that the wadding would protect the black powder from the hot metal.

The werewolf's growl was like that a mastiff might roar out, if he were the size of a bull.

Sir Stanley yelled out and fired pointblank, as the beast suddenly burst through a shattered window. The remnants of medieval glass tore at its hairy flesh, inflicting as little harm as did Sir Stanley's bullets.

It reared there for a moment amidst the debris, snarling at them – its wolfish muzzle showing carrion-smeared fangs. It was like a great hairy ape with a wolf's head – and yet, there was a red glow of depraved humanity in its eyes. It regarded its three victims, taking in their positions as a diner selects a slice of meat from a buffet, then rushed for Sir Stanley.

The heavy .44 calibre slugs from Sutton's Adams revolver staggered the creature momentarily, but they had no further effect. Unable to run, Sutton swore and flung the useless weapon at the charging beast.

Jacqueline ran toward him with a pair of firebrands.

Becker charged the chambers with powder and rammed home the silver bullets. He had learned well to reload quickly while riding with Quantrill, and the percussion caps were already in place on the revolver's cylinder.

Jacqueline threw herself between the werewolf and Sir Stanley – thrusting the blazing firebrands into its face.

Roaring more in rage than fear, the werewolf reeled back for an instant, striking away the firebrands with one taloned paw. Jacqueline spun away, just avoiding its claws. Sutton shoved her clear. The werewolf reached out for him.

"Bertrand!" Becker shouted.

As the creature turned at his shout, Adrian Becker shot him three times through the heart. There had not been time to load the other chambers. It wasn't necessary.

Putrid smoke boiled forth from the werewolf's chest as the silver bullets tore into him. Flame gushed from the wounds, suddenly setting his entire mass of flesh on fire. Bertrand howled hideously – his bestial roar rising into a human scream. Staggering backward, the creature lurched across the ruined cathedral, crimson flames eating through its flesh. Blackened bones were already poking forth from charred skin as it pitched backward like an obscene sacrifice into the crypt.

Becker and the others gazed down upon the creature. In a short time there was little more than ashes.

"I told you we must have silver," Becker said.

By daylight the shelling had stopped, and most of the fighting had moved to another quarter of Paris. Sir Stanley was still weak from loss of blood, but he insisted that he could walk with assistance. Becker thought they had best press on, before either the French or the Prussians restored order here.

As they passed through the churchyard, they met an aged priest. The tears on his face testified to his feelings upon viewing this scene of massacre and ruin. Nonetheless, he greeted them –

then gazed curiously at Jacqueline's petticoats, exposed beneath Sutton's coat.

Sir Stanley noticed his look. Always the gentleman: "She was attacked by the Communards, Father. We were able to drive them away in time to spare her, and sought refuge here. As for me, my wound is nothing."

"Bless you, my children. Such bravery is rare in these terrible days." The old priest gestured toward the massacred victims, then wiped away tears.

"God has gathered these in. Stones may be restored. But here in the crypts of this ancient cathedral is said to be hidden the Holy Grail – the very cup from which Our Lord drank before his betrayal – a silver chalice won by the blood of the crusaders and kept here in secret throughout the centuries."

His age-worn face implored them. "Will you not help me search this ruin for it? Those who guarded its secret are all slain. Perhaps its power could bring an end to all this senseless slaughter."

Adrian Becker exchanged glances with Sir Stanley Sutton.

"Yes," said Becker. "To some of it, certainly."

Brian Mooney

SOUL OF THE WOLF

Brian Mooney's first professional short story sale was "The Arabian Bottle", which appeared in the London Mystery Selection *in 1971. Since then his work has been published in such anthologies and magazines as* The 21st Pan Book of Horror Stories, Dark Voices 5, Shadows Over Innsmouth, The Anthology of Fantasy & the Supernatural, Fantasy Tales, Final Shadows, Kadath, Dark Horizons *and* Fiesta.

He explains that the idea for the following story came to him while he was watching a nature programme about wolves on television:"One of the wolf experts was an elderly American Indian who, in passing, mentioned an old superstition about cutting a dead animal's throat to release the soul. It was one of those all too rare instances where the plot just leapt into my mind almost the way it came out on paper ..."

Prelude: Trophies

There was an abundance of trophies, heads with frozen eyes which stared down upon Nugent as he sat at his desk in the weapons room. Almost every game animal in the world was represented there; some had been obtained expensively under licence, most had been killed illicitly and even more expensively. Many of the animals were drawing near to extinction but Nugent cared not a jot. He would begin to worry when there was nothing left to hunt.

On this evening, Nugent was smugly content. Sipping from his crystal glass of very old malt whisky, savouring the liquor's smokiness on his tongue, he reached out his other hand to touch, caress even, the laminated card which lay exactly in the centre of the desk's exquisite antique leather surface.

That card, a licence to kill yet another animal of a rapidly dwindling species, had taken him many years to obtain, years of sucking up to sleazy politicians and their fixers, years of bribery and blackmail and corruption.

Taking his whisky, Nugent arose and began to stroll around the huge room, looking at the trophies gracing the panelled walls, admiring his extensive collection of weapons in their display cases. Here an ancient Malay kris, there an early AK47, next to it a stone axe-head. Doc Holliday's Greener shotgun, used to cut down Frank McLaury at the OK Corral, nestled side-by-side with a rusted Saxon shortsword. Nugent smiled at one favourite: a well-honed, ivory-handled open razor, reputedly owned by an early twentieth century gang-leader in the Scottish city of Glasgow. There was a time when he had taken that razor and … well, never mind, that was history. A smile flitted across Nugent's hard face as he reminisced.

And there, on a small side-table, was the leather case which contained his latest hunting rifle, the one which he would use for this new kill. Nugent ran a fingertip along the hard, polished surface of the case and felt a small thrill in his breast.

Christ damn the Greens, he thought. Bastards just about had the world sewed up these days. But not completely, as that licence showed. What harm was he doing? He was genuinely puzzled. Animals have killed each other since time began. Hell, a man had all the money in the world and more, he should be able to do what he wanted. Right?

There were times Nugent wondered what it would be like to hunt men. He would love to take a party of those namby-pamby bastards out into the wild and show them how much better life could be when the adrenalin flowed and you knew that each minute might be your last. The hunt, oh the hunt …

*   *   *

(The pack ran free in the mountain forests and plains, wisps of grey mist loping steadily in pursuit of their prey, revelling in the wind and the scents on the air and the sheer exuberance of life …)

Item: Wolfhunt

The huge timber wolf was majestic, still and quiet against the gloaming as if it was a sculptured part of the slab-like boulder on which it stood.

The animal's head tilted back slightly as it delicately sniffed the evening air, redolent with the scent of the ubiquitous pine forest. The great body sloped down from the shoulders to where the bushy tail rested between muscular hind legs. Nugent slightly adjusted the telescopic sight and the image of the beast became sharper.

Although almost choking with excitement, Nugent compelled himself to the state of relaxation necessary for a perfect shot. The Remington's weight was comforting, the walnut stock cool and silky against his cheek, its touch as sensuous as a woman's fingertips sliding gently on bare skin.

Behind and to the right of where the wolf stood the sun was sliding into daily oblivion. Soon, probably, white, damp mist would creep down through the forest, impenetrable and seemingly alive, to fill the valley far below. But for the moment the air remained clear and sharp enough to sting the cheeks and ears.

The man's thumb reached out to ease the safety catch forward and his breathing shallowed. His nostrils wrinkled as he caught an acrid whiff of body odour from the Chinook lying beside him. Nugent could feel the Indian's humid warmth, had an instinct to flinch away. Christ, someone should drag these goddam primitives into the twenty-first century.

Nugent swallowed his distaste. If it wasn't for the Indians, it was unlikely that he would have gotten anywhere near the wolf. And this trophy had become a near obsession with him.

The cross-hairs of the scope centred on a spot just below the wolf's ear and Nugent's finger took first pressure on the trigger. A final slow exhalation and then the second pressure. There was no recoil as the killing missile, a tiny hypodermic filled with a destructive potpourri of toxins, sped from the rifle's muzzle.

The wolf just crumpled as if sinew and bone had dissolved. Nugent breathed in and then exhaled again, a fierce, triumphant grunt. At last, at last … The coveted wolf, and with neither mark nor injury on the handsome carcass. And then Nugent let out an angry yell, "*What the hell's Two-trees doing?*"

The second Chinook, the younger one who had been so self-effacing, so quiet in the background, was now running at full tilt towards the fallen animal, a long-bladed hunting knife in one hand. As he ran, moccasined feet kicking up dirt and pine needles, the Indian cried out, a weird, mourning ululation.

Nugent scrambled to his feet to give chase but already the older Indian, Jackson, was ahead of him. "What's he doing?" cried Nugent again, "Stop the bastard!"

When the wheezing Nugent reached the Indians, the senior was restraining his companion. The two were having a frenzied argument in their own tongue.

"All right, what is it?" gasped Nugent.

Jackson looked embarrassed. "Two-trees wants to cut the wolf's throat, boss."

"Is he crazy?" Nugent spat to clear his mouth and wiped sweat from his face. "What does he want to do that for?" He turned a snarling face to the younger man. "*Well, why?*"

A sullen Two-trees muttered briefly in his own language. Jackson shrugged. "It's an old superstition, boss, common to a lot of tribes. It's to release the wolf's soul. You've got to understand – our people revere the wolf, look on it as a brother hunter. It's okay to kill the wolf, but you must honour it as a warrior. You cut the throat straight away, it releases the soul for the hunt in the other world. Don't release the soul, in time the wolf will take revenge somehow."

"No way." Nugent prodded Two-trees in the chest. "*No goddamed way!* I paid a hundred thousand credits for the hunt licence and I paid another thirty thousand for this specially adapted Remington so that I wouldn't make a mess of the skin. You are not going to cut its throat, sonny, not for some damned crazy superstition."

Two-trees expostulated angrily with the elder Chinook. Jackson grimaced. "He says it's almost too late now, boss. Let him do it immediately, things might be okay."

Nugent hefted the Remington slightly. "Tell this damned savage that if he goes anywhere near that wolf, I'll shoot him."

Mouth twisted in disgust, the young Chinook thrust his knife back into its sheath. As he turned away, he said in English, "Your responsibility, Mr Nugent. This damned savage tried to do what was right. I just hope you can live with what you've done."

(*The mountains and the forest were dappled silver and black as full moon and smothering darkness vied for supremacy. A young Indian stood on a vast platform of rock which dominated a timber-free clearing, naked and unadorned save for strange splashes of paint which gave an animal-like appearance to his stringy body. Around the rock, still and uncanny in their watchfulness, sat the grey shadows of the wolf pack.*

The Indian drew breath and began a low, keening wolf howl, gradually lifting and throwing back his head until, as his howl reached its crescendo, he was staring straight into the face of the moon. The circling wolves, too, threw back their elongated heads as they joined the dirge …)

Item: Ceremony

In a small cave amid the towering mountains, five Indians gathered in conclave around a smoky fire. Two were dressed in denims and mackinaws, were shod in stout climbing boots. One, the elder, was ill-at-ease, the other inflexible and determined. The remaining Indians were old men, leathery bodies naked save for necklaces of bone and teeth. One of them clutched a small drum, as yet silent, between his knees.

In accordance with the old ways, a pipe was being passed around the men, from hand to hand, lip to lip, a pipe which contained something more than tobacco, something which dilated eyes and lightened heads and limbs.

When all had drawn upon the pipe several times, it was laid to the ground with reverence by the most wrinkled of the three naked men. He turned to the disquieted man, deferring to him as the senior visitor.

"This white man, this Nugent, you say he offended against the laws of the hunt?"

Jackson looked embarrassed. "I didn't say anything like that, the guy was just ignorant of our ways. He didn't mean no harm."

"Listen to yourself, Jackson," snarled Two-trees, "you might as well be a goddamned white-eyes, the way you try to make excuses for the bastards. Listen, Old Father—" turning to Jackson's questioner, "—I told this Nugent of the law, of our ways. He sneered, called us savages. Threatened to kill me if I did what was right. So Brother Wolf's soul has no resting place, it cries out for vengeance. Hear me, that night I went back into the forest to mourn, and the grey brothers, they all came to where I was. They offered me no harm, instead they wept with me. Help Brother Wolf's soul, Old Father, help it."

The old men drew closer together, muttered to each other in a tongue so old and strange that neither of the guides could understand it. Finally, hatchet faces grim in the orange and yellow flicker of the firelight, they nodded.

The one with the drum began to tap a rhythm, a steady thumping beat that inexorably enveloped the senses until it threatened to dominate the mind. The second old man took handfuls of the tobacco and drug mixture, casting them onto the fire which flared and emitted thickened skeins of acrid-smelling fumes. Within several inhalations. Jackson and Two-trees could feel themselves expanding, minds and bodies drifting like leaves on a fickle breeze.

Old Father began to chant, a strange, low song which despite its softness was soon vying with the power of the drumbeat. Like primitive paintings daubed onto the cave walls, shadows cast by the old men writhed and stretched and lengthened into monstrous shapes of an almost tangible blackness.

Then Two-trees nudged his companion and pointed with slightly trembling finger towards the fire. Awed, the two men watched the smoke twirling and dancing as it formed the unmistakable image of Brother Wolf ...

*   *   *

(In a luxurious apartment amid the towering blocks of the city, a sleeping man twitched and fidgeted. For a moment, despite the efficiency of the air-conditioning, there was the slightest suggestion of acridity in the bedroom's atmosphere, and the man's nostrils twitched in irritation as if someone nearby was smoking a mixture of tobacco and narcotics.)

Item: Preservation

"Perfect, quite perfect." Wallace Plumtree ran a pudgy hand over the magnificent carcass, his touch delicate and loving. "It will be a pleasure to prepare this one for you, Mr Nugent. Why, it must have been a giant amongst its kind."

"Guess so," said Nugent. He kept his tone matter of fact, concealing the gloating which tightened his stomach and threatened to swell in his throat. His years of badgering congressmen and the Secretary of State, his years of making certain generous donations to party and private funds, his years of threatening those with less than pure private lives before the precious licence had been agreed, all had been worthwhile.

"I see so few truly magnificent specimens these days," sighed Plumtree. "These damned conservationists, they're making life so awkward for such as you and I. We are anachronisms." He shook his head as if in despair, the mop of white curls flopping about his collar. With a huge spotted handkerchief he polished the old-fashioned eyeglasses he affected.

"We're a dying breed, we hunters, Plumtree," grunted Nugent, "There's no appreciation for the stalk and the kill these days."

The taxidermist raised an ironic eyebrow. "You're right there, sir. Unless you're some lowlife predator stalking and killing men on the streets. Then who cares what you do?"

Nugent nodded. "Yeah, run in a pack with switch-blades or Saturday night specials and you can rape and maim and kill as many of your own kind as you want. Nobody gives a good goddam. The cops don't often bust a gut, and if they do the courts just give the bad guys a slap on the wrist. But you want to kill a wild animal, hell, you're worse than Jack the Ripper.

"You know, Plumtree, there are nights when I walk the streets, the really bad streets, just hoping that some of these punks will try me. I want to see how they'd be when they meet a real predator. But nothing ever happens, know what I mean?"

Plumtree put his eyeglasses on, appraised the big, chunky man before him. He had heard of Nugent's skill at martial arts, of the wealthy socialite's collection of exotic weapons, of his sheer enjoyment of violence. "You don't look like a victim, I guess, Mr Nugent."

He added, "Now, as to the wolf, how would you like me to deal with him?"

Nugent stood, hand stroking chin, considering the question. "I wondered … Do you think perhaps mounted standing, threatening maybe, with a snarl?"

Wallace Plumtree shook his head a little. "So very passé, don't you think, Mr Nugent? And dare I say, a modicum vulgar? All very well for a school child visiting a museum but not for a person of taste. Why, it would be an insult to the nature of this lovely beast. If I may suggest …"

Nugent motioned the other man to continue.

"Well, sir, I recommend flaying, save for the head which would be treated and remain intact. Then the fur prepared so that the body, with legs and tail, are supple and soft, able to spread out. The whole would then make a beautiful rug or wall display."

"I don't want the fur damaged in any way," warned Nugent.

"Of course not, Mr Nugent. As you know, I use the very latest techniques, including laser technology. I guarantee that despite the opening out, no harm will come to the fur itself."

(*The night janitor was young and a nineteen-sixties freak. That night he was stoned, as he so often was, flying high, away in his own previous century world. He cleaned Wallace Plumtree's outer office but when he tried the inner door to the workshop he found it to be locked. This wasn't unusual, it generally meant the old dude had something special in there. Hey man, imagine stuffing dead animals for a living. Guess it paid well, though, that Plumtree cat didn't look like he'd worried about his next meal for decades. And the rents in this block didn't come cheap.*

Just as the janitor was about to turn away from the door, he thought that he heard something. It was low and distant and sounded a bit like an animal of some kind, dog maybe, alternately whimpering and howling. Might even have heard the sound of scrabbling, like clawed feet trying to gain purchase on a polished stone floor. Not possible, all those creatures in there, they were dead, man. The janitor pulled out the remains of the toke he'd been smoking earlier and studied it. Hey, powerful shit, man ...)

Interlude: Dreamplace

Nugent was back at that place of death in the mountains. He sprawled there with the ground hard beneath him and the Remington, aimed steadily at the timber wolf, weighty in his arms. The sun must have been setting, for the sky behind the animal was the bright scarlet of freshly-spilled arterial blood.

Nugent was aware that two Indians stood behind him, although neither one came into his line of sight. He could hear, or perhaps feel, a throbbing as of drums, or of rushing life filling veins and arteries. He thought that he could smell wood-smoke and tobacco, and beneath that something else, something narcotic.

Nugent knew that Two-Trees was trying to tell him something, but he could never quite catch the Indian's words. He understood the gist to be something concerning the wolf's soul, but he knew too that such a concept was ridiculous.

He closed his mind to those unheard entreaties and concentrated on making his shot good. He took first pressure. The telescopic sight was better, clearer than he had ever known it. It focused in upon the wolf's head and each hair in the coarse fur stood out sharp and plain. He took the second pressure.

And as he released death, as it became too late for him to stay his action, the wolf's noble head turned and through the 'scope Nugent found himself staring into human eyes, dark blue eyes like his own, which pleaded with him.

Nugent jerked up in his bed screaming ...

(In her penthouse room, the best in the apartment from which she had a wonderful panoramic view of city and sky, Marianna shifted

uneasily in bed. She awoke briefly, confused, thinking that she had heard an animal howling. How could she have done? This was the city. Muttering sleepily, she turned over and drifted off once more …)

Item: Display

Wallace Plumtree looked around him with interest. 'It looks a little different from when I was last here," he said.

"You've got sharp eyes," acknowledged Nugent, "I like change, I get bored easily. I've arranged things now so that the trophy can be displayed to better advantage. I thought here." He indicated an area of highly-polished wooden floor in front of the huge fireplace with its heap of artificial logs.

"Perfect." Plumtree motioned to his chauffeur to lay down the bulky parcel. When the man had left the room, his employer removed the lid from the box and tenderly lifted out the contents. "There, Mr Nugent, I'm as proud of that as of anything I've ever done."

The wolf's head lived. Plumtree had prepared it to seem that the beast was at rest, lazily satisfied, with a glint of knowing wisdom in the glass eyes. The pelt shone from the loving attention which had been paid to it, silver highlights glistening in the matt greyness.

Going to his knees, the taxidermist arranged the wolf-skin then looked to Nugent for approval.

The hunter nodded. "Thank you, Mr Plumtree. I am very pleased." He grinned. "Our finest work, I think."

(In the strange lambency of another dimension, something stirred, a patch of darkness which stretched itself into a long and slender lupine shape. Created of vengeance from nothingness, its sole need was to destroy.

With a silent snarl, the ethereal creature set out to find its prey …)

Item: Shame

With only the most perfunctory of knocks, Marianna strode into the trophy room, a swirl of white-blonde hair and lithe body and silken robe. Nugent was sitting, whisky in hand, contemplating the remains of the great wolf with satisfaction.

"What do you want?" asked the man without looking up. "More money, I suppose?"

"I want to go shopping," his mistress told him. "It's better than sitting around here on my butt while you spend all your time among these ... these masculine souvenirs of yours."

Nugent glared but said nothing. Although a violent man, he prided himself on never having raised a hand to a woman. Marianna pushed him, though, Jesus Christ did she push him. He pressed buttons on his desk computer, tore off the credit cheque it printed and thrust it towards her.

The woman took the check without a word of thanks. Instead, she stepped over to the wolf-skin and looked down at it with something like contempt.

She said, "Since this goddam thing came here, you've spent most of your time just gazing at it. What goes through your mind when you're doing that, Nugent? Wondering what it would be like to lay me on it? Fat chance of that, seeing that you can't get it up any more. Hell, I might as well be a nun for all the action I'm getting."

She wandered to one of the weapons cases and tapped her fingers on the glass lid. "Guess that's why you collect all these guns and things," she added. "And why you enjoy killing. It's all about penis substitutes and feeling macho, isn't it?"

Nugent drained his glass and poured himself another Glenlivet. "Why do you stay here, Marianna? There's nothing left between us and you can't stand me any more."

"Remember our cohabitation agreement, honey?" she mocked. "If I go voluntarily, I get nothing. And I've had enough of nothing in my life. You want rid, you send me away – and pay for it. God knows you can afford it. Or are you afraid I'll tell the world that the mighty hunter is impotent? It'd take a lot of killing to rid yourself of that particular shame, wouldn't it, Nugent? Well, must go, thanks for the cheque. Hey, maybe I'll buy you a present. How about a set of ivory splints for your dick?"

As Nugent watched the woman leave the room, his fist tightened slowly until the whisky glass crushed, driving long splinters into his fingers and palm. Blood spurted, but Nugent paid no heed. He noticed neither the pain of the cuts, nor the sting of the spirit as it seeped into his wounds.

(*Somewhere on another plane, the ebon, prowling wolf-shape stopped and raised its head, nostrils flaring. It had caught the whiff of something to lead it to its eagerly sought goal, the mingled odours of scorn and shame and hatred and blood …*)

Interlude: Dreamplace

Nugent stood on top of the rock, filling his lungs with the clean air of a mountain evening. Scents undreamed of called to him, told him tales of the forest, told him where the prey was, where the pack was, where his beloved mate, the alpha female, romped with their cubs. His greatly altered colour perception turned the landscape, the mountains and sky, the very rock on which he stood, into a bizarre and fascinating composition in monochrome.

He stretched, tensing and relaxing his powerful muscles, spread his great fanged jaws wide in a yawn. Never in his life had he felt so alive, so at one with the environment.

Without knowing why, he felt other presences in this place of peace. He turned his great head and saw the three man-creatures. Two of them were of the ancient race and he could feel the emanations of their admiration and awed respect. Then he realized what the third man-thing was about.

It looked at him over the barrel of a killing-stick, staring at him intently with its yellow wolf-eyes. Recognition of imminent death came to Nugent much too late, for the death dart struck him even as he was crying out, reaching out, to his brother …

(*Marianna jerked from slumber with a muffled cry. Some dreadful noise had awoken her, just like several nights ago. And there it was again, the howling of an animal, a dog perhaps. But dogs weren't common in this part of the city, in fact the weird and frightening noise seemed to have come from somewhere inside the building, even inside the apartment. But that was impossible … wasn't it?*

Marianna slipped from her bed, tiptoed quietly to her door and listened. She wasn't sure, but she had the impression that something was creeping around out there. She even thought that she heard a low snuffling, as if the skulking thing was trying to sniff her out. Despite the room's warmth, she shivered violently and felt her bare body crawl with goose-flesh. She pressed her thumb against the security reader and it locked the door in response.

Marianne ran back to the bed and hid her head beneath the topsheet. She slept badly for the remainder of the night ...)

Item: Nighthunt

Two cops stood in a doorway in a mean part of the city, smoking an illicit cigarette each. Their conversation was mainly precinct scuttlebutt, interspersed with derogatory comments about their captain, a dipshit with his nose stuck firmly up the Commissioner's ass.

One of them leaned out of the doorway to dispose of his cigarette butt and jerked back, cannoning into his partner. "Hell, what was that?"

"What was what?" said the other policeman, stepping out onto the sidewalk, "I don't see nothing."

The first cop joined him. "I'm not sure, I thought I saw something dash between those two alleys over there. Just a glimpse out the corner of my eye. I don't know ... it could have been a big dog, it could have been a man crouched down ..."

His partner was just saying, "Okay, so let's take a look," when the night was made hideous by several high, thin shrieks.

"*Christ Almighty!*" Pulling their machine-pistols, both cops rushed towards the source of the terrible noise. Covered by his partner, the first cop dived into the alley, flicked on his flashlight. There was nothing there save the remains of what could have been a cat, mangled and torn. Blood and guts everywhere, as they told the guys back at the station-house later.

It had got so bad that Old Weasel could smell himself, but he didn't give a shit. He'd found him a good, solid cardboard box, big enough to sit upright and lie down, plenty of newspapers for blankets and a fine spot over a warm air vent. A piece of sacking covering the front of the box, and his world was his castle. Okay, so he got a little gamey when warm, so what, any bastard didn't like it could stand downwind.

He itemized the gleanings from tonight's search among the garbage cans. A quarter loaf, a bit stale but at least it didn't have blue whiskers. Some chicken and burger scraps, a selection of throwout vegetables and fruit disposed of by a Chinese restaurant, in fact a feast. Why, he'd even found a paper bag with some stale donuts. And to wash it all down, a bottle of Weasel's special skullbuster, a litre jug of cheap Muscatel with a dash of Sterno to give it a lift, vintage this very evening.

Hey, whassat? There was somebody nosing around outside, probably after a hand-out. "Get lost, you bum! Go find your own booze!" yelled Weasel just as the curtain of sacking was wrenched aside.

Most people couldn't stand Weasel's stink. The thing that hauled him from his cardboard cave to rend him didn't seem to be all that fussy.

Slick Gerber took his latest girl into the park to make out. Slick fancied himself a hardcase, the thought of muggers and worse didn't worry him. He was well armed. As well as the essential packet of rubbers – hell, he didn't know who she'd pushed out to before, did he – he packed a switchblade and an old Iver Johnson .32, both of which he enjoyed using. He may have been well prepared for muggers but not for what found him and Rhonda in the bushes.

There were others … Mr Peters was an insomniac who liked to walk at night; Lucy Delgado thought her neighbourhood was safe to go jogging; Bill Brechner was sneaking home after an illicit liaison with a woman who was not his wife.

When the reports from various precincts were collated the next day, consensus was that some asshole had dumped a number of ageing, redundant and somewhat hungry fighting-mastiffs into the community.

And that was just the first night …

(Nugent awoke, his head limbs and eyeballs aching as if he'd been on the greatest bender of his life. Worse, his abdomen felt dreadfully distended, as if he had been force fed during the night. He practically fell from his bed and stumbled his way into the bathroom.

He pulled the lightcord and winced as he caught sight of his image in the floor-to-ceiling mirror. God, what had he been doing? And where the hell had that dirt all over his naked body come from?

Well, he had gotten stuck into the Scotch the previous evening but so he had on many other occasions. He'd always remembered what he'd done before. Feeling more sick than ever, Nugent relieved himself and vowed never again.)

Item: Bloodlet

It's always the cops who have to pick up the pieces, sometimes literally.

The bizarre and savage killings in the city had continued intermittently for several weeks. The official line was still that a pack of fighting dogs was on the loose, but in the privacy of the precinct bullpens, some detectives were beginning to wonder if there was a real nut somewhere out there, a nut who was just that bit worse than the run-of-mill nut. The tabloid press was beginning to speculate along the same lines.

The clincher for this unpublicized line of thought came with the late night slaughter of the Krazies. The rookie cop who found what was left of the street gang upchucked violently then lapsed into shock. His partner, older and generally more phlegmatic, slumped down on his butt in the gutter amid the mud and grime and garbage and worse. He drank the best part of the flask of good Irish whiskey he carried before calling in.

Soon, the place was crawling with uniformed men and detectives and paramedics. The reckoning was that there were at least four bodies, although it might take a series of autopsies to be sure.

Then back of a local store, somebody found a junior gang member intact but almost insane with terror. At the time, all they could get out of him was that he was called Zip. He was scrawny and underfed, his nose ran constantly and all around his mouth was the telltale rash of a solvent abuser.

Zip remained under heavy sedation for a couple of days before he could speak to the investigating officers.

STATEMENT OF CHARLES "ZIP" BELLINGER, MEMBER OF YOUTH GANG KNOWN AS "THE KRAZIES"

Me and some of the guys was hangin' out. There was Jocko, One eye, Tattoo Nick and Rammer as well as me. We was a little high, done some sniffin', figured that a bit of blood-lettin' would give us a buzz. We wandered the turf, hopin' that maybe we'd find us some guy from one of the spic gangs, carve him up good.

Didn't have no luck. Then Rammer spotted this creep, looked like some kinda loony. You believe it, he was naked? In this weather? Well, maybe not quite naked. He was wearin' some kinda coat and cap, made outa something furry. Thought we'd have some fun with him.

Didn't think there was nothin' to worry about, we was all carryin', you know? Knives, clubs, like that. We go over, get all around him. One-eye says somethin' like, "Hey man, you a crazy? We Krazies too." Like, One-eye, he enjoyed playin' with words.

Then Rammer, he says, "Only room on this turf for us Krazies, man, don't want no other crazies here. Guess we gonna have to teach you a lesson man, punish you real good."

Then, you know what happens? Don't mind tellin' ya, scared the shit outa me, man. This crazy guy, he looks around at us, then he smiles, real slow, like he's the one about to have fun and not us. Well, Rammer, he gets real pissed with this guy's grin and says, "First swing to me, fellers." Then he goes in with his club.

Man, that guy gutted Rammer. He moved so fast, I mean *fast*. One minute Rammer's there with his club so's the nails'll go right into the guy's skull, next the guy's ripped him from cock to throat, insides fallin' out, blood everywhere. You know what was worst? I think I saw the bastard pull somethin' out of Rammer and stuff it in his mouth.

One-eye goes in with his switchknife, this asshole tears his arm straight from the socket, starts to use it as a weapon. I saw him rip Jocko's head off, too.

That was when I chickened out, man. I ran, got to the alley, looked back. My buddies, they was all down. Bastard didn't pay me no heed, 'cos he was startin' to take them apart. And I don't think they was all dead, 'cos at least one of 'em was screamin', screamin' real loud. *Jesus, he was usin' his bare hands and teeth to take them apart.*

(A gigantic mirror graced one wall in the bathroom and Nugent looked in horror at his reflection. Where in the name of sweet God had all that dried blood come from, because he certainly didn't have any wounds. Suddenly his gut heaved and he staggered to the lavatory bowl, just making it before he spewed. He stared aghast at the reddish-brown mess his stomach had rejected, then he threw up again. His mouth and nostrils filled with the foul taste and odour of stale blood as spasm after spasm tore through him.

Nugent's physician examined him thoroughly, took a series of X-rays, asked a number of personal and pertinent questions. At the end of the session, the doctor was not sure that his patient was telling him the truth, that the man had vomited so much blood. Mr Nugent might have thought that he had done so, but the doctor doubted it.

"I can find nothing wrong physically. It's possibly some kind of psychosomatic illness. I'd like to refer you to a colleague of mine who understands more about these things.")

Interlude: Dreamplace

Nugent loped at a steady pace through the darkness, instinct carrying him over the lumpy and rock-strewn terrain without stumbling, helping him to avoid colliding with the tall trees which forested his habitat. All around and behind him he could sense his fellow pack members, companions whose loyalty and love were almost tangible in his new awareness. As he ran, he slitted his eyes against the light breeze blowing into his face, the breeze which carried the scent of fleeing prey ahead.

Nugent was in no great hurry to catch up with the prey. While the pack was driven by hunger to hunt, there remained a certain thrill in the chase which became anticlimactic when the quarry was eventually brought down.

He threw back his head and howled, howled to communicate with his mate, to communicate with the pack, howled as an expression of the sheer joy of living. Answering cries came from the pack, cries which were pitched at differing tones and levels to acknowledge position in the hierarchy.

Nugent came to a break in the tree-line, saw that the slope shallowed as it swept down to the valley far below. The moon-goddess dominated the crystal sky, her frosty light a welcome beacon for the pursuers.

Ahead, four or five hundred metres down the hillside, Nugent could see the victims, two of them, both man-creatures. He stopped momentarily and belled his triumph to the mountains. The other pack members, too, had stopped, their baying cries echoing his.

They stood awaiting his command, fierce grey animals with tongues lolling, panting breath steaming the night air. Nugent felt a rush of emotion such as he had never experienced in his life. He cried out again and leapt onwards, the other wolves close at his heels.

The man-things, male and female, must have realized that they were beaten, for they turned at bay, naked and helpless against the power of the ancient enemy, terror-riven faces illuminated by the icy and uncaring moon.

The man's face was that of Nugent himself, the woman's Marianna.

Nugent sprang at his alter ego, massive jaws clashing to tear away jugular and carotid. The rush of hot blood was wine to the beast, rich, intoxicating, life-giving.

Nugent stepped back, signalling to the pack that they could feast. As they jumped in to rend the helpless flesh, Nugent turned to stalk the woman …

★   ★   ★

(Previously, Nugent would have emerged from these nightmares in a state of gibbering terror. But after some weeks of therapy he was beginning to grasp why his sleeping mind played such dreadful pranks. He could understand the deep guilt of his subconscious.

There was something else, something he had not, probably would not, admit to Doctor Cudlipp. The dreams were becoming pleasurable, the chase, the kill, the piquancy of fresh warm blood, all were becoming things to be savoured. And Nugent was waking up with other lusts, renewed lusts …)

Item: Bloodlust

Doctor Cudlipp could well have afforded a suite of offices in one of the new blocks uptown, all glass and chrome, modern art and spindly, uncomfortable furniture. But he clung doggedly to a two-room office in the tired precinct where he had started out years before. The building was a gloomy old brownstone, shared with a sleazy gumshoe, two fortune tellers and a pornographer. It was as if Cudlipp was making a statement. "Hey, I'm successful and rich and so are my patients. I just don't need to prove it."

Many employees would have refused to work overtime in such a place. After dark, the streets outside became ill-lit, decaying canyons shunned by the wary. But Nancy Rhys lacked both imagination and a sense of caution. Besides, the returns for working late were worthwhile.

Only at one point during the evening had Nancy Rhys felt any apprehension. She was working in Doctor Cudlipp's office, which was dark save for an aura of light spilling onto the desk from his green-shaded banker's lamp. The door between the outer office and reception area, badly illuminated by an ancient lighting system, was ajar. Nancy had jumped when the thin bar of dull yellow extending across Cudlipp's floor was suddenly extinguished.

"Holy shit!" Calming herself with several deep breaths, she had gone into the outer office, had worked the switch several times. Either the damned bulb had gone or the old wiring was giving out. Even the stolid Nancy felt something oppressive in the impenetrable darkness. She also had a strange feeling that maybe she was no longer alone. Nancy was glad to get back to the doctor's desk and the friendly lamp-light.

Scattered on the desk were a large number of buff-coloured files marked "Confidential". Many of them were open, revealing dark, dark secrets. Nancy Rhys had been having a great time and now she picked up the doctor's telephone to share the fun with her friend Shirleen.

Nancy Rhys's presence in that place was a bad mistake. In fact, that whole day in Doctor Cudlipp's office had been a small series of misadventures which became one huge, tragic error.

Nancy Rhys should not have been placed in a position like this and normally the agency knew it. Unfortunately, the agency was using a stand-in day supervisor that morning. When the psychiatrist had telephoned asking for an emergency receptionist, only Nancy was available.

There was nothing wrong with Nancy's work, she was an efficient administrator. But she was a pry and a gossip.

Letitia, the doctor's regular nurse, had come into work determined not to let the incipient influenza beat her. For much of the morning she had worked in a desultory manner before giving in to her sickness. Almost her last action of the day was to answer a telephone call from a fairly new patient, Mr Smith.

Smith had asked for an evening appointment, his usual practice. Letitia had acknowledged the appointment but had failed to make a note of it. By the time she asked Cudlipp to excuse her, she was very ill and had forgotten all about Mr Smith.

When Nancy Rhys had arrived, the day's paperwork was well behind. Doctor Cudlipp had asked Nancy if she would mind staying on to finish up.

"I don't mind how late," he had instructed, "I'll clear it with your supervisor and pay for your over-time. Do a good job and I'll throw in a bonus, just between you and me."

Nancy Rhys needed the money and so she had jumped at the chance. The doctor gave her his keys, saying that they should be handed to the janitor when Nancy departed for the night.

Doctor Cudlipp left happily, unaware that he would never have to pay the bonus.

Recovering from her mild shock when the outer light had popped, Nancy became so engrossed with the files – "… such fun reading about this bunch of loonies …" she told Shirleen – that she failed to notice the passing of time. She continued to read the secrets of human despair and misery to Shirleen.

After a while, an odd noise distracted her.

"Anything wrong, honey?" asked Shirleen.

"I don't know, I thought I heard something out there … Hold the line, Shirleen." Nancy laid the handset aside, peered into the dark shadows surrounding her, futilely tried to see through the partly-open door into the outer office. She called out, "Hello, is anybody there?" The responding silence was stifling. Nancy tried again, more loudly, then shivered.

After a moment, she returned to her friend. "Hi, guess I'm imagining things. Shouldn't have read so many of these files. Now I've saved the best one for last, kid. Get this, the doctor's got a patient who thinks he's a wolf. Calls himself Smith, like who does he think he's kidding?" She listened with delight to Shirleen's shrieking laughter and tumbling words of disbelief. Nancy chuckled. "Yeah, that's right, a wolf."

Shirleen asked something. "Guess maybe he runs round howling at the moon, things like that," mused Nancy. Shirleen said something else and Nancy tittered. "I suppose he carries a poop-scoop."

Then, "Hey, I think I heard that noise again. Maybe there is somebody there. Could be the janitor. Better hang up, after all, the doctor's paying good rates. Call you later, honey.

"And hey, Shirleen, don't let the wolfman get you!" Still sniggering, she hung up.

And as she did so, Mr Smith partly stepped from the shadows. "Jesus! You scared me!" cried Nancy. And then she took a good look and realized she might have plenty of reason to be scared. There was something wrong with the man's indistinct shape. Maybe it was the odd fuzziness of his outline, or perhaps the way his shoulders hunched. And then there was the peculiar way his head thrust forward, as if he intended to sniff at her.

Nancy's breath caught in her throat. Then she tried to rationalize the situation. Maybe this guy wasn't a threat. Maybe this was some kind of sick joke. Yeah, that could be it, some kind of initiation prank to test the new girl on the block.

But there was something else very wrong, something about the man's eyes. In the dim light, those eyes were shining bright red. Nancy crammed knuckles into her mouth. People's eyes don't reflect light … do they?

Then the man smiled at her as he took a step forward, and Nancy began to weep. The smile was knowing, hungry, and marred by a thin line of drool depending from the bottom lip.

(The office door was jammed closed so tightly that Doctor Cudlipp had to summon the janitor to help him get it open. And when they had forced their way in, both men wished that the day hadn't even started.

The first thing they noticed was the charred smell, as if there had been a burning in the suite. In the middle of the floor was a metal waste-bin filled with burnt papers and the stiffer remnants of file covers.

Then their senses were assailed by the sight and slaughterhouse odour of the blood splashed all around the office, great gouts and pools on walls and floor and ceiling.

And finally, in Doctor Cudlipp's sanctum, they saw the human shambles which had been Nancy Rhys, a once-living being reduced to the slops of a butcher's tray. The very worst thing was the head, glued to the desk's top by a puddle of congealing blood. The face had been almost totally torn away, but the eyes were intact and they stared, mockingly, at the two men.

The janitor fainted and silent tears of anguish poured down Doctor Cudlipp's face.)

Item: Confession

Father Gálvez came through from the sacristy, being careful to secure the door behind him. Not even a church was safe now. The bad ones, they had no respect. He crossed the church, his progress making little noise save for the slight swish of his cassock's hem brushing against the stone flags. He paused in the presbytery to genuflect before the altar and make the sign of the cross.

Rising, the priest turned and looked down the nave towards the distant entrance which was barely visible in the dim illumination cast by the few low-powered light bulbs high in the vaulted ceiling. The air in the old church was thick with the mingled smell of candle-wax and polish and incense. Father Gálvez took a deep breath, enjoying the heady odours, to him a rich, olfactory wine.

As was common, the pews were empty, lending a hollowness to the church. Gálvez sighed. So few attended in this Godless age. Whereas once, in dead years past, the church was never quite empty, now it rarely saw a worshipper except for a handful of elderly parishioners on Sundays.

And yet despite this paucity, Gálvez was of the old school. The younger priests, the "moderns", would be out there with the street people, preaching their radical ideas and openly defying the Vatican. But he, Gálvez, maintained a punctilious adherence to the old and honoured routines.

Each evening at seven, he would occupy his stall in the confessional and wait for two full hours, reading his breviary with difficulty in the feeble glow of a small wall-lamp. When penitents did come, he heard the same so-called sins over and over in a variety of voices. Small, meaningless sins, petty tales of spite and jealousy and lust and weakness. How he wearied of them at times.

The priest smiled, a small, self-deprecating twitch of the lips. "Charity, Gálvez," he reminded himself as he walked to the far transept and took his seat in the confessional. Kissing his stole, he placed it around his shoulders and opened his prayer book. He prepared for a long, probably fruitless wait.

He must have dozed momentarily, for he was suddenly jerked awake by sounds of the other door closing and someone settling on the far side of the screen. Gálvez reached up and snapped out the light. The poor illumination from outside of the confessional revealed a black shadow pressing near to the screen.

"Father ... are you there, Father?" A man's voice, well-educated by the sound of it – odd in this neighbourhood – but low and hoarse. "I need help ..."

"Yes, my son, I'm here," Gálvez replied. The priest's appearance, stocky, swarthy, almond eyes and black hair heavily greyed at the temples, all proclaimed his Hispanic origins. But his voice, even when lowered and gentle, spoke harshly of the Lower East Side. "What is it you wish to tell me?"

"Father, I've done something so dreadful …" The other's voice trailed off, only to start again with hesitant words, as if the ritual was half-forgotten. "Bless me, Father, for I have sinned …

"It has been so many years since I last confessed, so many long years … years in which I thought I didn't need you. But now …" Gálvez heard a noise like a sob.

"Easy, my son," he soothed, "I have all the time that you need."

"I have sinned through the years, Father, many sins, some of them utterly vile sins." There was despair in the voice, and Gálvez felt a strong surge of pity. "I have no time to go through those sins," the hidden visitor continued, "Dammit, I've forgotten many of them, for my conscience is long dead. I guess that God will know of them, though. But now I carry a burden which I can't shed. I have taken a soul, and I've condemned that soul to restless wandering. And it's haunting me, Father, *it's haunting me to the point of insanity …*"

Father Gálvez made a small sign, an insignificant little gesture of the hand, as if the other could see him. "You have killed?"

"I … I think so. More than once, I think … but it's the soul, I cannot rid myself of the soul …"

"Whose was the soul which haunts you, my son?" the priest asked.

"The Indian warned me, he warned me … Whose soul, Father? Why, the wolf, the great, wonderful timber wolf which I destroyed in my lust for trophy."

"What is this you're saying?" demanded Gálvez. His voice was suddenly cold, compassion gone. "You are telling me that you are haunted by the soul of a wolf? Are you mocking me, man?"

"*No!*" Gálvez recognized the genuine anguish in the shouted protest. "I'm not mocking you. I need your help to rid me of this thing!"

"But animals do not have souls, my son."

"They do, Father, God knows that they do!"

The priest's voice became icy once more. "If you are Catholic, you will know Holy Mother Church's stance on this, that animals do not have souls. If you persist with this delusion, then I cannot help you."

"You must help me …" The other's voice now held a pleading note, almost a whine. "I tell you, Father, that the wolf has a soul and the soul cries for vengeance."

Gálvez frowned. "Have you considered seeking psychiatric help, my son?"

"I've tried that, damn you priest! It didn't work. And any way, I'm not mad. I may have said this thing is driving me to madness, but I'm not mad!"

"I didn't say you are mad. Disturbed, perhaps. Whatever is wrong with you, it seems to me to be a problem more for a doctor than a priest. If you have genuine sins to confess, I will hear you and give absolution if you are truly penitent. Other than that I can do nothing for you."

A stertorous breathing came from behind the screen, and below it another noise, like the grinding of teeth. And an unsure Father Gálvez thought that he heard a low growling sound.

"Go to a psychiatrist, my son," he urged, "My advice is offered in your best interests. I will pray for you, and God will help you."

"You fool, you holy idiot!" growled the other. There was a crashing noise as he kicked his way out of the confessional and then the priest's door was wrenched open. Father Gálvez started up, then gasped with shock as he saw what confronted him.

The priest's last thought – ironic in its certainty – was that God would not, could not help *him* …

(*An old woman came down the sidewalk towards All Souls, tottering slightly on chunky, varicosed legs. Mrs Jablonsky was ashamed, for that very afternoon she had reviled a neighbour, a poor silly woman of low intelligence who had meant no harm.*

Mrs Jablonsky had a soft heart and knew it would do her good to made reparation before Our Lord. It would be so comforting to see the good Father Gálvez …)

Item: Mating

The central heating in the apartment was kept high during the fall and winter, so high that Marianna habitually slept naked.

For some weeks now she had fallen out of the practice of locking her door at night, ever since noticing that Nugent was no longer behaving oddly, was no longer having the terrible dreams which made him cry out so hideously in the night.

Marianna's unclad form was sprawled face down on the counterpane on the midnight that Nugent came to her after such a long period of neglect. She was awakened by the weight of his body crushing down on top of her.

"Nugent, what the hell—"

"Quiet," he hissed, "Don't say anything."

Marianna became aware of the heat of a swelling penis thrusting against her. "Hey, Nugent," she purred, "what's come over you?" She tried to turn around, to welcome him with her arms.

"Don't move!" There was an odd, growling timbre to his voice, coupled with a note of urgency. "Stay as you are and keep quiet."

Marianna acquiesced, content to lie prone and let Nugent make all the play. She realized that unlike herself, the man was not fully naked. He was wearing some kind of robe, for she felt coarse fur caressing her skin as he moved about her. She began to purr and melted as fingers and tongue probed roughly at her private place, making her deeply moist.

Then Nugent lifted the woman's hips and took her savagely from behind, not making love but rutting. There was slight pain, but it was enjoyable and Marianna submitted to it. She felt only ecstasy and relief as the man's hardness pounded into her body. She yelled and sobbed aloud as Nugent brought her to orgasm once, twice, yet again. When the man climaxed, his cry was animal in its intensity.

He collapsed upon her, holding her to the bed. Gradually she relapsed into sleep.

(*Nugent opened his eyes slowly, aroused by the light which was shining in them. A full moon showed through the upper windows of the room, shedding illumination onto the dishevelled bed and onto Nugent's face. His eyes glinted redly and he felt a primitive urge to lift his head and bay to the silver orb.*

As he awakened more he became aware of Marianna's soft body lying beneath his. The pungent smell of woman-musk arose from her and Nugent could feel himself becoming aroused once more, but it was more than a sexual desire. There were other lusts, other passions, which overwhelmed him and took precedence over the urge to mate …)

Finale: Soul of the Wolf

Nugent came to, exhausted and stiff. He was curled up on the floor of his trophy room, almost naked. The room was not quite dark. Subdued early dawn light filtered through the fine drapes, providing some vision. The man raised his head with difficulty, feeling as much as seeing the artificial, disapproving glares of the beasts which he had killed. There was some kind of covering over him. He took a loose end in trembling fingers and stared at it.

It was the skin of the timber wolf, the head resting atop his own, forelegs draped and tied about his neck, the body fitting snugly to his back as if it belonged, the hind legs and tail falling down behind him.

Nugent struggled to hands and knees, rested there shaking his head, trying to get his thoughts into order. He recalled going to bed, overcome with the strange lethargy which was all too common now, maybe something to do with his medication. But no, he'd stopped taking that when he stopped going to Doctor Cudlipp. Why had he stopped going? He couldn't even remember that. So much eluded him now, so much …

Then there was something else, something to do with Marianna, what?

He remembered. He had gone to Marianna in the night and he had made love to her, had taken her with all the force and vigour which had once been his. But if he had slept with Marianna, then why did he end up here on the floor?

Still in a dazed state, Nugent crawled over to his desk and grasping the edge with both hands, hauled himself to his feet. There was a slight and unpleasant stickiness, either on his hands or on the edge of the desk.

Shuffling towards the door, Nugent found the switch and snapped the ceiling lights on. His hands and fingers were dyed with a partly dry, reddish mess which was also thick beneath his nails. Other stains blotched his torso and legs, while a glimpse in a polished silver wall-plate showed his face to be similarly smeared.

Darkening patches disfigured the floor at his feet. Trembling, Nugent opened the door and looked out into the hall. Mingled trails of drying drops and splashes meandered throughout the apartment.

With a feeling of sick horror in his heart, Nugent dashed up the stairway and flung open the door to Marianna's room, his hand leaping instinctively to flick on the light. He was unable to prevent himself from screaming when he saw the carnage.

Marianna, beautiful, vibrant, cold-hearted Marianna, was transformed into a shredded symphony in scarlet, an abstract canvas composed from gore and flesh and entrails.

Nugent threw back his head to scream a second time. Instead, the steadily rising croon of a wolf burst from his lips, filling the apartment with cold and lonely lamentation …

(*Nugent unlocked a weapons display case and selected the open razor, testing its keenness with the ball of his thumb. A bright pearl of blood oozed up.*

"*That'll do,*" *he muttered.*

He hurried into the bathroom and stood before the massive mirror. Regarding his reflection with sick loathing, he placed the edge of the razor beneath his left ear.

After a tentative jab or two, he pressed the blade home firmly and drew it swiftly to the right.)

Manly Wade Wellman

THE HAIRY ONES SHALL DANCE

Manly Wade Wellman (1903–1986) wrote more than seventy-five books and over two hundred short stories, many of which were published in the pulp magazines of the 1930s and '40s. He twice won the World Fantasy Award and some of the writer's best short fiction is collected in Who Fears the Devil? *(filmed in 1972),* Worse Things Waiting, Lonely Vigils *and* The Valley So Low.

The classic werewolf novella which follows was originally published over three issues of Weird Tales *in* January, February *and* March 1938 *under the pseudonym "Gans T. Field". One of the Virgil Finlay illustrations for the serial depicted Wellman (as Finlay imagined him) throwing a punch at the werewolf. The author didn't think it was a very good likeness, but then he and the artist had never met. Finlay gave the drawing to Wellman who, years later, passed it on to his friend Karl Edward Wagner.*

"The Hairy Ones Shall Dance" once again follows the exploits of occult investigator Judge Keith Hilary Pursuivant, whose adventures have previously appeared in both The Mammoth Book of Terror *and* The Mammoth Book of Vampires ...

Foreword

TO WHOM IT MAY CONCERN:

Few words are best, as Sir Philip Sidney once wrote in challenging an enemy. The present account will be accepted as a challenge by the vast army of skeptics of which I once made one. Therefore I write it brief and bald. If my story seems unsteady in spots, that is because the hand that writes it still quivers from my recent ordeal.

Shifting the metaphor from duello to military engagement, this is but the first gun of the bombardment. Even now sworn statements are being prepared by all others who survived the strange and, in some degree, unthinkable adventure I am recounting. After that, every great psychic investigator in the country, as well as some from Europe, will begin researches. I wish that my friends and brother-magicians, Houdini and Thurston, had lived to bear a hand in them.

I must apologize for the strong admixture of the personal element in my narrative. Some may feel that I err against good taste. My humble argument is that I was not merely an observer, but an actor, albeit a clumsy one, throughout the drama.

As to the setting forth of matters which many will call impossible, let me smile in advance. Things happen and have always happened, that defy the narrow science of test-tube and formula. I can only say again that I am writing the truth, and that my statement will be supported by my companions in the adventure.

Talbot Wills
November 15, 1937

I "Why must the burden of proof rest with the spirits?"

"You don't believe in psychic phenomena," said Doctor Otto Zoberg yet again, "because you *won't*."

This with studied kindness, sitting in the most comfortable chair of my hotel room. I, at thirty-four, silently hoped I would have his health and charm at fifty-four – he was so rugged for all his lean length, so well groomed for all his tweeds and beard and joined eyebrows, so articulate for all his accent. Doctor Zoberg quite apparently liked and admired me, and I felt guilty once more that I did not entirely return the compliment.

"I know that you are a stage magician—" he began afresh.

"I was once," I amended, a little sulkily. My early career had brought me considerable money and notice, but after the novelty of show business was worn off I had never rejoiced in it. Talboto the Mysterious – it had been impressive, but tawdry. Better to be Talbot Wills, lecturer and investigator in the field of exposing fraudulent mediums.

For six years I had known Doctor Otto Zoberg, the champion of spiritism and mediumism, as rival and companion. We had first met in debate under the auspices of the Society for Psychical Research in London. I, young enough for enthusiasm but also for carelessness, had been badly out-thought and out-talked. But afterward, Doctor Zoberg had praised my arguments and my delivery, and had graciously taken me out to a late supper. The following day, there arrived from him a present of helpful books and magazines. Our next platform duel found me in a position to get a little of my own back; and he, afterward, laughingly congratulated me on turning to account the material he had sent me. After that, we were public foemen and personal inseparables. Just now we were touring the United States, debating, giving exhibitions, visiting mediums. The night's program, before a Washington audience liberally laced with high officials, had ended in what we agreed was a draw; and here we were, squabbling good-naturedly afterward.

"Please, Doctor," I begged, offering him a cigarette, "save your charges of stubbornness for the theater."

He waved my case aside and bit the end from a villainous black cheroot. "I wouldn't say it, here or in public, if it weren't true, Talbot. Yet you sneer even at telepathy, and only half believe in mental suggestion. *Ach*, you are worse than Houdini."

"Houdini was absolutely sincere," I almost blazed, for I had known and worshipped that brilliant and kindly prince of conjurers and fraud-finders.

"*Ach*, to be sure, to be sure," nodded Zoberg over his blazing match. "I did not say he was not. Yet, he refused proof – the proof that he himself embodied. Houdini was a great mystic, a medium. His power for miracles he did not know himself."

I had heard that before, from Conan Doyle as well as Zoberg, but I made no comment. Zoberg continued:

"Perhaps Houdini was afraid – if anything could frighten so brave and wise a man it would assuredly come from within. And so he would not even listen to argument." He turned suddenly somber. "Perhaps he knew best, *ja*. But he was stubborn, and so are you."

"I don't think you can say that of me," I objected once more. The cheroot was alight now, and I kindled a cigarette to combat in some degree the gun-powdery fumes.

Teeth gleamed amiably through the beard, and Zoberg nodded again, in frank delight this time. "Oh, we have hopes of you, Wills, where we gave up Houdini."

He had never said that before, not so plainly at any rate. I smiled back. "I've always been willing to be shown. Give me a fool-proof, fake-proof, supernormal phenomenon, Doctor; let me convince myself; then I'll come gladly into the spiritist camp."

"*Ach*, so you always say!" he exploded, but without genuine wrath. "Why must the burden of proof rest with the spirits? How can you prove that they do not live and move and act? Study what Eddington has to say about that."

"For five years," I reminded him, "I have offered a prize of five thousand dollars to any medium whose spirit miracles I could not duplicate by honest sleight-of-hand."

He gestured with slim fingers, as though to push the words back into me. "That proves absolutely nothing, Wills. For all your skill, do you think that sleight-of-hand can be the only way? Is it even the best way?"

"I've unmasked famous mediums for years, at the rate of one a month," I flung back. "Unmasked them as the clumsiest of fakes."

"Because some are dishonest, are all dishonest?" he appealed. "What specific thing would convince you, my friend?"

I thought for a moment, gazing at him through the billows of smoke. Not a gray hair to him – and I, twenty years his junior, had six or eight at either temple. I went on to admire and even to envy that pointed trowel of beard, the sort of thing that I, a magician, might have cultivated once. Then I made my answer.

"I'd ask for a materialization, Doctor. An ectoplasmic apparition, visible and solid to touch – in an empty room with no curtains or closets, all entrances sealed by myself, the medium and witnesses shackled." He started to open his mouth, but I hurried to prevent him. "I know what you'll say – that I've seen a number of impressive ectoplasms. So I have, perhaps, but not one was scientifically and dispassionately controlled. No, Doctor, if I'm to be convinced, I must make the conditions and set the stage myself."

"And if the materialization was a complete success?"

"Then it would prove the claim to me – to the world. Materializations are the most important question in the whole field."

He looked long at me, narrowing his shrewd eyes beneath the dark single bar of his brows. "Wills," he said at length, "I hoped you would ask something like this."

"You did?"

"*Ja*. Because – first, can you spare a day or so?"

I replied guardedly, "I can, I believe. We have two weeks or more before the New Orleans date." I computed rapidly. "Yes, that's December 8. What have you got up your sleeve, Doctor?"

He grinned once more, with a great display of gleaming white teeth, and flung out his long arms. "My sleeves, you will observe, are empty!" he cried. "No trickery. But within five hours of where we sit – five hours by fast automobile – is a little town. And in that town there is a little medium. No, Wills, you have never seen or heard of her. It is only myself who found her by chance, who studied her long and prayerfully. Come with me, Wills – she will teach you how little you know and how much you can learn!"

II "You can almost hear the ghosts."

I have sat down with the purpose of writing out, plainly and even flatly, all that happened to me and to Doctor Otto Zoberg in our impromptu adventure at psychic investigation; yet, almost at the start, I find it necessary to be vague about the tiny town where that adventure ran its course. Zoberg began by refusing to tell me its name, and now my friends of various psychical research committees have asked me to hold my peace until they have finished certain examinations without benefit of yellow journals or prying politicians.

It is located, as Zoberg told me, within five hours by fast automobile of Washington. On the following morning, after a quick and early breakfast, we departed at seven o'clock in my sturdy coupé. I drove and Zoberg guided. In the turtle-back we had stowed bags, for the November sky had begun to boil up with dark, heavy clouds, and a storm might delay us.

On the way Zoberg talked a great deal, with his usual charm and animation. He scoffed at my skepticism and prophesied my conversion before another midnight.

"A hundred years ago, realists like yourself were ridiculing hypnotism," he chuckled. "They thought that it was a fantastic fake, like one of Edgar Poe's amusing tales, *ja*? And now it is a great science, for healing and comforting the world. A few years ago, the world scorned mental telepathy—"

"Hold on," I interrupted. "I'm none too convinced of it now."

"I said just that, last night. However, you think that there is some grain of truth to it. You would be a fool to laugh at the many experiments in clairvoyance carried on at Duke University."

"Yes, they are impressive," I admitted.

"They are tremendous, and by no means unique," he insisted. "Think of a number between one and ten," he said suddenly.

I gazed at my hands on the wheel, thought of a joking reply, then fell in with his mood.

"All right," I replied. "I'm thinking of a number. What is it?"

"It is seven," he cried out at once, then laughed heartily at the blank look on my face.

"Look here, that's a logical number for an average man to think of," I protested. "You relied on human nature, not telepathy."

He grinned and tweaked the end of his beard between manicured fingers. "Very good, Wills, try again. A color this time."

I paused a moment before replying, "All right, guess what it is."

He, too, hesitated, staring at me sidewise. "I think it is blue," he offered at length.

"Go to the head of the class," I grumbled. "I rather expected you to guess red – that's most obvious."

"But I was not guessing," he assured me. "A flash of blue came before my mind's eye. Come, let us try another time."

We continued the experiment for a while. Zoberg was not always correct, but he was surprisingly close in nearly every case. The most interesting results were with the names of persons, and Zoberg achieved some rather mystifying approximations. Thus, when I was thinking of the actor Boris Karloff, he gave me the name of the actor Bela Lugosi. Upon my thinking of Gilbert K. Chesterton, he named Chesterton's close friend Hilaire Belloc, and my concentration on George Bernard Shaw brought forth a shout of "Santa Claus." When I reiterated my charge of psychological trickery and besought him to teach me his method, he grew actually angry and did not speak for more than half an hour. Then he began to discuss our destination.

"A most amazing community," he pronounced. "It is old – one of the oldest inland towns of all America. Wait until you see the houses, my friend. You can almost hear the ghosts within them, in broad daylight. And their Devil's Croft, that is worth seeing, too."

"Their what?"

He shook his head, as though in despair. "And you set yourself up as an authority on occultism!" he sniffed. "Next you will admit that you have never heard of the Druids. A Devil's Croft, my dull young friend, used to be part of every English or Scots village. The good people would set aside a field for Satan, so that he would not take their own lands."

"And this settlement has such a place?"

"*Ja wohl*, a grove of the thickest timber ever seen in this over-civilized country, and hedged in to boot. I do not say that they believe, but it is civic property and protected by special order from trespassers."

"I'd like to visit that grove," I said.

"I pray you!" he cried, waving in protest. "Do not make us unwelcome."

* * *

We arrived shortly before noon. The little town rests in a circular hollow among high wooded hills, and there is not a really good road into it, for two or three miles around. After listening to Zoberg, I had expected something grotesque or forbidding, but I was disappointed. The houses were sturdy and modest, in some cases poor. The greater part of them made a close-huddled mass, like a herd of cattle threatened by wolves, with here and there an isolated dwelling like an adventuresome young fighting-bull. The streets were narrow, crooked and unpaved, and for once in this age I saw buggies and wagons out-numbering automobiles. The central square, with a two-story town hall of red brick and a hideous cast-iron war memorial, still boasted numerous hitching-rails, brown with age and smooth with use. There were few real signs of modern progress. For instance, the drug store was a shabby clapboard affair with "Pharmacy" painted upon its windows, and it sold only drugs, soda and tobacco; while the one hotel was low and rambling and bore the title "Luther Inn." I heard that the population was three hundred and fifty, but I am inclined to think it was closer to three hundred.

We drew up in front of the Luther Inn, and a group of roughly dressed men gazed at us with the somewhat hostile interrogation that often marks a rural American community at the approach of strangers. These men wore mail-order coasts of corduroy or suede – the air was growing nippier by the minute – and plow shoes or high laced boots under dungaree pants. All of them were of Celtic or Anglo-Saxon type.

"Hello!" cried Zoberg jovially. "I see you there, my friend Mr. Gird. How is your charming daughter?"

The man addressed took a step forward from the group on the porch. He was a raw-boned, grizzled native with pale, pouched eyes, and was a trifle better dressed than the others, in a rather ministerial coat of dark cloth and a wide black hat. He cleared his throat before replying.

"Hello, Doctor. Susan's well, thanks. What do you want of us?"

It was a definite challenge, that would repel or anger most men, but Zoberg was not to be denied. He scrambled out of the car and cordially shook the hand of the man he had called Mr.

Gird. Meanwhile he spoke in friendly fashion to one or two of the others.

"And here," he wound up, "is a very good friend of mine, Mr. Talbot Wills."

All eyes – and very unfriendly eyes they were, as a whole – turned upon me. I got out slowly, and at Zoberg's insistence shook hands with Gird. Finally the grizzled man came with us to the car.

"I promised you once," he said glumly to Zoberg, "that I would let you and Susan dig as deeply as you wanted to into this matter of spirits. I've often wished since that I hadn't, but my word was never broken yet. Come along with me; Susan is cooking dinner, and there'll be enough for all of us."

He got into the car with us, and as we drove out of the square and toward his house he conversed quietly with Zoberg and me.

"Yes," he answered one of my questions, "the houses are old, as you can see. Some of them have stood since the Revolutionary War with England, and our town's ordinances have stood longer than that. You aren't the first to be impressed, Mr. Wills. Ten years ago a certain millionaire came and said he wanted to endow us, so that we would stay as we are. He had a lot to say about native color and historical value. We told him that we would stay as we are without having to take money from him, or from anybody else for that matter."

Gird's home was large but low, all one storey, and of darkly painted clapboards over heavy timbers. The front door was hung on the most massive handwrought hinges. Gird knocked at it, and a slender, smallish girl opened to us.

She wore a woolen dress, as dark as her father's coat, with white at the neck and wrists. Her face, under masses of thunder-black hair, looked Oriental at first glance, what with high cheekbones and eyes set aslant; then I saw that her eyes were a bright gray like worn silver, and her skin rosy, with a firm chin and a generous mouth. The features were representatively Celtic, after all, and I wondered for perhaps the fiftieth time in my life if there was some sort of blood link between Scot and Mongol. Her hand, on the brass knob of the door, showed as slender and white as some evening flower.

"Susan," said Gird, "here's Doctor Zoberg. And this is his friend, Mr. Wills."

She smiled at Zoberg, then nodded to me, respectfully and rather shyly.

"My daughter," Gird finished the introduction. "Well, dinner must be ready."

She led us inside. The parlor was rather plainer than in most old-fashioned provincial houses, but it was comfortable enough. Much of its furniture would have delighted antique dealers, and one or two pieces would have impressed museum directors. The dining room beyond had plate-racks on the walls and a long table of dark wood, with high-backed chairs. We had some fried ham, biscuits, coffee and stewed fruit that must have been home-canned. Doctor Zoberg and Gird ate heartily, talking of local trifles, but Susan Gird hardly touched her food. I, watching her with stealthy admiration, forgot to take more than a few mouthfuls.

After the repast she carried out the dishes and we men returned to the parlor. Gird faced us.

"You're here for some more hocus-pocus?" he hazarded gruffly.

"For another séance," amended Zoberg, suave as ever.

"Doctor," said Gird, "I think this had better be the last time."

Zoberg held out a hand in pleading protest, but Gird thrust his own hands behind him and looked sternly stubborn. "It's not good for the girl," he announced definitely.

"But she is a great medium – greater than Eusapia Paladino, or Daniel Home," Zoberg argued earnestly. "She is an important figure in the psychic world, lost and wasted here in this backwater—"

"Please don't miscall our town," interrupted Gird. "Well, Doctor, I agree to a final séance, as you call it. But I'm going to be present."

Zoberg made a gesture as of refusal, but I sided with Gird.

"If this is to be my test, I want another witness," I told Zoberg.

"*Ach*! If it is a success, you will say that he helped to deceive."

"Not I. I'll arrange things so there will be no deception."

Both Zoberg and Gird stared at me. I wondered which of them was the more disdainful of my confidence.

Then Susan Gird joined us, and for once I wanted to speak of other subjects than the occult.

III "That thing isn't my daughter—"

It was Zoberg who suggested that I take Susan Gird for a relaxing drive in my car. I acclaimed the idea as a brilliant one, and she, thanking me quietly, put on an archaic-seeming cloak, black and heavy. We left her father and Zoberg talking idly and drove slowly through the town.

She pointed out to me the Devil's Croft of which I had heard from the doctor, and I saw it to be a grove of trees, closely and almost rankly set. It stood apart from the sparser timber on the hills, and around it stretched bare fields. Their emptiness suggested that all the capacity for life had been drained away and poured into that central clump. No road led near to it, and I was obliged to content myself by idling the car at a distance while we gazed and she talked.

"It's evergreen, of course," I said. "Cedar and a little juniper."

"Only in the hedge around it," Susan Gird informed me. "It was planted by the town council about ten years ago."

I stared. "But surely there's greenness in the center, too," I argued.

"Perhaps. They say that the leaves never fall, even in January."

I gazed at what appeared to be a little fluff of white mist above it, the whiter by contrast with the black clouds that lowered around the hill-tops. To my questions about the town council, Susan Gird told me some rather curious things about the government of the community. There were five councilmen, elected every year, and no mayor. Each of the five presided at a meeting in turn. Among the ordinances enforced by the council was one providing for support of the single church.

"I should think that such an ordinance could be set aside as illegal," I observed.

"I think it could," she agreed, "but nobody has ever wished to try."

The minister of the church, she continued, was invariably a member of the council. No such provision appeared on the town records, nor was it even urged as a "written law," but it had always been deferred to. The single peace officer of the town, she continued, was the duly elected constable. He was always commissioned as deputy sheriff by officials at the county seat, and his duties included census taking, tax collecting and similar matters. The only other officer with a state commission was the justice; and her father, John Gird, had held that post for the last six years.

"He's an attorney, then?" I suggested, but Susan Gird shook her head.

"The only attorney in this place is a retired judge, Keith Pursuivant," she informed me. "He came from some other part of the world, and he appears in town about once a month – lives out yonder past the Croft. As a matter of fact, an ordinary experience of law isn't enough for our peculiar little government."

She spoke of her fellow-townsmen as quiet, simple folk who were content for the most part to keep to themselves, and then, yielding to my earnest pleas, she told me something of herself.

The Gird family counted its descent from an original settler – though she was not exactly sure of when or how the settlement was made – and had borne a leading part in community affairs through more than two centuries. Her mother, who had died when Susan Gird was seven, had been a stranger; an "outlander" was the local term for such, and I think it is used in Devonshire, which may throw light on the original founders of the community. Apparently this woman had shown some tendencies toward psychic power, for she had several times prophesied coming events or told neighbors where to find lost things. She was well loved for her labors in caring for the sick, and indeed she had died from a fever contracted when tending the victims of an epidemic.

"Doctor Zoberg had known her," Susan Gird related. "He came here several years after her death, and seemed badly shaken when he heard what had happened. He and Father became good friends, and he has been kind to me, too. I remember his saying, the first time we met, that I looked like Mother and that it was apparent that I had inherited her spirit."

She had grown up and spent three years at a teachers' college, but left before graduation, refusing a position at a school so that she could keep house for her lonely father. Still idiotically mannerless, I mentioned the possibility of her marrying some young man of the town. She laughed musically.

"Why, I stopped thinking of marriage when I was fourteen!" she cried. Then, "Look, it's snowing."

So it was, and I thought it time to start for her home. We finished the drive on the best of terms, and when we reached her home in midafternoon, we were using first names.

Gird, I found, had capitulated to Doctor Zoberg's genial insistence. From disliking the thought of a séance, he had come to savor the prospect of witnessing it – Zoberg had always excluded him before. Gird had even picked up a metaphysical term or two from listening to the doctor, and with these he spiced his normally plain speech.

"This ectoplasm stuff sounds reasonable," he admitted. "If there is any such thing, there could be ghosts, couldn't there?"

Zoberg twinkled, and tilted his beard-spike forward. "You will find that Mr. Wills does not believe in ectoplasm."

"Nor do I believe that the production of ectoplasm would prove existence of a ghost," I added. "What do you say, Miss Susan?"

She smiled and shook her dark head. "To tell you the truth, I'm aware only dimly of what goes on during a séance."

"Most mediums say that," nodded Zoberg sagely.

As the sun set and the darkness came down, we prepared for the experiment.

The dining room was chosen, as the barest and quietest room in the house. First I made a thorough examination, poking into corners, tapping walls and handling furniture, to the accompaniment of jovial taunts from Zoberg. Then, to his further amusement, I produced from my grip a big lump of sealing-wax, and with this I sealed both the kitchen and parlor doors, stamping the wax with my signet ring. I also closed, latched and sealed the windows, on the sills of which little heaps of snow had begun to collect.

"You're kind of making sure, Mr. Wills," said Gird, lighting a patent carbide lamp.

"That's because I take this business seriously," I replied, and Zoberg clapped his hands in approval.

"Now," I went on, "off with your coats and vests, gentlemen."

Gird and Zoberg complied, and stood up in their shirt-sleeves. I searched and felt them both all over. Gird was a trifle bleak in manner, Zoberg gay and bright-faced. Neither had any concealed apparatus, I made sure. My next move was to set a chair against the parlor door, seal its legs to the floor, and instruct Gird to sit in it. He did so, and I produced a pair of handcuffs from my bag and shackled his left wrist to the arm of the chair.

"Capital!" cried Zoberg. "Do not be so sour, Mr. Gird. I would not trust handcuffs on Mr. Wills – he was once a magician and knows all the escape tricks."

"Your turn's coming, Doctor," I assured him.

Against the opposite wall and facing Gird's chair I set three more chairs, melting wax around their legs and stamping it. Then I dragged all other furniture far away, arranging it against the kitchen door. Finally I asked Susan to take the central chair of the three, seated Zoberg at her left hand and myself at her right. Beside me, on the floor, I set the carbide lamp.

"With your permission," I said, and produced more manacles. First I fastened Susan's left ankle to Zoberg's right, then her left wrist to his right. Zoberg's left wrist I chained to his chair, leaving him entirely helpless.

"What thick wrists you have!" I commented. "I never knew they were so sinewy."

"You never chained them before," he grinned.

With two more pairs of handcuffs I shackled my own left wrist and ankle to Susan on the right.

"Now we are ready," I pronounced.

"You've treated us like bank robbers," muttered Gird.

"No, no, do not blame Mr Wills," Zoberg defended me again. He looked anxiously at Susan. "Are you quite prepared, my dear?"

Her eyes met his for a long moment; then she closed them and nodded. I, bound to her, felt a relaxation of her entire body. After a moment she bowed her chin upon her breast.

"Let nobody talk," warned Zoberg softly. "I think that this will be a successful venture. Wills, the light."

With my free hand I turned it out.

All was intensely dark for a moment. Then, as my eyes adjusted themselves, the room seemed to lighten. I could see the deep gray rectangles of the windows, the snow at their bottoms, the blurred outline of the man in his chair across the floor from me, the form of Susan at my left hand. My ears, likewise sharpening, detected the girl's gentle breathing, as if she slept. Once or twice her right hand twitched, shaking my own arm in its manacle. It was as though she sought to attract my attention.

Before and a little beyond her, something pale and cloudy was making itself visible. Even as I fixed my gaze upon it, I heard something that sounded like a gusty panting. It might have been a tired dog or other beast. The pallid mist was changing shape and substance, too, and growing darker. It shifted against the dim light from the windows, and I had a momentary impression of something erect but misshapen – misshapen in an animal way. Was that a head? And were those pointed ears, or part of a headdress? I told myself determinedly that this was a clever illusion, successful despite my precautions.

It moved, and I heard a rattle upon the planks. Claws, or perhaps hobnails. Did not Gird wear heavy boots? Yet he was surely sitting in his chair; I saw something shift position at that point. The grotesque form had come before me, crouching or creeping.

Despite my self-assurance that this was a trick, I could not govern the chill that swept over me. The thing had come to a halt close to me, was lifting itself as a hound that paws its master's knees. I was aware of an odor, strange and disagreeable, like the wind from a great beast's cage. Then the paws were upon my lap – indeed, they were not paws. I felt them grip my legs, with fingers and opposable thumbs. A sniffing muzzle thrust almost into my face, and upon its black snout a dim, wet gleam was manifest.

Then Gird, from his seat across the room, screamed hoarsely. "That thing isn't my daughter—"

In the time it took him to rip out those five words, the huddled monster at my knees whirled back and away from me, reared for a trice like a deformed giant, and leaped across the intervening space upon him. I saw that Gird had tried to rise, his chained wrist hampering him. Then his voice broke in the midst of what he was trying to say; he made a choking sound and the thing emitted a barking growl.

Tearing loose from its wax fastenings, the chair fell upon its side. There was a struggle and a clatter, and Gird squealed like a rabbit in a trap. The attacker fell away from him toward us.

It was all over before one might ask what it was about.

IV "I don't know what killed him."

Just when I got up I do not remember, but I was on my feet as the grapplers separated. Without thinking of danger – and surely danger was there in the room – I might have rushed forward; but Susan Gird, lying limp in her chair, hampered me in our mutual shackles. Standing where I was, then, I pawed in my pocket for something I had not mentioned to her or to Zoberg; an electric torch.

It fitted itself into my hand, a compact little cylinder, and I whipped it out with my finger on the switch. A cone of white light spurted across the room, making a pool about and upon the motionless form of Gird. He lay crumpled on one side, his back toward us, and a smudge of black wetness was widening about his slack head and shoulders.

With the beam I swiftly quartered the room, probing it into every corner and shadowed nook. The creature that had attacked Gird had utterly vanished. Susan Gird now gave a soft moan, like a dreamer of dreadful things. I flashed my light her way.

It flooded her face and she quivered under the impact of the glare, but did not open her eyes. Beyond her I saw Zoberg, doubled forward in his bonds. He was staring blackly at the form of Gird, his eyes protruding and his clenched teeth showing through his beard.

"Doctor Zoberg!" I shouted at him, and his face jerked nervously toward me. It was fairly cross-hatched with tense lines, and as white as fresh pipe-clay. He tried to say something, but his voice would not command itself.

Dropping the torch upon the floor, I next dug keys from my pocket and with trembling haste unlocked the irons from Susan Gird's wrist and ankle on my side. Then, stepping hurriedly to Zoberg, I made him sit up and freed him as speedily as possible. Finally I returned, found my torch again and stepped across to Gird.

My first glance at close quarters was enough; he was stone-dead, with his throat torn brutally out. His cheeks, too, were ripped in parallel gashes, as though by the grasp of claws or nails. Radiance suddenly glowed behind me, and Zoberg moved forward, holding up the carbide lamp.

"I found this beside your chair," he told me unsteadily. "I found a match and lighted it." He looked down at Gird, and his lips twitched, as though he would be hysterical.

"Steady, Doctor," I cautioned him sharply, and took the lamp from him. "See what you can do for Gird."

He stooped slowly, as though he had grown old. I stepped to one side, putting the lamp on the table. Zoberg spoke again:

"It is absolutely no use, Wills. We can do nothing. Gird has been killed."

I had turned my attention to the girl. She still sagged in her chair, breathing deeply and rhythmically as if in untroubled slumber.

"Susan," I called her. "Susan!"

She did not stir, and Doctor Zoberg came back to where I bent above her. "Susan," he whispered penetratingly, "wake up, child."

Her eyes unveiled themselves slowly, and looked up at us. "What—" she began drowsily.

"Prepare yourself," I cautioned her quickly. "Something has happened to your father."

She stared across at Gird's body, and then she screamed, tremulously and long. Zoberg caught her in his arms, and she swayed and shuddered against their supporting circle. From her own wrists my irons still dangled, and they clanked as she wrung her hands in aimless distraction.

Going to the dead man once more, I unchained him from the chair and turned him upon his back. Susan's black cloak lay upon one of the other chairs, and I picked it up and spread it above him. Then I went to each door in turn, and to the windows.

"The seals are unbroken," I reported. "There isn't a space through which even a mouse could slip in or out. Yet—"

"I did it!" wailed Susan suddenly. "Oh, my God, what dreadful thing came out of me to murder my father!"

I unfastened the parlour door and opened it. Almost at the same time a loud knock sounded from the front of the house.

Zoberg lifted his head, nodding to me across Susan's trembling shoulder. His arms were still clasped around her, and I could not help but notice that they seemed thin and ineffectual now. When I had chained them, I had wondered at their steely cording. Had this awful calamity drained him of strength?

"Go," he said hoarsely. "See who it is."

I went. Opening the front door, I came face to face with a tall, angular silhouette in a slouch hat with snow on the brim.

"Who are you?" I jerked out, startled.

"O'Bryant," boomed back an organ-deep bass. "What's the fuss here?"

"Well—" I began, then hesitated.

"Stranger in town, ain't you?" was the next question. "I saw you when you stopped at the Luther Inn. I'm O'Bryant – the constable."

He strode across the door-sill, peered about him in the dark, and then slouched into the lighted dining room. Following, I made him out as a stern, roughly dressed man of forty or so, with a lean face made strong by a salient chin and a similar nose. His light blue eyes studied the still form of John Gird, and he stooped to draw away the cloak. Susan gave another agonized cry, and I heard Zoberg gasp as if deeply shocked. The constable, too, flinched and replaced the cloak more quickly than he had taken it up.

"Who done that?" he barked at me.

Again I found it hard to answer. Constable O'Bryant sniffed suspiciously at each of us in turn, took up the lamp and herded us into the parlour. There he made us take seats.

"I want to know everything about this business," he said harshly. "You," he flung at me, "you seem to be the closest to sensible. Give me the story, and don't leave out a single bit of it."

Thus commanded, I made shift to describe the séance and what had led up to it. I was as uneasy as most innocent people are when unexpectedly questioned by peace officers. O'Bryant interrupted twice with a guttural "Huh!" and once with a credulous whistle.

"And this killing happened in the dark?" he asked when I had finished. "Well, which of you dressed up like a devil and done it?"

Susan whimpered and bowed her head. Zoberg, outraged, sprang to his feet.

"It was a creature from another world," he protested angrily. "None of us had a reason to kill Mr Gird."

O'Bryant emitted a sharp, equine laugh. "Don't go to tell me any ghost stories, Doctor Zoberg. We folks have heard a lot about the hocus-pocus you've pulled off here from time to time. Looks like it might have been to cover up some kind of rough stuff."

"How could it be?" demanded Zoberg. "Look here, Constable, these handcuffs." He held out one pair of them. "We were all confined with them, fastened to chairs that were sealed to the floor. Mr Gird was also chained, and his chair made fast out of our reach. Go into the next room and look for yourself."

"Let me see them irons," grunted O'Bryant, snatching them.

He turned them over and over in his hands, snapped them shut, tugged and pressed, then held out a hand for my keys. Unlocking the cuffs, he peered into the clamping mechanism.

"These are regulation bracelets," he pronounced. "You were all chained up, then?"

"We were," replied Zoberg, and both Susan and I nodded.

Into the constable's blue eyes came a sudden shrewd light. "I guess you must have been, at that. But did you stay that way?" He whipped suddenly around, bending above my chair to fix his gaze upon me. "How about you, Mr Wills?"

"Of course we stayed that way," I replied.

"Yeh? Look here, ain't you a professional magician?"

"How did you know that?" I asked.

He grinned widely and without warmth. "The whole town's been talking about you, Mr Wills. A stranger can't be here all day without his whole record coming out." The grin vanished. "You're a magician, all right, and you can get out of handcuffs. Ain't that so?"

"Of course it's so," Zoberg answered for me. "But why should that mean that my friend has killed Mr Gird?"

O'Bryant wagged his head in triumph. "That's what we'll find out later. Right now it adds up very simple. Gird was killed, in a room that was all sealed up. Three other folks was in with him, all handcuffed to their chairs. Which of them got loose without the others catching on?" He nodded brightly at me, as if in answer to his own question.

Zoberg gave me a brief, penetrating glance, then seemed to shrivel up in his own chair. He looked almost as exhausted as Susan. I, too, was feeling near to collapse.

"You want to own up, Mr Wills?" invited O'Bryant.

"I certainly do not," I snapped at him. "You've got the wrong man."

"I thought," he made answer, as though catching me in a damaging admission, "that it was a devil, not a man, who killed Gird."

I shook my head. "I don't know what killed him."

"Maybe you'll remember after a while." He turned toward the door. "You come along with me. I'm going to lock you up."

I rose with a sigh of resignation, but paused for a moment to address Zoberg. "Get hold of yourself," I urged him. "Get somebody in here to look after Miss Susan, and then clarify in your mind what happened. You can help me prove that it wasn't I."

Zoberg nodded very wearily, but did not look up.

"Don't neither of you go into that room where the body is," O'Bryant warned them. "Mr Wills, get your coat and hat."

I did so, and we left the house. The snow was inches deep and still falling. O'Bryant led me across the street and knocked on the door of a peak-roofed house. A swarthy little man opened to us.

"There's been a murder, Jim," said O'Bryant importantly. "Over at Gird's. You're deputized – go and keep watch. Better take the missus along, to look after Susan. She's bad cut up about it."

We left the new deputy in charge and walked down the street, then turned into the square. Two or three men standing in front of the "Pharmacy" stared curiously, then whispered as we passed. Another figure paused to give me a searching glance. I was not too stunned to be irritated.

"Who are those?" I asked the constable.

"Town fellows," he informed me. "They're mighty interested to see what a killer looks like."

"How do they know about the case?" I almost groaned.

He achieved his short, hard laugh.

"Didn't I say that news travels fast in a town like this? Half the folks are talking about the killing this minute."

"You'll find you made a mistake," I assured him.

"If I have, I'll beg your pardon handsome. Meanwhile, I'll do my duty."

We were at the red brick town hall by now. At O'Bryant's side I mounted the granite steps and waited while he unlocked the big double door with a key the size of a can-opener.

"We're a kind of small town," he observed, half apologetically, "but there's a cell upstairs for you. Take off your hat and overcoat – you're staying inside till further notice."

V "They want to take the law into their own hands"

The cell was an upper room of the town hall, with a heavy wooden door and a single tiny window. The walls were of bare, unplastered brick, the floor of concrete and the ceiling of whitewashed planks. An oil lamp burned in a bracket. The only furniture was an iron bunk hinged to the wall just below the window, a wire-bound straight chair and an unpainted table. On top of this last stood a bowl and pitcher, with playing-cards scattered around them.

Constable O'Bryant locked me in and peered through a small grating in the door. He was all nose and eyes and wide lips, like a sardonic Punchinello.

"Look here," I addressed him suddenly, for the first time controlling my frayed nerves; "I want a lawyer."

"There ain't no lawyer in town," he boomed sourly.

"Isn't there a Judge Pursuivant in the neighborhood?" I asked, remembering something that Susan had told me.

"He don't practise law," O'Bryant grumbled, and his beaked face slid out of sight.

I turned to the table, idly gathered up the cards into a pack and shuffled them. To steady my still shaky fingers, I produced a few simple sleight-of-hand effects, palming of aces, making a king rise to the top, and springing the pack accordion-wise from one hand to the other.

"I'd sure hate to play poker with you," volunteered O'Bryant, who had come again to gaze at me.

I crossed to the grating and looked through at him. "You've got the wrong man," I said once more. "Even if I were guilty, you couldn't keep me from talking to a lawyer."

"Well, I'm doing it, ain't I?" he taunted me. "You wait until tomorrow and we'll go to the county seat. The sheriff can do whatever he wants to about a lawyer for you."

He ceased talking and listened. I heard the sound, too – a hoarse, dull murmur as of coal in a chute, or a distant, lowing herd of troubled cattle.

"What's that?" I asked him.

O'Bryant, better able to hear in the corridor, cocked his lean head for a moment. Then he cleared his throat. "Sounds like a lot of people talking, out in the square," he replied. "I wonder—"

He broke off quickly and walked away. The murmur was growing. I, pressing close to the grating to follow the constable with my eyes, saw that his shoulders were squared and his hanging fists doubled, as though he were suddenly aware of a lurking danger.

He reached the head of the stairs and clumped down, out of my sight. I turned back to the cell, walked to the bunk and, stepping upon it, raised the window. To the outside of the wooden frame two flat straps of iron had been securely bolted to act as bars. To these I clung as I peered out.

I was looking from the rear of the hall toward the center of the square, with the war memorial and the far line of shops and houses seen dimly through a thick curtain of falling snow. Something dark moved closer to the wall beneath, and I heard a cry, as if of menace.

"I see his head in the window!" bawled a voice, and more cries greeted this statement. A moment later a heavy missile hit the wall close to the frame.

I dropped back from the window and went once more to the grating of the door. Through it I saw O'Bryant coming back, accompanied by several men. They came close and peered through at me.

"Let me out," I urged. "That's a mob out there."

O'Bryant nodded dolefully. "Nothing like this ever happened here before," he said, as if he were responsible for the town's whole history of violence. "They act like they want to take the law into their own hands."

A short, fat man spoke at his elbow. "We're members of the town council, Mr Wills. We heard that some of the citizens were getting ugly. We came here to look after you. We promise full protection."

"Amen," intoned a thinner specimen, whom I guessed to be the preacher.

"There are only half a dozen of you," I pointed out. "Is that enough to guard me from a violent mob?"

As if to lend significance to my question, from below and in front of the building came a great shout, compounded of many voices. Then a loud pounding echoed through the corridor, like a bludgeon on stout panels.

"You locked the door, Constable?" asked the short man.

"Sure I did," nodded O'Bryant.

A perfect rain of buffets sounded from below, then a heavy impact upon the front door of the hall. I could hear the hinges creak.

"They're trying to break the door down," whispered one of the council.

The short man turned resolutely on his heel. "There's a window at the landing of the stairs," he said. "Let's go and try to talk to them from that."

The whole party followed him away, and I could hear their feet on the stairs, then the lifting of a heavy window-sash. A loud and prolonged yelling came to my ears, as if the gathering outside had sighted and recognized a line of heads on the sill above them.

"Fellow citizens!" called the stout man's voice, but before he could go on a chorus of cries and hoots drowned him out. I could hear more thumps and surging shoves at the creaking door.

Escape I must. I whipped around and fairly ran to the bunk, mounting it second time for a peep from my window. Nobody was visible below; apparently those I had seen previously had run to the front of the hall, there to hear the bellowings of the officials and take a hand in forcing the door.

Once again I dropped to the floor and began to tug at the fastenings of the bunk. It was an open oblong of metal, a stout frame of rods strung with springy wire netting. It could be folded upward against the wall and held with a catch, or dropped down with two lengths of chain to keep it horizontal. I dragged the mattress and blankets from it, then began a close examination of the chains. They were stoutly made, but the screw-plates that held them to the brick wall might be loosened. Clutching one chain with both my hands, I tugged with all my might, a foot braced against the wall. A straining heave, and it came loose.

At the same moment an explosion echoed through the corridor at my back, and more shouts rang through the air. Either O'Bryant or the mob had begun to shoot. Then a rending crash shook the building, and I heard one of the councilmen shouting: "Another like that and the door will be down!"

His words inspired additional speed within me. I took the loose end of the chain in my hand. Its links were of twisted iron, and the final one had been sawed through to admit the loop of the screw-plate, then clamped tight again. But my frantic tugging had widened this narrow cut once more, and quickly I freed it from the dangling plate. Then, folding the bunk against the wall, I drew the chain upward. It would just reach to the window – that open link would hook around one of the flat bars.

The noise of breakage rang louder in the front of the building. Once more I heard the voice of the short councilman: "I command you all to go home, before Constable O'Bryant fires on you again!"

"We got guns, too!" came back a defiant shriek, and in proof of this statement came a rattle of shots. I heard an agonized moan, and the voice of the minister: "Are you hit?"

"In the shoulder," was O'Bryant's deep, savage reply.

My chain fast to the bar, I pulled back and down on the edge of the bunk. It gave some leverage, but not enough – the bar was fastened too solidly. Desperate, I clambered upon the iron framework. Gaining the sill, I moved sidewise, then turned and braced my back against the wall. With my feet against the edge of the bunk, I thrust it away with all the strength in both my legs. A creak and a ripping sound, and the bar pulled slowly out from its bolts.

But a roar and thunder of feet told me that the throng outside had gained entrance to the hall at last.

I heard a last futile flurry of protesting cries from the councilmen as the steps echoed with the charge of many heavy boots. I waited no longer, but swung myself to the sill and wriggled through the narrow space where the bar had come out. A lapel of my jacket tore against the frame, but I made it. Clinging by the other bar, I made out at my side a narrow band of perpendicular darkness against the wall, and clutched at it. It was a tin drainpipe, by the feel of it.

An attack was being made upon the door of the cell. The wood splintered before a torrent of blows, and I heard people pushing in.

"He's gone!" yelled a rough voice, and, a moment later: "Hey, look at the window!"

I had hold of the drainpipe, and gave it my entire weight. Next instant it had torn loose from its flimsy supports and bent sickeningly outward. Yet it did not let me down at once, acting rather as a slender sapling to the top of which an adventuresome boy has sprung. Still holding to it, I fell sprawling in the snow twenty feet beneath the window I had quitted. Somebody shouted from above and a gun spoke.

"Get him!" screamed many voices. "Get him, you down below!"

But I was up and running for my life. The snow-filled square seemed to whip away beneath my feet. Dodging around the war memorial, I came face to face with somebody in a bearskin coat. He shouted for me to halt, in the reedy voice of an ungrown lad, and the fierce-set face that shoved at me had surely never felt a razor. But I, who dared not be merciful even to so untried an enemy, struck with both fists even as I hurtled against him. He whimpered and dropped, and I, springing over his falling body, dashed on.

A wind was rising, and it bore to me the howls of my pursuers from the direction of the hall. Two or three more guns went off, and one bullet whickered over my head. By then I had reached the far side of the square, hurried across the street and up an alley. The snow, still falling densely, served to baffle the men who ran shouting in my wake. Too, nearly everyone who had been on the streets had gone to the front of the hall, and except for the boy at the memorial none offered to turn me back.

I came out upon a street beyond the square, quiet and ill-lit. Along this way, I remembered, I could approach the Gird home, where my automobile was parked. Once at the wheel, I could drive to the county seat and demand protection from the sheriff. But, as I came cautiously near the place and could see through the blizzard the outline of the car, I heard loud voices. A part of the mob had divined my intent and had branched off to meet me.

I ran down a side street, but they had seen me. "There he is!" they shrieked at one another. "Plug him!" Bullets struck the wall of a house as I fled past it, and the owner, springing to the door with an angry protest, joined the chase a moment later.

I was panting and staggering by now, and so were most of my pursuers. Only three or four, lean young athletes, were gaining and coming even close to my heels. With wretched determination I maintained my pace, winning free of the close-set houses of the town, wriggling between the rails of a fence and striking off through the drifting snow of a field.

"Hey, he's heading for the Croft!" someone was wheezing, not far behind.

"Let him go in," growled another runner. "He'll wish he hadn't."

Yet again someone fired, and yet again the bullet went wide of me; moving swiftly, and half veiled by the dark and the wind-tossed snowfall, I was a bad target that night. And, lifting my head, I saw indeed the dense timber of the Devil's Croft, its tops seeming to toss and fall like the black waves of a high-pent sea.

It was an inspiration, helped by the shouts of the mob. Nobody went into that grove – avoidance of it had become a community habit, almost a community instinct. Even if my enemies paused only temporarily I could shelter well among the trunks, catch my breath, perhaps hide indefinitely. And surely Zoberg would be recovered, would back up my protest of innocence. With two words for it, the fantasy would not seem so ridiculous. All this I sorted over in my mind as I ran toward the Devil's Croft.

Another rail fence rose in my way. I feared for a moment that it would baffle me, so fast and far had I run and so greatly drained away was my strength. Yet I scrambled over somehow, slipped and fell beyond, got up and ran crookedly on. The trees were close now. Closer. Within a dozen yards. Behind me I heard oaths and warning exclamations. The pursuit was ceasing at last.

I found myself against close-set evergreens; that would be the hedge of which Susan Gird had told me. Pushing between and through the interlaced branches, I hurried on for five or six steps, cannoned from a big tree-trunk, went sprawling, lifted myself for another brief run and then, with my legs like strips of paper, dropped once more. I crept forward on hands and knees. Finally I collapsed upon my face. The weight of all I had endured – the séance, the horrible death of John Gird, my arrest, my breaking from the cell and my wild run for life – overwhelmed me as I lay.

Thus I must lie, I told myself hazily, until they came and caught me. I heard, or fancied I heard, movement near by, then a trilling whistle. A signal? It sounded like the song of a little frog. Odd thought in this blizzard. I was thinking foolishly of frogs, while I sprawled face down in the snow.

But where was the snow?

There was damp underneath, but it was warm damp, like that of a riverside in July. In my nostrils was a smell of green life, the smell of parks and hot-houses. My fists closed upon something.

Two handfuls of soft, crisp moss!

I rose to my elbows. A white flower bobbed and swayed before my nose, shedding perfume upon me.

Far away, as though in another world, I heard the rising of the wind that was beating the snow into great drifts – but that was outside the Devil's Croft.

VI "Eyes of fire!"

It proves something for human habit and narcotic-dependence that my first action upon rising was to pull out a cigarette and light it.

The match flared briefly upon rich greenness. I might have been in a subtropical swamp. Then the little flame winked out and the only glow was the tip of my cigarette. I gazed upward for a glimpse of the sky, but found only darkness. Leafy branches made a roof over me. My brow felt damp. It was sweat – warm sweat.

I held the coal of the cigarette to my wrist-watch. It seemed to have stopped, and I lifted it to my ear. No ticking – undoubtedly I had jammed it into silence, perhaps at the séance, perhaps during my escape from prison and the mob. The hands pointed to eighteen minutes past eight, and it was certainly much later than that. I wished for the electric torch that I had dropped in the dining room at Gird's, then was glad I had not brought it to flash my position to possible watchers outside the grove.

Yet the tight cedar hedge and the inner belts of trees and bushes, richly foliaged as they must be, would certainly hide me and any light I might make. I felt considerably stronger in body and will by now, and made shift to walk gropingly toward the center of the timber-clump. Once, stooping to finger the ground on which I walked, I felt not only moss but soft grass. Again, a hanging vine dragged across my face. It was wet, as if from condensed mist, and it bore sweet flowers that showed dimly like little pallid trumpets in the dark.

The frog-like chirping that I had heard when first I fell had been going on without cessation. It was much nearer now, and when I turned in its direction, I saw a little glimmer of water. Two more careful steps, and my foot sank into wet, warm mud. I stooped and put a hand into a tiny stream, almost as warm as the air. The frog, whose home I was disturbing, fell silent once more.

I struck a match, hoping to see a way across. The stream was not more than three feet in width, and it flowed slowly from the interior of the grove. In that direction hung low mists, through which broad leaves gleamed wetly. On my side its brink was fairly clear, but on the other grew lush, dripping bushes. I felt in the stream once more, and found it was little more than a finger deep. Then, holding the end of the match in my fingers, I stooped as low as possible, to see what I could of the nature of the ground beneath the bushes.

The small beam carried far, and I let myself think of Shakespeare's philosophy anent the candle and the good deed in a naughty world. Then philosophy and Shakespeare flew from my mind, for I saw beneath the bushes the feet of – of what stood behind them.

They were two in number, those feet; but not even at first glimpse did I think they were human. I had an impression of round pedestals and calfless shanks, dark and hairy. They moved as I looked, moved cautiously closer, as if their owner was equally anxious to see me. I dropped the match into the stream and sprang up and back.

No pursuer from the town would have feet like that.

My heart began to pound as it had never pounded during my race for life. I clutched at the low limb of a tree, hoping to tear it loose for a possible weapon of defense; the wood was rotten, and almost crumpled in my grasp.

"Who's there?" I challenged, but most unsteadily and without much menace in my voice. For answer the bushes rustled yet again, and something blacker than they showed itself among them.

I cannot be ashamed to say that I retreated again, farther this time; let him who has had a like experience decide whether to blame me. Feeling my way among the trees, I put several stout stems between me and that lurker by the waterside. They would not fence it off, but might baffle it for a moment. Meanwhile, I heard the water splash. It was wading cautiously through – it was going to follow me.

I found myself standing in a sort of lane, and did not bother until later to wonder how a lane could exist in that grove where no man ever walked. It was a welcome avenue of flight to me, and I went along it at a swift, crouching run. The footing, as everywhere, was damp and mossy, and I made very little noise. Not so my unchancy companion of the brook, for I heard a heavy body crashing among twigs and branches to one side. I began to ask myself, as I hurried, what the beast could be – for I was sure that it was a beast. A dog from some farmhouse, that did not know or understand the law against entering the Devil's Croft? That I had seen only two feet did not preclude two more, I now assured myself, and I would have welcomed a big, friendly dog. Yet I did not know, that this one was friendly, and could not bid myself to stop and see.

The lane wound suddenly to the right, and then into a clearing.

Here, too, the branches overhead kept out the snow and the light, but things were visible ever so slightly. I stood as if in a room, earth-floored, trunk-walled, leaf-thatched. And I paused for a breath – it was more damply warm than ever. With that breath came some strange new serenity of spirit, even an amused self-mockery. What had I seen and heard, indeed? I had come into the grove after a terrific hour or so of danger and exertion, and my mind had at once busied itself in building grotesque dangers where no dangers could be. Have another smoke, I said to myself, and get hold of your imagination; already that pursuit-noise you fancied has gone. Alone in the clearing and the dark, I smiled as though to mock myself back into self-confidence. Even this little patch of summer night into which I had blundered from the heart of the blizzard – even it had some good and probably simple explanation. I fished out a cigarette and struck a light.

At that moment I was facing the bosky tunnel from which I had emerged into the open space. My matchlight struck two sparks in that tunnel, two sparks that were pushing stealthily toward me. Eyes of fire!

Cigarette and match fell from my hands. For one wild half-instant I thought of flight, then knew with a throat-stopping certainty that I must not turn my back on this thing. I planted my feet and clenched my fists.

"Who's there?" I cried, as once before at the side of the brook.

This time I had an answer. It was a hoarse, deep-chested rumble, it might have been a growl or an oath. And a shadow stole out from the lane, straightening up almost within reach of me.

I had seen that silhouette before, misshapen and point-eared, in the dining room of John Gird.

VII "Had the thing been so hairy?"

It did not charge at once, or I might have been killed then, like John Gird, and the writing of this account left to another hand. While it closed cautiously in, I was able to set myself for defense. I also made out some of its details, and hysterically imagined more.

Its hunched back and narrow shoulders gave nothing of weakness to its appearance, suggesting rather an inhuman plenitude of bone and muscle behind. At first it was crouched, as if on all-fours, but then it reared. For all its legs were bent, its great length of body made it considerably taller than I. Upper limbs – I hesitate at calling them arms – sparred questingly at me.

I moved a stride backward, but kept my face to the enemy.

"You killed Gird!" I accused it, in a voice steady enough but rather strained and shrill. "Come on and kill me! I promise you a damned hard bargain of it."

The creature shrank away in turn, as though it understood the words and was momentarily daunted by them. Its head, which

I could not make out, sank low before those crooked shoulders and swayed rhythmically like the head of a snake before striking. The rush was coming, and I knew it.

"Come on!" I dared it again. "What are you waiting for? I'm not chained down, like Gird. I'll give you a devil of a fight."

I had my fists up and I feinted, boxerwise, with a little weaving jerk of the knees. The blot of blackness started violently, ripped out a snarl from somewhere inside it, and sprang at me.

I had an impression of paws flung out and a head twisted sidewise, with long teeth bared to snap at my throat. Probably it meant to clutch my shoulders with its fingers – it had them, I had felt them on my knee at the séance. But I had planned my own campaign in those tense seconds. I slid my left foot forward as the enemy lunged, and my left fist drove for the muzzle. My knuckles barked against the huge, inhuman teeth, and I brought over a roundabout right, with shoulder and hip driving in back of it. The head, slanted as it was, received this right fist high on the brow. I felt the impact of solid bone, and the body floundered away to my left. I broke ground right, turned and raised my hands as before.

"Want any more of the same?" I taunted it, as I would a human antagonist after scoring.

The failure of its attack had been only temporary. My blows had set it off balance, but could hardly have been decisive. I heard a coughing snort, as though the thing's muzzle was bruised, and it quartered around toward me once more. Without warning and with amazing speed it rushed.

I had no time to set myself now. I did try to leap backward, but I was not quick enough. It had me, gripping the lapels of my coat and driving me down and over with its flying weight. I felt the wet ground spin under my heels, and then it came flying up against my shoulders. Instinctively I had clutched upward at a throat with my right hand, clutched a handful of skin, loose and rankly shaggy. My left, also by instinct, flew backward to break my fall. It closed on something hard, round and smooth.

The rank odor that I had known at the séance was falling around me like a blanket, and the clashing white teeth shoved nearer, nearer. But the rock in my left hand spelled sudden hope.

Without trying to roll out from under, I smote with that rock. My clutch on the hairy throat helped me to judge accurately where the head would be. A moment later, and the struggling bulk above me went limp under the impact. Shoving it aside, I scrambled free and gained my feet once more.

The monster lay motionless where I had thrust it from me. Every nerve a-tingle, I stooped. My hand poised the rock for another smashing blow, but there was no sign of fight from the fallen shape. I could hear only a gusty breathing, as of something in stunned pain.

"Lie right where you are, you murdering brute," I cautioned it, my voice ringing exultant as I realized I had won. "If you move, I'll smash your skull in."

My right hand groped in my pocket for a match, struck it on the back of my leg. I bent still closer for a clear look at my enemy.

Had the thing been so hairy? Now, as I gazed, it seemed only sparsely furred. The ears, too, were blunter than I thought, and the muzzle not so—

Why, it was half human! Even as I watched, it was becoming more human still, a sprawled human figure! And, as the fur seemed to vanish in patches, was it clothing I saw, as though through the rents in a bearskin overcoat?

My senses churned in my own head. The fear that had ridden me all night became suddenly unreasoning. I fled as before, this time without a thought of where I was going or what I would do. The forbidden grove, lately so welcome as a refuge, swarmed with evil. I reached the edge of the clearing, glanced back once. The thing I had stricken down was beginning to stir, to get up. I ran from it as from a devil.

Somehow I had come to the stream again, or to another like it. The current moved more swiftly at this point, with a noticeable murmur. As I tried to spring across I landed short, and gasped in sudden pain, for the water was scalding hot. Of such are the waters of hell …

I cannot remember my flight through that steaming swamp that might have been a corner of Satan's own park. Somewhere along the way I found a tough, fleshy stem, small enough to

rend from its rooting and wield as a club. With it in my hand
I paused, with a rather foolish desire to return along my line
of retreat for another and decisive encounter with the shaggy
being. But what if it would foresee my coming and lie in wait?
I knew how swiftly it could spring, how strong was its grasp.
Once at close quarters, my club would be useless, and those
teeth might find their objective. I cast aside the impulse, that
had welled from I know not what primitive core of me, and
hurried on.

Evergreens were before me on a sudden, and through them
filtered a blast of cold air. The edge of the grove, and beyond it
the snow and the open sky, perhaps a resumption of the hunt by
the mob; but capture and death at their hands would be clean
and welcome compared to—

Feet squelched in the dampness behind me.

I pivoted with a hysterical oath, and swung up my club in
readiness to strike. The great dark outline that had come upon
me took one step closer, then paused. I sprang at it, struck and
missed as it dodged to one side.

"All right then, let's have it out," I managed to blurt, though
my voice was drying up in my throat. "Come on, show your
face."

"I'm not here to fight you," a good-natured voice assured me.
"Why, I seldom even argue, except with proven friends."

I relaxed a trifle, but did not lower my club. "Who are you?"

"Judge Keith Pursuivant," was the level response, as though I
had not just finished trying to kill him. "You must be the young
man they're so anxious to hang, back in town. Is that right?"

I made no answer.

"Silence makes admission," the stranger said. "Well, come
along to my house. This grove is between it and town, and
nobody will bother us for the night, at least."

VIII "A trick that almost killed you."

When I stepped into the open with Judge Keith Pursuivant, the
snow had ceased and a full moon glared through a rip in the
clouds, making diamond dust of the sugary drifts. By its light I

saw my companion with some degree of plainness – a man of great height and girth, with a wide black hat and a voluminous gray ulster. His face was as round as the moon itself, at least as shiny, and much warmer to look at. A broad bulbous nose and broad bulbous eyes beamed at me, while under a drooping blond mustache a smile seemed to be lurking. Apparently he considered the situation a pleasant one.

"I'm not one of the mob," he informed me reassuringly. "These pastimes of the town do not attract me. I left such things behind when I dropped out of politics and practice – oh, I was active in such things, ten years ago up North – and took up meditation."

"I've heard that you keep to yourself," I told him.

"You heard correctly. My black servant does the shopping and brings me the gossip. Most of the time it bores me, but not today, when I learned about you and the killing of John Gird—"

"And you came looking for me?"

"Of course. By the way, that was a wise impulse, ducking into the Devil's Croft."

But I shuddered, and not with the chill of the outer night. He made a motion for me to come along, and we began tramping through the soft snow toward a distant light under the shadow of a hill. Meanwhile I told him something of my recent adventures, saving for the last my struggle with the monster in the grove.

He heard me through, whistling through his teeth at various points. At the end of my narrative he muttered to himself:

"The hairy ones shall dance—"

"What was that, sir?" I broke in, without much courtesy.

"I was quoting from the prophet Isaiah. He was speaking of ruined Babylon, not a strange transplanted bit of the tropics, but otherwise it falls pat. Suggestive of a demon-festival. 'The hairy ones shall dance there.' "

"Isaiah, you say? I used to be something of a Bible reader, but I'm afraid I don't remember the passage."

He smiled sidewise at me. "But I'm translating direct from the original, Mr Wills is the name, eh? The original Hebrew of the prophet Isaiah, whoever he was. The classic-ridden compilers of the King James Version have satyrs dancing, and the prosaic

Revised Version offers nothing more startling than goats. But Isaiah and the rest of the ancient peoples knew that there were 'hairy ones.' Perhaps you encountered one of that interesting breed tonight."

"I don't want to encounter it a second time," I confessed, and again I shuddered.

"That is something we will talk over more fully. What do you think of the Turkish bath accommodations you have just left behind?"

"To tell you the truth, I don't know what to think. Growing green stuff and a tropical temperature, with snow outside—"

He waved the riddle away. "Easily and disappointingly explained, Mr Wills. Hot springs."

I stopped still, shin-deep in wet snow. "What!" I ejaculated.

"Oh, I've been there many times, in defiance of local custom and law – I'm not a native, you see." Once more his warming smile. "There are at least three springs, and the thick growth of trees makes a natural enclosure, roof and walls, to hold in the damp heat. It's not the only place of its kind in the world, Mr Wills. But the thing you met there is a trifle more difficult of explanation. Come on home – we'll both feel better when we sit down."

We finished the journey in half an hour. Judge Pursuivant's house was stoutly made of heavy hewn timbers, somewhat resembling certain lodges I had seen in England. Inside was a large, low-ceilinged room with a hanging oil lamp and a welcome open fire. A fat blond cat came leisurely forward to greet us. Its broad, good-humored face, large eyes and drooping whiskers gave it somewhat of a resemblance to its master.

"Better get your things off," advised the judge. He raised his voice. "William!"

A squat negro with a sensitive brown face appeared from a door at the back of the house.

"Bring in a bathrobe and slippers for this gentleman," ordered Judge Pursuivant, and himself assisted me to take off my muddy jacket. Thankfully I peeled off my other garments, and when the servant appeared with the robe I slid into it with a sigh.

"I'm in your hands, Judge Pursuivant," I said. "If you want to turn me over—"

"I might surrender you to an officer," he interrupted, "but never to a lawless mob. You'd better sit here for a time – and talk to me."

Near the fire was a desk, with an armchair at either side of it. We took seats, and when William returned from disposing of my wet clothes, he brought along a tray with a bottle of whisky, a siphon and some glasses. The judge prepared two drinks and handed one to me. At his insistence, I talked for some time about the séance and the events leading up to it.

"Remarkable," mused Judge Pursuivant. Then his great shrewd eyes studied me. "Don't go to sleep there, Mr Wills. I know you're tired, but I want to talk lycanthropy."

"Lycanthropy?" I repeated. "You mean the science of the werewolf?" I smiled and shook my head. "I'm afraid I'm no authority, sir. Anyway, this was no witchcraft – it was a bona fide spirit séance, with ectoplasm."

"Hum!" snorted the judge. "Witchcraft, spiritism! Did it ever occur to you that they might be one and the same thing?"

"Inasmuch as I never believed in either of them, it never did occur to me."

Judge Pursuivant finished his drink and wiped his mustache. "Skepticism does not become you too well, Mr Wills, if you will pardon my frankness. In any case, you saw something very werewolfish indeed, not an hour ago. Isn't that the truth?"

"It was some kind of a trick," I insisted stubbornly.

"A trick that almost killed you and made you run for your life?"

I shook my head. "I know I saw the thing," I admitted. "I even felt it." My eyes dropped to the bruised knuckles of my right hand. "Yet I was fooled – as a magician, I know all about fooling. There can be no such thing as a werewolf."

"Have a drink," coaxed Judge Pursuivant, exactly as if I had had none yet. With big, deft hands he poured whisky, then soda, into my glass and gave the mixture a stirring shake. "Now then," he continued, sitting back in his chair once more, "the time has come to speak of many things."

He paused, and I, gazing over the rim of that welcome glass, thought how much he looked like a rosy blond walrus.

"I'm going to show you," he announced, "that a man can turn into a beast, and back again."

IX "To a terrified victim he is doom itself."

He leaned toward the bookshelf beside him, pawed for a moment, then laid two sizable volumes on the desk between us.

"If this were a fantasy tale, Mr Wills," he said with a hint of one of his smiles, "I would place before you an unthinkably rare book – one that offered, in terms too brilliant and compelling for argument, the awful secrets of the universe, past, present and to come."

He paused to polish a pair of pince-nez and to clamp them upon the bridge of his broad nose.

"However," he resumed, "this is reality, sober if uneasy. And I give you, not some forgotten grimoire out of the mystic past, but two works by two recognized and familiar authorities."

I eyed the books. "May I see?"

For answer he thrust one of them, some six hundred pages in dark blue cloth, across the desk and into my hands. "*Thirty Years of Psychical Research*, by the late Charles Richet, French master in the spirit-investigation field," he informed me. "Faithfully and interestingly translated by Stanley De Brath. Published here in America, in 1923."

I took the book and opened it. "I knew Professor Richet, slightly. Years ago, when I was just beginning this sort of thing, I was entertained by him in London. He introduced me to Conan Doyle."

"Then you're probably familiar with his book. Yes? Well, the other," and he took up the second volume, almost as large as the Richet and bound in light buff, "is by Montague Summers, whom I call the premier demonologist of today. He's gathered all the lycanthropy-lore available."

I had read Mr Summers' *Geography of Witchcraft* and his two essays on the vampire, and I made bold to say so.

"This is a companion volume to them," Judge Pursuivant told me, opening the book. "It is called *The Werewolf*." He scrutinized the flyleaf. "Published in 1934 – thoroughly modern, you see. Here's a bit of Latin, Mr Wills: *Intrabunt lupi rapaces in vos, non parcentes gregi.*"

I crinkled my brow in the effort to recall my high school Latin, then began slowly to translate, a word at a time: " 'Enter hungry wolves—' "

"Save that scholarship," Judge Pursuivant broke in. "It's more early Scripture, though not so early as the bit about the hairy ones – vulgate for a passage from the Acts of the Apostles, twentieth chapter, twenty-ninth verse. 'Ravenous wolves shall enter among you, not sparing the flock.' Apparently that disturbing possibility exists even today."

He leafed through the book. "Do you know," he asked, "that Summers gives literally dozens of instances of lycanthropy, things that are positively known to have happened?"

I took another sip of whisky and water. "Those are only legends, surely."

"They are nothing of the sort!" The judge's eyes protruded even more in his earnestness, and he tapped the pages with an excited forefinger. "There are four excellent cases listed in his chapter on France alone – sworn to, tried and sentenced by courts—"

"But weren't they during the Middle Ages?" I suggested.

He shook his great head. "No, during the Sixteenth Century, the peak of the Renaissance. Oh, don't smile at the age, Mr Wills. It produced Shakespeare, Bacon, Montaigne, Galileo, Leonardo, Martin Luther; Descartes and Spinoza were its legitimate children, and Voltaire builded upon it. Yet werewolves were known, seen, convicted—"

"Convicted on what grounds?" I interrupted quickly, for I was beginning to reflect his warmth.

For answer he turned more pages, "Here is the full account of the case of Stubbe Peter, or Peter Stumpf," he said. "A contemporary record, telling of Stumpf's career in and out of wolf-form, his capture in the very act of shifting shape, his confession and execution – all near Cologne in the year 1589. Listen."

He read aloud: " 'Witnesses that this is true. Tyse Artyne. William Brewar. Adolf Staedt. George Bores. With divers others that have seen the same.' " Slamming the book shut, he looked up at me, the twinkle coming back into his spectacled eyes. "Well, Mr Wills? How do those names sound to you?"

"Why, like the names of honest German citizens."

"Exactly. Honest, respectable, solid. And their testimony is hard to pass off with a laugh, even at this distance in time, eh?"

He had almost made me see those witnesses, leather-jerkined and broad-breeched, with heavy jaws and squinting eyes, taking their turn at the quill pen with which they set their names to that bizarre document. "With divers others that have seen the same" – perhaps too frightened to hold pen or make signature …

"Still," I said slowly, "Germany of the Renaissance, the Sixteenth Century; and there have been so many changes since."

"Werewolves have gone out of fashion, you mean? Ah, you admit that they might have existed." He fairly beamed his triumph. "So have beards gone out of fashion, but they will sprout again if we lay down our razors. Let's go at it another way. Let's talk about materialization – ectoplasm – for the moment." He relaxed, and across his great girth his fingertips sought one another. "Suppose you explain, briefly and simply, what ectoplasm is considered to be."

I was turning toward the back of Richet's book. "It's in here, Judge Pursuivant. To be brief and simple, as you say, certain mediums apparently exude an unclassified material called ectoplasm. This, at first light and vaporescent, becomes firm and takes shape, either upon the body of the medium or as a separate and living creature."

"And you don't believe in this phenomenon?" he prompted, with something of insistence.

"I have never said that I didn't," I replied truthfully, "even before my experience of this evening went so far toward convincing me. But, with the examples I have seen, I felt that true scientific control was lacking. With all their science, most of the investigators trust too greatly."

Judge Pursuivant shook with gentle laughter. "They are doctors for the most part, and this honesty of theirs is a professional failing that makes them look for it in others. You – begging your pardon – are a magician, a professional deceiver, and you expect trickery in all whom you meet. Perhaps a good lawyer with trial experience, with a level head and a sense of competent material evidence for both sides, should attend these seances, eh?"

"You're quite right," I said heartily.

"But, returning to the subject, what else can be said about ectoplasm? That is, if it actually exists."

I had found in Richet's book the passage for which I had been searching. "It says here that bits of ectoplasm have been secured in rare instances, and that some of these have been examined microscopically. There were traces of fatty tissue, bacterial forms and epithelium."

"Ah! Those were the findings of Schrenck-Notzing. A sound man and a brilliant one, hard to corrupt or fool. It makes ectoplasm sound organic, does it not?"

I nodded agreement, and my head felt heavy, as if full of sober and important matters. "As for me," I went on, "I never have had much chance to examine the stuff. Whenever I get hold of an ectoplasmic hand, it melts like butter."

"They generally do," the judge commented, "or so the reports say. Yet they themselves are firm and strong when they touch or seize."

"Right, sir."

"It's when attacked, or even frightened, as with a camera flashlight, that the ectoplasm vanishes or is reabsorbed?" he prompted further.

"So Richet says here," I agreed once more, "and so I have found."

"Very good. Now," and his manner took on a flavor of the legal, "I shall sum up:

"Ectoplasm is put forth by certain spirit mediums, who are mysteriously adapted for it, under favorable conditions that include darkness, quiet, self-confidence. It takes form, altering the appearance of the medium or making up a separate body. It is firm and strong, but vanishes when attacked or frightened. Right so far, eh?"

"Right," I approved.

"Now, for the word *medium* substitute *wizard*." His grin burst out again, and he began to mix a third round of drinks. "A wizard, having darkness and quiet and being disposed to change shape, exudes a material that gives him a new shape and character. Maybe it is bestial, to match a fierce or desperate spirit within. There may be a shaggy pelt, a sharp muzzle, taloned paws and rending fangs. To a terrified victim he is doom itself. But to a brave adversary, facing and fighting him—"

He flipped his way through Summers' book, as I had with Richet's. "Listen: '… the shape of the werewolf will be removed if he be reproached by name as a werewolf, or if again he be thrice addressed by his Christian name, or struck three blows on the forehead with a knife, or that three drops of blood should be drawn.' Do you see the parallels, man? Shouted at, bravely denounced, or slightly wounded, his false beast-substance fades from him." He flung out his hands, as though appealing to a jury. "I marvel nobody ever thought of it before."

"But nothing so contrary to nature has a natural explanation," I objected, and very idiotic the phrase sounded in my own ears.

He laughed, and I could not blame him. "I'll confound you with another of your own recent experiences. What could seem more contrary to nature than the warmth and greenness of the inside of Devil's Croft? And what is more simply natural than the hot springs that make it possible?"

"Yet, an envelope of bestiality, beast-muzzle on human face, beast-paws on human hands—"

"I can support that by more werewolf-lore. I don't even have to open Summers, everyone has heard the story. A wolf attacks a traveler, who with his sword lops off a paw. The beast howls and flees, and the paw it leaves behind is a human hand."

"That's an old one, in every language."

"Probably because it happened so often. There's your human hand, with the beast-paw forming upon and around it, then vanishing like wounded ectoplasm. Where's the weak point, Wills? Name it, I challenge you."

I felt the glass shake in my hand, and a chilly wind brushed my spine. "There's one point," I made myself say. "You may think it a slender one, even a quibble. But ectoplasms make human forms, not animal."

"How do you know they don't make animal forms?" Judge Pursuivant crowed, leaning forward across the desk. "Because, of the few you've seen and disbelieved, only human faces and bodies showed? My reply is there in your hands. Open Richet's book to page 545, Mr Wills. Page 545 … got it? Now, the passage I marked, about the medium Burgik. Read it aloud."

He sank back into his chair once more, waiting in manifest delight. I found the place, underscored with pencil, and my voice was hoarse as I obediently read:

" 'My trouser leg was strongly pulled and a strange, ill-defined form that seemed to have paws like those of a dog or small monkey climbed on my knee. I could feel its weight, very light, and something like the muzzle of an animal touched my cheek.' "

"There you are, Wills," Judge Pursuivant was crying. "Notice that it happened in Warsaw, close to the heart of the werewolf country. Hmmm, reading that passage made you sweat a bit – remembering what you saw in the Devil's Croft, eh?"

I flung down the book.

"You've done much toward convincing me," I admitted. "I'd rather have the superstitious peasant's belief, though, the one I've always scoffed at."

"Rationalizing the business didn't help, then? It did when I explained the Devil's Croft and the springs."

"But the springs don't chase you with sharp teeth. And, as I was saying, the peasant had a protection that the scientist lacks – trust in his crucifix and his Bible."

"Why shouldn't he have that trust, and why shouldn't you?" Again the judge was rummaging in his book-case. "Those symbols of faith gave him what is needed, a strong heart to drive back the menace, whether it be wolf-demon or ectoplasmic bogy. Here, my friend."

He laid a third book on the desk. It was a Bible, red-edged and leather-backed, worn from much use.

"Have a read at that while you finish your drink," he advised me. "*The Gospel According to St John* is good, and it's already marked. Play you're a peasant, hunting for comfort."

Like a dutiful child I opened the Bible to where a faded purple ribbon lay between the pages. But already Judge Pursuivant was quoting from memory:

" 'In the beginning was the Word, and the Word was with God, and the Word was God. The same was in the beginning with God. All things were made by him; and without him was not anything made that was made …' "

X "Blood-lust and compassion."

It may seem incredible that later in the night I slept like a dead pig; yet I had reason.

First of all there was the weariness that had followed my dangers and exertions; then Judge Pursuivant's whisky and logic combined to reassure me; finally, the leather couch in his study, its surface comfortably hollowed by much reclining thereon, was a sedative in itself. He gave me two quilts, very warm and very light, and left me alone. I did not stir until a rattle of breakfast dishes awakened me.

William, the judge's servant, had carefully brushed my clothes. My shoes also showed free of mud, though they still felt damp and clammy. The judge himself furnished me with a clean shirt and socks, both items very loose upon me, and lent me his razor.

"Some friends of yours called during the night," he told me dryly.

"Friends?"

"Yes, from the town. Five of them, with ropes and guns. They announced very definitely that they intended to decorate the flagpole in the public square with your corpse. There was also some informal talk about drinking your blood. We may have vampires as well as werewolves hereabouts."

I almost cut my lip with the razor. "How did you get rid of them?" I asked quickly. "They must have followed my tracks."

"Lucky there was more snow after we got in," he replied, "and they came here only as a routine check-up. They must have visited every house within miles. Oh, turning them away was easy. I feigned wild enthusiasm for the man-hunt, and asked if I couldn't come along."

He smiled reminiscently, his mustache stirring like a rather genial blond snake.

"Then what?" I prompted him, dabbing on more lather.

"Why, they were delighted. I took a rifle and spent a few hours on the trail. You weren't to be found at all, so we returned to town. Excitement reigns there, you can believe."

"What kind of excitement?"

"Blood-lust and compassion. Since Constable O'Bryant is wounded, his younger brother, a strong advocate of your immediate capture and execution, is serving as a volunteer guardian of the peace. He's acting on an old appointment by his brother as deputy, to serve without pay. He told the council – a badly scared group – that he has sent for help to the county seat, but I am sure he did nothing of the kind. Meanwhile, the Croft is surrounded by scouts, who hope to catch you sneaking out of it. And the women of the town are looking after Susan Gird and your friend, the *Herr Doktor*."

I had finished shaving. "How is Doctor Zoberg?" I inquired through the towel.

"Still pretty badly shaken up. I tried to get in and see him, but it was impossible. I understand he went out for a while, early in the evening, but almost collapsed. Just now he is completely surrounded by cooing old ladies with soup and herb tea. Miss Gird was feeling much better, and talked to me for a while. I'm not really on warm terms with the town, you know; people think it's indecent for me to live out here alone and not give them a chance to gossip about me. So I was pleasurably surprised to get a kind word from Miss Susan. She told me, very softly for fear someone might overhear, that she hopes you aren't caught. She is sure that you did not kill her father."

We went into his dining room, where William offered pancakes, fried bacon and the strongest black coffee I ever tasted. In the midst of it all, I put down my fork and faced the judge suddenly. He grinned above his cup.

"Well, Mr Wills? 'Stung by the splendor of a sudden thought' – all you need is a sensitive hand clasped to your inspired brow."

"You said," I reminded him, "that Susan Gird is sure that I didn't kill her father."

"So I did."

"She told you that herself. She also seemed calm, self-contained, instead of in mourning for—"

"Oh, come, come!" He paused to shift a full half-dozen cakes to his plate and skilfully drenched them with syrup. "That's rather ungrateful of you, Mr Wills, suspecting her of patricide."

"Did I say that?" I protested, feeling my ears turning bright red.

"You would have if I hadn't broken your sentence in the middle," he accused, and put a generous portion of pancake into his mouth. As he chewed he twinkled at me through his pince-nez, and I felt unaccountably foolish.

"If Susan Gird had truly killed her father," he resumed, after swallowing, "she would be more adroitly theatrical. She would weep, swear vengeance on his murderer, and be glad to hear that someone else had been accused of the crime. She would even invent details to help incriminate that someone else."

"Perhaps she doesn't know that she killed him," I offered.

"Perhaps not. You mean that a new mind, as well as a new body, may invest the werewolf – or ectoplasmic medium – at time of change."

I jerked my head in agreement.

"Then Susan Gird, as she is normally, must be innocent. Come, Mr Wills! Would you blame poor old Doctor Jekyll for the crimes of his *alter ego*, Mr Hyde?"

"I wouldn't want to live in the same house with Doctor Jekyll."

Judge Pursuivant burst into a roar of laughter, at which William, bringing fresh supplies from the kitchen, almost dropped his tray. "So romance enters the field of psychic research!" the judge crowed at me.

I stiffened, outraged. "Judge Pursuivant, I certainly did not—"

"I know, you didn't say it, but again I anticipated you. So it's not the thought of her possible unconscious crime, but the chance of comfortable companionship that perplexes you." He stopped laughing suddenly. "I'm sorry, Wills. Forgive me. I shouldn't laugh at this, or indeed at any aspect of the whole very serious business."

I could hardly take real offense at the man who had rescued and sheltered me, and I said so. We finished breakfast, and he sought his overcoat and wide hat.

"I'm off for town again," he announced. "There are one or two points to be settled there, for your safety and my satisfaction. Do you mind being left alone? There's an interesting lot of books in my study. You might like to look at a copy of Dom Calmet's *Dissertations*, if you read French; also a rather slovenly *Wicked Bible*, signed by Pierre De Lancre. J. W. Wickwar, the witchcraft authority, thinks that such a thing does not exist, but I know of two others. Or, if you feel that you're having enough of demonology in real life, you will find a whole row of light novels, including most of P. G. Wodehouse." He held out his hand in farewell. "William will get you anything you want. There's tobacco and a choice of pipes on my desk. Whisky, too, though you don't look like the sort that drinks before noon."

With that he was gone, and I watched him from the window. He moved sturdily across the bright snow to a shed, slid open its door and entered. Soon there emerged a sedan, old but well-kept, with the judge at the wheel. He drove away down a snow-filled road toward town.

I did not know what to envy most in him, his learning, his assurance or his good-nature. The assurance, I decided once; then it occurred to me that he was in nothing like the awkward position I held. He was only a sympathetic ally – but why was he that, even? I tried to analyze his motives, and could not.

Sitting down in his study, I saw on the desk the Montague Summers book on werewolves. It lay open at page 111, and my eyes lighted at once upon a passage underscored in ink – apparently some time ago, for the mark was beginning to rust a trifle. It included a quotation from *Restitution of Decayed Intelligence*, written by Richard Rowlands in 1605:

> ... *were-wolves are certaine sorcerers, who hauvin annoynted their bodyes, with an oyntment which they make by the instinct of the deuil; and putting on a certain inchanted girdel, do not only*

> *vnto the view of others seeme as wolues[??290], but to their own*
> *thinking have both the shape and the nature of wolues, so long as*
> *they weare the said girdel. And they do dispose theselves as uery*
> *wolues, in wurrying and killing, and moste of humaine creatures.*

This came to the bottom of the page, where someone, undoubtedly Pursuivant, had written: "Ointment and girdle sound as if they might have a scientific explanation." And, in the same script, but smaller, the following notes filled the margin beside:

Possible Werewolf Motivations

I.   *Involuntary lycanthropy.*
    1. Must have blood to drink (connection with vampirism?).
    2. Must have secrecy.
    3. Driven to desperation by contemplating horror of own position.

II.   *Voluntary lycanthropy.*
    1. Will to do evil.
    2. Will to exert power through fear.

III.   *Contributing factors to becoming werewolf.*
    1. Loneliness and dissatisfaction.
    2. Hunger for forbidden foods (human flesh, etc.).
    3. Scorn and hate of fellow men, general or specific.
    4. Occult curiosity.
    5. Simon-pure insanity (Satanist complex).

Are any or all of these traits to be found in werewolf? Find one
and ask it.

That was quite enough lycanthropy for the present, so far as I was concerned. I drew a book of Mark Twain from the shelf – I seem to remember it as *Tom Sawyer Abroad* – and read all the morning. Noon came, and I was about to ask the judge's negro servant for some lunch, when he appeared in the door of the study.

"Someone with a message, sah," he announced, and drew aside to admit Susan Gird.

I fairly sprang to my feet, dropping my book upon the desk. She advanced slowly into the room, her pale face grave but friendly. I saw that her eyes were darkly circled, and that her cheeks showed gaunt, as if with strain and weariness. She put out a hand, and I took it.

"A message?" I repeated William's words.

"Why, yes." She achieved a smile, and I was glad to see it, for both our sakes. "Judge Pursuivant got me to one side and said for me to come here. You and I are to talk the thing over."

"You mean, last night?" She nodded, and I asked further, "How did you get here?"

"Your car. I don't drive very well, but I managed."

I asked her to sit down and talk.

She told me that she remembered being in the parlor, with Constable O'Bryant questioning me. At the time she had had difficulty remembering even the beginning of the séance, and it was not until I had been taken away that she came to realize what had happened to her father. That, of course, distressed and distracted her further, and even now the whole experience was wretchedly hazy to her.

"I do recall sitting down with you," she said finally, after I had urged her for the twentieth time to think hard. "You chained me, yes, and Doctor Zoberg. Then yourself. Finally I seemed to float away, as if in a dream. I'm not even sure about how long it was."

"Had the light been out very long?" I asked craftily.

"The light out?" she echoed, patently mystified. "Oh, of course. The light was turned out, naturally. I don't remember, but I suppose you attended to that."

"I asked to try you," I confessed. "I didn't touch the lamp until after you had seemed to drop off to sleep."

She did recall to memory her father's protest at his manacles, and Doctor Zoberg's gentle inquiry if she were ready. That was all.

"How is Doctor Zoberg?" I asked her.

"Not very well, I'm afraid. He was exhausted by the experience, of course, and for a time seemed ready to break down. When the trouble began about you – the crowd gathered at the town hall – he gathered his strength and went out, to see if he could help defend or rescue you. He was gone about an hour and then he returned, bruised about the face. Somebody of the mob had handled him roughly, I think. He's resting at our place now, with a hot compress on his eye."

"Good man!" I applauded. "At least he did his best for me."

She was not finding much pleasure in her memories, however, and I suggested a change of the subject. We had lunch together, egg sandwiches and coffee, then played several hands of casino. Tiring of that, we turned to the books and she read aloud to me from Keats. Never has *The Eve of St. Agnes* sounded better to me. Evening fell, and we were preparing to take yet another meal – a meat pie, which William assured us was one of his culinary triumphs – when the door burst open and Judge Pursuivant came in.

"You've been together all the time?" he asked us at once.

"Why, yes," I said.

"Is that correct, Miss Susan? You've been in the house, every minute?"

"That is right," she seconded me.

"Then," said the judge. "You two are cleared, at last."

He paused, looking from Susan's questioning face to mine, then went on:

"That rending beast-thing in the Croft got another victim, not more than half an hour ago. O'Bryant was feeling better, ready to get back on duty. His deputy-brother, anxious to get hold of Wills first, for glory or vengeance, ventured into the place, just at dusk. He came out in a little while, torn and bitten almost to pieces, and died as he broke clear of the cedar hedge."

XI "To meet that monster face to face!"

I think that both Susan and I fairly reeled before this news, like actors registering surprise in an old-fashioned melodrama. As for Judge Pursuivant, he turned to the table, cut a generous wedge of the meat pie and set it, all savory and steaming, on a plate for himself. His calm zest for the good food gave us others steadiness again, so that we sat down and even ate a little as he described his day in town.

He had found opportunity to talk to Susan in private, confiding in her about me and finally sending her to me; this, as he said, so that we would convince each other of our respective innocences. It was purely an inspiration, for he had had no idea, of course, that such conviction would turn out so final. Thereafter he made shift to enter the Gird house and talk to Doctor Zoberg.

That worthy he found sitting somewhat limply in the parlor, with John Gird's coffin in the next room. Zoberg, the judge reported, was mystified about the murder and anxious to bring to justice the townsfolk – there were more than one, it seemed – who had beaten him. Most of all, however, he was concerned about the charges against me.

"His greatest anxiety is to prove you innocent," Judge Pursuivant informed me. "He intends to bring the best lawyer possible for your defense, is willing even to assist in paying the fee. He also swears that character witnesses can be brought to testify that you are the most peaceable and law-abiding man in the country."

"That's mighty decent of him," I said. "According to your reasoning of this morning, his attitude proves him innocent, too."

"What reasoning was that?" asked Susan, and I was glad that the judge continued without answering her.

"I was glad that I had sent Miss Susan on. If your car had remained there, Mr Wills, Doctor Zoberg might have driven off in it to rally your defenses."

"Not if I know him," I objected. "The whole business, what of the mystery and occult significances, will hold him right on the spot. He's relentlessly curious and, despite his temporary collapse, he's no coward."

"I agree with that," chimed in Susan.

As for my pursuers of the previous night, the judge went on, they had been roaming the snow-covered streets in twos and threes, heavily armed for the most part and still determined to punish me for killing their neighbor. The council was too frightened or too perplexed to deal with the situation, and the constable was still in bed, with his brother assuming authority, when Judge Pursuivant made his inquiries. The judge went to see the wounded man, who very pluckily determined to rise and take up his duties again.

"I'll arrest the man who plugged me," O'Bryant had promised grimly, "and that kid brother of mine can quit playing policeman."

The judge applauded these sentiments, and brought him hot food and whisky, which further braced his spirits. In the evening came the invasion by the younger O'Bryant of the Devil's Croft, and his resultant death at the claws and teeth of what prowled there.

"His throat was so torn open and filled with blood that he could not speak," the judge concluded, "but he pointed back into the timber, and then tried to trace something in the snow with his finger. It looked like a wolf's head, with pointed nose and ears. He died before he finished."

"You saw him come out?" I asked.

"No. I'd gone back to town, but later I saw the body, and the sketch in the snow."

He finished his dinner and pushed back his chair. "Now," he said heartily, "it's up to us."

"Up to us to do what?" I inquired.

"To meet that monster face to face," he replied. "There are three of us and, so far as I can ascertain, but one of the enemy." Both Susan and I started to speak, but he held up his hand, smiling. "I know without being reminded that the odds are still against us, because the one enemy is fierce and blood-drinking, and can change shape and character. Maybe it can project itself to a distance – which makes it all the harder, both for us to face it and for us to get help."

"I know what you mean by that last," I nodded gloomily. "If there were ten thousand friendly constables in the neighborhood, instead of a single hostile one, they wouldn't believe us."

"Right," agreed Judge Pursuivant. "We're like the group of perplexed mortals in *Dracula*, who had only their own wits and weapons against a monster no more forbidding than ours."

It is hard to show clearly how his constant offering of parallels and rationalizations comforted us. Only the unknown and unknowable can terrify completely. We three were even cheerful over a bottle of wine that William fetched and poured out in three glasses. Judge Pursuivant gave us a toast – "May wolves go hungry!" – and Susan and I drank it gladly.

"Don't forget what's on our side," said the judge, putting down his glass. "I mean the steadfast and courageous heart, of which I preached to Wills last night, and which we can summon from within us any time and anywhere. The werewolf, dauntlessly faced, loses its dread; and I think we are the ones to face it. Now we're ready for action."

I said that I would welcome any kind of action whatsoever, and Susan touched my arm as if in endorsement of the remark. Judge Pursuivant's spectacles glittered in approval.

"You two will go into the Devil's Croft," he announced. "I'm going back to town once more."

"Into the Devil's Croft!" we almost shouted, both in the same shocked breath.

"Of course. Didn't we just get through with the agreement all around that the lycanthrope can and must be met face to face? Offense is the best defense, as perhaps one hundred thousand athletic trainers have reiterated."

"I've already faced the creature once," I reminded him. "As for appearing dauntless, I doubt my own powers of deceit."

"You shall have a weapon," he said. "A fire gives light, and we know that such things must have darkness – such as it finds in the midst of that swampy wood. So fill your pockets with matches, both of you."

"How about a gun?" I asked, but he shook his head.

"We don't want the werewolf killed. That would leave the whole business in mystery, and yourself probably charged with another murder. He'd return to his human shape, you know, the moment he was hurt even slightly."

Susan spoke, very calmly: "I'm ready to go into the Croft, Judge Pursuivant."

He clapped his hands loudly, as if applauding in a theater.

"Bravo, my dear, bravo! I see Mr Wills sets his jaw. That means he's ready to go with you. Very well, let us be off."

He called to William who at his orders brought three lanterns – sturdy old-fashioned affairs, protected by strong wire nettings – and filled them with oil. We each took one and set out. It had turned clear and frosty once more, and the moon shone too brightly for my comfort, at least. However, as we approached the grove, we saw no sentinels; they could hardly be blamed for deserting, after the fate of the younger O'Bryant.

We gained the shadow of the outer cedars unchallenged. Here Judge Pursuivant called a halt, produced a match from his overcoat pocket and lighted our lanterns all around. I remember that we struck a fresh light for Susan's lantern; we agreed that, silly as the three-on-a match superstition might be, this was no time or place to tempt Providence.

"Come on," said Judge Pursuivant then, and led the way into the darkest part of the immense thicket.

XII "We are here at his mercy."

We followed Judge Pursuivant, Susan and I, without much of a thought beyond an understandable dislike for being left alone on the brink of the timber. It was a slight struggle to get through the close-set cedar hedge, especially for Susan, but beyond it we soon caught up with the judge. He strode heavily and confidently among the trees, his lantern held high to shed light upon broad, polished leaves and thick, wet stems. The moist warmth of the grove's interior made itself felt again, and the judge explained again and at greater length the hot springs that made possible this surprising condition. All the while he kept going. He seemed to know his way in that forbidden fastness – indeed, he must have explored it many times to go straight to his destination.

That destination was a clearing, in some degree like the one where I had met and fought with my hairy pursuer on the night before. This place had, however, a great tree in its center, with branches that shot out in all directions to hide away the sky completely. By straining the ears one could catch a faint murmur of water – my scalding stream, no doubt. Around us were the thick-set trunks of the forest, filled in between with brush and vines, and underfoot grew velvety moss.

"This will be our headquarters position," said the judge. "Wills, help me gather wood for a fire. Break dead branches from the standing trees – never mind picking up wood from the ground, it will be too damp."

Together we collected a considerable heap and, crumpling a bit of paper in its midst, he kindled it.

"Now, then," he went on, "I'm heading for town. You two will stay here and keep each other company."

He took our lanterns, blew them out and ran his left arm through the loops of their handles.

"I'm sure that nothing will attack you in the light of the fire. You're bound to attract whatever skulks hereabouts, however. When I come back, we ought to be prepared to go into the final act of our little melodrama."

He touched my hand, bowed to Susan, and went tramping away into the timber. The thick leafage blotted his lantern-light from our view before his back had been turned twenty seconds.

Susan and I gazed at each other, and smiled rather uneasily.

"It's warm," she breathed, and took off her cloak. Dropping it upon one of the humped roots of the great central tree, she sat down on it with her back to the trunk. "What kind of a tree is this?"

I gazed up at the gnarled stem, or as much of it as I could see in the firelight. Finally I shook my head.

"I don't know – I'm no expert," I admitted. "At least it's very big, and undoubtedly very old – the sort of tree that used to mark a place of sacrifice."

At the word "sacrifice," Susan lifted her shoulders as if in distaste. "You're right, Talbot. It would be something grim and Druid-like." She began to recite, half to herself:

> *That tree in whose dark shadow*
> *The ghastly priest doth reign,*
> *The priest who slew the slayer*
> *And shall himself be slain*

"Macaulay," I said at once. Then, to get her mind off of morbid things, "I had to recite *The Lays of Ancient Rome* in school, when I was a boy. I wish you hadn't mentioned it."

"You mean, because it's an evil omen?" She shook her head, and contrived a smile that lighted up her pale face. "It's not that, if you analyze it. 'Shall himself be slain' – it sounds as if the enemy's fate is sealed."

I nodded, then spun around sharply, for I fancied I heard a dull crashing at the edge of the clearing. Then I went here and there, gathering wood enough to keep our fire burning for some time. One branch, a thick, straight one, I chose from the heap and leaned against the big tree, within easy reach of my hand.

"That's for a club," I told Susan, and she half shrunk, half stiffened at the implication.

We fell to talking about Judge Pursuivant, the charm and the enigma that invested him. Both of us felt gratitude that he had immediately clarified our own innocence in the grisly slayings, but to both came a sudden inspiration, distasteful and disquieting. I spoke first:

"Susan! Why did the judge bring us here?"

"He said, to help face and defeat the monster. But – but—"

"Who is that monster?" I demanded. "What human being puts on a semibestial appearance, to rend and kill?"

"Y – you don't mean the judge?"

As I say, it had been in both our minds. We were silent, and felt shame and embarrassment.

"Look here," I went on earnestly after a moment; "perhaps we're being ungrateful, but we mustn't be unprepared. Think, Susan; nobody knows where Judge Pursuivant was at the time of your father's death, or at the time I saw the thing in these woods." I broke off, remembering how I had met the judge for the first time, so shortly after my desperate struggle with the point-eared demon. "Nobody knows where he was when the constable's brother was attacked and mortally wounded."

She gazed about fearfully. "Nobody," she added breathlessly, "knows where he is now."

I was remembering a conversation with him; he had spoken of books, mentioning a rare, a supposedly non-existent volume.

What was it? … the *Wicked Bible*. And what was it I had once heard about that work?

It came back to me now, out of the sub-conscious brain-chamber where, apparently, one stores everything he hears or reads in idleness, and from which such items creep on occasion. It had been in Lewis Spence's *Encyclopedia of Occultism*, now on the shelf in my New York apartment.

The *Wicked Bible*, scripture for witches and wizards, from which magic-mongers of the Dark Ages drew their inspiration and their knowledge! And Judge Pursuivant had admitted to having one!

What had he learned from it? How had he been so glib about the science – yes, and the psychology – of being a werewolf?

"If what we suspect is true," I said to Susan, "we are here at his mercy. Nobody is going to come in here, not if horses dragged them. At his leisure he will fall upon us and tear us to pieces."

But, even as I spoke, I despised myself for my weak fears in her presence. I picked up my club and was comforted by its weight and thickness.

"I met that devil once," I said, studying cheer and confidence into my voice this time. "I don't think it relished the meeting any too much. Next time won't be any more profitable for it."

She smiled at me, as if in comradely encouragement; then we both started and fell silent. There had risen, somewhere among the thickets, a long low whining.

I put out a foot, stealthily, as though fearful of being caught in motion. A quick kick flung more wood on the fire. I blinked in the light and felt the heat. Standing there, as a primitive man might have stood in his flame-guarded camp to face the horrors of the ancient world, I tried to judge by ear the direction of that whine.

It died, and I heard, perhaps in my imagination, a stealthy padding. Then the whining began again, from a new quarter and nearer.

I made myself step toward it. My shadow, leaping grotesquely among the tree trunks, almost frightened me out of my wits. The whine had changed into a crooning wail, such as that with which dogs salute the full moon. It seemed to plead, to promise; and it was coming closer to the clearing.

Once before I had challenged and taunted the thing with scornful words. Now I could not make my lips form a single syllable. Probably it was just as well, for I thought and watched the more. Something black and cautious was moving among the branches, just beyond the shrubbery that screened it from our fire-light. I knew, without need of a clear view, what that black something was. I lifted my club to the ready.

The sound it made had become in some fashion articulate, though not human in any quality. There were no words to it, but it spoke to the heart. The note of plea and promise had become one of command – and not directed to me.

I found my own voice.

"Get out of here, you devil!" I roared at it, and threw my club. Even as I let go of it, I wished I had not. The bushes foiled my aim, and the missile crashed among them and dropped to the mossy ground. The creature fell craftily silent. Then I felt sudden panic and regret at being left weaponless, and I retreated toward the fire.

"Susan," I said huskily, "give me another stick. Hurry!"

She did not move or stir, and I rummaged frantically among the heaped dry branches for myself. Catching up the first piece of wood that would serve, I turned to her with worried curiosity.

She was still seated upon the cloak-draped root, but she had drawn herself tense, like a cat before a mouse-hole. Her head was thrust forward, so far that her neck extended almost horizontally. Her dilated eyes were turned in the direction from which the whining and crooning had come. They had a strange clarity in them, as if they could pierce the twigs and leaves and meet there an answering, understanding gaze.

"Susan!" I cried.

Still she gave no sign that she heard me, if hear me she did. She leaned farther forward, as if ready to spring up and run. Once more the unbeastly wail rose from the place where our watcher was lurking.

Susan's lips trembled. From them came slowly and softly, then louder, a long-drawn answering howl.

"*Aooooooooooooooo! Aoooooooooooooooooooooo!*"

The stick almost fell from my hands. She rose, slowly but confidently. Her shoulders hunched high, her arms hung forward as though they wanted to reach to the ground. Again she howled:

"*Aoooooooooooooooooooooo!*"

I saw that she was going to move across the clearing, toward the trees – through the trees. My heart seemed to twist into a knot inside me, but I could not let her do such a thing. I made a quick stride and planted myself before her.

"Susan, you mustn't!"

She shrank back, her face turning slowly up to mine. Her back was to the fire, yet light rose in her eyes, or perhaps behind them; a green light, such as reflects in still forest pools from the moon. Her hands lifted-suddenly, as though to repel me. They were half closed and the crooked fingers drawn stiff, like talons.

"Susan!" I coaxed her, yet again, and she made no answer but tried to slip sidewise around me. I moved and headed her off, and she growled – actually growled, like a savage dog.

With my free hand I clutched her shoulder. Under my fingers, her flesh was as taut as wire fabric. Then, suddenly, it relaxed into human tissue again, and she was standing straight. Her eyes had lost their weird light, they showed only dark and frightened.

"Talbot," she stammered. "Wh— what have I been doing?"

"Nothing, my dear," I comforted her. "It was nothing that we weren't able to fight back."

From the woods behind me came a throttling yelp, as of some hungry thing robbed of prey within its very grasp. Susan swayed, seemed about to drop, and I caught her quickly in my arms. Holding her thus, I turned my head and laughed over my shoulder.

"Another score against you!" I jeered at my enemy. "You didn't get her, not with all your filthy enchantments!"

Susan was beginning to cry, and I half led, half carried her back to the fireside. At my gesture she sat on her cloak again, as tractable as a child who repents of rebellion and tries to be obedient.

There were no more sounds from the timber. I could feel an emptiness there, as if the monster had slunk away, baffled.

XIII "Light's our best weapon."

Neither of us said anything for a while after that. I stoked up the fire, to be doing something, and it made us so uncomfortably warm that we had to crowd away from it. Sitting close against the tree-trunk, I began to imagine something creeping up the black lane of shadow it cast behind us to the edge of the clearing; and yet again I thought I heard noises. Club in hand, I went to investigate, and I was not disappointed in the least when I found nothing.

Finally Susan spoke. "This," she said, "is a new light on the thing."

"It's nothing to be upset about," I tried to comfort her.

"Not be upset!" She sat straight up, and in the light of the fire I could see a single pained line between her brows, deep and sharp as a chisel-gash. "Not when I almost turned into a beast!"

"How much of that do you remember?" I asked her.

"I was foggy in my mind, Talbot, almost as at the séance, but I remember being drawn – drawn to what was waiting out there." Her eyes sought the thickets on the far side of our blaze. "And it didn't seem horrible, but pleasant and welcome and – well, as if it were my kind. You," and she glanced quickly at me, then ashamedly away, "you were suddenly strange and to be avoided."

"Is that all?"

"It spoke to me," she went on in husky horror, "and I spoke to it."

I forbore to remind her that the only sound she had uttered was a wordless howl. Perhaps she did not know that – I hoped not. We said no more for another awkward time.

Finally she mumbled, "I'm not the kind of woman who cries easily; but I'd like to now."

"Go ahead," I said at once, and she did, and I let her. Whether I took her into my arms, or whether she came into them of her own accord, I do not remember exactly; but it was against my shoulder that she finished her weeping, and when she had finished she did feel better.

"That somehow washed the fog and the fear out of me," she confessed, almost brightly.

It must have been a full hour later that rustlings rose yet again in the timber. So frequently had my imagination tricked me that I did not so much as glance up. Then Susan gave a little startled cry, and I sprang to my feet. Beyond the fire a tall, gray shape had become visible, with a pale glare of light around it.

"Don't be alarmed," called a voice I knew. "It is I – Otto Zoberg."

"Doctor!" I cried, and hurried to meet him. For the first time in my life, I felt that he was a friend. Our differences of opinion, once making companionship strained, had so dwindled to nothing in comparison to the danger I faced, and his avowed trust in me as innocent of murder.

"How are you?" I said, wringing his hand. "They say you were hurt by the mob."

"*Ach*, it was nothing serious," he reassured me. "Only this." He touched with his forefinger an eye, and I could see that it was bruised and swollen half-shut. "A citizen with too ready a fist and too slow a mind has that to answer for."

"I'm partly responsible," I said. "You were trying to help me, I understand, when it happened."

More noise behind him, and two more shapes pushed into the clearing. I recognized Judge Pursuivant, nodding to me with his eyes bright under his wide hat-brim. The other man, angular, falcon-faced, one arm in a sling, I had also seen before. It was Constable O'Bryant. I spoke to him, but he gazed past me, apparently not hearing.

Doctor Zoberg saw my perplexed frown, and he turned back toward the constable. Snapping long fingers in front of the great hooked nose, he whistled shrilly. O'Bryant started, grunted, then glared around as though he had been suddenly and rudely awakened.

"What's up?" he growled menacingly, and his sound hand moved swiftly to a holster at his side. Then his eyes found me, and with an oath he drew his revolver.

"Easy, Constable! Easy does it," soothed Judge Pursuivant, his own great hand clutching O'Bryant's wrist. "You've forgotten that I showed how Mr Wills must be innocent."

"I've forgotten what we're here for at all," snapped O'Bryant, gazing around the clearing. "Hey, have I been drunk or something? I said that I'd never—"

"I'll explain," offered Zoberg. "The judge met me in town, and we came together to see you. Remember? You said you would like to avenge your brother's death, and came with us. Then, when you balked at the very edge of this Devil's Croft, I took the liberty of hypnotizing you."

"Huh? How did you do that?" growled the officer.

"With a look, a word, a motion of the hand," said Zoberg, his eyes twinkling. "Then you ceased all objections and came in with us."

Pursuivant clapped O'Bryant on the unwounded shoulder. "Sit down," he invited, motioning toward the roots of the tree.

The five of us gathered around the fire, like picnickers instead of allies against a supernormal monster. There, at Susan's insistence, I told of what had happened since Judge Pursuivant had left us. All listened with rapt attention, the constable grunting occasionally, the judge clicking his tongue, and Doctor Zoberg in absolute silence.

It was Zoberg who made the first comment after I had finished. "This explains many things," he said.

"It don't explain a doggone thing," grumbled O'Bryant.

Zoberg smiled at him, then turned to Judge Pursuivant. "Your ectoplasmic theory of lycanthropy – such as you have explained it to me – is most interesting and, I think, valid. May I advance it a trifle?"

"In what way?" asked the judge.

"Ectoplasm, as you see it, forms the werewolf by building upon the medium's body. But is not ectoplasm more apt, according to the observations of many people, to draw completely away and form a separate and complete thing of itself? The thing may be beastly, as you suggest. Algernon Blackwood, the English writer of psychic stories, almost hits upon it in one of his 'John Silence' tales. He described an astral personality taking form and threatening harm while its physical body slept."

"I know the story you mean," agreed Judge Pursuivant. "*The Camp of the Dog*, I think it's called."

"Very well, then. Perhaps, while Miss Susan's body lay in a trance, securely handcuffed between Wills and myself—"

"Oh!" wailed Susan. "Then it was I, after all."

"It couldn't have been you," I told her at once.

"But it was! And, while I was at the judge's home with you, part of me met the constable's brother in this wood." She stared wildly around her.

"It might as well have been part of *me*," I argued, and O'Bryant glared at me as if in sudden support of that likelihood. But Susan shook her head.

"No, for which of us responded to the call of that thing out there?"

For the hundredth time she gazed fearfully through the fire at the bushes behind which the commanding whine had risen.

"I have within me," she said dully, "a nature that will break out, look and act like a beast-demon, will kill even my beloved father—"

"Please," interjected Judge Pursuivant earnestly, "you must not take responsibility upon yourself for what happened. If the ectoplasm engendered by you made up the form of the killer, the spirit may have come from without."

"How could it?" she asked wretchedly.

"How could Marthe Beraud exude ectoplasm that formed a bearded, masculine body?" Pursuivant looked across to Zoberg. "Doctor, you surely know the famous "Bien Boa" séance, and how the materialized entity spoke Arabic when the medium, a Frenchwoman, knew little or nothing of that language?"

Zoberg sat with bearded chin on lean hand. His joined brows bristled the more as he corrugated his forehead in thought. "We are each a thousand personalities," he said, sententiously if not comfortingly. "How can we rule them all, or rule even one of them?"

O'Bryant said sourly that all this talk was too high-flown for him to understand or to enjoy. He dared hope, however, that the case could never be tied up to Miss Susan Gird, whom he had known and liked since her babyhood.

"It can never do that," Zoberg said definitely. "No court or jury would convict her on the evidence we are offering against her."

I ventured an opinion: "While you are attempting to show that Susan is a werewolf, you are forgetting that something else was prowling around our fire, just out of sight."

"*Ach*, just out of sight!" echoed Zoberg. "That means you aren't sure what it was."

"Or even that there was anything," added Susan, so suddenly and strongly that I, at least, jumped.

"There was something, all right," I insisted. "I heard it."

"You thought you heard a sound behind the tree," Susan reminded me. "You looked, and there was nothing."

Everyone gazed at me, rather like staid adults at a naughty child. I said, ungraciously, that my imagination was no better than theirs, and that I was no easier to frighten. Judge Pursuivant suggested that we make a search of the surrounding woods, for possible clues.

"A good idea," approved Constable O'Bryant. "The ground's damp. We might find some sort of footprints."

"Then you stay here with Miss Susan," the judge said to him. "We others will circle around."

The gaunt constable shook his head. "Not much, mister. I'm in on whatever searching is done. I've got something to settle with whatever killed my kid brother."

"But there are only three lanterns," pointed out Judge Pursuivant. "We have to carry them – light's our best weapon."

Zoberg then spoke up, rather diffidently, to say that he would be glad to stay with Susan. This was agreed upon, and the other three of us prepared for the search.

I took the lantern from Zoberg's hand, nodded to the others, and walked away among the trees.

XIV "I was – I AM – a wolf"

Deliberately I had turned my face toward the section beyond the fire, for, as I have said repeatedly, it was there that I had heard the movements and cries of the being that had so strongly moved and bewitched Susan. My heart whispered rather loudly that I must look for myself at its traces or lack of them, or forever view myself with scorn.

Almost at once I found tracks, the booted tracks of my three allies. Shaking my lantern to make it flare higher, I went deeper among the clumps, my eyes quartering the damp earth. After a few moments I found what I had come to look for.

The marks were round and rather vague as to toe-positions, yet not so clear-cut as to be made by hoofs. Rather they suggested a malformed stump or a palm with no fingers, and they were deep enough to denote considerable weight; the tracks of my own shoes, next to them, were rather shallower. I bent for a close look, then straightened up, looked everywhere at once, and held my torch above my head to shed light all around; for I had suddenly felt eyes upon me.

I caught just a glimpse as of two points of light, fading away into some leafage and in the direction of the clearing, and toward them I made my way; but there was nothing there, and the only tracks underfoot were of shod human beings, myself or one of the others. I returned to my outward search, following the round tracks.

They were plainly of only two feet – there were no double impressions, like those of a quadruped – but I must have stalked along them for ten minutes when I realized that I had no way of telling whether they went forward or backward. I might be going away from my enemy instead of toward it. A close examination did me little good, and I further pondered that the creature would lurk near the clearing, not go so straight away. Thus arguing within myself, I doubled back.

Coming again close to the starting-point, I thought of a quick visit to the clearing and a comforting word or two with Susan and Zoberg. Surely I was almost there; but why did not the fire gleam through the trees? Were they out of wood? Perplexed, I quickened my pace. A gnarled tree grew in my path, its low branches heavily bearded with vines. Beyond this rose only the faintest of glows. I paused to push aside some strands and peer.

The fire had almost died, and by its light I but half saw two figures, one tall and one slender, standing together well to one side. They faced each other, and the taller – a seeming statue of wet-looking gray – held its companion by a shoulder. The other gray hand was stroking the smaller one's head, pouring grayness thereon.

I saw only this much, without stopping to judge or to wonder. Then I yelled, and sprang into the clearing. At my outcry the two fell apart and faced me. The smallest was Susan, who took a step in my direction and gave a little smothered whimper, as though she was trying to speak through a blanket. I ran to her side, and with a rough sweep of my sleeve I cleared from her face and head a mass of slimy, shiny jelly.

"You!" I challenged the other shape. "What have you been trying to do to her?"

For only a breathing-space it stood still, as featureless and clumsy as a half-formed figure of gray mud. Then darkness sprang out upon it, and hair. Eyes blazed at me, green and fearsome. A sharp muzzle opened to emit a snarl.

"Now I know you," I hurled at it. "I'm going to kill you."

And I charged.

Claws ripped at my head, missed and tore the cloth of my coat. One of my arms shot around a lean, hairy middle with powerful muscles straining under its skin, and I drove my other fist for where I judged the pit of the stomach to be. Grappled, we fell and rolled over. The beast smell I remembered was all about us, and I knew that jaws were shoving once again at my throat. I jammed my forearm between them, so far into the hinge of them that they could not close nor crush. My other hand clutched the skin of the throat, a great loose fistful, drew it taut and began to twist with all my strength. I heard a half-broken yelp of strangled pain, felt a slackening of the body that struggled against me, knew that it was trying to get away. But I managed to roll on top, straddling the thing.

"You're not so good on defense," I panted, and brought my other hand to the throat, for I had no other idea save to kill. Paws grasped and tore at my wrists. There was shouting at my back, in Susan's voice and several others. Hands caught me by the shoulders and tried to pull me up and away.

"No!" I cried. "This is it, the werewolf!"

"It's Doctor Zoberg, you idiot," growled O'Bryant in my ear. "Come on, let him up."

"Yes," added Judge Pursuivant, "it's Doctor Zoberg, as you say; but a moment ago it was the monster we have been hunting."

I had been dragged upright by now, and so had Zoberg. He could only choke and glare for the time being, his fingers to his half-crushed throat. Pursuivant had moved within clutching distance of him, and was eyeing him as a cat eyes a mouse.

"Like Wills, I only pretended to search, then doubled back to watch," went on the judge. "I saw Zoberg and Miss Susan talking. He spoke quietly, rhythmically, commandingly. She went into half a trance, and I knew she was hypnotized.

"As the fire died down, he began the change. Ectoplasm gushed out and over him. Before it took form, he began to smear some upon her. And Mr Wills here came out of the woods and at him."

O'Bryant looked from the judge to Zoberg. Then he fumbled with his undamaged hand in a hip pocket, produced handcuffs and stepped forward. The accused man grinned through his beard, as if admitting defeat in some trifling game. Then he held out his wrists with an air of resignation and I, who had manacled them once, wondered again at their corded strength. The irons clicked shut upon one, then the other.

"You know everything now," said Zoberg, in a soft voice but a steady one. "I was – I am – a wolf; a wolf who hoped to mate with an angel."

His bright eyes rested upon Susan, who shrank back. Judge Pursuivant took a step toward the prisoner.

"There is no need for you to insult her," he said.

Zoberg grinned at him, with every long tooth agleam. "Do you want to hear my confession, or don't you?"

"Sure we want to hear it," grunted O'Bryant. "Leave him alone, judge, and let him talk." He glanced at me. "Got any paper, Mr Wills? Somebody better take this down in writing."

I produced a wad of note-paper and a stub pencil. Placing it upon my knee, with the lantern for light, I scribbled, almost word for word, the tale that Doctor Zoberg told.

XV "And that is the end."

"Perhaps I was born what I am," he began. "At least, even as a lad I knew that there was a lust and a power for evil within me. Night called to me, where it frightens most children. I would slip out of my father's house and run for miles, under the trees or across fields, with the moon for company. This was in Germany, of course, before the war."

"During the war—" began Judge Pursuivant.

"During the war, when most men were fighting, I was in prison." Again Zoberg grinned, briefly and without cheer. "I had found it easy and inspiring to kill persons, with a sense of added strength following. But they caught me and put me in what they called an asylum. I was supposed to be crazy. They confined me closely, but I, reading books in the library, grew to know what the change was that came upon me at certain intervals. I turned my attention to it, and became able to control the change, bringing it on or holding it off at will."

He looked at Susan again. "But I'm ahead of my story. Once, when I was at school, I met a girl – an American student of science and philosophy. She laughed at my wooing, but talked to me about spirits and psychical phenomena. That, my dear Susan, was your mother. When the end of the war brought so many new things, it also brought a different viewpoint toward many inmates of asylums. Some Viennese doctors, and later Sigmund Freud himself, found my case interesting. Of course, they did not arrive at the real truth, or they would not have procured my release."

"After that," I supplied, writing swiftly, "you became an expert psychical investigator and journeyed to America."

"Yes, to find the girl who had once laughed and studied with me. After some years I came to this town, simply to trace the legend of this Devil's Croft. And here, I found, she had lived and died, and left behind a daughter that was her image."

Judge Pursuivant cleared his throat. "I suspect that you're leaving out part of your adventures, Doctor."

Zoberg actually laughed. "*Ja*, I thought to spare you a few shocks. But if you will have them, you may. I visited Russia – and in 1922 a medical commission of the Soviet Union investigated several score mysterious cases of peasants killed – and eaten." He licked his lips, like a cat who thinks of meat. "In Paris I founded and conducted a rather interesting night school, for the study of diabolism in its relationship to science. And in 1936, certain summer vacationists on Long Island were almost frightened out of their wits by a lurking thing that seemed half beast, half man." He chuckled. "Your *Literary Digest* made much of it. The lurking thing was, of course, myself."

We stared. "Say, why do you do these things?" the constable blurted.

Zoberg turned to him, head quizzically aslant. "Why do you uphold your local laws? Or why does Judge Pursuivant study ancient philosophies? Or why do Wills and Susan turn soft eyes upon each other? Because the heart of each so insists."

Susan was clutching my arm. Her fingers bit into my flesh as Zoberg's eyes sought her again.

"I found the daughter of someone I once loved," he went on, with real gentleness in his voice. "Wills, at least, can see in her what I saw. A new inspiration came to me, a wish and a plan to have a comrade in my secret exploits."

"A beast-thing like yourself?" prompted the judge.

Zoberg nodded. "A *lupa* to my *lupus*. But this girl – Susan Gird – had not inherited the psychic possibilities of her mother."

"What!" I shouted. "You yourself said that she was the greatest medium of all time!"

"I did say so. But it was a lie."

"Why, in heaven's name—"

"It was my hope," he broke in quietly, "to make of her a medium, or a lycanthrope – call the phenomenon which you will. Are you interested in my proposed method?" He gazed mockingly around, and his eyes rested finally upon me. "Make full notes, Wills. This will be interesting, if not stupefying, to the psychic research committees.

"It is, as you know, a supernormal substance that is exuded to change the appearance of my body. What, I wondered, would some of that substance do if smeared upon her?"

I started to growl out a curse upon him, but Judge Pursuivant, rapt, motioned for me to keep silent.

"Think back through all the demonologies you have read," Zoberg was urging. "What of the strange 'witch ointments' that, spread over an ordinary human body, gave it beast-form and beast-heart? There, again, legend had basis in scientific fact."

"By the thunder, you're logical," muttered Judge Pursuivant.

"And damnable," I added. "Go on, Doctor. You were going to smear the change-stuff upon Susan."

"But first, I knew, I must convince her that she had within her the essence of a wolf. And so, the séance."

"She was no medium," I said again.

"I made her think she was. I hypnotized her, and myself did weird wonders in the dark room. But she, in a trance, did not know. I needed witnesses to convince her."

"So you invited Mr Wills," supplied Judge Pursuivant.

"Yes, and her father. They had been prepared to accept her as medium and me as observer. Seeing a beast-form, they would tell her afterward that it was she."

"Zoberg," I said between set teeth, "you're convicted out of your own mouth of rottenness that convinces me of the existence of the Devil after whom this grove was named. I wish to heaven that I'd killed you when we were fighting."

"*Ach*, Wills," he chuckled, "you'd have missed this most entertaining autobiographical lecture."

"He's right," grumbled O'Bryant; and, "Let him go on," the judge pleaded with me.

"Once sure of this power within her," Zoberg said deeply, "she would be prepared in heart and soul to change at touch of the ointment – the ectoplasm. Then, to me she must turn as a fellow-creature. Together, throughout the world, adventuring in a way unbelievable—"

His voice died, and we let it. He stood in the firelight, head thrown back, manacled hands folded. He might have been a martyr instead of a fiend for whom a death at the stake would be too easy.

"I can tell what spoiled the séance," I told him after a moment. "Gird, sitting opposite, saw that it was you, not Susan, who had changed. You had to kill him to keep him from telling, there and then."

"Yes," agreed Zoberg. "After that, you were arrested, and, later, threatened. I was in an awkward position. Susan must believe herself, not you, guilty. That is why I have championed you throughout. I went then to look for you."

"And attacked me," I added.

"The beast-self was ascendant. I cannot always control it completely." He sighed. "When Susan disappeared, I went to look for her on the second evening. When I came into this wood, the change took place, half automatically. Associations, I suppose. Constable, your brother happened upon me in an evil hour."

"Yep," said O'Bryant gruffly.

"And that is the end," Zoberg said. "The end of the story and, I suppose, the end of me."

"You bet it is," the constable assured him. "You came with the judge to finish your rotten work. But we're finishing it for you."

"One moment," interjected Judge Pursuivant, and his fire-lit face betrayed a perplexed frown. "The story fails to explain one important thing."

"Does it so?" prompted Zoberg, inclining toward him with a show of negligent grace.

"If you were able to free yourself and kill Mr Gird—"

"By heaven, that's right!" I broke in. "You were chained, Zoberg, to Susan and to your chair. I'd go bail for the strength and tightness of those handcuffs."

He grinned at each of us in turn and held out his hands with their manacles. "Is it not obvious?" he inquired.

We looked at him, a trifle blankly I suppose, for he chuckled once again.

"Another employment of the ectoplasm, that useful substance of change," he said gently. "At will my arms and legs assume thickness, and hold the rings of the confining irons wide. Then, when I wish, they grow slender again, and—"

He gave his hands a sudden flirt, and the bracelets fell from them on the instant. He pivoted and ran like a deer.

"Shoot!" cried the judge, and O'Bryant whipped the big gun from his holster.

Zoberg was almost within a vine-laced clump of bushes when O'Bryant fired. I heard a shrill scream, and saw Zoberg falter and drop to his hands and knees.

We were all starting forward. I paused a moment to put Susan behind me, and in that moment O'Bryant and Pursuivant sprang ahead and came up on either side of Zoberg. He was still alive, for he writhed up to a kneeling position and made a frantic clutch at the judge's coat. O'Bryant, so close that he barely raised his hand and arm, fired a second time.

Zoberg spun around somehow on his knees, stiffened and screamed. Perhaps I should say that he howled. In his voice was the inarticulate agony of a beast wounded to death. Then he collapsed.

Both men stooped above him, cautious but thorough in their examination. Finally Judge Pursuivant straightened up and faced toward us.

"Keep Miss Susan there with you," he warned me. "He's dead, and not a pretty sight."

Slowly they came back to us. Pursuivant was thoughtful, while O'Bryant, Zoberg's killer, seemed cheerful for the first time since I had met him. He even smiled at me, as Punch would smile after striking a particularly telling blow with his cudgel. Rubbing his pistol caressingly with his palm, he stowed it carefully away.

"I'm glad that's over," he admitted. "My brother can rest easy in his grave."

"And we have our work cut out for us," responded the judge. "We must decide just how much of the truth to tell when we make a report."

O'Bryant dipped his head in sage acquiescence. "You're right," he rumbled. "Yes, sir, you're right."

"Would you believe me," said the judge, "if I told you that I knew it was Zoberg, almost from the first?"

But Susan and I, facing each other, were beyond being surprised, even at that.

Adrian Cole

HEART OF THE BEAST

Adrian Cole's recent books include the dark fantasy novel Blood Red Angel *and* Oblivion Hand, *the latter a novelization of some of the stories featuring his heroic fantasy character, the Voidal. His series "The Omaran Saga"* (A Place Among the Fallen, Throne of Fools, The King of Light and Shadows *and* The Gods in Anger) *and "Star Requiem"* (Mother of Storms, Thief of Dreams, Warlord of Heaven *and* Labyrinth of Worlds) *have been published on both sides of the Atlantic, and recent short story appearances include* Dark Voices 2, The Year's Best Fantasy and Horror Fourth Annual Collection, The Anthology of Fantasy & the Supernatural *and* Shadows Over Innsmouth.

As the writer explains: "I originally intended to write a werewolf novel using the title Heart of the Beast, *and a year or two ago I started on a draft manuscript. After about 100 pages I decided it wasn't working out, so shelved it and went on to write something else, although the idea of a werewolf theme persisted. In the end I came up with a variant on my original with creatures called cyberwolves. They run their particular course in the new book,* Armageddon Road.

"I still had it in mind to write another werewolf novel and sketched out a plot, characters and a few themes. This was sitting on the back boiler for a while, until the opportunity came to write a short story for this collection. So the title survived, the main character (initially called simply, Arnoth) has partially survived, and elements of the novel have resurfaced. Perhaps such transformations are apt.

"I still intend to develop Heart of the Beast, *although the working title of the new novel will be the name of the main protagonist,* John Vigilant."

In the end there was only the terror. There was no other way he could have described it. And just as they said, it was cold, icy: he shivered with it, struggling to control his hands. He had the advantage, the primed shotgun. He should have been able to draw on other emotions: after all, they had fuelled him earlier. Disgust, anger, frustration, fury, the blind determination to exact justifiable retribution. These had shaped him and his companions into what they thought would be an irresistible force. The moment had come to exercise that potential power. Briefly he had known another emotion: exultation. The joy of the anticipated kill. Its feral grip had been almost sublime.

Down below him in the shadows his prey skulked. Trapped. Like a fish in a barrel. All he had to do was go down there and finish this. It should be easy. Just go down and end it.

Down into terror.

Grainger lived alone, but he was not a loner. He had many friends in the town and any time there was a party or a gathering, he was always included. He'd come close to marrying once, ten years ago, but the affair had broken off; at the time he wasn't sure if he should have given it more time, a better chance, but now he knew they had been right to end it. These days he was too set in his ways to look for a partner, though he sensed there were still a few interested parties. And God knew his friends had tried hard enough to pair him off. His real friends had stopped trying, or at least, the men had. The wives still hoped he would find a mate. They meant well, but at times it irritated him. He wasn't sure why.

They were not a closely-knit community, not a closed shop, but they drew a lot of comfort from knowing that they could depend on each other when the going got a little rough. The suburbs sprawled, one district blurring into another, but they had their own invisible divides. Grainger had adapted to their ways eagerly. He had lived in the hub of the city before moving, and there he had been truly alone. Out here he had become protective of his new place in society. Just how protective he could not have realized.

Maybe they had been lucky here: the media bawled ceaselessly about crime, vandalism, brutality. Grainger wasn't blind to it, nor was he careless. The dark side of humanity was quite capable of poking its indiscriminate snout anywhere. It was just that here things seemed to be under control. The kids were okay, thieving was minimal, mugging almost unheard of and killing didn't happen, or at least, not often.

So when it began, no one understood what it would lead to, not at first.

Ed Carlyon had disappeared. It didn't make a lot of sense. Ed was a car salesman who'd upset a few people in his time as was the way of car salesmen, but he had a reputation for being fair, and he looked after his friends. He had a wife and three kids. Not a marriage made in heaven, but they were happy. If Ed had been having an affair, it was the best kept secret in history. No money troubles, no problems with drink or gambling. Ed was just a steady guy. But one night he didn't come home.

The police couldn't locate him. Helen, his wife, was going crazy with grief and fear. No trace. They found his car parked at work, no sign of a struggle, no clues. After six weeks, the police filed the case, defeated. Grainger and others knew that they were assuming he'd taken off. Some of the locals who didn't know Ed that well assumed the same.

Then it was Lou Irlam's turn. He was fifty-four, a few years older then Ed Carlyon, but otherwise lived the same kind of life. His two sons had left home a few years before, heading for secure jobs and their own lives, but his marriage was fine. He liked a game of cards, but knew the limits. Another steady guy.

Again, no trace. Walked out of the office where he worked one afternoon, to pick up some groceries. Never seen again. The police gave it their best shot. Another fat zero.

In eight months, five men disappeared. All in the same district. No clues, no signs of foul play, no suggestion of discontent at home, infidelity, personal crisis. None of them had any reason to up and go. And not one of them had taken money from a bank or anything else. They had no more than what they were dressed in.

The police, embarrassed at their inability to learn anything whatsoever about the disappearances, refused to consider the possibility that the men had been murdered. They didn't say as much, but they suspected a conspiracy. They were up against a brick wall and were fed up banging their heads against it. They eased off their investigation.

Five families mourned. And a lot more people got angry. Afraid, but angry. Grainger was one of them. The five men had all been friends. And like other friends, Grainger thought of himself as a survivor. A potential victim.

Because something was hunting them.

No one could say anything that would convince the police that the men had been somehow taken. They paid lip service to the idea, but the file stopped growing, became just another wad of papers in a steel cabinet. The newspapers made a big thing of it at first: Grainger did a good job getting them involved. But the stories and the conjecture got wilder. By the time the media had worn out the "alien invaders" theory and had given voice to all the cranks and weirdos this side of Hell, the public had lost interest.

Tony Garcia had been the first one to come up with the idea. A unit, a defence mechanism. "I won't be the next," he said. "I'll shoot first."

The men, sequestered in Grainger's flat, talking deep into the night, looked singularly haggard.

"If the police can't protect us, it's up to us to do it for ourselves," said Garcia.

"You sayin' we should carry guns all the time?" said Ray Probin nervously. "That ain't goin' to be easy, Tony."

"Maybe not. But we're agreed on one thing. Someone is doing this. We don't know who, or why. But they're out there. Waiting for a chance to do it again. I say it's our turn to react."

"To do what?" said Al Hayes, a huge, bearded man who should have been afraid of no one. But like the rest, he was full of unease.

"Find them before they find us," said Garcia.

"How will we know?" said Probin.

"They'll make a mistake—"

"And then what?"

Garcia mimicked using a shotgun, pulling back his trigger finger.

Hayes snorted. "Hell, Tony, you gotta be sure about this. Can't just shoot every snooper in town."

"No. But we need to show our intentions. Let this bastard know we mean to defend ourselves."

"The law says this killer doesn't exist," said Grainger with a wry smile. "So they won't miss him if we do deal with him."

There were smiles at that, and in them a silent acquiescence. They would become hunters.

They set up midnight patrols, rotating every few nights in groups of threes and fours. Their wives and families, those that had them, argued, for when it came to it, they didn't want their men at risk. But they knew the families of the five missing men, shared their torments. They didn't want the reality. The risk was worth it.

The police found out about it, but they turned a blind eye. Maybe they assumed it wouldn't last. Let these people blow off steam, they told themselves. A few wasted nights and they'll soon get tired chasing shadows, or stumbling over drunks. Put their goddamed guns away.

For a few weeks nothing happened. The patrols went out, did their agreed rounds and saw only the excesses of youth mingled with the sad decay of an underclass structure that inevitably seeped outwards even here. It depressed them to realize that there was more dissatisfaction and more resentment in their society than they had perceived. Walking the streets was a very different reality to the cushioned experience of artificial images on a television screen: the pain out here was alive.

Grainger met Al Hayes one night after both had been discreetly traversing their patches. They huddled in shadows,

Hayes offering a flask of hot coffee which Grainger gladly accepted.

"Think it's time to quit this?" said the big man. In the darkness he was like a bear, his bulk a deterrent to any potential assailant.

Grainger sipped from the plastic cup. "Maybe whoever it was has moved on. Maybe they only take out so many from each district. Could be in another town by now."

"Yeah. Once they saw us, maybe it's been enough to scare them off. You reckon?"

It was what they wanted to believe. The group was tiring of the night work. Grainger nodded. "We better talk to the others—"

Hayes stiffened, his whole bulk quivering for a moment. He dropped the flask and coffee gushed out of it, splattering the pavement. Nothing seemed to move, apart from the upwardly curling tendrils of steam.

Grainger followed the big man's gaze, drawing in his breath, fingers crushing the plastic cup. Across the road, beneath a tree something was watching them. They knew they were in deep shadow, but the figure's eyes seemed to pierce the darkness: it was obvious they saw clearly.

Hayes swore obscenely, the words cutting the night air as though it were a curtain. The figure hunched up its shoulders, turned and moved swiftly away down the sidewalk. It seemed to be injured, as if it had damaged a leg: its flight was awkward, unnatural.

Grainger had released his cup, was now gripping the big man's arm. "Christ, Al, did you see who that was? Did you see the *face*?"

"I think so—"

"Al, it was Ed, Ed Carlyon! I swear to God—"

"No," Hayes murmured, but he knew Grainger was right.

For a moment they gaped at each other. Neither wanted to admit the sudden shudder of fear that went through them.

"We have to catch up with him. Ask him—" began Grainger, but Hayes cut him short with a curt nod. Without saying anything, they both checked their shotguns.

They ran, relieved to be doing something. Their footfalls broke the night silence. Somewhere ahead of them they thought they glimpsed movement, the imperfect flight of their former friend. They had said nothing about the changes in the face they had seen, but in both their minds those images burned. It was not the Ed Carlyon they had known. The man had changed inexplicably. They were almost afraid to catch up with him.

There was a park, its gates partly open. The locks had been snapped off long ago, never repaired. The fugitive had gone this way. Hayes squinted, pointing with his gun barrel to a cluster of trees and the slope beyond. "Lou Jaeger's breaker's yard is down there. Plenty of places for Ed to hole up. Think that's where he's been all this time?"

Grainger grunted. It was too confusing, the implications too bizarre. Why the heck should Ed Carlyon want to quit his home and hide out in a landscape of mangled machinery and autos?

They heard a shout ahead of them, but it wasn't the fleeing figure. Someone else had emerged from the trees. It was Tony Garcia, another of the night watch, and he was moving across the grass, intent on cutting off Carlyon's flight. The latter had bent almost double now, loping along in an ungainly way.

Grainger and Hayes were some fifty yards from Carlyon as Garcia stepped out directly in front of him, gun lowered. They had all moved well away from the park's pattern of pathways and the light out there was poor. Grainger and Hayes slowed, walking forward, the big man's chest heaving, his breath coming in rasps. If they thought that Carlyon would stop for Garcia, they were wrong.

Instead, the loping figure raised an arm, an arm which the night somehow seemed to distort, to elongate, and brought it crashing down across the man confronting him. Garcia's gun tumbled aside, there was a brief scream, then Carlyon was running down the slope again, this time moving more quickly.

Grainger and the big man broke into a trot, more concerned about Garcia than the runaway. They came upon him in moments and were staggered to find him floundering about like a man in a pool, one hand at his throat, the other beating pathetically at the grass in a desperate bid for help. His chest was wet.

Hayes bent down and gently pulled at the fingers, but he gasped. "How the hell did he do this?" The throat was ripped open, the top of Garcia's chest also torn.

"Ed did *that*?" said Grainger, gazing in stupefaction at the figure in the distance. As he looked, it leapt over a wire fence at the bottom of the park and was lost to sight down the slope beyond. Almost mesmerised, as if he had been watching a phantom, Grainger was suddenly aware of Hayes beside him, shaking him.

"He's dead. *Dead*, for Chrissake!" the huge man was shouting, his whole body shuddering with anger, fear, confusion. "Tony's dead!"

Grainger snapped out of his own confusion, staring at the inert form of Garcia. "Al, you want to take care of him? Get the police or something?"

"What are you going to do?"

"One of us has got to track Ed Carlyon, or whatever the hell it is we saw. If he gets away tonight, chances are we'll lose him. I'm going down there."

Terror twisted the big man's face. He looked as if he wanted to cry. "I'll get help."

"Do it." Grainger raced off across the park without looking back. Another moment and he would have gone with Hayes, back to safety, to sanity. But he had to finish this.

It had been much easier than he had thought. Beyond the park, standing on the slope that led to the waste region of the breaker's yard, he had felt the stirring of an animal reaction. The hunt. The potential kill. Ed Carlyon, or whatever he had become, was fair game. He had killed. The law was with Grainger.

Silently he prowled along the upper slope, watching the huge mounds of scrap metal and wasted automobiles below. Heaped and packed, they offered no immediate bolt hole. Carlyon would have had to burrow through a solid wall to hide. He must have traversed the perimeter of the yard, at least for a while.

Then Grainger saw it, and knew he had found the place. A huge shed, a patchwork of corrugated iron sheeting, fused into the landscape. One of its twin doors hung askew, hinges torn, to reveal a black maw. A burnt-out engine sprawled half in, half out of the shadows of the doorway, a collapsed robot, congealing in its rust shroud.

He was in there. Grainger knew it for sure. He could almost feel Carlyon's eyes on him, as he had done across the street when he first saw him. And the terror surged.

He began the descent.

Standing beside the rotting engine, Grainger stared into the darkness ahead of him, shotgun lifted, finger tensing on the trigger. Too dark to go in.

"Ed," he whispered, but it was a croak, smothered by fear. He called again, louder, but there was no response. The silence was supernatural, nothing stirring. He heard his own breathing, felt his whole system shaking. As he reached for the leaning door, something sputtered inside the vast shed.

A pool of light leaked towards him. But it revealed little of the interior.

"Ed, I know you're in there." Dumb words, but he needed the sound of his own voice. He edged forward, just through the line of the doors. Squinting, he saw an old oil lamp burning several yards ahead of him. It sat on a workbench that hadn't been used in years. Redundant machinery filled the shed, chains hanging from overhead, wrapped in thick cobweb nets. Parts of engines and discarded tools littered the dusty floor.

Grainger's eyes were getting used to the light; his circle of vision widened. But there was no sign of an occupant, other than the lamp. But Ed must have lit it.

"You don't have to be scared, Ed. It's Grainger." He tried to take a degree of comfort from the words, but his heart lurched as he caught movement near the shell of an old auto. He swung the gun a round. Beyond its snout he saw the figure. It was motionless and for a moment he thought it was no more than an old suit hanging up. But then the light mapped the face, danced in the wild eyes.

It was Ed Carlyon, but he was a sick man. Crazy, maybe.

"Ed. What the hell happened to you?"

"He doesn't understand you." The voice was a whisper, emanating from the shadows behind the lamp glow.

Grainger swung to face it, but saw nothing clearly. "Who are you? What's happening here?" The sound had come as such a shock that he had almost emptied the shotgun in its direction.

"Put down the gun. You won't need it." The voice was remarkably calm, incongruously so for the situation.

"Get into the light where I can see you," snapped Grainger, aiming the gun deliberately.

"Very well." As the shadow began to coalesce, Grainger heard a heavy tread behind him and swivelled at once. He wasn't going to fall for that old trick—

But he gaped, almost dropping the gun. In the doorway, hunched over and clutching at the frame for support was Garcia. Al Hayes had been wrong about him: he hadn't been dead at all.

"Tony—" said Grainger, stepping forward, but realized his error at once. Garcia looked up and the light from the lamp gleamed on the open neck wound, the sheen of blood across his chest. No one could have sustained such a wound and *walked* here.

A low rumble, animal-like, frothed on Garcia's lips. And his eyes were wild, wild like Ed Carlyon's. *Beast* eyes. Again, Grainger stumbled back. His muscles locked, prisoners finally of the terror. Something brushed past him, a dark shape, and faced Garcia. The latter looked as though he would spring, regardless of the horrific injury, but instead the wild eyes drooped, like the eyes of someone who'd been drugged. He leaned against the door stiffly, all fight gone out of him.

The man turned and Grainger saw him for the first time. He was tall, his pale face marked with a kind of cold arrogance, almost disdain. His overcoat was cut from a heavy, expensive, dark material, the lapels pulled up tight to the man's neck. In spite of the mildness of the night, he wore thin gloves.

"I am here to help you," he said and Grainger now noticed the voice had no accent, at least not one he recognized.

"What's happening? Tony needs help. So does Ed." He swung around, but Carlyon had not moved, frozen like a dummy, except for the eyes. They were filled with something alien, hellish.

"You've seen what your friends have become. You call them werewolves."

Grainger's face twisted in a grimace. "Don't take me for a fool—"

"All right. Call it what you like. But they are no longer what they were. None of them."

"The others are the same?"

The stranger nodded calmly, as though it made no difference to him. "Six of them now. All here."

"You said you want to help. How?"

"You have formed a group of vigilantes. You guessed that your friends had been hunted. You were right. But you have no idea what hunted them."

Grainger was conscious that he had raised his shotgun. Its mouth was no more than a few inches from the stranger's chest, but the man ignored it. "You trying to tell me they were hunted by a werewolf? That it did this to them – changed them?"

"I am. And you need help to destroy it. The gun is useless. All your powers are useless, your technology inadequate."

"But you can help?"

"I can. I have powers that your people don't have—"

"My people? What do you mean, my people? Who the hell are *your* people?"

"We don't belong here. The other, the werewolf, he fled here from the purges. My race seeks their extinction. He intends to contaminate enough of you to serve him, to make a sanctuary of your world. You can see he has already begun."

Grainger flashed a look at Garcia, another at Carlyon. "You're controlling them, is that it? Stopping them from attacking?"

"Yes. Their master has gone to ground. Before we begin the hunt, there is work to be done here. Unpleasant work."

Grainger was very still. This guy was completely nuts. Maybe he was some kind of mesmerist: he'd hypnotized Ed and Tony, that had to be it. There must be some kind of logical explanation.

Outside, there came a sudden distant howl. Grainger almost cried out in fear, his gut freezing up on him. The stranger merely turned, going to the door. He ignored Garcia and looked up the slope beyond the fence to the park.

"You doubt me. I expected that," he said. "Stay in the shadows and take notice." He moved back inside, waiting.

Presently there was another howl, much closer. Grainger realized that it was a dog of some kind, probably a police dog, put on the scent by the cops that Al Hayes must have contacted. Its feet scratched in the dirt outside the shed, its snuffling loud in the night. In another moment Grainger saw its black snout questing through the ope doors, saliva dripping from the gums as if the beast was eager to attack.

As it padded into the shed, ignoring Garcia, the stranger gently pushed the door to, shutting out the night. In the lamplight, Grainger could see that the black hound was huge. It faced him, barring its fangs, its intent clear. But before it could spring, the stranger called something aloud and at once the dog turned, snarling. It began to turn around and around, rolling over, twisting and convulsing, spittle flying from it in streamers.

Grainger's eyes bulged: *the dog was changing shape*.

It was true. In minutes its legs had stretched and thickened. Its neck was twice as large, the face pulled forward into a monstrous, vulpine snout, yellow fangs like sabres. And it dragged itself up on to its hind legs, front claws pulled up to its chest. Its scarlet eyes turned to the stranger, awaiting instruction.

"I have powers your people do not have," said the stranger. "So does the one I hunt."

Grainger could hardly stand, the shotgun hanging uselessly at his side. "Okay," he breathed. "So you have powers. Jeeze, but what do you want with us?"

"Will you trust me? Will you employ me?"

"*Employ* you?"

"I ask only one thing. The heart of the beast you seek. I must be certain that it dies. Your race are slaves to curiosity. They would capture it. I want its heart. I want to be sure of my kill."

Grainger nodded. "Far as I'm concerned, you can have what you like." His eyes were still fixed on the upright hound.

The stranger said something to it and it dropped on all fours and slunk into the shadows, out of sight.

"My friends," said Grainger uneasily, looking at them. "Can they be – helped? Changed back to what they were."

The stranger's face was unreadable, but he shook his head. "Once contaminated, the damage is permanent. I can keep them in check, but that is all."

"So what happens to them, for Chrissakes! They can't be left like this—"

"You have no choice. You cannot let them go back to their families. Or would you do that?"

"There must be something! Surely a hospital—"

"There's no hope for them. If you return them to your kind, you run the risk of contaminating others."

Grainger looked at Garcia. He had seen how quickly he had been transformed. Could that go on happening, spreading like a virulent disease?

"There is only one thing you can do," said the stranger. He indicated the oil lamp.

"*Burn* them? You're out of your mind—"

There were more sounds from the embankment outside, voices mingled with fresh barking.

"The pursuit. I have to lead them away, take them off the scent. You must destroy your former friends, using fire. There is a brand behind you. And the other four men are there."

Grainger watched, utterly confused, as the stranger snapped his fingers at where the dog had been stretched out. At once it rose and came into the light, mercifully restored. Had its shape-changing been an illusion? But no, Grainger could not stomach the thought of seeing it again.

The man eased the door open and spoke softly to the dog. It bolted silently into the night. The stranger turned.

"You must do it. I will lead the hunt far away. In the morning, the police will find this place, the bodies. They won't know what really happened. I will call you. Talk to your friends. Tell them I can help. Remember the price I ask." His eyes held Grainger's for a moment, but Grainger wasn't conscious of anything probing his mind, controlling it.

Then the man was gone. Outside there were brief shouts, but they began to fade quickly, as did the last of the howls of the dogs eager to give chase.

Grainger was torn. Should he go out to his friends, call the police? But what if the stranger had been right? He couldn't let Garcia and the others be found, not like this.

He picked up the oil lamp by its curved handle. It daubed Carlyon in an eerie glow, igniting the eyes, so filled with hatred, hatred that could not have been human. Grainger wondered about the stranger. Had it been *him*? Had he, after all, been the one who had contaminated the men? But if so, why show himself?

I have to do this, Grainger told himself. *These men have to die.*

He walked a little way into the shed, lifting the lamp. By its wavering glow he saw the others, the four missing men. Like Carlyon and Garcia, they were wretched, hunched, animals restrained by an invisible barrier. Grainger found the brand, made from an oil-soaked cloth wrapped tightly around a metal spar. He picked it up and ignited it: it flamed instantly, the heat dazzling him.

At once the four men began to snarl, hands held up like talons, their faces horribly changed. Grainger turned to see Carlyon and Garcia staggering forward, standing beside their companions.

And Grainger knew that once the light went out, they would leap forward, unrestrained. Only the threat of fire held them back now. He really did have no choice but to kill them.

The irrational drive to survive spurred him in his awful work.

He reached out and thrust his brand at the chest of the first of the creatures. Flames belched, fire catching as if the man were made of dry tinder, a scarecrow. The mouth opened to scream, but only a cloud of smoke emerged.

Now that he had begun, Grainger gritted his teeth and torched another two. They fell back, more flames erupting. Arms waved frantically, uselessly. Grainger stepped away, sensed someone closing with him. He twisted, bringing the still flaming brand down across the shoulder of the mutilated Garcia. The result was just as immediate.

Grainger was backing towards the door. Only Ed Carlyon remained on his feet. He lumbered forward, and for an instant Grainger paused, the memories flashing, but Carlyon's fangs gleamed in the torchlight. Grainger struck and the beast toppled backwards, enveloped.

It was over. Grainger turned to leave, but a shadow moved into the light by the door. There was one left to destroy. In his haste he had miscounted. He raised the brand he had been about to toss aside. And almost dropped it in horror.

The figure illuminated by the flames was a mirror image.

It held out its hand for the torch. "You've done enough," said a voice he recognized all too clearly as his own.

He wasn't fast enough to react, to understand. The creature before him took the torch easily. Grainger moved at last, stepping forward, mouth open to speak, but the torch jabbed at him, once, twice, and the flames caught hold quickly. Grainger burst through the doors, but his shins smacked into the discarded engine. He crashed over it, locked in a parody of an embrace, the flames leaping.

The figure tossed the torch into the shed, adding to the fires that were already threatening to turn it into an inferno.

The voice on the end of the phone said, "Is that Grainger?"

"Yes."

"You know who I am?"

It was impossible to mistake the voice with no accent. "Yes."

"You've heard the radio?"

"About the fire? Yes."

"You did well. The police found enough to assume that your missing friends had been recovered. Of course, they'll want to question you."

"That's okay, I think I can handle it."

"Once they leave you alone, I'll contact you again. This isn't over yet."

"I'll be waiting." The creature that called itself Grainger put down the phone. *And I'll be ready for you. Oh, yes, more than ready.*

On the sketch pad by the phone there was a single, idle doodle, the shape of an innocuous valentine heart.

Les Daniels

WEREMAN

In 1968, Les Daniels graduated with honours in English literature from Brown University in Providence, Rhode Island. Since then he has been a freelance writer, composer, film buff and musician. He has performed with such groups as Soop, Snake and The Snatch; The Swamp Steppers, and The Local Yokels.

His first book was Comix: A History of Comic Books in America *(1971), since when he has written a number of non-fiction studies, including* Living in Fear: A History of Horror in the Mass Media, Marvel: Five Fabulous Decades of the World's Greatest Comics *and* DC Comics: Sixty Years of the World's Favorite Comic Book Heroes. *He also edited the oversized anthology* Dying of Fright: Masterpieces of the Macabre, *illustrated by Lee Brown Coye. Daniels' debut novel,* The Black Castle, *was published in 1978 and introduced readers to enigmatic vampire-hero Don Sebastian de Villanueva. It was followed by* The Silver Skull, Citizen Vampire, Yellow Fog, No Blood Spilled *and* White Demon.

Although I've read a number of werewolf tales that used the same basic inversion of the myth as the following story, I think Daniels handles the theme better than almost anybody else …

He had no name (few wolves do) and little enough of memory. And when he remembered anything at all, it was not the cold sharp air of the forest piercing his nostrils, nor the musky scent of frightened prey, for there is no need to recall what is so often there. Instead his recollections were of stranger scents: flaming bits of bodies with the blood burned out of them, and beings trapped in rolling iron boxes, each one spewing forth cloud upon cloud of deadly fumes instead of sweetly pungent droppings. These odours haunted him, along with visions of pale hairless things that staggered on their fat hind legs, their paws wrapped in dried skins stolen from other creatures. Such things were monstrous, as were the celebrations in airless wooden boxes that did not move, where there was nothing to breathe but smoking weeds and the stink of fermented fruits and grains. There might be howling in such a box, but it came from another box, and it was marred by the sound of lightning forced through scraping metal wire, and wind forced through dried dead reeds.

He dreamed of these things when the moon was round, and had he been able he might have spoken of them to his fellows in the pack. Yet he was grateful that he had no words, and wondered why he knew of them at all. They were one of his dreams.

He slept in a den with his mate and her pups; he coupled with her when she gave him the scent; yet still he dreamed of nuzzling loins that reeked of mint or even strawberry. Horror possessed him. He trembled and howled, and all the more because his tiny forebrain knew as much of the truth as it could contain: when the light in the sky became a circle, he became a man.

He whimpered and snuggled into the musty fur of his mate, wondering all the while if it was her beauty or his own bestiality that was only a fragment of his troubled sleep. He wondered where he was.

Then he was free, loping through the snow in the deep track that had been plowed for him by a wandering moose, hearing nothing but the whisper of the wind and the touch of his feet on the ice beneath them. Hunger bit at his belly, almost like another animal attacking him; perhaps that was what had started the dreams and then driven him out into the night. His pack was starving, all of them, and they could not range free from the den while the pups were new. They would not survive much longer without food, and so he hunted, on and on for more than a dozen miles, pausing only to mark the trail with his leg lifted.

It was when he lowered his leg that he realized the change

was coming, for the pads on his foot turned suddenly tender, and the cold cut through them. He had lost the talent, which all wolves possess, of regulating his own body temperature, and by this sign he could tell that he was turning into a monster.

He began to shiver in the frigid air, rearing up on his hind legs to snap at nothing, a growl in his throat as he felt his teeth drawn painfully back into his head until he had only thirty-two little stumps, hardly enough to fill the muzzle being crushed back into his face. Everything was pulling back into him and everything was agony; he experienced each individual hair as it was absorbed into his stinging flesh.

And then he bloated, bulking up into a pink and swollen thing more than twice his proper weight, a thick and weak and hairless thing that feared the gentle dark. It fled shaking and screaming through the snow, and it took him with it.

With feeble, bleeding, clawless forepaws, the man he had become turned over a rock made slippery with a transparent glaze, and found the cache of clothes beneath it. He could not remember how they came to be there, but when he crawled into them the cold could not hurt him as much. Everything about him had changed except his hunger. He staggered on in search of food, his numb feet stuffed into the skin of slaughtered cows.

Much of the night had given way to his slow progress through the snow before he topped a rise and let his eyes confirm the truth his ears and nose had told him long ago: he was about to enter the other world. Below him was an endless stream of poison gas, floating over a strip of ground that looked like a dry river bed, and through that raced a succession of the iron boxes with humans caught inside. These beings seemed to be following the moon the way he was; in fact, each one of their boxes was in pursuit of two bright yellow disks of light that it could never catch. He saw that much almost at once, but decided he would follow the lights too. This was what men did. Perhaps there was food at the mouth of the empty river.

Dragging his feet through the piles of the grey slush that spattered at him, he paced behind the headlights (he began to to know their name), staying carefully to one side as it came back to him that cars could kill.

Finally he realized where they were going. It was not the moon they were pursuing after all, but a big red star whose outline glowed against the sky. There were red squiggles beside it, and somehow he knew that they meant RED STAR too, although that made no sense when the red star was right there beside them anyway. And they didn't look like what they said; they looked like splashes of blood on black snow.

Then he saw that the RED STAR was another box, but so much bigger than the others that he could not look around it. Most of it seemed to be made of ice: it glistened in vast sheets, and light came shining through to fall on him. The cars opened, and those who had been caught inside rushed away like sensible creatures but then gravitated at once toward the giant trap that looked like fire enclosed in ice. He sensed their hunger, and despite his fear he followed them. A good hunter could steal food even from a snare.

He was startled by the glare inside, brighter than sunlight and colder than moonlight. He closed his eyes against it as death filled his nostrils. Hundreds of animals had perished here, and their bodies had not been consumed. The overwhelming sense of slaughter and of waste filled him with dread even as he felt himself begin to drool.

Someone shoved against him; he snarled and raised his upper lip before he remembered that he had no fangs to bare. Dozens of humans had gathered here, but they were not a pack. Each one was like a lone wolf without a territory of its own; each one was angry and aggressive and afraid. They had hold of other little boxes that moved like the cars did, and they pushed them at each other as they passed. Some of them put things in these small boxes, and just the sight of that made his head swim. Everything in this world was inside something else; nothing ran free.

The noise he had dreamed about washed over him again: wires and reeds, and skins struck by sticks, with the scraping of hair against gut wailing over them. He found himself humming along with it against his will; he was becoming more like the humans with every minute he spent among them. He took a shopping cart and did with it what the others were doing.

The light was so intense it almost blinded him, just as darkness would blind a man, and the music made him deaf. Only the stubby pink nose he had been cursed with told him anything at all. It spoke of meat.

He was in an aisle filled with meat. The floors were meat and the walls were meat, and they stretched out before him as far as his dazzled eyes could see.

The sight should have brought him joy, but there was terror in it, too, the terror that only excess can bring. Had there ever been a time when so many animals had died at once? What could have killed them all, and what had stopped it from eating them? The fur on his back would have stood on end if it had not vanished hours ago.

He could smell cattle and sheep and pigs, chickens and turkeys and ducks, a few kinds of fish he recognized and many more that he did not. He could smell hundreds of dead creatures, thousands of them, and on each of them was the stench of decay. This was not fresh meat, still quivering with the hot pulse of blood; this was something sliced and drained and spoiled.

It was cold, too. He felt the chill of death seep into his hand as he clutched involuntarily at part of a cow. The meat had already been chewed up, like what he regurgitated to feed his cubs, and it was enclosed in transparent ice like the stuff that made up the walls of the BIG STAR. With trembling fingers he dropped it into his cart. Nearby lay pigs which had been masticated and then stuffed into their own intestines, even though such parts of an animal were not good to eat. He passed them by, but he could not resist the chance to sweep three chickens into the cart, even though they were as cold and hard as stone.

Then he was on a rampage, grabbing with numb fingers at the ribs of a hog, the leg of a lamb, the brain of a calf. He snatched at a cluster of chicken livers, still swimming in chilled blood, and felt the sticky liquid squirt out over his hand. He licked at it and saw a female staring at him. He growled at her.

It was time to go, time to escape with this meat before he joined it in those frigid walls that surrounded him. Panic surged through him when he saw that the way out was blocked, and then he recognized the checkout line for what it was. This standing in a row was something only humans did, and he was delighted by his cleverness in understanding it. Perhaps he would get away after all.

He followed a metal cage that had been loaded with the icy fragments of dead animals. Humans stood before him and behind him, similarly laden, their wire traps having captured creatures that were already corpses, but it was not this ugly image that made him shiver. Instead, he was possessed by the idea of taking these broken bodies to a place where he could expose them to a flame and watch the fat and juices flare into the sky, leaving him nothing but a dried husk to chew. The very thought made him gag, but he knew he would carry out this mad plan unless something stopped him. He tried to hold on to a picture of his pups, waiting in the burrow he had dug with his own paws, but somehow they seemed very far away, and he knew that they might die without seeing any of this meat he had hunted down for them.

Squinting against the glare around him, he watched those ahead of him file out into the night. Some sort of ritual seemed to be involved. They had to pass before a young female, hardly more than a cub herself, and they had to let her touch each one of their treasures as they greeted her. And there was something else. Each one made an offering to her, passing her something that looked like a green leaf, and sometimes more than one. But where could they have found green leaves in the winter? At this time of the year they were scarcer than prey. His twitching hands were empty, and the clothes he wore began to itch. He laid out his catch before the female and allowed her to touch it.

"Forty-two forty-nine," she said.

He had no idea what these sounds meant. She looked at him. He suddenly felt dizzy.

"Forty-two forty-nine," she said.

He thought of green leaves, and of summer, and of plentiful game. He dropped to his knees.

The human behind him saw what was happening and sprinted for the dairy section at the back of the store.

The cashier leaned over her register to get a better look just as he rose again on his hind legs. His slavering jaws closed on her face.

He fed, and not on putrid, juiceless carrion. He experienced the taste of living blood splashing in his mouth, the feel of hot flesh throbbing against his tongue. The purity, the truth of it. His throat was full.

He shrugged off the last of his clothing and ran. The BIG STAR opened up its glistening wall of ice and set him free. He danced around a stream of rolling traps and capered across the unbroken snow until he reached the shelter of the trees.

The chunks of the young cashier were safe inside him, ready to be coughed up when he was home at last. His children would eat tonight.

Nicholas Royle

ANYTHING BUT YOUR KIND

Nicholas Royle was born in Manchester in 1963. He is the author of five novels – Counterparts, Saxophone Dreams, The Matter of the Heart, The Director's Cut *and* Antwerp – *and two novellas* – The Appetite *and* The Enigma of Departure. *He has published around 120 short stories and to date has one collection to his name,* Mortality.

Widely published as a journalist, with regular appearances in Time Out *and the* Independent, *he has also edited thirteen original anthologies, including two volumes of* Darklands, Darklands 2, The Tiger Garden: A Book of Writers' Dreams *and* '68: New Stories From Children of the Revolution.

Since 2006 he has been teaching creative writing at Manchester Metropolitan University. He has won three British Fantasy Awards and the Bad Sex Prize once. His short story collection was shortlisted for the inaugural Edge Hill Prize.

About the background to the following story, the writer reveals: "In the UK we're used to the idea of there being very few wild animals – where once we had wolves and wild boar roaming free we now have domesticated Alsatians and farmyard pigs – so the many sights of big cats in recent years have really captured the public imagination. Virtually every species has been reported in many areas of the country, though the black panther crops up most frequently . . ."

It wasn't until the Rugby radio masts came into view on the right-hand side of the train that Gary felt he had really left London behind. They marked a psychological half-way point for him and once past them he was nearer his native north country than the city in which he'd spent the last ten tears, drifting in and out of dull jobs and dangerous relationships.

When the polytechnics were converted into universities practically overnight, new courses sprang up everywhere, and Gary had applied to teach the creative writing MA at what had once been his local poly without seriously considering what he'd do if they actually offered him the job. So when they did, he looked around, decided he'd miss the East End supply teaching like he'd miss having raw chillis rubbed on the inside of his eyelids; considered the answer machine at his flat, its tape worn thin with whining messages from Estelle, the last brooding hysteric he'd made the mistake of chatting up during a cigarette break in a Forest Gate staffroom; ran his finger along the spines of his own series of south London detective novels, whose anti-hero he'd killed off in the last book through sheer boredom; he looked around at all of this and opened up the job acceptance template on his Toshiba.

The flat was a rented one-bed hard-to-let affair in the unfriendliest corner of Dalston – a fiercely contested honour – so moving out was hardly a wrench and, once he'd had time to think about the idea, he was so glad to be returning up north he didn't care about losing a month's rent. It was all pretty much last minute, which included the setting up of the course itself: in short, it hadn't been, and it would be more or less up to Gary to do what he wanted. He supposed the Government – or more likely private sponsors – had been throwing money at the new universities and they hadn't known what to do with it. The Faculty of Arts and Letters, McDonald's Building; English Department, Scottish Widows Wing. Who cares, he thought as the train crawled through Stafford, it's a job, it gets me away from London and I'll be surrounded by students. He'd been feeling old lately and figured some new blood was just what he needed.

He stood on the platform and took a deep breath of wintry air. He half convinced himself he could taste the dark-red, flash-strobed excitement of his youth, then had a dry chuckle at his own expense and swung his bag over his shoulder. The man on the barrier returned his smile: yes, he was home again. Stepping out into the street he was about to hail a cab when he had second thoughts and began the long walk down the hill towards the bus station. Estelle had said many times he should pack his bags and go back up north if he hated London so much, but for some reason he'd never taken the idea seriously. As he looked about him now at the familiar street names and road signs he knew he should have done it long ago. He felt like a kid again, running out of school into a wide leaf-strewn playground. He only hoped the north would accept him back after so long.

The first surprise was the trams, their muffled klaxons honking like foghorns in the sharp white gaps between redbrick edifices. He'd read about the return of the trams, of course, but his was a generation that was more used to trams that were metallic shrieks cutting through the smells of fresh coffee, sausage vendors and Gitanes in Brussels, Cologne and Zürich. Manchester was a different matter, with its Waddingtons, chippies and Capstan Full Strength, but as soon as he saw the trams – a horn brought him to an abrupt halt and he watched the grey-green snake slink by – he felt they belonged. The bus station held another shock: gone was the criss-cross, Bridget Riley repetition of orange and white, to be replaced by a pantone chart of bus liveries. When he'd left, the Tories had only recently seized power and so were still a long way from their deregulation of the buses with its riot of colour and chaos of timetable.

He picked up a copy of the *Manchester Evening News* which had fresh sightings of the big cats splashed over the front page. He remembered when the *MEN* was a broadsheet and his parents were proud to take it, but the big cats story had captured his imagination.

As the bus bounced and creaked through the city's northern outskirts, Gary plugged in his Walkman and listened to an old compilation tape. He asked the jolly rosy-cheeked conductor for a single to his early twenties and his soundtrack was The Fall, Joy Division, Performance, The Passage. The copper-bright Rochdale canal cut through the industrial wasteland like a rusty wire through cheesy nostalgia.

He opened the *Evening News* and read about the big cats.
Although there had been rumours and reports for some years
about animals roaming free in the British countryside – jungle
cats in North Wales and Shropshire, a black panther in north
Devon, the "Fen Tiger" and the "Surrey Puma" – and a man
in Worcester even shot some video film of what looked like
a melanistic leopard, these sightings in the north-west had
captured the nation's imagination with their frequency: over 50
sightings had been reported since mid-summer. Nothing had
yet been recorded on film but photographers and TV crews
were coming from as far afield as Caithness and Cornwall to
hang around shivering on Black Hill at the Lancashire/West
Yorkshire border. In Gary's earphones The Passage sang their
ironic tribute to James Anderton, God's policeman. A party of
hikers from Chadderton, Gary read, had been confronted on
their path across Saddleworth Moor by a black cat the size of an
Alsatian. It had growled at them once and a Chester zoologist
wrote that they had probably been saved by their very fear
which rooted them to the spot. The hikers spoke of the animal
flicking its tail and vanishing behind a peat bank. "Needless
to say," Gary read, which made him wonder why the reporter
had bothered to say it, "the party returned the next day with
cameras but the Moors Mauler failed to reappear."

Gary couldn't see the name catching on. For, although
nocturnal livestock losses had been reported by farmers, no
humans had yet been attacked in this series of sightings, and,
in any case, the cats had been spotted throughout the region
from Brighouse to Warrington, Blackburn to Wilmslow. For the
rest of the journey he looked out of the window at the changing
landscape: more space opened out between the clusters of
houses, and the moors loomed sullen as stormclouds.

The first creative writing class took place four days later.
In that time Gary had found a flat and moved in, sampled a
few local pubs but found them a bit slow (he would find out
where the students went drinking), and been for an enjoyable
but unproductive walk on the moors. His flat had a cylinder
gas fire, the smell of which reminded him of the newsagent's

where he'd worked for a spell after giving up his paper round. He thought about travelling across the city to see if the shop was still standing, but decided it could wait.

One of the reasons Gary had been surprised to get the job was because of his lack of experience. He'd worked on and off with local schools in the East End, though more off than on, and taught English as a foreign language to diplomats' sons in Kensington for six months. His natural approach was more laidback and informal than had been appropriate – "The principal is a little concerned about your earring," one of the suits had informed him – for the tutelage of young Kuwaiti gentlemen in W8, but he still spent half an hour trying on clothes before the first creative writing seminar, finally settling on a pair of baggy black trousers, white T-shirt and check overshirt. "How do I look?" he asked his mirror. Young, free and desperate.

He gave the students five minutes in which to arrive before him then rolled in, looking back through the closing door as if to wave goodbye to someone in the corridor, affecting an air of distraction and nonchalance and thinking it was all quite pathetic.

"Hi," he said, brushing his floppy blond fringe out of his eyes. "Everyone here?"

A boy and a girl who sat close to each other like a couple looked around at the others, one guy looked at them, another looked straight at Gary and a girl in a big bobbly blue jumper stared over his shoulder straight out the window. Five of them. Good, there had been talk of a sixth, but he'd only been able to get hold of five copies of Geoff Dyer's *The Search* which he was going to send them all away with to read at the end of the seminar. For the time being the books were in his bag which he placed on the floor by his chair. Everyone sat around a big desk; Gary's seat was on the far side from the door, just by the window.

"OK," he said, trying to hide his nerves because he already sensed a slight atmosphere, "Let's introduce ourselves. I'm Gary ..."

The couple were Jim and Vicky, both had long blond hair and a sort of spacey aura; the guy next to them was Thom, who looked dauntingly serious with his Malcolm X specs and goatee beard – "That's Thom with an H, as in Thom Gunn"; the boy who'd been looking straight at Gary introduced himself as Con, he had a prominent brow, soft grey eyes and pretty much the same clothes on as Gary; and finally Catriona, bluey-green jumper, greeny-blue eyes, nice-looking girl. Gary clapped his hands and rubbed them together without realizing how stupid it made him look until he'd been doing it for four or five seconds.

"So, let's talk about writing," he said, thinking about anything but, as he looked at Catriona. "Catriona, what have you written or what do you want to write? Why are you here? What made you apply for the course? I'll shut up now," he added.

How old was she, he wondered as she murmured something about short stories he didn't quite catch. Twenty-three, twenty-four? If that. She'd had a couple of stories published, but really wanted to write poetry. Jim and Vicky were interested in drama and wanted to do a Mike Leigh-type thing with the college dramatic society: lots of improvisation, not much writing. Con had sold one or two pieces to literary journals but had found his favourite science fiction magazine a tough nut to crack, indeed, so far, "cast-iron walnut"; and Thom had written a novel which took as its subject the very act of creation, the process of novel writing, much as Dyer had in the book Gary had brought for them all to read. The difference being that Dyer's novel was published, and Thom's more than likely was a crock.

He told them a little about what he'd written, so they wouldn't think they'd been landed with a total loser, then took out the Dyers and asked them all to read it before the next seminar. "I know this is supposed to be about writing rather than reading," he said, "but it's very short and it's the only thing I'll ask you to read that isn't by a member of the group. See you all on Thursday."

Was it his imagination or did Catriona seem to take slightly longer than the others to pack up so that she was the last one in the room with him? He had to bite his tongue, which wanted to ask her to go for a drink. It would be stupid, especially right at the beginning.

Then she lifted her head and used her whole arm to sweep

her long, thick hair out of her face. "I read one of your books," she said.

Shocked, Gary couldn't think what to say.

"The one about the murders in the Bengali community."

"Really?" Gary asked. His fourth novel, it featured a racist villain brought to justice by Gary's unnamed private eye hero who learned a few things about his own prejudices during the course of the hunt.

"Good on racism but the sexual politics were a bit out of date, weren't they?"

Gary was intrigued. "You mean because he's always on the look-out?"

"He screws around."

"If he gets a chance, yeah," Gary said. "It doesn't make him that unusual."

"See you on Thursday," she said and she was gone, slipped through the door before he had a chance to come back at her.

For the next couple of days Gary hung around the students' union, strolled – in sub-zero temperatures – through the campus to the halls of residence, and generally came on like a "sad fuck", Estelle's choice of words and she was a fine one to talk. In the union bar he spotted Jim and Vicky all over each other in the corner and later, grabbing lunch in the refectory, he passed Thom who had the Dyer novel propped up against his sugar bowl. He hesitated a moment too long and Thom looked up, offered the facing seat to Gary who couldn't really say no.

"It's a bit transparent," Thom said of the novel. "It's like, you can see the skeleton through the skin of the prose, you know."

Like, when are you due back on the mother ship, Thom? Only Gary didn't say it; he nodded, stroked his chin, wondered why he couldn't have bumped into Catriona instead.

That evening, waiting for a bus to head back to his flat in town, Gary stamped his feet on the frosty pavement to keep warm. His breath froze in the air like the little clouds on the weather map; he tightened his scarf. On his own at the stop, he looked up the empty road and suddenly, for no reason other than something picked up by his sixth sense, he felt as if he wasn't alone. He was scared to look behind at the chain-link fence and the patch of scrubland beyond it. The halls were 300 yards away, mere furniture draped in dust-sheets of fog.

A smell was gathering around him in the freezing air, a hot, meaty smell that made his scalp prickle and his stomach lift. White shreds of frosted breath drifted between his legs which threatened to give way beneath him. Then he heard a muted sound and the smell was gone, quick as a jogger's sweaty draught. He listened for any sound but could hear only the bus approaching, poking shaky white rods of light into the damp gloom. He jumped on board with relief, and, as he sat down upstairs, rubbed clear a circle on his window to see if he could spot anything between the scrub and the halls. But it was too dark and misty. As the bus rumbled towards town he wondered if he should report his experience in case of danger to the students, but decided against it because he didn't wish to appear foolish: new kid in town is taken in by press hysteria and imagines big cat on campus, that sort of thing.

During the night, however, an animal, something "very large and very strong", killed three sheep belonging to a farmer whose land abutted the campus. Gary listened to the story on the local radio news as he got dressed, hopping about trying to keep his balance in front of the sputtering gas fire. He would know better next time, and he was relieved it had only attacked sheep. He tried to imagine how he would have felt if it had gone for any of the students. Then he felt sick as he realized how vulnerable he had been himself.

They talked about it in the seminar. Apart from Thom they were all quite excited by the reports. Thom just wanted to talk about the Dyer. "We will, Thom, in a minute, but shouldn't writers respond to events like this?" He held back from telling them about his own brush with the beast.

Jim and Vicky constantly shook their long manes of hair out of their faces and said it was cool that there was a lion roaming around campus.

"They didn't say it was on campus," said Catriona, looking slightly concerned. "There's a fence at the edge of the farm land. It could be contained on the farmer's territory."

Con scoffed at that and immediately apologized as Catriona shot him a look.

"They didn't say it was a lion either," Thom said, with an air of superiority. "Previous eye-witnesses described what sounded like a black panther."

"Melanistic leopard," Catriona corrected him, concerned, Gary thought, more with undermining Thom than with pedantry about the animal's identification. He hoped the group were going to get on. Although, Gary thought, some tension could spark off creativity and might make it easier for them to criticize each other's work. Thom was holding up his copy of Dyer's novel. Gary took the hint.

"Thom's right: we should be discussing the novel I asked you to read." Gary pulled his chair forward. "But Cat raised an important point …" – he used the abbreviated name self-consciously having seen that she'd written it on the front of her notebook. "We can choose, when we write, to use formal, precise language like melanistic leopard, or we can use more everyday forms like black panther. Chances are, more people will know what you mean if you say black panther. But if we persist in using the familiar, the correct terms become so rarely heard that they slip out of usage and language dies a little."

They nodded and he felt pleased, as if he'd actually got them on his side as a group. "Let's talk about the book," he said, brushing his hair out of his eyes, aware that Catriona was looking at him intently from behind her own blonde curtain. She wasn't just cute, Catriona – he thought to himself as he pressed on with discussion of the novel – she was deep as well. Something serious going on behind those eyes.

He packed up quickly at the end of the seminar, hoping to catch up with Catriona in the corridor. He could hear the voices of Thom and Jim as they faded away down the hall arguing some point raised by the discussion. He stood just behind the door, bag packed, giving it another moment before heading out, and of course when he did turn into the corridor he stopped short: Catriona was ten yards away looking at the noticeboard.

"You never know what you'll find," she said as he approached her. "Sometimes I think I should move out of hall and get a room in town."

"I think I might go for a drink," Gary said, scanning the notices. "Do you fancy one?"

"I don't think so," she said, taking a packet of Silk Cut out of her multicoloured patchwork bag and slipping one between her lips. She lit up using a bright pink Bic lighter and took a long drag, blowing the smoke towards the floor. "But a few of us are going to the union bar later. Why don't you come along?"

"I might do that," he said, furiously calculating the odds against this being a veiled come-on. Whatever, it was definitely worth turning up at the union bar.

"About half six," she said, swinging her shoulder away from the wall and looking back at him briefly as she padded down the polished corridor in her green Dr Marten's and fake fur coat.

Entering the union bar Gary stamped his feet to get warm and brushed the season's first snow off the arms of his leather jacket. There was a hum of activity, rugby players with turned-up collars and ruddy cheeks leaving the bar laden with pint after pint, an old Christmas single on the juke box. As he advanced slowly he looked around for Catriona, his eyes trailing over the main seating area, then he stood stock still, a gallon of ice water sloshing in his belly. He turned suddenly hot, as if standing next to a raging furnace. A pack of animals sprawled in the middle of the bar, legs playfully swiping at bewhiskered heads, incisors flashing. Gary blinked, feeling something loosen in his stomach, and Catriona was beckoning to him. "Over here," she seemed to be saying. The vision had vanished, replaced by a shifting sea of mohair jumpers, dreadlocks, straggly beards, cigarettes, and Catriona shaking her hair back, waving at Gary. She was sitting next to a scruffy boy in a khaki jacket who had his hand on her arm. Gary rubbed his eyes, shook his head and picked his way through the crowd towards her group.

He offered to buy a round but no one was drinking. Catriona disengaged herself from the scruffy boy, who snarled and turned his back on her, and she touched Gary's elbow. "We're going on somewhere," she said. The others were laughing at something Gary hadn't understood. They looked at him at one point and laughed. He turned to Catriona for support; she was suppressing a grin. The vision had cleared in a second but its effect stuck around. He was confused, out of his depth. Someone used the word "Granddad" and he knew he was being paranoid. Slade's "Merry Christmas Everybody" came on the juke box and he worked out that although he clearly remembered dancing around the lounge to the sound of what was still the best Christmas record ever, probably none of Catriona's friends had been born when it was first released. If they'd heard of Slade at all it would be as slightly disappointing heavy rockers.

"Cool record," he heard one of them say and wondered if he was taking the piss. Gary started to think that he should leave, get out before he did something he'd regret later, but Catriona gave him a look and a smile as she took out another Silk Cut. He stayed. They smoked so much these days. Maybe young people always had done, but they seemed different to how he'd been at their age. More Suede than Slade.

"Are you sure you don't want a drink?" he asked Catriona. "I'm going to the bar. If you want anything …"

She shook her head slowly and he got himself a pint, cradling it in his left hand while his right was splayed on the seat only a hair's breadth from Catriona's left hand. She wore a couple of ornate silver rings with complicated designs.

She turned to look at him from under her fringe. "We're going to a club," she said. "That's why we're not drinking."

"You'll be drinking there?"

"Drinking's not cool, Teach," she teased him, touching his hand with a soft finger.

"So where's this club then? The Hacienda, is it? I've heard of that. Do you know who Joy Division were?"

She stroked his hand and smiled. "You can't drink and take Es," she said. "You'd flip out, you could die."

He looked at his pint, his head swimming, tummy tying itself in knots with desire, frustration – she let go of his hand, puffed on her cigarette, shook her hair back. He glimpsed a soft nest of tiny curls behind her ear.

"What about tomorrow?" he asked her. "We could do something tomorrow."

"Breakfast?" she joked.

★   ★   ★

But it turned out she hadn't been joking.

Gary was turning in his bed, dreaming of a log cabin deep in the woods. The trees were huge firs which made him think it was Canada. He had a cold, but every time he took a tissue from the box to blow his nose it turned into a set of tiny antlers and he threw them down in disgust. Every sound was the approach of wild moose but when he turned to the iced-over window all he could see was snow and tree trunks. Something scratched at the door. He retreated into his bed, pulling the thin blankets over his head, but the scratching continued. He knew he mustn't open the door whatever happened. His life depended on it. So as he rose from the bed, powerless to prevent his feet heading for the door, he felt dread spreading through him like a bloodstain on a sheet.

"Who is it?" he asked sleepily, rubbing his eyes, having realized what was going on and got up.

There was renewed scratching but no one spoke. Gary opened the door a fraction and a weight on the other side pushed it out of his hand. A large dark furry ball unrolled on to the carpet, head lolling, and Gary jumped half out of his skin. The image blurred before his eyes before he recognized Catriona's thick coat. He got down on his hands and knees to support her.

"Hi," she said thickly. "Breakfast?" The effort of speaking knocked her out again and Gary picked her up carefully and carried her over to his bed. He unlaced her boots and removed her fur coat before tucking his quilt up to her chin and gently brushing the hair away from her forehead.

After showering and getting dressed he sat with her while he had his breakfast. It seemed better to let her sleep. When he came back up to the flat from fetching a paper she had turned on to her side and curled up. She had a light dusting of perspiration just below her hairline but she looked peaceful. Outside it had been snowing all night and it was at least three inches thick on the ground. There was a class scheduled for after lunch; he didn't know if they would make it to the campus. It might be better to try to contact the other students and cancel it. He realized with a start that Catriona had woken up and was watching him as he stared out of the window at the gusting flurries of snow.

"How are you feeling?" he asked. "Did you have a bad trip?" They probably didn't call it that but it didn't seem to matter any more: she lifted up the edge of the quilt high enough for him to get in.

Around one o'clock he realized he'd done nothing about cancelling the class.

"Are you worried about what they'll think?" she said between giggles.

He grinned at her, kissed her again and lay down beside her. Together they listened to the snow patting against the window. He leaned across to switch on his tape player. She screwed up her face at the music.

"What's this old crap, Granddad?" She tickled him.

He squirmed away then sat astride her. "Fad Gadget. Quite a hit when I was your age."

She leaned over and ejected the cassette. "Soon get rid of that," she said, reaching into the pocket of her coat which was hanging on the back of Gary's chair by the bed. She produced a tape and put it on.

"What's this?" he asked her.

"This is the real thing," she said, "Curve," throwing him back on the bed and mouthing "I'm anything but your kind" along to the girl singer's voice. Then without warning she let fly at him with her hands, long fingernails brushing the soft skin on his throat, fists punching him in the chest as she straddled him. Catching on, once he'd got over the initial shock, Gary fought back, trying to hold her arms, but she was strong. It was the hot, animal smell which radiated from her that turned him on most of all. Soon they formed a ball of flesh and fur, glistening teeth and dangling drool, sharp nails, long strong tongues and burning eyes, rolling over on the bed and falling on to the floor where they play-fought until mere exhaustion stilled their sweating bodies. As they were lying still enclosed in each other's embrace there came a muffled knock on the door. Gary would have ignored it, but Catriona seemed anxious.

"Ssh," he said to her. "They'll go away."

Then a voice spoke: "Catriona, let's go. The others are waiting for you."

Gary looked at her. She was twitching, head held high in the air. "Who is it?" he asked her.

"From the union," she said. "Graham. He was sitting next to me when you came in."

"Catriona, come on" – the voice again.

Gary remembered the scruffy kid in the khaki jacket, the hurt look that had smeared his features when Gary had turned up.

"I'm staying here, Graham." Her voice betrayed no anxiety, but Gary could see the fear in her eyes.

"Fuck him, Catriona. Come on, let's go." Graham sounded desperate.

"Leave me alone, Graham."

Gary was about to add his own voice to the argument, he was just drawing air when Catriona's hand snapped across his lips. "Don't get involved," she whispered, and louder, "Go away, Graham."

There was no more sound from the other side of the door. After a few minutes she said, "He's gone. It's OK."

"How do you know? I didn't hear anything."

"I can't smell him any more. He's gone."

Gary had a look out of the window but couldn't see anyone. He noticed it had stopped snowing, but the ground was still uniformly white. Catriona had got back into bed. He joined her and they lay quietly for a while. The day was silent in the way only a heavy snowfall can make it. Before long they were both asleep.

Gary came awake slowly, his dreams meshing with the real world like an Escher diagram which he had to pick at gently before it came apart. His head hurt and his mouth ached but a smile spread across his face as he remembered Catriona. It had only been six months or so since he'd last woken up after sleeping with someone new, but the feelings were bright and surprising as freshly minted coins. His mind still furred with dream dust, he searched for shadows and anxieties, but there didn't seem to be any. The tape was playing again – Catriona must have switched it on – and it had come round to the song that had been on when she'd initially switched cassettes. The singer's velvety voice closed around his mind like a glove: *You can say anything to contain my mind /You can try and strip me bare / Till you think you know my kind / But I will never be yours.* He turned over to look at Catriona.

She wasn't there.

I'm anything but your kind.

"Catriona?" he called, his voice falling like a stone into snow. He got up and looked around. It was cold in the flat and she wasn't there. Pulling on his jeans he looked at the time: 11.30 p.m. He hoped none of the students had turned up for the seminar. A glance out of the window revealed a set of tracks leaving the front of his building and heading in the direction of town. When he got downstairs he noticed they were twin tracks, one set of human footprints – about the size of Catriona's Dr Marten's – and one set of animal tracks, presumably a dog. *Or a fucking big cat.* He set off. Few people had ventured out at all, so it was easy to keep sight of the footprints. At the next junction they turned left, away from the town centre and towards the railway station. He buttoned his greatcoat and took his black woolly hat out of the pocket and pulled it down over his ears.

The tracks disappeared inside the railway station, which was deserted. The Curve song was still running through Gary's head. He stepped on to an empty platform. The sheltered part stretched away in both directions, beyond its limits a white carpet on which any fresh tracks would be quite clear. Gary wandered down the platform trying to look casual. He passed the Photo-me booth, peered into the standard class waiting room – a few plastic chairs and ashtrays in the lobby outside the ladies' loo – and the first class passenger lounge – carpeted, no-smoking signs and a television set, unplugged. The door was locked with a combination device. Gary reached the end of the awning and stepped into the snow, which was otherwise undisturbed. Across the line was a double platform.

He retraced his steps and crossed the footbridge to the other platforms, moving as quietly as possible and keeping a keen lookout. On the far side of the station a huddle of electric locomotives waited in sidings. The night's hush was broken by the insectile clucking and ticking of transformers and the buzzing of the overhead wires, each of which bore a thin line of snow. Gary squinted into the gloom between the locomotives. Had something moved against the mound of ballast or was he seeing things again? A noise made him jump: a crackle followed by a hissing sound coming from above. He looked up to catch the final graceful movement of a pantograph coming to rest on top of one of the locomotives after it had disconnected from the wires. The other locomotives remained connected to the power, their pantographs eager and still as praying mantises. Then he saw something which turned him to ice, rooting him to the platform. Draped across two sets of overhead wires was something that looked like a large black cat. As big as a leopard. With careful, slow movements he withdrew behind the corner of another waiting room and watched from there. It didn't move. He circled the outside of the waiting room and approached the far corner, twenty yards nearer to the cat.

It wasn't a cat.

It was Catriona's fur coat.

He ran forward in panic, looking closer to check he'd been right. It was definitely her coat. Just the coat. On the track beneath the wire was a small crumpled tissue which had fallen out of one of the pockets. He climbed down on to the line and picked his way across to the sidings, slipping between two locomotives. Snow-melt dripped from the wires. He stood between two lines of ticking hulks, looked both ways and saw a dark blur run across the open space at the far end. He ran, not caring how much noise he made now. He even called her name. But when he got to the end of the line of engines there was no sign of anyone, or anything.

Pressure was growing inside his chest. He hardly knew the girl, but there was a special vulnerability about a relationship that was only a night old. Having slept with her once it was as if he'd given her a part of himself for safekeeping, knowing she wouldn't run off with it, because it hadn't felt like a one-night stand.

Looking around frantically, determined to find her, he decided to search the whole station. He crossed the footbridge back to platform one and turned left.

Crossing the snow near the end of the platform was a set of paw prints. They led to a door. Gary approached slowly, hand outstretched. He listened but there was nothing to hear. He opened the door quickly. Curled up on the floor just a few feet inside the door was Catriona, freezing without her coat. Her eyes were like two moons.

"Catriona, it's okay. It's me," he said, bending down and moving towards her.

"Keep away," she said tearfully. "Go away, Gary. I can't be with you."

"It's okay. I'm here now. I'll take you back." He stroked her hair. "I don't know what's going on. Whether it's that boy Graham, or what. But it doesn't matter. I'll take you back and get you warm."

She stared at him sorrowfully. "I can't, Gary," she said quietly. "They want me to join them."

These words sent a chill through him.

"Catriona, what are you saying?"

Then he heard a noise behind him and instantly he saw a change in her eyes. They flashed once, clouded over, seemed to become yellow, and in a split-second that for the rest of his life would seem like an eternity he saw her turn. One moment she was frightened Catriona, the girl who'd been in his arms only hours before, the next she was snarling and spitting, no longer playing an erotic game, her pale soft flesh crisping to sleek black fur as she streaked past him and bounded through the open doorway.

He'd been knocked over and by the time he picked himself up and stepped back outside on to the platform she was gone, prints disappearing as the snow gave way at the start of the sheltered section. Outside the Photo-me booth he found her bright pink cigarette lighter and he sat in the booth playing with it until it was too cold to sit still any longer. If he'd thought she might come back for the lighter he was disappointed. He left the station and crossed the road bridge over the tracks, stopping to look down. Beyond the patient lines of waiting locomotives a large group of dark shapes flitted in and out of focus as they were gradually obscured by the trees that marked the border between the town and the moors.

Dennis Etchison

THE NIGHTHAWK

Just as I used Dennis Etchison's story "It Only Comes Out at Night" in The Mammoth Book of Vampires *because it could be interpreted as a vampire story, so some readers will have to read "The Nighthawk" carefully to discover why I've included it in the present volume.*

To reiterate what I said in my introduction to that previous book, I consider Etchison one of America's foremost short story writers (either inside or outside the so-called horror genre), and I'm proud to publish his work whenever I have the opportunity.

His stories have been collected in The Dark Country, Red Dreams, The Blood Kiss, The Death Artist, Talking in the Dark *and* Fine Cuts. *The title story of the first volume won the World Fantasy Award in 1982 (tied with Stephen King), as well as the British Fantasy Award that same year – the first time one writer received both major awards for a single work. He has also published several novels, including* The Fog, Darkside, Shadowman, California Gothic *and* Double Edge.

However, for now, prepare to be dazzled by a master of the short form ...

The little girl stood gazing north, toward the rich houses and the pier restaurant that was still faintly outlined through the mist. The high windows captured the white light of the sky in small squares, like a row of mirrors for the gulls; the pilings and struts underneath could have been stiff black legs risen from the sea and frozen in the November wind, never to walk again.

Is Maria coming? she wondered.

She had hurried to the corral first thing, of course, but Pebbles was gone. Maria must have come home early and taken him out, down past the big rocks to the Sea Manor, maybe, or up under the pier to the tidepools by the point at the edge of the Colony. She did not know what time Maria's school let out, had never asked, but still had always managed to be the first one home; she would be laying out the bridles or patching a break in the fence with driftwood from under the burned-out house by the time Maria came running – always, it seemed. Yes, always. Every time.

She began to wander back along the wet sand, found a stick and paused to block out a word in the sand – C-O-P-P-E-R – turning round over each letter and humming to herself to keep the chill away. But the fog came settling in now, a thick, tule fog it looked like, and she saw her breath making more fog in front of her face and so hastened the rest of the way with her head down, hearing only the cold breaking of the waves out on the dark, musseled rocks.

She stayed with Copper for as long as she could, leaving extra feed for Pebbles, too, so that Maria would not have to bother when she brought him back. Copper seemed restless, bobbing and pawing the sand, eager to be taken out. She tried to explain that it was too late now for a real ride and instead walked her out and around the cliffside and back, over the leach line creek that trickled from the cottages to the ocean. The tiny rivulet with its sculptured and terraced bed – she and Maria, trotting the ponies carefully from one crumbling tier to the other, liked to imagine that it was the Grand Canyon. But the truth was that she had no heart for riding, not now. Not with the dark coming on so soon and the fog all around. Not alone.

She was cold and growing colder as she climbed the wooden stairway and let herself in through the side door, the one to the storage room, and then slipped into the house as quietly as she could. She started to close the door on the fog, but decided to leave it ajar for Grandfather, who would probably be coming in soon.

She heard the television voices from the living room, the same ones she always heard when she went into the house after school. They laughed a lot, though there was an edge to the voices whenever they were interrupted by the music or the buzzer, which was almost all the time, it seemed. They were probably pretty nervous, too, about being kept on the program for so long, day after day, week after week; sometimes, of course, one of the voices would say the right things and win enough money to buy its freedom, and then they would have to let it go home and the next afternoon there would be another voice, a new one, to take its place. They always sounded excited and happy when they said a right answer, and then the audience would not laugh and the buzzer would not buzz.

She padded over the jute-covered floor and slipped around the doorway into the kitchen. She stopped with her hand on the refrigerator door. She looked back at the rattan chair and couch, the sandbag ashtrays, the clock and the flying metal geese on the wall, the shiny black panther on the table, the lamp shaped like a Hawaiian dancer, the ivy planter, the kissing Dutch girl and boy, the picture of the crying clown and the ones of the father and mother in the stand-up frames. She turned away. She opened the refrigerator and poured a glass of Kool-Aid.

"Is that you, Darcy?"

"Ye-es," she called sweetly, *Grandma*, but would not say it.

"Have you seen Maria yet?" She heard the grandmother climbing out of her chair, not waiting for an answer. "I must talk with you, dear. This morning we received a most disturbing telephone call …"

The grandmother was coming, even though the TV was still on. It must be something bad, she thought.

On the other side of the kitchen window the fog was descending heavily, almost like rain. In fact she heard a tapping begin on the low roof – but no, that would be Grandfather, hammering with his short strokes, scraping his slippers on the rough tar paper. *Just a minute, I have to talk to Grandfather.* Would that be good enough? She turned from the window to watch the doorway for the black walking shoes, the hem of the flowered dress. Another kind of movement caught her eye, down low by the floor, but she knew that would only be the fog.

There was the hammering on the roof, the plinking of the wind chimes by the geraniums out on the railing of the sun deck, the fog deepening until it, too, could almost be heard settling over the house. There was the slow, unsteady pursuit of the grandmother, nearly upon her now.

And something else, something else.

A dull, familiar thumping.

She looked quickly and saw, through the window, a moving shape approaching along the beach. She knew at once that it was Pebbles. The pony hesitated, breathing steam, and the vapor thinned around him momentarily so that his markings showed clear and unmistakable, like a cluster of moonstones through the white water of a pool at low tide, far out by the broken sea wall.

"Got to go," she yelled, *Grandma.* "Maria's got Copper. Ooh, that girl—!"

She darted out and, by the time the refrigerator door had swung shut and before the grandmother could object, had dropped from the deck and was sprinting toward Maria and the pony. It wasn't true, of course; of course not. Maria was riding Pebbles. But it had worked.

"Hey," she called. Then, again, when there was no answer, "He-ey!"

Maria, small and dark atop her pony, reined and turned Pebbles, his hooves slapping the slick, packed sand. She had kept near the water, had not even come close to Darcy's house; but she had had to pass by on the way back, and now she held her body tense and distant, almost as though afraid she might meet something there on the beach – herself, say – with which she knew she would not be able to cope. "Hey, yourself," she said, because she had to say something. But her face did not change.

"Did you stay home today?" tried Darcy. She waited and, trying to make it look like she was not, had not been waiting, leaned forward and watched her feet as they dug down into the sand. She stepped back, and the imprints of her toes began to fill up with water. "Well, were you sick or something?"

"I got to go now," answered Maria.

She was like that. Once, when they were playing and Darcy had said something wrong – it must have been something she had said because nothing had happened, they had only been sitting with their knees up, molding little houses in the sand with a paper cup – Maria had stopped and stared over the water with that smooth, flat face of hers, as if hearing what no one else on the beach or in the world could hear. And then she had said that, the same thing, *I got to go now*, and she had jumped up, brushed off her hands and started running – and not even toward her own house, so that Darcy knew Maria hadn't been called home, even if she couldn't hear it herself. Maria was like that.

The pony started walking.

"You better not ride him anymore today, Maria," yelled Darcy. "Ma-ri-a, he'll get all sweaty and sick for sure, you'll see!"

Maria kept riding.

"Well," said Darcy, staring after, "*I* waited."

At the corral Maria dismounted but did not raise her eyes when her friend finally caught up.

"What do you care about Pebbles," Maria said to her.

Only then did Darcy notice the scratches, fresh and deep, on Pebbles' right flank. Three parallel lines sliced into flesh that was still pink and glistening.

Darcy sucked in her breath. "Maria!" She forgot everything else. "Who did *that*?"

Maria walked away. She trailed her fingers over the makeshift fence, the tarp that covered the hay, and went to sit in the ruins, in the shadows, under the starfish that someone had nailed crucifixion-style to the supports of the big house years ago, before it burned; now the hard, pointille arms, singed black at the tips, still clutched tight to the flaking, splintery wood. She put her elbows on her knees and her face in her arms and started to cry.

Copper had sidled over to Pebbles, but the other pony shied away, protecting his flank. Copper snorted and tried to nuzzle.

Darcy reached for a blanket to throw over Pebbles, but hesitated because of the wound.

She joined her friend under the house.

After a time Darcy said, "I'll tell Grandfather. He'll get the vet to come over. You'll see."

"No."

Maria was crying deep down inside herself, from a place so protected that there were no sounds and nothing to show, nothing but the tears.

"Well, I'll go get some Zephiran right now from my house. And we'll fix it ourselves. I will, if you want me to, Maria."

"No!"

"Maria," she said patiently, "what happened?"

Maria's narrow lips barely moved. "It came. In the night, just like you said."

"What did?"

"You know what. The–the—"

"Oh no." Darcy felt a sinking inside, like an elevator going down too fast; she hadn't felt it for a long, long time. The last had been when she was very small, about the time that the mother and father went away. She couldn't remember the feeling very clearly; in fact, she couldn't even be sure what it was about; surely, she knew, it was about something she did not and could not understand. "Don't you be silly. It wasn't really real." That was right. It wasn't, it wasn't. "Maria, that was only a story. Ma-*ri*-a."

"That was what my Daddy said," the dark girl went on. "But he said you were still evil to make me scared of it." She was beginning to rush the words, almost as though afraid she might hear something and have to go away before she could finish. "You were the one, the one who told me about him, about how he comes at night and sees in your window and if you were bad, then – you know. You know what he does, the Nighthawk."

The Nighthawk. Of course she remembered the story. It had always been just that, a story to scare children into being good, the kind of story thought up by grandmothers to stop too much running in the house and laughing and playing games in bed. But it was also a story you never forgot, and eventually it became a special late kind of story for telling on the beach, huddled close to a campfire, under the stars, seeing who could scare the other the worse, all shivery in sleeping bags, hidden from the unknowable mysteries of a sudden falling star or the sound of wings brushing the dark edge of the moon.

She didn't know what to say.

The two of them sat that way for a while.

"Well, I'll help you take care of him," she offered at last. "You know that."

"It doesn't matter."

"He'll be good as new. You'll see."

"Maybe. But not because of you."

Darcy looked at her friend as though seeing her for the first time.

Maria let out a long sigh that sounded like all the breaths she had ever taken going out at once. "My Daddy's getting a better place. Up in the canyon, by the real stables. He said Pebbles can't stay here till we find out what hurt him. And he says I can't play with you anymore."

"Why?"

"Because."

"But *why*?"

"Because you're the one who scared me of those stories." Her brown eyes were unreadable. "You can't tell me about the Nighthawk, Darcy," she said. "Not anymore, not ever again."

Darcy was stunned. "But I didn't make it happen," she said, her own eyes beginning to sting. "I don't even know what happened to Pebbles. Maybe he – well—" But she was confused, unable to think. She remembered the story from the mouth moving above her in the darkness as she huddled close to her big brother, a long, long time ago, it must have been. "Th-there isn't any real Nighthawk, don't you get it? Come on, I thought you were big! You know it, don't you? Don't you?"

"Don't *you*?" said Maria mockingly. "I don't want to have those dreams, like last night. Darcy, I don't want to!"

Darcy's mouth was open and stayed open as she heard a new sound, and it was not the blood pulsing in her ears and it was not the waves smashing out by the sea wall and it was not her own heartbeat. She looked over and saw Maria hunch down quickly, struggle to cover her eyes, then jerk herself up – almost wildly, Darcy thought later – as the sound became loud, louder. Darcy moved her lips, trying to be heard, trying to say that it was only one of those big Army helicopters somewhere above the fog, cruising low over the coastline – they were so much louder than the Sheriff's 'copter, their huge blades beating the air like some kind of monster – but Maria was already running. Just like that. In a few seconds she had disappeared completely in the fog.

Grandfather was sorting his tools when Darcy came up. She moved slowly, as though underwater, absently poking at a pile of ten-penny nails, at the chisel, at the claw of the hammer. She had been trying to think of where to begin, but it was no use.

"Well, how goes it today, sweetheart?" he said, when she made no move to go inside.

She knew he would wait to hear her story for today, whatever it might be, before getting around to the next part: the something that might be wrapped clean and special in a handkerchief in his jacket or lying inside on the kitchen table or, if it were another article about horses he had clipped from a magazine, folded and waiting in his shirt pocket. Then and only then would he get on to the serious part. She looked up at him and knew that she loved him.

"Oh—" She wanted to tell. Maybe if she started with a teacher story or a recess story; but she couldn't feel it. "Oh, same old stuff, I guess," she said.

He glanced at her, pausing perhaps a beat too long, and said, "The pictures came, the ones we sent away for in the Sunday *Times*. Those prints of the white stallions." He fixed her with his good eye. "Remember?"

She felt a smile beginning in spite of herself. She reached over to help him.

"And I believe your grandmother would like a word with you, Darcy, before you go downstairs."

"I know," she said quickly.

He latched his toolbox, wiped his hands on a rag.

Reluctantly she started inside.

"See you at dinner," he said. "Afterwards, we can measure them for frames and figure where they should go. All right?"

She turned back.

"Grandpa?"

"Yes?" He waited.

"What—what does it mean when somebody says you're 'evil'?"

He laughed easily.

"Well, Darcy," he said, "I'd have to say it just means that somebody doesn't really know you."

She felt her way downstairs. *Now do as you're told.* She made sure to land each foot squarely in the middle of each step. *I'm sure her father knows what's best, leaving it open to the air like that.* That way no part of her would touch the edge. *Remember – but of course you couldn't –* She was aware of a pressure at her heels. *Now why would you ask a thing like that, child? Why can't you leave well enough –* She knew what she would see were she to look back. *You'd better watch yourself, young lady. You're not too old to forget the –* She would see – *I didn't mean anything.* I didn't mean anything! *Your Mama and Daddy, rest their souls –* She would see the fog. *Say it.* Curling close. *Say it.* About her ankles. *Say it.* Say it—

"Help me."

She started.

Joel stood there in the semidarkness, one hand extended. The other hand was on the knob to the door next to hers, the door to his room. When her eyes adjusted, she saw that he held something out to her in his stubby fingers.

Without thinking, she took it. A pair of ringed keys, new and shiny. She studied them uncertainly.

Joel picked at a splinter along the doorjamb. As she watched, Darcy made out the bright brass gleam of a new lock.

"It's a dead-bolt," he said, as if that would explain everything. "Can't be forced, not unless you break the frame. The hinges are on the right side, too."

"But—"

"I want you to keep the keys in a safe place. Really safe. Got it?" When she nodded, he added with deceptive casualness,

"You want to come in? You hardly ever do anymore, you know."

He opened the door and led her inside, looking like someone who had something terribly valuable to give away but could hardly remember where he had hidden it.

She hadn't seen the inside of her brother's room in weeks, maybe months. Since before she had met Maria. Usually they talked (more correctly, she listened while he talked) in her room, anyway, though, or else she managed to avoid him altogether to lie on her bed, playing her records or writing in her diary or thinking about the horses, the ones in the movie Grandfather had taken her to see, the wild ones leaping through water and fire on a seashore somewhere. It was very much like a dream.

While her own room seemed to be in a perpetual state of redecoration, Joel's remained the same jail-like no-color; where she had posters and cutouts to cover her walls, Joel had science and evolution charts and black felt-tip drawings she couldn't understand, marked up and shaded so dark that she couldn't see how he was able to make any sense of them. Still, it all reminded her of something, as it always did: she found herself thinking again about a house with unlocked doors and huge, loving faces bobbing in and out of the darkness over her. And fire, and water, and something else, something else.

The main thing she noticed, of course, was the statue on the shelf over the headboard of Joel's unmade bed. And, as before, it fascinated and frightened her at the same time.

It was a glazed plaster sculpture a couple of feet high, the paint brushed on real fast and sloppy, probably so that it could be sold cheap in the kind of stores that have pillows and ashtrays with words and pictures of buildings printed on them. Some kind of snake, a cobra, she thought, and it was coiled around what was supposed to be a human skull. Maybe it had come out of the skull, out of one of the eyes; she wasn't sure. But crawling out of the other eye was an animal that looked like a mouse. It was about to attack the snake, to try to bite it on the neck, or maybe to charm it, to hold its attention so that it would do no harm; she didn't know which. The snake was poised, squinting down, his fangs dripping. There was no way of telling which one would win. She had seen another like it once, in the window of a shop in the Palisades where they sold old-looking books and those sticks like Fourth of July punks that smell sweet when you light them. She wondered where Joel had gotten it and why and how much it cost, had even asked him one time, but he had only looked at her funny and changed the subject.

She sat on the edge of the bed.

"Joel," she began, knowing he would jump in about his locks and keys, whatever they were for, if she did not. There were things on her mind now, questions that were as yet only half-formed but which needed answers before she would be able to listen and really hear him. "Joel," she said again, trying to find a way to ease into it. "Was – was our house always this way? I mean, the way it is now? Or did Grandpa build it over when we were little?"

She glanced around the room, pretending interest in the cluttered walls and cramped ceiling.

" 'Course it was," he said, casually condescending. "You're thinking about the other place."

"What other place is that, Joel?"

"The first house, the one over by your corral. The place where we lived with Mother and—"

He stopped himself, shot one of his sudden, funny looks at her, as if she had caught him off-guard.

She had an odd feeling then, as if they had begun to talk about something they were not supposed to, and her not even knowing. The feeling attracted her and scared her at the same time.

"You don't go poking around in there, do you?" he asked in a controlled voice. "Not all the way in there, where the house used to be?"

"Anyone can go, Joel. It's right there on the beach. What's left of it."

"You've been in there, underneath there? You've been there before?"

"I've *always* been there before. So what?"

He straightened, his back to her. "You shouldn't, you know. It's not safe."

"What do you mean? Of course it's—"

"There was an explosion once, you know," he said, cutting her off with more information than he had planned to give. "The gas lines are probably still there. Anyway, I don't want you remembering a thing like that. And," he added, as if to cover up, "you ought to stay home more."

"Oh."

She felt a laugh coming on, one of those wild, high ones that she didn't want to stop. She threw herself backwards on the bed, her arms over her head. His bed was so bouncy, mounded with all the quilts the grandmother had made for him.

"Safe, not safe," she sang. "Oh Joel, you're just on another one of your *bummers*. I know why you have such bad dreams. You pile on so many blankets, your body heats up at night like a compost heap!"

"Don't you taunt me, Darcy. Don't, or I'll—"

There, she had caught him again. *Or you'll what? Send the Nighthawk?*

He turned and stared at her for too long a time, until she stopped laughing and they both grew uneasy. Then he began moving about the room, picking at things, his compass and protractor, the lens cover to his telescope, putting them down again, pacing. It was an unnatural pause; Joel never ran out of crazy things to talk to her about, which was why she always had to be the one to leave.

He faced her again.

"I hear Grandma's pretty mad at you, Darcy." This time he was doing the taunting. The tension was gone from his face now, hidden again just below the surface like one of those sharp, crusted rocks when the tide changes. "What's it about this time?"

"Oh, who knows?" It was almost true; the grandmother was pretty nearly always mad at her about something. "I don't know, why is a mouse when it screams? That probably makes about as much sense." Then, when he didn't laugh, "It was about the ponies, I guess."

"What about the ponies?"

"What do you care?"

"I had a dream about them," he said tightly.

Another one of his dreams. She sighed. She didn't want to hear about it so she went ahead and told about Pebbles. But not the part about Maria. She was not ready to talk about that part yet, least of all to him.

But then she stopped and said, "It was about the corral, your dream, wasn't it? That was where you went. In your dream. *Wasn't* it?"

Sometimes, she did not know why, Joel tried to make himself look like a stone boy; this was one of those times.

"Darcy, I tried to warn you. All of you." And, surprisingly, tears of rage came to his eyes. "I told him, I told *her* to tell him, but she must've thought she could take care of—"

A new thought struck her, cold and fully shaped as a steel bit, and it stayed and would not let go. Perhaps it had been there all along and only now was she able to feel it fully, its chill, and begin to know what it was.

She said, "What was it that hurt Pebbles?"

There was a ringing silence.

"You know, don't you, Joel. I think you know."

She saw him start to shake. She went on, oddly detached, as if she were watching what was happening through the wrong end of his telescope.

"You know what else I think? I–I think that maybe Mama and Daddy got hurt the same way, a long time ago. I already know they didn't just 'go away', like everybody says."

She waited.

He did not try to answer. He lost his balance and hunkered close to the floor, by the edge of the bed. His hands clawed into the quilt and pulled it down with him.

Now she did begin to feel afraid. She felt a nervous jolt enter her body, sort of like a charge of static electricity from the air, but she strained to keep breathing, to draw energy from the feeling and not be smothered by it. She had to know.

"Say something!" she said to him.

She saw his face press into the pillow, heard his shallow, rasping sobs. She felt a terrible closeness in her own chest as her breath caught and took hold again. She thought of touching him but could not. Because she never had. Not like that.

"What about—" she began, and this was the hardest part, but it had to be said, " —what about the fire? Tell me about the fire, Joel. Tell me about Mother and Father."

I'll help you, I will, she thought, *and never, ever ask again. If only you'll tell me.* And then an answer came, slowly at first and then like something icy melting far away and rushing down to meet the sea. And whether it was his voice or her own she did not know just then, but could only focus on the pictures that appeared in her mind. And the pictures showed the big old house bursting upward into the sky and the boards falling back down again into a new and meaningless configuration on the sand, and she thought of charred pick-up-sticks. And before that: within the house a woman, breathing on her knees by the range, the oven open, the burners flickering and the image rising in a watery, gaseous mirage, and she thought *Mama.* And before that: a man dying in a hospital bed, his body laced with fresh scars, pink and glistening, and Mama weeping into her closed fists, her hair tumbling forward like brackwater and a little girl watching, and she thought *Daddy.* And before that: Daddy's face outside the window the night he brought Copper for her, smiling secretly and then the smile fading, shocked, as something, *something* moved against him beyond the glass, and she turned, turned for her brother who was not there, and she thought *the Nighthawk.* And before that: another face, dream-spinning over them both in the dark when Mama and Daddy were not home, an old face that went on storytelling long after she had fallen asleep, a face she had not let into her room since she had been old enough to lock it out, and again she thought *the Nighthawk.*

She stayed her hand in the air, near his head. Her voice was almost kind; her touch would have been almost cruel.

Outside, the tide was shifting. A single wave, the first of many, rolled and boomed against the retaining wall beneath the house. The bed throbbed once under her, and a pane of dirty glass in the one tiny window shook and rattled.

His head jerked up.

"No!"

"Shh," she said, "she'll hear you."

But of course it didn't matter. The grandmother wouldn't mind. She didn't mind anything Joel did, but only coddled him more. She waited on him, even in the middle of the night sometimes, with soothing cups of soup and those gray-and-red pills that were supposed to be hidden in the back of the top shelf of the medicine cabinet. And if Grandfather heard or cared, he wouldn't do anything about it, either. He left the boy alone, no matter what, to dream his dreams and become what he would. Of course it was silly to think that Grandfather would be – what? afraid of him? Of course it was. He was only a boy. He was only her brother Joel.

She followed his gaze to the window. The water was rolling in long, slow curls, tipped at the ebb with a pearly-white phosphorescence. But Joel wasn't seeing that.

For the first time she noticed the window sill.

It was scored with dozens, hundreds of vertical cuts and scratches; the marks shifted and deepened as she watched, as Joel's shadow undulated over the scarred wood. Then she glanced back and saw the burning aureole of the high-intensity lamp behind him, across the room, the one the last tutor, who had stayed the longest, had left on his final visit.

Without warning, Joel lurched up. He stood a moment, turned around, around again, in the manner of an animal who has awakened to find himself trapped in a room with the door shut and the air being sucked from his lungs. Whatever he was looking for he did not see, or even, probably, know how to name it, because just then he did a strange thing, really: he shrank down until he was sitting on the floor, right where he had been standing, without having moved his feet at all. She had seen something like that only once before. It had been the day the grandmother came home from what Darcy knew had been the funeral for the father and mother; it was as if she now had permission to remember. The grandmother had come in cradling two armloads of groceries. She had stood in the middle of the kitchen, scanning the walls like that, not seeing any of it, least of all the little girl there in the doorway, because Darcy was not what she was looking for, any more than the walls or ceiling or the table and chairs. And she had moved from side to side, turning from the waist, and then the expression had come over her face and she had sunk down onto the linoleum, the bags split and the contents rolling, forgotten, a collapsed doll with its strings cut. She had probably not even known that Darcy was there.

"Use the key," he said to her, "now."

"Why?"

"Do it, Darcy."

She stepped around him carefully and backed to the door.

She saw the way the light played over the sculpture above the bed. The way its eyes shone, forever straining but unable to see the most important thing of all. The way the shadow had grown behind the hood, so that it had come to be larger, darker, more like the monster from a bedtime story than she had ever noticed. She found herself staring into the eyes until she seemed to recognize something; yes, she herself remembered the way it felt, the need to lash out and hurt. What would have happened to her those times if she had not had Grandfather there to help? And there was something else, too, about a snake she had seen in a book, one that had gotten so mad or afraid that it had actually tried to swallow its own tail …

The eyes held her longer than she liked. The sharp eyes that missed nothing, not the other creatures that had come close enough to threaten, not the head that had nurtured it but which was now too old and empty to protect it, not anything but itself, what it had become, the very thing it feared most, the creature of its dreams, the most difficult thing of all to know when the dreams it is given are all nightmares.

She was standing between the door and the lamp. The shadow of Joel's head and body moved and distorted. She drew back involuntarily and, behind her back, her hand brushed the cold doorknob.

She shuddered.

She imagined the fog creeping down the steps from outside, hissing over the floor and pooling by the edges. She pushed the door shut and moved away.

As she moved, her own shadow merged with the other, rendering it somehow less frightening. But the eyes on the headboard shimmered and burned out of the blackness, and she wanted to say, *Does it see, Joel?*

He gestured at her imploringly.

She wished she could say *I got to go now*, the way Maria would have said it, and simply run away as fast as she could. But there was the dark outside, and the fog that followed her down the stairs, waiting to slither under doors and between cracks. There was the grandmother, she knew, waiting at the top of the stairs with her words, her stories that would not soothe but only bring more nightmares. She wondered whether the grandmother knew that; probably not, she realized, and that was the most frightening thought of all.

She went to him.

"What do you want me to do, Joel?"

Suddenly she felt her wrist taken in a death grip.

"No, Joel, not me!" she cried, wrenching free. She lunged for the door. "I'm doing it, see, I'm …"

She reached up to lock the door, thinking, *Why did he give me both keys?* But it was a good idea to lock it now, yes, she would—

She stared at the door.

Where was the lock? The mechanism was on the outside, as were the hinges. So the keys could not be used to keep anything out.

They could only be used to lock something in.

Very slowly she came back to him, his unblinking eyes following her.

"What do you see, Joel?" she said softly.

There was the room. The window. The luminous waves, aglow now with the pale, dancing green of St Elmo's fire rippling below the surface. The sky ablaze with a diffused sheen of moonlight above the fog. The glass chill and brittle now, and if she placed her fingers on it they would leave behind five circles imprinted in mist, the record of a touch that would remain to return each time someone sat close and breathed at the night.

Then she was listening to the slapping of the surf, the trembling in the close room, the sound of a sob and the high, thin weeping of the wind, that might have been the keening of an animal left too long alone.

"Do you hear that, Joel? Is that Copper?"

And she saw the room and that it was only her brother's, and she heard the crying and knew that it came from her own lips, and she reached out her hand to him and felt his moist hair, the bristles at the back of the neck, the fuzz at his temple and the quivering in his cheek and the wetness running to and from his tender mouth and the shaking of his body.

Closing her eyes, she said, "How do you feel?"

He would have told her to go away, just to go away and lock the door and not open it until the morning. But she placed herself between him and the window and said:

"I'm going to stay, Joel. I want to. I'll watch and listen from here and if anyone – if Copper – needs me, I'll know it. Do you understand?"

"No," he said pitifully, after some time had passed.

She kept her eyes shut tight against the fog and the world as she said, "It's all right. I'm only waiting, Joel, for you to go to sleep."

Because, she thought, somebody has to.

And that was the way their first real night together began.

David Case

THE CELL

David Case was born in upstate New York but first moved to Britain in 1960, where he divided his time between lengthy sojourns in Greece (he claims he once saw a werewolf there!).

His first two collections of macabre stories, The Cell and Other Tales of Horror *(1969) and* Fengriffen and Other Stories *(1971), were favourably compared to the classic weird fiction of Algernon Blackwood, and Arkham House published his occult Egyptian novel* The Third Grave *in 1981. He has also written more than three hundred books under at least seventeen pseudonyms, and his Western novel* Plumb Drillin' *(1976), which was originally optioned for Steve McQueen, now looks set to finally make it to the screen. Two of his stories, "Fengriffen" and the classic werewolf thriller "The Hunter", were filmed as—* And Now the Screaming Starts *(1973) and* Scream of the Wolf *(1974) respectively.*

Described as "a frightening psychopathic view of lycanthropy", "The Cell" was the author's first horror story, and Ramsey Campbell has said that Case's work "… can hold its own against the most extreme of today's horror fiction", as you will discover in the disturbing novella which follows …

When my old Aunt Helen died I inherited her house. I was the only relative. I wasn't sad about her death because I hardly knew her, and I wasn't overjoyed about the house because it was an ancient thing, ugly and dilapidated and unpleasant. I suppose that it had been a decent enough house in its day, but Aunt Helen had lived there all alone for many years, ever since her husband disappeared. She was slightly crazy and never left the house. The house and the old woman sort of fell apart together. Sometimes she could be seen rocking on the front porch, cackling or laughing or moaning. It was a singular sound and rather hard to define. No one knows just how crazy she was, and no one cared. She seemed to be harmless enough and they left her alone and in the end she died quite peaceably of old age. So the house was mine.

I went there one miserable afternoon to look it over and see if there was anything that I wanted to keep before putting it up for auction. There was nothing. I would have left after the first ten minutes if the rain had not increased. But it increased. It came down very heavily and I had only a light coat with me. I decided to wait and see if it would let up presently. There was nothing else to do so I continued to poke around those damp and dirty rooms. Nothing seemed of the slightest value on the ground floor. I opened the basement door, thinking there might be something stored down there, but a gust of foul air belched out and I shut the door again. I was certain there would be nothing worth going down for. Instead, I went upstairs and looked through the bedrooms. They were all just skeletons of rooms, except the one that Aunt Helen must have used. There was some furniture there but it was broken and worthless. I was ready to leave and it was only some whim of chance that made me open one of the bureau drawers. That was where I found the book.

It was mouldy with age. It had been torn and then repaired with tape. When I opened it the binding groaned stiffly and the pages crackled. They were dry and stained and creased, but I could still read the writing on them. It was in a man's hand, small and precise and neat and careful. The hand of a boring person, I thought. It appeared to be a diary or journal of some sort. I read a line or two, started to toss it back in the drawer, read another line. I opened it towards the middle and read a few more words. Then I closed the book and took it downstairs and sat in the front room, by the window. The light was dull and the pages brittle, but I began to read that extraordinary journal. I didn't stop ... I didn't pause ... until I had read it all. I couldn't. I was glued to the chair. My spine seemed fixed and my flesh fluid and creeping around it. The light grew dimmer but my eyes would not leave those pages. Beside my chair the rain was drumming against the glass, the sky was dark with clouds unbroken, and the wind rushed across the unkept lawn. It was the right day to read such a book.

This is the book:

May 4

God! It was horrible last night.

Last night it was the worst that it has been to date. I wish that I could remember the other times more clearly. I should have started keeping a record earlier, I know that now. But it took a great effort to begin this book that will show what I am, and I could not bring myself to do it before. At any rate, I am sure that last night was much worse than ever before. Perhaps that is why I feel that I must start this record now. Perhaps I must drain my feelings off in some way. It makes me wonder if I will be able to force myself to go down to my cell again next month ...

But, of course I must. There can be no doubt of that, and I must never attempt to rationalize about it. No excuse will do. What I must do is to go down earlier next month. I can never leave it too late, or who knows what might happen? I suppose I could control it, but ... I left it just a bit too long last night, I think. I didn't mean to, but it is so difficult to tell. When I know that the thing is going to begin soon I get nervous and anticipate the first signs, and it is often impossible to tell the anticipation from the beginnings. The change starts with a certain nervous feeling and when I am already nervous it can begin before I realize it. That frightens me. I shall have to be more careful in the future.

I am in my room now. I am trying to remember all the details. This record will be useless if it is not completely accurate. It will be of no value to me, or to anyone else. I have not yet decided if anyone else will ever see it. Under the circumstances that is a terrible decision to be forced to make. I know that if I ever offer this record, I must also offer proof. That is the terrible part. I don't want anyone to think I am mad ...

Last night my wife began to get agitated just after dinner. We were in the front room. She kept looking at her wrist-watch and then glancing sideways at me. I didn't like the way she let her eyes slide towards me without moving her head. I can't blame her, of course, and I pretended not to notice. I dreaded the thought of going down, and wanted to put it off as long as possible. It wasn't really very late and the sky was still light. I was sitting beside the window where I would be able to know when it was time. I pretended to be absorbed in the evening paper, but I was much too restless to read. I just saw the print as a blur. But I don't think that was a symptom. All the lights were on in the room and I was careful not to let Helen see me looking out of the window. I didn't want to make her any more troubled than she already was, poor thing. But, at the same time, I can remember feeling a strange sense of pleasure as I noticed the frightened look in her eyes. It was almost a sexual pleasure, I think. I don't know. Perhaps it was a preliminary sign of my disease, or perhaps it is a reaction normal to men. I can't tell, because I am not like other men. Still, I felt disgusted with myself as soon as I recognized that feeling, and so I knew that nothing had really started to take effect.

The bad part at that time was the contrast. Sitting there in that comfortable living-room with the bright lights and the leather chairs and the new carpet and, at the same time, knowing what was coming in an hour or so ... it was grotesque. Leading a completely normal life most of the time, and trying to pretend that it was normal, made the change so much more repulsive. It made me almost hate myself, even though I fully understand that it is a sickness and no fault of my own. Perhaps no fault of anyone's, possibly the fault of a distant ancestor, I don't know. But certainly I am not to blame. If I were I would kill myself, I think ...

I kept stealing glances at the gilt-framed mirror on the wall and expecting to see some sign, although I knew that it was too early. It had to be too early, or else it would have been too late. Even if I were able to control myself in the first stages it would have been too horrible for my wife. I doubt that I could have borne it myself, if I saw it begin. If I looked in that normal, gilt-framed mirror, and actually saw it …

That is why there is no mirror in the cell.

At nine o'clock I stood up. The sky was darkening outside the window. The window was bordered by pretty lace curtains. My wife looked quickly at me, then looked away. I carefully folded the newspaper and put it down in the chair. I looked normal and calm.

"Well, it's time," I said.

"Yes, I suppose so," she said, and I could hear the struggle to keep relief out of her voice.

We went into the hallway and down the dark stairs to the basement. My wife went down first. They are old wooden stairs with the clammy basement wall on one side and a handrail on the other. This is an old house and although I have kept the upstairs in good repair the basement is ancient and gloomy. I cannot seem to force myself to go down there at normal times. But that is understandable enough, under the circumstances. And, in a way, it seems proper that it should be dank and unkept. It at least lessens the contrast at the last minute.

The stairs groaned underfoot. The dead air seemed to climb the steps to meet us, and suddenly I felt dizzy. I put one hand against the mouldy wall for support. My foot slipped and I had to clutch at the handrail. I caught myself, but my foot passed one step and banged down on the next. My wife turned at the noise. Her face was terrible. Her eyes were white and wide. Her mouth was open. For a long instant she could not control that expression. I have seldom seen more fear and horror in a face. Never without cause, certainly. And certainly she had no cause. She must know that I would never hurt her. Still, I cannot blame her for being afraid. It was the horror that hurt me. I hated to see the horror that I could inspire in one I loved. And then the expression vanished and she smiled, a little lip-biting smile. I think that she was ashamed that she had shown her fear. I smiled back at her, and that was when I realized that I had left it to the very last moment. My mouth was stiff and my teeth felt too large. I knew that my control was going.

The cell is at the far end of the basement. I went ahead of her and opened the door myself. She stood back a bit, I walked in and looked out of the door and smiled again. Her face was very pale, almost illuminated, in the dark basement. She moved forward and it was as if her face were floating, disembodied. Her throat was the whitest part of all, and I could see the veins in her neck. I looked away from the veins in her neck. She tried her best to look as though she regretted having to close the door. I suppose she did, in a way. Then she closed it and I heard the key turn in the lock and the heavy bar slide into place. I listened behind the door and for a few moments there was no sound. I knew that she was waiting outside. I could picture her standing there, looking at the barred door with a mixture of relief and regret on that phosphorescent face. And then I heard her footsteps very faintly as she went back to the stairs, I heard the upstairs door close. I felt sorry for both of us.

I sat down in the bare corner and buried my face in my hands. It was still my face. But it was very stiff. I could tell that it would not be long. It seems to be getting quicker and easier for the change to come each month. It is not as painful. I wonder if that is a good sign or a bad sign?

But I can't really talk about that yet. It would be too hard to write about the details. It would be almost as hard as it is for me to go into that cell, knowing the agonies to come …

When my wife knocked at the door in the morning I was still very weak. But I was all right. I was surprised that it was morning already. There is no way to tell time inside the cell, of course. I do not take my watch with me.

Helen did not hear me answer the first time, and knocked again before she opened the door. She opened it a crack and I saw one big eye peering in. Then she saw that everything was all right, and she opened the door wide. I am glad that she is cautious, of course, but still it hurts me. Damn this disease!

She didn't ask how I was. She knows that I can't talk about it. I wonder if she is curious? I suppose she must be. She doesn't know that I am keeping this journal. I am going to keep it locked in the desk in my study. I'm sitting at the desk now, looking out of the window at the trees. Everything is very peaceful today, and last night is more nightmare than memory. If it only were! It is strange the way that the memories come through to me, after I have become myself again. I must think about that and try to describe it later. I don't know why, though. I don't know why I feel compelled to keep this record. It must be some form of release. I feel more relaxed now, at any rate. I am going to rest now. My body suffers the damage that the other thing infllicts on itself. We share the same body and I am exhausted. I will write later.

May 6

I have been thinking about the disease. I thought about it all day yesterday. It is hard to do this clearly, because when I am … not myself … I seem to have no thoughts. Or, if I do, I don't remember them after I have become myself again. I suppose that, at those times, my mind must work much as an animal's does. I am left with only a vague, general impression of how I felt. How it felt. I do not know if I and it are the same, but we share the same body. Anyway, there is certainly no reasoning involved when I am changed. It must be purely instinct that motivates the thing, and instinct does not fit well into the pattern of the human brain. Or does my brain also change? The impressions are very strong. I can recall the impressions, almost to the point of summoning them up again. But this is simply a matter of remembering what the other thing was feeling at that time, not what it was doing, or what it looked like. It is a matter of recalling an emotion without the circumstances that caused it. But what a powerful emotion! It is always hard to express a feeling in words, and this is a very complex feeling.

I think it was need, most of all. Need and frustration. But there is all that violence and hatred and lust mingled with it. I don't suppose any normal man could ever feel it in quite the same way. Perhaps emotion is always stronger when it is instinctive and when there is no rational force working on it. It all came from within and seemed to have nothing to do with the actual physical action. It burned like an inferno within the thing. That was what drove it to its wild ferocity. That was what it felt like at the time.

As far as what actually happens ... I see that objectively, divorced from the emotion and impressions, as though I were a separate person who had been in the cell and had witnessed the whole thing. (God help any person who ever had! It would surely drive him mad ... although I doubt that there would be time for madness, locked in that cell with the thing that I became.)

I can clearly see the scene within that cell. It flings itself at those padded walls, tearing at them with talons and ripping with terrible fangs. It drops to the floor, crouches for a moment, snarling, then springs at the walls again. It is driven by that rage within, again and again, in a frenzied passion. It pauses only to summon renewed rage, and then springs again, more savagely than before, until at last its energy is spent and it grovels, panting and waiting. Last night it attempted to batter the door down, but the door is too strong.

I wonder if my wife can hear the sounds that it makes as it attacks the walls? Or worse, far worse, the sounds that come from its snarling lips? That would be ghastly. They are very revolting sounds.

At dinner yesterday I noticed the way that she looked at me as I ate. We had steak. I have always liked my steak rare. But she looked at me as though she expected I would tear at the meat like some wild beast. Perhaps she does hear ... Thank heavens that she can never see it! It takes her several days to recover as it is ... to become normal again.

I am quite normal now, of course.

May 7

I am completely sane.

It occurs to me that I have not yet stated that, and it is necessary. If anyone ever reads this, they must understand that I am not crazy. It is not a disease of the mind, it is a disease of the body. It is purely physical. It must be, to cause the physical change that it does. I haven't yet written about the change. That will be very hard, although I can see it objectively. I can see my hands and body, and feel my face, I cannot see my face, of course, because there is no mirror. I don't know if I could bear it if I had a memory of what my face must become. And I don't know if I can describe it honestly, or honestly describe it. Perhaps some night I shall bring this book into my cell with me and write as long as I can – describe the changes as they occur in my body, until my mind can no longer cope with the effort ... until it is no longer my body.

The question that plagues me most in this is whether any other human being has ever suffered from the same disease. Somehow I think it would be easier to bear up to it, if I knew that I was not the only one. It is not a case of misery enjoying company; it is just that I want the reassurance that it is not peculiar to me, that it is in no way my fault that I suffer with it. I can be patient under this trial only so long as I know that it could not have been prevented.

I have tried to find a case similar to mine. I have done a great deal of research ... enough to make the librarian suspicious, if she were of a superstitious nature. But she is not. She is an old maid and she is fat. I believe she thinks that lycanthropy is the study of butterflies. But the research has turned up nothing. The mouldy old volumes and the big, leather-bound psychological books record legends and myths on the one hand, and madness on the other. There are cases that are similar in the recorded details, but in each of these the subject was mentally ill. There were no physical changes, although sometimes the poor madman thought that there were. And yet ... there must be a basis for the legends. All legends have some anchor in the truth. I cling to that belief. I must cling to something.

My grandfather on my father's side came from the Balkans. Somewhere in the Transylvanian Alps. I don't know if that has any relevance, but most of the legends seem to have begun in that area. It is surely a diseased area. And, too, I feel sure that it must be an inherited disease. It is nothing that I could have caught. I have always been a temperate and clean-living man.

I practise moderation in all things. I neither drink nor smoke nor womanize, and my health has always been good. So I am certain that the disease was congenital. I suffer for the sins of my forebears through some jest of fate – some terrible jest of a wicked fate that punishes the innocent for the crimes of the guilty.

The disease must be carried in the blood or, more likely, in the genes. I suppose that it is passed on to one's children in a recessive state, waiting, lurking latently in man after man down through the generations until, once every century … once every thousand years perhaps … there is the proper combination to turn it into a dominant trait. And then it becomes a malignant, raging disease, growing stronger as the victim grows older, gaining strength from the body that it shares, and tries to destroy …

I must believe this, and I do.

I must not think that I am unique, or that I could be in any way, no matter how indirectly and innocently, responsible for it. I must know that it was a curse born with me as surely as my brown hair or greenish eyes, and that it was predestined from the time – who knows how many generations ago? – when my ancestor committed some vile act that brought him into contact with the germs of the sickness. I hate my ancestors for this, but I am grateful that it is their sin and not my own. If I thought that any action of my life had brought about this affliction, the thought would surely drive me mad. It would destroy my mind. I have a great fear of that. It is a rational fear. This thing that I suffer from is enough to drive anyone to insanity …

June 2

Last week I thought seriously about going to a doctor. It is out of the question. I knew that all along, of course, but the fact that I even considered it shows how desperate I have become. I am ready to clutch at straws; to take any risk that has the slightest chance of saving me. But I know that I must cure myself; any salvation must come from within.

It was my wife who put the idea into my head; indirectly, of course. She mentioned something about psychiatrists –

something that she had read in the newspaper, I think – just some vague statement so that she could use the term while talking with me, and suggest it without saying so. Well, her plan worked, because I did think about it, but it is quite impossible.

I was hurt that she mentioned a psychiatrist instead of a medical doctor. She knows as well as I that it is a physical affliction. I have told her that often enough. Still, she has a point. No doctor would believe me. They would think me insane, and refer me to a psychiatrist anyway. And the psychiatrist would be useless because he would try to cure a non-existent concept. The only way that I could prove that the disease is physical would be to have them actually witness the change, and that must never be.

That thought gave me the first laugh that I have had for a long, long time. I can picture myself in the psychiatrist's office. It is at night. The night. I am lying on my back on his leather couch and he is sitting in a chair beside me. I have just finished telling him all about my illness while he listened patiently, nodding from time to time. When I finish explaining he begins to talk in his low, confident tones. He is a very professional type with a bald head and gold-rimmed spectacles. He sits with his legs crossed, his notebook on his knee. He is not looking at me while he speaks, he is looking down at his notes. And I am not looking at him. I am looking at the window. I see the whole scene so clearly. I can even see his degrees framed on the wall. They are on the wall opposite the window, where the moonlight glitters on the gold seals. There are rows of huge and heavy books and a large desk. I see everything and then I look at the window again. The change always comes much more quickly and smoothly when I can see the moon than when I am in the cell. I feel it begin. The doctor talks on, softly. Perhaps he tells me that it is all nonsense, that it is impossible; that it is merely a figment of my imagination, a delusion of a sick mind. He turns towards me to impress his point. He looks into my eyes. And his face … this is what makes me laugh … his face would break and shatter. That cold, scientific, intelligent face would plunge down through all the long aeons of time, and become the primitive and superstitious and terrified face of his ancestors. And then …

I don't suppose that it is really so funny, but it is pleasant to laugh again.

June 3

Tonight I must go to the cell.

I dread it. So does my wife. Yesterday I detected signs of nervousness in her. She is getting worse. She hinted again that I should get help. Help! What help is there for me? But she doesn't seem to understand. Perhaps she is blocking the terrible truth from her mind. Perhaps she would prefer it if I were mad. But it is her sanity I worry about at these times, not my own. For myself I can only hope that it does not get worse, and that I shall be able to live my life out this way, normal but for that one night each month … But how I dread that night, that cell! Even when I am no longer myself, I am still me to the extent that we share the same body and that the emotions and the impressions remain with me and hurt me. Even now, a month later, I can still recall the feeling, not objectively the way that I can remember the way that the thing moved and acted, but deep inside me as one recalls a great pain from the past. It is unbearable to think of a future like this. I can bear the present, but not the thought of the future. And if it should get worse …

But perhaps it may get better. That is possible. Diseases can cure themselves, bodies can develop tolerances and antibodies and immunity. I can only hope for that as I face the future – hope that some day the month will pass and it will not happen and I will know that I am on the way to recovery.

I must never have children, of course. Even if I recover there can be no children. The disease must never be passed on. My wife is sorry about this. She wants children. She doesn't seem to understand why it is impossible, why it would be a monstrous act. I think that she truly might prefer it if I were insane. Sometimes I even think that she doubts me … that she thinks that I am not quite right. Well, of course I am not all right. But I mean … sometimes she seems to think that I am insane. There! I have stated that for this record. But perhaps I am being overly sensitive.

I have a right to be.

I have neglected this record during the month. I meant to write every day, but I found it too oppressive to write about it when it was not imminent. I prefer to forget it as long and as often as I can. Thinking about it only reminds me that the night must come again. This night I intend to bring this notebook into the cell with me. I want to record as much as I can ... perhaps the record will prove valuable. Perhaps it will only be disgusting. But I must try, I must gain all the possible knowledge that I can. It is my only hope that I may find a cure.

I must rest now. Tonight will be exhausting. It is a lovely clear day and I know that the sky will be sparkling. It will be an effort to go to the cell.

June 3 (night)

Well, the door is locked and barred. I listened until her footsteps went up the stairs, and the door closed at the top. Now I am alone in the cell. I feel all right. I came down earlier tonight. I was afraid to wait any longer. It was a good idea to bring this book with me. It is something to do, something to occupy myself with while I wait. Anything is better than just sitting here and waiting for it to happen.

I keep watching my hands as I write; my fingernails. They are all right. Nothing has begun. My fingers are long and straight and my nails are clipped. I must watch carefully so that I can detect the very first signs. I want to be able to describe everything in complete detail.

There is no furniture here in the cell. Furniture would only be destroyed. I am sitting in one corner with my knees drawn up and the notebook on them. The pages look slightly tinted, I should have thought to put a brighter bulb in the light. The light is in a recess in the ceiling and covered by a wire netting. The netting is a little twisted, but I don't remember doing that. I wouldn't, probably. It is light enough to observe the cell, anyway. I have never really noticed it before. I suppose that I was always too concerned with myself to notice my surroundings. But it is earlier tonight ...

The cell is concrete. The walls are thick and the door is metal with large bolts. The walls are heavily padded on the inside. Helen and I did the padding ourselves, of course. It might have been difficult to explain to the contractor why we wanted a padded cell in our basement. I think that we told him the concrete structure was for our dog. He didn't seem curious about it. We don't have a dog really. Dogs don't like me. I frighten them. I suppose that they can sense my affliction even when I am normal. That is further proof that it is a physical disease. I killed a dog once, but it was a vicious dog and I had to.

The smell is stifling and musty, I expect that the walls are damp under the pads, and the stuffing has begun to moulder. We shall have to replace the padding soon. I must try to make the cell as bearable as possible. The pads are ripped in places and the stuffing is running out and curling to the floor. The cover of the padding is tough and thick and smooth, so I know that my … its … talons must be very powerful and sharp. They must be able to slice through those pads like a knife through butter. I wonder if I have ever broken a nail tearing at the walls? I should look in the ripped places to see. It would be evidence of an actual change. I will look later; it seems likely that I will find something. I know the terrible rage that drives the thing at those walls, the unbelievable strength that it possesses, and it seems that even those heavy nails would be splintered by the force that is behind them.

Those wicked claws! I shudder when I think of them, moving at the ends of constricted and hooked fingers. The way that they can rend and tear those heavy pads … think what they could do to the softness of flesh! Think what they would do to a man's throat! It makes me tremble all over to imagine it. I can almost feel what it would be like and the feeling sickens me. But it persists. It wants to be recognized. I can see how those fingers would close, drawing the white skin up in little trails until the skin parted and the fingers sank into the bubbling, pulsing throat. I can see the talons disappear, the fingers themselves gouge in, feel the heat of the blood as it comes spurting out into my face. Taste the hot, salty blood, smell it until my head reels and everything fades away and there is only the stricken face beneath me. I can see that face change and hear the death that would gurgle in his throat as my fangs … as I bring myself … soft throat as my fangs … close … soft, hot flesh and they sink in … and … tear …

June 4

I have just finished patching this book together. I had to use tape where it was torn. I must have ripped it last night, during the sickness. I don't remember doing it. I don't think that it was deliberate, it is just that anything within reach is destroyed in the blind fury. The book was not methodically torn in half or quarters, but just mutilated at random. The front cover was torn to shreds, but the pages are all still readable. My fountain pen had been snapped in two, like a twig. It is hard to imagine such unleashed energy and power. I have always been a strong man, and I have always kept myself in perfect fitness through exercise and moderation, but the strength that comes with the change is beyond comprehension. It seems that the very muscles and sinews of my body must change, that it must be internal as well as external. Perhaps we do not share the same body, but the same small part of the brain that remembers. That would be encouraging, to be able to think of the thing as a different entity. And yet my own body bears the bruises and the marks of the tortured flesh. The two bodies cannot exist at the same time. It is very confusing, it is beyond my powers of reasoning, and I am as rational as any man and more so than most. How many other men could face this thing that I struggle with and retain their sanity? I am proud of that. I am not a vain man, but of that strength of mind I am proud.

I didn't write about the change. I remember feeling it start, and it seems that I was writing, but somehow it is not recorded. The last few lines of what I wrote are scribbled and blurred and do not look at all like my handwriting, and I suppose that was a symptom. I was writing about how strong the thing's hands were and then it just seems to come to an end, in the middle of a sentence. I imagine that my fingers had started to contract while

I wrote, and that would account for the different style. But there is nothing there about the change.

The change seemed different last night. Not greater, but different somehow. I think that I have reached a new stage in the disease, and that the disease is changing … perhaps modifying.

The thing is beginning to think more. Or else I am beginning to remember more. Whichever it is, I can distinctly recall certain thoughts along with the impressions this time. I remember all that frustration and need and hatred, but I also remember snatches of vague thought. Not my thoughts. Its thoughts. They are closer to the human thoughts in that they would be. It is hard to envisage human thoughts in that monstrous body. Disturbing. I do not want to share my mind with it. But I remember that it was reasoning, trying to figure some way to get out of the cell. I remember a pause in the violence while it crouched and rolled its white eyes around, seeking some weak point in the walls, the door. Perhaps it was seeking some deception to get Helen to open the door. There was no escape, of course. We have taken all necessary precautions. Even if it were able to reason as well as I, it could figure no way to get out of the cell.

But that is the change in the disease, that reasoning power. It is possible that the thing is becoming more normal, more human. It is possible that I and the thing that I become are drawing closer together. But it is impossible to say which of us is moving towards that closer relationship, whether the disease is conquering me, or I am beginning to cure myself, I cannot decide if this new development is a good thing or a bad thing … It makes me tremble. I am sweating profusely and my stomach is knotted with fright.

I am calmer now. I lay down for a few minutes. I can still taste the blood and foam on my lips, although I have brushed my teeth several times. I bit my lip last night. It is swollen and painful. I cannot get the taste from my mouth – I suppose that it is all in my mind. It was nauseating to awaken this morning and swallow and know that I could not brush my teeth and rinse my mouth until Helen came and let me out. It seemed as if I waited a very long time, but there was no way to tell. Time seems to stand still when it is enclosed in that cell. Time is surely a concrete dimension, and relative to the other dimensions. Perhaps it is affected by my disease. It would be interesting if there were some way to measure it.

I am sure that it lasted longer last night. It certainly seemed to. It may be that it seemed longer because there were more impressions and memories, but my wife said that when she knocked at the usual time this morning there was no answer from the cell. I always call out that everything is all right before she opens the door, and this morning I did not call at the usual hour. She said that she heard … certain sounds … but that there was no answer. She did not say what the sounds were like.

So she went back upstairs and waited another hour. I can imagine how frightened and worried she must have been during that time, wondering what had happened. Poor woman. She loves me so, and she cannot really understand. She did not know about the illness when she married me, and it was a terrible shock. I am grateful that she has stood up under the strain so well. She must worry and suffer as much as I, in a different, woman's way.

After another hour had elapsed she came down and knocked at the cell door again. I answered this time, and she opened the door. She opened it very slowly, and I could hear her intake of breath when she first looked in. She must have been half mad with fear for me. I don't think she would be afraid of me.

I don't remember her knocking the first time. I was surprised when she told me. I do have an indistinct impression of crouching beside the door with my thighs tensed and taut and my hands open in front of me, as though I were waiting for something to open that door. But it is very vague. It could have been at any time. I know that I would never wait that way for my wife.

June 6

I have been very worried, thinking about how it lasted longer than usual this month. Longer than it ever did before, I think. I am trying to get the history of my illness in context, from the beginning, so that I can follow the progress and the process.

I feel that there is definitely a change coming, and pray that it may be the first step towards recovery. Up until now it has merely become worse time after time. It would seem that since it lasted longer the last time it is just another step in the same direction, but there was also the fact that I remembered the thing's thoughts this time. That has never happened before, not since I really began to change. That is much closer to how it was when it first began. It may be the first sign that I am on the way back, that a cure has begun. It may have taken longer this time because it was less intense. I don't really see how it can get any worse than it is now ...

Thinking back on my life, I find that I cannot tell when it first began. It must have been very gradual. I surely would remember if it came on me suddenly, all at once. A weaker mind might block the memory out to save itself from the knowledge, but I am sure that I would have faced it.

Had I only known the truth in those days there might have been some way to prevent it. I doubt it, but there might have been. But how was I to know? I was never a superstitious child. I did not even believe in ... the thing that I become. I did not believe in Santa Claus, or fairies, or witches, or the elves that leave money under a pillow and take away the baby teeth. My parents would have none of that nonsense, and told me the truth from the first. So how was I to believe in the existence of ... I will not write the word. I know what I am doing, that I have a block about admitting what I know to be true, as though the admission would condemn me more than the fact. But I cannot help that, and it is not the mental block of a weak man whose mind denies the truth, it is just that I rebel at putting the word on paper. I know the word. I think it. It dances in my thoughts, and I am strong enough to recognize it there, and make no effort to deny it. I live with the knowledge as best I can. I know that, all along, through all my life, the inherited sickness was there inside my blood, being carried to every capillary of my body, taking hold and growing stronger as I myself grew, waiting, lurking ... I know that now, but how could anyone have predicted it? It was no fault of mine.

I was always a rather tempestuous child. I used to get angry, to throw tantrums. But many children do. It is common enough. There was never any physical change in me. No warnings. And yet ... my bursts of violence, when I would fight with other children or break my favourite playthings ... those outbursts did not seem to stem from any recognizable fact. They were not the result of something that angered or frustrated me; they seemed to come on for no reason, at any time, whether I was happy or unhappy at the moment they began. I can remember one time when a neighbour, a boy my own age but smaller, threw a rock and hit me over the eye. It hurt awfully. It broke the skin and a trickle of blood ran down the side of my face. The boy was frightened then, because he had hit me for no reason, and because I was much stronger and could have easily punished him. But I did not. I did not even get angry, which amazed him, because he knew my reputation for flaring up. I simply looked at him with the blood running down and I felt no anger at all. I can remember licking the blood from the corner of my mouth where it had gathered. I felt a bit dizzy, from the blow I suppose, and I just stood there and licked the blood away and did nothing. The other boy must have thought that I was afraid of him because I did not retaliate, because after that he persecuted me. He would wait for me after school and throw stones at me and push me and sometimes he would hit me with his fist. I never became angry with him. I never wanted to punish him or hurt him and I took his abuse without any resentment. He used to boast about how I was terrorized and all the other children used to make fun of me about this, but I didn't care. I have never cared what other people thought. This was an example of how my temper was not aroused at times when it would have been fully justified.

And at other times ... for no apparent reason ... I can recall one evening, towards dusk, when I was playing with my favourite toy, a clockwork train. I had been playing with it for some time and was quite happy. And then, suddenly, I picked it up from the tracks and smashed it against the floor until it was broken to pieces. I continued to smash it, over and over again. My mother came into my room and was very angry that I had broken it, and threatened never to buy me another toy, but I didn't seem to care. Even later, the next day, I did not regret the loss of my train. When I thought of it I merely felt as though it had been a good thing to break it. I felt glad that I had done it. It seemed satisfying.

It was inconsistencies like those two that made me different from other temperamental children. I realize, now, that the outbursts must have followed the same cycle as the illness follows now, but at that time I had no reason to think about any regularity, or detect any rhythm. Neither did my parents. They must have supposed it was merely the storms of adolescence, and I don't think that it worried them unduly.

I don't remember very much about my mother. I suppose that she was overshadowed by my father. He was a big man, straight and broad-shouldered and strict. He was religious and very moral, and I have him to thank for the fact that I was brought up right, and that I have always avoided all vices and corruption. Many a time he lectured me, in his deep voice, one forefinger pointing towards my heart, giving me the benefit of his age and experience and, more vital, of the experiences that he had avoided. I was overawed by him, by his knowledge and his goodness and his strength and I always tried to live a life of which he would have been proud. And I believe that I have done that, except for the disease. It is almost impossible to realize that my father himself must have carried the disease in his blood – that that good and strict man had passed the curse on, unknowingly, to his son. It is further proof that it is no fault of my own, that even such a fine man as my father did not know, that he could have been the one whom it affected as it does me.

Only once can I remember my father being unjust and unreasonable. It was the only time that he was ever angry with me. That was when I had to kill the neighbours' dog and I have never been able to understand why my father did not see that it was necessary.

The dog belonged to my enemy, the boy who constantly persecuted me. I do not remember his name. He was an insignificant creature and hardly worth remembering. But I remember his dog. It was a large and vicious brute, a mongrel with a great deal of Alsatian in it. It was often with the boy when he tormented me, and it added its snarls to its master's jibes. It would watch with its yellow eyes while the boy plagued me. Its tongue hung out and its muzzle twitched as though it were very satisfied that I was being tormented. I never paid any attention to the dog at those times. I ignored it and its master, but of the two I believe I hated the dog more. I know it a fallacy to believe that dog is man's best friend. It is a stupid statement made by sentimental and ignorant people, who have been deceived by the brutes. And this dog was a particularly foul beast, with a filthy mottled hide and yellow teeth. It had never attacked me, but I could tell that it would have liked to.

One evening I was coming home from town rather late. Our house was in the country, a few miles from the town. I forget what I was doing out at that hour, but at any rate it was dark as I walked towards our house. It must have been a moonlit night, because everything was very clear. It was necessary to pass our neighbours' house on the way to my own, for we lived on the same road. To avoid passing their house I would have had to go through the woods, and I saw no reason for this.

Well, I was passing their house, minding my own business, when my enemy suddenly appeared. He began to throw stones at me as usual, and I ignored him. I walked on. He hit me in the back with one stone, and it hurt. I knew that it would leave a bruise. I walked on a little way and then I must have sat down beside the road. I know that I thought about the boy, and wondered why he hated me so, and after a while I began to hate him. I had never felt that way towards him before, and it must have been the sum total of all his injustices and attacks that finally added up to the whole of hatred. The longer I sat there the more I hated him. I remembered everything that he had done to me. I remembered the first time, when he had cut my head and I had tasted my own blood. For some reason the taste of that blood came back to me more strongly then than it had seemed when it happened. I knew that he would torment me for ever, unless I put a stop to it, and I got up and walked back towards his house.

He was in the yard, by the woodshed. He saw me coming and picked up a stone and began to yell tauntingly, calling me unmentionable names. It enraged me to hear him use those foul words, and I knew for the first time how truly evil he was. I didn't understand why I had tolerated him before, how I could have let such a wicked person annoy me. I wanted to punish him for annoying me but, more strongly, I wanted to punish him for being a deplorable creature, a foul-mouthed and evil-minded creature. He had to be taught a lesson.

I walked right up to him. He continued to taunt me until I was quite close, and then he must have realized with his slow, dim mind that this was not the same as the other times, because he began to back away. I went after him, walking slowly. When he threw the stone it struck me in the face, but I hardly felt it. He ran backwards to the woodshed and I moved between him and the house. I remember how his eyes darted around as he looked for help, for a path to escape. I was much bigger and stronger than him – I was bigger than anyone else of my age at school – and he became very frightened. His fear did not satisfy me; for some reason it made me all the more anxious to punish him … I felt he realized that he must be punished, that he knew he was evil and, if he were not punished, he would think that it was all right to do as he did. I would not have that. I went at him and he tried to run, but I am very fast and nimble even now, and in those days I could move like a cat. I caught him with both hands. I caught him by the neck and threw him down on the ground. He tried to kick me but I brushed his feet aside and fell over him. He hit me in the face with his small fists but it was less than an insect sting. I got my hands very firmly around his neck and began to punish him. I intended to punish him greatly, in proportion to his sins. I squeezed, and his eyes got very large and that made me feel satisfied. Or almost satisfied – as if satisfaction were on the way, and the harder I squeezed the more rapidly it came. It seemed to run up from my fingertips to my shoulders, and then diffuse throughout my body. He stopped hitting me. His small hands were wrapped around my wrists, but they could do nothing. I put all my weight into my arms and pressed.

It was then that the savage brute attacked me.

I had not seen it sneak up behind me. It was sly and vicious and the first that I was aware of it was when it pounced at me.

I had to release the boy, and the dog and I rolled over. It was a powerful creature, but it was no match for me in an equal struggle. I got over it and got my hands under its collar and twisted. I turned the collar right round, choking the brute. It had torn my forearm with its teeth and the blood ran down my arm and splattered over the dog. The sight of the blood drove me in a frenzy. I realized then how dangerous that animal was, and how necessary it was that it should be destroyed. I twisted the collar around again and it bit into the hairy throat. The tongue slid from its muzzle and I banged its head against the ground so that its own teeth buried themselves in that laughing tongue that was no longer laughing so slyly. The look in the creature's eyes was delightful! It knew that it was going to die then. It knew that it was going to pay for its viciousness, and the eyes rolled and bulged out like two yellowish hard boiled eggs. It made me laugh to see that, but I did not laugh so much that I had to release my grip. I did not let the dog go until it was very dead.

When I stood up finally I saw that the boy had recovered and run away. He must have gone into his house. I would have followed him, but for some reason I no longer hated him. Perhaps I felt that he had been punished enough. I was sure that he would torment me no more. The dog was like a limp and oil-stained rag in the moonlight and I felt very good. A good job well done. I felt warm and satisfied and I turned and walked home. My arm did not begin to hurt until later.

In the morning the boy's father came to our house and talked with my father. After he had gone my father spoke to me. He seemed angry. I explained to him that it had been self-defence, and that the beast had tried to kill me, but he had the strange idea that I had attacked the boy first, and that the dog had died protecting its master. Even my father was fooled by that common lie about dogs being faithful and true, and I could not make him understand. I showed him the slash in my forearm, but it made no difference. He seemed to really believe that I had tried to kill the boy, ridiculous though it seems. But that was the only time that my father was ever unjust, and he forgot about it after a while.

And no one ever taunted me or threw rocks at me again.

June 7

I am up early today and intend to work on this journal until lunchtime. I read what I wrote yesterday, about the dog. I don't think that it is really relevant to the disease. I was, after all, forced into killing it to save myself, and any man would have done the same. But it does show a bit of the violence of which I am capable, and also the tolerant attitude that I take at normal times, so I will leave it in the record, for what it is worth, and continue with my efforts to get the beginnings of the illness sorted out clearly in my mind, in sequence and intensity, so that they can help me to foresee what the next change will be.

My strongest impression of those early years concerns the woods. We lived in a large old house in the country and the woods were behind it. The house was draughty and chilly and damp and I did not like it, but I was always happy in the woods – except when those feelings took possession of me. I liked to go into the woods alone. I always felt safer when there were no other people about. I can still picture just how it looked there. I always seem to picture it in the moonlight, however. The impression of it in the day is not strong. But this may be because there were more distractions in the daylight, and fixed memories yielded to immediate sensations. But at night! Is it one night that I remember, or many nights so similar that they have blended into the same memory?

I was standing in a small clearing with the tall pine trees on every side. It was on a slight hill, and at the bottom of the hill our house nestled in the shadows. I could just see the top of the roof and the chimney against the sky because the land rose a little to the far side as well. It was dark in the clearing but the tops of the trees were white in the moonlight; silver needles under the wind. It was very quiet. A few fluffy cotton clouds avoided the moon. Standing in this place I felt a great yearning, a vague and indistinct need. It was very much the same as spring fever when one had to sit in school and could look out of the window at the flowers and grass, but it was much, much stronger. I had to do something, and there was nothing to do. I suppose that I thought it was a sexual need, at the time. That must have been why I took my clothing off. I took everything off, even my shoes and socks, and stood there completely naked in the trees. It wasn't cold, but I was shivering. One shaft of light penetrated straight down the side of a tree, and it seemed to give off a cold glow that turned me to ice. And I just stood there, with my head thrown back and my mouth wide open, staring up at the sky and trembling as though every vein and every nerve of my body had become charged with electric current. I don't know how long I stood like that. It must have been some time because the heavens had shifted position. And then, suddenly, it was over. Suddenly the need had left me, and I realized that I was shouting. Not shouting ... it was more like a howl, a bay. I stopped. Everything was silent and dark and I felt very strange, very naked, and very much alone and slightly ashamed at what I had done. I still supposed that it had been sexual, I imagine. But I also felt a great relief. I dressed and walked back to the house and everything was all right for the rest of that month. Everything was fine. I was very much at peace. As I say, I don't know if this was a single memory or a combination of many months and many nights. I must have been quite young ...

I have been pondering for a while over what I have just written. I think that it must have happened more than once. I have glimpses of myself running through the woods naked, and crouching and hiding behind trees and rocks. These are very objective memories. They come back to me in the same way as the actions of the thing in the cell, as opposed to the impressions and emotions. I don't think that I was running from anyone, or hiding from anyone, however. I am sure that I was all alone in the woods. I am also sure that there was no physical change. Quite sure. And, strangely enough, I cannot remember the first time that I did change, or the first time that I became aware of changing. It must have come very gradually, so that there was no shock that would remain in my memory.

The first recollection that I have of changing took place in my own bedroom, not in the woods. This must have been later. I was sitting on my bed, bent over and watching my hands. The bed was beside the window and the moon was right there so that the bedroom was all black and white. My hands were in my lap, and a shaft of light passed over them. I was naked. My backbone felt more naked than the rest of me, as though even the skin had been peeled away. I watched my hands. This couldn't have been the first time, because I seemed to know exactly what I was looking for. And I remember how my fingernails began to grow, and my hands trembled and drew up ...

I don't remember what I did after that.

June 8

Helen is a good wife.

Few women would have put up with what she has. I must be honest, she is not a good-looking woman. Perhaps she married me as a last resort, but I don't think so. I believe that she loves me. Sometimes it annoys me when she cannot seem to understand about my sickness, but apart from that she is a good wife. And she must know that I would never hurt her. I don't think that I would ever hurt anyone. I go out of my way not to hurt anyone. I am basically a shy and gentle person, and that is what makes the contrast so hard to imagine when one doesn't realize that it is a physical disease, and that I actually become something different, something dangerous. But I have managed to control it, and so I have never hurt anyone.

I have promised Helen that I will take her out for dinner this evening. She is very happy about it. We do not go out much, I do not care for a frivolous social life and prefer to stay at home, but once in a while it does no harm. Helen enjoys it, although she agrees that I am right in limiting such evenings to two or three times a year. She is dressing now. I may write more when we get home, if it is not too late.

Well, what a fiasco this night has been!

We have just returned and Helen has gone directly to her room. She appears to be annoyed with me. I should have known better than to go out, than to cater to the whims of a woman. Women do not understand much of life.

To begin with, to start the evening off on the wrong foot, Helen put on a dress that she knows I hate. It is an immodest dress that leaves her shoulders bare and makes her look like a tart. I tried to be pleasant about it, but she got annoyed when I told her the simple truth. Why do women get annoyed at the truth and not at deceptions? It is beyond me. Surely her own mirror would have told her the same thing that I did. She can't really think, after all this time, that I am a man who can be flattering without reason, or that I would care to have my wife dress like a tramp? But she put the dress on and we had a little argument even before we left the house. I finally let her wear it, but I should have known better; I should have known what an ill temper I would be in all night because of it.

When we got to the restaurant and got a table I could see several of the other patrons looking at Helen. She didn't seem to be aware of it. She sat, smiling happily and looking around the room. I'm sure that everyone thought that she was looking for someone to flirt with. What else would they think, the way she was dressed? I was mortified. I could just imagine their thoughts. She looked like some strumpet that I had just picked up off the street. She had too much lipstick on, and her knees were uncovered when she was seated. I would have got up and walked out right then if I had not been too embarrassed to leave my seat. I determined to destroy that dress as soon as we were home, so it would never disgrace me again. And, unbelievably, poor Helen seemed to have no idea what a stir she was causing. She is so innocent and inexperienced. She looked around as though she were really enjoying herself and I tried to pretend I did not notice anyone else. I did, though. Some of the other women in the room were dressed as bad, or worse, than my wife, and I realized then that it was not the proper place for us to be. We had never eaten there before, and it had a good reputation, and so I had been deceived. It was one of those gaudy places with plush walls and candles that pretend to be European and overcharge their customers for bad food. I hate any place or any person that pretends to be something other than they are.

When the waiter came he leaned over the table a little, from behind Helen. I'm sure that he was attempting to look down the front of her dress! It enrages me, even now, as I recall that greasy smile. He had a little moustache and wavy hair and he was some sort of foreigner, an Italian perhaps. He had an accent, or affected one. I was angry and miserable and it is little wonder that I lost my temper when he brought me the wrong order.

I hate fancy, foreign foods. I had ordered a plain steak with boiled potatoes and no salad. When my order arrived the steak was ruined with some slimy sauce and there were creamed potatoes and an oily salad. It was revolting. On top of all the other annoyances it was simply too much to take. Perhaps I should have controlled my temper, even though it was justified. Perhaps, as Helen says, I should not have thrown the plate at the waiter. But I don't regret it. These foreigners have to learn that they can't push everyone around. I acted on the spur of the moment, before I even thought about what I was doing. I lifted the plate on one open hand. The waiter was leaning towards me with that nasty smile, and I hurled the plate, food-first, directly into his face. I believe that I was as gentlemanly as possible under the circumstances. I did not shout or cause a scene or speak to him. I simply threw it in his face.

Well, we left after that. We weren't asked to leave, and I suppose that I was respected for sticking up for my rights, but we left anyway. Helen cried as we walked out and I kept my head up and looked about and saw that everyone in the place was looking at us. Or, more precisely, they were looking at that lewd dress that she wore. Some of them were snickering and some looked angry. But I didn't let it bother me. I kept my dignity through the whole affair.

Helen doesn't seem to realize that it was all her fault, and she has gone directly to her room and locked the door. I heard her lock it. She made sure of that. It was just a bit of feminine dramatics, of course. I never go to her room.

Anyway, perhaps this evening will serve one good cause. It may convince my wife that it is not a good thing to go out so often.

June 9

Helen was still angry this morning. For a while she did not speak to me. That was all right with me, I was still thinking about the wasted evening and that horrible restaurant that charged far too much and brought the wrong food. But then she mentioned how I had flared up for no reason! For no reason! She even suggested that it had been a symptom of my sickness! In the middle of the month! It shows that she still has no idea what it is. I had to grip the edge of the table to keep from shouting at her and I must have looked very angry because she went away without another word. She looked rather chastened.

I shall try to be more tolerant of her stupidity. It is, after all, a hard thing for a normal person to comprehend. And it was such a shock to her when I had to tell her about it. I often wonder if the shock did not unbalance her slightly? Not much, but enough to account for some of the things that she does that aren't reasonable … such as thinking that harlot's dress that she wore last night was attractive, and wanting to go out in the evenings like a teenager, and mistaking genuine and justified anger for a symptom of my disease. Yes, I must be more tolerant of her, poor thing.

It wasn't really bad when we were first married. It wasn't until afterwards that it got really bad, and the increase was slow enough so that I could see it coming and make plans to prevent any accidents. I didn't have the cell then – I didn't need it. There was plenty of time to have it made when I saw the need.

Oh, I changed. I changed, all right, but not nearly as much as now. Never completely. I still looked human. I remember how I looked in those early stages, before I was afraid to look in a mirror. My face looked unshaven, nothing more. As if I had gone a week without a shave. My teeth were long, but I was able to keep them covered with my lips so that they looked as though they protruded. It was the eyes that were the worst. They were definitely animal eyes; at least they were definitely not human eyes. But there was nothing that was really out of the ordinary to the extent that anyone who did not know what I normally looked like would have noticed. They would simply have thought that I was a singularly ugly person.

I never lost control in those days. The disease never took over, it just raged in me like a fever, and I was always at least partly myself. That was before we needed the cell, and before I told Helen about it. I suppose that it was wrong to marry her without telling her, but I did not expect it to get worse. And I am sure that it would have made no difference; she would have married me regardless.

On those nights when it happened I would go to bed early and turn the lights out. We had separate rooms, of course. I would tell Helen that I did not feel well and she would not bother me. She must have eventually noticed the regularity of the attacks, because once she made a very crude joke about monthly sickness, and I had to give her a stern lecture on what women did, and did not, mention, even to their husbands.

But then it continued to get worse, and finally I decided it was better to take no chances. I began to go out of town once a month. I told her that it was a business trip, and I suppose she believed me. She didn't act suspiciously, and she made no vulgar jests about it. She knew that I was not the type of creature who would keep a mistress, or go away for a gay night once a month, and so she trusted me and asked no questions.

I would go to some small town thirty or forty miles away. I went to a different town each month. I would check into some cheap little hotel (cheap, because no one would notice an unshaven man in a cheap hotel) and spend the long night in a dingy room. I would never leave that room, no matter how unpleasant it became through that night. And it certainly became unpleasant. I wanted so badly to go out. I needed … something. Perhaps it was the urge to run naked through the woods again. But I fought against it and conquered it and remained in the room. I always locked the door on the inside. It would have been better to have someone else lock me in, but I couldn't very well ask the clerk to do that. That would have been suspicious. So I had to rely on my willpower. Luckily I am a strong-minded man, and I managed. Although it was often very very bad, I managed.

Later, when I knew that it was getting progressively worse, it was necessary to have the cell constructed. It was a plan that I had long been considering. I had to tell my wife about the sickness then. That was the hardest part. Helen is not the most intelligent woman in the world, and at first she would not take me seriously. She would not believe me. She thought that I was joking. But then, when I had the contractor come in and build the cell and she realized that I was serious about it, she thought that I was losing my mind. Oh, she never said that, but I could tell by the way she looked at me. When we were putting the pads on the wall she kept shaking her head as though we were both being ridiculous and wasting our time. It is understandable; I cannot blame her for being dubious at first. She knows better now. She is beginning to realize, although she still makes stupid mistakes and cannot differentiate between the physical and the mental, the normal and the abnormal. It takes time.

We have had the cell for six months now. I have gone there every month and Helen has done her part without question. She is a good wife, all in all, and if she annoys me occasionally by her lack of intelligence and inability to grasp the facts, I suppose that that is only normal in most marriages when one partner is so vastly superior in mind.

I am satisfied with my wife. I shall try to be more tolerant of her faults. I would never hurt her in any way. I would never hurt anyone ...

June 9 (evening)

I have not been honest. It bothers me. I did not write anything untruthful, but I omitted writing about the drunkard in the hotel. I have to tell everything or else there is no point in keeping this journal, and so I must write about him. Anyway, nothing happened which I was to blame for.

It happened on the last night that I went out of town, before the cell was built. I had been thinking about making a cell, but had put it off because of Helen, because that would mean telling her all about my disease. I suppose that the episode with the drunkard was the thing that finally decided me about it. It did show me that I was liable to be dangerous, and that my control was weakening. All in all, it was just as well that it happened, since it turned out all right, as far as I was concerned. I was innocent and what happened to the drunkard was his own fault completely.

It was a very poor hotel. I remember it well, it was as poor as any I had stayed at. The entrance was just a narrow doorway on the street with a sign hanging over it. The sign was crooked. There was a maroon carpet in the corridor with all the threads showing, leading to the staircase. The reception desk was just an alcove in the hall. I had to ring a bell there and wait for the clerk to come out of a room under the stairs. It took him a long time and when he came he was rubbing his eyes, and his shirt was hanging out of his trousers. He went behind the desk and shoved the book at me and yawned right in my face. He was a horrid fellow. I tell these things to show what kind of a hotel it was, and what the people who stayed there must have been like; especially the drunkard. People like that are better off dead than alive.

The desk clerk did not look the least bit disgusted when he saw that I was unshaven. I always took the precaution of not shaving for a day or two before I went to a hotel, just in case someone were to see me when I was being ill. They might think it funny that a man's beard could grow so rapidly, grow in just a few hours. It was just one of the small details that I was so careful about. I am sure that no one ever suspected. But then, it is not a thing that one tends to think about in this day and age. In the day of the psychiatrist, I am a legend.

The clerk in that place was unshaven himself, and he acted as if all the guests at the place went without a razor. Even though I had a suitcase he asked for the money in advance. I went up to my room and closed and locked the door and turned all the lights out and lay down on the bed. I kept my clothing on. The only window was small and greasy and looked out on a brick wall so that I could not see the moon. It was always harder and more painful to change when I could not see it and had to imagine it, big and yellow and round in that black sky. I wanted so much to leave that horrible little room. I remember how I waited, almost wishing for the change to come so that I could get it over with I kept getting up and walking to the window, pacing the room, going to the filthy sink and splashing water on my face. And then I must have gone to the bed again, because the next thing I remember, I had already changed. I was lying on my back, tossing and turning and groaning. I was soaked with sweat. The bed was soaked. The grey sheets were all twisted beneath me and I gripped the brass bedstead with one hand. One changed hand. It was bad. It was like having a high fever and hallucinations. But I was strong and I stuck it out and all the while I was thinking that it had never been so bad before.

And then I heard the drunkard come down the corridor. I have always despised drunkards – anyone who has to seek artificial aids to life and cannot be content and happy without stimulants and drugs. This drunkard was singing loudly and his footsteps were clumping. I lay very still as he came near the door to my room. And he must have got the rooms confused, because he stopped outside my door. He tried it. I heard the knob turn and rattle. And then he tried to fit his key into the lock and I heard it scraping and clanking. I did not move at all. I lay there with my eyes rolling and the froth on my lips. I could hear him cursing and swearing and I hated him. I have never hated anyone as much as I hated that drunkard. And I had a terrible thought … suppose, in this cheap hotel, his key could open my door? Suppose he were to come into the room and see me? Rage and fear moved me. I leaped from the bed and was across the room, leaning with my ear against the door. I listened. I heard his laboured breathing and his muttered words. I pressed against the door so that he would not be able to open it. I am exceedingly strong when I have changed, and he could not have opened the door against me. The door felt hot and smooth against my bristly cheek and hands.

And then he began to pound on the door. He pounded very loudly, and I was afraid that he might awaken everyone, that there might be a dispute, that the night clerk might demand that I open up so that it could be settled. I waited, silently, while my insides boiled and bubbled, and he continued to bang on the door.

I think that I opened the door then.

I didn't really hurt him. But I will never forget the look on his face when he saw me! His eyes, his mouth, his skin ... He took a step backwards, and I wanted to go after him but I knew that I must not. I possibly might have struck out at him. I do not remember. But he collapsed very suddenly. He was just a bundle of rags on the floor with the horrible smell of alcohol and the other smell of blood. I stared for a moment, my fingers hooking at the air, and then I controlled myself and slammed the door and locked it again. I remember leaning against the door and panting. I must have been very frightened. I was sure that when he awoke he would get help and they would break into my room, and I knew that I must change back to myself before they did. Perhaps the fear acted as a catalyst, because very shortly after that I lay down and when I opened my eyes I was all right once more.

In the morning the clerk was very excited. Apparently they had just taken the body away. He asked me if I had heard any noise in the night and I told him that I thought I had heard someone singing in the hall – someone intoxicated. He told me that one of the residents had been found dead in the corridor by my room. I was very surprised and asked about it. Apparently the man had died of a heart attack. That seemed the obvious solution. The clerk told me that he had been drinking and had walked up the stairs and it must have been too much for him. Drinking is very bad on the heart. The man had had a large bruise on his temple, but that must have happened when he fell down. Anyway, that is what happened with the drunkard in the hotel, and so it wasn't really my fault. I didn't hurt him.

June 11

I am afraid that the librarian is suspicious of me! It came as a terrible shock. I had never considered her intelligent enough to suspect anything, but I see now that that was my mistake ... She is one of the types that are stupid enough to believe in the things that intelligent people laugh at. That makes her very dangerous. I don't know what I should do about her. I won't go back there, of course, but if she already suspects … I don't know. I would hate to suffer because of such a stupid woman.

I first began to distrust her when I went into the library today. I walked past her desk and nodded and she nodded back as usual, but I noticed that there was a calendar on her desk. It was right there in full view, as though she had been studying it. There had never been a calendar there before. Why should there be one now? If it was necessary in order to keep track of how long books had been out on loan she would have always had one. Anyway, the books are all stamped in the back or something. No, I am sure that she has the calendar to keep track of the full moons!

I thought that as soon as I saw it, but I wasn't sure. There was a chance that she might be innocent. I always give a person the benefit of the doubt. But then, when she followed me into the dark back room …

It is very silent and gloomy in the back, where the big research books are. No one seems to use that room much. I was looking through an old volume and suddenly the librarian came in. She had her arms full of books, and pretended that she had come to put them on the shelves, but she didn't fool me. She was watching me. When I turned and stared at her she blushed. She said something inane, and I kept staring, and she shoved the books in at random and hurried off. She has a disgusting way of walking, so that her bottom bounces suggestively. She is overweight and unclean looking. She is an old maid, although not really so old. I have often seen young men talking to her at the desk, pretending that they are interested in some books and leaning towards her. I am sure that she has foul habits. It is no wonder that she has never married. She doesn't look like a virgin, either. But I am afraid of what she suspects. She is dangerous. I don't know what she might try to do …

When I left she tried to strike up a conversation. I had not stayed long and she mentioned that, just to get me talking. She was smiling and flushed, pretending to be interested in me in ways other than she is. I gave her a crisp nod and went right past the desk without saying anything. I could feel her looking at my back until I had left the building. I know that she wants to get me into a conversation so that she can find out more about me. She pretends to be flirting with me, but she has other motives. That is a pretence. But it is a mistake on her part to imagine that I am the type of man who would be interested in a flirtation.

Still, I must admit it is a possibility that she is genuinely trying to strike up an acquaintance. I know that I am appealing to women, and she is quite wretched and probably has few friends. She is much homelier than Helen. If that is the case then I have nothing to fear from her, although I must feel disgusted that any woman should attempt to start something with a happily married man. Any woman who would do that is better off dead. They are not fit to live, to corrupt our society.

Perhaps it would be better not to suddenly stop going to the library. That might simply arouse any suspicions that she has. It might be better to talk to her, and see just how much she suspects …

June 15

I went back to the library today. She tried to strike up a conversation again. I talked to her for a few minutes this time, just to see how she reacted. It is hard to tell what she is thinking. I have never had much experience with women of that sort. She appeared to be trying to tempt me. It is monstrous, but I believe it may be true. I feel relieved that she did not ask me any questions that showed she was suspicious of me, but it sickened me to see the way that she carried on. I had all I could do from letting her see how angry I was. It was hard to keep from screaming at her when she twitched her hips and looked coy and leaned over the desk towards me. She had a disgustingly tight sweater on. It makes a man wonder what could have happened to turn a woman out that way? The calendar was still on the desk but I had a chance to look at it and saw that the stages of the moon were not marked on it. So I no longer think that I have anything to fear from her. She is more stupid than I supposed.

Afterwards I went to the poetry section and pretended to be reading some poems so that it would throw her off the trail. I hate poetry. It seems so useless. But I fooled the girl. I just hope that no one saw me talking to her and got the wrong impression.

June 24

Well, the librarian showed her hand today. It was just as I thought, she is an immoral woman. She suspected nothing of my disease, she merely lusted after me! I believe that she makes a practice of seducing men. She certainly seemed experienced.

She followed me into the back this afternoon. It was late and we were the only ones in the whole library. I didn't hear her approach, I was reading, concentrating because it was hard to see in the dim light between the high shelves, and all of a sudden she was right there beside me. When I moved, startled, she giggled. She asked if she had scared me, and then, before I could answer, she said that I needn't be frightened of her. She has very wicked eyes, they seem to reflect her soul. They gleam. I could not help but look into those terrible eyes. It was like staring at a flickering fire … it was hypnotic. Why is that? Why should a moral man be fascinated by evil and degradation and be unable to take his eyes away? Is the horror of seeing wickedness so strong? Try as I would I could not look away from her, and the creature mistook my loathing for interest. She moved closer to me. I forget what she said. It was meaningless, just something to say as she smiled. I think that she asked me why I was so shy and timid. I couldn't answer, I couldn't force myself to speak to her. I remember opening my mouth to tell her how I despised her, but words failed me. And then she reached out and touched my arm. Her fingers brushed my arm and it was like the touch of the Devil himself. An icy hatred moved from my arm to my heart itself, and everything faded away, the shelves and the books and the walls all vanished into a red haze and all I could see was her gruesome countenance, drawing closer and closer to mine.

I believe that she would have actually kissed me, if I had not struck her! I don't remember telling myself to slap her, so it must have been a purely reflex movement. Self-preservation works for the soul as well as the mortal life, and I had to stop her. I slapped her as hard as I could, in the face. I have never struck a woman before, but I do not regret it. That creature was less than a woman, less than a human. She was an abomination on life itself, a bloated parasite feeding on men's bodies.

After I struck her, I turned and walked away. She didn't pursue me. She did not say a word. I suppose that she was stunned by my blow. Perhaps she fell down, I did not wait to see. I just walked out of that library and came home. My hands are still trembling. It was a dreadful experience and I know that I shall never forget it. I only hope that I may have done some good; that my strength and resolve will show her that not every man can be ruined by her perverted desires.

June 24 (evening)

Well, I just had a shock. It was a remarkable coincidence, no doubt about that. I had just finished this afternoon's entry in this journal and gone downstairs to listen to the news on the radio. It appears that someone has murdered the librarian. The announcer said that she was found in the back room of the library, between two high bookshelves. Her neck had been broken by a tremendous blow to the side of the head. It must have happened in the very same place where she tried to work her evil designs on me. I expect that it was under much the same circumstances. She was undoubtedly in the habit of following men back there and approaching them without the slightest trace of modesty. Well, after being rebuffed by me she was most likely feeling frustrated or desperate or whatever it is that lewd women feel when they come up against a man strong enough to resist them, and I imagine that she tried harder with the next man that she managed to trap. The great coincidence of it is this man, the murderer, must have been a very moral person, the same as I, and he reacted to her foul advances with uncontrolled anger. He probably did not mean to kill her, although surely she is better off dead, but he must have hit her the same way that I did, except he had less control over himself and struck her too hard. That is what I think has happened. I may be wrong. But whatever it was, I cannot feel sorry for that woman. I am sure that it is better she is dead.

My wife heard the broadcast too, and asked me if I had not been at the library at the approximate time of the murder. I said that it must have happened just after I left, but I didn't tell her that I was sure I knew how it had happened. That would have been too embarrassing, and I'm sure that Helen could not conceive of such a woman and would only be confused. She said that I should go to the police, that I might be able to help them. But I saw no one else, there is nothing that I can do. I don't want to get involved and, besides, I cannot help but feel sympathy for the man. Murder is a dreadful crime, of course, but under certain circumstances it is justified, and when one's morals are outraged it is very easy to lose control and to do something that would normally be out of the question. I couldn't explain this to Helen. She is not intelligent enough to understand that, in certain instances, the letter of the law is not necessarily correct. I just told her that I was sure I could not be of any assistance to the law and she agreed, although I cannot help but feel she thinks I am shirking my duty to society.

Well, the police will undoubtedly apprehend the man. It seems likely that he will give himself up after he has had time to consider and realize that it was justifiable homicide or self-defence or with extenuating circumstances, and the law should not be too harsh with him once he has told his story. I suppose he must be punished in some way, because that is the law, but for myself I think that he is more to be admired than punished. His only crime was in failing to keep himself under control, as I did in similar circumstances. But, of course, I am a remarkable man and cannot expect everyone to be as strong-willed and restrained.

June 27

I had a rather curious conversation with Helen while we were taking coffee this morning. For several minutes she seemed to want to say something, but kept hesitating. I presumed that it was about the time of month (it draws near again) or the cell or, perhaps, about seeing a doctor. But it wasn't.

"They haven't caught that murderer yet," she said.

She meant the man who killed the librarian. The police had apparently found no clues. It must be difficult to solve an unpremeditated murder, since there is no motive, and in this case the man was most likely a complete stranger to the librarian. I find myself hoping that he will escape the written law, for his actions were ordained by the higher law of morality.

I said, "Perhaps they won't."

"Don't you think that you really should go to them and tell them that you were there?" she asked.

I asked her why.

"Well … you must have been there at almost the same time as the killer. She was murdered before you came home, apparently. There might be something you could tell them …"

"I've told you. I saw nothing."

"You aren't … afraid to go to the police, are you?" she asked me. She looked away when she said it. I don't know what could have given her that idea. What would I be afraid of? I repeated that I knew nothing, and then I told her that I hoped the man would escape punishment because the librarian had obviously been a bad woman. I did not tell her that the woman had tried to work her ways on me, but maybe she guessed it, because she looked at me in a very strange way and then left the table and went to her room. It was a funny way for her to behave. I suppose it is her upbringing. The middle classes have such a ridiculous idea that man-made laws have some higher right than man who is behind them. I cannot understand how people can be so dense, so easily led. How can they regard the rules of society as the rules of God? They make no distinction between descriptive laws and laws that are relative to the situation: between the eternal laws of nature and God and morality and the fluctuating and often wrong laws that men create to hinder themselves and others. It truly bothers me that this is so, that prejudice has made it so. Just think how it applies to myself … I would be scorned and hated and punished if anyone knew of my affliction. The authorities would most likely pass a law to make it illegal to have this disease. But what good would that do? Diseases are not governed by the laws of governments, and I would be thought a criminal although powerless to help myself.

That is why no one must ever know about it. The old, almost forgotten prejudices and fears and superstitions would join forces with the new power of the authorities and destroy me. It is a terrible thing. One sees it everywhere, and can do nothing to combat it. I feel very bitter about it. If I had lived three hundred years ago I would have at least been feared and acknowledged by anyone who knew. Now I would simply be legislated against. It is a good thing that I am a well-balanced man, or there is no telling what such stupidity would drive me to.

I often feel bitter like this when the time draws near. I hate that cell so much …

July 1

Tomorrow I must go to the cell once more.

I have tried to avoid thinking of it. I even neglected this journal in an attempt to think of other things, but it is quite impossible. I cannot avoid the thoughts, and the thoughts torment me. I feel that I shall not be able to bear it again. Even as I write this my hands tremble and I am perspiring. It seems so unjust to punish myself because I am ill. It seems so unfair to martyr myself for the sake of an uncomprehending, uncaring society. I don't know if I am thinking this way because it is so near or because I am right. I know that my thoughts could change as the disease begins the cycle; I admit that. And yet, my reasoning is flawless.

I wonder if the cell is making the illness worse? I have not considered this before; I suppose it occurred to me, but it seemed too close to rationalization and I did not think about it. But the fact remains that it was never so bad before I started going into the cell. I always had control of myself then. Even the last time that I stayed out, the time when the drunkard had the heart attack, I was able to restrain myself. The drunkard's death was the prime factor in my decision to have the cell built, but as I look back and realize that his death had nothing to do with me I see that it was a false factor; that I acted without properly reasoning, without seeing that the cell might affect me and punish me instead of keeping me safe. Now I wonder if possibly the cell has aggravated the disease. It seems reasonable. It was always easier when I could see the sky, and since I have been shutting myself off completely it has become worse. I really don't know. I would like to see, however.

I wonder if I dare to stay out of the cell tomorrow night?

July 3 (morning)

Nothing that I can write can possibly describe my feelings. I am in despair. I despise myself. I know that it was not my fault, but the knowledge cannot diminish the shame, the horror. I feel that the human body cannot stand this much mortification; that my heart will burst, my brain melt so that all the memories run molten together and I will die. But I am still alive. I would rather be dead. I have thought of suicide. I actually took my razor out and looked at the big blue veins in my wrists, and I think that I would have done it if it were not that the blood would remind me of what happened, and even as I felt my life drain away I would be remembering that fiendish night ... I cannot kill myself that way. If I had sleeping pills I know that I would use them, but I have none. I have never used them. I do not approve of using drugs.

I feel a little better now. I have been lying down. I think that I see things more clearly now that I am rested. It wasn't as though I were responsible. Suicide would punish me, not the disease that turned me into the thing that committed the terrible crime. But I am still on fire with self-abasement, I hate myself. If only I had gone to the cell ... but how was I to know? How could I have even imagined what was going to happen? I am a gentle person; it was impossible to know that my body could be used for ... what happened. I feel as if I should take a cleaver and chop my hands off at the wrist; should have my teeth torn out at the roots. God knows, if it were possible to change the past there would be no question of it. I would surely destroy myself rather than let it happen. But there is no question of that. What is done is done. But I am so ashamed ...

I tried to act normally when I came into the house this morning. I acted as though nothing had happened, although it was very hard. My wife didn't say anything, but I saw her look at me very closely. She didn't even ask where I had been all night, but I told her that I had been called away on business very suddenly. I don't know if she believed me. Neither of us mentioned that it had been … the night. Perhaps she thinks that nothing happened this month, or that I am beginning to control it better. Or perhaps … I hate to write this, but it is a possibility … perhaps she thinks that I forgot about it, and that it is my mind that causes it. I don't know. She acted as though she wanted to ask me, but she didn't. I will have to consider this … later, when I can think more clearly. My mind is still burning, and I can think of nothing except what happened last night … I keep seeing her face … all that I can do is to keep brushing my teeth and cleaning under my fingernails.

I have had to burn my shirt.

July 3 (afternoon)

It was in all the newspapers!

It never occurred to me. I suppose that I was so concerned and confused, that I was thinking so much of myself, that I forgot the rest of the world. But naturally it was on the front page of all the papers, and they had it all wrong!

When I went down to lunch my wife had the papers on the table. They were all folded back so that the story about last night was on top. She did not look at me while I read them. That was a good thing, because I could not help but show my anger and pain. It was enough to make even a strong man lose restraint. I'm certain that Helen knows I am the one. I only hope that she realizes that the newspapers have it all wrong. They have made it out to be much worse than it really was, although it was certainly bad.

They called it the work of a madman! A madman! They used all the most lurid words and the worse type of sensationalism, all the most violent terms and expressions and the most ghoulish descriptions and details. And each and every paper referred to it as an insane act. Newspapers are supposed to keep to the objective facts, and not feel obligated to formulate theories about which they know nothing. But they are all so eager for sales that they must make everything sound as obscene as possible. What evil-minded fiends they must be! They have even implied that it was a sex crime! That is the worst of all. Every paper implied that the girl had been sexually assaulted! It sickens me to the very heart. They go so far as to say that her clothing was disarranged, that her thighs had been torn and bleeding and her stomach gouged and mutilated; that her blouse had been torn off and her underclothes shredded and her private parts mangled! All facts designed to make it appear that she had been sexually interfered with. Can't they see that clothing must become disarranged when one struggles as she did? Are they so sick that they can never see beyond a sexual motive for any act? Or do they ignore the truth in order to sell more papers?

I am furious! It enrages me to see that the newspapers can be so irresponsible! And the public ... the terrible public ... to think that the way to increase circulation is to publish such complete lies, such sensationalism. What is wrong with our society that men and women actually enjoy reading such things? How can an ill person ever hope to be cured in such a society? It is so discouraging. It makes me lose hope.

I have the papers here in my room. They are all alike. The headlines differ but the lies are the same. The headlines range from MADMAN SLAYS GIRL IN WOODS to SEX FIEND MURDER to MANGLED CORPSE IN LOVERS' LANE. And nowhere in any of the stories is there any suggestion of a physical illness. Are they blind? Or do they fear to look at the truth? Do they prefer the mentally ill to the innocent? What can I do about it?

I have contemplated writing letters to each of the newspapers, explaining exactly how it was, and what the disease is. They would surely publish the letters, if only to increase sales, but who knows what alterations or omissions they would make? I am sure that they would destroy any truth that I wrote them. I have learned that they are not to be trusted. I would like to have the editors of those scandalous papers locked in a room with me ... locked in the cell with me on the night that it happens. I would like to see the way their faces change as they look upon the truth, as they realize how wrong and wicked and libellous they have been. That would be the way to show them, to teach them the truth and to teach them how to suffer for their errors at the same time. It would not be corrective punishment, but they would deserve it. They would be …

I should not be thinking this way. I can feel my heart begin to drum, my blood is hurtling through my veins. I suppose it must be some reaction left by last night, some after-effect of the disease. It is probably not well to let myself feel this way. It is yielding to the emotions of the sickness instead of combating it. I must never let it gain control when it is not necessary. But it is understandable why I should feel that way. I have been outraged and slandered without cause by men who care nothing for truth; men who deserve to suffer; men who would be better off dead.

I am too disgusted and angry to write any more now. Later I must write and cancel my subscriptions to those papers …

July 3 (night)

I feel obligated to tell what really happened, no matter how painful the effort is. I must write it all, objectively and truthfully. It may bring me relief to purge myself this way, or it may increase the despair … I can only do it and see, and do it regardless. I must show that it was the act of a sick person and not the disgusting crime of a pervert. That is what hurts me most, to be labelled a pervert. A sex pervert! I, of all people, to be so misunderstood.

I hope and pray that Helen does not believe the newspapers. She is not given to thinking for herself, she has a tendency to believe whatever she reads instead of forming her own opinions, and it drives me to frenzy to imagine that she might be thinking of me in that light, by that lie. What would she feel if she believed that I had raped a young woman? The possibility of being thought capable of such a fiendish act appals me. I would hate anyone who believed that I was capable of it, hate them terribly. I have always been very pure in mind and body. Even with my wife I have tried to limit our sexual relations to a minimum. I have never been guilty of feeling any great need for sex, and usually I do it simply to satisfy Helen. I believe that she is a bit over-sexed, but I have managed to regulate that, and to show her by my example that continence is the proper basis for health and purity. Over-indulgence in sexual acts is every bit as heinous as taking drugs, or drinking to excess.

Perhaps the fact that it happened in that lovers' lane gave those newspapers the wrong impression. But that was merely a coincidence. I swear that I did not touch her in any unclean manner. Even after I had changed, my moral code was strong enough to resist that temptation, even if it had occurred. But it did not. There was never the slightest urge towards it. It could just as well have been a man as a girl. The fact that it was a girl, and that she was young and rather pretty, in a cheap and painted fashion, had absolutely nothing to do with what happened. I swear that. I would never, under any circumstances, interfere with a woman.

I suppose that, in one way, I should be thankful that they have got it all wrong. It will throw the police off the trail. They will be searching for a madman, a sex pervert. There is no way that I could come under suspicion. My life has always been beyond reproach. The more they investigate, the further from the truth they seem to move. In the late news broadcast it was hinted that there might be a link between this crime and the librarian's murder. The poor benighted fools! How could they imagine that? It is beyond me. I suppose they are desperate to solve one crime or the other and find it less compelling if they are able to lump them together. Well, they will never find the truth, that is definite.

I see that I am still unable to write objectively. I am still a bit annoyed at the newspapers, and a little shaken by last night. Tomorrow I will write exactly how it was.

July 6

I have waited until I feel that I can explain everything calmly. I could not trust myself before. But now I am ready, and I will describe what really happened on that night, and show how wrong the newspapers were.

That afternoon I went for a long walk. I left the house just after lunch and there was plenty of time before darkness would set in. Helen did not seem to realize what night it was, or else she thought that I would only be gone a short while. She didn't question me when I went out, at any rate. I had not the faintest idea where I should spend the night, but I knew that I had to get away from that cell. I could not bear the thought of going there again. And I knew that I must get away from the town, away from people. I intended to take no chances. I thought … I had convinced myself … I truly believed that it was the confinement of the cell that had made the change so much greater in the past months. Being shut off from the air and the sky and the moon I had felt the change violently, and I believed that, since the change had to be more powerful to occur in the stifling cell, it had also been greater necessarily. I know now that that is not so, that the degree of change is not modified by the degree of struggle necessary to bring it about, but I firmly believed it then. I could not foresee any danger.

I walked around the streets aimlessly for some time, and then, in the late afternoon, I headed away from the populated areas. I walked west. I did not hurry, but I walked at a steady pace, and very soon the town was behind me and I was on the open road. It was a wide highway and motor cars roared by in clouds of dust and noise and it was very unpleasant. I have never cared for motor cars myself. I prefer to walk or to take a train. Perhaps I am somewhat oldfashioned, but I see no harm in that. I see it as a virtue in this day and age of idleness and laziness. Soon it began to grow dark and some of the cars had their headlights on. I knew that it was time to find seclusion then, and I turned up the first secondary road that I came to. This road was narrow and unpaved. It headed in a northerly direction. There were trees on both sides and I could see more trees ahead. The noise of the highway faded behind me. There was no traffic on the small road, although there were wheel tracks in the dust. I did not know that it was too early for traffic there, you see. And I certainly did not know that it led to the local lovers' lane. Such thoughts never occur to me, and I find them disgusting. I am not naïve; I know what goes on in parked cars before people are properly married. But I did not know that I was walking towards such a place.

It was uphill. The road turned and twisted as it rose and I suppose that I walked for an hour or more without seeing another human being. Several times I saw dogs. They snarled and yelped and when I made a quick motion they ran off with their tails tucked in between their legs, looking back over their shoulders at me. Dogs are always terrified of me. Even fierce dogs that attack postmen and delivery boys run from me. I find it amusing. Their owners can never understand why this is so. One very large mongrel stood its ground for a moment, in the centre of the road. It had very large teeth. I made a noise in my throat and moved quickly towards it and it went away very fast then, very chastened. It looked so humorous that I had to laugh.

Soon I had reached the top of the hill and the road ended in a quarry or pit of some kind. I don't know much about such things, but I believe that this one was deserted. It was growing dark by this time and I paused to rest. I sat on a flat stone and loosened my necktie. I was sweating a little from the climb but it was relaxing to be there in the open, all alone. It brought back memories of childhood. I felt quite sure that the change would be slight and that I would be satisfied to run through the woods as I had in the past. It never occurred to me that I might meet another person. Everything was so deserted and so quiet. The sounds of the woods are not like the sounds of the cities, they are a pleasant background, almost like music. I was content to sit there with my eyes closed, and I believe that I would have stayed right there all night and nothing terrible would have happened, if the car hadn't come.

I heard it when it was still a long way away. At first I thought that it was down on the highway, but then it seemed to be getting closer. It annoyed me. I didn't want to be disturbed and I could not see why a car should be coming to the deserted sandpit. I waited until I was sure that it was coming and then I left my rock and went into the woods. I went a few yards back into the brush, where I was sure I could not be seen, and knelt down. The ground was crisp and dry under my knee and smelled very rich. There was still a little light and I could see the dirt road and the pit from where I crouched. After a while the automobile drove up in a great cloud of dust. It drove to the end of the road and stopped. I waited, expecting the driver to see that it was a dead end and turn around, but he did not. He turned off the motor. That made me very angry. I felt as though he were trespassing on my land. I stared at the car from beneath a large clump of bushes, and that was when I realized what was happening. There was a girl in the car. Two men and one girl. I could not really see what was going on, but I heard a great deal of giggling and rustling and soft voices. I knew what was going on then. It filled me with great anger. I dug my hands into the soft earth and made noises in my throat and hoped that they would go away. Why wouldn't they go away? But they did not. The darkness fell suddenly and there was the moon, shining right down on that motor car with all the lewd sounds coming from within. I wanted to leave then, to run away as fast as I could, but something seemed to hold me there. I could not leave. I could not even look away from the motor car. I suppose that the change must have occurred at this time, but I was not even aware that it had started; even after I changed I did not realize it.

And then they got out of the car! The girl was laughing and flushed and her clothing was partially unfastened. She got out and stood beside the car and the two men got out. One of them had a blanket and he spread it on the ground. The other one kissed her. I saw his lips grind on hers, and I could tell that she liked it. She was not a good girl. I saw it all. I saw her take her undergarments off and lift her dress and lie down on the blanket, and then both of those men got down and they both … they took turns … Ah, I cannot write of that, there are some things that a normal man cannot face. But they did things to her and I crouched there in the woods and I saw everything that happened …

I controlled myself. Perhaps the horrible thing that I was witnessing had hypnotized me so that control was not hard. But I waited there, even though I wanted to spring at those execrable and detestable creatures, to punish them, to bring an end to their foul act. I waited and after a long time both men seemed to have sated their lust and they got up and put their clothing on. The girl was smiling. She remained on the blanket for a while. She actually seemed to be contented, as if she were satisfied with her wickedness! I looked at her, at that evil twisted smile on her mouth, at the way she lay with her head back and her knees raised. I looked at her throat and her arched back and her white thighs. Everything about her was flagitious and depraved. She was exposed in a beam of moonlight and made no attempt at all to cover her parts. Her legs were parted and her undergarments lay beside her on the ground. I have never imagined such base corruption.

A strange thing happened then. I do not pretend to understand it. The two men got in the motor car. They were laughing and one of them leaned out the window and said something to the girl. She looked startled and leaped to her feet. The car started and she tried to get in. She was very distressed and the men were looking pleased with themselves. They backed around and the car turned and she pleaded with them. But they drove off. One of them waved at her from the window, and she hurled a curse at them which no gentleman could ever repeat. She stood there, looking down the road after the car and muttering to herself. She had her hands on her hips, and the words that she mumbled were such as I have never heard before; I scarcely know the meaning of them, and I am a full-grown man. But they all had sexual reference, for even in her anger she was depraved. I have never known a greater sinner than that woman was. I presume that the two men, their lust satiated, had been appalled at what they had done, and left her to punish her for her part in their crime against nature. That is the only explanation that occurs to me, although I do not understand why they laughed as they drove off. There are some things that I do not understand about the relationships between men and women. But I do understand what is wrong and that girl was wrong. That girl needed to be punished.

I didn't intend to hurt her. I don't know what I intended. I waited until she had walked back to the blanket and then I got to my feet and moved out into the open. She had bent down to pick up her panties. I walked very quietly up behind her. She raised one leg and started to draw the panties over her foot and then I must have made some slight sound, because she turned towards me.

I don't know if she screamed. Her mouth was open but I heard no sound. Perhaps she was too frightened to scream, or perhaps my ears were not functioning. She staggered backwards a few steps, her hands raised, palms out towards me. Her panties were bundled around her ankle. The fear in her face was indescribable. I slowly moved after her, with my hands clawed in front of me and my teeth bared. I moved closer and she fell to the ground. Her eyes never once left my face. Even when I crouched over her she looked directly into my face. Her fear seemed to inspire me. I had only meant to frighten her, I am sure. But there is something about fear … the smell of fear … it made me lose control. Fear and blood have much the same smell. I could not help myself then, it was her fault; she drove me to it just as she must have driven those two men to that foul act. I remembered that as I saw her white thighs flash and her painted lips move and I wanted to rip and tear and destroy; to drive my talons into her flesh so that the blood jetted out and that evil life was ended.

That was when I sprang on her.

And all the while she looked directly into my eyes, until her own eyes clouded over. She seemed to remain conscious for an extraordinarily long time.

I don't remember what happened afterwards. I don't know how long I crouched over her corpse, or what I did to it. I must have been there for some time, if the newspapers have accurately reported the condition of her body. But then, they have reported nothing else correctly, and I am glad that I have been able to write this so that the truth is written somewhere.

This is the truth; this is exactly how it happened.

July 20

I have ignored this book for the past two weeks. I have not even read it. I think that I exhausted myself with my last entry, and it was a good thing to get my mind off the disease and to relax for a while. That is a serious trouble with modern civilization, it leaves so little time to relax. Luckily, I have never fallen into the habit of rushing madly after money and success and happiness. I am content to let it come to me if it will, or to do without it if it will not. I am stoical and reasonable and undoubtedly born several hundred years too late in history. But I do not complain. I have never been given to boasting, but I feel that eventually I shall be able to even reconcile myself to accepting my affliction on the same terms that I regard the other aspects of life. It is, after all, only one night per month, only twelve nights each year that I suffer. It could be so much worse. Many diseases are worse, it is just that they are common and taken for granted, whereas mine is unique and seems more horrible than it really is. It is not as bad, surely, as having cancer, or leprosy, or being blinded. Only vanity made me think it was so terrible, and I am happy to see that I have defeated such thoughts and now look at it in its true perspective. If it is a trial sent to judge me, I shall not be found lacking. I am happier now than I have been in a long while, because I am thinking clearly for the first time, thinking as clearly about my illness as I am in the habit of thinking about other things. I accept my agony in the same way as I accept my pleasures and my mild happiness. I have learned to live with the sickness just as I have learned to live with the cruelty of society, with the lesser mentality of my wife.

I have read what I wrote about that night. It is all very objective and true, and I believe it helped me to see myself more perfectly. One thing I noticed, which would have disturbed me a short time ago, but which now makes me understand better … In writing about what happened, I continually referred to myself, as myself, instead of to the thing that I become, or to it. I see that those words were a defence, that I used them instead of facing the truth. For, of course, it and I are the same. We are the same being, with changes and differences but basically the same. I can even face up to that now, and it shows how well I am thinking. I don't know if this change in my writing happened because I was trying so hard to remember all the details, or because I am drawing nearer to it, and it to me, or purely for literary ease and convenience, but whichever caused it, I feel it is a good symptom, and shows truthfulness and lack of inhibition. It was, after all, an unusual night ... an extraordinary night ... it is hardly strange that I remembered it differently than I remembered those terrible nights in the cell. I will have to wait and see how things are this month, when I return to the cell again. I will bring this book with me again, and go down in plenty of time. I won't take any chances on staying outside again. I must never allow another accident to take place. But ... I am not at all sure that, in this one instance, it was not rather a good thing. That may sound heartless, but many true thoughts do. And when one considers how many young men that woman would have debased, how many she would have led into sin and degradation and ruin ... well, perhaps I have saved a good many. And surely the girl herself is better off dead. She had nothing whatsoever to live for. Young as she was, she was already old with sin, and she could never have been happy in her depravity ...

To think that I actually considered suicide the day after it happened! I was so emotional, so out of character. But everything is all right now, and I have felt better for the last two weeks than I have felt for a long, long time. It is hard to give the reasons, it is almost as though I accomplished something ... as though I have suddenly achieved something or gained something that I have wanted for a long time, without knowing it. And yet, nothing is changed. I cannot see what it is. It must be something intangible, some frustration that I never realized I had must have been removed from my mind. It may be that the shock of what happened on that night broke up whatever was blocking my mind. It does seem to have something to do with it. I cannot trace the path through my thoughts and emotions, but it is there. It is not a new feeling, but it is a new depth of satisfaction. I can remember feeling this way when I was young. It is almost the way that I felt when I destroyed my favourite toy. It is close to how I felt when I destroyed that savage dog that had attacked me. It is a very curious phenomenon. It is very peculiar that three acts which were so completely different can give such a similar feeling. I find it quite interesting ...

July 28

The day approaches. I am quite resigned. I am in perfect physical health and my mind is clear and I live a pure life and if I must suffer one night it is hardly anything to complain of. I wish my wife would stop acting so peculiarly, however. All this month she has seemed very distant. Perhaps she actually took some stock of those false newspaper accounts, and is angry with me, but she has not mentioned it. She has never said a word about that. It is no longer front page news, new scandals and lies have displaced it, but each day there is a small paragraph reporting the progress of the police. Each day they claim that an arrest is imminent. It makes me chuckle. I do hope that they do not arrest some innocent man. But, still, I am sure that if they do arrest someone he will be a known pervert and will be guilty of far worse crimes than mine, and so I am not worried about it. Punishment for the wrong sin is quite just, if some other sin has been committed. As far as myself … and the man who struck the librarian down … I cannot feel any guilt.

July 29

When I was coming home from my afternoon stroll today I saw a workman leave our house. There was a lorry outside, and I believe he was from the same company that built the cell for us. I asked Helen about it, and she looked startled, and then she denied that he had been there. I was curious about that at first, and for a moment I actually wondered if she might have been unfaithful to me, she acted so strange and so nervous. But that was a terrible thought and I never should have had it for a moment. It was a sin to think such a thing. I have guessed what the truth is now. She has had something done to make the cell more comfortable for me. Perhaps she has had new padding put in, or a brighter light installed. I can't imagine what else it could be. She wanted to keep it as a surprise, of course. Something that she imagines will cheer me up when I have to go to the cell. Perhaps it will, at that. I do hope, however, that she was bright enough to give a logical reason for having the padding in the cell, if the workman saw the inside. Even unintelligent construction workers sometimes have imaginations … I suppose they sometimes read the newspapers, too. Still, we have a right to have a padded cell if we choose, and no one can question that.

I have just wondered if perhaps the man had come to install a stronger lock on the door. Helen has been strange … distant. It is possible that she is frightened. Poor thing. I can understand how it is. I must make an attempt to be more pleasant, and more tolerant of her weaknesses. I should give her some little token of my affection. Perhaps I should go to her bedroom this evening. She always seems very grateful when I do that, and I have not gone for some time now. But that is her fault. She does not give any indication that she wants me to, and I only do it for her. Perhaps she has come to see that it is better to abstain as much as possible.

July 30

Helen has changed remarkably.

Who can understand the workings of the female mind? There are depths to even the simplest and most unimaginative of women that can never be probed. I feel that I have as much insight as any man, that my logic is capable of plumbing any logical depths, and yet I have no conception of what has brought about this difference in my wife. It has been coming on for some time now, I think, but last night it was the most noticeable that it has been yet. Perhaps it is simply that there is no reason for it, that the basic motions of the female atoms are erratic. I hate to think that. I prefer a well-ordered concept of life. But I am open-minded to other possibilities. I have had to be open-minded; a closed mind would not have the scope to deal with life as a man in my circumstances must do. I would not be in the least surprised to know that I am the only man who has ever suffered with my affliction and still kept his sanity. Perhaps that seems like a vain statement, but still a man must recognize his virtues in order to capitalize on them. I am humble in my pride.

Last night I went to her room. She had gone to bed early and after a while I decided to go to her. But everything was different.

When I opened her bedroom door she sat up quickly, holding the covers up to her chin and looking at me with her eyes open wide. It was almost as though she had been lying there waiting, expecting me to come. That in itself is strange. And the way that she looked ... well, it was very much like fear. She cringed when I touched her. She said nothing at all but she trembled under my hand and searched my face. I hated to see that expression, that look in her eyes. It was as though she thought last night was the night of the change. Perhaps she had lost track of the date. But surely she knows that I will never forget it? How can my own wife fear me? Is it all a result of those atrocious lies in the newspapers, or is she breaking down under the strain – suffering, perhaps, in sympathy with me? It might be that. She does seem to be different when it is getting near the night when I must go to the cell. I have heard that often one suffers for a loved one. Men are reported to have labour pains when their wives are pregnant. It might possibly be something of that nature. I prefer to think that, because it is very unpleasant to think that she fears me.

When we were first married Helen used to be very affectionate. Even passionate. Far too much so, in fact, and several times I had to ask her to please exercise a bit of restraint. It is wrong for a woman to abandon herself to carnal pleasures. I am not sure if it is wrong to feel pleasure in a carnal act, but it certainly is wrong to give oneself up to it. Once Helen tried to take the initiative in the marriage act, and several times she came right out and asked me if I would not come to her bed. I had to lecture her quite firmly about that. She was not really to blame; she was innocent and had no experience and did not realize how wrong her behaviour was. She was undoubtedly trying to please me by her overt desire and undisguised lustings. It does seem that a proper young woman should know instinctively that it is wrong, but who am I to judge? I have never attempted to set myself up as a moralist, I am simply a moral man who tries to show others the proper way to live. I had to be a bit strict with Helen, of course, but that was for her own good.

Last night it was very different, however. She was not in the least demanding, and she seemed quite pleased when we had finished and I was ready to return to my own room. All through the act she had continued to stare up at me with that strange expression. It made me feel very uncomfortable. I am never quite comfortable while I am performing the marital duty, but this was worse. It was ... uncomfortable is not the word, but I know no word to describe it. It was an exceedingly troubling emotion. I hope that she never looks at me that way again. There is something about fear ... I don't know what it is ... it always makes me feel ... makes me imagine ... indefinite things. This is very difficult to express correctly. Vague things seem to be lurking just below the surface of my mind, unclear, clouded and dark and unsavoury. Dangerous things, somehow. Shrouded images. I cannot define it more closely than this.

July 31

I am waiting for tomorrow with the usual dread and disgust, but also with a certain curiosity. I wonder how last month has affected the disease. I have been so much at peace all during July; have come to terms with myself so well, that I would not be in the least surprised to find a definite change in the sickness. Last month may have acted as a catalyst and change the chemistry of the thing ... perhaps for the better. Whatever happens I feel that I will be able to accept it stoically.

I would tell Helen of my hopes if she did not seem so distant and unusual. But it is probably better not to, until I know. There is little benefit in raising false cheer. This morning she acted peculiarly again. I had gone out into the hall to fetch my gloves and when I turned around she was looking around the corner at me. Just her face was around the corner, and she ducked back. I went down and asked her if she wanted anything and, after mumbling for a moment, she said that she wondered whether I was going down to the basement. Why would she think that? She knows that I hate the basement, and that I never go down there until it is necessary. When I assured her of this she seemed relieved, so perhaps she is just overwrought as the day draws near. Perhaps she is afraid that it might begin sooner than usual, and that I shall have to spend more time, perhaps more than one night, in the cell. I can understand how that would bother her, and it shows her concern for me. But it also shows her complete lack of understanding of just what my disease is.

August 1

I am fairly bursting with energy today. I took a long, brisk walk after lunch. I stopped to watch some children playing in an empty lot. I seemed to share their enthusiasm for life. It made me regret the fact that I can never have children. They were so gay and carefree that I felt sorry they must grow up and face the troubles of life. My childhood was not happy; at least it does not seem happy in my memory, except for a few outstanding occasions. But I do not envy others in this respect, because my beginnings have carried me on to a proper manhood and I am able to look back at my whole life and regret no single thing that I have ever done. Any regrets that I feel are for things not my fault, things ordained before I was created. It is surely the greatest peace that man can know when he can see his whole existence running in one continuous sequence and find that at no point has there been any shame, anything to mar his past; that his total life has been exactly as he would have willed it, considering those things in which he has a choice.

I am almost looking forward to the change tonight, I feel so certain that there will be an improvement ... or is it that I know now that no improvement is necessary, that I understand my affliction is not nearly as bad as I believed it to be? I hope that the thing which I become can share my tranquillity.

August 1 (night)

Well, the door is barred now. Helen has gone upstairs and I am alone in the cell. Helen tried to be very pleasant today. She cooked my favourite dinner, simple wholesome food and she chattered away self-consciously and tried to be gay and to take my mind off what would soon happen. I appreciate her pitiful little efforts against a thing she cannot grasp. I came down quite early so that she did not have to worry about it. I was afraid that she would begin to be nervous and frightened, and wanted to spare her that ordeal … and spare myself witnessing it, too.

I have not noticed anything different about the cell. I was sure that she had had some improvement made, but the lock is the same and the padding is still torn in places. Perhaps she had the workman come to make an estimate and intends to have the work done next month. I wish that I had thought to put a brighter light in, however. It is difficult to write, and the corners are in shadow. If …

I have just made a horrible discovery. I am at a loss to understand what it means. A cold sliver is knifing up my backbone and my flesh is like ice. I was writing before and I glanced at the wall and … there is a hole through the wall! It is a small hole, and I didn't notice it immediately. It is in the corner by the door, and it is large enough for someone to look through … to look into the cell. The hole was not there before, and there is still some concrete dust on the floor, so I know that it was made recently. That must have been why the workman was here. But why did my wife have the hole made? Whatever has possessed her? Why would she do such a fiendish thing? She must be mad! She must intend to look into the cell after the change has occurred! But why would she want to? It is beyond belief, it is monstrous. The thought that she will see me … see me become … something other than a man. I am crouching against the wall with the hole and I cannot be observed from there, but I don't know what to do about later … after I change. The thing is not rational, or does not care about rationality. It will not remain here against the door where it cannot be seen. I have considered trying to plug the hole with my shirt, but I fear that the shirt will become torn loose when the disease is at its frenzied pitch. Or she might poke it free with a stick. There is nothing I can do. She is going to see me!

I am sick with dread. I feel that I shall vomit. My head is spinning. Why would Helen do this to me? Is it simply morbid curiosity? Has she some perverted twist to her nature that I have never before observed? Or is it that she still doubts me, and wants proof that I am not mad, that I do not imagine it all? I do not know. The thought that she will see the change is terrible, and God knows what effect it will have on her! I can only hope that she recognizes it as an illness, and that the truth will not drive her out of her mind. But her mind is not strong and I fear ... I have seen the look on other faces when they see me changed. The drunkard ... the girl ... There was a look of madness on those faces, and Helen is not strong ... I have seen the fear in her eyes even when I am normal. After she read those lies in the newspapers, those horrible tales of mutilation and dismemberment ... the other night in bed ... and that fear that makes her face glow white as the moon, makes it shift and tremble until I can see only that terror and everything else fades away and I look ... I feel ... I feel that such fear must not be left to survive ... How will I ever face her again after ... when I am normal ... when ...

I heard the door close.

I think she is coming down ...

August 2?

I presume it is morning. I am all right now, although I am exhausted. My clothing is torn to shreds. Helen will be down soon to open the door. How will she face me now, after last night? I begged her to go away and she would not even answer me, she just looked into the cell and waited. My agitation brought the sickness on sooner than it should have come, and I lost all control. She saw everything. I hate her. I hate her for what she has done to me. I am on fire with rage and shame and hatred! When she opens the door I shall have to exercise great control to keep from striking her. She deserves to be struck. She deserves worse. For what she has done to me there could be no punishment too great. She made it much much worse than it has ever been before. I can clearly remember raging against the wall, trying to tear my way out, trying to rip the hole apart, and all the while she was standing there, on the other side of that indestructible barrier, looking in at everything. She is a monster, a fiend, a devil! There are no words to describe her ...

August

I don't know the date. There is no way to tell the time. It seems an eternity. I no longer care about this record. It seems futile now. And my pen is nearly out of ink. The light seems to be growing dim too, and soon I shall be in darkness. I might be able to write with my own blood, but it hardly seems worth the effort … I don't like blood, it reminds me of too much. Still, trying to record something occupies my mind. It is an ally against madness. I can bear the hunger and the thirst but I could not bear to lose my mind.

I cannot understand why she has done this to me. I no longer hate her, I just cannot understand. She comes down and looks in once in a while. Once a day, once a week … I don't know. It is all the same here. She never says anything. She won't answer me when I speak to her. She makes a strange noise sometimes, a cackling sound. I suppose she is insane. When I plead with her she goes away …

?

I am so hungry.

I have tried to eat the padding from the walls, but it is no good. It makes my thirst greater. The light is nearly out now. Only by standing directly beneath it can I see to write. My vision is blurred as well. I am very weak and dizzy. I don't suppose that I will be able to write again.

I know now that I must die here. I am resigned to it. It seems proper that, if I must die, it is through no fault of my own. I have done nothing to bring this about. Like all the suffering of my life, I am innocent of the cause, I have suffered through the sins of my ancestors, and now I die through the madness of my wife. It is unjust, but proper. I must lie down now. I am sure that there will be nothing more to record.

I know it is night. I bit my arm …

That was the journal that I found in my aunt's drawer. There were some pages after the last entry that had been marked, but they were undecipherable. They may have been an attempt to write in the dark, or they may have been the heedless markings of something with the hand of a man. I did not look long at them. I closed the book slowly and stared out the window at the rain. A loud clap of thunder sounded and the big elm tree in the yard whipped under the wind and the wind rushed under the clouds. Somewhere a dog howled. I sat there for a long time and then I got up and put the journal in my pocket. It was getting late. I went into the hall and opened the door that led down to the basement. I had to go down there. I hesitated but I had to. The air was thick and foul and it was like walking into a grave, but I went down.

The cell was in the corner, as the book said. My footsteps were incredibly loud as I crossed the concrete floor. The door was barred and I lifted the bar quickly, without thinking about it. It groaned and rust flaked off. I tried the door but it would not move. It had been locked with a key as well. It was a large lock and the door was very strong. I stepped to the corner and after a moment found the hole. The edges had begun to crumble. I looked through it but I could see nothing within. It was black inside. I turned and walked very calmly across the basement and up the stairs. I had every intention of searching for the key to the cell. I knew that it must be somewhere in Aunt Helen's possessions. As I reached the top step it gave way under my weight. I had to leap to keep from falling. I landed off balance in the hallway and suddenly I was running. I went out of the front door and into the storm. I am as brave as the next man, I am fit and very strong, but that day I ran and kept on running until I was far away from the house and drenched with rain. I had forgotten my coat.

That was some time ago and I have never been back to the house that I inherited from Aunt Helen. Someday I shall. I am often curious as to what is in the cell now. Surely there could be nothing there that would harm me. It all happened long ago. And Aunt Helen must have been in herself at some time, because she had the book. I have checked the old newspapers carefully, and found a report of an unsolved murder that might have been the one he wrote about. Or it might not. He was surely mad, and perhaps it was all in his mind. Of course it was all in his mind. And yet … I cannot help but wonder what Aunt Helen saw when she looked into the cell that night. Did she realize then, for the first time, that he was insane, and leave him for that reason? Or did she see something else? Something that drove her mad?

I shall never know, at any rate. I don't expect that she kept a journal of her own. It doesn't really trouble me. Not really. I have never been a superstitious man. But I have determined that I must never have children. Because, you see, Aunt Helen was related to me by marriage. It was her husband who was related to me by blood. I have kept the book and sometimes I read it through again, trying to find the truth. Sometimes I read it on those long white nights when the moon is bright and round and I have nothing at all to do but sit alone by my window. I live alone. I would like to have a pet, but animals don't like me. Dogs are afraid of me. It is rather boring and I shall have to start keeping a diary to occupy my time on those nights. As it is I just sit, watching the moon, watching my hands …

Suzy McKee Charnas

BOOBS

Following her work with the Peace Corps in Nigeria and a drug abuse treatment team touring New York high schools, Suzy McKee Charnas' first novel, Walk to the End of the World, *was published in 1974 and was nominated for the John W. Campbell Award. She has followed it with* Motherlines, The Vampire Tapestry, Dorothea Dreams, The Furies *and such young adult novels as* The Bronze King, The Silver Glove, The Golden Thread *and* The Kingdom of Kevin Malone.

Her offbeat werewolf story "Boobs" gives a feminist slant on the age-old myth, and it won the Hugo Award for best science fiction story in 1990. The version published here (which originally appeared in Lisa Tuttle's anthology Skin of the Soul*) restores the original ending, as the writer explains:" 'Boobs' addresses a matter of concern to one half the human race (menstruation, not werewolfery), but it was not exactly suitable for* Redbook *or* Mademoiselle; Seventeen *wouldn't touch it, and* Ms *told me they weren't taking fiction. In the end Gardner. Dozois bought it for* Asimov's. *He asked for a minor rewrite of the ending, something to take a little of the chill off, so to speak. My stepdaughter had reacted in a similar fashion, objecting that Kelsey is too cold-blooded about wolfish violence.*

"I reminded her of: a) the tendency in the young toward a very narrow morality ('What hurts me is unforgivably awful and what I do is okay"); b) the surprising failures of empathy in children that can lead to the most shockingly loathsome behaviour committed in a very casual manner, for example, the true beastliness of teenage

boys in packs. Personally, I am pleased to see the original ending restored, for readers who may be disinclined to have their angry young heroines sweetened."

The thing is, it's like your brain wants to go on thinking about the miserable history mid-term you have to take tomorrow, but your body takes over. And what a body! You can see in the dark and run like the wind and leap parked cars in a single bound.

Of course you pay for it next morning (but it's worth it). I always wake up stiff and sore, with dirty hands and feet and face, and I have to jump in the shower fast so Hilda won't see me like that.

Not that she would know what it was about, but why take chances? So I pretend it's the other thing that's bothering me. So she goes, "Come on, sweetie, everybody gets cramps, that's no reason to go around moaning and groaning. What are you doing, trying to get out of school just because you've got your period?"

If I didn't like Hilda, which I do even though she is only a stepmother instead of my real mother, I would show her something that would keep me out of school forever, and it's not fake, either.

But there are plenty of people I'd rather show that to.

I already showed that dork Billy Linden.

"Hey, Boobs!" he goes, in the hall right outside Homeroom. A lot of kids laughed, naturally, though Rita Frye called him an asshole.

Billy is the one that started it, sort of, because he always started everything, him with his big mouth. At the beginning of term, he came barrelling down on me hollering, "Hey, look at Bornstein, something musta happened to her over the summer! What happened, Bornstein? Hey, everybody, look at Boobs Bornstein!"

He made a grab at my chest, and I socked him in the shoulder, and he punched me in the face, which made me dizzy and shocked and made me cry, too, in front of everybody.

I mean, I always used to wrestle and fight with the boys, being that I was strong for a girl. All of a sudden it was different. He hit me hard, to really hurt, and the shock sort of got me in the pit of my stomach and made me feel nauseous, too, as well as mad and embarrassed to death.

I had to go home with a bloody nose and lie with my head back and ice wrapped in a towel on my face and dripping down into my hair.

Hilda sat on the couch next to me and patted me. She goes, "I'm sorry about this, honey, but really, you have to learn it sometime. You're all growing up and the boys are getting stronger than you'll ever be. If you fight with boys, you're bound to get hurt. You have to find other ways to handle them."

To make things worse, the next morning I started to bleed down there, which Hilda had explained carefully to me a couple of times, so at least I knew what was going on. Hilda really tried extra hard without being icky about it, but I hated when she talked about how it was all part of these exciting changes in my body that are so important and how terrific it is to "become a young woman".

Sure. The whole thing was so messy and disgusting, worse than she had said, worse than I could imagine, with these black clots of gunk coming out in a smear of pink blood – I thought I would throw up. That's just the lining of your uterus, Hilda said. Big deal. It was still gross.

And plus, the *smell*.

Hilda tried to make me feel better, she really did. She said we should "mark the occasion" like primitive people do, so it's something special, not just a nasty thing that just sort of falls on you.

So we decided to put poor old Pinkie away, my stuffed dog that I've slept with since I was three. Pinkie is bald and sort of hard and lumpy, since he got in the washing machine by mistake, and you would never know he was all soft plush when he was new, or even that he was pink.

Last time my friend Gerry-Anne came over, before the summer, she saw Pinky laying on my pillow and though she didn't say anything, I could tell she was thinking that was kind of babyish. So I'd been thinking about not keeping Pinky around any more.

Hilda and I made him this nice box lined with pretty scraps from her quilting class, and I thanked him out loud for being my friend for so many years, and we put him up in the closet, on the top shelf.

I felt terrible, but if Gerry-Anne decided I was too babyish to be friends with any more, I could end up with no friends at all. When you have never been popular since the time you were skinny and fast and everybody wanted you on their team, you have that kind of thing on your mind.

Hilda and Dad made me go to school the next morning so nobody would think I was scared of Billy Linden (which I was) or that I would let him keep me away just by being such a dork.

Everybody kept sneaking funny looks at me and whispering, and I was sure it was because I couldn't help walking funny with the pad between my legs and because they could smell what was happening, which as far as I knew hadn't happened to anybody else in Eight A yet. Just like nobody else in the whole grade had anything real in their stupid training bras except me, thanks a lot.

Anyway I stayed away from everybody as much as I could and wouldn't talk to Gerry-Anne, even, because I was scared she would ask me why I walked funny and smelled bad.

Billy Linden avoided me just like everybody else, except one of his stupid buddies purposely bumped into me so I stumbled into Billy on the lunch-line. Billy turns around and he goes, real loud, "Hey, Boobs, when did you start wearing black and blue make-up?"

I didn't give him the satisfaction of knowing that he had actually broken my nose, which the doctor said. Good thing they don't have to bandage you up for that. Billy would be hollering up a storm about how I had my nose in a sling as well as my boobs.

That night I got up after I was supposed to be asleep and took off my underpants and T-shirt that I sleep in and stood looking at myself in the mirror. I didn't need to turn a light on. The moon was full and it was shining right into my bedroom through the big dormer window.

I crossed my arms and pinched myself hard to sort of punish my body for what it was doing to me.

As if that could make it stop.

No wonder Edie Siler had starved herself to death in the Tenth Grade! I understood her perfectly. She was trying to keep her body down, keep it normal-looking, thin and strong, like I was too, back when I looked like a person, not a cartoon that somebody would call "Boobs".

And then something warm trickled in a little line down the inside of my leg, and I knew it was blood and I couldn't stand it any more. I pressed my thighs together and shut my eyes hard, and I did something.

I mean I felt it happening. I felt myself shrink down to a hard core of sort of cold fire inside my bones, and all the flesh part, the muscles and the squishy insides and the skin, went sort of glowing and free-floating, all shining with moonlight, and I felt a sort of shifting and balance-changing going on.

I thought I was fainting on account of my stupid period. So I turned around and threw myself on my bed, only by the time I hit it, I knew something was seriously wrong.

For one thing, my nose and my head were crammed with these crazy, rich sensations that it took me a second to even figure out were smells, they were so much stronger than any smells I'd ever smelled. And they were – I don't know – *interesting* instead of just stinky, even the rotten ones.

I opened my mouth to get the smells a little better, and heard myself panting in a funny way as if I'd been running, which I hadn't, and then there was this long part of my face sticking out and something moving there – my tongue.

I was licking my chops.

Well, there was this moment of complete and utter panic. I tore around the room whining and panting and hearing my toenails clicking on the floorboards, and then I huddled down and crouched in the corner because I was scared Dad and Hilda would hear me and come to find out what was making all this racket.

Because I could hear them. I could hear their bed creak when one of them turned over, and Dad's breath whistling a little in an almost snore, and I could smell them too, each one with a perfectly clear bunch of smells, kind of like those desserts of mixed ice-cream they call a medley.

My body was twitching and jumping with fear and energy, and my room – it's a converted attic-space, wide but with a ceiling that's low in places – my room felt like a jail. And plus, I was terrified of catching a glimpse of myself in the mirror. I had a pretty good idea of what I would see, and I didn't want to see it.

Besides, I had to pee, and I couldn't face trying to deal with the toilet in the state I was in.

So I eased the bedroom door open with my shoulder and nearly fell down the stairs trying to work them with four legs and thinking about it, instead of letting my body just do it. I put my hands on the front door to open it, but my hands weren't hands, they were paws with long knobby toes covered with fur, and the toes had thick black claws sticking out of the ends of them.

The pit of my stomach sort of exploded with horror, and I yelled. It came out this wavery "wooo" noise that echoed eerily in my skullbones. Upstairs, Hilda goes, "Jack, what was that?" I bolted for the basement as I heard Dad hit the floor of their bedroom.

The basement door slips its latch all the time, so I just shoved it open and down I went, doing better on the stairs this time because I was too scared to think. I spent the rest of the night down there, moaning to myself (which meant whining through my nose, really) and trotting around rubbing against the walls trying to rub off this crazy shape I had, or just moving around because I couldn't sit still. The place was thick with stinks and these slow-swirling currents of hot and cold air. I couldn't handle all the input.

As for having to pee, in the end I managed to sort of hike my butt up over the edge of the slop-sink by Dad's workbench and let go in there. The only problem was that I couldn't turn the taps on to rinse out the smell because of my paws.

Then about three a.m. I woke up from a doze curled up in a bare place on the floor where the spiders weren't so likely to walk, and I couldn't see a thing or smell anything either, so I knew I was okay again even before I checked and found fingers on my hands again instead of claws.

I zipped upstairs and stood under the shower so long that Hilda yelled at me for using up the hot water when she had a load of washing to do that morning. I was only trying to steam some of the stiffness out of my muscles, but I couldn't tell her that.

It was real weird to just dress and go to school after a night like that. One good thing, I had stopped bleeding after only one day, which Hilda said wasn't so strange for the first time. So it had to be the huge greenish bruise on my face from Billy's punch that everybody was staring at.

That and the usual thing, of course. Well, why not? *They* didn't know I'd spent the night as a wolf.

So Fat Joey grabbed my book bag in the hallway outside science class and tossed it to some kid from Eight B. I had to run after them to get it back, which of course was set up so the boys could cheer the bouncing of my boobs under my shirt.

I was so mad I almost caught Fat Joey, except I was afraid if I grabbed him, maybe he would sock me like Billy had.

Dad had told me, Don't let it get you, kid, all boys are jerks at that age.

Hilda had been saying all summer, "Look, it doesn't do any good to walk around all hunched up with your arms crossed, you should just throw your shoulders back and walk like a proud person who's pleased that she's growing up. You're just a little early, that's all, and I bet the other girls are secretly envious of you, with their cute little training bras, for Chrissake, as if there was something that needed to be *trained.*"

It's okay for her, she's not in school, she doesn't remember what it's like.

So I quit running and walked after Joey until the bell rang, and then I got my book bag back from the bushes outside where he threw it. I was crying a little, and I ducked into the girls' room.

Stacey Buhl was in there doing her lipstick like usual and wouldn't talk to me like usual, but Rita came bustling in and said somebody should off that dumb dork Joey, except of course it was really Billy that put him up to it. Like usual.

Rita is okay except she's an outsider herself, being that her kid brother has AIDS, and lots of kids' parents don't think she should even be in the school. So I don't hang around with her a lot. I've got enough trouble, and anyway I was late for math.

I had to talk to somebody, though. After school I told Gerry-Anne, who's been my best friend on and off since Fourth Grade. She was off at the moment, but I found her in the library and I told her I'd had a weird dream about being a wolf. She wants to be a psychiatrist like her mother, so of course she listened.

She told me I was nuts. That was a big help.

That night I made sure the back door wasn't exactly closed, and then I got in bed with no clothes on – imagine turning into a wolf in your underpants and T-shirt – and just shivered, waiting for something to happen.

The moon came up and shone in my window, and I changed again, just like before, which is not one bit like how it is in the movies – all struggling and screaming and bones snapping out with horrible cracking and tearing noises, just the way I guess you would imagine it to be, if you knew it had to be done by building special machines to do that for the camera and make it look real: if you were a special effects man, instead of a werewolf.

For me, it didn't have to look real, it was real. It was this melting and drifting thing, which I got sort of excited by it this time. I mean it felt – interesting. Like something I was doing, instead of just another dumb body-mess happening to me because some brainless hormones said so.

I must have made a noise. Hilda came upstairs to the door of my bedroom, but luckily she didn't come in. She's tall, and my ceiling is low for her, so she often talks to me from the landing.

Anyway I'd heard her coming, so I was in my bed with my whole head shoved under my pillow, praying frantically that nothing showed.

I could smell her, it was the wildest thing – her own smell, sort of sweaty but sweet, and then on top of it her perfume, like an ice-pick stuck in my nose. I didn't actually hear a word she said,

I was too scared, and also I had this ripply shaking feeling inside me, a high that was only partly terror.

See, I realized all of a sudden, with this big blossom of surprise, that I didn't have to be scared of Hilda, or anybody. I was strong, my wolf-body was strong, and anyhow one clear look at me and she would drop dead.

What a relief, though, when she went away. I was dying to get out from under the weight of the covers, and besides I had to sneeze. Also I recognized that part of the energy roaring around inside me was hunger.

They went to bed – I heard their voices even in their bedroom, though not exactly what they said, which was fine. The words weren't important any more, I could tell more from the tone of what they were saying.

Like I knew they were going to do it, and I was right. I could hear them messing around right through the walls, which was also something new, and I have never been so embarrassed in my life. I couldn't even put my hands over my ears, because my hands were paws.

So while I was waiting for them to go to sleep, I looked myself over in the big mirror on my closet door.

There was this big wolf head with a long slim muzzle and a thick ruff around my neck. The ruff stood up as I growled and backed up a little.

Which was silly of course, there was no wolf in the bedroom but me. But I was all strung out, I guess, and one wolf, me in my wolf body, was as much as I could handle the idea of, let alone two wolves, me and my reflection.

After that first shock, it was great. I kept turning one way and another for different views.

I was thin, with these long, slender legs but strong, you could see the muscles, and feet a little bigger than I would have picked. But I'll take four big feet over two big boobs any day.

My face was terrific, with jaggedy white ripsaw teeth and eyes that were small and clear and gleaming in the moonlight. The tail was a little bizarre, but I got used to it, and actually it had a nice plumey shape. My shoulders were big and covered with long, glossy-looking fur, and I had this neat colouring, dark on the back and a sort of melting silver on my front and underparts.

The thing was, though, my tongue, hanging out. I had a lot of trouble with that, it looked gross and silly at the same time. I mean, that was *my tongue*, about a foot long and neatly draped over the points of my bottom canines. That was when I realized that I didn't have a whole lot of expressions to use, not with that face, which was more like a mask.

But it was alive, it was my face, those were my own long black lips that my tongue licked.

No doubt about it, this was *me*. I was a werewolf, like in the movies they showed over Halloween weekend. But it wasn't anything like your ugly movie werewolf that's just some guy loaded up with pounds and pounds of make-up. I was *gorgeous*.

I didn't want to just hang around admiring myself in the mirror, though. I couldn't stand being cooped up in that stuffy, smell-crowded room.

When everything settled down and I could hear Dad and Hilda breathing the way they do when they're sleeping, I snuck out.

The dark wasn't very dark to me, and the cold felt sharp like vinegar, but not in a hurting way. Every place I went, there were these currents like waves in the air, and I could draw them in through my long wolf nose and roll the smell of them over the back of my tongue. It was like a whole different world, with bright sounds everywhere and rich, strong smells.

And I could run.

I started running because a car came by while I was sniffing at the garbage bags on the curb, and I was really scared of being seen in the headlights. So I took off down the dirt alley between our house and the Morrisons' next door, and holy cow, I could tear along with hardly a sound, I could jump their picket fence without even thinking about it. My back legs were like steel springs and I came down solid and square on four legs with almost no shock at all, let alone worrying about losing my balance or twisting an ankle.

Man, I could run through that chilly air all thick and moisty with smells, I could almost fly. It was like last year, when I didn't have boobs bouncing and yanking in front even when I'm only walking fast.

Just two rows of neat little bumps down the curve of my belly. I sat down and looked.

I tore open garbage bags to find out about the smells in them, but I didn't eat anything from them. I wasn't about to chow down on other people's stale hotdog-ends and pizza crusts and fat and bones scraped off their plates and all mixed in with mashed potatoes and stuff.

When I found places where dogs had stopped and made their mark, I squatted down and pissed there too, right on top. I just wiped them *out*.

I bounded across that enormous lawn around the Wanscombe place, where nobody but the oriental gardener ever sets foot, and walked up the back and over the top of their BMW, leaving big fat pawprints all over it. Nobody saw me, nobody heard me, I was a shadow.

Well, except for the dogs, of course.

There was a lot of barking when I went by, real hysterics, and at first I was really scared. But then I popped out of an alley up on Ridge Road, where the big houses are, right in front of about six dogs that run together. Their owners let them out all night and don't care if they get hit by a car.

They'd been trotting along with the wind behind them, checking out all the garbage bags set out for pickup the next morning. When they saw me, one of them let out a yelp of surprise, and they all skidded to a stop.

Six of them. I was scared. I growled.

The dogs turned fast, banging into each other in their hurry, and trotted away.

I don't know what they would have done if they met a real wolf, but I was something special, I guess.

I followed them.

They scattered and ran.

Well, I ran too, and this was a different kind of running. I mean, I stretched, and I raced, and there was this joy. I chased one of them.

Zig, zag, this little terrier-kind of dog tried to cut left and dive under the gate of somebody's front walk, all without a sound – he was running too hard to yell, and I was happy running quiet.

Just before he could ooze under the gate, I caught up with him and without thinking I grabbed the back of his neck and pulled him off his feet and gave him a shake as hard as I could, from side to side.

I felt his neck crack, the sound vibrated through all the bones of my face.

I picked him up in my mouth, and it was like he hardly weighed a thing. I trotted away holding him up off the ground, and under a bush in Baker's Park I held him down with my paws and I bit into his belly, that was still warm and quivering.

Like I said, I was hungry.

The blood gave me this rush like you wouldn't believe. I stood there a minute looking around and licking my lips, just sort of panting and tasting the taste because I was stunned by it, it was like eating honey or the best chocolate malted you ever had.

So I put my head down and chomped that little dog, like shoving your face into a pizza and inhaling it. God, I was *starved*, so I didn't mind that the meat was tough and rank-tasting after that first wonderful bite. I even licked blood off the ground after, never mind the grit mixed in.

I ate two more dogs that night, one that was tied up on a clothesline in a cruddy yard full of rusted out car-parts down on the South side, and one fat old yellow dog out snuffling around on his own and way too slow. He tasted pretty bad, and by then I was feeling full, so I left a lot.

I strolled around the park, shoving the swings with my big black wolf nose, and I found the bench where Mr Granby sits and feeds the pigeons every day, never mind that nobody else wants the dirty birds around crapping on their cars. I took a dump there, right where he sits.

Then I gave the setting moon a goodnight, which came out quavery and wild, "Loo-loo-loo!" And I loped toward home, springing off the thick pads of my paws and letting my tongue loll out and feeling generally super.

I slipped inside and trotted upstairs, and in my room I stopped to look at myself in the mirror.

As gorgeous as before, and only a few dabs of blood on me, which I took time to lick off. I did get a little worried – I mean, suppose that was it, suppose having killed and eaten what I'd killed in my wolf shape, I was stuck in this shape forever? Like, if you wander into a fairy castle and eat or drink anything, that's it, you can't ever leave. Suppose when the morning came I didn't change back?

Well, there wasn't much I could do about that one way or the other, and to tell the truth, I felt like I wouldn't mind; it had been worth it.

When I was nice and clean, including licking off my own bottom which seemed like a perfectly normal and nice thing to do at the time, I jumped up on the bed, curled up, and corked right off. When I woke up with the sun in my eyes, there I was, my own self again.

It was very strange, grabbing breakfast and wearing my old sweatshirt that wallowed all over me so I didn't stick out so much, while Hilda yawned and shuffled around in her robe and slippers and acted like her and Dad hadn't been doing it last night, which I knew different.

And plus, it was perfectly clear that she didn't have a clue about what *I* had been doing, which gave me a strange feeling.

One of the things about growing up which they're careful not to tell you is, you start having more things you don't talk to your parents about. And I had a doozie.

Hilda goes, "What's the matter, are you off Sugar Pops now? Honestly, Kelsey, I can't keep up with you! And why can't you wear something nicer than that old shirt to school? Oh, I get it: disguise, right?"

She sighed and looked at me kind of sad but smiling, her hands on her hips. "Kelsey, Kelsey," she goes, "if only I'd had half of what you've got when *I* was a girl – I was flat as an ironing board, and it made me so miserable, I can't tell you."

She's still real thin and neat-looking, so what does she know about it? But she meant well, and anyhow I was feeling so good I didn't argue.

I didn't change my shirt, though.

That night I didn't turn into a wolf. I laid there waiting, but though the moon came up, nothing happened no matter how hard I tried, and after a while I went and looked out the window and realised that the moon wasn't really full any more, it was getting smaller.

I wasn't so much relieved as sorry. I bought a calendar at the school book sale two weeks later, and I checked the full moon nights coming up and waited anxiously to see what would happen.

Meantime, things rolled along as usual. I got a rash of zits on my chin. I would look in the mirror and think about my wolf-face, that had beautiful sleek fur instead of zits.

Zits and all I went to Angela Durkin's party, and the next day Billy Linden told everybody that I went in one of the bedrooms at Angela's and made out with him, which I did not. But since no grown-ups were home and Fat Joey brought grass to the party, most of the kids were stoned and didn't know who did what or where anyhow.

As a matter of act, Billy once actually did get a girl in Seven B high one time out in his parents' garage, and him and two of his friends did it to her while she was zonked out of her mind, or any way they said they did, and she was too embarrassed to say anything one way or the other, and a little while later she changed schools.

How I know about it is the same way everybody else does, which is because Billy was the biggest boaster in the whole school, and you could never tell if he was lying or not.

So I guess it wasn't so surprising that some people believed what Billy said about me. Gerry-Anne quit talking to me after that. Meantime Hilda got pregnant.

This turned into a huge discussion about how Hilda had been worried about her biological clock so she and Dad had decided to have a kid, and I shouldn't mind, it would be fun for me and good preparation for being a mother myself later on, when I found some nice guy and got married.

Sure. Great preparation. Like Mary O'Hare in my class, who gets to change her youngest baby sister's diapers all the time, yick. She jokes about it, but you can tell she really hates it. Now it looked like it was my turn coming up, as usual.

The only thing that made life bearable was my secret.

"You're laid back today," Devon Brown said to me in the lunchroom one day after Billy had been especially obnoxious, trying to flick rolled up pieces of bread from his table so they would land on my chest. Devon was sitting with me because he was bad at French, my only good subject, and I was helping him out with some verbs. I guess he wanted to know why I wasn't upset because of Billy picking on me. He goes, "How come?"

"That's a secret," I said, thinking about what Devon would say if he knew a werewolf was helping him with his French: *loup, manger.*

He goes, "What secret?" Devon had freckles and is actually kind of cute-looking.

"A *secret*," I go, "so I can't tell you, dummy."

He looks real superior and he goes, "Well, it can't be much of a secret, because girls can't keep secrets, everybody knows that."

Sure, like that kid Sara in Eight B who it turned out her own father had been molesting her for years, but she never told anybody until some psychologist caught on from some tests we all had to take in Seventh Grade. Up till then, Sara kept her secret fine.

And I kept mine, marking off the days on the calendar. The only part I didn't look forward to was having a period again, which last time came right before the change.

When the time came, I got crampy and more zits popped out on my face, but I didn't have a period.

I changed, though.

The next morning they were talking in school about a couple of prize miniature Schnauzers at the Wanscombes that had been hauled out of their yard by somebody and killed, and almost nothing left of them.

Well, my stomach turned a little when I heard some kids describing what Mr Wanscombe had found over in Baker's Park, "the remains," as people said. I felt a little guilty, too, because Mrs Wanscombe had really loved those little dogs, which somehow I didn't think about at all when I was a wolf the night before, trotting around hungry in the moonlight.

I knew those Schnauzers personally, so I was sorry, even if they were irritating little mutts that made a lot of noise.

But heck, the Wanscombes shouldn't have left them out all night in the cold. Anyhow, they were rich, they could buy new ones if they wanted.

Still and all, though. I mean, dogs are just dumb animals. If they're mean, it's because they're wired that way or somebody made them mean, they can't help it. They can't just decide to be nice, like a person can. And plus, they don't taste so great, I think because they put so much junk in commercial dog-foods-anti-worm medicine and ashes and ground-up fish, stuff like that. Ick.

In fact after the second Schnauzer I had felt sort of sick and I didn't sleep real well that night. So I was not in a great mood to start with; and that was the day that my new brassiere disappeared while I was in gym. Later on I got passed a note telling me where to find it: stapled to the bulletin board outside the Principal's office, where everybody could see that I was trying a bra with an underwire.

Naturally, it had to be Stacey Buhl that grabbed my bra while I was changing for gym and my back was turned, since she was now hanging out with Billy and his friends.

Billy went around all day making bets at the top of his lungs on how soon I would be wearing a D-cup.

Stacey didn't matter, she was just a jerk. Billy mattered. He had wrecked me in that school forever, with his nasty mind and his big, fat mouth. I was past crying or fighting and getting punched out. I was boiling, I had had enough crap from him, and I had an idea.

I followed Billy home and waited on his porch until his mom came home and she made him come down and talk to me. He stood in the doorway and talked through the screen door, eating a banana and lounging around like he didn't have a care in the world.

So he goes, "Whatcha want, Boobs?"

I stammered a lot, being I was so nervous about telling such big lies, but that probably made me sound more believable.

I told him that I would make a deal with him: I would meet him that night in Baker's Park, late, and take off my shirt and bra and let him do whatever he wanted with my boobs if that would satisfy his curiosity and he would find somebody else to pick on and leave me alone.

"What?" he said, staring at my chest with his mouth open. His voice squeaked and he was practically drooling on the floor. He couldn't believe his good luck.

I said the same thing over again.

He almost came out onto the porch to try it right then and there. "Well, shit," he goes, lowering his voice a lot, "why didn't you say something before? You really mean it?"

I go, "Sure," though I couldn't look at him.

After a minute he goes, "Okay, it's a deal. Listen, Kelsey, if you like it, can we, uh, do it again, you know?"

I go, "Sure. But Billy, one thing: this is a secret, between just you and me. If you tell anybody, if there's one other person hanging around out there tonight—"

"Oh no," he goes, real fast, "I won't say a thing to anybody, honest. Not a word, I promise!"

Not until afterward, of course, was what he meant, which if there was one thing Billy Linden couldn't do, it was keep quiet if he knew something bad about another person.

"You're gonna like it, I know you are," he goes, speaking strictly for himself as usual. "Jeez. I can't believe this!"

But he did, the dork.

I couldn't eat much for dinner that night, I was too excited, and I went upstairs early to do homework, I told Dad and Hilda.

Then I waited for the moon, and when it came, I changed.

Billy was in the park. I caught a whiff of him, very sweaty and excited, but I stayed cool. I snuck around for a while, as quiet as I could – which was real quiet – making sure none of his stupid friends were lurking around. I mean, I wouldn't have trusted just his promise for a million dollars.

I passed up half a hamburger lying in the gutter where somebody had parked for lunch next to Baker's Park. My mouth watered, but I didn't want to spoil my appetite. I was hungry and happy, sort of singing inside my own head, "Shoo, fly, pie, and an apple-pan-dowdie …"

Without any sound, of course.

Billy had been sitting on a bench, his hands in his pockets, twisting around to look this way and that way, watching for me – for my human self – to come join him. He had a jacket on, being it was very chilly out.

He didn't stop to think that maybe a sane person wouldn't be crazy enough to sit out there and take off her top leaving her naked skin bare to the breeze. But that was Billy all right, totally fixed on his own greedy self and without a single thought for anybody else. I bet all he could think about was what a great scam this was, to feel up old Boobs in the park and then crow about it all over school.

Now he was walking around the park, kicking at the sprinkler-heads and glancing up every once in a while, frowning and looking sulky.

I could see he was starting to think that I might have stood him up. Maybe he even suspected that old Boobs was lurking around watching him and laughing to herself because he had fallen for a trick. Maybe old Boobs had even brought some kids from school with her to see what a jerk he was.

Actually that would have been pretty good, except Billy probably would have broken my nose for me again, or worse, if I'd tried it.

"Kelsey?" he goes, sounding mad.

I didn't want him stomping off home in a huff. I moved up closer, and I let the bushes swish a little around my shoulders.

He goes, "Hey, Kelse, it's late, where've you been?"

I listened to the words, but mostly I listened to the little thread of worry flickering in his voice, low and high, high and low, as he tried to figure out what was going on.

I let out the whisper of a growl.

He stood real still, staring at the bushes, and he goes, "That you, Kelse? Answer me."

I was wild inside, I couldn't wait another second. I tore through the bushes and leaped for him, flying.

He stumbled backward with a squawk – "What!" – jerking his hands up in front of his face, and he was just sucking in a big breath to yell with when I hit him like a demo-derby truck.

I jammed my nose past his feeble claws and chomped down hard on his face.

No sound came out of him except this wet, thick gurgle, which I could more taste than hear because the sound came right into my mouth with the gush of his blood and the hot mess of meat and skin that I tore away and swallowed.

He thrashed around, hitting at me, but I hardly felt anything through my fur. I mean, he wasn't so big and strong laying there on the ground with me straddling him all lean and wiry with wolf-muscle. And plus, he was in shock. I got a strong whiff from below as he let go of everything right into his pants.

Dogs were barking, but so many people around Baker's Park have dogs to keep out burglars, and the dogs make such a racket all the time, that nobody pays any attention. I wasn't worried. Anyway, I was too busy to care.

I nosed in under what was left of Billy's jaw and I bit his throat out.

Now let him go around telling lies about people.

His clothes were a lot of trouble and I really missed having hands. I managed to drag his shirt out of his belt with my teeth, though, and it was easy to tear his belly open. Pretty messy, but once I got in there, it was better than Thanksgiving dinner. Who would think that somebody as horrible as Billy Linden could taste so *good*?

He was barely moving by then, and I quit thinking about him as Billy Linden any more. I quit thinking at all, I just pushed my head in and pulled out delicious steaming chunks and ate until I was picking at tidbits, and everything was getting cold.

On the way home I saw a police car cruising the neighborhood the way they do sometimes. I hid in the shadows and of course they never saw me.

There was a lot of washing up to do in the morning, and when Hilda saw my sheets she shook her head and she goes, "You should be more careful about keeping track of your period so as not to get caught by surprise."

Everybody in school knew something had happened to Billy Linden, but it wasn't until the day after that that they got the word. Kids stood around in little huddles trading rumors about how some wild animal had chewed Billy up. I would walk up and listen in and add a really gross remark or two, like part of the game of thrilling each other green and nauseous with made-up details to see who would upchuck first.

Not me, that's for sure. I mean, when somebody went on about how Billy's whole head was gnawed down to the skull and they didn't even know who he was except from the bus pass in his wallet, I got a little urpy. It's amazing the things people will dream up. But when I thought about what I had actually done to Billy, I had to smile.

It felt totally wonderful to walk through the halls without having anybody yelling, "Hey, Boobs!"

There are people who just plain do not deserve to live. And the same goes for Fat Joey, if he doesn't quit crowding me in science lab, trying to get a feel.

One funny thing, though, I don't get periods at all any more. I get a little crampy, and my breasts get sore, and I break out more than usual – and then instead of bleeding, I change.

Which is fine with me, though I take a lot more care now about how I hunt on my wolf nights. I stay away from Baker's Park. The suburbs go on for miles and miles, and there are lots of places I can hunt and still get home by morning. A running wolf can cover a lot of ground.

And I make sure I make my kills where I can eat in private, so no cop car can catch me unawares, which could easily have happened that night when I killed Billy, I was so deep into the eating thing that first time. I look around a lot more now when I'm eating a kill, I keep watch.

Good thing it's only once a month that this happens, and only a couple of nights. "The Full Moon Killer" has the whole State up in arms and terrified as it is.

Eventually I guess I'll have to go somewhere else, which I'm not looking forward to at all. If I can just last until I can have a car of my own, life will get a lot easier.

Meantime, some wolf nights I don't even feel like hunting. Mostly I'm not as hungry as I was those first times. I think I must have been storing up my appetite for a long time. Sometimes I just prowl around and I run, boy do I run.

If I am hungry, sometimes I eat from the garbage instead of killing somebody. It's no fun, but you do get a taste for it. I don't mind garbage as long as once in a while I can have the real thing fresh-killed, nice and wet. People can be awfully nasty, but they sure taste sweet.

I do pick and choose, though. I look for people sneaking around in the middle of the night, like Billy, waiting in the park that time. I figure they've got to be out looking for trouble at that hour, so whose fault is it if they find it? I have done a lot more for the burglary problem around Baker's Park than a hundred dumb "watchdogs", believe me.

Gerry-Anne is not only talking to me again, she has invited me to go on a double-date with her. Some guy she met at a party invited her, and he has a friend. They're both from Fawcett Junior High across town, which will be a change. I was nervous, but finally I said yes. We're going to the movies next weekend. My first real date! I am still pretty nervous, to tell the truth.

For New Year's, I have made two solemn vows.

One is that on this date I will not worry about my chest, I will not be self-conscious, even if the guy stares.

The other is, I'll never eat another dog.

Neil Gaiman

ONLY THE END OF THE WORLD AGAIN

Neil Gaiman is one of the most acclaimed comics writers of his generation, most notably for his epic World Fantasy Award-winning Sandman *series (collected into various volumes) and his numerous graphic novel collaborations with artist Dave McKean (*Violent Cases, Black Orchid, Signal to Noise, Mr. Punch, The Day I Swapped My Dad for Two Goldfish *and* The Wolves in the Walls*).*

He is the author of such best-selling novels as Good Omens *(with Terry Pratchett),* Neverwhere, Stardust, American Gods, Coraline, Anansi Boys, Odd and the Frost Giants, Interworld *(with Michael Reaves) and* The Graveyard Book.

Angels & Visitations: A Miscellany *is a collection of his short fiction that won the International Horror Guild Award. It was followed by* Smoke and Mirrors, Adventures in the Dream Trade, Fragile Things *and* M is for Magic.

He created the BBC mini-series Neverwhere *(with Lenny Henry) and scripted the English-language version of* Princess Mononoke, *an episode of* Babylon 5 *("Day of the Dead"), Dave McKean's* MirrorMask *and Robert Zemeckis' 3-D epic* Beowulf *(with Roger Avary). Mathhew Vaughn's movie* Stardust *and Henry Selick's* Coraline *are adapted from the author's work.*

The following is one of two stories that Gaiman has written about "Lawrence Talbot" – the name of the character originally played by Lon Chaney, Jr. in the 1941 Universal movie The Wolf Man *– who is re-imagined as a lycanthropic "Adjustor" in this tale of Lovecraftian monsters. It is dedicated to the late Fritz Leiber.*

It was a bad day: I woke up naked in bed, with a cramp in my stomach, feeling more or less like hell. Something about the quality of the light, stretched and metallic, like the colour of a migraine, told me it was afternoon.

The room was freezing – literally: there was a thin crust of ice on the inside of the windows. The sheets on the bed around me were ripped and clawed, and there was animal hair in the bed. It itched.

I was thinking about staying in bed for the next week – I'm always tired after a change – but a wave of nausea forced me to disentangle myself from the bedding, and to stumble, hurriedly, into the apartment's tiny bathroom.

The cramps hit me again as I got to the bathroom door. I held on to the door-frame and I started to sweat. Maybe it was a fever; I hoped I wasn't coming down with something.

The cramping was sharp in my guts. My head was swimming. I crumpled to the floor, and, before I could manage to raise my head enough to find the toilet bowl, I began to spew.

I vomited a foul-smelling thin yellow liquid; in it was a dog's paw – my guess was a Doberman's, but I'm not really a dog person; a tomato peel; some diced carrots and sweet corn; some lumps of half-chewed meat, raw; and some fingers. They were fairly small, pale fingers, obviously a child's.

"Shit."

The cramps eased up, and the nausea subsided. I lay on the floor, with stinking drool coming out of my mouth and nose, with the tears you cry when you're being sick drying on my cheeks.

When I felt a little better I picked up the paw and the fingers from the pool of spew and threw them into the toilet bowl, flushed them away.

I turned on the tap, rinsed out my mouth with the briny Innsmouth water, and spat it into the sink. I mopped up the rest of the sick as best I could with washcloth and toilet paper. Then I turned on the shower, and stood in the bathtub like a zombie as the hot water sluiced over me.

I soaped myself down, body and hair. The meagre lather turned grey; I must have been filthy. My hair was matted with something that felt like dried blood, and I worked at it with the bar of soap until it was gone. Then I stood under the shower until the water turned icy.

There was a note under the door from my landlady. It said that I owed her for two weeks' rent. It said that all the answers were in the *Book of Revelations*. It said that I made a lot of noise coming home in the early hours of this morning, and she'd thank me to be quieter in future. It said that when the Elder Gods rose up from the ocean, all the scum of the Earth, all the non-believers, all the human garbage and the wastrels and deadbeats would be swept away, and the world would be cleansed by ice and deep water. It said that she felt she ought to remind me that she had assigned me a shelf in the refrigerator when I arrived and she'd thank me if in the future I'd keep to it.

I crumpled the note, dropped it on the floor, where it lay alongside the Big Mac cartons and the empty pizza cartons, and the long-dead dried slices of pizza.

It was time to go to work.

I'd been in Innsmouth for two weeks, and I disliked it. It smelled fishy. It was a claustrophobic little town: marshland to the east, cliffs to the west, and, in the centre, a harbour that held a few rotting fishing boats, and was not even scenic at sunset. The yuppies had come to Innsmouth in the 1980s an bought their picturesque fisherman's cottages overlooking the harbour. The yuppies had been gone for some years, now, and the cottages by the bay were crumbling, abandoned.

The inhabitants of Innsmouth lived here and there in and around the town, and in the trailer parks that ringed it, filled with dank mobile homes that were never going anywhere.

I got dressed, pulled on my boots, put on my coat and left my room. My landlady was nowhere to be seen. She was a short, pop-eyed woman, who spoke little, although she left extensive notes for me pinned to doors and placed where I might see them; she kept the house filled with the smell of boiling seafood: huge pots were always simmering on the kitchen stove, filled with things with too many legs and other things with no legs at all.

There were other rooms in the house, but no-one else rented them. No-one in their right mind would come to Innsmouth in winter.

Outside the house it didn't smell much better. It was colder, though, and my breath steamed in the sea air. The snow on the streets was crusty and filthy; the clouds promised more snow.

A cold, salty wind came up off the bay. The gulls were screaming miserably. I felt shitty. My office would be freezing, too. On the corner of Marsh Street and Leng Avenue was a bar, "The Opener", a squat building with small, dark windows that I'd passed two dozen times in the last couple of weeks. I hadn't been in before, but I really needed a drink, and besides, it might be warmer in there. I pushed open the door.

The bar was indeed warm. I stamped the snow off my boots and went inside. It was almost empty and smelled of old ashtrays and stale beer. A couple of elderly men were playing chess by the bar. The barman was reading a battered old gilt-and-green-leather edition of the poetical works of Alfred, Lord Tennyson.

"Hey. How about a Jack Daniels straight up?"

"Sure thing. You're new in town," he told me, putting his book face down on the bar, pouring the drink into a glass.

"Does it show?"

He smiled, passed me the Jack Daniels. The glass was filthy, with a greasy thumb-print on the side, and I shrugged and knocked back the drink anyway. I could barely taste it.

"Hair of the dog?" he said.

"In a manner of speaking."

"There is a belief," said the barman, whose fox-red hair was tightly greased back, "that the *lykanthropoi* can be returned to their natural forms by thanking them, while they're in wolf form, or by calling them by their given names."

"Yeah? Well, thanks."

He poured another shot for me, unasked. He looked a little like Peter Lorre, but then, most of the folk in Innsmouth look a little like Peter Lorre, including my landlady.

I sank the Jack Daniels, this time I felt it burning down into my stomach, the way it should.

"It's what they say. I never said I believed it."

"What *do* you believe?"

"Burn the girdle."

"Pardon?"

"The *lykanthropoi* have girdles of human skin, given to them at their first transformation, by their masters in Hell. Burn the girdle."

One of the old chess-players turned to me then, his eyes huge and blind and protruding. "If you drink rain-water out of warg-wolf's paw-print, that'll make a wolf of you, when the moon is full," he said. "The only cure is to hunt down the wolf that made the print in the first place and cut off its head with a knife forged of virgin silver."

"Virgin, huh?" I smiled.

His chess partner, bald and wrinkled, shook his head and croaked a single sad sound. Then he moved his queen, and croaked again.

There are people like him all over Innsmouth.

I paid for the drinks, and left a dollar tip on the bar. The barman was reading his book once more, and ignored it.

Outside the bar big wet kissy flakes of snow had begun to fall, settling in my hair and eyelashes. I hate snow. I hate New England. I hate Innsmouth: it's no place to be alone, but if there's a good place to be alone I've not found it yet. Still, business has kept me on the move for more moons than I like to think about. Business, and other things.

I walked a couple of blocks down Marsh Street – like most of Innsmouth, an unattractive mixture of eighteenth-century American Gothic houses, late nineteenth-century stunted brownstones, and late twentieth prefab grey-brick boxes – until I got to a boarded-up fried chicken joint, and I went up the stone steps next to the store and unlocked the rusting metal security door.

There was a liquor store across the street; a palmist was operating on the second floor.

Someone had scrawled graffiti in black marker on the metal: JUST DIE, it said. Like it was easy.

The stairs were bare wood; the plaster was stained and peeling. My one-room office was at the top of the stairs.

I don't stay anywhere long enough to bother with my name in gilt on glass. It was hand-written in block letters on a piece of ripped cardboard that I'd thumb-tacked to the door.

LAWRENCE TALBOT
ADJUSTOR

I unlocked the door to my office and went in.

I inspected my office, while adjectives like *seedy* and *rancid* and *squalid* wandered through my head, then gave up, outclassed. It was fairly unprepossessing – a desk, an office chair, an empty filing cabinet; a window, which gave you a terrific view of the liquor store and the empty palmist's. The smell of old cooking grease permeated from the store below. I wondered how long the fried chicken joint had been boarded up; I imagined a multitude of black cockroaches swarming over every surface in the darkness beneath me.

"That's the shape of the world that you're thinking of there," said a deep, dark voice, deep enough that I felt it in the pit of my stomach.

There was an old armchair in one corner of the office. The remains of a pattern showed through the patina of age and grease the years had given it. It was the colour of dust.

The fat man sitting in the armchair, his eyes still tightly closed, continued, "We look about in puzzlement at our world, with a sense of unease and disquiet. We think of ourselves as scholars in arcane liturgies, single men trapped in worlds beyond our devising. The truth is far simpler: there are things in the darkness beneath us that wish us harm."

His head was lolled back on the armchair, and the tip of his tongue poked out of the corner of his mouth.

"You read my mind?"

The man in the armchair took a slow deep breath that rattled in the back of his throat. He really was immensely fat, with stubby fingers like discoloured sausages. He wore a thick old coat, once black, now an indeterminate grey. The snow on his boots had not entirely melted.

"Perhaps. The end of the world is a strange concept. The world is always ending, and the end is always being averted, by love or foolishness or just plain old dumb luck.

"Ah well. It's too late now: the Elder Gods have chosen their vessels. When the moon rises ..."

A thin trickle of drool came from one corner of his mouth, trickled down in a thread of silver to his collar. Something scuttled down into the shadows of his coat.

"Yeah? What happens when the moon rises?"

The man in the armchair stirred, opened two little eyes, red and swollen, and blinked them in waking.

"I dreamed I had many mouths," he said, his new voice oddly small and breathy for such a huge man. "I dreamed every mouth was opening and closing independently. Some mouths were talking, some whispering, some eating, some waiting in silence."

He looked around, wiped the spittle from the corner of his mouth, sat back in the chair, blinking puzzledly. "Who are you?"

"I'm the guy that rents this office," I told him.

He belched suddenly, loudly. "I'm sorry," he said, in his breathy voice, and lifted himself heavily from the armchair. He was shorter than I was, when he was standing. He looked me up and down blearily. "Silver bullets," he pronounced, after a short pause. "Old-fashioned remedy."

"Yeah," I told him. "That's so obvious – must be why I didn't think of it. Gee, I could just kick myself. I really could."

"You're making fun of an old man," he told me.

"Not really. I'm sorry. Now, out of here. Some of us have work to do."

He shambled out. I sat down in the swivel chair at the desk by the window, and discovered, after some minutes, through trial and error, that if I swivelled the chair to the left it fell off its base.

So I sat still and waited for the dusty black telephone on my desk to ring, while the light slowly leaked away from the winter sky.

Ring.

A man's voice: *Had I thought about aluminum siding?* I put down the phone.

There was no heating in the office. I wondered how long the fat man had been asleep in the armchair.

Twenty minutes later the phone rang again. A crying woman implored me to help her find her five-year-old daughter, missing since last night, stolen from her bed. The family dog had vanished too.

I don't do missing children, I told her. *I'm sorry: too many bad memories.* I put down the telephone, feeling sick again.

It was getting dark now, and, for the first time since I had been in Innsmouth, the neon sign across the street flicked on. It told me that Madame Ezekiel performed Tarot Readings and Palmistry. Red neon stained the falling snow the colour of new blood.

Armageddon is averted by small actions. That's the way it was. That's the way it always has to be.

The phone rang a third time. I recognised the voice; it was the aluminum – siding man again. "You know," he said, chattily, "transformation from man to animal and back being, by definition, impossible, we need to look for other solutions. Depersonalisation, obviously, and likewise some form of projection. Brain damage? Perhaps. Pseudoneurotic schizophrenia? Laughably so. Some cases have been treated with intravenous thioridazine hydrochloride."

"Successfully?"

He chuckled. "That's what I like. A man with a sense of humour. I'm sure we can do business."

"I told you already. I don't need aluminum siding."

"Our business is more remarkable than that, and of far greater importance. You're new in town, Mr Talbot. It would be a pity if we found ourselves at, shall we say, loggerheads?"

"You can say whatever you like, pal. In my book you're just another adjustment, waiting to be made."

"We're ending the world, Mr Talbot. The Deep Ones will rise out of their ocean graves and eat the moon like a ripe plum."

"Then I won't ever have to worry about full moons anymore, will I?"

"Don't try and cross us," he began, but I growled at him, and he fell silent.

Outside my window the snow was still falling.

Across Marsh Street, in the window directly opposite mine, the most beautiful woman I had ever seen stood in the ruby glare of her neon sign, and she stared at me.

She beckoned, with one finger.

I put down the phone on the aluminum-siding man for the second time that afternoon, and went downstairs, and crossed the street at something close to a run; but I looked both ways before I crossed.

She was dressed in silks. The room was lit only by candles, and stank of incense and patchouli oil.

She smiled at me as I walked in, beckoned me over to her seat by the window. She was playing a card game with a tarot deck, some version of solitaire. As I reached her, one elegant hand swept up the cards, wrapped them in a silk scarf, placed them gently in a wooden box.

The scents of the room made my head pound. I hadn't eaten anything today, I realised; perhaps that was what was making me light-headed. I sat down, across the table from her, in the candlelight.

She extended her hand, and took my hand in hers.

She stared at my palm, touched it, softly, with her forefinger.

"Hair?" She was puzzled.

"Yeah, well. I'm on my own a lot." I grinned. I had hoped it was a friendly grin, but she raised an eyebrow at me anyway.

"When I look at you," said Madame Ezekiel, "this is what I see. I see the eye of a man. Also I see the eye of a wolf. In the eye of a man I see honesty, decency, innocence. I see an upright man who walks on the square. And in the eye of wolf I see a groaning and a growling, night howls and cries, I see a monster running with blood-flecked spittle in the darkness of the borders of the town."

"How can you see a growl or a cry?"

She smiled. "It is not hard," she said. Her accent was not American. It was Russian, or Maltese, or Egyptian perhaps. "In the eye of the mind we see many things."

Madame Ezekiel closed her green eyes. She had remarkably long eyelashes; her skin was pale, and her black hair was never still – it drifted gently around her head, in the silks, as if it were floating on distant tides.

"There is a traditional way," she told me. "A way to wash off a bad shape. You stand in running water, in clear spring water, while eating white rose petals."

"And then?"

"The shape of darkness will be washed from you."

"It will return," I told her, "with the next full of the moon."

"So," said Madame Ezekiel, "once the shape is washed from you, you open your veins in the running water. It will sting mightily, of course. But the river will carry the blood away."

She was dressed in silks, in scarves and cloths of a hundred different colours, each bright and vivid, even in the muted light of the candles.

Her eyes opened.

"Now," she said. "The Tarot." She unwrapped her deck from the black silk scarf that held it, passed me the cards to shuffle. I fanned them, riffed and bridged them.

"Slower, slower," she said. "Let them get to know you. Let them love you, like … like a woman would love you."

I held them tightly, then passed them back to her.

She turned over the first card. It was called *The Warwolf*. It showed darkness and amber eyes, a smile in white and red.

Her green eyes showed confusion. They were the green of emeralds. "This is not a card from my deck," she said, and turned over the next card. "What did you do to my cards?"

"Nothing, ma'am. I just held them. That's all."

The card she had turned over was *The Deep One*. It showed something green and faintly octopoid. The thing's mouths – if they were indeed mouths and not tentacles – began to writhe on the card as I watched.

She covered it with another card, and then another, and another. The rest of the cards were blank pasteboard.

"Did you do that?" She sounded on the verge of tears.

"No."

"Go now," she said.

"But—"

"*Go*." She looked down, as if trying to convince herself I no longer existed.

I stood up, in the room that smelled of incense and candle-wax, and looked out of her window, across the street. A light flashed, briefly, in my office window. Two men, with flashlights, were walking around. They opened the empty filing cabinet, peered around, then took up their positions, one in the armchair, the other behind the door, waiting for me to return. I smiled to myself. It was cold and inhospitable in my office, and with any luck they would wait there for hours until they finally decided I wasn't coming back.

So I left Madame Ezekiel turning over her cards, one by one, staring at them as if that would make the pictures return; and I went downstairs, and walked back down Marsh Street until I reached the bar.

The place was empty, now; the barman was smoking a cigarette, which he stubbed out as I came in.

"Where are the chess-fiends?"

"It's a big night for them tonight. They'll be down at the bay. Let's see: you're a Jack Daniels? Right?"

"Sounds good."

He poured it for me. I recognised the thumb-print from the last time I had the glass. I picked up the volume of Tennyson poems from the bar-top.

"Good book?"

The fox-haired barman took his book from me, opened it and read:

"Below the thunders of the upper deep;
Far, far beneath in the abysmal sea,
His ancient dreamless, uninvaded sleep
The Kraken sleepeth ..."

I'd finished my drink. "So? What's your point?"

He walked around the bar, took me over to the window. "See? Out there?"

He pointed toward the west of the town, toward the cliffs. As I stared a bonfire was kindled on the cliff-tops; it flared and began to burn with a copper-green flame.

"They're going to wake the Deep Ones," said the barman. "The stars and the planets and the moon are all in the right places. It's time. The dry lands will sink, and the seas shall rise …"

"For the world shall be cleansed with ice and floods and I'll thank you to keep to your own shelf in the refrigerator," I said.

"Sorry?"

"Nothing. What's the quickest way to get up to those cliffs?"

"Back up Marsh Street. Hang a left at the Church of Dagon, till you reach Manuxet Way and then just keep on going." He pulled a coat off the back of the door, and put it on. "C'mon. I'll walk you up there. I'd hate to miss any of the fun."

"You sure?"

"No-one in town's going to be drinking tonight." We stepped out, and he locked the door to the bar behind us.

It was chilly in the street, and fallen snow blew about the ground, like white mists. From street level I could no longer tell if Madame Ezekiel was in her den above her neon sign, or if my guests were still waiting for me in my office.

We put our heads down against the wind, and we walked.

Over the noise of the wind I heard the barman talking to himself:

"*Winnow with giant arms the slumbering green,*" he was saying.
"*There hath he lain for ages and will lie*
Battening upon huge seaworms in his sleep,
Until the latter fire shall heat the deep;
Then once by men and angels to be seen,
In roaring he shall rise …"

He stopped there, and we walked on together in silence, with blown snow stinging our faces.

And on the surface die, I thought, but said nothing out loud.

Twenty minutes' walking and we were out of Innsmouth. The Manuxet Way stopped when we left the town, and it became a narrow dirt path, partly covered with snow and ice, and we slipped and slid our way up it in the darkness.

The moon was not yet up, but the stars had already begun to come out. There were so many of them. They were sprinkled like diamond dust and crushed sapphires across the night sky. You can see so many stars from the seashore, more than you could ever see back in the city.

At the top of the cliff, behind the bonfire, two people were waiting – one huge and fat, one much smaller. The barman left my side and walked over to stand beside them, facing me.

"Behold," he said, "the sacrificial wolf." There was now an oddly familiar quality to his voice.

I didn't say anything. The fire was burning with green flames, and it lit the three of them from below; classic spook lighting.

"Do you know why I brought you up here?" asked the barman, and I knew then why his voice was familiar: it was the voice of the man who had attempted to sell me aluminum-siding.

"To stop the world ending?"

He laughed at me, then.

The second figure was the fat man I had found asleep in my office chair. "Well, if you're going to get eschatological about it …" he murmured, in a voice deep enough to rattle walls. His eyes were closed. He was fast asleep.

The third figure was shrouded in dark silks and smelled of patchouli oil. It held a knife. It said nothing.

"This night," said the barman, "the moon is the moon of the Deep Ones. This night are the stars configured in the shapes and patterns of the dark, old times. This night, if we call them, they will come. If our sacrifice is worthy. If our cries are heard."

The moon rose, huge and amber and heavy, on the other side of the bay, and a chorus of low croaking rose with it from the ocean far beneath us.

Moonlight on snow and ice is not daylight, but it will do. And my eyes were getting sharper with the moon: in the cold waters men like frogs were surfacing and submerging in a slow water-dance. Men like frogs, and women, too: it seemed to me that I could see my landlady down there, writhing and croaking in the bay with the rest of them.

It was too soon for another change; I was still exhausted from the night before; but I felt strange under that amber moon.

"Poor wolf-man," came a whisper from the silks. "All his dreams have come to this; a lonely death upon a distant cliff."

I will dream if I want to, I said, *and my death is my own affair*. But I was unsure if I had said it out loud.

Senses heighten in the moon's light; I heard the roar of the ocean still, but now, overlaid on top of it, I could hear each wave rise and crash; I heard the splash of the frog people; I heard the drowned whispers of the dead in the bay; I heard the creak of green wrecks far beneath the ocean.

Smell improves, too. The aluminum-siding man was human, while the fat man had other blood in him.

And the figure in the silks …

I had smelled her perfume when I wore man-shape. Now I could smell something else, less heady, beneath it. A smell of decay, of putrefying meat, and rotten flesh.

The silks fluttered. She was moving toward me. She held the knife.

"Madame Ezekiel?" My voice was roughening and coarsening. Soon I would lose it all. I didn't understand what was happening, but the moon was rising higher and higher, losing its amber colour, and filling my mind with its pale light.

"Madame Ezekiel?"

"You deserve to die," she said, her voice cold and low. "If only for what you did to my cards. They were old."

"I don't die," I told her. "*Even a man who is pure in heart, and says his prayers by night*. Remember?"

"It's bullshit," she said. "You know what the oldest way to end the curse of the werewolf is?"

"No."

The bonfire burned brighter now, burned with the green of the world beneath the sea, the green of algae, and of slowly-drifting weed; burned with the colour of emeralds.

"You simply wait till they're in human shape, a whole month away from another change; then you take the sacrificial knife, and you kill them. That's all."

I turned to run, but the barman was behind me, pulling my arms, twisting my wrists up into the small of my back. The knife glinted pale silver in the moonlight. Madame Ezekiel smiled.

She sliced across my throat.

Blood began to gush, and then to flow. And then it slowed, and stopped ...

— The pounding in the front of my head, the pressure in the back. All a roiling change a how-wow-row-now change a red wall coming towards me from the night
— I tasted stars dissolved in brine, fizzy and distant and salt
— my fingers prickled with pins and my skin was lashed with tongues of flame, my eyes were topaz I could taste the night

My breath steamed and billowed in the icy air.

I growled involuntarily, low in my throat. My forepaws were touching the snow.

I pulled back, tensed, and sprang at her.

There was a sense of corruption that hung in the air, like a mist, surrounding me. High in my leap I seemed to pause, and something burst like a soap bubble ...

I was deep, deep in the darkness under the sea, standing on all fours on a slimy rock floor, at the entrance of some kind of citadel, built of enormous, rough-hewn stones. The stones gave off a pale glow-in-the-dark light; a ghostly luminescence, like the hands of a watch.

A cloud of black blood trickled from my neck.

She was standing in the doorway, in front of me. She was now six-, maybe seven-feet high. There was flesh on her skeletal bones, pitted and gnawed, but the silks were weeds, drifting in the cold water, down there in the dreamless deeps. They hid her face like a slow green veil.

There were limpets growing on the upper surfaces of her arms, and on the flesh that hung from her ribcage.

I felt like I was being crushed. I couldn't think any more.

She moved towards me. The weed that surrounded her head shifted. She had a face like the stuff you don't want to eat in a sushi

counter, all suckers and spines and drifting anemone fronds; and
somewhere in all that I knew she was smiling.

I pushed with my hind-legs. We met there, in the deep, and we
struggled. It was so cold, so dark. I closed my jaws on her face, and
felt something rend and tear.

It was almost a kiss, down there in the abysmal deep ...

I landed softly on the snow, a silk scarf locked between my jaws.

The other scarves were fluttering to the ground. Madame
Ezekiel was nowhere to be seen.

The silver knife lay on the ground, in the snow. I waited
on all fours, in the moonlight, soaking wet. I shook myself,
spraying the brine about. I heard it hiss and spit when it hit
the fire.

I was dizzy, and weak. I pulled the air deep into my lungs.

Down, far below, in the bay, I could see the frog people
hanging on the surface of the sea like dead things; for a handful
of seconds they drifted back and forth on the tide, then they
twisted and leapt, and each by each they *plop-plopped* down into
the bay and vanished beneath the sea.

There was a scream. It was the fox-haired bartender, the pop-
eyed aluminum-siding salesman, and he was staring at the night
sky, at the clouds that were drifting in, covering the stars, and he
was screaming. There was rage and there was frustration in that
cry, and it scared me.

He picked up the knife from the ground, wiped the snow
from the handle with his fingers, wiped the blood from the blade
with his coat. Then he looked across at me. He was crying. "You
bastard," he said. "What did you do to her?"

I would have told him I didn't do anything to her, that she
was still on guard far beneath the ocean, but I couldn't talk any
more, only growl and whine and howl.

He was crying. He stank of insanity, and of disappointment.
He raised the knife and ran at me, and I moved to one side.

Some people just can't adjust even to tiny changes. The
barman stumbled past me, off the cliff, into nothing.

In the moonlight blood is black, not red, and the marks he left
on the cliffside as he fell and bounced and fell were smudges of

black and dark grey. Then, finally, he lay still on the icy rocks at the base of the cliff, until an arm reached out from the sea and dragged him, with a slowness that was almost painful to watch, under the dark water.

A hand scratched the back of my head. It felt good.

"What was she? Just an avatar of the Deep Ones, sir. An eidolon, a manifestation, if you will, sent up to us from the uttermost deeps to bring about the end of the world."

I bristled.

"No, it's over, for now. You disrupted her, sir. And the ritual is most specific. Three of us must stand together and call the sacred names, while innocent blood pools and pulses at our feet."

I looked up at the fat man, and whined a query. He patted me on the back of the neck, sleepily.

"Of course she doesn't love you, boy. She hardly even exists on this plane, in any material sense."

The snow began to fall once more. The bonfire was going out.

"Your change tonight, incidentally, I would opine, is a direct result of the self-same celestial configurations and lunar forces that made tonight such a perfect night to bring back my old friends from Underneath ..."

He continued talking, in his deep voice, and perhaps he was telling me important things. I'll never know, for the appetite was growing inside me, and his words had lost all but the shadow of any meaning; I had no further interest in the sea or the cliff-top or the fat man.

There were deer running in the woods beyond the meadow: I could smell them on the winter's night's air.

And I was, above all things, hungry.

I was naked when I came to myself again, early the next morning, a half-eaten deer next to me in the snow. A fly crawled across its eye, and its tongue lolled out of its dead mouth, making it look comical and pathetic, like an animal in a newspaper cartoon.

The snow was stained a fluorescent crimson where the deer's belly had been torn out.

My face and chest were sticky and red with the stuff. My

throat was scabbed and scarred, and it stung; by the next full moon it would be whole once more.

The sun was a long way away, small and yellow, but the sky was blue and cloudless, and there was no breeze. I could hear the roar of the sea some distance away.

I was cold and naked and bloody and alone; ah well, I thought: it happens to all of us, in the beginning. I just get it once a month.

I was painfully exhausted, but I would hold out until I found a deserted barn, or a cave; and then I was going to sleep for a couple of weeks.

A hawk flew low over the snow toward me, with something dangling from its talons. It hovered above me for a heartbeat, then dropped a small grey squid in the snow at my feet, and flew upward. The flaccid thing lay there, still and silent and tentacled in the bloody snow.

I took it as an omen, but whether good or bad I couldn't say and I didn't really care any more; I turned my back to the sea, and on the shadowy town of Innsmouth, and began to make my way toward the city.

Kim Newman

OUT OF THE NIGHT, WHEN
THE FULL MOON IS BRIGHT . . .

Kim Newman is a multiple award-winning writer. His 1993 novel
Anno Dracula *(which started out as a novella in* The Mammoth
Book of Vampires*) became a bestseller on both sides of the Atlantic
and has attracted plenty of interest from movie-makers.*

*A former semi-professional kazoo player and cabaret performer,
he is now a freelance writer, film critic and broadcaster. His non-
fiction studies include* Nightmare Movies: A Critical History
of the Horror Film Since 1986, Ghastly Beyond Belief *(with
Neil Gaiman), the Bram Stoker Award-winning* Horror: 100 Best
Books *(with Stephen Jones), and* Wild West Movies. *Amongst his
other books are* In Dreams *(co-edited with Paul J. McAuley), the
novels* The Night Mayor, Bad Dreams, Jago, The Quorum *and*
The Bloody Red Baron, *a series of gaming adventures under the
pseudonym "Jack Yeovil", and such recent collections as* The Man
from the Diogenes Club *and* Secret Files of the Diogenes Club.

*As the author explains: "Having done an intricate vampire story
for* The Mammoth Book of Vampires, *I was hunting around for
an idea to work up a similarly ambitious piece for this volume when
I hit upon the immediate inspiration for this story, the Cordettes'
record of the* Zorro *theme song, from which the title comes. I must
also credit three invaluable books for crystallizing my feelings
about Los Angeles, California history and Zorro: Mike Davis'*
City of Quartz: Excavating the Future in Los Angeles, *Carey
McWilliams'* North from Mexico: The Spanish Speaking People
of the United States, *and Bill Yenne's* The Legend of Zorro."

Given his encyclopaedic knowledge and eclectic tastes, it should come as no surprise to those who know the author's work that Newman expertly integrates the legendary swashbuckling hero and near-future LA riots in the following novella about a mythic shapeshifter ...

Oppression – by its very nature – creates the power that crushes it. A champion arises – a champion of the oppressed.
The Mark of Zorro (1920)

I

"Stuey," Officer García began, "how about this for *high concept*?"

The idea bulb above his cop cap practically turned the inside of the windscreen into a silver-black mirror.

"These two cops in East LA, man ..."

García grinned at Officer Scotchman, who kept eyes on the street, hands on the wheel.

"... and they're really *werewolves* ..."

The hispanic officer half-turned in the patrol car's front passenger seat. Neck-twisting, he looked back at Stuart with glittering, amused steel eyes.

"... and the title of the *cho* is ..."

The cruiser eased over a speed-bump, unsettling Stuart's jet-lagged stomach.

"*Prowl Car.*"

Maybe it wasn't a speed-bump. Maybe it was something lying in the road.

García snickered at his high concept, repeating his projected title like a mantra. Stuart shrugged in the shadow of the rear compartment, blackly invisible to the cops up front. Scotchman's face, impassive in reflection, slid up the windscreen as they cruised under one of the rare functioning streetlights.

When García first introduced the other cop, Stuart assumed his name was Scotch, man. He sussed Scotchman thought his movie crazy partner was a prick.

"How d'ya like it, Stuey? Think it'll play in Peoria?"

Stuart shrugged again. Last night, García had come up with a dozen movie ideas. Cop movies.

"Take it to New Frontier, man," García insisted. "*Prowl Car*, man. Will be *the* werewolf cop movie. Be boffo boxo. Can write it together. Like a *collaboration*, man. Split credit."

García's eyes rolled like the comedy Chicano he pretended to be when he wasn't beating someone. He howled at the moon. It was nearly full tonight, a sliver away from a perfect circle.

The cop had a Cheech Marín moustache, but was skinnier in the body than the straighter half of Cheech and Chong. He had overdeveloped forearms like Popeye's. He would look proportioned if his torso were Schwarzeneggered out by kevlar body armour.

"Werewolf *cho*, man. Everybody loves *el hombre lobo*. Specially when he wrestle with *El Santo*. Those were great *chos*, man. Scotchman, you get yours when the moon is full and bright?"

Scotchman's eyes swivelled to one side and back again. Reflection cut in half by shadow, his eyes shone in the dark upper half of his face. He looked like Batman.

Or Zorro.

His hair was gathered at the back of his head into a Steven Seagal ponytail which seemed to pull his face flat into lizard-like impassivity. The officer worked at being scary. He had the kind of hardness and smarts they called "onstreet" this year.

This was the second night of Stuart's three-week ridealong with García and Scotchman. The LAPD had good relations with New Frontier; Ray Calme, the so-called studio head, had been able to arrange this tour of duty with no hassle.

There was the usual jaw-drop when the Brit writer turned out to be black, but it passed. Most cops he'd met so far were black, latino or Asian. The city had just appointed its first Japanese-American Police Chief, Yasujiro Ryu. Whites, actual *anglo* Angelinos, were a minority, barricaded in secure enclaves, hiding behind "Armed Response" signs on their lawns.

They passed through dark streets. Stuart had the impression of people scurrying away from the cruiser's path. Every building was tattooed, each block with its own style of graffiti. The overlapping scrawls were an endless layering of tag upon tag. Some called it art, but the coloured chaos looked to him like a canvas signed so many times there was no room for a painting.

He was supposed to pick up background for the *Shadowstalk* script. The book (Soon To Be A Major Motion Picture) was set in a North London council estate, but the movie (the *cho*, García would say) was relocating to Any*barrio*, USA. He was now learning what an American hellhole looked like from the inside. He'd have been happy enough to spend a long weekend with tapes of *Boyz N the Hood, South Central* and a couple of PBS social problem documentaries, then make it all up. It was more or less how he had done the novel.

Scotchman slowed the cruiser as he turned a corner off Van Ness Avenue. Kids in highly-coloured windbreakers stood outside a barricaded liquor store, conversing with what looked like sign language. Even through armoured glass, Stuart heard savage scratchrap rhythms from boomboxes. García craned to clock faces, but Scotchman looked without seeming to look. The white cop had a billion dollar brain for mug shots and rap sheets.

Scotchman shook his eyes without moving his head. No one worth busting. The kids were black or somewhere thereabouts, and they all wore badges even Stuart could identify as gang colours. Back in Britain, he'd heard of the Crips and Bloods, but they were Old Hat, long split into other factions, superseded by newer waves of ethnicity and criminality. Last night's lecture on the nomenclature and uniforms of Los Angeles gangs had been about as intricate and dull as an account of the dissolution of the Austro-Hungarian Empire.

Stuart knew he should be writing another novel, not traipsing around the Big Car Park (which was what LA looked like from the air when he first saw it) with a cowboy film company trying to wring some sort of commercial movie out of *Shadowstalk* (Soon To Be A Minor Video Release).

This year, black writers were onstreet; even a company as low down on the Hollywood food chain as New Frontier needed to buy one. Black and Brit was a whole new spin; Ray Calme was congratulating himself on having hooked a live one in Stuart Finn.

Raymond Chandler, one of Stuart's idols, said: "If my books had been any worse, I should not have been invited to Hollywood. If they had been any better, I should not have come."

The roof was suddenly thumped. The interior of the patrol car rang like a bell.

"Bee-bee, man," García laughed. "Onstreet shot. Feel up there, Stuey."

Stuart ran his hand over the roof. It was armour-plate covered with thinning and holed foam rubber.

"Can you find a bump?"

Stuart couldn't.

"What was that?" he asked.

"A steel ball-bearing," Scotchman said. "Kids fire them from pistolgrip catapaults like miniature crossbows. They're for hunting birds. You can punch through a crash helmet if you aim at the visor. Go through a skull like a walnut through wet ricepaper."

"Fockin' kids, man," García said, tolerantly.

"Someone shot the car?"

"Don't call it a shot unless there's a dent. No time for paperwork."

Neither of the cops seemed to care about the attack. Stuart was sure a London copper would mind very much if someone propelled a steel missile at him with killing force. This was a different culture; he had to keep notes until he knew it well enough to translate *Shadowstalk* into its language.

Scotchman scoped out the roofs of the single-storey buildings lining the street. The Catapault Kid was up there, somewhere. It might not be worth filing a report, but the cop was certainly filing a grudge. One night, he'd get his payback.

Thanks to jetlag, Stuart was perfectly adapted to the ridealong life. He was awake at night and sleepy in the day, just like the cops. Only he felt lousy about it.

"You got Projects back in England, man?" García asked.

Projects? Oh yes, housing estates. Council houses.

"We have Projects."

"Like in your book?"

"Yeah."

"Onstreet book, man."

When he found out his ridealong was a writer, García read *Shadowstalk*. Stuart, interviewed to death on publication, didn't have anything more to say about the novel, but García kept bringing it up.

"Must be heavy, man. What you say the name of that Project was, Bridgwater Farm?"

"Broadwater Farm."

"Yeah, heavy."

"Certainly is."

Actually, Stuart had spent about four afternoons in his life trudging around Broadwater Farm, visiting his uncles with Mum and Dad. In Autumn, the place was boring rather than threatening. Kids made fun of his school uniform, but that was it. No guns, no knives, no ball-bearings. He had noticed all the concrete litter bins had had fires lit in them and been rained out, leaving streaks of sooty sludge. He'd used that in *Shadowstalk*.

"You like that, Scotchman? They got a *barrio* in Britain. Drive-bys, man. Gangstas, zonk houses, riots. Whole *enchilada*. It's in Stuey's book. Should read it, man."

Scotchman, who only read rap sheets and law enforcement magazines, made no answer.

Shadowstalk was about killings on a North London Estate, and the young black policeman (a convenient author's stand-in, as everybody rightly said) who realizes the murderer isn't just a psycho but the voodoo incarnation of all the social misery abroad in the land. It wasn't exactly a thriller, more a portrait of life in the dead end of the twentieth-century United Kingdom. Ray Calme saw it as about a younger (i.e., cheaper) Wesley Snipes or Denzel Washington tracking down and totaling a bad-ass monster motherfucker. It could certainly be read that way, Stuart admitted, but he hoped to keep some content in the screenplay.

"Where Stuey comes from is just as onstreet as the Jungle, man," García said. "Only with a different accent."

Stuart didn't mention that his Dad was a doctor in Bath, and that he'd been a day boy at a private school. There were plenty of blacks and Asians at Sexey's (yes, that was the real name, by Damballah); members of Royal Families or the sons of coup-elevated Third World army officers.

No one could say it hadn't been tough, though. He always wished he had gone to an inner city Comprehensive. At least, then, he might not now be a twenty-three year old virgin.

"Real riots in Britain, man. They kill cops just like here. Stuey, in the last LA riots, me and Scotchman got cut off in the Jungle. Crowd turned the car over, started kicking in the windows ..."

He tapped the reinforced glass with his knuckles.

"... only they couldn't crack it. Tried to get in the gas tank to fry us up, only it's got a bullet-proof combination lock. The end, they just got bored and went away. Scotchman, though, he remember the faces."

Stuart was a member of the Charlie Aziz Group, founded in memory of a Pakistani killed in police custody. They were still trying to get some lads who had been fitted up for assaulting police officers out of prison. He signed petitions and wrote letters to his MP but deplored direct action. When one of the CAG was suspected of throwing a petrol bomb at a police station, he personally made the resolution calling for his immediate expulsion and censure.

"We ran into some of those *cholos* from the riot. Scotchman, he make them strip naked and walk down a corridor, whistling the *Andy Griffith Show* theme while me and other officers beat on them with rubber flashlights, man. Was real payback."

Stuart had heard similar stories about London police, who apparently made you whistle *Dixon of Dock Green*. That was a weird international police tradition.

"The Jungle out there, man," García said, proudly. "We're the *beasts*. We're the *kings* of the Jungle. Gotta be, to survive. Put that in your screenplay, man. Give the cop guy claws that cut like razors and a roar that chills the blood of evildoers. Like us."

If he couldn't write for the movies, García would like to act in them. He said he became a cop because the first thing he could remember on TV was Erik Estrada in *CHIPS*. That was culture for you. For Stuart, it was *Fawlty Towers* repeats.

The patrol car had its route marked out, but Scotchman put his own random spin on the detail. He had explained that it was important in the jungle not to be predictable, so he superimposed his own course. They started out and finished up where they were supposed to be and hit certain points along the way, but there were any number of deviations he made sure to work into the schedule. Scotchman called it a *skedule*, of course.

They were covering the LA grid, taking as many cross-streets as possible. Names which sounded exotic in Bath (Sepulveda, Pico, Figueroa) had turned out to be nondescript thoroughfares stretching for miles, for all the world like Surbiton High Street with more palm trees and fewer pedestrians. This route was away from those names, threading from Downtown to the South-East, through the bitterly-contested territory called the Jungle. The neighbourhoods were mainly Chicano, most blacks having been driven out. A wave of Koreans was coming, García said. Stuart wondered where the people who were driven out went.

Most cross-streets were dark, streetlights shot out and businesses shuttered up behind graffiti-covered steel rollers. Scotchman drove slower, and Stuart felt the crunching caltrop-like obstructions under the armoured tyres. The roads were very poorly maintained, far worse than in Britain.

To the left, a shutter rolled up like a broken blind, and light flooded out of a garage. Stuart flinched: the shutter reminded him of flaps going up over a pirate ship's gunports as the cannons delivered a broadside.

A sleek black van slid swiftly out, crossing a forecourt in a liquid instant like a panther. The van *nudged* the patrol car's nose as it took possession of the street. Stuart felt the impact in his teeth as Scotchman braked.

García swore in rapid Spanish.

The van slipped into the night, at once beyond sight. With its one-way black windows and reflective paint-job, it could be swallowed by shadow. Stuart had seen no visible license plate.

"Shouldn't we go after that?" he suggested.

Neither cop said anything. Light from the garage still filled the car.

"Should check for damage," García said, at last.

Scotchman nodded. He unlocked his driver's side door, and stepped out, hand easy on his gun.

"Stay here, Stuey," García said, also leaving the car.

Stuart bridled. He couldn't pick up much from sitting in the back while the world went on outside. Then again, he wasn't sure how much he wanted to pick up.

The cops examined the hood, where the van had side-swiped. They talked intensely, maybe argued, but Stuart couldn't lip-read. He looked at the garage. It seemed floodlit and yellow light poured down the forecourt. In the yellow were trickles of red that gave him a bad turn. Knowing he'd regret it, he opened the door and got out.

II From the *Corrido* of Diego

"I was born within a day's ride, as distances were measured then, from *El Pueblo de Nuestra Senora de la Reyna de los Angeles de Rio Porciunculo*. My mother was an Indian, my father was a Jesuit. They were, of course, not married. Such arrangements were common in our neglected corner of the Empire.

"My father baptised me Diego, and finally, grudgingly, left me his family name. My mother birth-named me Fox, for her totem animal. You may know me by the Spanish form of my Indian name, *Zorro*.

"This was 1805; five years before the *Grito de Dolores*, Father Hidalgo y Costilla's call for revolt against Spain; sixteen years before the end of the rule of Madrid over Mexico; forty-three years before California was ceded to the United States by the Treaty of Guadalupe Hidalgo; forty-five years before the territory attained statehood ...

"Had I merely lived out my expected years, I should have experienced history enough for any man. As things happened, history and I have become intertwined until we are each inseparable from the other.

"Mine is not a story, as an *anglo* would have it, but a *corrida*, a song. What is true and what is not have long ceased to matter. From the very beginning, I have been a legend as much as a living creature. Often, I lose myself inside the legend.

"Sometimes, I am Diego, masked as Fox; sometimes, I am Fox, hiding inside Diego. In this, what you know from motion pictures and television, is true. Little else is.

"I was born hispanic if not a Spaniard, and I shall die an American if not an *anglo*. Stories represent me as of the *ricos*, strutting around a *hacienda* in absurdly embroidered finery, galloping over peon-tilled land on a purebred Castilian steed, elegantly dueling with a Toledo blade. Such men were fewer than stories would like, and rarely made themselves evident. I was of the *pobres*, the nameless thousands who were born, dug out goods from the ground with their hands, and, in the normal course, died.

"The *ricos* left behind their names (the streets of this city bear them still), but the *pobres* passed utterly from the land, leaving not even a memory.

"Except mine."

"The *viejo* had changed me. That I knew from his last touch, which struck like lightning. I thought myself dead but trapped in my body. I felt the weight of my limbs but could not make them move. Then I realized my body merely had an unfamiliar shape. With a little concentration, I could move.

"I was different.

"Since early childhood, my back had been bent in field labour, my hands had fought earth and rock. Pain was as much a part of my body as the taste of spit in my mouth. Now the pain was gone. For the first time, I had pleasure in movement. Simply raising my hand to my face was an exhilaration.

"Against sky, I saw my long-fingered, sharp-nailed hand. It was dark and thinly furred. The knuckle of my forefinger burned with pain. My finger lengthened, joints popping. See, my forefingers are as long as my middle fingers. That is part of the old stories.

"I no longer felt the cold of the night. My clothes were stretched in some places and loose in others, and confined me intolerably. I looked at the full moon and saw not the familiar silver disc, but a ball of light brighter than the sun, containing all colours of the rainbow.

"As I looked about, the dark was banished. Each rock, each plant, was as plain as if under a frozen streak of lightning. Bright, moving forms were animals. I saw movement as well as colour, and could discern a grey rabbit which would by day have been hidden in similarly-coloured scrub.

"I rent apart my shirt, my thick pelt bristling as I let night air at my rough skin, and brought down the rabbit. The animal moved slowly as a muddy stream and I was swift as a hawk.

"Swift as a fox.

"The rabbit's blood was like a pepper exploding on my tongue, like *peyote* blazing in my brain. My powerful jaws, lined with sharp teeth, could crunch through bone; my mouth was wide enough to finish the rabbit in three bites.

"Sights and smells and tastes blossomed. I was lost in a new world. I could stand straight-backed, as never by day; and I could run swiftly on all fours, my claws striking sparks from stone.

"The *viejo* lay in the moonlight, body dry, limbs like black sticks. The Indian, who my mother said was of the People Before Our People, might have been buried in the desert and unearthed after ages. His face had turned from leather to parchment. Dead for only a few moments, it seemed life had fled from him many years ago.

"As he died, something had passed from the tired old man to me. I, Diego, ran under the moon and fought beasts for my food. Soon, I would fight beasts for my people."

III

Thin blue smoke swirled hypnotically under the striplights. Thick smell stung his nose and eyes like teargas.

A pedantic copy editor at Real Press had told him not to call it cordite (the stuff wasn't used any more), but couldn't suggest an up-to-date alternative term for the afterstench of discharged guns. Something Stuart had never smelled before, it was unmistakable.

The garage was filled with people. There was no doubt about how dead they were. The far wall was pocked with bullet-holes and splashed with bright blood. A line of young men slumped where the skirting board would have been, limp arms overlapping, surprised heads lolling on chests. It was his Dad's usual suggested solution to industrial disputes; they'd been put against the wall and shot.

The predictable thing to do was bend over double and bring up his doughnuts and coffee. Stuart, in this case, was highly predictable.

García and Scotchman found him on his knees, coughing into a pool of chyme. Clear, bitter fluid hung in ropes from his mouth. His head was whirling.

Scotchman whistled and García swore.

Stuart shut his eyes, but his mind's instamatic developed polaroids in his head. Gouting wounds in colourful jackets, puckered out and leaking meat stuffing. Criss-cross trails of blood like raffia strands on a concrete floor. One man, a boy, hanging from chains, stripped not only to the waist but almost to muscle and bone.

"This fool got special treatment," Scotchman said.

The hanging boy had been chubby; pockets of fat stood out in his flayed torso. Stuart was carrying around about half a stone more than he should have been.

His gut twisted again, but there was nothing left inside.

"Stuey, man," García said, not unkindly, "clean yourself."

He found a handkerchief and wiped his wet face. He tried to lick the ghastly taste out of his mouth.

Now he had stopped being sick, he had time to get scared.

When he opened his eyes, it wasn't so bad. He told himself it was special effects. In movies, he had seen worse.

The hanging boy's arms were wrenched upwards, probably out of his shoulder sockets to judge by the stretched tendons, and fastened to the chain above his head. His wrists were cinched together like beercans by one-piece plastic cuffs. Whoever had worked on him had known what they were doing.

Scotchman whispered a report into his wafer-phone, glancing over each of the dead. He mentioned that all the boys had been given a just-to-make-sure head shot. That was where a lot of the mess came from. García rooted around on a work-surface. He found some car mechanic tools, and a large chemistry set.

"Looks to be a zonk house, man."

Zonk was the latest packaging of the product, cocaine. It came in squeezable plastic bulbs, like tomato-shaped ketchup containers. A single oily drop on the tongue was a force ten hit. Connoisseur zonkbrains preferred to drip it into their nostrils or onto their corneas. Chief Ryu had declared War on Zonk.

As well as taking out the zonk krewe, the killers had raked their equipment with gunfire. The chemistry set was smashed and odorous. Pools of different coloured liquids mixed and steamed on the bench-top.

"Party favours," García commented, flipping open a deep Samsonite to reveal densely-packed zonk squeezers. "Couple of hundred K, easy."

Scotchman had made his report. He folded up his wafer-phone and slipped it back into his top pocket.

"Gang activity," he diagnosed. "These are Caldiarres. They've been warring over turf with the Eyes."

All the dead people flew colours. Scarves and symbols and jackets and headbands. The Caldiarres' badge was a red, angry demon face. From the tribalism, you'd have sworn the Indians had won in the Americas.

"Wouldn't another gang take the drugs?" Stuart asked.

García looked into the face of the hanging boy and said "Think I recognize this fool. Esquiverra, Escalante, Esca-something …"

Scotchman looked around, crossing names off his mental wanted list.

García picked out a squeezer and felt the weight of it. A single hundred dollar pellet of zonk was inside, diluting in liquid.

"Feels like a tit, man. Really does."

Zonkbrains called their poison Mother's Milk, and talked about "sucking Diablo's Teat".

García gave an experimental squeeze and a tiny gusher of whitish fluid dribbled from the nipple.

"Ever wonder what it's like, Stuey?"

Stuart had a particular horror of drugs. When his sister was fourteen and Stuart eleven, Dad had caught Brenda with a joint and gave them both a scarifying tour of a rehab clinic. Neither of the Finn kids so much as smoked cigarettes; Stuart worried about the amount of coffee he drank.

"Let's post the Crime Scene: Keep Out notice and be on the road," Scotchman said. "The clean-up will be here in minutes."

"You just leave these people?" Stuart said, astonished.

"They're not going anywhere. And nobody is going to mess with them."

Scotchman took a last look around the garage. The smoke had dissipated.

"A message has been delivered," he said. "Let's hope it gets to the right people."

IV From the *Corrido* of Diego

"My mother had fourteen babies that I know of, at least five with my father. By my twenty-fifth year, I alone still lived. My brothers and sisters were taken by illness and the land.

"My father wished to give me work at the mission. Don Esteban would not hear of a peon being taught to read and write. I was in all but name a slave of the *patrón*. Under the Spanish statutes of California, I was prohibited from tilling earth or raising livestock for my own table. I was paid six *reales* (twelve cents, American money) a day. Obliged by law to buy food from Don Esteban, I never saw a coin. Like all peons, I inherited the debt of my family. The debts of my dead brothers and sisters, which fell upon my shoulders, were numbered in thousands of *reales*.

"This was the way things had been under Spain; this was the way things were under Mexico; this was the way things would be in the United States.

"The mission collected its tithe from Don Esteban, who deducted it from the earnings of the peons. My father taught us to be devout and dutiful, for we would receive our reward in Heaven."

"One night of the full moon, soon after the change, I hunted down and killed Don Esteban.

"In the stories, Don Esteban might be a tyrant, lashing about with a whip, striping the backs of the peons. Perhaps one of my sisters survived to young girlhood and became beautiful. Or maybe one of the daughters of my neighbours was comely and promised to me in marriage. From his steed, the *patrón* espied beauty under dust and carried her back to his *hacienda* to be abused. Or the priest might raise gentle protest against the lot of the peons and be turned away roughly by Don Esteban, falling dead in the dirt with a throwing knife buried to its hilt in his godly back. One night, Don Esteban and his men might become distracted with wine and, as a sport, ride through the village, pulling down the one-room *jacales* in which we lived, emptying one-shot pistols at random at any human shadow.

"None of these things were the case. By his own lights, Don Esteban was a pious man. He treated his peons as he treated other beasts that he owned, strictly but with care. His wealth was founded upon our work, and you do not slaughter a good horse or ox until it is too old to work.

"Killing Don Esteban was something that came to my animal mind. He was not the first man to feed my night hungers, but he was the first whom I sought out.

"If the *patrón*'s home was a *hacienda*, it was a modest one. It was made of stone but its floors were beaten earth. My feet made no sound as I entered. Don Esteban was reading his Bible by firelight. As I stalked towards him, he gripped a rosary tight and stared.

"At the first sight of me, Don Esteban fouled himself. To my snout, the smell was intense and exciting.

"With my long fingers, I gripped the *patrón*'s head firmly as I tore out his throat. I chewed through the fine lace of his collar. My teeth hurt as I bit down on a silver button. His muttered prayer cut off sharply.

"When finished, I found my hooked thumbnail had cut a zig-zag-zig into Don Esteban's cheek as he struggled. A red letter stood out in the brown skin above his beard. The letter Z.

"A servant found me squatting over Don Esteban. As often after tasting human blood, I had fallen into a reverie, distracted by patterns in the flames of the hearth. The servant gave the alarm and I was chased into the hills."

"Next morning, when I returned exhausted to my *jacale*, the peons mourned the passing of the *patrón*. Many loved Don

Esteban as a dog loves its master. The mission bells tolled for his death. By this time, my father was dead of fever and a young Jesuit, Fray Molina, had taken his place.

"A cousin of Don Esteban sold his lands, and we had a new *patrón*, Don Luis. He was much like the old *patrón* and, after some years passed, I took the opportunity to kill him also. Of course, there would always be *patrónes*. This was understood. I could not exterminate the breed. Also, I killed Fray Molina, whom I knew troubled the young boys of the village. And I killed *Capitán* Cordoba, who hanged Tío Pancho for speaking against the Church. I killed many. Still, I kill many.

"With my long finger, I took to leaving my zig-zag-zig on my kills. Others took to using my mark. Often, I saw it cut into the bark of trees or the adobe of a wall.

"By now, there was much talk of a curse and a demon. The old women, more Indian than Spanish, said the curse was always upon the land. In the times before the *conquistadores*, when the Apache preyed upon the Pueblos, the demon fought the raiders. It was a fox, a wolf, a bear, a wild man …

"Some said the demon was an angel, that only the unjust were struck down by its hand. I *was* drawn to certain men: cruel officers, venal priests, murderous bandits, harsh overseers. If I chanced upon one such by daylight in the period just before the full moon, their flesh seemed to glow like the moon through my altered eyes. I would be certain our paths would cross by night.

"By day, I took a wife, Dolores, Lolita. She grew old and died in short years. I did not grow old and die. My sons seemed to me like my brothers, then like grandfathers, then they too died. Few remarked upon my situation, but other peons kept their distance from me. After I buried my Lolita, I could find no other to wed me. My grandchildren avoided me. I was no longer welcome at the mission.

"Eventually, I would have been driven from the land. Those who sang of the Fox of the Night wished to deny the Diego of the Day. I became as a phantom, entirely invisible to those among whom I lived. If I did not work the land, no overseer reprimanded me. If I found my sustenance by night, no one questioned my well-fed appearance. My *jacale* fell into disrepair, but that did not trouble me.

"Each month, the Fox had five or six nights, immediately before, during and after the full moon. Only then did I live. I hunted, I found lovers, I struck. Sometimes I wished Diego would disappear forever into the Fox. Then I could depart for the hills, there to live away from the cares of man."

V

"Be a blue moon tomorrow, man," García said, thumbing up at the sky.

Stuart looked up through the wide window, puzzled. The moon above was silver, as usual.

"A moon can be called blue when it's full twice in a month," Scotchman explained. "It was full on the first and we've a couple of days to go 'til September."

So that was what "once in a blue moon" meant. Stuart guessed you got a better education on the streets of LA than at Sexey's School for Boys. Maybe night patrol was so boring, you picked up all this trivia.

Of course, tonight hadn't been boring.

García and Scotchman were known at the Coffee Stop. An 80-year-old counter girl with a jet-black beehive served them without being asked. She might have been eighteen when the sun set and aged through a long graveyard shift. No greeting, no conversation.

They didn't talk about the zonk house. Stuart, stomach empty, was hungry but found the idea of food repulsive. He dunked a doughnut, then sucked coffee out of it.

Stuart felt gimlet eyes on his back. Now he knew what it was like to be with the Heat. Even at 4.30 a.m. the Stop was crowded. Thin old people and restless young ones. Night people. One or two teenagers wore discreet colours, almost as quiet as AIDS remembrance ribbons. Scotchman was the only *anglo* in the room. Stuart wasn't quite the only black guy, but he was the only one who felt as though he were from outer space.

He could tell the night people knew he wasn't a cop. He sensed eyes searching for a gun bulge under his pullover. Not being a cop wouldn't be any protection if that black van cruised down the street and someone rolled down one of the reflective black windows to spray automatic gunfire at the Coffee Stop, shattering the window and perforating García and Scotchman as inconvenient semi-witnesses. Stuart would get just as many bullets.

A screen-fronted sphere above the counter gave out a smog forecast in Spanish. The golden-skinned weather-girl was one of the CGI simulacra so popular this season. It had only taken America fifteen years to catch up with Max Headroom. Traffic and crime stats stuttered across the image, those with an immediate effect highlighted in pulsing red.

A young Chicano walked over to the cops. He wore silver-tipped cowboy boots and tight black jeans. His hair was covered by a tied-at-the-back black bandana. If he slipped the bandana over his eyes, he would look like a masked avenger. Though clean-shaven, his eyebrows were slicked and teased like a Douglas Fairbanks moustache.

"*Buenas noches*, Vega," Scotchman said, quietly. No doubt Vega merited his own file card.

The kid said something to Officer García and the cop inclined his head to think. Remembering GCSE Spanish, Stuart gathered the cops were invited to talk with someone called the Alcalde. "Alcalde" meant "Mayor", but Stuart guessed Vega didn't mean Krystina Jute, the controversial Mayor who wanted to change the city's name to Las Angelas.

"The Alcalde is concerned about what went down this night with the Carriares," Vega explained, diplomatic but forceful like an ambassador of an overconfident superpower. "He would like to discuss this matter."

García looked at Scotchman, who gave no signal. As one, the cops stood.

"Who is this Alcalde?" Stuart asked.

"Could call him a community leader," García said.

As they all walked across the checkerboard floor, people at the tables cringed to give them air-space. The cops had a special saunter, probably from lugging all the iron around on their belts. The Colt Police Python on one hip was balanced by the multi-use stunstick on the other. Stuart, taller than García and within an inch of Scotchman, felt he was trotting in their wake like a tolerated younger brother.

At a table in the farthest alcove, the Alcalde held court. He was a white-haired man whose unlined face was adorned with a neatly-trimmed goatee beard, black but undyed. He wore a white jacket over a sparkly black shirt, and had a necklace with an animal-tooth fetish. Clustered around him were serious-looking kids like Vega, sharply dressed but without obvious gang colours. All were latino, save a girl with oriental eyes and a braided queue who might be half-Korean or Vietnamese.

If the Alcalde's party had eaten or drunk anything, the waitresses had long ago cleared away the washing-up. The Alcalde smoked a thin cigar. He smiled at the cops and, speaking Spanish so slowly Stuart could follow with no trouble, invited them to sit with him.

Stuart found himself crammed on a squeaky seat between Scotchman and the half-oriental. He was aware of the cop's holstered gun, pressing into his thigh as he was crowded against the girl.

"This is a bad thing that has happened," the Alcalde declared. "Blood spilled, lives wasted ..."

Stuart expected Scotchman to comment on the occupation of the dead kids, but the cop said nothing.

"The Eyes are evil fools," García said. "This was coming for months."

The Alcalde waved the comment away. "This was not the work of the Eyes. They themselves suffered a similar attack three nights ago. A black van was seen."

"We saw ..." Stuart began, then halted as Scotchman tapped his knee.

"The Caldiarres and the Eyes have made cases to me," the Alcalde continued. "They say there will be no war."

"As long as they're in the zonk business, there's war," Scotchman said.

The Alcalde shook his head. "This is regrettable. This zonk is a poison, the Devil's Milk. It is right that your Chief Ryu should wish it vanished from our streets."

Vega nodded, eyes on the Alcalde. The kid reminded Stuart of Deal, the boy in *Shadowstalk*. The boy who shows the policeman where the evil comes from.

"But there are other poisons."

Dawn seeped into the Coffee Stop, dispelling the grubby corpse light of crackling ceiling panels. Shadows appeared on the Alcalde's face. Back in Britain, it was getting near bed-time. Stuart was exhausted to the point of dropping.

García and Scotchman stood, ending the audience. Stuart, reluctant to unbend from the soft seat, got up too. Formal farewells were exchanged. The cops walked to the door and the patrol car outside.

For an odd instant, Stuart stayed behind, looking at the faces of the Alcalde's entourage. Vega, the oriental girl, others. He saw an intensity that touched a chord. Something he could use for the script.

Throughout the audience, the Alcalde had not seemed to notice Stuart. His followers, though, took turns to stare at him until he had nowhere to look away. Now the Alcalde looked straight at him and said, in precise English, "Take care, black man. This is a jungle."

VI From the *Corrido* of Diego

"On February the 2nd, 1848, at the end of the Mexican-American War, the Treaty of Guadalupe Hidalgo was executed. Mexico ceded to the United States territory greater in size than Germany and France combined. Aside from giving up claim to the Republic of Texas, which was taken promptly into the Union, Mexico yielded New Mexico, Arizona and California.

"By that time, I had walked away from my village. Runaway peons were traditionally hunted down and punished, returned in chains like the slaves of the Southern States. But the *patrón*, like everyone else, had come to regard me as invisible. I left the graves of my family and the ruin of my *jacale* to the dust and wind and followed the paths of the beasts. I drifted from place to place, never settling. Diego lived long months of hunger for the nights of the moon.

"I was greeted with suspicion by those I chanced across. I still saw the strange glow and I made my kills. Bandits, mostly; *renegados*, bad men. Some understood my situation; I was given shelter and food in the homes of the *pobres*, but never for long. For some years, I was with the Pueblo Indians, my mother's people. They were less unsettled by my presence. A few even commented upon my situation with humour.

"Fox was known to them of old.

"Some moon nights, young girls would couple with Fox. With Diego, these girls were respectful and obedient, as if with the father or elder brother of a lover, but with Fox, they were passionate, enthusiastic, delighted. They wore zig-zag-zig scratches like badges of honour. I noticed some old women wore similar, long-healed marks, and thought occasionally of the *viejo*.

"In giving away California, Mexican negotiators believed they were disposing of an Indian-plagued wilderness inhabited by only 7,000 Christian souls and an indeterminate number of savages. They were unaware that *nine days earlier* an *anglo* by the name of James Marshall had struck gold in the Sacramento Valley. Within three years, 200,000 people had flooded into the territory. Not all the newcomers were *anglos* from the States; many were *gambussinos*, experienced Mexican prospectors who headed North from Sonora to swell the population of the gold-fevered land.

"The anglo story has Marshall rushing into Fort Sutter shouting 'gold, gold, gold!' In truth, the word he used was 'chispa', Spanish for 'bright speck'. In everything concerning gold, the *anglos* followed the Spanish. *Conquistadores* named California for the gold they believed they would find, and Mexicans were prising precious poisons from dirt long before Marshall got on his mule. In Nevada, the *anglo* Comstock was about to abandon an unsuccessful gold strike when a passing Mexican miner told him the bluish stuff he'd been discarding signalled that he'd hit upon the richest silver mine in the world.

"Gold and silver are poisons. This I know; once, much later, an Americano named Reid put a silver bullet in Fox. Sometimes, I limp still, after more than a century.

"Like a sudden wind rising, the empty lands were crowded. Rarely was I alone on the trails. I fell in with *gambussinos*, and, from boredom rather than need, took to prospecting.

"Many speak proudly of their 'Spanish heritage', as if their ancestors were *ricos*, born on silk sheets in Madrid and sent to the colonies to win fortunes. It is a fact that when California became a state in 1850, over one-half of the Spanish-speaking population had arrived within the previous two years, *gambussinos* in search of gold. To be Chicano has nothing to do with the Dons of Aragon and Castile; it is to be the sons of miners and peons and Indians.

"I have been a miner, a peon and an Indian.

"With gold came guns. The rich flow of metal attracted men and women whose business was to dig their goods out of the purses of the men who had dug it from the ground. Mining camps bristled with vice and violence, then turned to ghost towns as a strike petered out. Cities were founded and abandoned. Deserts were littered with possessions cast away when they became too heavy.

"Eventually, there were more miners than could be supported by the wealth of the earth. At many strikes, *gambussinos* were more successful than anglos who left Philadelphia or Kentucky for fabulous riches without troubling to discover, for instance, what fresh-mined gold actually looked like. Many expected to unearth shining bricks, brush off a little dirt and take them to the bank.

"It was from these men that I first heard the expression 'greaser'. It was to these men that I first applied the expression '*gringo*'. Both words cannot be said without a snarl of hate.

"The new-born State Legislature, flexing *anglo*-dominated muscle, passed laws with official names like the Greaser Act of 1851, which limited the rights of the *pobres* to stake mining claims, raise livestock or buy land. Of course, laws only applied selectively. *Rico* and *anglo* embraced like long-lost cousins, each searching for the other's purse. Don *Patrón* was never a greaser to his face.

"It was to be expected that ill-educated *anglos* would be unable to comprehend the finer points of our new laws. Documents subtly worded to weight a balance in their favour were interpreted in the field as bestowing the legal right to murder Mexicans and steal their goods. Towns appointed Sheriffs and Vigilance Committees to do the murdering and thieving.

"Under the light of the full moon, gold shines pale like silver, like the faces of those I must kill. Fox was almost blinded by shining silver-white faces in an ocean of *gringos*. Diego learned quickly that he could not visit all who deserved the zig-zag-zig on their cheek.

"But I still had to try."

"There was a man, surnamed Murieta, called Joaquin. He lived, he died, he did few of the things ascribed to him. He was a miner, then he was a bandit. Driven from his claim by *anglos*, he raided the makeshift banks of the mining camps for the gold he was no longer allowed to dig with his hands. There were very many like him. Sheriffs put up posters offering a reward for anyone by the name of Joaquin. There were many Joaquins, and many were bandits. When the *gringos* said Joaquin, they meant upwards of five men who were called by that name.

"I was myself a notorious Joaquin.

"Another man, named Salomon Maria Pico, was a bandit also. Often, it could not be decided whether a thing had been done by a Joaquin or by Pico. To the *gringos*, we were all one. When they pickled the head of Joaquin Murieta, they were satisfied. He had come to stand for us all, a legend more than a man. The head of 'the renowned bandit' was exhibited at various places throughout California. As an added attraction, the hand of another 'notorious robber and murderer', Three Fingered Jack, was also exhibited.

"But a legend cannot be killed like a man. This, I know. Many were convinced that Joaquin Murieta lived still. And there were many called Joaquin, ready to take his place."

VII

It was hard to believe Millennium Plaza, a cross between a high-tone shopping mall and a Japanese Garden, was part of the same city as the Jungle. It was impossible to believe the hanging dead boy was in the same California demographic as the ornamental creatures grazing all around.

Everything was new in this Pastel Inferno. Men and women wore *chinoiserie* robes over swimming costumes and ambled with remote, beatific smiles. A few retro sharpies in shoulderpad suits moved faster than the herd. Discreet public speakers inside statuettes of Buddha and the Tasmanian Devil broadcast whale songs and purred reminders that smoking was illegal outside the red-marked areas.

After less than three hours of hotel sleep, Stuart was in a headachy fug. The Plaza's air of reassurance and safety was subtly aggravating. He was sure the security guards registered his black face and typed him as a zonkbrain, marking him for a back-clap with a palm-pad stun-gun.

High above the walk-ways, sun-screens stretched across sky, a parasol for the Plaza. *Parasol*, that was another one. Stuart was noticing the number of Spanish loan-words in California English. Millennium Plaza was a controlled environment, with musical fountains and an artificial, rose-scented breeze. Finally, a Californian dream was achieved: outdoor air conditioning.

The smiling security guards were bulked out in white *Star Wars* armour. A young black goon with a gold nostril-plug played with bejewelled kids, lumbering like Frosty the Snowman. Tan mothers in wide hats with scarf bands exchanged bleeping business cards by an *espresso* robot. Their children dressed like mini-adults, with child-sized Rolexes, Rodeo Drive harem outfits and thousand-dollar Nikes.

A street market for millionaires, Millennium Plaza was a subliminal laxative for the bank account. Tasteful products were displayed on stands, like art objects in an exhibition. A card in a slot and a tapped-in code number could make payment in a second. The purchase would automatically be delivered to your upscale address.

All buildings were identical so he couldn't find New Frontier. He was twenty-five minutes late for the meeting and wasn't one of the personnel in whom tardiness was permitted. He was to be kept waiting, not to keep others waiting.

He queued by a free-standing mapscreen. A console listed companies, individuals and institutions he might wish to visit. If you pressed a stud next to the name, a path-way lit up from this spot to the address. A father and son team were taking advantage of the mapscreen's general function to decide which film to see. Pressing "Movie Theaters", they made the grid light like an electrified web. There were over a hundred screens at six locations in Millennium Plaza, offering upwards of forty movies. The map could access information on films by classification (automatically excluding NC-17), start time, finish time, genre category (teenage zombie comedy), box office gross, and star rating averaged from a poll of ninety nationally-syndicated critics. Stuart felt as if he were in a Post Office with one small parcel, stuck behind a pensioner who hadn't talked to anyone since last week and needed a full half-hour of therapy with the bewildered counter clerk.

The family unit (a divorcé spending court-ordered quality time with his son) finally opted for the film which had made the most money: if so many others had seen it, they must know something the crix didn't. Stuart, trying not to be desperate, returned the father's shrug-and-grin combo and stepped casually up to the console, then ran his eyes up and down columns. There were dozens of companies called New Something; he found New Frontier between New Front and New Fruitz. A tiny squiggle appeared by the pulsing You Are Here dot. The New Frontier offices were just across the Square.

Alerted, he could see the NF logo on a building's shield-like marker-plate. The quickest path was through the crowded grass-and-pool area.

As he force-walked, Stuart saw a lot of white armour. Goons gathered around a group of chanting women in black. Old and young, the women didn't fit with Millennium Plaza: their clothes were not only an unfashionable colour but shapeless. Bodies deviated from the emaciated ideal: some had light moustache furrings, others wore unsubtle face paint. Thick ankles, barrel-waists, angry faces. They chanted in sing-song Spanish. A young woman hooded like an agonized nun held a placard which listed, in micro-letters, hundreds of names, almost all obviously latino.

The guards were antsy, armour plates shifting in insectile clicking. A young man with a rank insignia on his breastplate argued reasonably with an emotional spokeswoman. Stuart didn't have time to find out what it was about, but a wide woman blocked the walkway and chattered at him in rapid Spanish he couldn't follow, presenting a clipboard and a pen. On the board was a sheet half-covered with signatures.

This was all to do with *Los Disaparidos*, the Disappeared Ones. That usually meant political dissidents "vanished" by the apparatus of a police state. He knew about these women: mothers, wives, sisters, sweethearts, daughters. This must be some Latin American protest. He looked about for an Argentine Consulate or a Paraguayan Trade Commission.

The woman would not let him by, so he scribbled his name on the petition. The goon he'd seen earlier, with the gold in his nose, glared as if he were giving succour to the enemy. Once Stuart had signed, he became the large woman's best friend. He was embraced and passed on to the other women.

A banner was held up. *Comité de los Disaparidos de los Angeles*, Committee of the Disappeared of the Angels. No, Committee of the Disappeared of *Los Angeles*.

He was uncomfortable. The chanting was louder, the goons' smiles set in concrete. The black guard forced his gauntlet palms close together and an arc crackled between them. The spokeswoman gave up arguing with the ranking guard and joined her voice with the chant.

Stuart managed to get out from between the factions. The officer spoke into a throat-mike which amplified his voice to a Crack of Doom, instructing the women to "kindly disperse and clear the square." One woman fell on him and stabbed his armoured chest with something black and stubby, a marker-pen. In a swift movement, she scarred the officer with a thick black streak. It looked like the Mark of Zorro, a zig-zag-zig ...

The officer made a pass by the woman's scarved head with his open hand, as if to cuff her ear. There was a crackle, and the woman fell, twisting and spasming, to the ceramic tiles.

"Will you *please* kindly disperse and clear the square!"

Shaking and queasy, Stuart got away from the action. The building recognized his temporary tag and automatically opened for him. The doors were tinted, soundproof glass. When they hissed shut, he saw white guards, ungainly like marooned spacemen, tussling with crow-black protestors, but could not hear the kerfuffle.

Tansey, a tiny girl introduced days ago as a "personal expediter", greeted him in the foyer. She was eye-candy, a knock-out blonde who decorated New Frontier as a bikini extra decorates a beach party movie. She put a paper cup of decaf in his hand and escorted him to the elevator. She ordered him to have a good time and sent him up to the conference suite.

There was no table in the conference suite, and few items of furniture recognizable as chairs. Stuart was invited to loll on an inflated beanbag. Electronic equipment towers rose between the cushions, like hookahs in a cyberpunk Arabian Nights. A spherescreen revolved, quietly playing a video clip whose images stuttered along with scratchrap vocals.

Ray Calme, President of New Frontier, knelt on a karate mat, white robe tented about him. Its thong-laced neckline disclosed a scrub of grey chest hair and a tan, corded throat. On his chest, a penphone, a slimline tabulator and other gizmos hung like a *generalissimo*'s medal cluster. The company fortune was founded on pictures like *Gross* and *The Cincinatti Flamethrower Holocaust*, but New Frontier had climbed to mini-major status with franchises: the *Where the Bodies Are Buried* horror films and the *Raptylz* urban youth comedies. Nestled securely in a portfolio of media interests, New Frontier was shooting its wad on hard-edged genre merchandise, to wit: *Shadowstalk*.

There were two others: the haggard bikette with an enormous trollcloud of bleached hair was Ellen Jeanette Sheridan, soon to sign as director of *Shadowstalk*; the fat boy in the one-piece orange skinsuit was Brontis Machulski, the richest teenager

Stuart had met since school. Ellen Jeanette had gone from Metalhead promos to a *Where the Bodies Are Buried* sequel to A-list star vehicles, working with hot comedy and action names. Machulski designed interactive software and had invested his obscene profits by buying into New Frontier (in effect, he was Calme's boss), developing movie projects to tie in with computer games. Synergy was the watchword: a movie might bomb, but the ancillaries (games, merchandizing, spin-off, cable, laser) could turn over major money.

While Calme talked script ideas, Machulski tapped keys on a personal note-pad. He could have been making a shopping list or zapping flying saucers for all Stuart knew. Ellen Jeanette sniffled badly as if she had flu coming. On being introduced to Stuart, she'd offered him a demi-squeeze and told him it was important to stay onstreet if he was to keep his creative *cojones* pumping story sperm. García told him Beverly Hills zonk was so diluted as to be barely illegal.

Machulski had brought *Shadowstalk* to New Frontier. Though Stuart had never got up the nerve to raise it, he was sure the kid was also the only person involved who'd *read* the book rather than glanced at coverage. Ellen Jeanette refused to read anything: scripts, treatments, contracts and even personal mail had to be recorded on micro-cassettes she could playback through helmetphones while tooling around the Secure Zones on her "hundred thousand dollar hog", a vintage Harley motorcycle.

Calme had word of last night's escapade from his LAPD fixer. When he commiserated with Stuart, Ellen Jeanette perked interest. Stuart haltingly went through the story, trying to balance the onstreet callousness they expected from the author of *Shadowstalk* with his genuinely conflicted feelings about patrols through the heart of darkness. Much as he hated to say it, he felt it was equipping him to write better, if not this script then the next book.

"Hung up like meat?" Ellen Jeanette squirmed, "*Guh-ross!*"

"I saw that footage on *CrimiNews*, Channel 187," Machulski said. "The kid looked like he'd been crucified, with his arms stuck out."

Machulski's arms rose as if he were pretending to be an aeroplane.

"We should get *Zonk War* shooting soon, Ray," Ellen Jeanette told Calme. "Before we're eclipsed by events. The script is nearly whipped. A few more tweaks, and Muldoon will commit."

Muldoon Pezz was a black comedian looking for a serious role. *Zonk War* was a project Ellen Jeanette was more enthusiastic about than *Shadowstalk*.

Calme showed the ad that was going in *Daily Variety* and the *Hollywood Reporter*, announcing that the project was in development. Stuart thought they'd taken artwork from an old *Where the Bodies Are Buried* and retouched it to fit his story. Maybe they would retouch his story to fit the art.

Stuart, almost bursting, asked if anyone had notes on his four page treatment, which they'd all had for three days. Ellen Jeanette pinched her nose and looked out of the panoramic window. Calme admitted his reader hadn't finished going through the document yet. Machulski pressed a button on his gadget and a tickertape chittered out in a coil. His comments were about the game, which demanded a multiplicity of scenarios, rather than the film, which needed a single plot. One thing about the game business was that no script draft was ever discarded, it simply became another path the player could take through the maze of the story.

"Know this," Calme began, "English is a minority language in the Los Angeles school system. I've had to send my kids to some rich brat academy so they don't come home spieling Spanish. I mean, it's snazz they can talk to the maid, but it's getting so they can't talk to me. Sometimes, I feel like the last white man in my neighbourhood."

Calme realized what he had said and swallowed. Stuart was fed up with having to speak for an entire race, anyway. The British reviewers had gone on about his blackness, and his publishers tried to make him seem a lot more onstreet than he actually felt. Whenever he was profiled in the press, his parents would chide him for trying to come on like a tough kid from a broken home, battering a word-processor because it was either that or push zonk.

"It's what *Shadowstalk* should have," Calme continued, recovering. "The sense of *threat* of the *barrio*, the way it swallows the city, dragging it down. Like a monster, like a disease. You know now why they call it the Jungle, Stuart. It's a great image, the jungle getting thicker, growing over everything, everyone. That's what I love about this project, the chance to say something about the way the city is going. We're not after Academy Awards, but maybe we can make a difference."

"Look," Ellen Jeanette said, suddenly, "isn't that pretty."

Columns of pink and blue smoke jetted towards the sun-screens and swooped down again like the exhaust trails of an invisible jet. Calme was aghast. He talked into a gizmo.

"Tansey, shut off the a-c and seal the building. They're gassing again."

Stuart looked out of the window, down at the Square. Everything was blurry and silent. The goons wore snoutlike masks now and were spreading coloured smoke over the protesters, who shook and fell as if speaking in tongues. Millennium people fled, or produced mouth-and-nose breathers from inside robes. Some of the protesters were hauled out, twitching but manageable, and piled onto an electric cart like an old-fashioned milkfloat. The large woman with the petition could hold her breath long enough to fight back and had to be stunned with a palm-touch, then have her wrists plastic-noosed behind her back. The petition clipboard probably got lost in the melée.

"I wish they'd find the goddamned Disappeared and get those harpies off our necks," Calme said. "It's the third time this month. There ought to be a law."

Stuart's eyes followed the smoke as it pooled around the writhing protesters, layering pastel over black.

VIII From the *Corrido* of Diego

"Chispa del Oro was like any other mining camp. It was strung out along the banks of a creek, where men, women and children panned for sparkles among the sands.

"It was an hour before true sun-down. I was at the creek, circling the grit in water, holding my *batea* up to the light, hoping the last red rays would coax a gleam my eyes had missed. As the moon neared the underside of the horizon, my sight changed. The water swirled heavily, like quicksilver.

"Fox crept up on Diego. At first, there had been pain with the moonchange. Now I could pull on Fox as easily as one pulls on a cloak. If I concentrated, Diego could resist Fox and pass a moon night in human form, if with considerable discomfort.

"I had a woman and children, then. At least one of the children, the youngest, was mine. The baby boy's elder brothers were fathered by a man who had been killed, one of numberless Joaquins. The woman, Julietta, was part-Indian, like almost all of us. She loved Fox but lived with Diego, even became fond of him. She came to me because I killed the men who murdered her true husband. I marked them with my zig-zag-zig.

"A trickle of gold was coming in and I fed my family. In evenings when there was no moon, I would listen to Julietta play the flute with another woman who played the guitar. This was all a man could want; I wished to grow old and die like others, mourned by my children ...

"Diego could almost pretend Fox had fled. Except on moon nights. Mostly, then, I hunted rabbits.

"One of my son's brothers pulled at my sleeve and pointed. The creek ran through a valley, washing gold down from the mountains. Up on the lip of the valley were seven white men, five or horses. Chispa del Oro had no problems with *anglos*. We were too removed from the big strikes, our yield was too meagre. We panned mainly for placer, the thin sand from which gold could be distilled only with more patience and skill than most *anglos* could summon.

"With the red of the dying sun behind them, the seven men were shadow figures. But I saw their faces as blobs of gloomy light. I told the boy to fetch a gun. He was barely ten yards from me when a bloody gobbet exploded in the back of his neck. One man had a long rifle, and was a fine shot with it.

"I stood, howling my rage and felt a *push* in my chest, the force spinning me off my feet. I dropped my *batea* and fell backwards into the creek. Water ran all around me, soaking through my clothes, trailing my hair away from my face.

"The horsemen passed me, cold shadows washing across my face.

" 'Greaser ain't kilt,' one said.

" 'I allus has to finish your leavin's,' another replied, voice close.

"A man knelt over me, face upside-down over mine. The glow on his skin was so bright I couldn't make out his features. A shining blade passed below my chin, cutting. I choked blood out through the hole in my neck.

" 'A clean job, Hendrik,' the rifleman said. 'Crick'll bleed him dry 'fore sun-down.'

" 'Clean and quiet,' said Hendrik.

"I lay still, hearing and feeling, unable to move. The current kept open the throat wound. Water streamed in as if through the gills of a fish, gulping out of my mouth.

"Hendrik stood up and doffed his wide hat. From inside his placket shirt, he produced a hood which he slipped over his head. Ragged scarecrow eyeholes shone like candleflames in the night. All were hooded now, night-riders.

" 'Gotta run them greasers off,' someone said. 'They dirty up the crick. Dang Meskins.'

"The night-riders moved on. In time, I heard more shots, and whoops, and the slow crackle of fire."

"The moon rose, and the hole in my throat closed. Fox slipped out of Diego's wet clothes and padded towards Chispa del Oro.

"The shacks were ablaze, casting a circle of light. The dead lay in heaps. Fray Juniperro, our *gambussino* priest, was slumped dead on his knees, bleeding from the gashes in the side of his head. His ears had been cut off. Juan Ochoa, who had fled North from Santa Anna's soldiers, was several times gutshot and dying slowly. The night-riders had staked out my Julietta and torn her clothes. They took turns to violate her.

"Fox leaped from the dark and closed daggered fingers in the throat of a man who was holding a firebrand. I threw him at the feet of the others. With a clawed swipe, I stripped a zig-zag-zig of skin from the side of one of the horses, exposing ribs and vitals. The beast neighed and collapsed, gore gouting around my ankles.

"Pistols were discharged into my chest and I felt mosquito stings. I tore the hooded head off the man who knelt between Julietta's legs, working with his bowie knife. My woman had been dead for minutes. I crushed the head like a rotten grapefruit.

" 'Well, if it ain't a weirdwoof,' Hendrik said, calm.

"I killed two others and howled, the blood of my kills bubbling in my throat. I had meat scraps between my teeth.

"One of the night-riders was down on his knees praying and sobbing and tearing at his hood. I grasped his chest with my feet, crushing ribs with my barbs, and I ate out his eyes, chewing through the cloth of his hood.

" 'Look at him *feed*,' said Hendrik.

"Only Hendrik and the man with the rifle still stood. The rifleman was tamping powder in the barrel. His hood was up over his nose, a powderhorn dangled by a string from his mouth. I stood up, flexing my limbs and growling.

"The rifleman was a cool hand. He got a ball into his weapon and packed it down, then brought the gun up and pointed it at me. I laid a hand on the barrel and held its aperture to my forehead. With my animal's snarling mouth, I called him an accursed *gringo*, a killer of women and children, a man with no honour . . .

"He fired and the ball flattened against my skull. I smelled the singe of my furred face, but felt no pain.

"The rainbow ecstasy of killing was on me.

"I made a hole in his head with my thumb, then jammed his powder-horn into the hole and held his head in one of the fires. The explosion was satisfying, scenting the air with burned powder and blood.

"I dropped the rifleman's body and looked at Hendrik. He was clapping, slowly.

" 'Savage critter, ain't ye?'

"As I bounded towards him, he slipped off his hood. His eyes still glowed, but his skin was rough and dark, angry fur swarming across his face.

"I must have frozen in the air.

" 'What be matter, fox. Ain't ye never met a wolf afore?'

"Hendrik's mouth was misshaping as teeth crowded out of it. As his body expanded, his clothes split along their seams. Bony knives burst through the fingers of his gloves. I howled and threw myself at him, tearing and gouging and rending. Powerful claws ripped my hide.

"We fought to the death, only neither of us could die.

"Hendrik chewed clean through my shoulder until one arm was hanging off on a thread of gristle. I wrestled his jaw free of the skull, yanking it to one side. We both healed within minutes, struggling still.

"Hendrik was a bigger beast than I, and master of the creature he became. Finally, he bested and humiliated me. He ground my face into dirt soaked with the blood of my woman, and sprayed me with a jet of thick piss. I smelled him on me for years.

"At sun-up, we both changed. The killing frenzy was gone from me, though daylight disclosed more atrocities done my family and my people. My baby son hung from a post by his ankle.

"Hendrik and I didn't talk, but we sat opposite each other in the burned village. I heard the rushing of the stream and the settling of the embers.

" 'I'm sorry for ye, greaser, that I am,' Hendrik said, before leaving. 'I've got what I've got and it's my way, but you've got the *curse* ...'

"Still, I didn't understand."

IX

"And this baby is the Leveller," said Muldoon Pezz. "State-of-the-art all-in-one burpgun, grenade launcher and flamethrower. An ideal Riot Weapon."

The comedian, whose sculpted hair made his head look like a sugar loaf mountain, hefted the Leveller and posed with it. His arm disappeared entirely inside the weapon. He might be auditioning for *Black Terminator*.

Stuart looked into his half-coconut of fruit-filled exotic alcohol as guests oohed and ahhed over the array of gleaming steel deathware. He had thought the guns and knives mounted on the display wall were movie props, but Pezz was eager to explain how real they were.

"Is that loaded?" gasped Leitizia Six, the coffee-skin starlet. She was stapled into a brief flame-red dress.

"What the use of a gun that ain't loaded, child?"

Pezz shimmie-jerked with his metal partner, hip-thrusting at the girl. He wore a leather codpiece, decorated with a sequinned roaring lion, over a pair of the baggily diaphanous harem pants popular (and costly) this year. He made a dakka-dakka-dakka sound and raked imaginary death at his laughing guests.

Welcome to the Black Pack, Stuart thought.

This was the Ethnic Elite: scratchrappers, foulmouth comics, Spike Lee or Wesley Snipes gottabes, colour-coded execs, MC-DJ alpha beta soupers, lower echelon politicos, transvestite TV anchors. Instead of eye candy, the party had chocolate drops, like Leitizia Six. It was impossible not to imagine five earlier Leitizias who hadn't worked out so well.

Stuart wandered out of the gun room into a sunken area where a jacuzzi full of young black writer-directors waiting for their first credits passed around a smoky crystal ball. They sucked the ball's nipples and described projects, competing yarns of how onstreet the hoods they'd left behind were.

The wri-dies wore nothing but gold: necklaces, bracelets, armlets, cock-rings, nose-plugs, belts. Extras from a black porn *Cleopatra*.

"Homes," shouted the wri-die of *Mama Was a Crack Ho*, "get in on the bubbles, man. Anyone can write *Shudderslash* and get out of the hood has earned bubbles."

Stuart wasn't sure whether the bubbles were in the jacuzzi or the crystal ball. He certainly wouldn't be comfortable stripping to his Marks & Sparks boxers and hanging with this crowd. His worst teenage experiences had been on a rugby pitch.

"I'll take a rain check," Stuart said, using an expression from his English-American phrase book.

"Don't know what yo missing, my man."

Back in the gun room (which was where people ended up chatting at this party, rather than the kitchen) Pezz was ranting.

When "the next time" came, he'd be onstreet with the Leveller, "protectin my home, my people."

Having missed the set-up, Stuart didn't know whether Pezz would be protecting his people from rioters or cops. One of the wri-dies, who had read a synopsis of *Shadowstalk*, shoved him in a corner and preached at him for quarter of an hour: Stuart had to change his hero from a cop to a gangsta. "The cop is the natural-born enemy of the black man, Finn. We gotta stop makin cops heroes."

The wri-die got sidetracked by a diatribe against all the performers who had sold out to the man by playing cop heroes: Poitier, Whoopi, Murphy, Washington. The wri-die was rapping along to "Cop Killer" when someone reminded him Ice-T played a cop in *New Jack City*.

Pezz was weighed down with more weapons. Chocolate drops draped him with guns as if he were a terrorist Christmas Tree. Stuart had seen *Pixie Patrol*, Pezz's last hit, and not thought much of it. His catch-phrase was "*bitch, fuck* that *shit!*", also the title of his best-selling comedy CD and scratchrap single. Pezz played a cop in *Pixie Patrol*; he maliciously thought of mentioning it to the wri-die on the next pass around.

Now Pezz was completely tooled up – his display case was empty, and he was *wearing* all his weapons – he wanted to party. One of the girlies, a bald freeway shaved through her hair, climbed up on a stool with an eye-dropper and squeezed fluid-smidgens into both his eyes.

Stuart didn't think zonking up a walking armoury was too clever. Pezz yelled encouragement and jiggled his guns, clanking like a junk-cart. Sooner or later, he was going to go off. If he wasn't too zonked, he'd do it in the yard because this was his house; if he *was* too zonked, he could afford to replace a ceiling or a wall. Maybe even a guest.

"Yez hear about the time Muldoon dropped a frag grenade in Mike Ovitz's swimming pool?" Leitizia asked.

Leitizia was very friendly whenever Stuart got near. She was the star of the *Velvet* series of "erotic thrillers", rated NC-17 on the top shelf at a video store near you. In his blazer pocket,

Stuart had Leitizia's card: it was plastic with a chip set into it that breathed her name and number when caressed.

Last night: a garage full of dead kids. Now: swimming pools, movie stars. Los Angeles was disorienting. Mood Change City.

"Stuart Finn?" said a young man with goldwire-rimmed glasses.

As they shook hands, Stuart realized the young man wore surgeon's gloves. He'd seen that in the last few days. It was a health fad, ANSC: Absolutely No Skin Contact.

"Ouesmene Collins," he said.

Leitizia's scarlet-tipped fingers slipped up and down Stuart's shirt buttons. He had the idea she *believed* in skin contact.

"I'm with Reality Programming, Channel 187. *CrimiNews*. We understand you were at the Obregon Street Crimescene?"

"Obregon Street?"

"The garage."

Stuart knew where Collins meant.

"We're doing a follow-up newsbite, and would like to schedule an interview."

Collins spoke in a monotone and had no expression. Stuart thought he was squirmy.

"I'm afraid I signed a contract with LAPD," Stuart shrugged. "One of the conditions of my ridealong is that I not discuss anything with the media."

"Indeed. But there are ways around contracts."

"I've another five nights to go," he said, looking at his watch. "In fact, I should be leaving. The patrol starts at midnight."

"There are serious questions about Obregon Street," Collins continued, intent. "Ryu has stated that there are no concrete suspicions."

Something warm and wet slipped into Stuart's ear. Leitizia's tongue. He'd waited twenty-three years for this and now had to skip out. Would the Velvet Vulva, as she introduced *herself*, "take a rain check"?

"It was the van, surely," Stuart said. "The men in the van."

"What van?"

"The black van leaving the garage."

"There's no van in the reports."

"Ouesmene," Leitizia purred out of the side of her mouth, "disappear, would you."

Collins, still thinking *van*, vanished.

"You British guys," Leitizia said, "you've just got *it*."

A tiny thought (shouldn't have mentioned the van: *contract violation*) shrivelled in his mind. Other thoughts loomed larger, more pressing.

"Yo," shouted Pezz, "Velvet Vulva, all the waayyyy!"

One of his smaller guns went off, putting a thumb-hole dent in the wall. Everybody laughed.

Stuart made excuses.

X From the *Corrido* of Diego

"If I could change, others must too. I was not greatly surprised to learn I was not the only creature of my kind. The old stories had come from somewhere. But what Hendrik said about a *curse* disturbed me greatly. I realized I did not understand my condition. Then again, who among us can say he fully understands his condition?

"Maybe ten years later, I crossed trails with a wagon train. Its cargo was women: mail order brides for California miners, paid-for wombs to yield a harvest of *anglo* babies. Many were from far corners of Europe. Irish, German, Dutch, Hungarian. Gypsy, even. Few spoke English, let alone Spanish.

"For a while, I rode with the wagon-master. It was a harsh trail, across a desert that burned by day and froze by night. There was disease and hardship and privation and accident. As a month passed, I saw a glow growing in the face of one of the trail-hands, who took to what he called 'breaking in' the brides. If the wagon-master hadn't hanged him, I would have killed him.

"Among the women was a Serbian girl who was also a cat, a big cat. From the first I saw her, I knew she could change. Her monthly cycle and mine did not jibe, so Fox never met Cat. In her centuries, Milena had learned languages; this skill made her special, not her ability to change. She was the interpreter, between the women and the trail-hands, and with whoever we chanced across.

"I asked Milena what Hendrik had meant by my *curse*, but she could not help me understand though she thought she understood herself. I knew it was something quite apart from the moon-change, something that marked me as different from the rest of the changing kind.

" 'Men call us the creatures of darkness,' Milena explained, 'and they have good reason. Many, perhaps most, of us are like this Hendrik, animals in human skin. Our place is the dark, our strength is the night. But your strength is the moon. The light of the moon is the light of a sun shining back from a silver mirror. You are a creature of the light, perhaps even a prisoner of the light. I hunt where I will, for cats know no rules. The path you walk is narrow and lonely, for you must always hunt the evil in men, must always protect your people. Yet you can never be truly with your people, for you change. I do not envy you, Diego, and yet I accept that you are better than I, perhaps better than us all.'

"Soon after, I killed a German woman without knowing why. Her face had glowed like a ghost-flame, as sickly and bright as the face of the worst ravager or tyrant I had ever slaughtered. It turned out the woman had stifled two of her children and taken their water rations for herself. During the desert crossing, a dozen women died who might have been saved by a few drops of water.

"The wagon-master said the woman must have been mauled to death by a mountain lion or a coyote. Gypsies and Hungarians muttered that they knew better. I left the next night, racing off as Fox.

"Later I heard a tall tale about a wagon train who turned on one of their womenfolk and skinned her alive to prove her hide was furred on the inside."

XI

"Got another high concept, man," García said. "This cop becomes a Mexican wrestling star, *El Demonio Azul*, and goes undercover ..."

A whining shriek cut through García's movie idea, the public address system's way of saying "Listen Up". The cops in the locker room all looked to the wall-screen. Like all public buildings in LA, the police station had its own interactive TV station, narrowcasting from a top floor studio suite. There were commercials: cop insurance and pension schemes, special bilingual coaching for promotion boards, holiday-camp descriptions of faraway stations that needed personnel to transfer in, new brands of body armour. Then the sergeant of the watch, outlined in frizzy blue against a blurry slo-mo explosion, gave a cop news round-up.

Mug-shots flashed by. Scotchman paid attention, nodding slightly at each face he recognized. The sergeant downloaded new charges to his patrol teams: some players were climbing, from rape to armed robbery to murder one; others were slipping down the leagues, narco beefs diminishing as they lost territory to the comers.

"As a result of last night's Obregon Street incident, the Caldiarres are Off The Board," the sergeant announced, to general cheers. What looked like home video footage of the garage came on, the camera circling around the hanging boy. Arms outstretched and head hung, he did look as if he had been crucified. A crude computer graphic represented the angry face Stuart had seen on the dead boys' jackets, and a big black X crossed through it. "This investigation is closed. Chief Ryu has commended the officers on the scene for the speedy mop-up."

ID photos of García and Scotchman appeared in an iris, and cops gathered to josh the patrol team.

"They found the van?" Stuart asked.

"What van?" García said, fighting off a hug-happy *hermano*.

"The black van," Stuart insisted, feeling dumb. Something about Obregon Street was nagging the edge of his mind. "From last night, remember?"

"Didn't see no van, man," García said, eyes swiveling towards an angling security camera. Its directional mikes could pick up what he was saying, but his face was out of shot. García shook his eyes from side to side.

Stuart gathered he should drop the subject.

★   ★   ★

Plenty of people wore sunglasses at night, especially those who also carried white canes. But this blind girl was waving a snub-nosed pistol. Far less aesthetically stimulating than anything on Muldoon Pezz's wall, it could still put a dent in a person. García yanked the gun out of her paw and whipped the heavy glasses from the suspect's eyes. They were red marbles, with tiny yellow irises like pus in pimples.

This one was far gone, a tertiary zonkbrain.

The girl's friends backed off and let the officers make an arrest. They were piling out of a club in the Jungle, having made enough trouble to prompt a call to the cops. Probably, they'd just run out of money and the management dropped the dime to bring round the garbage collectors.

Through windows as thin as arrow-slits, strobe-lights pulsed. A band named Dire Tribe did a scratchrap take on "Heart Attack and Vine". A sumo wrestler in combat armour barred the door, watching García and Scotchman take care of business.

When Scotchman shoved the zonkbrain against the patrol car and pulled disposable cuffs from his belt, the penny dropped. Stuart realized what bothered him about Obregon Street.

The zonkbrain, mad eyes leaking blood, twisted and kicked out blindly. She wore a ra-ra skirt and combat boots. Scotchman got out of the way of the kick and jabbed his stun-stick into her side. There was a crackle and the smell of ozone. She was so zonked she didn't feel the charge.

"The Caldiarre in the garage was cuffed," Stuart said aloud, recalling the horror-flash image. "His arms were fixed over his head. In the news footage, his arms are loose, stuck out like a scarecrow's. Someone uncuffed him."

"Case closed," García said. "Don't think on it, man."

García waded in and pummeled the zonkbrain. He took her head by a beaded scalplock and slammed it against the hood of the car. The fight went out of her. Scotchman got his ratcheted plastic noose around the perp's wrists and pulled tight. It would have to be clipped off with special shears.

Some clean-up cop must have cut the cuffs in Obregon Street. They were disposable, so they'd been disposed of.

The zonkbrain's boyfriend stood back, astonished but not appalled. He seemed to find it all quite entertaining. Struggling with the cuffs, she fell in a fetal ball, leaking foam. The sidewalk where she twitched was patterned with overlapped and faded spray-paint body outlines.

"Too far gone for detox," García said as she rolled into a gutter clogged with concaved zonk squeezers, take-out food McLitter, and empty shell cases. Scotchman helped the girl stand and wiped off her mouth.

The boyfriend laughed and left at a run, taking off with his buddies for the next club. Some night, it would be him dribbling strawberry froth on the sidewalk.

Why would cops cut the cuffs? Because *cuffs* meant *cops*?

Cops covered cops, that was the first thing Stuart had seen onstreet: Scotchman distracting him while García popped pills. García was right: he shouldn't think about it, he'd only get his brain hurt.

A combat ambulance arrived. Zonkbrains fell between offender and casualty, and rated secure hospital facilities. A Paramedic, a Chinese guy in dark coveralls, hit the street.

"Why the camouflage?" Stuart asked.

"Whites make too good a target," the Paramedic said.

García helped the Paramedic sling the zonkbrain in the back. Scotchman threw her white cane and dark glasses in after her.

As the ambulance turned a corner, Stuart noticed it was the same model vehicle as the van on Obregon Street, jungle-striped rather than dead black.

The sumo guardian looked up at the sky, weary shoulders weighted down by armourpads.

"It's always like this in the Jungle when the moon is full," he said. "It gets to their rotted brains. Moonlight is like a drug."

"Gone quiet back there, Stuey? What's going down?"

Stuart was thinking hard. He couldn't help it; in his mind, he was putting together a jigsaw. The picture that emerged was scary, but he couldn't stop himself from fitting in the pieces.

They were driving down a well-lit strip. There were clubs and allnight shops. Pedestrians wandered onstreet, drifting between cars.

The banner with the names of the Disappeared of Los Angeles. Copissue cuffs on the Caldiarre kid. A garage full of dead zonk dealers. The closed investigation. A van so black it fades into the night.

There were shots in the night. García sighed.

Every time Stuart turned on the television in his hotel, Chief Ryu was talking about the War on Zonk. Ryu reminded him of Gomez Addams, a shark-smiling little man in pinstripes. Mayor Jute was always behind the Chief, voting more funds to special Zonk Task Forces.

Stuart wasn't thinking Task Force. He was thinking *Death Squad*.

"Fuckin' Jungle," Scotchman said, hitting the brakes.

A car was overturned in the street. A couple of kids with guns crouched behind it, dodging and returning fire from a low rooftop.

A slug spanged against the windscreen, but didn't shatter the armoured glass. The shot came from the roof faction.

"Shoot 'em in the brain," Scotchman muttered, unslinging a pump-action shotgun. He got out of the car, bent low, and ran across the street. García radioed for back-up.

Scotchman straightened and fired at the roof, not apparently aiming at anything in particular.

García finished his call-in.

"This time, man, stay here. Hollywood can't afford to lose you. Needs all the talent it can get."

García drew his Colt Python and slipped out of the side door.

García and Scotchman didn't come back. Stuart heard gunfire, shouts and sirens. The patrol car's radio crackled, but no messages came through. He shifted on the squeaky seats and thought of the Disappeared, remembering crowd control smoke settling on the protesters in Millennium Plaza.

If, for some reason Stuart couldn't fathom, you *wanted* Millennium Plaza, you had to have the Jungle as well. It was how the city worked. All the folks at Muldoon Pezz's party were standing on the backs and heads of the onstreet scavengers who scuttled away when the shooting started. If Pezz stepped out into a riot, even toting his precious Leveller, he would last about seven seconds before someone drew a bead on his unprotected hairstyle and pre-empted his last punchline. And Stuart Finn didn't kid himself he was any fitter to survive out in Darwin City.

The street was clear now, as if cordoned off to be a movie set. The skirmish had shifted. García and Scotchman must be in pursuit. Everyone else had made a policy decision to get out of the way.

Stuart had enough background for his script now, and wanted to go home. He could work in Bath and fax the pages to New Frontier. The council might complain about the spare change brigade, but even the rabid right didn't suggest rounding them up and putting bullets through their eyes.

A pebble-tap hit the window near his head, startling him. He looked out and saw a black-uniformed cop chest. A gauntleted hand made a beckoning motion.

Stuart was puzzled, then realized he was invited to get out of the car. He nodded, and pushed the door. It wouldn't give. There was a green light on the inside handle. Like a London taxi, the rear doors could be locked from the dashboard. To prevent prisoners making a break. Last night, in Obregon Street, the lock hadn't been on; that was how he had been able to wander into the garage and see what he shouldn't have seen.

He shrugged an apology at the uniform. The green light cut out and the door pulled open. The lock was overriden by remote control. Stuart stepped out and looked into a silver-visored crash helmet. His own face was fish-eye reflected. Other uniforms, García's back-up, stood about. They wore no insignia, just black jump-suits and crash helmets. Stuart could tell they were cops by the gizmo-weighted belts. And the walk, the stand, the attitude. Actors couldn't fake that.

Stuart pointed in the direction that García and Scotchman had taken off. The uniform shook his helmet and laid a gauntlet on Stuart's shoulder, then spun him around to face the patrol car.

Something bit Stuart's right wrist, like the jaws of a dog, and he heard a familiar rasp. He was being cuffed.

Over the top of the car he saw the black van the uniforms had come in and his knees became water. He fell down before the uniform could cuff his other wrist, and realized he was yelping.

He was a writer, not some hero. He was not going to survive. He would be one of the Disappeared.

Still squealing, he shrank and writhed under the car. He shut his eyes, but nothing changed. He saw boots. Other boots joined them. There was a buzz of communication.

They were being cautious, Stuart realized. He hadn't been searched so no one wanted to lie down and take a shot in case he was nestling his own gun, ready to hole a visor. The patrol car weighed a few tons, so they couldn't lift it. By accident or instinct, he had gone to ground.

Something small and white had fallen out of his pocket and lay on the gritty asphalt next to his cheek. It was Leitizia Six's card. It recited Leitizia's name, address, phone and fax, representation and major credits.

He raised his head and banged it against the underside of the car. Pain jammed through his skull.

Those cop bastards had set him up for this. García and Scotchman. How was that for high concept? That wri-die was right: the cop was the natural enemy of the black man, even a black man who'd been to public school and wasn't in the least onstreet or zonkbrained or even bloody American.

Boots shifted, heels clicking on the street. He heard the car door opening. The floor was armoured, so they couldn't shoot through it. This moment, he was turtle safe. It wouldn't last. They could pour petrol in the street and drop a match.

Maybe his Dad would be like Jack Lemmon in *Missing*, and bust the LA Death Squad story in a fit of grief-stricken political outrage. It didn't seem likely, though.

The engine engaged, loud near his head. They were going to drive a few yards and expose him to the air, like lifting a rock off a worm. He twisted to look at his feet. Moonlight fell on them as the car moved. He pulled in his hand so his fingers wouldn't be squashed under a wheel and banged his elbow on armour-plate.

Lying like an animal, extremities tucked in, he waited for bullets. The boots stood around, in a circle, examining him. He looked up black-clad legs, past weapon-heavy belts to flak-armoured chests and expressionless silver screens.

He remembered the boy in Obregon Street, who had seemed crucified. Suddenly, he prayed for a bullet. The alternative was to be hung up and worked on.

One of the squad popped a stud in his helmet and pulled it off. He was young, of indeterminate race, with long hair tied back.

"I always like to be face to face," he said.

XII From the *Corrido* of Diego

"This city grew, encompassing the village of my birth, spreading fingers across the state. Wherever I wandered, I would find myself back in Los Angeles.

"In 1919, my *corrido* caught up with me.

"I was fighting still, striking owners of canning factories and fruit orchards who treated my people as cruelly as any of the *patrónes* of old. Indeed, many were far worse: with a superfluity of labour, wastage was acceptable. If a union organizer was whipped or an overworked family starved, there were many in line for the job vacancies.

"It was the year of the Great Influenza Epidemic. In a few months, a disease cut down more of my people than the worst sweatshop tyrant could in a lifetime. And what could I do? I could not kill a disease.

"For ninety years, I killed the enemies of my people. But I was alone. The tide of death swept around me, rushing faster. I recognized how little I could do, but each moon night I fought harder, killed more.

"That year, I left my zig-zag-zig in scores of hides."

"As grapes ripened, itinerant pickers gathered and were signed up for work. I was among their number. We moved into shanty towns near the vineyards, dormitory shacks.

"During the harvest, I found a magazine under my cot at the dormitory, left by one of the few *anglos* who worked the vineyards. It was *All Story Weekly*, and it contained the third instalment of "The Curse of Capistrano", a serial by Johnston McCulley.

"The action was laid in an Old California that never was, a scramble of different times: the time of the mission, the time of Mexican rule, the time of the Gold Rush.The hero of this idiotic fiction was Don Diego de la Vega, a young noble who masked himself and rode as a renegade. This defender of maidenly virtue and justice called himself Zorro, the Fox. In this Zorro, I heard echoes of Joaquin Murieta and Salomon Pico. But in his mark, carved elegantly with the point of a blade rather than slashed with a claw, I saw myself.

"As a people, we tell stories and sing songs. Nothing happens which does not become a story or a song. I had plainly crept into these legends, and in retelling they had seeped through to this *anglo* writer. I do not know where McCulley heard of the zig-zag-zig.

"I was shocked for a moment, but assumed this obscure story would pass and be forgotten. It was, as even I could judge, not very good."

"The next year, I was running. For the first time, the night-work of Fox was not written off as that of an animal. The name of Diego came up in police investigations, and my description circulated to Pinkertons in the pay of those I killed.The science of the century nipped at my heels.

"I took shelter in the centre of the growing city. In the old district around the fresh, new railroad station. Many thronged to California, looking for work in motion pictures. Cowboys and beauty queens paraded the streets, hoping to be discovered. Thousands had been employed by D.W. Griffith for *Intolerance*, whose sets still dominated a backlot.

"In a mission (at last, I had returned to the world of my father), I heard a film company was looking for men of my people.They paid up to fifty cents a day.

"Between moons I need to eat as anyone else, so I turned up at the United Artists studio. A crowd of red-headed Irishmen and cornfed Swedes were all shouting *caramba* and *arriba* at the tops of their voices. With many others, I was picked as an 'extra' in the new Douglas Fairbanks picture.

"On my first day, I was singled out as a 'type' by an assistant director in knickerbockers and a knit cap. A costume was found for me, a carnival parody of the dress of the *ricos*, and a moustache gummed to my lip. I was given a hat and a sword and sent to the set.

"These films are now called silent pictures, but the studio was noisier than a factory or battlefield. The air rang with the din of construction, the rattle of cameras, the shouting of directors, the chatter of extras and the boom of powder-puff explosions. Instrumental combos competed and clashed, supplying "mood music" for scenes of love, violence, tragedy and comedy.

"The Fairbanks set represented an Old California *hacienda* or some such nonsense. Doug, as he was called by all, appeared – a notably diminutive hero, which explained why many taller men as qualified by looks as myself were unable to secure employment on his set. He was dressed in black, with a mask and a broad hat.

"Short and tubby as he was, Doug Fairbanks was a hero who looked like a hero. His face, I was relieved to say, did not glow unnaturally. I have never killed anyone famous, which may account for my longevity.

"In the scene being shot under the blazing arc-lights, Doug fought a villainous officer (a type I remembered too well) to a stand-still, humiliating his defeated opponent by leaving a sword-mark on the man's neck.

"After the fight was filmed several times, a make-up man came on set and worked on the actor who played the dastardly officer. I stood nearby, momentarily fascinated as the make-up man drew in and elaborated a fresh scar. He stood back to admire his handiwork. Doug came over and grinned famously at the wound he was supposed to have inflicted.

"It was a zig-zag-zig. *My* zig-zag-zig.

" 'What's the name of this picture?' I asked another 'extra'.

" '*The Mark of Zorro*,' I was told."

XIII

The breath was forced out of Stuart's lungs as the killer cop knelt on Stuart's chest, padded knee coming down hard. He slipped a knife from a sheath on his utility belt. Its serrated blade shone silver in moonlight.

The knife would be the last thing Stuart ever saw.

He had published a novel. That was something. A year ago, he'd have said he could die happy after the achievement.

The cop raised the knife for a backhand slash. At the top of the arc, he paused for the briefest instant.

He would have liked to have had sex.

Stuart forced himself to look not at the blade but into the eyes of his murderer. He saw nothing.

"Any last thoughts, nigger?"

This was one time he wouldn't think of the right thing to say twenty minutes after the moment passed.

Then, in a rush, the weight was off him. An animal – a big dog? – barreled out of nowhere and struck the cop in the side, wrenching him off Stuart, carrying him across the street and sidewalk. They crashed against the chain-link shutters of a pawnshop.

Under the three ball sign, the animal dropped the cop and trampled with barbed feet. There were scatters of blood.

Stuart sat up, too astonished to hurt. The Death Squad stood about, stunned. The animal moved too swiftly for the mind to develop the eye's photographs. It wasn't a dog, it wasn't a man.

It picked up the cop by the throat and rammed him against the pawnshop shutter. The cop's boots dangled inches above the sidewalk. A sharp thumb gored into his neck. Blood squirted like juice from an orange.

With its free hand – it was more hand than paw, long fingers tipped with horny razors – the animal tore its prey's flak-jacket out through his uniform, exposing a white torso, hairless and untattooed. With three passes of its hand, it left a mark.

Zig-zag-zig.

The animal squeezed harder, and the cop's head popped off his spine. The creature dropped its kill.

The Death Squad brought up firearms and emptied them into the animal. It jitter-slammed against the shutter, explosions bursting against stiff, red fur. Stuart's ears were assaulted by the intolerable blurt of close-up gunfire. Forgotten, he pulled himself to his feet.

He should run.

... but he needed to see what happened next.

After a continuous burst of co-ordinated fire, the Death Squad shut off the bullet-spray to examine their kill.

Hey man, should've seen the beast we brought down last night. Freak must've got loose from a zoo or something ...

The animal still stood, scorched and smoking. Its ragged clothes were holed and afire. But it wasn't dead, didn't seem even to be hurt.

Stuart looked at its eyes. It was not an animal, not entirely.

"Take a head-shot," someone ordered.

A rifle came up, and a red dot wavered against the beast-man's forehead. There was a bone-snap as the rifle discharged.

"On the button."

There was a blackened patch above the thatch of darker eyebrow fur, but the eyes were still alive.

"Mother ..."

The hunter pushed away from the pawnshop, and attacked. Besides the dead killer, there were seven men in the squad. Within twenty seconds, they were all dead or dying.

Stuart couldn't look away. The hunter was fast and sure, a graceful yet deadly dancer. Smooth muscle shifted under a thick pelt. Eyes, teeth and claws shone silver. A red veil splattered across silver.

Several cops got off more shots. Others tried to get away. It was all useless. Uniforms came apart. Screams bubbled through cracked helmets. Limbs wrenched from trunks like twigs from branches, ropy coils of gut pulled through claw-holes.

All the dead were marked with the zig-zag-zig.

It was over so quickly Stuart's ears still ached from the gunfire. He had not got used to the fact that he was saved from the descent of the knife.

Saved, but for how long?

The beast-man who had executed the Death Squad rooted on all-fours among his kill, shutting off voices that still moaned. Satisfied, mouth stuffed with flesh, he stood erect and bipedal. Surrounded by dead, this was the ruler of the Jungle. A broad chest inflated and the hunter howled at the moon.

The howl was an animal sound, but the song of a man was mixed in. Stuart knew eyes were looking, from behind shutters, through windows, from alleys. In the Jungle, they knew about the hunter. They just hadn't told the Man.

The hunter's song ended. With sharp nyctalopic eyes, he glanced about the street. Somewhere above, a helicopter's muffled blades cut through thick air. More back-up coming down.

Stuart was against the abandoned patrol car. The hunter looked at him, full mouth curving wickedly, more and more teeth exposed.

Having fought for it, the hunter was entitled to this scrap of food. This time, Stuart was calm before death.

The hunter's mouth grew wider still. The shark-grin was a smile. The whole snouted head shook as the hunter swallowed what he was chewing. He padded towards Stuart, interest in his intelligent eyes.

The eyes were familiar.

Stuart knew the beast-man wasn't going to kill him. This hunter bore down only on those who deserved death.

The hunter was close, now. Stuart saw a human face buried under the animal's skin, and just failed to recognize it. The beast-man breathed heavily through his snout. He reached out to touch Stuart's face. Stuart saw a leathery, hairless palm; short, ruffled bristles running down each finger; polished, sharp oval knife-nails.

The hunter laid his hand against Stuart's face. Stuart tried not to flinch. They looked at each other, each seeing something.

The beast-man pulled away, almost whirling in the air. He extended a long, clawed forefinger and etched a swift zig-zag-zig into the roof of the patrol car, then bounded away.

Stuart was alone on the street with eight torn and bleeding corpses.

A wave of people appeared and swept across the street, descending on the dead squad like vultures. The black van was hot-wired and driven off. Bodies were stripped of guns, knives, radios, flak-jackets, boots, belts, everything. Stuart was manhandled away from the patrol car, and five young men with gang colours and power tools got to work on it, disassembling the vehicle like a factory team in reverse motion.

He stumbled through the carrion-stripping crowd, thinking of the eyes of the beast-man. For him, the world had changed; he shared the earth with creatures of wonder and moonlight.

A helicopter lowered, and light brighter than the sun raked across the street. Stuart's eyes stung as if he stared into a nuclear fireball. A call-to-attention signal whined.

Someone fired single shots at the huey, which responded with a rain of strafing. Holes pocked in the asphalt, puncturing legs and vehicles, as a chaingun raked the crowd.

Stuart remembered Muldoon Pezz's apocalypse talk. And the negro spiritual quoted by James Baldwin.

"God gave Noah the rainbow sign,
No more water, the fire next time …"

Things were moving too fast to keep up.

"LAPD," announced a robocop voice from the huey. "Cease and desist …"

The helicopter touched down daintily between bodies. Cops hit the street, firing indiscriminately …

"Cease and desist …"

This time, Stuart ran.

XIV From the *Corrido* of Diego

" 'Hoy, *pachuco*,' I was greeted outside the bar.

"Miguel Ynostrosa whirled down the boulevard, dancing as much as walking, pleated pants flapping. He wore 'drapes': high-waisted pants with loose legs and tight cuffs; wide-brimmed hat with a velvet band; jacket a yard across at the shoulders, cinched tight in the middle; a loop of watchchain; pointed-toes and highly polished shoes.

"My outfit was no less outlandish. We were both zoot-suiters. I raised my hand to receive the slap of greeting.

" 'Papers come through, Diego,' he said. 'You lookin at a private, first class.'

"Everybody was enlisting. I wondered if there was a way round my lack of birth papers. Throats in Berlin and Tokyo which would be the better for Fox's attention. I had always been a lone predator. It was probable I could not survive unnoticed in the services.

" 'Maybe soon you're lookin at a *seriente*,'Ynostrosa grinned.

"He was a good kid, an epitome of *pachucismo* but with a streak of the political. We met collecting for the Sleepy Lagoon Defence Fund.

"To be young and have a Spanish surname in the early '40s was to be branded a gangster by the yellow press. When a murder was committed near a swimming hole the Hearst papers tagged 'the Sleepy Lagoon', seventeen youths were convicted. The 'evidence' consisted of confessions beaten out of the defendants. The case was fought through appeal after appeal. What the Scottsboro Boys were to blacks and Sacco and Vanzetti to union men, Sleepy Lagoon was to the *chicano*.

"Roosevelt promised to be a 'Good Neighbour' to Latin Americans abroad, but his policies had no influence with the Los Angeles police, courts and city council.

"We strolled down the boulevard. The bars were full of sailors, in town on leave from the Chavez Ravine Armory. Everyone was waiting to go overseas. The city was bustling to a swing beat. Panicky citizens had been known to imagine Japanese subs in the municipal plunges and bombers over the La Brea Tar Pits.

"Ynostrosa suggested we go to the movie theatre. There was a re-release double bill: *The Mark of Zorro*, with Tyrone Power, and *The Wolf Man*, with Lon Chaney. I'd seen both, but there were always people at the theatre, zoot-suiters and their girls. Afterwards, we could get a crowd together and go to one of the night-clubs that admited coloureds and 'Mexicans'.

"It was early June, a clear night. The breeze smelled of oranges. The moon was past full.

"A sailor slouched at the corner of an alley, dragging on a Lucky, looking up and down the street. I could tell he was look-out. His buddies were probably among the garbage cans with a whore.

"As the sailor saw us, he tossed his butt and looked over his shoulder. There was a faint glow on his face, which shocked me. At this time of the month, my strange sight was at its weakest.

"In the alley, someone was being beaten up. We stopped by the sailor and looked past him. Five of his comrades, caps askew, were beating and kicking a boy who wore a zoot-suit.

"The sailor called; his shipmates left off work and rushed out. We were surrounded by a white wall.

" 'Fuckin' zooters,' the smallest sailor spat.

" 'Zooter' was the 1943 synonym for 'greaser'.

"A zoot-suit was seen by *anglo* service-men as a challenge to uniformed manhood. Unjustifiably, zoot-suiters were reckoned draft-dodgers, seducers of left-behind sweethearts, sons of fascist Spain, black marketeers.

" 'Strip your drapes,' a sailor said, shoving me hard in the chest.

"I snarled, Fox struggling inside me. The moon-time was just past.

" 'Fuckin' animals. Look at the hair-oil on this nance, Costigan.'

" 'Strip your drapes,' Costigan repeated.

"The sailors began to rip our clothes. We fought, but there were reinforcements. Word got into the bars that the Navy was giving zoot-suit hoodlums a lesson. More sailors, plus soldiers and marines, rushed to join in.

"Ynostrosa fought harder than I. For so long, I had relied on Fox; now, there was only Diego. Fox was a month away.

"We were stripped to our skivvies, bloodied and battered and left in the street. Then the police came and arrested us. As we were man-handled into a paddy wagon, I saw the uniformed mob roll down the boulevard, seizing another young zoot-suiter. Four were required to hold back a girl as twenty or thirty heroes trampled her beau. As she spat and kicked, hair coming loose from her high pompadour, soldiers made jokes about Mexican spitfires.

"An *anglo* rushed up to the wagon, protesting. He was a bar-owner, and his place had been smashed up by sailors. A zoot-suiter had been thrown through a window.

" 'It's a matter for the Shore Patrol,' a cop told him, turning away."

"That night, and for about a week afterwards, hordes of servicemen charged into town, hired fleets of taxicabs, and cruised the streets in search of zooters. Girls were raped, boys were killed, but only *pachucos* were arrested. No sailor, soldier, or marine was charged with any crime. The police adopted a policy of driving meekly in the wake of the mobs and arresting their battered victims. Newspaper editorials praised servicemen who took action against 'lawlessness'. Many openly lamented that the raids were stopped, on orders from on high, before 'the zoot-suit problem' was subjected to a final solution.

"Miguel Ynostrosa never went into the army; he lost the use of his legs.

"In the lock-up, I healed fast and was at least safe from further brutality. Enraged, I heard of the cripples and mothers beaten by the cops when they protested arrests. The Los Angeles City Council adopted a resolution which made the wearing of a zoot-suit a crime.

"I sweated out a long month, knowing the moon nights were approaching. The bars of my cell seemed strong, maybe strong enough to hold Fox. The faces of men around me began to glow. I knew I would have to resist the change.

"I remembered the sailors in the alley. Some faces had glowed, some hadn't. Some believed they were doing the right thing; perhaps they were worse than the men who relished the chance to go out and beat someone up without suffering consequences.

"I was released after three weeks, no charges laid against me. During the moon-nights, I prowled the streets, searching for glowing faces and sailor suits. I found prey, but never saw any of the men who crippled Ynostrosa. I killed drunken servicemen, whom I found alone. Once, I found two Military Policemen raping a girl, and exulted in killing them. The girl saw me up close, but never told.

"At the end of the full moon, I was exhausted. I had done nothing, though the press screamed at the police for failing to catch the 'Zorro Killer' who left the zig-zag-zig on his victims. Those who had attacked the zoot-suiters were mainly overseas, directing aggression against the Japanese; within a few years, most would probably be dead. It was not up to me which would live through Guadalcanal or Midway; just and unjust, good and bad, all would fall in this War."

"I was tired and I knew what Hendrik had meant by my *curse*. No matter how I fought and killed for my people, no matter how many zig-zag-zigs I left, I could do nothing.

"I was one creature, alone and unaided. Evil was too vast, a mob with no true leaders. I couldn't even protect friends like Ynostrosa, let alone an entire race, an entire country. But still I saw the glow in the faces of those who deserved to die, still I changed on moon-nights and left my zig-zag-zig.

"I got into the War, working in a defence plant. In October, 1944, the convictions of the Sleepy Lagoon defendants were reversed by the Court of Appeals. By then, they had served two years in jail. When released, several youths of previous good character turned in bitterness to crime and were swiftly returned to prison.

"When men with Spanish names came back from the Just War minus limbs or with medal ribbons and insisted they be served in 'No Mexicans' bars and restaurants, things began to change a little, on the surface.

"I began to feel old."

XV

Firefights lit up the Jungle. The War on Zonk had just passed Def Con 4. A row of window-fronts exploded as fire raked across them. Next to tonight's police action, the Rodney King beating was a misfiled parking ticket.

Stuart jogged through the pre-emptive riot reprisal, running with the fox as hounds made steady progress down wide streets. No arrests were being made, but instant sentences were carried out.

If he had a gun, he would shoot back.

There'd be nothing worth looting in the burning stores. People were too busy fleeing to take advantage of excellent terms offered on electrical goods.

This all couldn't be some crazy scheme to trap the beast-man. This was way too big, way too organized. Even for a wonder like the hunter Stuart had seen, there was no need to send in an army. This had the feel of something long in the planning.

From helicopters, soothing voices assured those on the ground that they should lay down their arms and surrender.

"You will not be harmed."

Nobody believed that. There were no innocent bystanders any more. If you got shot: sorry, but you must have been guilty.

What the hell was this all about?

Stuart made a bad decision, and took a left into a cross-street that turned out to be a blind alley. A wire-topped wall came up in front. He could never get over it.

He turned and pain caught up with him. His lungs and knees hurt. He was seven years away from his last rugby match; the only exercise he had taken since was climbing stairs.

"Shit," he breathed.

A cop came into the alley, a flash-light fixed to his helmet like a miner's lamp. That gave him both hands free to hold his gun.

Stuart reached into his jacket pocket and pulled out his passport.

"British citizen," he said. "Diplomatic Immunity," he lied. "*Civis romanus sum*," he tried, desperately.

"Who ya got?" someone shouted from outside the alley.

"Nigger on zonk," the cop said over his shoulder.

As the someone advised "waste him", Stuart pushed himself away from the wall and at the cop.

He felt the gunbarrel slam against his shoulder, and was sure he'd been shot. The cop, surprised, collapsed backwards. His gun skittered away into garbage.

Stuart felt his wound. The barrel had just gouged at him, not even ripping his clothes.

Angry, he dug into the cop's chest with his knees and wrestled off the lamp-helmet. A face appeared. Young, white, freckles. Stuart made a fist and smashed the cop's nose, over and over.

Policemen Are Your Friends, he'd been taught in infants' school. Cop is the natural-born enemy of the black man, he'd been told at a party.

Something animal inside made it necessary Stuart break this killer cop's skull. He was becoming acclimatized to the Jungle.

A slim shadow fell on Stuart and the cop. Stuart looked up.

"Stop fuckin' around and ice the pig," a girl said.

Anger froze.

Ice, waste, *kill* …

"Pussy," the girl said, kneeling. In the lamp-circle, Stuart recognized the half-oriental who had been with the Alcalde. She had a little silver gun, which she fired into the cop's forehead.

Stuart felt the cop die, the last writhe of his body like a hobby-horse between his legs.

He stood up, shuddering, cold.

"Come on, gangsta," the girl said, "let's get offstreet."

She led him out of the alley and along the sidewalk to a door. Mop-up crews were proceeding ruthlessly down the boulevard.

The girl got the door open and shoved Stuart through. They were in a hallway, lit only by searchbeam passes over a skylight.

"Esperanza," said a weak voice. "That you?"

Stuart looked at her. She shrugged and said "Esperanza Nguyen. Some call me Warchild, but that's kidshit."

The girl shouted back, identifying herself.

A door was opened and Esperanza marched Stuart into a room. Computers and desk-top publishing equipment on desks, framed covers of Spanish language periodicals on the walls.

One of the boys from the Coffee Stop, side soaked with blood, jittered around.

"How is he?" Esperanza asked.

"Bad, man, *muy* bad."

In a baggy leather chair slumped the Alcalde, face drained white. He looked as if he'd been beaten extensively. On a desk by him was an old-style square TV set, with news coverage. There were aerial views of the burning Jungle.

Irises showed ID photos of García and Scotchman.

"What is this about?" Stuart asked.

"You, gangsta," Esperanza said.

The iris showed Stuart's passport shot. He hated it; he was wearing his old school tie.

"They say you've been taken out by a zonk gang," she said, translating the garble of the newscast. "Two cops are dead, you just missing. There's an "orgy of cop killing" going down, and Chief Ryu is sending in Special Tactical Groups."

The TV cut to Mayor Jute, improbably well-groomed for someone hauled out of bed in the middle of the night.

"Genfems of the press," she said, "the officers who've fallen will be honoured. The sympathies of the city are for the significant partners and offspring of the law enforcement casualties."

"What about the ridealong?" a non-CGI journo asked.

"Every effort is being exerted to recover Stuart Finn. I have just interfaced with Prime Minister Heseltine and assured him our best non-gender specific operatives are onstreet ..."

"I didn't vote for *him*," Stuart blurted.

"At this temporal juncture, it seems decreasingly likely that Mr Finn is still living. The Zonk Gangs have demonstrated in the past their savage ruthlessness."

Back in the studio, the news-anchor summed up, "Following an unprovoked attack by gangs, two LAPD officers are confirmed dead ..."

Grainy homevideo footage showed two burned bodies hanging from cuffed wrists. The camera focused on a boiled face. It was García.

"... and a British writer on a ridealong is missing ..."

García and Scotchman had set Stuart up, then been set up themselves. This was a stage-managed riot.

But why?

"Chief Ryu has vowed ..."

The Alcalde spasmed with coughing. Stuart thought the man had a couple of broken ribs, at least.

"They're coming down like a hard rain," the boy said. "Soon as this shit started, they got the Alcalde. It was deliberate, man. On radio, I got word others have been taken out. Not just gangstas, man. Others like the Alcalde. That commie priest, he's dead. And a couple of women from the Committee for the Disappeared. It was a surgical strike. Shut up the trouble-makers, man."

Esperanza was thoughtful.

"All this community spirit garbage is over," the boy waved around. There were anti-zonk posters, schedules for educational drives, portraits of positive ethnic role models. "The Caldiarres were right, Warchild. We should just've fought back."

The Alcalde died.

Esperanza thought it over. The boy hefted a machine pistol, itching to get onstreet and take out some cop butt. Finally, the girl nodded agreement.

"Gangsta," she said, pointing at Stuart, "we dead by dawn, dead or disappeared. You, you have to live, live to show the lie. You a writer, right? Tell this story. Tell them all how it went down."

It seemed a fair bet to say Stuart would not be working on the *Shadowstalk* script any more.

"You a hero, man," the boy said. "I can see it on you."

He was alone. The explosions had died down, though there were still bursts of gunfire. The TV chattered quiet lies, and repeated shock footage of edited truth. There was talk of arrested zonk gangstas, but not of slain community leaders.

The Alcalde was under a dust-sheet. Stuart gathered he had tried to give his people an example, tried to keep them out of the gangs, off the drugs. Something about the waste of effort chilled Stuart to despair.

There were kids out onstreet who had hung with the Alcalde, studied hard and tried their best; they were just as dead as the zonkbrains and gangstas.

He wondered where the beast-man was in this fight. Lost, probably. In a city-wide battle, one small impossible wonder counted for little.

The office door opened.

"Fuck shit death," Stuart said.

A young man staggered in. It was Vega, one of the Alcalde's boys. His clothes were a ruin. He had been in a fight.

"Black man," he said, looking at Stuart. "I'm spent."

His eyes shone. Stuart recognized them and staggered back against a desk.

Vega smiled; the smile became a snarl. The hunter's snout surfaced in Vega's face and receded again.

Now Stuart knew Vega's secret, could the beast-man let him live? The whole of Los Angeles had reasons for finding it more convenient if Stuart Finn were dead.

"What did I do?" he said. "I wrote a book? Hollywood called, I took the money. Do I deserve to die for it?"

"Depends on the movie," Vega said, grinning.

XVI From the *Corrido* of Diego

"So, black man, that is what I am, what I have done, what I have been, what I have learned.

"Some call me monster, some call me hero. They will call you the same things. I know truly I am neither. I am merely a fool. I know I can make no difference, can change nothing but myself, but I have been compelled to try. Many are deservedly dead by my hand, but many more equally as deserving never crossed my path. I have felled tiny trees in an ever-expanding jungle.

"That poor dead man, the Alcalde, was better than I. He was a man of peace, of learning, of love. His way was best. And yet he has been killed. Others, men and women of good will, are slaughtered. This is as bad a time as I have known and it wearies me more than I can tell. I am near the end of my days and I am not sorry.

"At first, I understood that I killed for my *people*. I was wrong, I killed for my *kind*. Chicano, black, white, whatever. My kind is all colours. I am of the *pobres*, the poor, the oppressed, the neglected, the inconvenient. I am the cry of the sad, the true *grito de dolores*. My task has been futile, but I have not abandoned it until now.

"You are different from me. You will understand the *curse*. You will tilt at windmills, for you have no choice. You will stand knee-deep in the sea and cry 'go back, waves.' I am truly sorry for you, but I have no choice, as I have never had a choice. Your face shines, not as the faces of those I kill shine, but with a rainbow brilliance. The *viejo* must have been that rainbow in my own face.

"Live long with your legend, black man ..."

XVII

"What do you mean?" Stuart asked.

"This," Diego Vega said, holding out a frail hand. Pain passed across his face. His eyes were ancient.

Diego struck out, and touched Stuart's face.

It was an electric jolt. Stuart convulsed and fell, banging his head against a deskleg. His body throbbed as something coursed through his flesh.

After a time, his mind came back together. He did not know how long he had been space-voyaging inside his skull. The *corrido* Diego Vega had told him was imprinted in his brain, as if the man's memories had passed from his mind to Stuart's at the moment of the jolt.

Scrambling across the floor, he found a body. Diego Vega was dead; an old man, withered to a husk. There was no particular expression of peace on his face. Nobody was home.

Stuart stood, wondering how he was changed.

As Diego had spoken, the noise from the Jungle had changed. Fewer shots and explosions, more sirens and helicopters. They had ignored the TV as the flickering images of violence became pacified. Onstreet, the Tactical Squads were taking control.

Stuart knew he should get out of the office. People were looking for him. He had to find the right way of coming out of the Jungle. It had to be public, preferably televised. Mayor Jute had said he was probably dead, and many of her subordinates wouldn't hesitate to turn her supposition into a statement of fact.

The door was kicked open and three cops with shotguns piled in, levelling gleaming barrels.

Stuart, in the throes of a change he couldn't understand, was still going to die. He would die before he had achieved his potential.

"It's him," a cop said. "Finn, the Brit."

They paraded him, half-captive and half-trophy. An officer made a comprehensive report into a wafer-phone,

The Jungle was tamed. The dead had been disappeared. Now, things were being cleaned up. Teams shifted the burned-out cars, searched for survivors and culprits, even picked up empty shell-cases like litter collectors.

Stuart was still too high on the jolt he had taken to be tired. Last night, several times, he'd thought he was a changed man. Now, he truly was. He remembered Diego's voice, at once urgent and discursive, and the *corrido* that had been an education and a preparation.

Small businessmen sighed outside smoking wrecks. Crying mothers searched for missing sons. Floral tributes lay on corpse outlines. Cops stood around with paper cups of coffee. Newsteams scavenged for interviews with firefighters and cops.

Everyone would want Stuart's story.

He was hustled to an intersection where a tangle of newsies pointed cameras and mikes at a knot of officials. There were uniform cops, faces grimed from the action, and serious, smiling dignitaries. He recognized Chief Ryu and Mayor Jute.

Their faces glowed like moonlight.

The gleam made Stuart sick. He clenched fists, and felt his sharp, strong nails breaking his skin. His forefingers were lengthening, strange aches in their knuckles. The pain was not unpleasant, and made him aware of the growing reconfigurations of his nerves and senses.

The crowds parted and Stuart was welcomed. Hundreds of questions were asked, but a suit Stuart had never seen explained "Mr Finn is exhausted from his grueling ordeal but will answer all serious inquiries later."

Stuart knew he'd rate a debriefing before he was allowed to say anything.

Chief Ryu and the Mayor competed to shake his hand. The Mayor, a head taller, won. Dazed by the almost-opaque wasp's nest of light around her head, Stuart accepted Mayor Jute's grip.

He left her palm bloody, and smiled.

"I'm sorry," he apologized.

"This atrocious situation will not be repeated," Chief Ryu insisted to the media. "When the moon comes out tonight, things will be different."

"That's true," Stuart said. Reaching out as if dazed, he wiped his bloody hand on the hood of a police armoured car. It was warm in August sunlight.

Diego Vega had talked most of the day away, invisibly dying all the while, something inside him gathering to make a *leap*. Now, evening was rushing on, and night was creeping after.

As Stuart's smile stretched, he ran his tongue over his teeth and felt an unfamiliar sharpness.

"Regardless of the bleats of the bleeding heart bunch," Ryu said, arms extended, "there is Evil all around us. And Evil must be suppressed. Wrong-doers must be punished."

"I couldn't agree more," Stuart said.

He looked at the car he had smeared. His mark was drying. His mark in blood.

Zig-zag-zig.

Jo Fletcher

BRIGHT OF MOON

Jo Fletcher is associate publisher at British book imprint Gollancz. She co-edited the World Fantasy Convention *anthologies* Gaslight & Ghosts *and* Secret City: Strange Tales of London *(both with Stephen Jones), and contributed to the macabre poetry collection* Now We Are Sick. *Her own verse is collected in* Shadows of Light *and* Dark. *The first recipient of the British Fantasy Karl Edward Wagner Award, she has also won the World Fantasy Award: Professional.*

The dark of moon,
The torment born
For those the gods have marked.

Slow swell of moon
Presages doom;
The change has now been sparked.

The bright of moon,
A change of form –
The Children roam the land.

Howl at the moon
And shun the dawn,
Ravenous and damned.

The wane of moon,
The Feeding done,
In shadows spurn the sun.

'Til pull of moon
The Frenzy spawns –
The Children once more run.